Warning!

Violence and the Supernatural

This book may be inappropriate for young readers.

The fictional World of Mystic China™ is violent, deadly and filled with supernatural monsters. Magic, monsters, demons, gods, demigods, immortals, dragons, combat, insanity and the supernatural are all elements in this book.

Some parents may find the violence and supernatural elements of the game inappropriate for young readers/players. We suggest parental discretion.

Please note that none of us at Palladium Books condone nor encourage the occult, the practice of magic, the use of drugs, or violence. Although parts of **Mystic China™** has been inspired by Chinese myths and legends, it is a *fictional* work. The magic, powers, monsters and characters depicted in this book are NOT real.

A massive sourcebook for use with Heroes Unlimited™, Ninjas & Superspies™, and Beyond the Supernatural™. Compatible with Rifts® and the entire Palladium Books® Megaverse®!

Dedication

Dedicated, in far too slight a measure of felial piety, to my scholarly mother, Nora Evarian Wujcik, and to my self-sainted father, Joseph St. Wujcik, with great love and affection.

Erick Wujcik

A very special thank you to the original, 1989, play-testers of Mystic China: Marvin Allen, Todd Bake, Kevin Lowry, Reg Roehl, John Speck, and Don Woodward.

Thanks for valued assistance go to Don Anderson, Yi-Mei Chng, Paul Deckert, Larry Feinstein, Stephanie Itchkawich, Chuck Knakal, Alan Moen, Tony Townson, Diane Vogt-O'Connor, and Roger Zelazny.

Thanks for the books go to Lisa Leutheuser, Julius Rosenstein, Joe Saul, Steve Wujcik and, of course, my main source, for which I am forever grateful, The Main Branch of the Detroit Public Library.

Erick Wujcik

Coming in 1995!
Mystic China™ Sourcebook

Other Palladium RPG titles include:
Ninjas & Superspies™
Beyond the Supernatural™
Heroes UNlimited™
Rifts® RPG
The Palladium® RPG
Robotech® RPG
Macross II™ RPG
RECON®
The Compendium of Weapons, Armor and Castles™
The Compendium of Contemporary Weapons™

First Printing — February 1995

Copyright © 1995 Palladium Books Inc.

All rights reserved, worldwide, under the Universal Copyright Convention. No part of this book may be reproduced in part or whole, in any form or by any means, without permission from the publisher, except for brief quotes for use in reviews. All incidents, situations, institutions, governments and people are fictional and any similarity, without satiric intent, of characters or persons living or dead, is strictly coincidental.

Palladium Books®, Megaverse®, and Rifts® are registered trademarks owned and licensed by Kevin Siembieda and Palladium Books® Inc. Mystic China™, Ninjas & Superspies™, Heroes Unlimited™, Beyond the Supernatural™ and other names and titles are trademarks owned by Kevin Siembieda and Palladium Books® Inc.

Mystic China™ is published by Palladium Books Inc., 12455 Universal Drive, Taylor, MI 48180.
Printed in the USA.

PALLADIUM BOOKS® PRESENTS:

MYSTIC CHINA™

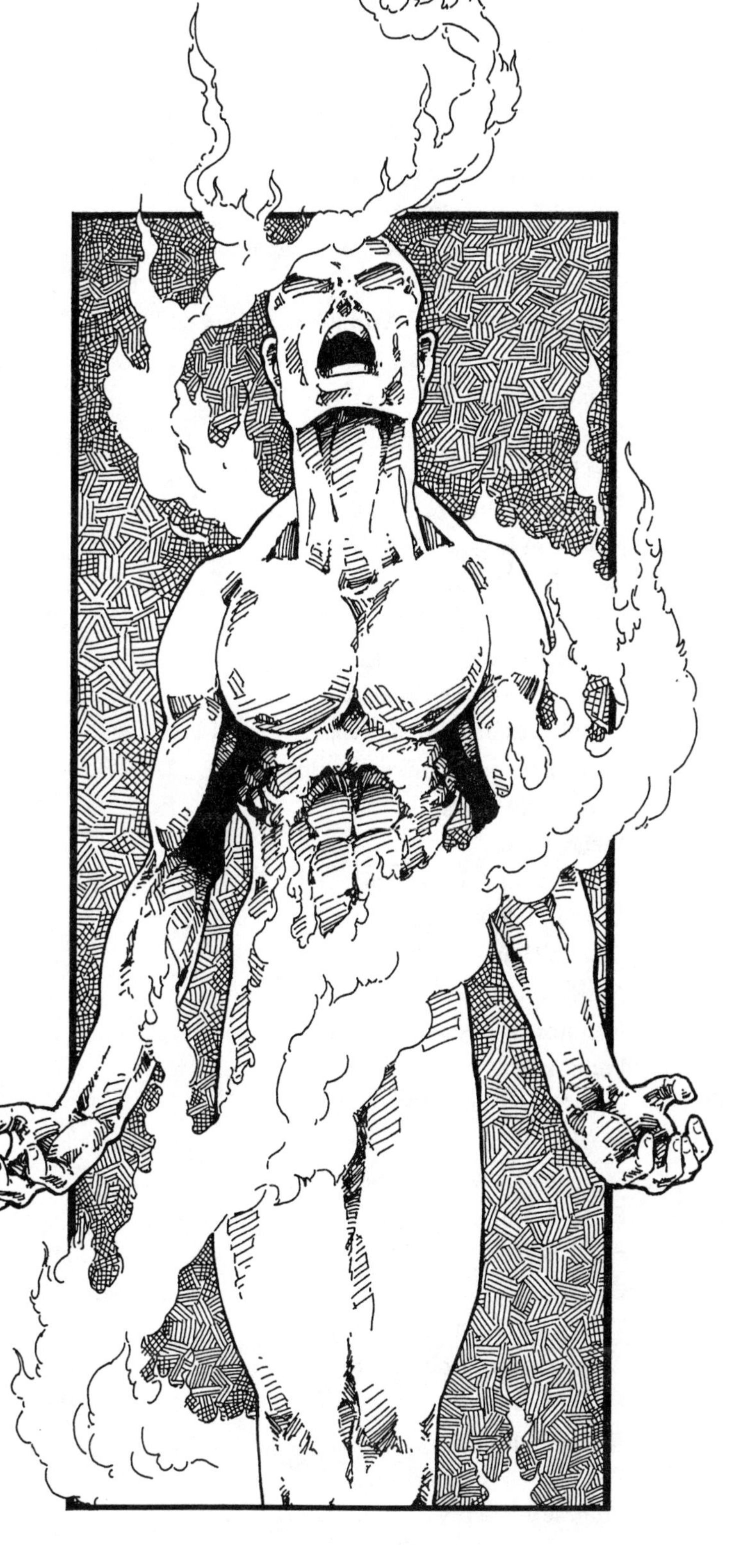

Written By: **Erick Wujcik**

Additional Text & Concepts: **Kevin Siembieda**

Senior Editor: **Kevin Siembieda**

Editors: **Alex Marciniszyn**
James A. Osten
Kevin Kirsten
Julius Rosenstein

Cover Painting: **James Steranko**

Interior Artists:
Vince Martin
Wayne Breaux Jr.
Kevin Long
Roger Petersen

Art Direction & Keylining: **Kevin Siembieda**

Typography: **Maryann Siembieda**
Michael O'Connor

Special Thanks to James Steranko for a fantastic cover painting (and for his patience). Erick for another great book. Vince, Wayne and Rog for more tremendous artwork! And to Maryann, Alex, Steve, Thom, Mike and the usual gang of Palladium Immortals.

Kevin Siembieda

Table of Contents

Quick Find Table

Introduction

"Why bother with those people? As a Buddhist, you ought rather to avoid those who enjoy making a display of spectacular powers. Taoist hermits delight in all sorts of childish antics far removed from the exalted teachings of their ancient sages, Lao Tsu and Chuang Tsu. Haven't you seen their pictures? Immortals disporting themselves with music, chess and wine among the purple mountains of Fairyland. Drunk with eternal youth, they fly upon the backs of cranes or ride their many-coloured steeds — unicorns, griffins and even dragons!" His lips met in a thin line of disapproval...

A quote from the abbot of a Buddhist Monastery, as recorded, circa 1932, by John Blofeld, in his biography, **The Wheel of Life**.

Taoists!

I can't remember ever being carried away with a project as much as with this one, **Mystic China**. Mostly because I've found myself enchanted by the Taoists.

Taoism is something like a philosophy, something like a religion, and more than a little like some kind of formal insanity. Don't expect me to explain it — according to the foremost Taoists of the ages, Taoism can't be taught, nor can it even be explained — but I can tell you that Taoism is the only major religion that I know of that believes in dragons and fairies. Even their villains, from evil Immortals, to island-sized sea monsters, are cool.

For hundreds of years Buddhists and Confusianists, along with the more recent missionaries of Islam and Christianity, have all condemned Taoism. It's silly they say, or they criticize it for being filled with fanciful superstitions. Why, the other religions seem to be asking, why can't the Chinese take religion *seriously?*

How could I help but be bewitched?

So, much of this book is based on my own role-playing-centered version of Taoism.

It's also based on China, and most of the material deals with Chinese people and places. If you like, you can base a role-playing adventure or a whole campaign in Hong Kong or wandering around mainland China.

However, given that there are more Chinese than any other people on Earth, and that they're distributed just about everywhere (I can't think of too many places without a Chinese restaurant nearby), you should find the material suitable for **any** role-playing campaign!

Everywhere the Chinese people go, they carry a bit of their ancient culture with them. Anywhere on the planet; in a local Chinatown, displayed in a museum, or hidden away in the private horde of a collector, are the preserved mysteries of *Mystic China.*

For example, do you know you could have a **Mystic China** adventure set in the American West? Remember, during the building of the transcontinental railway, thousands upon thousands of Chinese laborers were brought in through San Francisco, and from there were scattered all over the West, until they were just as common as cowboys or indians.

Anyway, here's hoping this book inspires you, excites you, and provides you with some new directions in role-playing.

Oh! One last thing. Much of what is in **Mystic China** came about because of feedback from the fans of **Ninjas & Superspies**. So, if you'd like to see more, write me a letter and tell me what you want. It may take awhile, but if you don't ask, you don't get! I can tell you that I'm already working on a second **Mystic China** sourcebook which *should* quickly follow this one.

Erick Wujcik, the 4,701st Year since the Ascension of the Yellow Emperor (1994)

Mystic China™ Character Creation

Here's a quick eight-step review on rolling up a character for *Mystic China*. For more details about character creation, check out a copy of **Revised Ninjas & Superspies**, **Beyond the Supernatural**, **Revised Heroes Unlimited**, or even **Teenage Mutant Ninja Turtles & Other Strangeness**.

Step #1: Determine Attributes. Roll 3D6 for each of the eight Attributes. If the roll is a 16, 17 or 18, roll another 1D6 to add to that Attribute.

Step #2: Select an O.C.C., P.C.C. or R.C.C. In addition to those listed here in *Mystic China*, you can also choose from any of the O.C.C.s in **Revised Ninjas & Superspies**. With the Game Master's permission, you may also be able to select from the Psychic Character Classes (P.C.C.s) in **Beyond the Supernatural**. Note: R.C.C. is Racial Character Class, primarily applicable to inhuman characters.

Step #3: Determine P.P.E. Points. Unless the Potential Psychic Energy (P.P.E.) is listed with the character's O.C.C., P.C.C. or R.C.C., roll 2D6 for the total P.P.E.

Step #4: Determine Hit Points. Add 1D6 to the character's Physical Endurance (P.E.) attribute number.

Step #5: Select Martial Art Forms, Martial Art Abilities, Skills and Equipment. Follow the guidelines under your character's O.C.C., P.C.C., or R.C.C.

Step #6: Look up Attribute Bonuses. Once all the changes and additions have been made to the attributes, look up the bonuses on the *Attribute Bonus Table*.

Attribute Bonus Chart

Step #7: Determine Chi Points. Unless otherwise listed with the O.C.C., P.C.C. or R.C.C., a character's *base* Chi is equal to the Physical Endurance (P.E.) attribute, after all the skill and martial art form bonuses have been added to the P.E. For a complete description of Chi, see the section on *Chi Mastery*.

Step #8: Select Alignment. Use the description of the Alignments in **Ninjas & Superspies** where the Disciplines of Honor are also described. Or players can use those described in **Beyond the Supernatural** or from *any* Palladium rule books, except for *Revised Recon*. Also, check out the section called "*One Hundred and Twenty-Nine Chinese Characters*" for a fun way to roll up your character's name.

	17	18	19	20	21	22	23	24	25	26	27	28	29	30
I.Q. add to all skills. One time bonus	+3%	+4%	+5%	+6%	+7%	+8%	+9%	+10%	+11%	+12%	+13%	+14%	+15%	+16%
M.E. save vs psychic attack/insanity	+1	+2	+2	+3	+3	+4	+4	+5	+5	+6	+6	+7	+7	+8
M.A. trust or intimidate	45%	50%	55%	60%	65%	70%	75%	80%	84%	88%	92%	94%	96%	97%
P.S. Hand to Hand Combat: Damage	+2	+3	+4	+5	+6	+7	+8	+9	+10	+11	+12	+13	+14	+15
P.P. parry, dodge and strike bonus	+1	+2	+2	+3	+3	+4	+4	+5	+5	+6	+6	+7	+7	+8
P.E. save vs coma/death	+5%	+6%	+8%	+10%	+12%	+14%	+16%	+18%	+20%	+22%	+24%	+26%	+28%	+30%
P.E. save vs poison and magic	+1	+2	+2	+3	+3	+4	+4	+5	+5	+6	+6	+7	+7	+8
P.B. charm and impress	35%	40%	45%	50%	55%	60%	65%	70%	75%	80%	83%	86%	90%	92%
Speed: No special bonuses.														

Taoist Alignment (Good)

Taoist characters are rather eccentric. They are **not** selfish, in that they care nothing for wealth, riches, or any personal gain, but they are self-centered in that they'd rather have fun than be bothered by serious obligations. Ultimately, the Taoist is always torn. On the one hand, the character should work for the good of others. However, the attainment of wisdom, insight, and even Immortality are also the goals of the Taoist. Also, since a Taoist takes the long view, the character is willing to let people suffer if it's possible they'll learn from the experience.

A good example of Taoist behavior is the story of the Taoist and the young thief:

While drinking in a low dive, a young man was complaining about his lack of funds. "If only," said the delinquent, "I knew the secrets of the thief, I'd never lack for money in this town."

"Would you like to learn how to be a thief?" asked the Taoist. "Just come with me tonight. I'll break into the richest house in town and you'll learn everything you need to know to be an excellent thief."

The young man agreed and they met late that night. Everything went splendidly, as the Taoist showed the young man how to hide his smell so he wouldn't alarm the animals, how to move quietly, how to hide in the shadows, and how to break open the gate. Finally, once they were inside, the Taoist proceeded to pick the lock of the family's treasure chest.

"Quick," whispered the Taoist, "hop inside."

Thinking that he was to search the inside of the chest for hidden riches, the young thief did as he was told.

At which point the Taoist slammed down the lid of the chest, locked it, and then loudly began singing and rummaging around among the wine cabinet of the house. Before slipping out the front door, wine jar in hand, the Taoist even lit a candle in the room with the chest.

Terrified, the youngster huddled in the chest, which was locked from the outside, while the inhabitants of the house flew into an uproar. Seeing only the flickering of the candle, and a few shapes passing by, the young thief could only wait in horror.

However, after a few minutes, when most of the armed men of the house seemed to have gone outside, the thief started to scratch the inside of the chest, making just a small amount of noise.

Then, when one of the ladies opened the lock, he sprang out, blew out the candle, and ran panic-stricken into the night.

Outside, there was little hope of escape, with family members, police, and neighbors all in pursuit. So the young thief had no choice but to dive into a nearby well, hoping that he would be overlooked.

Sure enough, the ruse worked, and the young thief managed to stay hidden all the night, and all through the next day, until the following midnight.

Shivering with cold and fright, the youngster started to climb out of the well, when suddenly a hand reached out to grab him, and pull him out.

"Ho, ho," said the Taoist, laughing at the young thief's shocked expression.

"Why... why did you trap me there last night?" said the thief.

"Well," said the Taoist, "you did say you wanted to learn everything about being a thief..."

Taoist Characters Will...

1. Intend to keep their word of honor, when they give it. However, if things change, well...
2. Avoid Lies (except in fun).
3. Cheat whenever necessary.
4. Will not kill an unarmed foe (but will take advantage of the situation).
5. Never harm an innocent.
6. Not use torture unless absolutely necessary.
7. Never kill for pleasure.
8. Usually help those in need.
9. Refuse to take any position of leadership or authority, except in a short-term emergency.
10. Ignore the law and the rules, whenever they feel they can get away with it. However, they will never violate the law for personal gain.
11. Usually make fun of authority.
12. Usually, but not always, stick by a friend.

A Select List of Skills for Mystic China

While some of the skills listed are duplicates of those found in **Revised Ninjas & Superspies** and in other Palladium rule books, there are a number of new entries, each marked (New!).

Skills Listed by Category

Chinese Cultural Skills
Artistic Calligraphy
Calligraphic Forgery (new)

Game Skills
Tiao Qi or Chinese Checkers (new)
Wei Qi or Go
Xiang Qi or Shogi (new)

Chinese Swindler Espionage Skills
Shell Game (new)
Yarrow Stick Counting (new)

Chinese Science Skills
Archaeology (new)
Chemistry - Chinese Alchemical

Chinese Technical Skills (Languages)
Chinese Antiquarianism (new)
Chinese Calligraphic Codes & Code Breaking (new)
Chinese Classical Studies (new)
Chinese History (new)
Chinese Language & Literacy (new)
Chinese Mythology - Taoist (new)
Chinese Mythology - Buddhist
Language (Other Oriental; new)
Language Dialects (new)

Temple Philosophies & Skills
Begging
Fasting
Feng Shui or Geomancy (new)
Meditation (new)
Oriental Philosophies (new)

Ancient Weapon Proficiencies
W.P. Paired Weapons
W.P. Axe (new)
W.P. Blunt
W.P. Chain
W.P. Forked
W.P. Knife
W.P. Polearm (new)
W.P. Spear
W.P. Staff
W.P. Large Sword
W.P. Short Sword
W.P. Whip (new)

Projectile Weapons (not guns)
W.P. Mouth Weapons (new)
W.P. Small Thrown Weapons
W.P. Bow
W.P. Cross bow
W.P. Slingshot
W.P. Weapon Improvisation (new)

Chinese Cultural Skills

Artistic Calligraphy: (The equivalent of 'Calligraphy' in *Ninjas & Superspies*) This is the skill needed to produce beautiful letters, using a brush, ink stone, and paper. Taken along with skill in Chinese Language & Literacy (see Technical Skills, below), the character can create variations on any of the Chinese characters. For example, there are over 200 ways to render the character for 'longevity.' **Base Skill:** 35%+5% per level of experience.

Calligraphic Forgery (New!): A special skill that allows the character to imitate the calligraphy of the ancients and to reproduce copies of exotic styles. This is an advanced version of artistic calligraphy, and the character must take both skills. To successfully pass off a forgery as an ancient work requires a roll under the base skill on percentile. Attempting to forge the penmanship of a particular author is more difficult (-25% penalty on the roll). **Base Skill:** 25%+5% per level of experience.

Qi (Game) Skills

Tiao Qi or Chinese Checkers (New!): The skill involves being able to play Chinese Checkers (with marbles, on a six-cornered board, where the object is to get all your pieces to the opposite side), at a professional level. There is also an *advanced*, or *blitz* version of the game where the rules are a bit more complex, where entire groups of marbles can be moved simultaneously. **Base Skill:** 24%+4% per level of experience.

Wei Qi or Go: As chess is the most widely accepted intellectual game of the west, so Go is accepted as the most "enlightening" game of the eastern world. On a more practical level, the oriental world is filled with villains who will spare the life of a good Go player. And, for many martial artists, the prospects of an intelligent game of Go easily outweigh any desire for combat. **Base Skill:** 30%+5% per level of experience.

Simulating a game of Wei Qi: A truly expert game involves many hours and many rituals. First there should be a series of three quick "test" games to determine the weaker player's handicap; figure that for every 5% of difference between the players' skills, the weaker player starts with an extra 'stone' (playing piece). Once the players begin in earnest, the game can take hours, especially since true masters of the game allow their opponents to take back however many moves they like. That's because the true object of *Wei Qi* is not supposed to be winning, but playing a 'perfect' game.

Xiang Qi or Shogi (New!): The Chinese version of chess, where each side, red and black, received two *Ju*, or Chariots; two *Ma*, or Horsemen; two *Pao*, or Cannons; five *Zu*, or Pawns; two *Xiang*, or Ministers; and two *Shi*, or Officers. The piece corresponding to the King is called a General, but the red General is called *Shuai*, and the black General is called

Jiang. Unlike the checkerboard used in chess, the board for *Xiang Qi* is played on 90 intersections of vertical, horizonal and diagonal lines, and the board contains special domains for each general, as well as a "river" that separates the two sides. **Base Skill:** 15%+5% per level of experience.

Chinese Swindler Espionage Skills

Shell Game (New!): It's the same the world over. All the character needs is a flat surface, three shells (or cups, or bowls), a pea, and a gullible customer. The idea is to keep moving the shells around and let the customer bet on where the pea will appear. Missing the roll (getting over the base skill on percentile) means that a customer has a genuine chance of spotting the correct shell and wins. Or, if the pea was hidden or palmed, the customer is likely to see the trick. **Base Skill:** 20%+4% per level of experience.

Yarrow Stick Counting (New!): This is a fraudulent form of fortune telling, or divination, where one *pretends* to cast the Yarrow Sticks for an *I Ching* reading. However, the con artist will "count" the sticks, so as to arrive at a desired set of lines (usually the particular interpretation is memorized from the book, right before the reading, so the character will seem to know the whole *I Ching* by heart). Not unlike "card counting," an expert can arrive at any desired Hexagram (by rolling under the skill on percentile). Even if the character fails the roll, it's still possible to move the sticks around quickly enough so that the customer won't see the deception. **Base Skill:** 24%+3% per level of experience.

Chinese Science Skills

Archaeology: (from *Beyond the Supernatural*) Scientific study of relics by excavation and analysis of artifacts and their sites. Studies include proper excavation techniques (digs), preservation, restoration and dating (including carbon dating) methods, as well as rudimentary history and anthropology background. The skill can be used to excavate/recover and clean/restore ancient artifacts and ruins, more accurately determine age/date of the artifact, establish authenticity and identify the likely time period, place of origin, and people. **Base Skill:** 35%+5% per level of experience.

Note: Excavations are extremely time consuming and laborious, requiring weeks, months, or even years of work and study. Restoration and accurate dating processes require the proper chemicals, equipment, facilities and time. Determining an accurate date of an artifact will place the object under several tests to establish its age. The length of time and level of accuracy under scientific conditions is listed on the following chart. Scientific determination of an item's age can be conducted by the character (if proper facilities are available), or an item can be sent to a laboratory that specializes in it. The latter is expensive, costing as little as $1,000 for items only a few hundred years old, and from $10,000 to $60,000 for an object which is thousands or millions of years old. Items that can be age-tested include man-made items, organic material, rocks, dirt, and/or fossils.

Age in Years — Level of Accuracy

300 years or less — Within 2D4 years
301 to 500 years — Within 2D6 years
501 to 1,000 years — Within 3D6 years
1,001 to 2,000 years — Within 6D6 years
2,001 to 5,000 years — Within 1D6×10 years
5,001 to 10,000 years — Within 2D6×10 years

Chemistry - Chinese Alchemical: A combination of modern chemistry (organic and analytical), botany (a lot of elixirs require different herbs, flowers and roots), and history, with a little cryptography thrown into the mix. The character can interpret ancient alchemical texts, formulas and directions, and knows how to substitute modern ingredients for their ancient counterparts, and can use high-tech versions of the primitive equipment. A successful roll means the character succeeds in interpreting an alchemist's formula (even if written in code). Depending on the complexity of the procedure, it could take from one to six additional rolls to accurately reproduce an actual elixir. **Note:** Classical Chinese Literacy, Chemistry and Biology skills are all required prerequisites. **Base Skill:** 25%+5% per level of experience.

Chinese Technical Skills (Languages)

Chinese Antiquarianism (New!): Knowledge of the value and rarity of Chinese artistic, historical and ancient artifacts. The character can attempt to appraise the dollar value of any item. In addition, the character knows how to buy and sell antiques, and will be able to locate customers for any given item. The character can also attempt to determine fakes and frauds, based on both the quality of the item, as well as whether or not it fits correctly into the knowledge of the period. Also includes a basic understanding of precious stones and metals, and the ability to do simple quality tests. For example, the character can do a simple test for the purity of gold, or examine a gem and determine its size (carats), clarity and luster. **Base Skill:** 35%+5% per level of experience.

Chinese Calligraphic Codes & Code Breaking (New!): This very special form of Cryptography involves training in Chinese mythology, the classics of Chinese literature, plus an extensive investigation into the different styles and techniques of Chinese calligraphy. Chinese codes usually involve two levels of deception. First, the characters are altered, substituted, or invented, so that the code-breaker will have to figure out a whole new "alphabet." Second, the messages are usually cryptic references to historical or mythic figures, so the code-breaker has to have a good knowledge of books and legends. **Base Skill:** 10%+2% per level of experience.

Chinese Classical Studies (New!): The character is a master of the four categories of classics of China, including *Ching* (classics), *Shih* (history), *Tzu* (philosopher's writing), and *Chi* (miscellany). In addition, the character has committed to memory (to the point where they could pass one of the fabled Imperial examinations) the **Five Sacred Books** — the *I Ching*, the *Shih Ching* (Book of Odes), the *Shu Ching* (Book of History), the *Li Chi* (Book of Ritual), and the *Ch'un Ch'iu* (Spring & Summer Annals) — **and** the four books of Confucian thought — *The Great Learning, The Doctrine of the Mean, Analects of Confucius,* and *The Works of Mencius.* **Base Skill:** 40%+5% per level of experience.

Chinese History (New!): Extensive knowledge of the history of China. The character can, based on architecture, materials, technology, artistic form, and style of calligraphy, identify objects or sites associated with the various dynasties and pre-dynastic periods. The character will know the names, and at least a brief history, of all the various rulers of China, the various kingdoms and provinces, and important neighboring nations, as well as the works of such important writers as Confucius, Mencius, Lao Tzu, and Sun Tzu. **Note:** In order to have the Chinese History skill, the character must have an O.C.C. skill in Chinese Language. **Base Skill:** 45%+5% per level of experience.

Chinese Language & Literacy (New!): Chinese, as a language, is unique in the world. That's because the language has been in continuous use, both in the spoken and written form, for over three thousand years. And, because the written language is based on abstract characters (ideas), rather than phonetics (sounds), it has become more and more complex as it evolved. Here are the four "levels" of literacy available to characters, depending on which skills they select.

Stage 1 - Thousand Character Literacy. This applies only to characters who take Chinese as a *Secondary Skill.* The character can read simple instructions, write notes, and knows how to use a Chinese dictionary (something that a character with no skill in Chinese could not do). The character knows only one dialect, either Mandarin or Cantonese. **Base Skill:** 40%+5% per level of experience.

Stage 2 - Chinese Literacy. Applies to native speakers (those raised in a Chinese-speaking household) and to characters who take Chinese as an O.C.C. skill. The character can read and write around 3,000 ideograms, and can quickly learn more when they need to. Reading and writing are fully fluent and it's possible to read all modern newspapers, magazines and popular books. The character knows both Mandarin and Cantonese dialects. **Base Skill:** 55%+5% per level of experience.

Stage 3 - Advanced Chinese Literacy. The character must have an O.C.C. skill in Chinese Language (or be a native speaker) and either Chinese Antiquarianism, Chinese Classical Studies, Chinese History, or Chinese Mythology (any one will do). The character has a mastery of from 15,000 to 50,000 characters, which means that anything printed in the late Twentieth Century is readable. With reference books and dictionaries, the character can attempt to decipher ancient manuscripts and inscriptions. Knows both Mandarin and Cantonese, and can also read and write Chinese cursive script. **Base Skill:** 60%+5% per level of experience.

Stage 4 - Classical Chinese Literacy. The character must have an O.C.C. in the Chinese Language (or be a native speaker) plus Chinese Classical Studies, Chinese History, and Chinese Mythology. This allows the character to be able to read and write in just about any version of the Chinese characters, including the pre-dynastic pictographs. The character can speak Mandarin and Cantonese and, if exposed to a speaker of ancient Chinese, could easily pick up the spoken language. **Base Skill:** 60%+5% per level of experience.

Chinese Mythology - Taoist (New!): Includes extensive knowledge of the vast library of works on Chinese myths relating to gods, ghosts, demons, monsters, dragons, Immortals, and the undead. Since there are such a vast array of mythic entities (it is said, for example, that every star in the sky corresponds to a named deity in Chinese Mythology), characters are very skilled at locating written references on any given subject. This is all further complicated by the legends of Immortals becoming gods, of gods becoming mortal, and of virtually any mythic figure dying and being reincarnated as some "other" mythic figure. Characters will, given a few hours of research time and access to a decent library, be able to come up with a variety of legends (unfortunately, often contradictory) on any given named mythic entity or related to any particular place or period of history. **Base Skill:** 35%+5% per level of experience.

Chinese Mythology - Buddhist: This skill is pretty much the same as the Taoist version, except that it deals with the equally crowded hordes of Chinese Buddhist entities. A separate skill. **Base Skill:** 35%+5% per level of experience.

Language (Other Oriental; New!): Speaking, reading and writing a language other than the one the character grew up with. The skill can be selected as often as desired. Each selection counts as a language skill. **Base Skill:** 55%+5% per level of experience. If taken as a secondary skill, start at 40%+5% per level of experience. Here are some of the likely languages one will find in *Mystic China:*

Mongolian is the language of Mongolia (north of China). Its speakers are found scattered all around China, as well in many parts of the former Soviet Union. By the way, Mongolian is part of the Altaic family of languages, which also includes Japanese and Korean.

Tibetan, the language of Tibet, can be found in many of the mountainous regions of southwest China.

The **Miao** are a tribal people, who have been alternately warring with, and living peacefully with, the Chinese for thousands of years. Their language is still found in many wilderness areas.

Thai is not only the language of Thailand, but also of many ethnic groups scattered across southern China and most southeast asian countries.

Kazakh, Kirghiz, Uighur and Urianghai are all **Turkic** dialects (related to Turkish) and are found in the far west and northwest of China.

There are even more exotic languages, but most are spoken only in remote regions. **Note:** See *Chinese Language* above, which is treated differently.

Language Dialects (New!): Taking this skill for a particular language means the character will be able to communicate in *all* of the dialects of that language. Unlike English, where the language has only had a few hundred years to develop regional mutations, the oriental languages have been evolving separately for thousands of years! In the case of Chinese, some of the dialects are as different from one another as Italian is to Spanish (i.e. you could say that Italian and Spanish are both dialects of Latin).

A character with the Chinese dialects skill would be able to communicate in Mandarin (the "official" language of mainland China), Cantonese (Hong Kong and most Chinese-speakers in North America), Amoy (Taiwan), Hakka, Hunana, and Suzhou (also known as Wu), and would be able to quickly pick up any of the dozen or so other regional dialects. There are also ten different Tibetan dialects, and a half dozen Mongolian. **Base Skill:** 50%+5% per level of experience.

Temple Philosophies & Skills

Begging: Although learned as a monk, this skill can be particularly useful, either as a disguise, or to collect emergency money when things are desperate. The base skill determines the chance of collecting a donation from each passerby. On a crowded street it could be pretty lucrative. The amount of money depends on the economy of the country and city where the begging is taking place. **Base Skill:** 8%+1% per level of experience.

Fasting: The ability to go for long periods of time without food. So long as the character has sufficient water, two weeks without food will be pretty easy. After that the character will have to roll under the base skill to avoid becoming weakened or sick. **Base Skill:** 54%+4% per level of experience.

Feng Shui or Geomancy: (*Modified* from *Ninjas & Superspies*) This skill allows the character to evaluate the amount of Chi in any area. Some places will have a large amount of positive Chi, others will have substantial negative Chi. If the area has a *natural* flow of Chi (between zero and eight points), then the character will be able to measure it exactly. As far as rolling is concerned, it's useful for finding places with exceptionally high or low Chi of either flavor. **Base Skill:** 15%+5% per level of experience.

Meditation (New!): Involves engaging the mind and body so that the body remains motionless, but without fatigue or pain, and the mind stays in a clear, calm and rested state. While meditating a character recovers Chi, I.S.P., P.P.E. and other internal resources at an accelerated rate. Although it is not a substitute for sleeping, characters will usually feel alert and refreshed after any period of meditation. When in a meditative state they character is, at a subconscious level, well aware of what is happening in the environment and can instantly leave the meditation position with no combat penalties. **Note:** Meditation is required for any character wishing to learn Mudra.

Base Meditation Skill: Regardless of the experience level of the character, any rolls based on meditation should use only the number provided by the character's Mental Endurance (M.E.) attribute.

Base Meditation Time: The amount of time that a character can continue to meditate: One hour at first level, with an additional fifteen minutes at 2nd, 3rd, 4th and 5th levels. At 6th level the meditation time jumps to three hours, and the character picks up another half hour after advancement into 7th level and beyond.

Oriental Philosophies: (*Modified* from *Ninjas & Superspies*) Characters educated in monasteries or temples can learn one philosophy (additional philosophies are available by taking the skill more than once). Chinese Philosophies include Taoism, Confucianism, Legalism (a very hard-line, dictatorial-government philosophy), or Chinese Buddhism. Japanese choices include Shinto, Buddhism or Zen. Another possibility is that of Tibetan Lore, which includes a special sect of Buddhism. **Base Skill:** 70%+2% per level of experience.

Weapon Proficiencies

There are three categories of weapon proficiencies (W.P.): Ancient, Projectile and Modern (guns). Modern weapon skills can be found in **Ninjas & Superspies, Heroes Unlimited** and others.

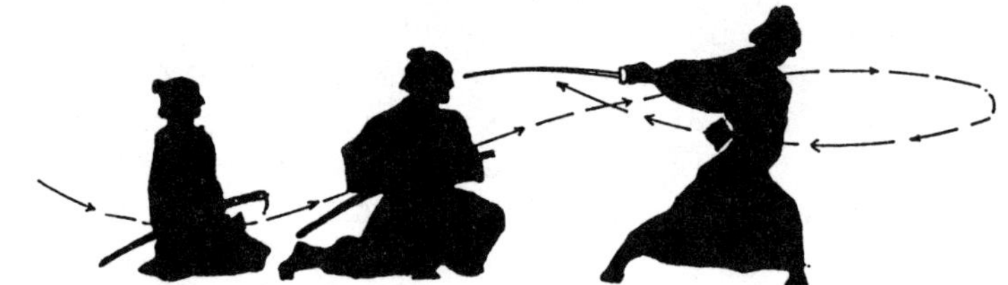

Ancient Weapon Proficiencies

Each skill area provides combat training with a particular type of weapon. The result is hand to hand combat bonuses to strike and parry, but only when that weapon is used. Each W.P. counts as one skill. The character may select several W.P.s **Note:** Characters without a W.P. CAN use any weapon, but without bonuses.

W.P. Paired Weapons: This is an extra skill that, combined with an ancient weapon proficiency, allows for the use of two weapons simultaneously.

W.P. Axe (New!): One- or two-handed weapons with handles, and with one or two bladed striking surfaces. Bonuses: Start with +1 to strike and +1 to damage at level one. +1 to strike at 3rd, 6th, 9th, 12th, and 15th levels. +1 to damage at 4th, 7th, 11th, and 14th levels. +1 to throw at 2nd, 5th, 8th, 10th and 13th levels.

W.P. Blunt: A skill with any type of blunt weapon, including mace, hammers, cudgels, pipe, staff and clubs. Bonuses: Start with +1 to strike at level one. +1 to strike at 3rd, 5th, 8th, 11th and 14th levels. +1 to parry at 2nd, 6th, 9th, 12th and 15th levels. +1 to throw at 4th, 7th, 10th and 13th levels.

W.P. Chain: Includes ordinary lengths of chain, mace and chain, flail, nunchaku, etc. Bonuses: Start with +1 to strike and +1 to entangle at level one. +1 to strike at 3rd, 5th, 8th, 11th, and 14th levels. +1 to parry at 4th, 7th, 10th, and 13th levels. +1 to throw at 6th, and 12th levels. +1 to entangle at 2nd, 5th, 8th, 11th, and 14th levels.

W.P. Forked: Includes Sai, Tiger Forks, Tridents, and other weapons with tines. Bonuses: Start with +1 to strike and +2 to entangle. +1 to strike at 3rd, 5th, 8th, 12th and 15th levels. +1 to parry at 5th, 9th, and 13th levels. +1 to throw at 3rd, 7th, 11th and 15th levels. +1 to entangle at 4th, 6th, 8th, 10th, 12th and 14th levels.

W.P. Knife: Combat skill with all types of knives. Bonuses: Start with +1 to throw at level one; +1 to strike at 2nd, 4th, 7th, 10th and 13th levels. +1 to parry at 3rd, 5th, 8th, 11th and 14th levels. +1 to throw at 2nd, 4th, 6th, 9th, 11th, 13th and 15th levels.

W.P. Polearm (New!): This is a combat skill that covers very large spears and polearms, which are really spears mounted with sword, axe, or pickaxe hardware. Bonuses: Start with +1 to strike and parry at level one: +1 to strike at 5th, 8th, 11th and 14th levels. +1 to parry at 4th, 6th, 10th, and 15th levels. +1 to Damage at 3rd, 7th, 9th, and 13th levels.

W.P. Spear: Combat with long weapons, usually tipped with metal points or blades. Bonuses: Start with +1 to strike and parry at level one; +1 to strike at 4th, 7th, 10th, and 13th levels. +1 to parry at 3rd, 6th, 9th, 12th, and 15th levels. +1 to throw at 2nd, 5th, 8th, 11th, and 14th levels.

W.P. Staff: Combat skill with large and small staffs. Bonuses: Start with +1 to strike and parry at level one. +1 to strike at 4th, 7th, 10th and 14th levels. +1 to parry at 2nd, 4th, 6th, 8th, 10th, 12th and 14th levels. +1 to throw at 3rd, 7th, 11th, and 15th levels.

W.P. Large Sword: Combat skill with large swords. Bonuses: Start with +1 to strike at level one. +1 to strike at 3rd, 6th, 9th, 12th, and 15th levels. +1 to parry at 2nd, 3rd, 5th, 7th, 9th, 11th, and 14th levels. +1 to throw at 5th, 10th and 14th levels.

W.P. Short Sword: Combat skill with short swords. Bonuses: Start with +1 to strike and +1 to parry at level one. +1 to strike at 3rd, 6th, 9th, 12th, and 15th levels. +1 to parry at 4th, 7th, 11th, and 15th levels. +1 to throw at 2nd, 6th, 10th and 13th levels.

W.P. Whip (New!): Skill at "whipping" or snapping with long, flexible, light weapons. Bonuses: Start with +1 to strike at level one. +1 to strike at 3rd, 5th, 7th, 9th, 11th and 13th levels. +1 to damage at 4th, 8th, and 12th. +1 to entangle at 2nd, 6th, 8th, 10th, and 14th levels.

Projectile Weapons (not guns)

Includes Bows, Crossbows, Slingshots and small thrown Weapons. The number of shots per melee is totally independent of the character's attacks per melee round.

W.P. Mouth Weapons (New!): Includes blowpipes, mouth darts, and other weapons that depend on a person's lungs and that aim out of the mouth. Bonuses: Start with +1 to strike at 1st level. Add +1 to strike at 4th, 8th and 12th levels. An extra shot per melee round is added at 3rd, 7th and 11th levels.

W.P. Small Thrown Weapons: Includes shuriken, throwing spikes, etc. Bonuses: Start with a rate of fire of three per melee round. +1 to throw at 4th, 7th, 10th and 13th levels. Extra shot per melee at 2nd, 3rd, 5th, 6th, 8th, 9th, 11th, 12th, 14th and 15th levels.

W.P. Bow: Includes short bow, long bow, Samurai bow, Mongol bow, and Ninja bow, as well as modern compound bows. Bonuses: Start with +1 to strike and two shots per melee round. Add +1 to strike at 2nd, 3rd, 5th, 7th, 9th, 11th, 13th and 15th levels. An extra shot per melee round is added at 2nd, 4th, 5th, 8th, 10th, 12th and 14th levels.

W.P. Crossbow: Includes both heavy and light crossbows. Bonuses: 1 shot per melee at first level. +1 to strike at 2nd, 4th, 6th, 8th, 10th, 12th and 14th. An extra shot per melee round is added at 2nd, 3rd, 5th, 7th, 9th, 11th, 13th and 15th levels.

W.P. Slingshot: Includes both ancient slings and modern slingshots. Bonuses: +1 to strike and 2 shots per melee at first level. +1 to strike and an extra shot per melee at 2nd, 4th, 6th, 8th, 10th, 12th and 15th levels.

Weapon Improvisation: Any object, no matter how humble, can be turned into a weapon. Masters of this form are capable of doing extra damage, getting a bonus to strike with the object, and a bonus to parry, a bonus to throw, or a bonus to entangle (pick one). In other words, improvised weapons can only do one thing well and everything else badly. Note that most improvised weapons tend to take as much S.D.C. damage as they deliver. Therefore, weapons like this usually fall apart after a melee round or two. Bonuses (one of the following): +1 to strike, parry, damage, entangle or throw at first level. +1 to strike or parry at 3rd, 6th, 9th, 12th and 15th levels. +1 to damage at 2nd, 4th, 6th, 8th, 10th, 12th and 14th. +1 to throw or entangle at 2nd, 3rd, 5th, 6th, 8th, 9th, 11th, 12th, 14th and 15th levels.

Game Master Section

Tips on good Game Mastering

Game Mastering, like any art, is a mix of science and instinct carefully blended with planning and spontaneous decision-making. There is no "right" way to Game Master, any more than there is a "right" way to paint, sculpt, or write.

It's hard to give you any specific advice, mostly because everybody runs their campaigns a little differently. That's one of the things that makes role-playing such a unique and enjoyable experience. Some people depend on a lot of action with fight scenes every few minutes, others like to have a great deal of character interaction, and others are more "trap" and "puzzle" oriented. In order to figure out what kind of Game Mastering is right for you and for your role-players, it's a good idea to ask yourself some of the following questions:

1. How much action do you want? Most role-players love the big battles, the times when they can live through the excitement of their character's triumphs. However, it's also possible to have too much action. In a perfect role-playing campaign every battle should be important, either as a stepping-stone on the way to final victory, or as a way for the players to gain important information or objectives.

When the player characters don't seem to care about a particular battle, then, chances are, it shouldn't have been in the campaign. In addition, an important battle is probably the end result of a series of minor skirmishes, information gathering, intrigue and mystery.

2. How much interaction do you want? In other words, how much conversation between the player characters and the non-player characters? It's the conversations that make the difference between excellent role-playing and a high-action computer game. Most players really enjoy interaction. It's such interplay that also creates a sense of urgency, danger, friendship and suspense.

However, as much as I like a lot of interaction, sometimes it can turn into too much of a good thing. If a group goes for too long without resolving anything or really accomplishing anything, there's a danger of the campaign slowing down into boredom, there's too much attention to details, and it's lost direction. Generally, when the players seem restless, there's too much interaction, and not enough action. *Pacing* is a delicate balance of ALL the elements of role-playing.

3. How much problem-solving do you want? When role-players (not their characters) have to figure things out by piecing together clues presented in the campaign, that's problem-solving. Every good campaign should present the players with enough problems to keep them guessing and interested, and not be boringly repetitive, too simple, or imposing. Problem-solving should provide challenge and intrigue that leaves the players with a sense of accomplishment when they do figure things out. After all, it's much more satisfying to win through teamwork, knowledge of the villain's weaknesses, and clever strategies than by simply outslugging the enemy.

Of course, too much problem-solving can bring a campaign to a screeching halt and replace enjoyment with frustration. If the players can't seem to move past a puzzle or problem, spend too much time asking detailed questions, or if the action is slowed down by constant confusion, then the Game Master should feel free to add more clues, or a little help from knowledgeable non-player characters.

I'll confess to being guilty of getting all three of these things *wrong* more frequently than I'd like. Even though I've been Game Mastering for many, many years and I get a lot of compliments on the way I run, I still try to keep my eyes and ears open in an attempt to figure out how I can better balance my Game Mastering skills and keep things exciting. It's a challenge I enjoy.

Tips on creating the right atmosphere for Mystic China

Part of the attraction, for me, in running **Mystic China**, is the atmosphere of the place, and the unconventional characters that are found there. Here are some guidelines for helping your campaign seem authentic and unique.

Three differences between Chinese & Japanese Culture. First, make sure you aren't confusing China with other oriental cultures, like Japan (I know I did that a lot when I first started play-testing!). From here in the U.S. it's easy to get notions of China mixed up with images of Japan. Here are three BIG differences that every Game Master should know:

1. The Chinese generally use western-style furniture, including chairs and tables, except in rural temples and monasteries. The Chinese do NOT sit on Japanese-style floor mats and cushions.

2. Traditional clothing for Chinese almost always includes long pants, NOT the kimono-style garb of the Japanese. The only Chinese who wear robes in public are certain monks and religious figures, although richly embroidered jackets or robes may be worn *over* pants.

3. The Chinese do NOT share the Japanese fetish about bowing to each other. Martial art students or members of religious orders may bow to their teachers, but bowing is not a routine greeting in China.

Just to be on the safe side, I'd recommend that Game Masters take a trip to the library and/or the local used book store. Get a couple of picture books or magazines on China and compare them with something similar from Japan. It just a takes a few minutes to figure out the different "looks" of the two cultures. **Note:** *National Geographic* can be an excellent reference. A

copy typically costs a quarter or less at used book stores and flea markets.

A Little Chinese Goes a Long Way. As a Game Master, it's not your job to speak Chinese, only to get across a little extra flavor. Adding just a word or two (or even an accent) can make a lot of difference.

Don't overdo it! The real trick is to make it sound authentic. That works best if you (1) practice words a few times before using them in front of the players, (2) integrate it into the non-player character's "voice," and (3) slur it together. Since you have a lot of choices, don't try using words that give you trouble.

Consider the following examples:

1. "Yes, my friends, you are right! This is a place filled with many evil influences."

2. "Yes, my friends, you are right! This is a place filled with *Hai*, with evil influences."

3. "Yes, my friends, you are right! There is much *Sha Chi* here, what a *Fang Shih* would call a hurtful flow of Chi, many evil influences."

In general, I wouldn't recommend introducing more than a couple of Chinese words per role-playing session. However, if you *aren't* comfortable with using Chinese words, then don't! Just like with the first example (#1), there are other ways of getting across the right atmosphere without tripping over your own tongue.

Consider the common Chinese expression/insult, "Seven Parts Good!" This is something like our English expression, "nine out of ten," except that it means "seven out of eight," and it's a good-natured criticism since it means that getting even a single part wrong means failure. Here are some variations on the same phrase:

"Seven parts good!"

"Only the eighth part counts!"

"Seven parts are the same as no parts at all!"

"The water may be seven parts heated, but it is the eighth part that brings it to a boil. Without the eighth part you have no tea!"

Exaggerating Personalities

Humility & Arrogance:

"I, Po Ling, ignorant as a stone, weak as a fly's larvae, am unworthy of the honor you have bestowed upon me. For example, I have never been able to meditate more than forty hours continuously without having my mind wander. You may be sure that I will weep tears of gratitude when I think upon your kindness in years to come."

Attitude, Attitude, Attitude. Part of the reason that Mystic China can be so much fun to play is the contrast between the extremes. On the one hand you've got the most arrogant, self-centered, egotistical beings on the face of the Earth, Infernals/demons. They love posturing, bellowing, and making stupid pronouncements of their infinite superiority. With demons, lean forward, clench your fists tightly (pounding on a table occasionally is permitted) and speak as deeply as you can (a rumble in your voice can do wonders!). For example, instead of just saying, "Insignificant Worm," try putting in the following emphasis; "IN-sig-NI-fi-CANT WOormmmm!"

Consider these examples:

"Foolish mortal! ———— Kneel and grovel before me, and I will reward you by carving your large bones into flutes, so that your soul will be less troubled by the pain of your death!"

"A demon!?! You merely call me a demon? I am more than any mere demon! I am one of the thirty demons that make the exalted guardians of the Gates of Hell! To call me demon is to call the greatest among you a monkey! One of a race of gibbering primates!! I am no mere demon!"

"Show me the source of your power and I will reduce it to pretty motes of dust, visible only in the beams of the morning sun!"

On the other hand, to get across the whispering, self-effacing, and humble posture of certain monks, try holding your hands together, close to your chest, and bowing your head down slightly. Also, speak softly, whispering when you have something important to say. If the players can't quite hear you, you're likely doing it just right.

Pause frequently. Instead of just saying "I am unworthy," try "I (pause, swallow) am (another pause) un-worthy."

Don't worry about players interrupting you. Monks are used to being interrupted. These rude interruptions are, after all, beneath contempt and their words are "as meaningless as the fluttering of a butterfly's wings."

For really, really deep humility, avoid saying "I" or "me." Instead of "I have failed," or "you should chastise me for my weakness," try "This miserable monk has failed," and "you should chastise this worthless monk."

Imagine, for example, that the local Taoist Priest has offered to let his daughter practice martial arts with one or two of the player characters. Inserting a few of the following phrases into the conversation can definitely add atmosphere to the encounter:

"This weak and helpless maiden begs that you forgive her womanly frailty and will honor her with a small lesson in the martial arts. Please feel free to laugh at my presumption."

"Great warrior, Po Ling is grateful for your restraint. I am certain that my powerless female form would have shattered had you not held you strength and skill in check."

"Po Ling humbly thanks you for your kindness. Her clumsiness is inexcusable. Had not this clumsy, talentless body gotten in your way, you would not have had to injure yourself in order to save me from harm. Please, I beg you, in future do not try so hard to prevent me from being injured. My body should suffer for such ineptness."

Chinese Hours of the Day

Although most people in China have switched to standard western clocks and watches for keeping time, people still refer to the traditional twelve "hours" of the day. Likewise, ancient Immortals and Infernals will usually use the old way of measuring time.

1. The Hour of the Rat – 11:00 PM until 1:00 AM
2. The Hour of the Ox – 1:00 AM until 3:00 AM
3. The Hour of the Tiger – 3:00 AM until 5:00 AM
4. The Hour of the Hare – 5:00 AM until 7:00 AM
5. The Hour of the Dragon – 7:00 AM until 9:00 AM
6. The Hour of the Snake – 9:00 AM until 11:00 AM
7. The Hour of the Horse – 11:00 AM until 1:00 PM
8. The Hour of the Sheep – 1:00 PM until 3:00 PM
9. The Hour of the Monkey – 3:00 PM until 5:00 PM
10. The Hour of the Rooster – 5:00 PM until 7:00 PM
11. The Hour of the Dog – 7:00 PM until 9:00 PM
12. The Hour of the Pig – 9:00 PM until 11:00 PM

So, for example, the "Middle of the Hour of the Rat" would be Midnight, and the "Middle of the Hour of the Horse" would be Noon.

The Calendar of Chinese Astrology

The Chinese New Year begins on the second New Moon after the Winter Solstice, so it's a different day every year. For example, it will be February 19th in 1996, February 7th in 1997, January 28th in 1998, February 16th in 1999 and February 5th in the year 2000.

Here's a table that can be used to look up every year from 1880 until 2119:

1880/1940/2000/2060 Metal Dragon
1881/1941/2001/2061 Metal Snake
1882/1942/2002/2062 Water Horse
1883/1943/2003/2063 Water Sheep
1884/1944/2004/2064 Wood Monkey
1885/1945/2005/2065 Wood Rooster
1886/1946/2006/2066 Fire Dog
1887/1947/2007/2067 Fire Pig
1888/1948/2008/2068 Earth Rat
1889/1949/2009/2069 Earth Ox

1890/1950/2010/2070 Metal Tiger
1891/1951/2011/2071 Metal Rabbit
1892/1952/2012/2072 Water Dragon
1893/1953/2013/2073 Water Snake
1894/1954/2014/2074 Wood Horse
1895/1955/2015/2075 Wood Sheep
1896/1956/2016/2076 Fire Monkey
1897/1957/2017/2077 Fire Rooster
1898/1958/2018/2078 Earth Dog
1899/1959/2019/2079 Earth Pig

1900/1960/2020/2080 Metal Rat
1901/1961/2021/2081 Metal Ox
1902/1962/2022/2082 Water Tiger
1903/1963/2023/2083 Water Rabbit
1904/1964/2024/2084 Wood Dragon
1905/1965/2025/2085 Wood Snake
1906/1966/2026/2086 Fire Horse
1907/1967/2027/2087 Fire Sheep
1908/1968/2028/2088 Earth Monkey
1909/1969/2029/2089 Earth Rooster

1910/1970/2030/2090 Metal Dog
1911/1971/2031/2091 Metal Pig
1912/1972/2032/2092 Water Rat
1913/1973/2033/2093 Water Ox
1914/1974/2034/2094 Wood Tiger
1915/1975/2035/2095 Wood Rabbit
1916/1976/2036/2096 Fire Dragon
1917/1977/2037/2097 Fire Snake
1918/1978/2038/2098 Earth Horse
1919/1979/2039/2099 Earth Sheep

1920/1980/2040/2100 Metal Monkey
1921/1981/2041/2101 Metal Rooster
1922/1982/2042/2102 Water Dog
1923/1983/2043/2103 Water Pig
1924/1984/2044/2104 Wood Rat
1925/1985/2045/2105 Wood Ox
1926/1986/2046/2106 Fire Tiger
1927/1987/2047/2107 Fire Rabbit
1928/1988/2048/2108 Earth Dragon
1929/1989/2049/2109 Earth Snake

1930/1990/2050/2110 Metal Horse
1931/1991/2051/2111 Metal Sheep
1932/1992/2052/2112 Water Monkey
1933/1993/2053/2113 Water Rooster
1934/1994/2054/2114 Wood Dog
1935/1995/2055/2115 Wood Pig
1936/1996/2056/2116 Fire Rat
1937/1997/2057/2117 Fire Ox
1938/1998/2058/2118 Earth Tiger
1939/1999/2059/2119 Earth Rabbit

According to Chinese Astrology, a character's personality is partly based on the year of their birth. Here are some rough, brief interpretations of the different signs:

Rat – Quick of Wit.
Ox – Strong & Steady.
Tiger – Honorable & Powerful.
Rabbit – Talented & Fast.
Dragon – Filled with Energy.
Snake – Opportunistic.
Horse – Hard Working.
Sheep – Patient.
Monkey – Thinks Ahead.
Rooster – Punctual & Precise.
Dog – Loyal & Reliable.
Pig – Comfortable & Friendly.

The Chinese Five Elements:

Wood – Personal growth, health and a concern for living things.
Fire – Filled with energy, but also restless.
Earth – Leadership qualities, but can also mean someone who is never satisfied.
Metal – Quiet, contained, and capable of understanding evil.
Water – Flexible and capable of deep thoughts.

So, for example, a character born in 1970, would be associated with both the element of Metal, and the sign of the Dog (Jin Dou). The character might be expected to be loyal, but also secretive.

A Couple of Notes on the Language of China

1. There are entire books devoted to arguing about how to express the sounds of Chinese in English. For example, "Peking" and "Beijing" are two versions of one city's name, and "Hong Kong" is spelled "Xiang Gang" in Pinyin, and "Hsiang Kang" in Wade-Giles.

Then there's the problem with pronunciation. Whose pronunciation? Mandarin? Cantonese? Or one of the dozen or so other Chinese dialects?

Beats me. So I took the easy way out. Rather than trying for accuracy, I went for simplicity. If a familiar English version of a word or a name exists, that's what I used. Otherwise, I've tried to substitute Chinese-sounding words for each written Chinese character. For *"Yüan-liu K'ao,"* a three-character phrase, I've written *"Yuan Liu Kao."* I break this rule only when it comes to quoting from some other author.

So, having begged off on all the controversies, I'll just make two little comments. The words *Tao* and *Taoism* are pronounced so the "t" sounds more like a "d". The word *Chi* (also seen as *Ch'i* and *Qi*), sounds like "key."

2. When it comes to translating words from Chinese to English, I've mostly gone along with the main reference books. However, whenever possible, I've tried to make the words gender neutral. In other words, many authors translate "*Sheng*" into "the superior man," where I'd rather use "sage" or "wise one."

I'm not doing this because of any feminist leanings (although I do lean toward most feminist arguments), but because Chinese characters are, mostly, gender neutral to begin with. In the original Chinese, the descriptions for alchemists, wizards, warriors, and hermits apply equally to men and women (and, in fact, historically there were plenty of female alchemists, wizards, warriors and hermits in ancient China). For example, the word *Jen*, doesn't mean monk *or* nun, but both at the same time.

Just another example of how the Chinese were a couple of thousand years ahead of their time.

Name Generation One Hundred and Twenty-Nine

Chinese Symbols

Aside from the obvious use for the following tables, generating names for new player and non-player characters, it's also handy for coming up with Chinese nicknames for existing characters.

In English we have relatively few words that sound "alike," such as night and knight, through and threw, and most are spelled differently. There are very few words that are spelled the same and sound the same, but have totally different meanings (strike an opponent, strike out down the road, a strike at the factory, strike a pose, strike a light, and strike oil, not to mention the fact that a strike is a miss in baseball and a hit in bowling).

Chinese, on the other hand, is very rich in confusing similarities. There are words that sound like other words, but have different characters, and there are characters that can mean different words depending on their context.

Then, just to make matters even more confusing, remember that Chinese characters are actually little pictures. Sometimes the picture will represent two things with different words. So, in addition to being able to make fun of someone's name by how it sounds, the Chinese can also make fun of the name by examining how the written character might look like other written characters. In other words, the Chinese can make fun of anyone's name with a little work. Fortunately, just about any name generated from this list can also be perverted, allowing friends and villains to occasionally insult just about anybody's character.

A good way of creating authentic-sounding Chinese names is by rolling percentile dice twice on the following table, to come up with a two-part name. If the name seems incomplete, or unsatisfactory, then consider rolling for a third word or for an additional number-name on the next table.

Note: Rolling for a name and getting the same word twice in a row should be regarded as very lucky! Do not discard the result, but instead double up the name. For example, rolling "47" twice would result in the name "Long Long," or "Double Dragon."

Please note that this is an incredibly simple-minded list. Each of the words was selected because 1) it is represented by a single character, and 2) it sounded cool. A little research with an Chinese-English dictionary should enable any Game Master to come up with a thousand different variations on this list.

Chinese Symbol & Name Table

Roll Percentile Dice

1. An – Tranquility/Peaceful/Quiet/Harmony. A name that gets across spiritual values, like the feeling of being in a remote monastery or religious retreat. Another character with the same sound is the word for "Quail."

2. Bai – White/Pallid. On its own, this would be considered a very unlucky, very dangerous name (of course, some characters might like that!). White is the color of death, things old and aging, and the west, but it is also the color of purity.

3. Bao – Leopard. In contrast to the tiger, leopards are considered quicker and more skillful. A very strong name element.

4. Bi – Writing Brush/Pen. Since the writing brush is the symbol of an educated person, this name is often translated as "Student," "Scholar" or "Artist."

5. Bing – Ice. A symbol of clarity and strength. Bai Bing could be "Ice Purity" or "Pure Ice."

6. Chen – Dust. This can also mean "Transition" or "Change" (the expression "dust to dust" would fit well in Taoism). The name also denotes humility and a sensible precaution;

some superstitious Chinese will give their children very ugly, or very humble names, so that spirits will pass them by.

7. Chi – Energy. This is the same as the "Chi" used in the martial arts and studied by Feng Shui and geomancers. Chi is also called "Breath" or "Divine Breath." Other symbols with the same sound are "Flute" and "Machine."

8. Chih – Ambition/Motivation. It describes someone who is driven to succeed. "Hard-Driving," "Pushy," or "Determined" are other words that could be used as this part of the name. Other characters with the same sound are "Lard" and "Lake."

9. Chin – Clarity/Clear. Used to describe someone who is clear-headed. A character with the same sound means "Gold" or "Metal."

10. Chung – Loyalty/Loyal. A good name indicating humility. Another symbol with the same sound is the word for "Bell" or "Clock".

11. Deng – Lantern. As a person's name, Lantern would describe someone who is helpful, or someone willing to teach or learn.

12. Di – Earth. One of the five elements. A very forceful name.

13. Dong – Cave/Cavern. Since caves are the places of Negative Chi, this is a rather inauspicious name. Caves are also where hermits go to receive divine enlightenment, so they also imply wisdom.

14. Dou – Bean. A good luck name! Since beans are a valued food, as well as being a way of describing something commonplace, it can have a meaning of humility, but also of being an important member of a larger group.

15. E – Goose. While the goose isn't noted for any particular skills or abilities (although geese are considered watchful and are more trusted as watch animals than dogs, since they quack at any disturbance), a goose is considered a sign of very good luck.

16. Fei – Flying. The words "Fast-Moving" or "Dynamic" are easy substitutes.

17. Feng – Wind. One of the five elements. The name Feng Shui means "Wind Water."

18. Fu – Axe. Aside from being an important traditional weapon and a sign of military might, the axe is also one of the primary symbols of imperial power. Another character with the same sound means "Bat," and flying bats are considered signs of incredible good fortune.

19. Gong – Bow/Archer. As in archery.

20. Gou – Dog. Until relatively recently, the Chinese would always include the character for "Dog" when describing anyone not ethnically Chinese.

21. Gu – Drum. A good name for a loud character or someone who insists on telling the truth.

22. Gua – Trigram. The eight Trigrams are considered a very powerful symbol.

23. Guan – Hat. In addition to the common meaning, the word "Hat" also describes anyone official, a bureaucrat, or someone in authority. A term of respect. Another symbol with the same sound is the name for a Taoist Monastery.

24. Gui – Spirit. Gui can be used as a name for any dweller in the Spirit World, including "Wandering Souls," "Ghosts," "Demons" and others.

25. He – Crane. Powerful symbol of strength and skill.

26. Hei – Black/Ebony. The color black is the symbol of "Water," the "North," "Death," and also of "Honor."

27. Hong – Red/Crimson/Scarlet/Ruby/Vermilion. Red is the luckiest color. It also represents "South."

28. Hou – Monkey. Monkeys are considered the most clever animals.

協

29. Hsieh – Unity/Union/Unification.

30. Hu – Tiger. Sign of strength and power.

31. Huan – Badger. In China the badger isn't considered fierce. Instead it's the animal associated with being "Jolly," "Happy," and "Content."

32. Huang – Yellow/Saffron. The color representing China itself, as well as the Emperor. A very lucky name.

33. Huo – Fire. One of the five elements. Combined with something else it can also be "Flaming," "Burning" or "Blaze."

34. Hui – Ashes. Since ash is what remains after a sacrifice (usually the burning of paper money for the dead), it is considered a way of keeping away dangerous ghosts and spirits. A lucky name, but can also be humble.

35. I – Righteousness/Righteous. Another symbol with the same sound could be "Will," "Mind" or "Intent."

36. Jiang – Ginger. One of the most important spices in Chinese cooking. A symbol of prosperity. Another symbol with the same sound means "Spicy."

37. Jiao – Glue. In a more abstract sense, the name can refer to someone who helps keep families and communities together, acting as a social "Glue." Can also use the word "Sticky."

38. Jin – Metal. One of the five elements and a very strong name. Sometimes other metals, such as "Lead," "Tin" or "Silver," can be used in its place.

39. Jing – Mirror. Mirrors are powerful tools for channeling Chi and for deflecting demons and other evil spirits.

40. Ju – Chrysanthemum. This is the flower of autumn and long life.

41. Kai – Open/Expanding.

42. Lan – Blue/Azure/Sapphire. Since this color is considered very unlucky, the words "Unlucky," "Luckless," "Jinx," or "Unfortunate" can be used as part of the name. Good for a little dose of humility.

43. Lang – Waves.

44. Lei – Thunder.

45. Li – Carp. The very luckiest of names. The same as calling someone "Lucky." Another character with the sound "Li" refers to the quality of great social grace and proper ritual, so nicknames might be "Cordial" or "Propriety."

46. Lin – Forest/Grove/Woodland.

47. Long – Dragon. The ultimate symbol of power! Tian-Long is the "Heaven Dragon," Shen-Long is the "Spirit Dragon," Di-Long is the "Earth Dragon," and Long-Wang is the "Dragon King."

48. Lu – Green/Emerald. The color green represents the "East," and the season of "Spring." Green is also the color of jade, a material held in high esteem by the Chinese, so frequently a name will change from (for example) "Green Tiger" to "Jade Tiger."

49. Ma – Horse. Horses are considered strong, valuable, and good workers.

50. Mao – Cat.

51. Mei – Beauty. Another character, also pronounced "Mei," stands for "Eyebrow," which is another way of describing beauty. Another character with the same sound means "Plum" or "Plums".

52. Meng – Dream.

53. Mi – Honey. Can also refer to "Bee" or "Bees." Since honey is rare, expensive and highly sought after, it is considered very good luck. Bees are considered the most honorable and intelligent of insects.

54. Nai – Milk.

55. Nan – Man. In Chinese, unlike English, most titles are not specifically male or female. In other words, Tao Jen means Taoist Nun or Taoist Monk, and a Fa Shih (Shaman) is just as likely to be a man as a woman. Adding Nan (or Nu) makes the character's gender clear.

56. Niu – Ox. Another way of saying, "Strong."

57. Nu – Woman. One meaning is to make it clear that the character is female. However, it can also be used to modify other names, emphasizing their Female/Yin/Dark aspect. For example, combined with Hu (Tiger), the name Nu Hu might be "Tigress," "Dark Tiger" or "Night Tiger."

58. Pao – Cannon/Catapult. Another way of interpreting this word is as "shooting" or "exploding."

59. Pen – Bowl. A lucky name, it also can mean "Stomach."

60. Ping – Peace/Balance of Forces.

61. Qian – Money/Cash. A lucky name, usually meaning riches and wealth, but also implying a character who is greedy and/or money hungry.

62. Qiao – Bridge.

63. Ri – Sun. The sun is considered a powerful Yang, or male symbol. Also refers to the "Three-legged raven," the supernatural incarnation of the sun.

64. Shan – Mountain.

65. She – Snake/Serpent.

66. Shen – Spirit/god. The word is also used to describe someone very skilled.

67. Sheng – Sage/Holy One. Denotes wisdom, but also enlightenment. Another symbol with the same sound is the word for a Chinese musical instrument played in the mouth, "Harmonica" or "Mouth Organ".

68. Shih – Scholar. Usually more of a title than a name, so a "Tao Shi" is a *Wise Man of Taoism* (or, just as likely, a *Wise Woman of Taoism*), "Gong Shi" would be a *Master of Archery*, and "Bi Shi" could refer to a *Professor of Calligraphy*.

69. Shu – Rat. Another symbol with a similar sound means "Book," "Text," or "Volume."

70. Shui – Water/Stream. One of the five elements.

71. Shun – Gentle/Gentleness/Favorable. The picture in the character is of a leaf in a stream.

72. Song – Pine Tree. A good luck sign, also represents someone "Independent."

73. Su – Clean/Clear. Also, in food, the word "Crispy" has a different symbol but the same sound.

74. Suan – Garlic. Another important spice. The plant is considered lucky and an antidote to poison or disease.

75. Tao – Peach. The symbol of immortality. Another symbol that sounds the same is Tao, as in Taoism.

76. Tian – Heaven/Paradise. Another symbol with the same sound is that for "Sweet-one of the five tastes" or "flavors of cooking," so nicknames like "Sweetie," "Candy," "Sugar" and "Honey" are possible.

77. Tieh – Iron. Another character with a similar sound means "Butterfly."

78. Tong – Copper. Also can mean "Bronze" or "Brass," or even "Coin" or "Coins."

79. Tu – Bald Head. Since monks are shaved bald, the name can refer to a monk or someone with monk-like qualities. Or just as "Bald." Another symbol with the same sound means "Rabbit," "Hare" or "Bunny."

80. Wa – Frog. A sign of luck.

81. Wan – Ten Thousand. For the Chinese, this is the most common word used to describe a really big number (sort of like saying "million" in English). It also refers to richness. Another symbol with the same sound means "Bay" or "Lagoon."

82. Wang – King. Another character with the same sound means "Illegitimate" or "Bastard."

83. Xian – Immortal. Another symbol with the same sound is that for "Salt," one of the five flavors of cooked food and also a very valuable substance.

84. Xiang – Elephant.

85. Xiao – Filial Piety. Possibly *the* most important quality in a moral Chinese person. It means someone who really, really respects their parents.

86. Xin – Heart.

87. Xing – Constellation.

88. Xue – Blood.

89. Ya – Duck. Another character with the same sound means "Crow" or "Raven."

90. Yan – Smoke.

91. Yang. In the Yin-Yang of the universe, Yang represents the light, maleness, and positive chi. Another symbol with the same sound means "Goat."

92. Yin. In the Yin-Yang of the universe, Yin represents shadow, the female aspect, and negative chi.

93. Ying – Eagle. There is another character, also pronounced "Ying," which stands for "Courage." Another character with the same sound means "Apricot."

94. Yue – Moon. The moon is the symbol of Yin and powerful female forces. The three-legged toad is the animal deity of the moon.

95. Yun – Clouds. A name of very good fortune.

96. Yung – Eternity/Eternal/Forever.

97. Zhong – Middle. Since China is called Zhong Guo or the "Middle Kingdom," this is a very propitious name. It can also mean "Mark" or "Target."

98. Zhu – Bamboo. A very useful material. Also means "Fast-Growing" and "Resilient." Another symbol with the same sound means "Pig" or "Hog."

99. Zi – Purple/Violet. The color of the imperial court and also the color of heaven.

00. Roll part of the name from the "Numbers" table, below.

Numbers

Roll Percentile Dice

01-10. Yi – One. The most unlucky number, but it also means "Undivided" or "Perfect." The unity of the Tao.

11-20. Er – Two. The ultimate number of Yin and femaleness. It also refers to the Primeval Pair of Yin and Yang, the broken and unbroken lines of the I Ching. It's also a lucky number that means "Easy."

21-30. San – Three. The principle number of Yang and maleness. A lucky number that implies fertility.

31-40. Si – Four. The Four Forms, Heaven, Earth, Man and Woman, of the I Ching.

41-50. Wu – Five. A very important number (the Five Elements, etc.).

51-60. Liu – Six. A lucky number meaning "Long-Life" or "Longevity."

61-70. Qi – Seven.

71-80. Ba – Eight. The next most important number after five (the Eight Trigrams, the Eight Pillars of Wisdom, etc.). A very lucky number meaning "Prosperity."

81-90. Jiu – Nine. The luckiest number, meaning "Perpetual Luck" or "Eternity."

91-00. Shi – Ten. A very lucky number.

Counting Past Ten

To count from eleven to nineteen, just make simple combinations: Shi Yi (11), Shi Er (12), Shi San (13), etc. The numbers from twenty to ninety are also simple combinations like Er Shi (20), San Shi (30), Si Shi San (43), etc. Bai is the root word for the hundreds, so we get Er Bai (200), Wu Bai (500) and numbers like Qi Bai Ba Shi San (783). Qian is the root for thousand; Yi Qian Si Bai Jiu Shi (1,490) or Liu Qian Shi Wu (6,015). Wan is then the root for ten thousand; San Wan San Qian San Bai San Shi San (33,333).

More Notes on Numbers as Names

Numbers as part of a character's name can be interpreted in different ways. "Er" could be "Two," but it can also be "Double," or "Twofold," or "Pair," or "Couple," or "Duo," depending on what it describes.

For example, in Barry Hughart's terrific fantasy novel, *Bridge of Birds*, the main character, Lu Yu, is called "Number Ten Ox" (Shi Niu), because he was the tenth of his father's sons and because he was very strong. By the way, the character usually introduces himself by saying, "My surname is Lu and my personal name is Yu, but I am not to be confused with the eminent author of *The Classic of Tea*. Everyone calls me Number Ten Ox."

With a little work, a name like Ba Bao (no kidding! I just rolled this up!), can be made into a nifty piece of role-playing background:

"I am Ba Bao, or Eight-Ways-Like-a-Leopard! Those who would win my favor call me Ba Bao because I am fortunate to share the five beneficial qualities of the leopard. I am quick and strong, quiet in movement, clever, and skillful with sharp implements. Others call me Ba Bao because I share two neutral qualities with my namesake, that I am watchful and that I am very careful. Finally, with regard to the last quality that I share with the leopard, I would recommend that no one make light of my problem skin!"

"The Hundred Family Names"

A common Chinese expression when referring to all of the people of China is "The Hundred Family Names." Traditionally, there have been relatively few (compared to a population of hundreds of millions!) surnames. Remember that in China the surname, or family name, goes **first**, before the character's personal name.

In spite of the exact figure of 100, current Chinese Almanacs, while they still list the chapter "The Hundred Family Names," actually list 400 to 500 different family names. In each case, each name is identified according to its place of origin ("the family Chan comes from Wan Chuen County"), and according to some famous person who is considered one of the ancestors of the family name ("the Kung family is descended from Kung Sheng-Yen, or Confucius").

Here's a short list, with some of the most common names, allowing for the generation of a family name by rolling a twenty-sided die (1D20):

1. Chan	6. Chu	11. Kung	16. Wan
2. Chin	7. Deng	12. Lee	17. Wong
3. Ching	8. Fung	13. Lim	18. Yee
4. Cho	9. Hoi	14. Sung	19. Yim
5. Chow	10. Hung	15. Tse	20. Yu

Examples of Generated Names: Just as an experiment, I decided to get out some dice and roll up a few Chinese names:

1. Rolled 53 Twice, resulting in the name Mi Mi. While the obvious meaning, "Double Honey," might be appropriate for a court figure or a merchant, a fighter character could be called "Bee Swarm."

2. Rolled 46 and 21, resulting in the name Lin Gu, or "Forest Drum," the perfect name for a martial artist, a monk or, best of all, a hermit. While that sounds pretty cool, just for the fun of it I rolled a 1D10 on the Number Table and came up with 9 (Jiu). So the name could be Jiu Lin Gu, "Number Nine Forest Drum," or "Nine Forest Drums" or "Ninefold Forest Drum."

3. Rolled 58 and 01, resulting in the name Pao An, or "Cannon of Tranquility." Probably my favorite name on this list, since the idea of a Cannon being "Tranquil" is rather contradictory, which means the character could also be contradictory.

4. Rolled 16 and 25, resulting in the name Fei He, or "Flying Crane." Since the Crane is one of the major animals represented in the martial arts (plus, it's a lucky symbol!), a flying crane would be viewed as something of awesome speed and power.

5. Rolled 01 and 46, resulting in the name An Lin, or "Tranquil Forest." Cool!

6. Rolled 97 and 83, resulting in the name Zhong Xiang, or "Middle Elephant." By itself this is pretty neat, since it has a wonderful combination of boastfulness ("I'm mighty as an elephant,") and modesty ("but I'm just the middle elephant."). Give the multiple meanings of Zhong, the character could also be "Elephant Defender of the Middle Kingdom" or, for a character with a sense of humor, "Target the size of an Elephant" ("Bozo! How could you miss me? I'm Zhong Xiang! Ha!").

7. Rolled 38 and 13, resulting in Jin Dong, or "Metal Cave." The natural nickname of the character would then be "Gold Mine!" Combining the idea of Metal, one of the five elements, with a cave, a strong symbol of Negative Chi, means the character is like a primal force.

8. Rolled 64 and 39, resulting in Shan Jing, or "Mountain Mirror." Which sounds like the kind of character who might be family oriented, so I rolled up a family surname. The result was Lim Shan Jing (the surname, in China, always goes first). *Lim Shan Jing*, I like the sound of that!

9. Rolled 18 and 66, resulting in Fu Shen, or "Axe Spirit." Other possible interpretations are "Skilled Axe" and "Truth Spirit."

10. Rolled 24 and 54, resulting in Gui Nai, or "Ghost Milk." This would be a very appropriate name for someone dabbling in Chi, or someone who is interested in the undead. While most common folks would consider it unlucky (and probably be a bit afraid of someone with such a spooky name), the character could let it symbolize courage.

English-to-Chinese Glossary

Please note that a spoken Chinese word may represent different written characters, and therefore may have several different meanings.

1 = Yi	8 = Ba
2 = Er	9 = Jiu
3 = San	10 = Shi
4 = Si	100 = Bai
5 = Wu	1,000 = Qian
6 = Liu	10,000 = Wan
7 = Qi	1,000,000 = Chao

Abundance = Jao
Adhesive/Sticky = Nien
Age = Ling
Alchemy = Tan
Alchemy, External/Chemical = Wai Tan
Alchemy, Internal/Yogic = Nei Tan
Ambition = Chih
Angel = E
Ant = Ma Yi
Apricot = Ying
Apricot Pits = Hsing Jen
Archer = Gong
Armor = Kai
Ashes = Hui
Atemi = Tien Hsueh
Atlas = Thu
Attack = Kung
Autumn = Qiu Tian
Axe = Fu

Badger = Huan
Bamboo = Zhu
Bastard = Wang
Bay = Wan
Bean = Dou
Beautiful = Luan
Bee/Bees = Mi
Bell, with clapper = To
Bell = Chung
Black = Hei
Blind = Mang
Blind Man or Blind Woman = Mang Jen
Blood = Xue
Blue (color) = Lan
Bone/Bones = Ku
Bottle/Jar = Lei
Bow (archer's) = Gong or Kun
Bow/Bowing (in respect) = Kou Tou
Bowl = Pen
Brass = Tou
Bridge = Qiao
Brother, Younger = Ti, or Ti Ti
Brother, Elder = Ke, or Ke Ke
Brush (paint brush, ink brush) = Bi
Burn = Jan
Butterfly = Tieh
Cannon = Pao
Carp (fish) = Li

Cash = Qian
Cat = Mao
Catalog = Yao
Catapult = Pao
Cauldron = Hu
Cave = Dong
Cavern = Dong
Centipede = Kung
Ceremony = Li
Chain = Lien
Chrysanthemum = Ju
Cinnabar = Chu Sha
Clam, Giant = Chan
Clamshells = Ko Pu
Clarity = Chih
Clear = Chih
Clock = Chung
Cloud/Clouds = Yun
Comet = Po
Conceal = Ni
Constellation = Xing
Copper = Tong
Courage = Ying
Crane = He (or Kuan)
Crispy = Su
Crocodile = Ngoh
Crossbow = Neu
Crow = Ya, or Wu
Dagger = Bi Shou
Dark = An
Deer = Lu
Demon = Kuei, or Mei
Devil = Mo (A Mo has more powerful magic than a Kuei or Mei).
Dice = Tou
Divination = Po
Doctrine = Chiao
Dog = Gou
Dollar = Yuan
Dove = Ko
Dragon = Long
Dragon Bones = Lung Ku
Dragonfly = Qing Ting
Dream = Meng
Drug/Drugs = Yao
Drum = Gu
Duck = Ya
Duke = Kung
Dust = Chen
Eagle = Ying
Earth = Di
East = Dong Feng
Eel = Shan
Egret = Lu
Eight = Ba
Elegant = No
Elephant = Xiang
Elf = Wang
Elixir = Fa
Elixir of Immortality = Tan
Emerald = Lu
Emperor = Ti
Energy = Chi
Epsom Salts = Hsiao Shih
Eternity/Eternal = Yung
Evil = Hai
Falcon = Ying
Fast-Growing = Zhu
Father = Ba, or Ba Ba
Female/Feminine = Yin
Filial Piety = Hsiao, or Xiao
Fire = Huo
Five = Wu
Flute = Chi, or Yo
Fly/Flying = Fei
Fly (the insect) = Cang Ying
Forest = Lin
Forever = Yung
Fortune Telling = Po Mai
Fortune Teller = Po Jen
Four = Si
Frog = Wa (see also, toad)
Garlic = Suan
Gentle = Shun
Ghost = Kuei
Ginger = Chiang
Girl = Niang
Glue = Jiao
Goat = Yang
God = Shen
Goddess = E
Gods, Profane or Evil = Su Shen
Gold = Chih
Gong = Lo
Good/Goodness = Jen
Goose = E
Green = Lu
Grove = Lin
Guerrilla Troops = Chi
Gun = Chiang
Hair, Human = Luan Fa
Hammer = Chui
Handcuffs = Liao
Hare = Tu
Harmony = An
Hat = Guan
Hawk = Chan
Healthy = Chuang
Heart = Xin
Heaven = Tian
Hell/Hades = Ming
Herb/Herbs = Yao
Hermit = Ou Ying
Hide = Ni
History = Shih
Hog = Zhu
Honey = Mi
Horse = Ma
Humble = Jang
Humility = Chien
Hunger = Ngo
Ice = Bing
Illegitimate = Wang
Immortal = Xian
Insult = Pang
Integrity = I
Iodine = Tieh
Iron = Tieh
Irony/Ironic = Feng
Jade = Yu
Jade, Powdered = Yu Fen
Jar/Bottle = Lei
Joke = Tsou
Judgement = Chih
Key = Yo
King = Wang
Laboratory = Tsao Wu
Lagoon = Wan
Lake = Chih
Lantern = Deng
Lard = Chih
Law = Ling
Lead (the metal) = Chien
Leopard = Bao
Lichen = Hsieh
Lie/Falsehood = Huang
Light = Yang
Lion = Shi Zi
Lock = Yo
Lotus/Lotus Root = Ngou
Loyal = Chung
Loyalty = Hsin
Lunatic = Feng
Machine = Chi
Mage/Magician = Wu
Male/Masculine = Yang
Man = Nan
Mercury/Quicksilver = Hung
Metal = Jin
Middle = Chung
Milk = Nai
Mirror = Jing
Mirror, Metal = Chien
Miscellaneous = Tsa Tsu
Mole (digging animal) = Yen
Money = Qian
Monkey = Hou
Moon = Yue
Mosquito = Wen Zi
Moss = Hsieh
Mother = Ma, or Ma Ma
Motivation = Chih
Mountain = Shan
Mouse = Hsi
Mudra = Yin
Never = Pu
Miss (as in Mr., Mrs. and Miss) = Niang

Officer = Kuan
Old Man = Lao Jen
One = Yi
Onion = Suan Chiu
Open = Kai
Orchid = Lan
Oriole = Li
Orphan = Ku
Owl = Chih
Ox = Niu
Parrot = Ying
Peace = Ping
Peaceful = An
Peach/Peaches = Tao
Peach Pits = Tao Jen
Pen/Pencil = Bi
Pewter = La
Philosopher = Tzu
New = Hsin
Nine = Jiu
No = Pu (Mandarin)
Noble/Nobleman = Chun
North = Bei Feng
Phoenix = Feng
Pig = Zhu
Pigeon = Ko
Pine Tree = Song
Pistol = Chiang
Plum/Plums = Mei
Pot = Lei
Powdered Jade = Yu Fen
Powdered Silver = Yin Fen
Prunes = Wu Mei
Purple = Zi
Quail = An
Quartz = Pai Shih Ying
Quiet = An
Rabbit = Tu
Rain = Yu
Rat = Shu
Raven = Ya
Red = Hong
Red, deep or dark = Chiang
Reform = Kai
Resilient = Zhu
Reveal = Kai
Riddle = Mi
Righteousness/Righteous = I
Ritual = Li
Roc (mythical giant bird) = Peng
Ruby = Hong
Rule = Ling
Rust = Hsiu
Sage = Sheng
Salt = Xian
Scholar = Shih
Schoolmate = Tong Tsu
Seagull = Ou
Secret Society = Hung Mun
Serpent = She
Seven = Qi
Shackles = Liao
Shadow = Yin
Shark = Sha
Shovel = Chan
Silk = Szu
Silver = Yin
Silver, Powdered = Yin Fen
Sister, Younger = Mei, or Mei Mei
Sister, Elder = Chieh, or Chieh Chieh
Six = Liu
Skeleton = Ku
Skull, if living = Tu
Skull, of dead = Lou
Slander = Pang
Smoke = Yan
Snake = She
Sorcerer/Sorceress = Wu
South = Nan Feng
Spear = Chiang
Spider = Chi Chu
Spirit = Gui, or Kuei
Spirit, godlike = Shen
Spirit, magical = Mo
Spirit, water = Shui Ling
Spring (the season) = Chun Tian
Sprite = Liang
Spy = Tieh
Staff (weapon) = Chang
Starvation = Ngo
Steel = Lou
Sticky = Nien
Stomach = Pen
Stork = Ho
Stove = Hao
Strong = Chuang
Student = Tzu
Sugar/Sweet = Tian
Sulphur = Liu
Summer = Xia Tian
Sun = Ri
Sword = Jen
Target = Zhong or Chung
Tea = Cha
Teacher = Lao Shih
Ten = Shi
Ten Thousand = Wan
Three = San
Thunder = Lei
Tiger = Hu
Tin (the metal) = Hsi
Toad = Min (see also frog)
Tortoise, of Divination = Kuei
Tortoise, Sea = Ao
Traitor = Tieh
Traitor = Kuei
Tranquility = An
Tree = Shu
Tree, Pine = Song
Trident = Bar
Trigram = Gua
Turtle, River = Pieh
Two = Er
Unicorn = Chi Lin
Unity/Union = Hsieh
Vinegar, Concentrated = Yen Tsu
Vinegar, Rice = Tsu
Violet (the color) = Zi
Vulture = Chiu
Water = Shui
Water, ritual or holy = Hsuan Chiu
Waves = Lang
Weasel = Yu
West = Xi Feng
Whale = Ching
White = Bai
Wind = Feng
Winter = Dong Tian
Woman = Nu
Woods = Lin
Worm = Qiu Yin
Yellow = Huang
Yes = Shi (Mandarin), or Hai (Cantonese)

Money in Mystic China

Personally, as a Game Master, I prefer to be fairly generous with my player characters. As I see it, **Mystic China** is mostly about encountering Infernal Demons, Epic Immortals, and supernatural evil. It's not about the nickel and dime expenses of the player characters. That said, there are plenty of good role-playing opportunities that involve money. Officials and criminals will want bribes, everyone would like to be truly rich, and there are always funny situations where player characters, finding themselves totally broke, have to struggle.

What I'm trying to say is, only use the rules for money when it seems like it's important, appropriate and/or fun! If the role-playing is getting bogged down in details or if things are getting boring, remember that role-playing is about adventure, not economics. On the other hand, being unreasonably generous can wreck the dynamics of a game and make the players careless and foolish in how their characters spend money, because the G.M. always works things out in their favor. Be reasonable and fair.

Symbols & Money

$ = Standard World Price, in U.S. dollars. Other prices may be more or less of a bargain, depending on the item and the seller. When characters buy their initial equipment, it should be with the U.S. dollar price.

¥ = Yuan, the currency of mainland China. This is the price one would expect to pay in the more remote areas of mainland China. While it often reflects a black market price and is usually expensive, some things are dirt cheap.

The small change units are called Jiao and Fen: ¥1 = 10 Jiao = 100 Fen. Paper currency consists of ¥100, ¥50, ¥20, ¥10, 5 Jiao, 2 Jiao, and 1 Jiao. Coins are 1, 2, and 5 Fen. *One U.S. dollar is usually worth around two Yuan ($1 = ¥2).*

HK$ = What you pay in Hong Kong, shopping for a bargain. Hong Kong dollars are printed and controlled by the city's two largest banks, **The Hong Kong and Shanghai Banking Corporation** and **The Standard Chartered**. Bills look more or less the same, except that the pictures will be one or the other's headquarter buildings. There are HK$1,000 (gold), HK$500 (brown), HK$100 (red), HK$50 (blue), HK$20 (orange) and HK$10 (green) bills. Coins are HK$0.05, HK$0.10, HK$0.20, HK$0.50, HK$1, HK$2 and HK$5, each with a picture of the Queen of England. *One U.S. dollar is usually worth around seven Hong Kong dollars ($1 = HK$7).*

Basic Exchange Rates

At Hong Kong Bank – $1 = ¥2.5 = HK$7
Tourist Desk/Hotel – $1 = ¥2 = HK$6.5
Mainland Official – $1 = ¥1.5 = HK$6
Black Market – $1 = ¥3.5 = HK$9

Random Fluctuations in World Exchange Rates:

01-15 Strong US$: Add ¥0.5 to all exchanges of dollars for Yuan. Add HK$1 to all exchanges of dollars for Hong Kong dollars. **Bank Rate:** $1 = ¥3 = HK$6.

16-25 Weak US$: Subtract ¥0.5 from all exchanges of dollars for Yuan. Subtract HK$1 from all exchanges of dollars for Hong Kong dollars. **Bank Rate:** $1 = ¥2 = HK$4.

26-45 Boom Times in Hong Kong: Subtract HK$2 from all exchanges of dollars for Yuan or Hong Kong dollars. **Bank Rate:** $1 = ¥2.5 = HK$5.

46-65 Growth in Mainland China: The Yuan is now worth more. Subtract ¥0.5 from all exchanges. **Bank Rate:** $1 = ¥1.5 = HK$7.

66-75 Troubles in Hong Kong: Big troubles in Hong Kong mean the money takes a dive. Add HK$1 to all exchanges. **Bank Rate:** $1 = ¥2.5 = HK$8.

76-90 Recession in Mainland China: The economy looks bad. Add ¥0.5 to all exchanges. **Bank Rate:** $1 = ¥3 = HK$5.

91-95 China Wobbles: Things look very bad. Yuan drops, so add ¥1.5 to ¥9 (3D6 times 0.5) to all exchanges. With things so unstable, another Yuan drop can happen every week (add another 1D6 times ¥0.5). **Bank Rate:** Varies, but an average (rolled 10 on 3D6) is $1 = ¥7.5 = HK$7.

96-98 China Suppresses Hong Kong: A military move, sending troops to seize the major facilities and banks of Hong Kong, sends the world economy into a panic. Eventually, if the Chinese economy remains stable (this could be the move that causes Balkanization, above), the result will be a loss of value of the Yuan, and a disastrous fall for the Hong Kong dollar. **Bank Rate:** $1 = ¥4 = HK$40.

99-00 China Balkanizes! The government of China falls apart completely. There is chaos on the mainland, while revolutionaries, factions and generals seize control of different provinces. The Yuan becomes nearly worthless. Hong Kong isn't too stable either, under these conditions, so add HK$1 to HK$6 to the Hong Kong dollar. **Bank Rate:** $1 = ¥101 to ¥600 (roll 1D6+Percentile) = HK$8 to HK$13 (1D6).

Examples of Cost of Living

A Frugal Week's Visit to Hong Kong. Staying at the YMCA or in some low dive, walking almost everywhere, and eating cheap. No souvenirs. **Cost:** $400/¥800/HK$2,800.

A Tourist Week in Hong Kong. Living in a decent hotel ($200/day), eating out every day, visiting the sights, participating in nightlife, and shopping, shopping, shopping. **Cost:** $3,000/¥6,000/HK$21,000.

Living Cheap for a Week in Hong Kong. Long-time residents will have figured out how to get by with very little money. Housing is usually in a dormitory or a room in a family house. Other possibilities are a small space in one of the alley way squatter areas, or part of a cabin on one of the innumerable sampans crowding the harbor area. Cooking for oneself, or paying to eat with a family, also cuts expenses. **Cost:** $100/¥175/HK$580.

Living Well for a Week in Hong Kong. An independent character or an experienced traveler may want a small apartment, either a private place on one of the islands or sharing with a single roommate in a larger place downtown. This means eating out much of the time, but in good-quality, low-priced restaurants. **Cost:** $500/¥1100/HK$3,000.

A Week's Touristing in Mainland China. Covers all the costs of hotels, meals, transportation, expenses, and even a few souvenirs. Usually involves seeing Peking, the Great Wall, and at least two or three other sights during the week. **Cost:** $1.000/¥2.000/HK$5,000.

A Week's Living Expenses in Mainland China. Sharing living space with a family or getting a tiny room in a dormitory. Food is simple and home-cooked, with no allowance for visiting restaurants. **Cost:** $25/¥45/HK$155.

One Week of a Foot or Bicycle Expedition. All the food and basic supplies necessary for a one week trip into the Chinese wilderness. **Cost:** $280/¥600/HK$2,000 per person.

One Week of a Motor Vehicle Expedition. Figuring in all that's needed, including gas for a single vehicle's week's travel.

Cost: $700/¥1,400/HK$5,000 for the group, plus $200/¥400/HK$1,500 for each participant.

Player Character Saving Options

Since the world of the player characters in **Mystic China** can be somewhat unsettled, they should decide how to keep their spare money. Basically the choices boil down to cash, bank accounts, traveller's checks, valuables or a combination.

Cash. Obviously, this is handy to have around. However, in large quantities it can attract trouble. If you lose it, it's gone. A lot of money in a particular currency could lose value depending on trade and other economic conditions. Player characters should decide in advance how much they'd like of each currency, whether it be US$, ¥, HK$, or other (don't worry about the exchange rate, just put down, for example, "$500 in Swiss money and $200 in Japanese Yen").

Traveller's Checks. While characters lose 1% of the value when buying traveller's checks, they gain the security of knowing that the money can be refunded if the checks are lost, stolen or destroyed. Furthermore, they can be converted at most banks and many government offices (post offices, etc.). Most traveller's checks are in U.S. dollars and are accepted as valuable currency at most places, even in remote areas of Tibet or Mongolia, although rates of exchange may vary.

Bank Accounts. Aside from the safety factor, a character with money in the bank can also get credit cards which make it easy to pay for stuff anywhere there are telephone connections. Also, an ATM (Automatic Teller Machine) card, provided by the bank, lets characters get at their money twenty-four hours a day, at least in urban centers where the bank has branches. Player characters should specify the *nationality* of their bank. Most large international banks have branches in Hong Kong. Hong Kong banks have branches overseas, as well as in mainland China.

Valuables/Trade Goods. Sometimes it makes more sense to carry your wealth in a portable form. The valuables listed here are generally easier to carry than cash, and are good for trading, bribing, etc. **Note:** Fake, counterfeit, or cheap knock-offs cost 75% less, but could lead to big trouble if discovered.

Containers are included in the total cost. **Pouches** are small bags, usually of cloth or leather, that can be easily concealed in clothing, or anywhere else. **Cases** are easy-to-handle briefcases or suitcases.

1. Antique Chinese Bronzes. Case of four durable, easy to carry, easy to sell, Chinese Bronze sculptures, each at least 200 years old. The longer you hold on to them, the more valuable they become. **Note:** These are worth 20% more *outside* of China. **Cost:** $10,000/¥15,000/HK$65,000.

2. Computer Processor Chips. Pouch of thirty (30) microprocessor chips or a case of three thousand (3,000) memory (RAM) chips. **Note:** These tend to lose their value over time, dropping to one-third the price in one year and becoming worthless within two years. **Cost:** $15,000/¥50,000/HK$125,000.

3. Gold Coins. One of the most popular ways of holding onto wealth. A pouch contains ten small gold coins. **Note:** In troubled, war-torn areas, the value of gold can skyrocket, up to ten times the usual value, but prices will fluctuate up and down 3D6% depending on the buyer.

Cost: $2,000/¥5,000/HK$12,000.

4. Handheld Electronic Games. Case of two dozen. Each comes with a half-dozen game cartridges and a pair of extra batteries. **Cost:** $4,800/¥15,000/HK$25,000.

5. Jade Miniatures. A pouch of three very rare jade antique miniatures, or a case of 24 collector quality pieces of carved jade. **Cost:** $12,000/¥20,000/HK$70,000. They are worth 10% more *outside* of China.

6. Jewels/Gemstones. Either a pouch of 24 precious stones (diamonds, emeralds or rubies, from ½ carat, to three carats), or a case of 500 semi-precious stones, of varying sizes. **Cost:** $20,000/¥40,000/HK$140,000. Prices will fluctuate up or down 4D6% depending on the buyer and the country (down in China).

7. Palladium Books T-Shirts. Case of 24 of these hot **Rifts®** T-Shirts, designed by Kevin Siembieda, with art by Kevin Long, make for great bribes, gifts, or trade goods. So do other similar "hot" American items.

Cost: $500/¥6,000/HK$9,000.

8. Pocket Pistols. Case of one dozen compact "personal protection" automatic pistols. High quality, with polished metal and wood, but low powered. Each includes two 7-round clips of 7.62 mm pistol ammunition (2D6 damage).

Cost: $7,500/¥17,000/HK$55,000. Prices will fluctuate up or down 10% depending on the buyer and the country.

9. Wei Qi (Go) Game Sets. Case of eight sets of exquisite stones (black & white), in sixteen (16) bowls, with eight (8) inexpensive folding boards. **Cost:** $4,000/¥9,000/HK$27,000.

10. Wristwatches. Case of 72 high-quality watches, or a pouch of six ultra-expensive designer watches. Prices will fluctuate up or down 10% depending on the buyer and the country. **Cost:** $30,000/¥75,000/HK$20,000.

Paperwork & Documents

Note: Fake documents can cost 10% to 60% more depending on the supplier, purchaser, situation and country.

Entry/Exit Visa. The paperwork that lets someone in or out of countries with restrictions. Even "free" border countries require entry/exit visas of particular classes of people, or for people from particular countries. For example, Canadians are freely admitted into the U.S.A., but those from Mexico or Europe are not. **Note:** The cost of counterfeit visas is about the same as the cost of obtaining genuine paperwork through bribery. **Cost:** $100/¥80/HK$400.

Export/Import Permits. The paperwork necessary to carry non-personal items across borders. Removing an archeological artifact or object of art from most countries requires an Export Permit. Taking expensive equipment (such as professional video equipment), or a commercial quantity (a dozen cameras) into most countries requires an Import Permit. Moving any kind of military hardware and/or weapons requires **both** Export and Import Permits. Costs for bribery and counterfeiting are about the same. **Cost:** $250/¥400/HK$1,200.

Fake Civilian I.D. All the paperwork needed to pass a character off as someone else (usually a local resident), including passport, driver's license, national I.D. card, etc.

Cost: $500/¥1,000/HK$2,000.

Military I.D. Includes passport, I.D. card, insignia of rank and unit, credentials and certifications, plus medals and commendations. **Cost:** $1,500/¥2,500/HK$7,000.

Set of fake government I.D. Includes all personal paperwork, plus papers necessary to identify the character as a high-ranking employee of that government. **Cost:** $3,000/¥5,500/HK$17,000.

Counterfeit Money. One million dollars, or Yuan, or Hong Kong dollars, or any other currency, in fraudulent bills. Not tremendously convincing, so those familiar with the type of money can examine a bill and detect the hoax (68% chance of recognizing fakes). However, for people not used to that kind of cash (for example, passing Hong Kong dollars in Wisconsin, or passing U.S. dollars in a remote village of China), it's sometimes possible to pass it off as genuine (only a 10% chance of being recognized as a fake). **Cost:** $15,000/¥30,000/HK$60,000.

Hell Money. Burning Hell Money, in the name of someone dead, is said to channel the money toward the departed soul. Package contains one hundred million Hell Money dollars in $10,000 bills. **Cost:** $1/¥1/HK$1; this is NOT real currency accepted by any country.

Apparel, Equipment & Supplies Price Lists

There are *three* prices for each item: $, ¥, and HK$. Prices reflect the "typical" going rate in that area. So, for example, $5/¥8/HK$30, means the item would probably cost $5 in the U.S., or an equivalent price in Canada and Western Europe, ¥8 (about $4) in mainland China, and HK$30 (a little less than $4).

Clothing

Character Outfits: All clothing "outfits" are sold in full sets. In other words, enough to go at least a week without doing the laundry. Each "outfit" includes underwear, shoes, hats and all other accessories that might be needed. Also includes a full set of appropriate (basic) luggage, sufficient to contain the entire wardrobe.

Temple Outfit: Simple robes, a cloak of heavier material, and sandals. **Cost:** $50/¥70/HK$200.

Poor Outfit: Clothing suitable for someone down on their luck. Everything will be used, older, and shabby. Includes mostly casual clothing, but with at least one threadbare dress-up suit or dress. **Cost:** $100/¥120/HK$400.

Casual Outfit: Blue jeans, casual pants, selection of shirts and sweaters, plus a pair of jackets, all of reasonable quality. **Cost:** $250/¥400/HK$1,250.

Exercise Outfit: Sweat pants, sweatshirt and jacket, with athletic shoes or simple Kung Fu outfit of cotton or silk. **Cost:** $500/¥800/HK$2,500.

Heavy Work Clothing: Suitable for a construction site, factory, or other blue collar work place. Includes steel-toed shoes, hard hat, and other protective gear, along with suitable work clothing. **Cost:** $750/¥1,200/HK$5,000.

Military Outfit: Includes three sets of fatigues, two semi-dress uniforms, one formal dress uniform, jackets for mild or cold weather, rain gear, and full overcoat. Includes gloves, ties/scarves, and insignia for one nation.

Cost: $1,000/¥1,800/HK$6,000.

Business Outfit: The character can dress for the bank, board meetings, and to impress potential clients.

Cost: $2,000/¥4,500/HK$11,000.

Prosperous Outfit: Clothing suitable for hanging out with rich, jet-set types. All items are expensive designer labels. Includes everything from fashionable swimsuit to formal wear (gown or tuxedo). **Cost:** $10,000/¥34,000/HK$60,000.

Clothing Gimmicks

Buying a gimmick means it gets installed in just one set of clothing, NOT in an entire outfit.

1. Reversible Suit. The character can simply turn the suit inside-out and completely change their appearance. For example, there could be a jumpsuit on one side, business suit on the other (with shirt, tie & pocket handkerchief).

Cost: $1,000/¥1,200/HK$5,000.

2. Bullet-Proofing. A layer of bullet-proof material is built in between layers of fabric. 40 S.D.C. and gives the character an A.R. of 13. **Cost:** $2,500/¥7,500/HK$15,000.

3. Nerve Gas Protection. To protect against gases that go in through the pores of the skin, the suit is made with a skintight underlayer or to be airtight with drawstrings at the ankles, wrists and neck. In either case, the character will still need protection for the feet, hands and head. **Cost:** $8,000/¥15,000/HK$40,000.

4. Designer Pockets. Special holders for just about anything. Even something the size of a sawed-off shotgun can be concealed in a pocket of the right piece of clothing. **Cost:** $100/¥150/HK$500 each.

5. Fake Wound Capsules. Plastic capsules filled with fake blood are placed in the suit. Each has a small explosive "cap." When triggered, the cap ruptures the capsule and blows a hole in the outer layer of the suit, causing the "blood" to splatter and then seep out. Two can be installed as a pair, one on each side of the body, to make it look like a bullet went all the way through. A small hand or radio control is included. **Cost:** $500/¥2,500/HK$3,000 each.

6. Wired. A garment, as small as a single glove, is wired so that a thin network of electronics is fitted between the layers of the material. When activated, the unit can be used to emit a homing signal, or be used as a listening device/radio transmitter. **Cost:** $4,000/¥11,000/HK$29,000.

Computers & Electronics Equipment

Portable (lap top) Computer. A state-of-the-art computer, battery operated, complete with built-in modem and pointing device. The hard drive contains a full range of software. **Cost:** $3,500/¥10,000/HK$20,000.

Personal Computer System. Includes computer, monitor, modem, black-and-white printer, optical scanner, keyboard and full software. **Cost:** $3,500/¥11,000/HK$21,000.

Desk Top Publishing Setup. Has everything included in the personal computer system, but with the added ability to create full-color publication quality books, pamphlets, magazines, I.D. cards, etc. Also includes a full selection of fonts, digitized color photographs, and graphic images, all on CD-ROM. **Cost:** $7,500/¥25,000/HK$50,000.

Video Camera. A lightweight, battery operated, portable video camera, suitable for both outdoor and indoor use. Includes a dozen blank tapes and a weatherproof metal carrying case. **Cost:** $1,000/¥2,700/HK$4,900.

Video Production Mini-Studio. One large suitcase has two monitors built-in, along with a two-tape video cassette recorder (VCR) and editing equipment. Designed to be plugged into a video camera. **Cost:** $4,000/¥14,000/HK$28,000.

Video Transmission Unit. A tiny television broadcast station, small enough to fit into the back seat of a car. Range varies according to antenna (one mile/1.6 km, line-of-sight, minimum). **Cost:** $15,000/¥45,000/HK$100,000.

Advanced Walkie-Talkies. Hand-held, or helmet-mounted units, each capable of two-way communication over a range of five miles (8 km); half that range in a big city with lots of tall building, traffic and interference. Built-in scrambler/decoder prevents eavesdropping. **Cost:** $2,800/¥8,800/HK$16,500.

Ear Mike Radio. A tiny device that fits in the ear like a hearing aid, capable of two-way, hands-free communications over a limited range (1 mile/1.6 km maximum).

Cost: $500/¥2,000/HK$3,000.

Two-Way Field Radio. A compact transmitter/receiver with a range of 60 miles (96 km), broad-band monitoring, and scrambler/decoder functions. Old style versions were the size of a backpack, but lately they've been reduced to the size of belt-pack. Also picks up AM/FM/TV Stations (audio only) and shortwave. **Cost:** $1,250/¥2,950/HK$4,150.

Portable Radio/Satellite Broadcast Setup. This backpack-sized unit can be used as a two-way field radio, or can function as a full broadcast radio, sending out a strong enough signal to either jam (up to ten miles/16 km), or override (up to two miles/3.2 km) a single frequency. This means that a character can either block (cause static), or replace a radio station's signal, so the listeners will hear the character's transmission. Hooking the unit up to a satellite dish will allow for communications with orbiting satellites, and full international capacity. **Cost:** $4,000/¥14,000/HK$28,000.

Medical Equipment

Medical Aid Kit. An eight pound (3.6 kg) bag filled with adhesive pads, bandages, gauze pads, adhesive tape, splints, sterile gloves, scissors, forceps, thermometer, needle, razor blades, pins, antibacterial/sterilization ointment, salt tablets, and some over-the-counter medications (anti-allergens, aspirin, etc.). The shoulder bag is available in camouflage, green, black or khaki. **Cost:** $275/¥425/HK$1,225.

Professional Medical Kit. A backpack filled with everything from the Medical Aid Kit, plus scalpels, probes, and everything needed for emergency surgery. Pharmaceuticals include enough antibiotics, anti-inflammatories, sedatives, painkillers, snake-bite reagents and other drugs, to treat 16 patients with each. **Cost:** $2,000/¥$3,500/HK$12,000.

Portable Bio-Lab. Contained in a large steel trunk is a portable laboratory, computer system and all the tools, instruments and chemicals needed to examine microbiological organisms, culture diseases, and do simple DNA testing, so as to identify new cells and viruses. **Cost:** $45,000/¥100,000/HK$600,000.

Optics/Sensing Gear

Binoculars. Good quality set. **Cost:** $500/¥1,000/HK$3,250.

Nightsight. "Starlight" image intensifier for night viewing of objects up to 2,000 feet (610 m) away.

Cost: $1,500/¥3,800/HK$9,000.

Hand-held Sonar Gear. Looks like a big gun; can be used to do sonar scans underwater and detects objects up to 2,500 feet (760 m) away. **Cost:** $2,000/¥7,000/HK$14,000.

Suitcase Radar Setup. Once it's unpacked, with the dish set up, it can do a line-of-sight radar scan, picking up objects in darkness or in dense fog. **Cost:** $80,000/¥250,000/HK$640,000.

Portable X-Ray Scanner. Fits in a suitcase and can be used to scan the insides of packages, containers, sculptures, walls, etc. **Cost:** $130,000/¥450,000/HK$800,000.

Miscellaneous Equipment

Shoulder Bag, Canvas. **Cost:** $50/¥50/HK$250.
Backpack, Nylon. **Cost:** $150/¥100/HK$300.
Sleeping Bag, Basic. **Cost:** $150/¥300/HK$750.
Handcuffs, Standard. **Cost:** $25/¥55/HK$100.
Lock Pick Set, Basic. **Cost:** $50/¥95/HK$300.
Flashlight, Utility. **Cost:** $20/¥10/HK$35.
Micro-Cassette Tape Recorder. **Cost:** $50/¥210/HK$200.
35 mm Camera, Tourist Quality. **Cost:** $200/¥450/HK$1,000.
Instant-Print Camera. **Cost:** $125/¥300/HK$800.

Chinese Calligrapher's Kit. Includes brushes, inkstone, solid inks, and a supply of paper, all in a compact case. **Cost:** $130/¥80/HK$500.

Smoke Grenade/Generator. When triggered it releases colored smoke for up to six melee rounds. Usually used as a signal for aircraft or at a distance. **Cost:** $35/¥55/HK$280.

Vehicles in China

Street Bicycle. The standard bike found filling the city streets and country roads of Mainland China and Korea. **Cost:** $150/¥300/HK$750.

Mountain Bicycle. Useful for getting around in cities, but can also be used for cross-country travel and rugged terrains. **Cost:** $1,000/¥2,500/HK$5,900.

Motorbike. Good for travelling around inside the crowded cities of East Asia. **Cost:** $3,000/¥10,000/HK$25,000.

Motorcycle. A rugged multi-purpose motorcycle that can be used for long-distance highway or cross-country travel. **Cost:** $8,000/¥20,000/HK$64,000.

Compact Car. Inexpensive transportation. Cramped for more than two people. Also anonymous in that the car won't be noticed among thousands of others just like it. **Cost:** $15,000/¥25,000/HK$90,000.

Luxury Car. A full-sized car. Six can be seated comfortably, and the trunk can hold a full load of gear (or a couple of bodies). **Cost:** $40,000/¥80,000/HK$340,000.

Sports Car. An expensive, flashy, very fast muscle car. Impresses people, but also stands out so it's remembered. Furthermore, it can't travel at high speeds in the streets of larger cities filled with thronging crowds of people and bicycles. **Cost:** $100,000/¥300,000/HK$750,000.

Utility Van. Big enough for a decent laboratory or repair center. Seating for from three to twelve, depending on other cargo. **Cost:** $25,000/¥40,000/HK$175,000.

Four-Wheel Drive Vehicle. Either a jeep, truck or land-rover, designed for rugged cross-country driving.

Cost: $35,000/¥50,000/HK$190,000.

Quarter Ton Truck. Large field truck capable of handling rough roads and hauling a huge amount of gear and supplies. **Note:** If purchased in mainland China, the truck will be a "deactivated" (or stolen) military vehicle.

Cost: $50,000/¥10,000/HK$300,000.

Rowboat/Dinghy/Inflatable. A small watercraft which relies on muscle-power (oars!) for getting around. Usually holds up to eight people, or four with heavy gear.

Cost: $1,000/¥1,600/HK$7,000.

Ocean-Going Sailboat or Yacht. A luxury vessel capable of holding up to eight in comfort, complete with three months of supplies. **Cost:** $500,000/¥1,000,000/HK$6,000,000.

Junk (sailing vessel) or Small Cargo Ship. All that's needed for a major expedition. Capable of carrying over twenty people, plus major cargo. **Cost:** $1,000,000/¥1,400,000/HK$5,500,000.

Single-Engine Airplane. A two-seater, only capable of carrying up to 600 pounds (272 kg) total.

Cost: $28,000/¥45,000/HK$200,000.

Twin-Engine Airplane. Utility aircraft with seating for four and can carry up to 1,200 pounds (544 kg) of cargo. **Cost:** $75,000/¥170,000/HK$500,000.

Cargo Aircraft. A large, twin-engine, propeller airplane. It can be used for hauling up to six tons (5440 kg) of cargo, or a large batch of people and gear. Well-used (i.e.: broken down) versions are available for much less.

Cost: $350,000/¥700,000/HK$2,100,000.

Private Jet. Capable of carrying six passengers and light cargo up to half a ton. It has a top speed of 500 mph (800 kmph) and a range of up to 1,200 miles (1920 km) without refueling. **Cost:** $800,000/¥2,000,000/HK$5,000,000.

Weapons

Note: See Palladium's **Compendium of Contemporary Weapons** for 400 additional weapons from around the world, plus ammunition, special rounds, body armor, grenades, riot control gear, armored vehicles, optional rules and more.

Ammunition Costs

Standard Pistol Ammunition. Rounds in standard sizes, such as .22, .32, .38, .45, 7.62 mm and 9 mm, are relatively easy to find, and fairly inexpensive. **Cost:** $0.20/¥1/HK$1 per bullet.

Standard Rifle Ammunition. 5.62 mm, 7.62 mm, and .30 caliber rifle bullets (which are much larger than pistol bullets). **Cost:** $0.40/¥2/HK$2 per bullet.

Chinese Military Ammunition. 7.62 mm pistol rounds (for automatic pistols and sub-machineguns) and 7.62 mm rifle rounds (for guns and sub-machineguns) are incredibly common, as poorly-paid soldiers often trade them for cigarettes, etc. Easy to buy on the black market, just about anywhere. **Cost:** $0.05/¥0.2/HK$0.5.

Rare Ammunition. Non-standard ammunition, such as the 7.65 mm rounds for a Chinese silenced pistol, and teflon bullets. **Cost:** Roughly $1/¥10/HK$5 per bullet.

Chinese Military Weapons

Since these weapons are made in such vast quantities (enough to support armies and militia numbering in tens of millions) and because soldiers and officers are often poorly paid, these weapons are inexpensive and plentiful on the black market.

.22LR Firing Combat Knife. Looks like a combat knife, but there are four (4) pre-loaded barrels on the back end. 1D8 damage/round, or 1D4 as knife. **Cost:** $35/¥50/HK$135.

7.62 mm Automatic Pistol. 8 round magazine. 1D8 damage. Incredibly common and easy to buy. Offer a trade and you could get one for a carton of cigarettes or a nice pair of sunglasses. **Cost:** $30/¥40/HK$85.

7.65 mm Silenced Automatic Pistol. 8 round magazine. 2D6 damage. **Note:** One problem with this gun is that it needs special ammunition, which is sometimes hard to find. **Cost:** $125/¥200/HK$600.

7.62 mm Type 64 Sub-machinegun. 30 round magazine. 2D6 damage. **Cost:** $200/¥400/HK$1,200.

7.62 mm Assault Rifle. 15 or 30 round magazines. 3D6 damage. **Cost:** $100/¥200/HK$650.

7.62 mm Type 67 Light Machinegun. 100 round belt. 6D6 damage. **Cost:** $500/¥1,000/HK$3,500.

7.92 mm Model 37 Medium Machinegun. Belt-fed. There are 50-round belts made out of durable material, which can be carried around, slung around a shoulder, or draped over the fender of a jeep. However, most ammo is in 500 round boxes, where the cloth holding the bullets together is much more fragile. 5D10 damage. **Cost:** $1,000/¥2,000/HK$7,000.

Imported Weapons

All of the following weapons can be bought and sold (illegally) in Hong Kong and in black markets throughout China. The price will be jacked up to double or triple the listed prices if there is any kind of major trouble. However, if it looks like there is going to be a big demand, chances are that small companies in Hong Kong will start manufacturing knock-offs, keeping the price stable.

.22 Magnum Advantage 422 (U.S.A.). A compact, four-barrelled pistol. Weighs just over one pound (0.45 kg) fully loaded. Total length is just 4.5 inches (11 cm). 1D8 damage. **Cost:** $165/¥500/HK$1,000.

.38 Special Single Shot Derringer (Various Countries). A very light, very easy to conceal, one-shot pistol. Loading Time: One full melee round, Barrel Length: 4.9 inches (12 cm) long. 2D6 damage. **Cost:** $115/¥300/HK$550.

.38 Revolver (Various Countries). 6-shot cylinder. Used by many military organizations, police forces, and private security firms. There are a lot of models manufactured, of varying quality. 2D6 damage. **Cost:** $250/¥500/HK$1,250.

Colt .45 Automatic Pistol (Used). 7 round magazine. Mostly the weapons available are left over from the Vietnam war when huge quantities were brought in by the U.S. military. 2D6 damage. **Cost:** $55/¥100/HK$300.

Beretta Model 92 9 mm Double-Action (Italy). 15 round magazine. 2D6 damage. **Cost:** $300/¥1,000/HK$2,750.

Browning High Power 9 mm (Belgium). 13 round magazine. 2D6 damage. **Cost:** $750/¥2,400/HK$6,000.

Glock 9 mm (Austria). 17 round magazine. 2D6 damage. **Cost:** $1,500/¥5,000/HK$10,000.

Heckler & Koch 9 mm VP70 (Germany). 18 round magazine. 2D6 damage. **Cost:** $1,000/¥3,500/HK$7,500.

New Nambu Model 57A 9 mm (Japan). 18 round magazine. 2D6 damage. **Cost:** $225/¥600/HK$1,500.

9 mm PA15 MAB (France). 15 round magazine. 2D6 damage. **Cost:** $450/¥1,500/HK$4,000.

Pindad 9 mm (Indonesia). 13 round magazine. Relatively cheap, and it fits the requirements for Triad use. 2D6 damage. **Cost:** $85/¥250/HK$550.

9 mm PM Model VII Sub-machinegun (Indonesia), 33 round magazine. 2D6 damage. **Cost:** $650/¥1,300/HK$3,000.

5.56 mm SAR80 Assault Rifle (Singapore), 20 or 30 round magazine. 3D6 damage. **Cost:** $800/¥1,900/HK$4,000.

Tube Guns and Derringers

Each of the following calibers is available in a simple device consisting of a barrel and a trigger mechanism. Can be built into a pistol stock (as a one-shot derringer), or installed in any device. The device can even be installed in the sleeve of a shirt, or strapped directly on someone's arm. Each device weighs about a quarter of a pound (0.11 kg) loaded. It also takes a full round to reload, or even longer if the device is covered by clothing or machinery.

9 mm – $335/¥300/HK$1,800 – 2D6 damage per round
.45 Magnum – $350/¥450/HK$2,000 – 4D6 damage per round
.30-06 Rifle – $370/¥500/HK$2,200 – 5D6 damage per round

Throw-Away Automatic Pistol

This smooth, toy-like automatic pistol is designed for ease of concealment. All parts are made of plastic, including the teflon bullets. It will not be sensed by a metal detector. It can't be reloaded, and must be thrown away when all of its seven (7) shots are expended. Range: 120 feet (36.6 m), 3D6 damage. **Cost:** $3,000/¥10,000/HK$30,000.

Weapons of Ancient China

While there are an enormous number of historical Chinese weapons (after all, even Confucius carried a sword), we present here those most likely to be used by characters in **Mystic China**.

Bi Shou (Dagger)

Traditional daggers come in a nearly infinite variety. **Weapon Proficiency Type:** W.P. Knife. **Cost:** $15 to $200. **Damage:** 1D4.

Bian (Hard Whip)

This is considered by the Chinese to be a "hard whip" (as opposed to a soft whip made out of flexible leather). The hard whip is used by police, martial art instructors, and military officers as a way of enforcing discipline, inflicting punishment, and a sign of authority. The size and shape of a short sword (though with no cross-piece), Bian are either bamboo, hard leather, wood or metal. **Weapon Proficiency Type:** W.P. Blunt. **Cost:** $15 to $100. **Damage:** 1D6.

Biau Dau (A Throwing Knife)

A curved throwing knife, designed with all edges and points, and no handle. There are three points and all the edges are sharpened. The curve of the blade makes it possible to throw the Biau Dau indirectly on a curved flight path (sort of like a boomerang). **Weapon Proficiency Type:** W.P. Knife. **Cost:** $50 to $150. **Damage:** 1D6. **Effective Throwing Range:** 60 feet (18.3 m)

Chang Bahn & Chang Bahn Jin (Staff)

A very long staff used both in sweeping and thrusting motions. An expert wielder will be able to stand off opponents from two directions, staying in the middle of the weapon. Although the standard length is 11 feet (3.4 m), this is based on the idea of the staff being twice the height of the wielder. Characters who are 5 foot, 10 inches, to 6 foot 2 inches (1.8 to 1.9 m) can get a 12 foot (3.7 m) Chang Bahn, and characters taller than that should seek to have one custom built for double their height. The diameter of the Chang Bahn should allow the character to encircle it with the thumb and forefinger of the left hand.

Chang Bahn are solid wood, where Chang Bahn Jin are metal. The metal version is hollow and comes with wooden plugs, as well as cloth wrappings for each end. Often the wielder will use the hollow area for storage of water, cooking oil, or other odds and ends. Fighting is usually done with the ends covered, but some Chang Bahn Jin wielders will sharpen the edges of the pipe ends, giving them a +2 to damage when thrusting (and uncovered).

Characters with a P.S. of 14 or less will find a Chang Bahn easier to use, while those with a P.S. of 15 or more can use the

Chang Bahn Jin (which weighs from 40 to 50 pounds/18 to 23 kg) with no penalty (-2 to strike and parry if P.S. is under 15).

Weapon Proficiency Type: W.P. Staff. **Cost:** $100 for Chang Bahn, $500 to $5,000 for Chang Bahn Jin (a makeshift Chang Bahn Jim, made of iron pipe is only $30, but will tend to bend or break). **Damage:** 2D6 for Chang Bahn, 3D6 for Chang Bahn Jin.

Chiang, Chiang Zhu, Mao Chiang & Chiang Chiang (Spear)

The most common Chinese weapon is the Chiang, or spear, typically eight to nine feet (2.4 to 2.7 m) long. The most popular model comes with an eight-inch (20 cm), double-edged blade, which has a three-inch (8 cm) hook (pointing back toward the handle). There is always a tassel, usually made of horsehair, edging the border of the metal with the wood. Aside from being useful as a guide to training or in distracting the enemy, the tassel is also important because it will stop blood from trickling down the shaft.

The best wood for the shaft is Bai La Gan (White Wax Wood), which must be imported from the far north. Treated properly (it should be soaked in oil occasionally), the shaft will last just about forever and will remain taut and flexible.

A Chiang Zhu is a simple spear made out of bamboo. One end is shaved off at an angle, making a sharp edge. While incredibly cheap and lightweight, Chiang Zhu usually don't last long and the wielder will usually have to shave off a few inches from the point after any combat.

The Mao Chiang is just like a Chiang, except that it comes with a wavy blade, up to a foot and a half (46 cm) long. Reserved for the true experts, it is said that a good Mao Chiang wielder can disable opponents by cutting the laces and threads of their clothing.

A Chiang Chiang is a double-headed spear with a wood shaft. One end has a large steel blade with the standard horsehair tassel, while the other end is tipped with a short steel blade (shaped like an arrowhead).

Weapon Proficiency Type: W.P. Spear. **Cost:** $200 for ordinary Chiang or Chiang Chiang, $300 for Mao Chiang, $500 for Chiang Zhu, $800 to $1500 for high quality Chiang, Mao Chiang, or Chiang Chiang made of wax wood. **Damage:** 2D6 for Chiang and Chiang Chiang, 2D4 for Chiang Zhu. **Effective Throwing Range:** Roughly 100 feet (30.5 m)

Da Kan Dau (Short Sword)

Commonly known as "Butterfly Knives," the Da Kan Dau are usually used as a pair. The blades are at least 3 inches (8 cm) wide, but are relatively short (18 inches/46 cm or so). The handle always comes equipped with a large, wraparound guard. **Weapon Proficiency Type:** W.P. Short Sword. **Cost:** $130 each. **Damage:** 1D6+1.

Er Neu & Gan Neu (Crossbow)

The Er Neu, or "Two-Trigger Crossbow," is a multi-shot version of a light crossbow. Either of two strings can be fired independently. Also, the crossbow is designed so that each string can fire one bolt or two bolts (side by side). Note that firing more than one bolt simultaneously is most effective at groups — a single human-sized target will only be hit with one of the bolts, no matter how many are fired; unless, of course, the crossbow is fired at point-blank range.

The Chinese also have a "Repeating Crossbow," the Gan Neu. While the repeater delivers volume (a good man on the lever can fire all twelve bolts in 15 seconds), the bolts do relatively little damage. That explains why the bolts in a Gan Neu were usually poisoned.

Weapon Proficiency Type: W.P. Crossbow. **Cost:** From $200 to $800 for the Two-Trigger model, and from $400 to $1,000 for the repeater. **Damage:** For the Er Neu it's 2D4 damage per bolt, or 4D4 if more than one bolt is fired at the same time. The repeating crossbow always does 1D4 damage per bolt. **Effective Range:** 500 and 400 feet (152 and 121 m) respectively.

Fu (axe)

The axe is one of China's most traditional ancient weapons. Not only does it appear in many historical battles, but the symbol for "Fu" is one of the twelve symbols of imperial power. They come in many sizes and shapes, including massive battle-axes and long-handled axes. Smaller axes are often used as paired weapons. **Weapon Proficiency Type:** W.P. Axe. **Cost:** $50 to $600. **Damage:** 2D4 for small or paired, 2D6 for battle-axe, 4D6+2 for long-handled battle-axe.

Gen (Sai)

Looking like oversized three-pronged forks, the Gen are designed to be used as a pair, with one in each hand. Skilled users can use the pair to entangle an opponent's weapon (they work well against swords, spears, etc.). Once an enemy's weapon is caught, one of the Gen will be used to continue pinning, while the other is used to strike, using either the main point (thrust), the pommel (usually with a side-strike) or, after "missing" with a thrust, quickly reversing the weapon and striking with one of the pointed tines. **Weapon Proficiency Type:** W.P. Forked. **Cost:** $50 to $200 for a pair. **Damage:** 1D6 per thrust or 1D4 for a pommel side strike.

Giau Chiz & Giau Chiz Jin (Staff)

A man-sized staff, generally tall enough to come up over the wielder's head and narrow enough so the thumb and forefinger can overlap. It can be used to sweep, thrust, or block. A favored martial art technique is to handle the weapon in the center, spinning it in a figure eight motion.

Characters with a P.S. of 11 or less will find a Giau Chiz easier to use, while those with a P.S. of 12 or more can use the Giau Chiz Jin with no penalty (-1 to strike and parry if P.S. is under 12).

Weapon Proficiency Type: W.P. Staff. **Cost:** $60 for wood, $100 to $500 for metal. **Damage:** 2D4 for Giau Chiz, 2D6 for Giau Chiz Jin.

Giau Tzu Jen (Sword)

The "Snake-Headed Sawtooth Sword" is designed to strike fear in opponents. First, by it's appearance. Both edges are serrated, like the teeth on a hacksaw, which gives it a nasty look. Even more terrifying for those unfamiliar with this weapon, is the sharp, loud, and high-pitched "hissing" sound the sword makes. This is caused by the "eyes" near the tip of the sword. These eyes are actually small holes, cunningly placed so even a gentle swinging of the sword will cause a disquieting "hiss." **Weapon Proficiency Type:** W.P. Large Sword. **Cost:** $375 to $3750, depending on quality. **Damage:** 2D6+2.

Gieh Bian (Whip)

A steel whip, used much like a leather whip, but with the added advantage of sharp blades and a nasty point at the end. The whip is usually as long as the wielder's height, but the number of sections can range from seven to twelve steel pieces. Aside from sweeps, slashes and high-speed circles, an expert can also attempt to "snap" the whip, driving the point directly into the victim. **Weapon Proficiency Type:** W.P. Whip. **Cost:** $175 to $500. **Damage:** 2D8 or 4D4.

Jiu Long Bar (Nine Dragon Trident)

Possibly the most difficult Chinese weapon of them all. The Nine-Dragon Trident comes equipped with nine different points, each with flanking twin blades. Relatively short (about the height of the wielder), an expert will be able to spin the weapon end over end while at the same time rotating it so the elaborate blade structure turns into a forest of deadly points and blades. **Weapon Proficiency Type:** W.P. Polearm. **Cost:** $1,000 for ordinary version, $1,500 with wax wood, $15,000 or more for a really outstanding weapon. **Damage:** 3D6+1. **Penalty:** -1 to strike and parry until the user is at least 3rd level.

Kun Gen & Kun Dan (Bow)

The Kun Gen is a Chinese bow made of either bamboo, wood or metal. The Kun Dan is similar but designed with a pouch in the string so it can fire balls or stones, instead of arrows. **Weapon Proficiency Type:** W.P. Bow. **Cost:** $100 to $150. **Damage:** 1D6 for arrows, 1D4 for stones. **Effective Range:** 300 feet (91 m).

Lieu Yeh Dau & Pok Dau (Sword)

The Lieu Yeh Dau, or "Willow Leaf Saber," is considered the easiest lethal weapon for the novice martial artist to learn. While weak in defensive maneuvers (it's difficult to block or parry), the weight and power of this two-handed weapon makes it difficult to be parried or blocked by others.

There was a time in China's history when carrying a Pok Dau was a pretty good way for a wandering martial artist to make a living. That's because a Pok Dau is known as the "executioner's blade," and smaller communities, not being able to afford a full-time executioner, would happily pay for killing services if there were any condemned prisoners in the local jail.

Weapon Proficiency Type: W.P. Large Sword. **Cost:** $150 to $750 for a Lieu Yeh Dau, while a decent Pok Dau costs at least $1,000. **Damage:** 2D6.

Mei Far Chen (Blowpipe)

Otherwise known as "Plum Flower Needles." These poison needles are built into a small tube which is designed to fit in the wielder's mouth. Using the tongue to manipulate the tube, the needles can then be blown, or spat, up to twenty feet (6.1 m) away. Up to five needles can be arranged in the "flower," and each can be shot separately. **Weapon Proficiency Type:** W.P. Blowpipe. **Cost:** $15 to $50. **Damage:** One point plus poison. **Effective Range:** 20 ft (6 m).

Pao Hsaio (Flute & Dart)

To all outward appearances and even to a detailed inspection, this would seem to be a metal flute. It can be played, producing excellent tones and all the keys function. It can even be partially disassembled or water poured through it without having its secrets revealed. However, the Pao Hsaio is a truly devious weapon.

First, it's built solidly, so it can be used as a blunt weapon and to parry attacks from other weapons.

Second, when a particular combination of keys are depressed, a tiny dart is "loaded" onto a spring-powered launch channel. Another key sets off the spring and fires the dart.

Finally, for its third trick, another combination of keys will cause a razor-sharp blade to protrude from an end of the flute.

Weapon Proficiency Type: W.P. Blunt for use as a club, W.P. Dartgun to fire darts, and W.P. Knife for use with the blade. **Cost:** $3,000 for single dart model, $3,500 for double dart, $5,000 for six-dart auto-loader. It's an additional $1,000 if it is to be equipped with double blades. **Damage:** 1D4 for each dart, 1D4 as blunt weapon, 1D6 as edged weapon. **Effective Dart Range:** 20 ft (6.1 m).

Pi Bian (Whip)

The Chinese version of a bullwhip. The whip is from 8 to 12 feet (2.4 to 3.6 m) long, with a solid handle. The most expensive types are made with animal tendons instead of leather, an alteration that gives the weapon more of a cutting impact (however, the tendons must be treated carefully and are more likely to break). **Weapon Proficiency Type:** W.P. Whip. **Cost:** $60 to $120, add $175 for tendon style. Another feature, a concealed dagger in the handle, costs an additional $150. **Damage:** 2D4, or 2D4+2 if made with tendons.

Shan Gieh Kun (Nunchuk)

Something like nunchuks, but with three rods and two chains. A complicated, difficult weapon, that is impossible to use as a pair. **Weapon Proficiency Type:** W.P. Chain. **Cost:** $150. **Damage:** 2D4+2.

Jen Chiang

This fusion of a sword ("Jen") and a spear ("Chiang") combines the two-foot (60 cm) wooden handle of a spear with a foot-long (30 cm) sword blade. It can also be used as a thrown weapon, but range is limited to twenty-five feet (7.6 m). Although the handle is large enough for two-handed use, the Jen Chiang is more commonly used as a paired weapon. **Weapon Proficiency Type:** W.P. Short Sword. **Cost:** $150 each. **Damage:** 1D10 or 2D4+2. **Thrown:** 1D8. **Effective Throwing Range:** 25 feet (7.6 m).

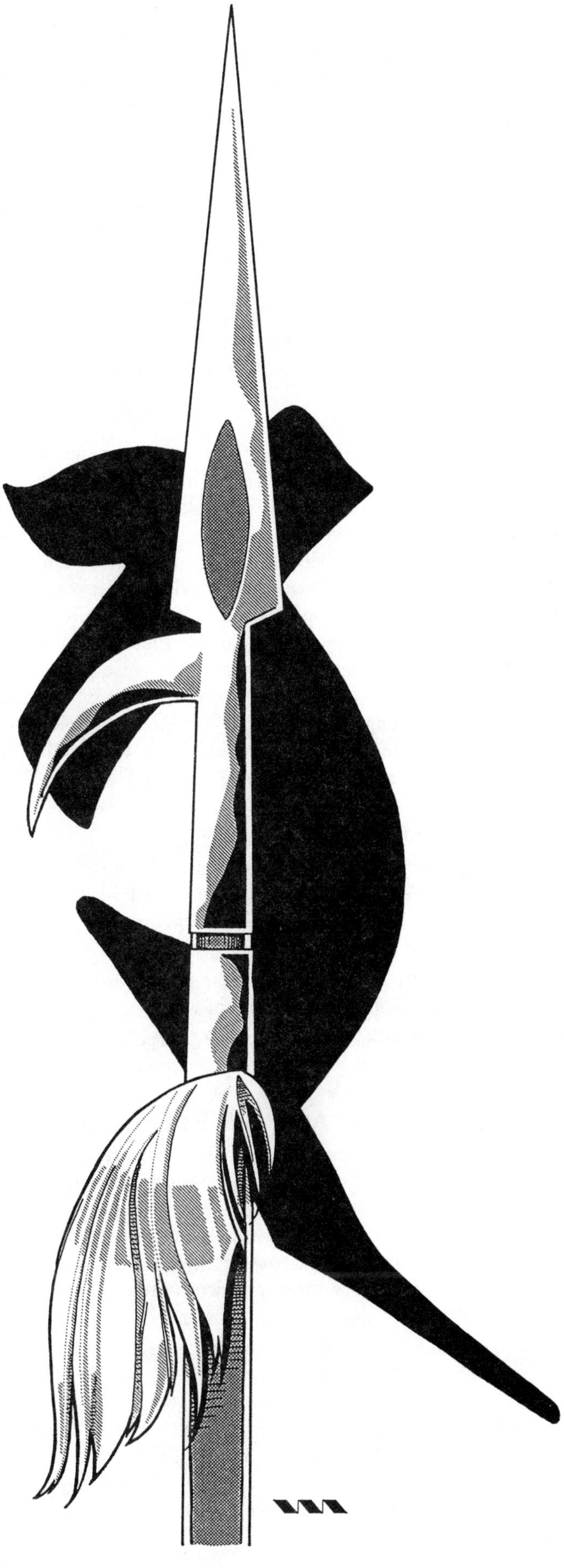

Lo Han Chain (Throwing)

Sharpened coins, easily concealed, that can be used as projectile weapons. It is said that it takes three years of practice to build the technique necessary to drive the coin through flesh. **Weapon Proficiency Type:** W.P. Small Thrown Weapons. **Cost:** Less than $10. **Damage:** 1D4. **Effective Range:** 30 feet (9.1 m).

Shao Tzu (Flail)

A Chinese version of the European flail. The handle part is usually the height of the user, while the chain connects with a swinging wood piece from two to three feet (0.3 to 0.6 m) long. Usually referred to as a "sweeper" because it's used to sweep men off their feet with low strikes. It's also effective in swinging over and around blocks and parries. **Weapon Proficiency Type:** W.P. Chain. **Cost:** $100 to $200. **Damage:** 2D6.

Shen Biau

Remember what it's like to whip a string around in a circle? The "Rope Dart" takes that idea to its logical extreme. At one end is a weight shaped like a broad-bladed arrowhead with very sharp edges. At the other end is a hollow handle, with the rope running through it. Take the handle in one hand and use it to swing the rope. You also use that hand to either squeeze, keeping the rope in place, or release, allowing the rope to move through the handle. Then, with the other hand, feed the rope, or pull the rope, through the handle. The result is a spinning weapon, but one where you control the size of the circle by changing the length of the rope. **Weapon Proficiency Type:** W.P. Shen Biau (unique!), +1 to strike at 1st, 3rd, 6th, 10th and 15th levels of experience. **Cost:** $20 to $60. **Damage:** 1D6.

Shi-Zi Jen (Sword)

The classic "Lion Head Sword" is a favorite of many martial art forms. Even those who have abandoned weapon styles and katas will still value the symbolism of this sword.

Both edges and the point are sharp. It is traditional to always have a brightly colored cord on the pommel, which is used in training and to show off the styles of various katas.

Weapon Proficiency Type: W.P. Large Sword. **Cost:** $250 to $15,000. **Damage:** 2D6 (3D6 for the highest quality).

Shou Gen (Sleeve Arrow) & Fa Gen (Back Arrow)

These are two weapons favored by assassins or those who like to have a real "stand-by." *The Shou Gen* consists of a tube hidden in a sleeve or strapped to the arm. A string connects the trigger to one of the fingers which can then release a spring, automatically firing an arrow or arrows (up to five can be packed in a single tube for simultaneous fire).

Even more treacherous is the *Fa Gen.* It is much larger and designed to be strapped to the wielder's back. When the wielder bows down (to a superior, or a captor, for example), the spring is automatically released and the arrow is fired at whoever is being "honored." **Weapon Proficiency Type:** W.P. Dartgun. **Cost:** $60 for simple Shou Gen and $15 for each arrow. $100 for the Fa Gen. **Damage:** The sleeve arrow does 1D4 damage, while the back arrow does 2D4. **Effective Range:** 20 feet (6.1 m) for both types.

Shou Li Jen (Sleeve Sword)

This is a weapon with two secrets. First, it is designed to be concealed up the sleeve of a traditional Chinese loose jacket. Second, the weapon, when first revealed, will seem to be relatively short, the length of a standard dagger. However, concealed in the hilt of the weapon is a spring. When activated, the blade is extended to its full length. **Weapon Proficiency Type:** W.P. Small Sword. **Cost:** $250 to $500. **Damage:** 1D4 in short form, 1D6 when lengthened.

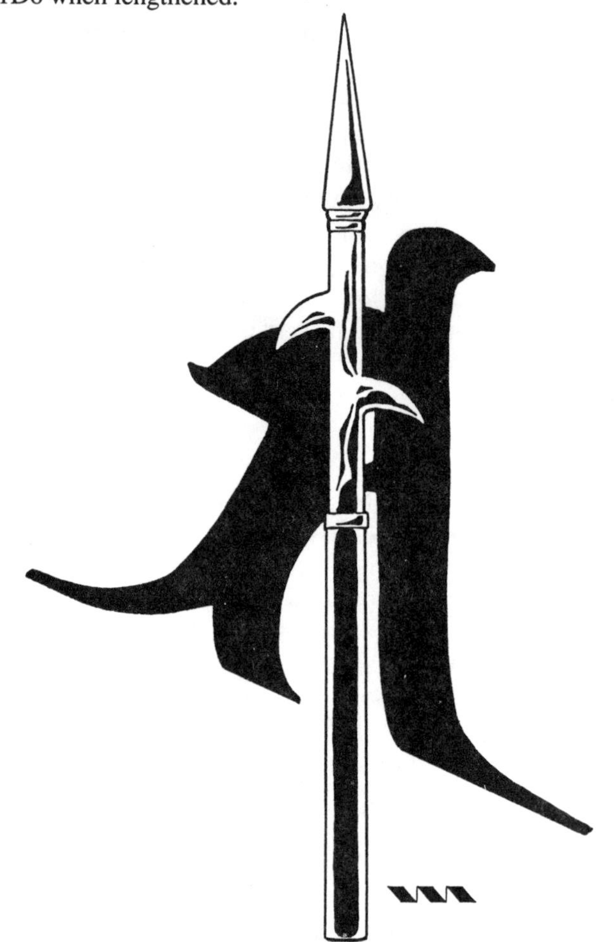

Shunn Gou Shih (Club/Sword)

Although the "Double Hook Arrow" looks like an oversized arrow (it looks like it was made for a really big crossbow or arbalest), it's actually a hand-to-hand combat weapon. The pointy parts include the arrowhead with a double-edged blade and two hooks spaced about four inches (10 cm) apart that are pointing in opposite directions. An expert can use two hands to throw the Shunn Gou Shih about thirty feet (9.1 m) but it's usually not thrown in combat. **Weapon Proficiency Type:** W.P. Small Sword. **Cost:** $100 to $200. **Damage:** 1D8, or 1D6 if thrown. **Effective Range:** 30 feet (9.1 m).

Tien Tzu (Club)

The name translates into "Iron Ruler" and it is used much like a baton or a nightstick. Although not designed for lethal combat, in the hands of an expert the Tien Tzu can be quite deadly. Officials and officers usually have a model equipped with a handle, while lower-ranking characters will just use a plain piece of iron. **Weapon Proficiency Type:** W.P. Blunt. **Cost:** $35 (without handle) to $225 (with handle). **Damage:** 1D4+1.

Ton Zen (Club)

One of the oddest looking weapons around, the Ton Zen is the statue of a man, made of brass, and measuring about three feet (0.9 m) long. Swinging the Brass Man by the ankles would take a pretty strong wielder (P.S. of 14 or better), but since it weighs over 200 pounds (91 kg), the Ton Zen does a hefty amount of damage. Unless the wielder has a specific Weapon Proficiency in Ton Zen, there is a -4 on all rolls to strike and parry, and **no** other combat bonuses to strike or parry can be considered. **Weapon Proficiency Type:** W.P. Blunt. **Cost:** $500 or more. **Damage:** 4D6 (plus P.S. bonus).

Wen Jen (Sword)

The lightest, most flexible swords are considered "Scholar's Swords." More similar to contemporary fencing swords, the Wen Jen were considered to be a good compromise between utility and lethality. A Wen Jen is considered a thing of beauty, to be admired, worn or carried and is not considered a dangerous weapon. At the same time, a Wen Jen, in the hands of an expert can be as deadly as it's less dainty cousins. **Weapon Proficiency Type:** W.P. Small Sword. **Cost:** $750 to $20,000. **Damage:** 2D4 or 2D4+2 depending on the quality of the blade.

Wu Grou Jen (Sword)

The sword most favored by ancient Chinese armies was this "hooked" version of the Lion Head Sword. It's when fighting another sword-wielder that the main advantage of the Wu Grou Jen comes into play. When parried, it's possible to slide the blades together (the point of contact moving toward each hilt), and then twist so that the hook could catch the opponent's hand or arm.

Instead of a conventional scabbard (the hook prevents it), the wielder of a Wu Grou Jen needs to either use a special sword case (like the case for a musical instrument), which means added time in drawing the weapon, or to carry it in hand. **Weapon Proficiency Type:** W.P. Large Sword. **Cost:** $100 to $500. **Damage**: 2D6.

Martial Art O.C.C.s

Chun Tzu O.C.C.: Philosopher Martial Artist
Demon Hunter O.C.C.: Fu Yao Da Chia
Jian Shih O.C.C.: Weapon-Based Marital Artist
Nei Chia Wu Shih O.C.C.: Meditative Martial Artist
Wai Chia Wu Shih O.C.C.: Open Hand Martial Artist

Characters in this category have no psychic powers or control over magic. They are basically ordinary human beings who have gained physical prowess, strength, mental focus and special abilities through their mastery of the mind and body in combat. The martial artist possesses incredible agility, fighting abilities and martial arts *powers* that put them a cut well above "normal" folks. Furthermore, they each have a passion that makes them seek out and deal with the mysteries of life, magic and the supernatural.

In addition to the characters on the following list, the *Dedicated Martial Artist O.C.C.* and the *Worldly Martial Artist O.C.C.* from **Ninjas & Superspies** (along with 41 martial arts styles of combat) can also be used in conjunction with **Mystic China** and vice versa.

Chun Tzu O.C.C.

Philosopher Marital Artist

The *Chun Tzu*, or "Seeker of Perfection," is an ancient tradition in China. This character's goal is to combine the lifelong dedication of the monk, a scholarly study of the classics of military philosophy, and the rigorous training of the martial artist.

Typically, a *Chun Tzu* believes that the best military officer is one who can lead by example.

In practical terms, that means the character is a jack-of-all-military-trades who thinks it's just as important to learn how to drive a tank, strip a machinegun, and practice a Martial Art Kata. When it comes to studying, the character is equally interested in a 3,000 year old classic, as Mao's writings on guerilla warfare, and an article on laser sights in the latest issue of *Special Warfare*.

As a character in **Mystic China**, the *Chun Tzu* is always looking for new challenges and new sources of information. The Chun Tzu is particularly fascinated with the prospect of encountering dragons, demons and other creatures of myth. First, because such entities may present a great challenge. Secondly, and even more importantly, because such epic beasts may have secret knowledge of combat systems, techniques, and strategies which he can learn.

Chun Tzu Requirements & Base Numbers:

Attribute Requirements: I.Q. 9 and P.P. 8.
Alignment Requirements: None
Base S.D.C.: 25
Base Hit Points: Standard (equal to P.E.), plus 1D6 per level of experience.
Base Chi: Standard (equal to P.E.)
Base P.P.E.: Standard (3D6)

Chun Tzu Advancement Bonuses: These bonuses are in addition to Martial Arts Combat.
1st: +3 to save vs pain, +2 to save vs possession, +1 to save vs horror factor.
2nd: Add 1D6 to hit points.
3rd: Add 1D6 to S.D.C. and select one new W.P.
4th: Select one new O.C.C. related skill.
5th: Add 1D6 to hit points and select one secondary skill.
6th: Select one new W.P. and +1 to save vs horror factor.
7th: Select one new O.C.C. related skill.
8th: Add 1D6 to hit points and add 1D6 to S.D.C.
9th: Select one new W.P. and +1 to save vs horror factor.
10th: Select one new O.C.C. related skill.
11th: Add 1D6 to hit points, and select one secondary skill.
12th: Select one new W.P. and +1 to save vs horror factor.
13th: Select one new O.C.C. related skill.
14th: Add 1D6 to hit points, and add 1D6 to S.D.C.
15th: Select one new W.P. and +2 to save vs possession.

Chun Tzu Martial Arts: Select any **one** of the following martial arts:
Ba Gua Kung Fu (Eight Trigrams)
Bok Pai Kung Fu (Crane Style)
Choy-Li-Fut Kung Fu (Boxing)
Fu Chiao Pai Kung Fu (Tiger Claw)
Gui Long Kung Fu (Dragon Spirit)
Han Yu Kung Fu (Chi Katas)
Hsien Hsia (Immortality)
Hsing-I Kung Fu (Mind Shaping)
Liang Hsiung Kung Fu (Demon Combat)
Shan Tung Kung Fu (Black Tiger)
Shih Ba Ban Wu Yi (Eighteen Weapons)
Pao Pat Mei Kung Fu (Leopard Style)
Shao-Lin Kung Fu (Classic Style)

Chun Tzu O.C.C. Skills:
Wei Qi, The Game of Go (+15%). To the *Chun Tzu* character, Wei Qi is much more than just a game. The elegance of play, where perfection is more important than winning, is meant to be an allegory of life. In addition, unlike the western game of chess (which can also teach valuable military lessons), Wei Qi teaches valuable tactical lessons about the importance of numbers and terrain.
Chinese Language: Stage 4/Classical Chinese Literacy (+5%).
Chinese Classical Studies (+10%). Specializes in ancient military writing. Can attempt to date, authenticate, and recognize the value of old manuscripts within the specialty (roll on skill).
Chinese History (+5%).
Detect Ambush (+5%).
Land Navigation (+5%).
Paramedic (+5%).
Wilderness Survival (+5%).
Radio: Basic Communications.
Artistic Calligraphy.

W.P. (Ancient Chinese): One of Choice.
W.P. (Modern): One of Choice.

Chun Tzu O.C.C. Related Skills: Select six skills from the following list:
Communications: Any
Computer: Any
Cultural/Domestic: Any (+5%)
Cultural Games: Any (+10%)
Electrical: Basic Only.
Espionage: Any (+5%)
Mechanical: Basic, Automotive and Locksmith Only.
Medical: None
Military: Any (+5%)
Physical: Any
Pilot Skills, Basic: Any
Pilot Skills, Advanced: Any
Pilot Related Skills: None
Science: Any
Swindler: None
Technical: Any
Temple: Any
W.P. Ancient: Any
W.P. Modern: Any
W.P. Military: Any

Chun Tzu Secondary Skills: Select any four from the list of Chun Tzu O.C.C. related skills. These do NOT get the advantage of the bonus listed in parentheses. All secondary skills start at base skill level.

Chun Tzu Finances: The Chun Tzu could care less about wealth, or poverty. Fully capable of living on the street, or retreating into the wilderness, riches mean nothing.

Cash: Start with $35,000. The Chun Tzu can spend any part of the money on initial equipment and save whatever is left.

Income: None. However, the character can always do freelance literary work or serve as a military consultant; typically makes at least $1,000 per week!

Special Chun Tzu Gear: Books: Modern reprints of at least two of the ancient Chinese military classics.

Weapons: Select any one (1) pistol or rifle.

Clothing/Personal Effects: Wardrobe includes a complete military outfit, plus personal and business attire.

Chun Tzu Heroes and Role Models:

1. Sun Tzu: Sun Tzu is, without a doubt, the most celebrated military thinker in the history of warfare. His book, **Sun Tzu's Art of War**, has been the main military text in Asia for over two thousand years. After the first French translation was used by Napoleon, it has been recognized worldwide.

In his first test, Sun Tzu is said to have trained and equipped the palace women of Ho Lu, the King of Wu, into a viable army (though it required cutting off the heads of the king's two favorite concubines). In the 5th Century B.C., Sun Tzu led Wu's armies to defeat two renegade generals and the powerful neighboring states of Chu, Chi, and Chin.

The thirteen short chapters of **Sun Tzu's Art of War** stress the importance of (1) gathering information and the use of spies, (2) using regular (*cheng*) forces to attack an enemy's weaknesses, and using unorthodox, guerilla (*chi*) forces to attack the enemy's strengths, and (3) using deception, disinformation, or whatever it takes to command the element of surprise. Here is Sun Tzu's advice on the five dangerous characteristics of a military leader:

1. A Chun Tzu who is willing to die is liable to get killed.
2. A Chun Tzu who is afraid to die is likely to get captured.
3. A Chun Tzu who gets angry when insulted is going to make mistakes.
4. A Chun Tzu who is obsessed with honor misses out on tactical advantages.
5. A Chun Tzu who loves his sword is apt to misuse it.

2. The Tai Kung Wang: His personal name was Chiang Shang. He was the military leader who made possible the Chou Dynasty in the 11th Century B.C. According to the legends, the Tai Kung feigned madness in order to escape service to a tyrant and retreated to the rugged ocean coast. Eventually, at the advanced age of 72, Tai Kung became the military advisor to the kings of the Chou (King Wen and later, King Wu) and spent nearly 30 years leading their forces in brilliant campaigns, constantly surprising his enemies with unorthodox plans. The book, **Tai Kung's Six Secret Teachings**, advances the idea of *Total Warfare*, where every element in society, including all classes of people, are to be organized and armed. The six books are **Civil Tao**, instructions on governing and rulership, **Martial Tao**, how to manipulate the enemy, **Dragon Tao**, military organization, **Tiger Tao**, the tactics of weapons and the battlefield, **Leopard Tao**, how to use difficult terrain effectively, and **Canine Tao**, coordinating heavy and light infantry and cavalry, as well as regular, elite and guerilla forces.

3. Wu Tzu: Also called Wu Chi (440-361 B.C.), was a model for Chun Tzu in that he always lived among the common troops, shared all their hardships, marched with the soldiers, and carried his own pack. He also put his military duty above everything, to the point of missing his mother's funeral rites (a horrible, horrible crime of filial irresponsibility, especially to Confucians), rather than abandoning his duty post. His book, known simply as *Wu Tzu*, emphasizes the selecting and training of soldiers, at all ranks, as well as the importance of the army's relationship to the society (for example, he thought it vital that the families of slain soldiers be provided for).

4. Others: Other role models for a Chun Tzu include Ssu Ma Fa, who wrote of *The Methods of the Ssu Ma*; and the author of *Three Strategies of Huang Shih Kung*. Three other important books are *Wei Liao Tzu*, *Questions & Answers of Tang Tai Tsung and Li Wei Kung*, and the *Wu Ching Tsung Yao* ("Essentials of the Martial Classics").

Demon Hunter O.C.C.

Fu Yao Da Chia ("Great Demon Catching Hero!")

Demon Hunters are usually written off as misfits and/or troublemakers who are unable to fit into the suit-and-tie (or mandarin-jacket-and-pants) world. If there was a job posting for a Demon Hunter, it would look something like this:

Wanted: Loud-Mouthed Big-Muscled Jerk. In need of someone who takes risks, bets against the odds, and is a good loser. Must be obnoxious, capable of blustering and/or pleading for mercy but also charming and fast-talking. Criminal record of gambling, drunkenness, vandalism and carousing required; skill with confidence games (i.e. "Con Artist") a plus. Please, no one with moral or ethical compunctions need apply, yet applicant must be ultimately honest in outlook and practice, and completely resistant to threats, bribery, coercion or blackmail. No job security, unpleasant travelling conditions, and very little hope of monetary compensation.

Of course there are no such advertisements. Demon Hunters hunt demons because they *love* doing it. It's the ultimate challenge, putting mountain-climbing, bungee-jumping, and alligator-wrestling to shame.

Finding the demons, though it may take decades, is the easy part. After all, it's not all that different from finding any kind of monster. Keep your ears open for stories, legends and myths. Then go tracking all over the place looking for demons. It may take years, but when you get close enough, all you have to do is follow the screams of the victims.

Once you find a demon, everything changes.

Demon Hunters aren't anything like their strong-jawed, monster-slayer cousins, who win by out-fighting or out-gunning their prey. No, Demon Hunters have to outsmart their quarry. For this character it's not good enough to simply defeat, exile, or kill, a demon in combat. Sooner or later the demon will come back, nastier than ever and probably hundreds of miles away, seeking a fresh batch of innocent victims.

Successful Demon Hunters understand that demons must be somehow bound, forced to submit, or utterly humiliated. Ideally, a Demon Hunter can even *rehabilitate* a demon. Of course, to do any of this you have to learn to *think* like a demon, to develop an understanding of how demons react and behave. So here's a briefing on what a Demon Hunter knows about demon weaknesses, and how to take advantage of them.

Demon Hunter Requirements & Base Numbers:

Attribute Requirements: I.Q. 11 and P.S. 12. A high M.A. and P.E. are good too, but not requirements.

Alignment Requirements: None, but is usually unprincipled or anarchist.

Base S.D.C.: 35

Base Hit Points: Standard (equal to P.E.), plus 1D6 per level of experience.

Base Chi: Standard (equal to P.E.).

Base P.P.E.: Standard (3D6).

Demon Hunter Knowledge of Demon Weaknesses:

1. Demon Ego. Demons are very egotistical. They imagine themselves to be tremendously superior in every way, particularly to any mere mortal. From a demon's point of view, humans are less than bugs, less than germs, less than dust. This means they tend to underestimate humans, and accept foolish challenges and duels.

2. Demon Greed. Demons are, by their very nature, greedy, power-hungry and selfish. If they want something, they want it NOW! Demons can usually be persuaded to want just about anything (a demon obsessed with the shopping channel is not out of the question).

3. Demon Groveling. When defeated or in the presence of their Infernal masters, demons turn into pathetic, fawning, servile, yes-demons. In other words, when the tables are turned, so do demons. Accustomed to taking arbitrary orders from their masters, all demons have had a few thousand years to get used to being an underling. Most demons regard their overlords with a combination of awe and dread.

4. Demon Laziness. While most demons are far from dumb, they are lazy. Given half a chance, they'll do no work at all, even putting off urgent assignments whenever there is the slightest excuse. This means they may try to get other lesser beings/slaves/lackeys to do their work for them, and are always looking for the easy way out (which can get them into trouble).

5. Demon Cowardice. Demons are nearly invulnerable. However, they are also ridiculously sensitive to certain types of pain. The hard part is figuring out *how* to inflict that pain. Demons are pretty invulnerable to many of the things that would hurt a human. For example, most demons don't even register the pain from cuts, puncture wounds, bullets, heat or cold, poison, dismemberment, etc. Frankly, you could gouge out an eyeball with a dull spoon and the demon wouldn't do much more than chuckle. However, there are things that can really *hurt* a demon, at least for as long as it is in physical form. The demon hunter strives to learn these weaknesses and exploit them. Often even the threat of pain will be enough to bluff or intimidate a Chinese demon (the fact that the hunter knows what its weakness is, sends shivers up the creature's spine). Remember, not all demons have the same vulnerability to pain.

6. Twisting & Pinching. Surprisingly, most demons can suffer hideous pain when their own body parts are constricted. Fingers, toes, ears, noses, lips, tongues, eyelids, and any other loose body parts are good possible targets. Don't try to grab the whole body or limb, the idea is to just pinch or twist a tiny amount, just enough to fit between the fingernails. Such attacks will startle, distract and bother the creature to such a point that the demon may lose the initiative and one melee action as a result of each pinch or twist (roll 20 sided die, high roll wins). Constant attacks of this nature can intimidate, confuse or chase away lesser demons, however, they tend to only annoy and enrage the more powerful ones.

7. Hangovers. After bouts of heavy drinking, usually within fifteen minutes of the last drink, demons are subject to horrible, horrible hangovers. While in the grip of the terrible pain, the demon will be sensitive to noises, smells, vibration, and bright lights (all of which do double damage or have double the effect). Furthermore, all of the creature's usual combat abilities, bonuses, attacks per melee, skill proficiencies and speed are reduced by *half* while hungover! Unfortunately, demons recover from a hangover in about 15 minutes (and typically need to consume eight to ten times more alcohol than a human to get drunk in the first place).

8. Tickling. *Some* demons are tremendously ticklish. This is also something that they are deeply ashamed of. Not only can such demons be rendered helpless by tickling, but threatening to reveal the demons' terrible secret may be a great way to bully them into submission. When tickled, the creature's combat abilities, bonuses, attacks per melee, and speed are reduced by 75%! Skill proficiency is zero (they just squirm and laugh)!! Constant, relentless tickling will completely incapacitate the demon — no attacks or melee actions are possible except for one strike (punch, push, kick, bite, etc.) to make the tickler stop, or an attempt to dodge per melee round. The dodge is an attempt to tumble or leap away from the tickler, but the demon is -4 to dodge, and -6 to strike while being tickled. A demon who is able to pull away from a tickle attack recovers immediately and will be extremely angry and/or embarrassed. He will seek to punish the perpetrator, but will also be cautious of future tickle attacks (or other tricks) and, as a result, is -2 on initiative and -1 to strike, parry or dodge when facing his tickler.

9. Demon Treason. Once conquered or defeated, demons are total turncoats. They'll squeal out every secret they know, betray all the plans of their former masters, and instantly kowtow to whoever commands them. For this reason, lesser demons are frequently told only what they need to know and those captured by the enemy may be slain by their retreating comrades or Infernal masters before they can talk. Of course, Demon Hunters who have demon servants should bear in mind that the reverse is also true, and that a demon stolen away from him will immediately spill its guts about all the Demon Hunter's plans, secrets and vulnerabilities.

10. Demon Superstition. Demons are very superstitious, gullible, and easily led into believing in legends, myths, rumors, etc. For example, while true *Demon Mirrors* are exceedingly rare, demons have a fright of ALL mirrors (H.F. 8). *See the I Ching mirror under Special Gear* for details about mirrors.

11. Demon Cruelty. It is in the nature of demons to torture their victims and subject them to degradation. However, most exhibit a surprising measure of restraint and control. Any demon knows, "living things suffer more than dead things," and "an arm dismembered is an arm that feels no pain." Also, "a victim's anticipation of torture is just as important as hunger before a meal." More than one Demon Hunter has survived by knowing these important demon maxims.

Demon Hunter Tricks & Tactics. Or, Trickery, and the Art of Binding Demons

1. Talking! The first step in conquering a demon is to get it to talk! Simply fighting demons is pretty useless since you'll either (1) start winning so that the demon will flee, or (2) lose, which means torture and/or death. A fleeing demon only means trouble down the road, and the latter alternative is too horrible to contemplate. So the trick is, talk first, fight later.

Getting the demon to talk is simply a matter of playing to its weaknesses such as its ego, greed or superstitions. Another possibility is to simply say something that confuses or interests the demon. Consider the following bit of name-dropping as an example:

Demon (to a cornered Demon Hunter): "Stupid human, I will now tear the limbs from your body..."

Demon Hunter: "So, how about that King Pien Cheng Wang? Is he a kidder, or what?"

Demon: "What?"

Demon Hunter: "You know, Cheng Wang, Yama King of the 6th Hell! A being who really appreciates a good joke."

Demon (suddenly cautious): "You know Cheng... I mean... you know the great King Pien?"

Demon Hunter: "Well, you know how it goes. You go to a couple of royal Yama functions, and one thing leads to another."

Suddenly the demon is more cautious. He doesn't want to evoke the wrath of a Yama King by slaying a friend or family member. Furthermore, if this apparently puny human is a friend of the King, then he may be much more than he appears. Ultimately, this all leads to some degree of confusion or hesitation which opens the door to opportunity for the Demon Hunter (he can strike, escape, bluff, trick or manipulate his opponent).

2. Entertaining Demons. Demons just aren't used to being treated all that well. In their native land (one of the Hells of the Yama Kings) they are usually kicked around, beaten, and forced to work for centuries at a time without so much as a coffee break. From a demon's point of view, an invitation to share a drink or a bite to eat is pretty inviting. Make it a part of a sit-down meal and the demon is probably hooked. Combining this tactic with compliments, praise and apparent appreciation or respect for the monster, and the demon becomes putty in the hands of the Demon Hunter. This is especially true of lesser demons. Ancient demons and lords tend to be more wary and quick to recognize lies, false praise and con-games, but they too can be swayed, or put at ease by (false) adoration and entertainment.

3. Gambling with Demons. Demons will gamble on anything. In their native land (one of the Hells of the Yama Kings), they are desperate enough to bet on the stupidest things imaginable, just to break the tedium. Winning a bet against a demon may not be enough to conquer it, but if a demon loses (especially repeatedly) it will definitely shake the monster's confidence (-1 on initiative and strike when up against the character it lost to). The demon is also more likely to believe, or be intimidated by a character it has lost many bets or contests to.

4. Challenging Demons. Ultimately, to truly subdue a demon, the Demon Hunter has to challenge it to some kind of contest, duel or game. A crude example, found in many fairy tales, is where the hero says something like, "Well, yes, you seem awfully mighty and powerful, but how could you possibly fit into this teeny-weeny, little bottle?" Here's a typical exchange for a Demon Hunter:

Demon Hunter: "Yes, I believe that you are the most powerful of demons. However, I wonder..."

Demon: "Wonder what? Do you doubt my power?"

Demon Hunter: "I was just wondering..."

Demon: "What!?! Speak, you meaningless thing!"

Demon Hunter: "Can you wrestle?"

Demon: "Wrestle? I can out-wrestle all of you! I can defeat the greatest human wrestler that ever lived! I could wrestle your entire nation into abject submission."

Demon Hunter: "Yes, but do you think you could out-wrestle me?"

Demon: "Of course, I could out-wrestle you any day of the year! I could out-wrestle you in any of the fourteen planes of hell! I could out-wrestle you in front of the celestial throne itself! There is no way that you could ever defeat me!"

Demon Hunter: "Ever?"

Demon: "Ever!"

Demon Hunter: "Mighty one, while you are awesome indeed, I think that you are exaggerating. Surely there must be some way, in the wide and infinite wonder of the world, that would allow me to wrestle you with some tiny chance of success..."

Demon Hunter Combat Abilities: There is no way that someone with the personality of a Demon Hunter would be able to stick around long enough to master an entire Martial Art Form. They just don't have that kind of patience. Instead, Demon Hunters tend to wander from school to school, picking up one ability at a time, and ending up with their own hodgepodge combat system (*see the Demon Hunter Advancement Bonuses*).

Demon Hunters automatically have the following martial art abilities:

Demon Wrestling and one Demon Hunter Body Hardening Exercise.

Sword Chi Technique, from Martial Art Techniques.

Weapon Kata: Demon Hunter Sword, from Specialty Katas.

Demon Hunter Advancement Bonuses: This character does not select a specific area of Martial Arts training.

1st Level: Two attacks per melee round, entangle, +1 to strike, +2 to roll with punch/fall/impact, +1 to pull punch, +1 to dodge, +2 to save vs pain, and +2 to strike and entangle with "Demon Snare."

2nd: Add 1D6 to hit points, +2D6 to S.D.C. +1 on initiative, +1 to maintain balance, and +2 to save vs horror factor.

3rd: +1 attack per melee round, and is able to do all kicks, leap attacks, and backward sweeps.

4th: Select one Demon Hunter Body Hardening Exercise, and knockout/stun on 19 or better, and +1 to save vs horror factor.

5th: +1 on initiative and select one new secondary skill.

6th: +1 to roll with punch/fall/impact, +1 to save vs horror factor, +2 to save vs possession and +2D6 to S.D.C.

7th: +1 to strike and parry, +1 to entangle with Demon Snare.

8th: +1 attack per melee round, and select +2 to break fall.

9th: Select one additional Demon Hunter Body Hardening exercise.

10th: Arm hold, leg hold, and select one new secondary skill.

11th: +1 to parry and dodge, +1 to entangle with Demon Snare.

12th: Double existing Chi, +1 to save vs horror factor, and +1 to roll with punch/fall/impact.

13th: +1 attack per melee round, and +1 to strike.

14th: Add 1D6 to hit points, +15 to S.D.C., and +1 to parry.

15th: Select one additional Demon Hunter Body Hardening Exercise, or One art of Invisibility, and select one new secondary skill.

Demon Hunter O.C.C. Skills:

Tiao Qi, the game of Chinese Checkers (+10%).
Chinese Language: Stage 1/Thousand Character Literacy.
Fasting (+10%)
Singing (+5%)
Tracking (+15%)
Wilderness Survival (+10%)
Desert Survival (+5%)
Mountaineering (+10%)
Spelunking (+10%)
Cook
Hunting — Snare
W.P. Long Sword: Proficient in, *Shi-Zi Jen* ("Lion Head Sword"), *Lieu Yeh Dau* ("Willow Leaf Saber"), *Pok Dau* ("executioner's blade") and *Giau Tzu Jen* ("Snake Headed Sawtooth Sword").

W.P. Demon Snare (Special!). Used exclusively as a weapon of entrapment to catch an opponent's neck, wrist, or ankle. A snare can *not* be used to parry and does no damage on impact. However, the snare is designed to pinch and gouge as it tightens, creating pain in susceptible demons. Also see the entangling combat skill.

This skill also includes training in braiding demon snares out of ordinary string or rope, or out of strips of cloth or leather.

Arm Wrestling Skill (New!). Distractions... need to beat the other guy's roll three times in a row: 1st successful roll steadies the grip, 2nd successful roll tilts the enemy's arm down, and the third successful roll slams the enemy's hand to the table! Roll 20 sided die (plus bonuses). High rolls win, ties mean no advantage for either side — stalemate, roll again. Every three points of a character's P.S. above 16 counts as a +1 bonus to win at arm wrestling. Furthermore, a character with the arm wresting skill gets an additional +1 bonus at 1st level, 5th, 10th and 15th levels. **Note:** This skill can be taken by other O.C.C.s but counts as two skill selections.

Demon Hunter O.C.C. Secondary Skills: Select ten from the following list. (No, the Demon Hunter has no O.C.C. *related* skills, but thanks for noticing). The numbers in parentheses are the Demon Hunter's bonuses for those skills.

Communications: Basic Radio Only.
Computer: None
Cultural/Domestic: Any
Cultural Games: Any (+5%)
Electrical: Basic Only
Espionage: Any
Mechanical: Any, but only as Secondary Skill.
Medical: First Aid or Paramedic Only.
Military: None
Physical: Any (+10%)
Pilot Skills, Basic: Any
Pilot Skills, Advanced: None
Pilot Related Skills: None
Science: None
Swindler: Any (+5%)
Technical: Any. **Note:** Demon Hunters have a +10% in any language or dialect skill they select.
Temple: Any
W.P. Ancient Chinese: Any
W.P. Modern: Any
W.P. Military: Any

Demon Hunter Finances: Overall, the Demon Hunter's finances waver somewhere between disaster and calamity. No matter how much they make, it seems like they're always spending/losing more. The fact that Demon Hunters don't really live for the future means they have a nasty habit of borrowing money from loan sharks.

Cash: Start with $5,000 for initial equipment, with the remainder as ready cash and/or valuables.

Income: None. If worse comes to worst and no work is available, the Demon Hunter can always fall back on dish washing in a restaurant for $250 per week.

Special Demon Hunter Gear: In order to really get going as a Demon Hunter, the character must have had some training from an older Demon Hunter. This "teacher" will give the player character the following items to help them on their way:

Book: Wan Gui Yao: Otherwise known as the "Essentials of the 10,000 Infernals," this book can be used to look up all kinds of information on various demons. Replacement Cost: $500. The trick is finding a copy, since only a few copies have ever been printed. There is only a 1% chance of finding one in a used bookstore, and a 15% chance that an Antiquarian can track down a copy.

Weapons: A Demon Hunter Sword, the equivalent to a "Lion's Head Sword." Comes with a long, straight blade, a short crossbar, and a Yin-Yang symbol. Sharp edges and a sharp point. Replacement Cost: $2,000. Damage: 2D6+2

I Ching Mirror: According to ancient legend, these eight-sided mirrors, decorated with the eight trigrams of the I Ching, are supposed to be able to entrap any demon foolish enough to be caught gazing into it. This is pure hogwash! However, demons are gossipy critters and they've all heard a few hundred years of rumors about how dangerous magical mirrors can be. Better safe than sorry, is how most demons think. So an I Ching Mirror can be pretty handy when it comes to threatening demons, especially if the Demon Hunter has a good reputation, an impressive name for the mirror, and a convincing story about it. To a demon, such mirrors will have a horror factor of 13 (+1 for every three levels of experience of the Demon Hunter; any mirror will have a horror factor of 8. Half for greater demons and lords). Most lesser and stupid demons will react to the I Ching Mirror similar to the reaction of the traditional vampire and the crucifix. The I Ching Mirror will hold the beast at bay (at least temporarily), and cause it to look away or cover its eyes (they try never to look into mirrors), and requires a roll to save vs horror factor 13 (or higher). If nothing else, the mirror should provide the player character a momentary distraction in which he can flee, hide, attack or take some action. Replacement Cost of an I Ching Mirror: $50 to $75

Jian Shih O.C.C.

Weapon-Based Martial Artist

A purist, the Jian Shih is a character who has found a lifelong hobby in the study of tools of combat. Like a swordsman from Ancient China, or the Medieval knight, the character attempts to forge the body and the tool of combat into one.

Their weapons are so deadly that many Jian Shih are reluctant to enter into a battle. Unlike other martial artists, when they do fight, they understand that they may well deal in death.

Since they are so dependent on the martial arts they practice, and the corresponding weapons they select, there are really four different kinds of Jian Shih, almost four different O.C.C.s.

Jian Shih Requirements & Base Numbers:

Attribute Requirements: P.P. 10 (or higher)

Alignment Requirements: None; can be any alignment.

Base S.D.C.: 25

Base Hit Points: Standard (P.E.), plus 1D6 per level of experience.

Base Chi: Standard (P.E.)

Base P.P.E.: Standard (3D6)

Chun Tzu Advancement Bonuses: This is in addition to bonuses gained from martial arts combat training.

1st: +1D6 hit points, +2 to save vs pain and +1 on initiative.
2nd: +1 to save vs horror factor, +1 to pull punch.
3rd: Add 2D6 S.D.C.
4th: Select one new W.P., +1 to strike with a thrown weapon.
5th: Select one secondary skill.
6th: +1 on initiative and +1 to pull punch/strike.
7th: Select one new W.P.
8th: Add 2D6 to S.D.C.
9th: +1 to roll with impact or fall and +1 to save vs pain.
10th: Select one secondary skill.
11th: +1 to strike with a thrown weapon.
12th: +1 on initiative, and add 2D6 to S.D.C.
13th: +1 to save vs pain, and +1 to save vs horror factor.
14th: Select one new W.P.
15th: Select one secondary skill.

Jian Shih Martial Arts. Select any **one** martial art form from the following. Each sends the character along a quite different pathway.

1. Gui Long Kung Fu. The ultimate Jian Shih martial art, Gui Long views the sword as the most perfect of weapons. Swords are also considered to have a mystical quality, such that extraordinary blades may even achieve a kind of "life." **Special Weapon:** A high-quality Lion Sword (does 3D6 damage), worth from $2,000 to $7,000 (1D6+1 times $1,000). This weapon should eventually be named by the character and is considered an extension of himself.

2. Liang Hsiung Kung Fu (Demon Combat). Characters who choose Liang Hsiung will tend to be the most fun-loving of all the Jian Shih. While these characters enjoy a good bash, whether in combat or a rousing game of street football, their humor takes on a more grim purpose when they don their suits of demon armor.

Special Weapons: The student of Liang Hsiung Kung Fu has three sets of spurs:

1. Exercise Spurs. Straps, each mounted with metal spurs, can be attached to the character's knuckles, palms, elbows, shoulders, knees and ankles, along with a light helmet fixed with twin horns. While designed for practice, these spurs inflict full spike and gore damage (see Liang Hsiung for details), but they are blunted enough so they won't penetrate exercise padding. Replacement Value: $450.

2. Combat Spurs. Identical to the exercise version, except the spurs have sharpened points, and serrated edges. Effectively they do the same damage, but they'll rip through clothing, exercise padding and light armor (padded and soft leather). Replacement Value: $750.

3. Full Demon Armor. A spectacular full-armor suit, painted and shaped to appear as an armored demon bristling with thorn-like spurs, horns and spikes, each with sharp points and serrated edges. Typically Demon Armor has an A.R. 14, 140 S.D.C. (see the section describing *Liang Hsiung Kung Fu* for full details). Replacement Cost: $3,500 to $5,000.

3. Shih Ba Ban Wu Yi (Eighteen Weapons). The ideal martial art for the character who wants to be able to use just about *any* hand-to-hand weapon. While not as powerful as some other martial arts, it does give unprecedented versatility. **Special Weapons:** The character can select up to ten weapons from the "Weapons of Ancient China" section, each is of the highest quality (any additional skill selections can include modern weapons).

4. Triad Assassin Training (Automatic Pistols). Having received the full training, the character has subsequently fled the Triad for some reason (perhaps because of a change in alignment). This means the character is now living under an assumed name and must be constantly alert to being discovered by the old organization. **Special Weapons:** The character starts with a *pair* of 9 mm pistols (choose either Beretta, Browning, Glock, Heckler & Koch, or the French PA15), fourteen magazine clips, and an extra 400 rounds of ammunition.

5. Optional. The Japanese martial art form *Zanji Shinjinken-Ryu*, from **Revised Ninjas & Superspies,** is another option, subject to the Game Master's approval. A Jian Shih with *Zanji* will start off with a high quality pair of swords, Katana (3D6 damage) & Wakizashi (2D6 damage), worth about $2,500 each.

Jian Shih O.C.C. Skills:

Chinese Language: Stage 2/Chinese Literacy.
Paramedic (+5%).
W.P.: Just those included in the martial art form and Chun Tzu advancement bonuses table.

Jian Shih O.C.C. Related Skills: Select a total of four skills from the following list:

Communications: Basic Radio Only
Computer: None
Cultural/Domestic: Any
Cultural Games: Any
Electrical: Basic Only
Espionage: Any
Mechanical: Any, but only as Secondary Skill.
Medical: None
Military: Any
Physical: Any (+10%)
Pilot Skills, Basic: Any
Pilot Skills, Advanced: Any
Pilot Related Skills: Any
Science: None
Swindler: Any (+5%)
Technical: Any
Temple: Any
W.P. Ancient Chinese: Any
W.P. Modern: Any
W.P. Military: Any

Jian Shih Secondary Skills: Select any four from the Jian Shih O.C.C. Related Skills. These do not get the advantage of the bonus listed in parentheses. All secondary skills start at base skill level.

Standard Jian Shih Gear: In addition to a full set of clothing and personal effects, the character gets a weapon, or weapons, according to the martial art form selected. See above.

Jian Shih Finances: Money isn't a pressing concern, but the Jian Shih usually tries to keep at least $2,500 around (in travellers' checks, or in some portable form), for "emergencies."

Cash: $20,000 to spend on initial equipment, or saved.

Income: Always a difficulty, jobs will depend on the O.C.C. related skills that the character selects. However, it is in the nature of a Jian Shih that they have difficulty staying anywhere very long, and they'll generally make about 20% less than usual for any given position.

Nei Chia Wu Shih O.C.C.

Meditative Martial Artist

Calm, clear, committed. The Nei Chia Wu Shih tends to be like a smooth rock in the river of life, allowing troubles and woes to flow across and around without disturbance. From this character's point of view, even more important than the martial arts is the art of Meditation. *Mudra*, the mystic positioning of the hands and body, over which the Nei Chia Wu Shih is a master, is considered a mere side-effect to the ultimate mastery of the mind.

Nei Chia Wu Shih are most committed to self-mastery, through the clarity of their own minds. However, one cannot advance uniformly by completely retreating from the world. There is also much to be learned by seeking out demons and other supernatural entities in the world of *Mystic China*.

Nei Chia Wu Shih Requirements & Base Numbers

Attribute Requirements: M.E. 12 or higher and a high M.A. is helpful but not required.

Alignment Requirements: None

Base S.D.C.: 20

Base Hit Points: Standard (P.E.), plus 1D6 per level of experience.

Base Chi: Standard (P.E.)

Base P.P.E.: 4D6

Nei Chia Wu Shih Mudra Mastery: Each Nei Chia Wu Shih has an understanding of all Mudra and how they work. However, the character, at the start, can perform the three basic Mudra plus an additional ten selections, as follows:

Mudra of Protection: Take the *Mudra of Silent Contemplation*, plus any four others.

Mudra of Evocation: Take the *Mudra for the Collection of Alms*, plus any three others.

Mudra of Self-Possession: Take the *Mudra of Tranquility and Collection*, plus any two others.

Mudra for the Manipulation of Objects: Select any one.

Note: Additional Mudra are available as the character advances in experience levels, according to the Advancement Bonuses table.

Nei Chia Wu Shih Advancement Bonuses: This is in addition to bonuses gained from martial arts combat training.

1st: +3 to save vs pain, +2 to save vs possession, and +1 to save vs horror factor.

2nd: Add 1D6 to hit points, and select one new Mudra of Protection.

3rd: +1 to save vs possession, and select one new Mudra of Evocation.

4th: Add +5 to Chi, select one new Mudra of Self-Possession.

5th: +1 to psionic attack/mind control, +1 to save vs horror factor, and select one new Mudra for the Manipulation of Objects.

6th: Add 1D6 to S.D.C, +1 to save vs possession, and select one new Mudra of Evocation.

7th: Select one new Mudra of Self-Possession.

8th: Add +5 to Chi, and select one new Mudra of Protection.

9th: Select one new Mudra of Evocation.

10th: +1 to save vs magic, and select one new Mudra of Self-Possession.

11th: Select one new Mudra for the Manipulation of Objects.

12th: Add 1D6 to S.D.C., add +5 to Chi, and select one new Mudra of Protection.

13th: +1 to save vs horror factor and +1 to psionic attack/mind control.

14th: +1 to save vs possession, and select one new Mudra of Self-Possession.

15th: Select one new Mudra for the Manipulation of Objects.

Nei Chia Wu Shih Martial Art Forms: Select any **one** martial art form from the following list:

Ba Gua Kung Fu (Eight Trigrams)
Ch'in-Na (Seizing)
Fu Chiao Pai Kung Fu (Tiger Claw)
Gui Long Kung Fu (Dragon Spirit)
Han Yu Kung Fu (Chi Katas)
Hsien Hsia (Immortality)
Hsing-I Kung Fu (Mind Shaping)
Lee Kwan Choo (Non-Violent)
Mien-Ch'uan Kung Fu (Cotton Fist)
Monkey Style Kung Fu (Monkey Katas)
Pao Chih (Animus Development)
Shan Tung Kung Fu (Black Tiger)
Pao Pat Mei Kung Fu (Leopard Style)
Shao-Lin Kung Fu (Classic Style)
Tai-Chi Ch'uan (Exercise Style)

Nei Chia Wu Shih O.C.C. Skills:

Meditation (+20%)
Chinese Language: Stage 4/Classical Chinese Literacy.
Other Languages: Character can select a total of three languages and/or dialects (+5% each).

Artistic Calligraphy (+5%): Copying old books and manuscripts is an occasional part of the character's duties, something that is still practiced in many Taoist and Buddhist monasteries and temples.
Wilderness Survival (+10%). The character knows how to live off the land.
Begging (+10%)
Fasting (+5%)
Oriental Philosophy: Taoism or Buddhism (+8%)

Nei Chia Wu Shih O.C.C. Related Skills: Select four other skills.
Communications: Basic Radio only (+5%)
Computer: Operations only
Cultural/Domestic: Any (+5%)
Cultural Games: Any (+5%)
Electrical: Basic Only
Espionage: Any
Mechanical: Any, but only as Secondary Skill.
Medical: Any
Military: None
Physical: Any (+10%)
Pilot Skills, Basic: Any
Pilot Skills, Advanced: None
Pilot Related Skills: None
Science: Any
Swindler: None
Technical: Any
Temple: Any (+5%)
W.P. Ancient Chinese: Any
W.P. Modern: Any
W.P. Military: None

Nei Chia Wu Shih Secondary Skills: Select any four from the previous list. These do not get the advantage of the bonus listed in parentheses. All secondary skills start at base skill level.

Nei Chia Wu Shih Finances: Most Nei Chia Wu Shih have taken a vow of poverty and deliberately avoid possessions of any kind.

Cash: Has $300 to spend on small personal possessions. The character rarely has more than $300 at any time; usually less than $50!

Income: Begging, just enough for the bare necessities, usually only spends a few hours per day to acquire money. The character would usually rather meditate than engage in any job, however any low-paying job with boring, repetitive motions can be handled with ease ($120 to $220 per week). Money is spent on food, essential items, or given to the poor and good causes.

Special Nei Chia Wu Shih Gear: The character starts with a simple set of temple garb, including a robe, a warm cloak, sandals, a begging bowl (also used for eating), and a meager assortment of personal effects (toothbrush, soap, small towel, etc.). In addition, the character can have a case containing a personal journal or notebook, writing implements, and room for another book or two. Instead of collecting any kind of library, the character prefers to borrow or trade books, never having more than one or two at a time.

Wai Chia Wu Shih O.C.C.

Open Hand Martial Artist

From the point of view of a Wai Chia Wu Shih, taking up any weapon, for any reason, is a sign of weakness and is a surrender to barbarism. Conflict, when it cannot be avoided, should be settled with the ultimate weapon: the human body itself. For that reason the character will NEVER learn any weapon proficiency or weapon Kata. However, the same unstinting devotion and single-mindedness that causes the character to spurn the use of weapons, also enables the character to master *two* different martial art forms.

In general, Wai Chia Wu Shih are skeptical of most modern innovations. That doesn't mean the character won't ride on a bus or an airplane, but it does mean that he/she will never own a motorized vehicle. Likewise, when it comes to any kind of tool or device, the character is usually happier with a manual version over a powered one, and happiest of all if the task can be completed with nothing more than hands, feet and muscle.

Wai Chia Wu Shih

Requirements & Base Numbers

Attribute Requirements: I.Q. 9 and M.E. 10
Alignment Requirements: None
Base S.D.C.: 30
Base Hit Points: Standard (P.E.), plus 1D6 per level of experience.
Base Chi: Standard (P.E.)
Base P.P.E.: Standard (3D6)
Chun Tzu Advancement Bonuses: This is in addition to bonuses gained from martial arts combat training.
1st: +1 to save vs horror factor, +2 to save vs pain, and +1 to save vs possession.
2nd: Add 1D6 to hit points, add 1D6 to Chi.
3rd: +1 to save vs horror factor and +1 to save vs possession.
4th: Select one new O.C.C. related skill.
5th: Add 1D6 to hit points, 2D6 to S.D.C. and 1D6 to Chi.
6th: Add 1D6 to P.P.E. and +1 on initiative.
7th: Select one new O.C.C. related skill.
8th: Add 1D6 to hit points and +1 to save vs pain.
9th: Add 1D6 to Chi and +1 to save vs possession.
10th: Select one new O.C.C. related skill.
11th: Add 3D6 to S.D.C., and add 1D6 to P.P.E.
12th: +2 to save vs pain and +1 to save vs horror factor.
13th: Select one new O.C.C. related skill.
14th: Add 1D6 to hit points and add 1D6 to Chi.
15th: Add 1D6 to P.P.E. and +1 to save vs possession.

Wai Chia Wu Shih Primary Martial Art Form: Select any **one** martial art form from the following list:
Bok Pai Kung Fu (Crane Style)
Hsing-I Kung Fu (Mind Shaping)
Lee Kwan Choo (Non-Violent)
Mien-Ch'uan Kung Fu (Cotton Fist)
Shao-Lin Kung Fu (Classic Style)
Snake Style Kung Fu (She Shen)
Tai-Chi Ch'uan (Exercise Style)

Tien-Hsueh Kung Fu (Touch Mastery)
Tong Lun Kung Fu (Praying Mantis)

Wai Chia Wu Shih Secondary Martial Art Form: Select any **one** martial art form from the following list:
An Yin Kung Fu (Meditative/Mudra)
Ch'in-Na (Seizing)
Drunken Style (Pu Kung Fu)
Kuo-Ch'uan Kung Fu (Dog Boxing)
Han Yu Kung Fu (Chi Katas)
Monkey Style Kung Fu (Monkey Katas)
Pao Chih (Animus Development)
Pao Pat Mei Kung Fu (Leopard Style)

Wai Chia Wu Shih O.C.C. Skills:

Bicycle (New!). Where most characters can ride a bicycle with minimal training, having the bicycle skill means the character can (1) ride a suitably tough bike over wilderness and rocky terrain, (2) attain speeds up to three times normal running speed, (3) travel cross-country at a speed equal to the character's full-out running speed (Spd. attribute), and perform jumps and tricks (roll under skill proficiency. A failed roll means a crash or fall). Speed can be maintained for a number of hours equal to half the character's Physical Endurance (P.E.). The skill also includes some basic bicycle mechanics/repairs, so the character can fix tires, reattach chains, and generally make sufficient field repairs to get a wounded bike to a garage. **Base Skill:** 44% +4% per level of experience. **Note:** This skill can be selected by other characters but counts as two skill selections.
Chinese Language: Stage 3/Advanced Chinese Literacy.
Language Dialects: Chinese (+10%).
Chinese Classical Studies (+5%).
Oriental Philosophies: Taoist or Buddhist.
Land Navigation (+5%)
Paramedic (+10%)
Mountaineering
Wilderness Survival (+5%)
Acrobatics
Athletics (General)
Climbing
Swimming: Advanced
Cooking (+15%)
Gardening (+6%)
Note: All Wai Chia Wu Shih are strict vegetarians, who often have to prepare their own meals.

Wai Chia Wu Shih O.C.C. Related Skills: Select four other skills from the following list.
Communications: Basic Radio Only
Computer: None
Cultural/Domestic: Any (+10%)
Cultural Games: Any (+5%)
Electrical: None
Espionage: None
Mechanical: None
Medical: First aid or paramedic Only (+5%).
Military: None
Physical: Any (+5%)
Pilot, Basic: Water Vehicle, Sail Only (+10%).
Pilot, Advanced: None
Pilot Related Skills: None
Science: Any
Swindler: Any
Technical: Any
Temple: Any (+15%)
W.P.: None

Wai Chia Wu Shih Secondary Skills: Select any four from the previous list. These do not get the advantage of the bonus listed in parentheses. All secondary skills start at the base skill level.

Wai Chia Wu Shih Finances: Not terribly concerned about money, the character can almost always find jobs. For one thing, as a martial arts teacher/expert, the character is respected as a devoted, honest, hard working person — a desirable employee from the point of view of many ex-students and acquaintances.

Cash: Starts with $5,000 in initial equipment and savings.

Income: Usually an outstanding martial artist, the character can always pick up extra money as a *part-time* martial arts instructor, or teacher of self-defense classes, for about $150 per week ($300 to $350 if full-time).

Special Wai Chia Wu Shih Gear: The character will have a full set of personal clothing and effects, but not much more than that. Usually starts out with an apartment, or sharing a dormitory house with other martial artists, typically from the same school.

Two Non-Combat O.C.C.s

Antiquarian O.C.C.: The scholarly collector of the Arcane
Capitalist Entrepreneur O.C.C.: Wealthy adventurer

Antiquarian O.C.C.

Gu Dong Chia

As a Game Master, I personally love playing this kind of character, complete with odd quirks, unique abilities, and an insatiable craving to collect the rare and unusual. Such characters are fun also because of where they are likely to live: crowded cities and musty old mansions, or shops, filled with bizarre curios and odd servants.

The character is typically eccentric and fascinated by the supernatural, antiquities and the unknown. Antiquarians are part historian, part archeologist, part archivist, and part dabbler in the mystic arts. While antiquarians have no particular psychic or mystic powers, their passion for knowledge and for collecting is downright awesome (and likely to give them a certain amount of arcane knowledge). While they are usually much older than the other player characters, they are interested in adventuring and obsessed with a desire to plumb the depths of the unknown.

More than anything else, the antiquarian is a *collector*. To illustrate the character's attitude, consider the following exchange with another character at the end of successful adventure:

Other Character (OC): "We need money! Can't we sell some of this stuff?"

Antiquarian: "I've already explained. Everything here is priceless. To sell any of it would be a horrible crime, an affront to science and history!"

OC: "Look, what about this book? Let's sell it..."

Antiquarian: "Oh no, we couldn't possibly sell this copy of the *Yuan Ying Chi*. It was printed by the Imperial Court, during the early Ming Dynasty."

OC: "Wait a minute, don't you already have a copy of that book?"

Antiquarian: "Yes! In fact I have, let's see... Hmmm... Eight copies of the *Yuan Ying Chi* in my collection. It is, after all, a very important book."

OC: "Eight copies! Then why can't we sell this one?"

Antiquarian: "I thought I had explained that already. It is an invaluable addition to the other *Yuan Ying Chi* in my collection. You see, my original copy was preserved in a dry climate, off in the desert. See the watermarks on *this* copy?"

OC: "The stains? Here? Does that mean it isn't worth anything? Is that why we can't sell it?"

Antiquarian: " Oh, no. The book is worth thousands to a collector. The water stains merely diminishes the value, but it also indicated this is an entirely different specimen, a valuable contrast to the one preserved in the desert, so it's all the more important to retain *both* copies in the collection..."

Antiquarian Requirements & Base Numbers:

Attribute Requirements: I.Q. 10 and P.P. 8.
Alignment Requirements: None
Base S.D.C.: 10
Base Hit Points: Standard (P.E.), plus 1D6 per level of experience.
Base Chi: Standard (P.E.).
Base P.P.E.: Standard (3D6).
Base Age (Special!): Antiquarians are not young characters. None will be younger than forty (optional: roll 4D6+40 years).
Antiquarian Advancement Bonuses:
1st: +1 to save vs pain, +1 to save vs possession, and +1 to save vs horror factor.
2nd: +2 to save vs psionic attack and mind control.
3rd: Select one new Mudra for the Manipulation of Objects.
4th: +1 to save vs horror factor and +1 to save vs magic.
5th: +5% to decipher calligraphy (celestial, cryptic and mundane).
6th: Add 1D6 to Chi and +1 to save vs possession.
7th: Select one new Mudra for the Manipulation of Objects.
8th: +1 to save vs horror factor and +1 to save vs pain.
9th: +5% to decipher calligraphy (celestial, cryptic and mundane).
10th: Add 1D6 to Chi and +1 to save vs magic.
11th: Select one new Mudra for the Manipulation of Objects.
12th: +1 to save vs horror factor and possession.
13th: +5% to decipher calligraphy (celestial, cryptic and mundane).
14th: Add 1D6 to Chi and +1 to save vs possession.
15th: Select one new Mudra for the Manipulation of Objects.
Antiquarian Knowledge of Mudra: While no expert, an antiquarian will have studied the mystic Mudra enough to have mastered the basics. Aside from being able to perform the *Mudra of Silent Contemplation*, the *Mudra for the Collection of Alms*, and the *Mudra of Tranquility and Collection*, the character's main interest is in the Mudra for the Manipulation of Objects (see Antiquarian Advancement Bonuses above).
Antiquarian Martial Arts (limited): An antiquarian is a *retired martial artist*. That means the character can select one of the following martial art forms, but that there will be NO advancement beyond 1D4 level (roll once to determine combat level)!

Ba Gua Kung Fu (Eight Trigrams)
Bak Mei Kung Fu (White Eyebrow)
Chi Hsuan Men (White Jade Fan)
Hsien Hsia (Immortality)
Shao-Lin Kung Fu (Classic Style)
Tai-Chi Ch'uan (Exercise Style)

Antiquarian Knowledge of Celestial Calligraphy: While incapable of creating a piece of Celestial Calligraphy (the character is **not** a psychic and has no control over P.P.E.), an Antiquarian has the knowledge to use existing Celestial Calligraphy, and can also attempt to interpret, or decipher any Celestial Calligraphy.

Antiquarian O.C.C. Skills:
Chinese Antiquarianism (+25%)
Archeology (+18%)
Chinese Classical Studies (+12%)
Chinese Language: Stage 4/Classical Chinese Literacy.
Chinese History (+5%)
Other Languages: Select Two (+10%)
Math: Basic (+12%)
Photography (+5%)
Writing
W.P. (Ancient Chinese): One of Choice.
W.P. Modern: One of Choice.

Antiquarian O.C.C. Related Skills: Select twelve from the following list:
Communications: Any (+10% for basic only)
Cultural/Domestic: Any (+10%)
Cultural Games: Any (+5%)
Electrical: Basic Only
Espionage: Any
Medical: Any one (+5%)
Pilot, Basic: Any
Pilot, Advanced: Any
Pilot Related Skills: Any
Science: All (+15%)
Technical: Any (+10%)
Temple: Any

Antiquarian Secondary Skills: Select any four from the following:
Cultural/Domestic: Any
Cultural Games: Any (+5%)
Mechanical: Any
Physical: Any
Pilot, Basic: Any
Swindler: Any (+5%)
Technical: Any
W.P. Ancient Chinese: Any
W.P. Modern: Any
W.P. Military: Any

Antiquarian Finances: In spite of the character's considerable financial resources, antiquarians are perpetually short of funds. That's because there is always some new treasure coming on the market, something that *must* be added to the collection. The character will rarely part with anything already in his possession.

Cash: Start with $25,000 which can be saved or spent on initial equipment, supplies and personal effects.

Valuables/Trade Goods: If needed, an antiquarian can assemble either a case of antique Chinese bronzes or books (worth 2D6×$1,000), or a pouch of rare miniature jade pieces (worth 4D6×$1,000) from his collection. However, it will pain the character deeply to have to part with such treasures.

Income: $40,000 to $240,000 (4D6 times $10,000) per year. Note that after expenses (maintenance and such on the mansion), and spending money on essential purchases (i.e., buying whatever priceless items come on the market, or to auction, every year), the character will usually have only about $100 per week in actual pocket money and seldom more that $25,000 in savings.

The Antiquarian's Steward (NPC)

This is usually an aged person, from ten to thirty years older than the antiquarian (5D6 years). The steward is likely to have been in the character's service for many years (frequently decades) and is a trusted confidant. The steward has interests (though less expertise) similar to those of the antiquarian's and is happy puttering around the collection during his master's extended absences.

Responsible for cataloging, organizing, and placing objects within the collection, the steward is far more likely to be able to locate any given item, or reference than the antiquarian.

The steward lives in the antiquarian's mansion/home, but is usually a native of the land where it is located.

The Antiquarian's Mansion

Every Antiquarian must have some place suitable for the storage and display of their vast array of books, valuables, antiques, specimens, and miscellaneous junk. In places like Hong Kong, London and Paris, the mansion will be a tall building, usually from five to eight stories tall, squeezed amid other buildings in an ancient part of the city. In other places, where room isn't at such a premium, the mansion will come with a few acres of walled grounds, will only be three stories tall, and a bit more spread out.

All mansions come with quarters, the area where the antiquarian, the steward, and any resident staff or family actually live. The quarters include bedrooms, bathrooms, personal studies, dining rooms, kitchens, etc. In addition to quarters, the character can select up to seven of the following chambers to be contained within their mansion (or, if preferred, roll seven times on 1D20):

1. Asylum: An inner room, windowless, usually accessible only by a secret door or passageway. Those objects collected that might be considered illegal, too rare and valuable, or simply too bizarre for public display, are usually kept here.

2. Auditorium: A large room, once used as a place for theatrical recitals, plays, etc. Now converted into a large gallery filled with cabinets, bookshelves, etc. Used for the lesser quality, lesser valuable items.

3. Catacombs: A set of underground rooms and passageways, with as much area as a floor of the mansion, and often several levels deep. Only the most accessible areas have been fitted with electric lights, which means the use of a lantern or flashlight will be necessary in the more remote areas. Often there will be exits to the surrounding city's underground subways, utility channels, sewers or drains, separated by a locked gateway.

4. Crypt: An underground chamber, usually the oldest part of the mansion, where the antiquarian's ancestors, relatives, and certain departed servants are entombed. While some are buried under the floor (carved marble slabs mark their graves), most are fitted into slots in the walls. The character may store or hide collected human remains, including skulls, skeletons, mummies and containers filled with ashes, or other valuables here in the crypt.

5. Drawing Room: A room suitable for guests, usually wood paneled, where many of the collection's weapons & armor are put on display.

6. Laboratory: Where once this room might have actually been used to carry out experiments, it has long since become all too crowded with specimens. Shelves and chests of drawers typically fill the room, and cover the old marble-topped tables. It may contain stuffed animals, organs and sea creatures preserved in formaldehyde-filled glass bottles, and drawer after drawer of fossils and small skeletons. Chemical containers and alchemical equipment is usually stored here as well. A small area may still be used to test specimens for authenticity and age.

7. Labyrinth: The attic equivalent of the catacombs. A set of tiny storage rooms and narrow corridors filling the upper floor, and under-roof areas at the top of the building.

8. Library: Usually a series of two to six rooms, each completely filled with shelving, such that there are just narrow aisles between the books. Here is where the vast majority of the antiquarian's books and manuscripts are found.

9. Mausoleum: A room where the walls and floor are covered in worked stone (usually marble). Typically a place where jade and other precious stones and jewels are kept and displayed.

10. Office: A somewhat smaller room usually with an antechamber; traditionally, the secretary's office. It is often at the front of the house, with a separate entrance. Contains a desk, filing cabinets, personal computer, clerical items, etc.

11. Parlor: One or more rooms set aside for the display of antique furniture and small items such as collections of games, cards, candleholders and small statuary.

12. Picture Gallery: Generally the walls are completely covered with paintings, drawings and pieces of artistic calligraphy. In the center of the room are several wooden cabinets and/or flat files, each with wide drawers, filled with stacks of artwork, or compartments filled with rolled-up scrolls. There will also be at least two bookcases where many of the reference works, catalogs and files on art will be kept.

13. Reading Room: A smaller library or den, filled with personal reading, journals, and reference books. Unlike the library, where there is barely room to move. The reading room is furnished with comfortable chairs, a desk or two, and at least one large table.

14. Salon: A favorite place for vases and other ceramics.

15. Sanctuary: An inside room, without windows. It is usually designed to be very dry and is typically used for the storage of dried plants, herbs, spices and seeds.

16. Sculpture Garden: A large room inside the mansion usually illuminated by a series of overhead windows/skylights. Larger items in the collection, including full-sized sculptures, vases, and carvings are generally displayed here.

17. Sepulcher: A small niche or room that once functioned as a private chapel. It usually contains a small altar and the windows are fitted with antique stained glass. This is where the collection's holy artifacts, religious pieces and related items are stored.

18. Solarium: A room fitted with huge windows, often (especially if the antiquarian is a botanist, or a collector of exotic plants) fitted out as a greenhouse.

19. Studio: A large room, usually on an upper floor, well-lit by many windows that face the north.

20. Vault: This is a large walk-in vault the size of a medium to large room. It is usually temperature controlled and heat/fire resistant. It is often located in the center of the mansion, on the main floor or in the basement. It is reinforced with steel walls and is accessible only by a heavy vault door which is often concealed. The antiquarian's most treasured, valuable and delicate artifacts are stored inside. Only the antiquarian and his steward (and possibly his attorney) have the keys and/or combination to enter the vault.

Note: Some antiquarians will live above or behind an antique or curio shop (some believe it gives them a greater opportunity to stumble across rare treasures. The stuff in the shop is considered to be mostly unimportant, modern junk and is not part of the character's personal collection). The shop can be squeezed among the buildings of a big city or be part of a home or mansion. It will also have seven of the special areas as described above.

Capitalist Entrepreneur O.C.C.

Shang Ren

The capitalist entrepreneur is one of the many financial wizards who ride the roller coaster of a booming city economy. They are very much a character of the cities such as *Hong Kong*.

Those who are interested in playing a *Shang Ren* (by the way, that's a slightly insulting description) should bear in mind that they will be severely under-powered compared to other **Mystic China** characters. Capitalists have no great martial art abilities, no special psychic powers or magic knowledge.

However, from the point of view of the Shang Ren, none of that matters, because the character has something even better; *a talent for making money!* Where other characters might scrounge for their daily meals, the Shang Ren has to agonize over choosing between taking a chauffeur-driven limousine to a top-notch restaurant, or staying in and taking advantage of the efforts of his own personal chef. A rooftop penthouse, vacation homes, a small fleet of vehicles, a yacht, plus control over various powerful corporations are all part of this character's range of "power."

Unfortunately, just because the capitalist entrepreneur has a talent for making money, that doesn't mean the character actually *has* a ton of money at his or her fingertips.

Why?

Well, you've got to take a look at the life-style of this kind of wheeler-dealer. Typically, our rich friends are going to either (1) have all their money tied up in investments, trying to take advantage of new opportunities, or (2) due to a downturn in their fortunes, the character is in a deficit position (they owe more than they own). Many of the Capitalist's possessions make for wonderful balance sheets and tax breaks and available cash is a matter of juggling the profit and loses. Consequently, the character rarely has a spare million rattling around, simply because a good entrepreneur always keeps his money hard at work.

You might ask, why can't the character just sell out, right when things are looking good, and keep the money? Well, any other character might do just that. But to the capitalist entrepreneur that would be giving up on living. It would be as if one of the world's greatest athletes, having just won the most-valued-player award, at the age of twenty-one, decided to retire! As the athlete would say, you don't play for trophies, you play because you love the game.

Some other axioms the character lives by include:

1. It takes money to make money.
2. Risk is part of the game. Don't play if you're not prepared to lose (well, at least sometimes).
3. Play to win, but keep sight of your goals, and know when to fold.
4. Growth means profit. You have extra money, but put most of those profits back into investments for continued growth.

Although much of the character's vast fortune may be tied up, he or she will always have the *appearance* of wealth. After all, everything from wearing the right clothing to entertaining the right people is essential for keeping investors satisfied. Furthermore, what the average blue collar and even white collar worker may consider to be a lot of money is often readily available funds to this high-powered businessman. The capitalist entrepreneur won't think twice about buying a thousand dollar suit, book or artifact, and can pay for it with a credit card, check or even cash. If the character ever really needs a large amount of money, say, for financing a major expedition into *Mystic China*, or the purchase of a major (mystic) artifact, he/she can always get the money the old-fashioned way, by borrowing it (but some part of the business or business holdings may have to be sold or put up for collateral).

Capitalist Entrepreneur Requirements & Base Numbers:

Attribute Requirements: I.Q. 11, M.E. 11, a high M.A. is also suggested but not required.

Alignment Requirements: None

Base S.D.C.: 20

Base Hit Points: Standard (P.E.), plus 1D6 per level of experience.

Base Chi: Standard (P.E.)

Base P.P.E.: 2D6

Capitalist Entrepreneur Advancement Bonuses:

1st: +1 on initiative; tends to be a quick thinker and resourceful.

2nd: Add 1D6 to S.D.C.

3rd: Select one new O.C.C. related skill.

4th: +1 to save vs horror factor.

5th: Special expertise: +10% on any one skill.

6th: Add 1D6 to S.D.C. and +1 on initiative

7th: Select one new O.C.C. related skill.

8th: +1 to save vs all forms of mind control.

9th: +1 to save vs possession.

10th: Select one new O.C.C. related skill.

11th: Select one secondary skill.

12th: Add 1D6 to S.D.C. and +1 on initiative.

13th: Select one new O.C.C. related skill.

14th: Select one secondary skill.

15th: Add 2D6 to S.D.C.

Note: Combat skills are limited to the basic types of hand to hand skills.

Capitalist Entrepreneur O.C.C. Skills:

Entrepreneurship (Special!): The mastery of business, finances and economics necessary to build companies from scratch, as well as management/running existing corporations, recognizing and solving problems, investment opportunities, and to the know-how buy out other businesses. Aside from management skills the character has to have the charm necessary to raise large amounts of investment money and direct both people and resources. **Base Skill:** 40% +4% per level of experience.

Chinese Language: Stage 2/Chinese Literacy.
Radio: Basic (+10%)
Math: Basic (+15%)
Computer Programming (+10%)
Athletics (General)
Running
Pilot Skills, Basic: Select any three (+10%).
Hand to Hand: Basic

Note: Hand to hand: basic can be changed to hand to hand: commando (agent) or martial arts (agent) at the cost of two other O.C.C. related skills.

Capitalist Entrepreneur O.C.C. Related Skills: Select eight other skills.

Communications: Any (+5%)
Computer: Any (+5%)
Electrical: Any
Espionage: Any
Pilot Basic: Any (+10%)
Pilot Advanced: Any (+5%)
Pilot Related Skills: Any (+5%)
Science: Any
Swindler: Any
Technical: Any (+5%)

Capitalist Entrepreneur Secondary Skills: Select any four from the previous list. These do not get the advantage of the bonus listed in parentheses. All secondary skills start at the base skill level.

Cultural/Domestic: Any
Cultural Games: Any
Medical: Any
Military: Any
Physical: Any
Pilot Skills, Basic: Any
Science: Any
Technical: Any
Temple: Any
W.P. Ancient Chinese: Any
W.P. Modern: Any

Capitalist Entrepreneur Finances:

Cash: $250,000 in available cash. An additional $150,000 can be raised in 48 hours through quick bank loans or the sale of stock.

Line of Credit: The character can borrow up to one million at any time (takes a week or two to cement the deal). However, the greater the sum, the more strain it puts on the character's business, and no other money can be borrowed until some portion of the loan money is paid back (only the paid back amount can be reborrowed).

Income: The character can usually come up with around $1,000 per week of spendable cash. On paper, the character actually earns more money (perhaps $10,000 per week), but repaying personal loans, investments, and the upkeep on various properties soaks up most of it.

Special Capitalist Entrepreneur Gear: The character starts with all the trappings of wealth, including a penthouse apartment, a country/vacation home, a yacht or luxury sailboat (usually large enough for extended trips for up to eight people), four luxury sedans, a limousine, 1D4 sports cars, a personal secretary, and servants. The character should also have a full wardrobe of leisure, business and formal clothing and personal effects necessary to fit into the rich and famous crowd.

Capitalist Entrepreneur's Major Corporate Holdings: Each capitalist entrepreneur can select from one to four of the following possible corporate holdings. Note that the more that are selected, the smaller each individual holding will be. For example, if the character selects just one corporate holding, say a daily newspaper (Mass Media), then that paper will be a dominant force in Hong Kong (or wherever it is based) and likely the most influential newspaper in town (second most influential if in a major city). If the newspaper is one of two or three of the character's holdings then it will be one of several competitors in the market. If the newspaper is one of four businesses, then it will be small and struggling to force its way into a crowded market filled with other similar businesses.

1. Banking Institutions. The character owns a major share of either (1) an international investment bank (with just a few offices, in major cities), or (2) a regional bank (with a chain of bank offices offering consumer services in the area).

2. Real Estate Investment Holdings. The major business of the company is buying and selling land, including office buildings, shopping centers, factories, warehouses, etc. Not a broker (real estate brokers merely act as selling agents), the company actually owns the land and properties that seem to have potential, developing them for lease or sale (building or refurbishing new structures), or sitting on land until the time is right to sell, lease (or trade) for a substantial profit.

3. Raw Materials. This is usually some kind of mining operation, whether it be digging for metals in Mainland China, or off-shore oil-rigs off Vietnam. The character often has to make deals directly with high-ranking government officials, in Mainland China, Vietnam, Laos, Thailand, etc.

4. Agribusiness. The company is involved in everything from the production of the raw food stuff (farming, cattle-raising, fishing), to processing, packaging, and marketing consumer brand products.

5. Heavy Industry. Corporate factories and foundries are involved in a major industry, producing construction steel (for building buildings, bridges, roads, etc.), vehicles (cars, trucks, etc.), or other major product (aircraft, ships, plastics, etc.).

6. Textiles. The company is big in producing clothing (which is a huge Hong Kong export industry), housewares (bedding, curtains, etc.), carpeting, or car seats.

7. High-Tech Electronics. Could be consumer electronics (select from audio equipment, TV/VCRs, telephones/faxes, radios, toys, etc.), microchips, microwave ovens, or some other electronic-based manufacturing company. Probably involved in the hottest areas of the current market.

8. Research & Development. A holding in an R&D corporation is something of a gamble, since it makes no money initially and soaks up all the character's excess earnings. It may be years or even decades before it pays off. Possibilities are bio-technology, virtual reality systems, pharmaceutical/human disease research, advanced computer systems, artificial intelligence, or robotics. **Note:** This must be one of two or more corporate holdings, since the character can't count on this company for a regular income.

9. Mass Media Corporation. The character has a daily newspaper, a weekly magazine, or a book publishing company. Another possibility is an entertainment venture, where the company has a major theater, television station, radio station, a movie/film production studio, videocassette production or a chain of movie theaters.

10. Computers. The company will be in either hardware or software and specialize in a particular area. Hardware possibilities include personal computers, printers, modems, monitors, keyboards/pointing devices, or network systems. Software specialists usually deal in one particular kind of programming such as business/accounting systems, inventory/bar-coding, games, word processing, office systems, etc.

Note: Small businesses, such as restaurants, bookstores, clinics, etc., are just too small for the capitalist to be interested. They have no particular equity, are extremely risky, and they take far too much of the character's time and money.

Racial Character Classes (Optional)

It's up to the Game Master to decide whether or not to allow either of the following two R.C.C.s into a campaign. Please be warned, playing a *Reformed Demon* can be difficult, and it's a character that's easy to lose control over. Players should try to work with the Game Master when portraying these kinds of characters. Likewise, don't give the G.M. a hard time if he or she does not allow them as player characters.

Fox Spirit (Hu Ching)
Reformed Demon (Shan Muo)

Fox Spirit R.C.C.

Hu Ching

Fox Spirits, or "Hu Ching," are supernatural creatures not even remotely human nor even really mortal. They can instantly shift from fox, to human, to a form of pure Positive Chi.

Most of the skills, abilities and powers of a Fox Spirit are instinctive. They are simply born able to do the things they do. While they are interested in human skills, they find them extremely difficult.

Known to be mischievous, Fox Spirits aren't truly evil. Most are just intensely curious about the affairs of mortal humans and often spend their early years taking on human form to travel and observe mortal society.

Fox Spirit Transformation Ability

All Fox Spirits can magically transform themselves, instantly, from fox to human, or to an entity of Pure Positive Chi. Each transformation costs a single point of Chi. While this is normally not a problem, a Fox Spirit drained of all Chi, or infected with Negative Chi, will be unable to transform.

1. Fox Form: While in this form, the Fox Spirit can travel virtually invisibly (to humans, anyway) and soundlessly. The fox form also conceals its Chi, as if wearing a Chi Mask of Zero Chi. However, since the Fox Form *smells* like a fox, it is still detectable to creatures like dogs, cats, and any other character or creature with advanced scent, heightened sense of smell, extraordinary sense of smell, or similar abilities. Professional hunters (like the **Heroes Unlimited** special training character; the Hunter/Vigilante) will have a "feeling" if they are observed by a fox form for more than a minute or two, and can roll on their detect concealment skill every five minutes in an attempt to locate/identify the Fox Spirit.

In fox form the character can't use weapons or tools. Nor is human speech possible. The only possible attack is its bite (1D4 damage). The character can, however, use any of its Chi Mastery Abilities, plus it can see and *talk* with any ghosts, demons, dragons, spirits, or other entities of Pure Chi, while in Fox Form.

Fox Form S.D.C.: 8

Fox Form Chi: Base Chi, minus 16.

Fox Form Bonus: While in animal form, the character always has an additional +3 to dodge.

Fox Form Appearance: The character looks like an ordinary fox, complete with bushy, white-tipped tail. In fox form the character is about the size and weight of an ordinary cat, or small dog.

2. Human Form: Only while in this form can the character perform human skills, use weapons or tools, talk, or do anything requiring hands or voice.

Human Form S.D.C.: 20

Human Form Chi: Base Chi, minus 40.

Human Form P.B. Attribute Bonus: Roll 3D6 for each of the eight attributes. The I.Q. is never less than 9 and Spd. is a minimum of 11 (adjust appropriately). If the character's P.B. is less than ten, add +9 to it. Otherwise, if the P.B. is ten or more, add +4 to it. Note that the P.B. bonus applies only to the human form, not to any other form or transformation.

Human Appearance: The character has just one human form and always looks the same every time it transforms (with the exception of age). The character's human looks, coloring and other features are that of an ordinary human, although a very good-looking one. The height and weight will be somewhat less than normal and is never more than five feet (1.5 m) tall, no heavier than one hundred pounds (45 kg), and is typically (but not always) Oriental looking. One thing that the Fox Spirit can alter is the human form's apparent age. Upon changing into human form (it is not possible to change its age while actually in human form), the Fox Spirit can seem as young as a teenager, as aged and frail (complete with wrinkles and thinning grey hair) as a centenarian, or anywhere in between.

3. Pure Positive Chi Form: Fox Spirits can shift to a completely intangible mass of Positive Chi. It is unaffected by any physical attacks while in this energy form, but the character is all too vulnerable to Chi-based attacks. Generally this form is used only for escaping, since Pure Positive Chi entities can move at great speed along the routes of natural Positive Chi in the earth, air and water. **Note:** While in Chi form, the character can use all Chi Mastery abilities. If in an area where there is a flow of Negative Chi, the character risks being attacked by an amount of Negative Chi equal to the prevailing flow every melee round.

Energy Form Chi: Total Base Chi.

Pure Positive Chi Form Appearance: An invisible mass of Positive Chi, detectable to anyone capable of sensing Chi, psychic sensitives, or those who can see spirits and other disembodied entities (in **Rifts** this would include shifters, psi-stalkers, dog boys and dragons).

Natural Fox Spirit Sensitivity

No matter what form it is in, the Fox Spirit always has supernatural senses and is able to *automatically* detect any of the following:

Chi: The character is always perfectly aware of the flow of Chi in an area, as well as any sources, persons or containers of strong Chi. Unless the character is in a Negative Chi environment (where everything looks the same), any intrusion of Negative Chi can be sensed from up to 100 feet (30 m) away.

Magic: Fox Spirits can sense for the presence of magic in any creature or artifact. Range 200 feet (61 m). Duration: automatic and continuous; basically the same as the spell or psychic ability.

Fox Spirit Requirements, Base Numbers & Bonuses.

Attribute Requirements: None; see various forms above.
Alignment Requirements: None
Base S.D.C.: 20 in Human Form, 8 in Fox Form.
Base Hit Points: None, Fox Spirits are made of pure Chi.
Base Chi: 5D6+50
Base P.P.E.: None, Fox Spirits are made of pure Chi.

Fox Spirit Advancement Bonuses: In addition to any hand to hand combat skill and/or ancient weapon proficiencies (W.P.).

1st: Three attacks per melee round, +2 to dodge, +2 to roll with punch, fall or impact, +2 to back flip, and is able to perform leap attack.
2nd: Add 1D6 to Chi and +1 to save vs horror factor.
3rd: +1 to roll with punch/fall/impact, Add one Chi Mastery ability (No Negative Chi allowed).
4th: +1 to back flip, +1D6 to Spd. attribute, add 1D6 to Chi.
5th: Add one additional Zenjorike Power.
6th: +1 to dodge, and add 1D6 to Chi.
7th: +1 to strike, ans add one Chi Mastery ability (No Negative Chi allowed).
8th: Add 1D6 to Chi, Add one additional secondary skill.
9th: Add one additional Zenjorike Power.
10th: +2D6 to Spd. attribute.
11th: +1 to back flip and add one Chi Mastery ability (No Negative Chi allowed).
12th: +1 to roll with punch/fall/impact and add 1D6 to Chi.
13th: Add one additional Zenjorike Power.
14th: Double existing Chi.
15th: Select one additional Secondary Skill and add one Chi Mastery Ability (No Negative Chi allowed).

Fox Spirit Human Martial Art Abilities: While Fox Spirits do not learn martial arts in the way of normal humans, they all have a natural instinct for combat that is quick, agile, and very flexible, and that could be called the "Art of the Fox."

In addition, the character starts out with the following Chi and Zenjorike Powers: *Dragon Chi*, and any other three *Positive Chi Mastery Abilities* and/or *Positive or Negative Chi Mastery Abilities* and one *Zenjorike Power*. A Fox Spirit can never learn any pure *Negative Chi Mastery Abilities*.

R.C.C. Skills: While Fox Spirits have no skills as a human would define them, the character does have a natural "ear" for languages. In addition to those listed here, the character can pick up a new language after just 2D6 days of living with/listening to native speakers (80% proficiency). When it comes to dialects, the Fox Spirit can usually learn a new version of a known language within one day (4D6 hours; 75% proficiency).

Chinese Language: Stage 0/Illiterate; unable to read or write.
Language Dialects: Chinese.

Secondary Skills: The Fox Spirit, being an other-worldly creature, has no O.C.C. skills. All it knows of the human world is what it observes. So, all the spirit can learn is a handful of secondary skills. Select four from the following choices:

Communications: Radio basic only

Computer: None
Cultural/Domestic: Any
Cultural Games: Any
Electrical: None
Espionage: None
Mechanical: None
Medical: None
Military: None
Physical: Any (+10%)
Pilot Skills: None
Science: None
Swindler: Any. **Note:** The Fox Spirit will have a +7% bonus on any swindler skill requiring physical dexterity.
Technical: Any
Temple: Any
W.P.: None

Fox Spirit Finances: The Fox Spirit starts with no money and virtually no possessions.

Special Fox Spirit Gear: *Spirit Garment.* This is a one-piece item of clothing, usually a dress for a woman, or a monk-style robe or work coverall for a man. A gift from the Fox Spirit's elders, this one piece of clothing transforms as the character changes into different forms. In human form it will appear as a human garment (although the Fox Spirit can control whether it will appear in any state ranging from perfectly new to tattered with age). When in Fox Form, the garment becomes just a few threads invisibly woven into the character's fur. When in Pure Positive Chi form, the garment travels along as an item with three points of Positive Chi.

The player character should describe the garment's color and appearance before putting it into play. While it is magical, it is not indestructible, but it can be washed and patched.

Fox Spirit's Allies & Enemies:

Allies: Among its true equals are other spirit creatures such as badgers, bears, turtles, winged rabbits, and the like.

Friends: Enlightened Immortals, who also hide among humans, always seem to be able to recognize Fox Spirits. Perhaps because they feel a certain kinship. Enlightened Immortals are usually very friendly toward Fox Spirits.

Enemies: True enemies, who are feared, are the spirits of the falcon, owl, and wolf. Any of these spirit creatures will attack, or kill a Fox Spirit if given any excuse.

Frights: To a Fox Spirit there are several entities that aren't actual enemies, but which are downright scary! Demons and creatures of Pure Negative Chi are dangerous and unpredictable. It is best to avoid them. That which Fox Spirits fear most is something capable of enslaving or consuming them. So the most threatening thing to them is a Yin Tiger (White Tiger) composed of Pure Negative Chi, yet still of the spirit world.

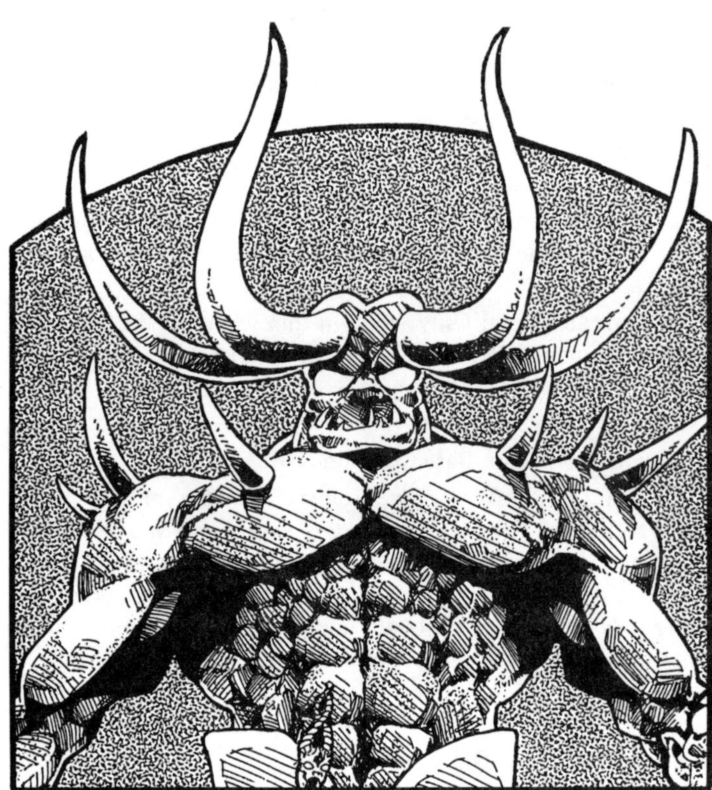

Reformed Demon R.C.C.

Shan Muo

Demons/Infernals, according to Chinese Mythology, are capable of being reformed or rehabilitated. It is exceedingly rare, but it does offer a great opportunity for a unique new Racial Character Class.

Here's what it's like from a Reformed Demon's point of view:

"Old habits die hard.

"Even though I am now striving to be "good" in my quest for personal enlightenment and fulfillment, I still have momentary lapses. I am, after all, as a demon, a creature of pure negative *chi*.

"For example, just the other day I was asked to speculate on the outcome of some event. I immediately started to respond with the logical answer, "What we need to do is sacrifice a virgin, and examine the entrails for portents of..."

"Well, you can imagine my embarrassment when I realized what I had said.

"It just goes to show, you can't put aside twelve thousand years of demonic behavior in a few short months."

Restrictions on the Reformed Demon: The Reformed Infernal starts out being hated by just about the entire population of the Ten Hells, all the way from the exalted Yama Kings down to the most humble Iron Dogs and Brass Snakes. All of them, from the highest to the low, would love to bring back the character for the most severe punishment, and to serve as an example to any other Infernals who might be considering escape.

However, so long as the character keeps away from the underworld and stays "straight," obeying the law, the Yama Kings and their minions can do little. Note, however, that the law of the Yama Kings is more a matter of "letter" than spirit. If the Reformed Infernal is caught breaking any rule, no matter how minor, the Yama Kings will be authorized to recapture the character.

In role-playing terms, this means the character has to be "good." If a Reformed Demon is ever recaptured and found guilty of crimes against the Yama King, then that character will be permanently out of the game!

The Rules of Hell: Here is a guideline to a Reformed Demon's behavior.

1. A Reformed Demon **must** keep his/her word of honor.
2. A Reformed Demon must not be **caught** in a lie.
3. A Reformed Demon must **never** attack first.
4. A Reformed Demon must **never** maim or kill a helpless foe.
5. A Reformed Demon must **never** harm an innocent.
6. A Reformed Demon must **never** harm, torture or kill for pleasure.
7. A Reformed Demon **must** obey local law.
8. A Reformed Demon **must** respect local authority.

Reformed Demon Transformation Ability.

All Reformed Infernals can magically transform themselves, instantly, from demon to human form, or to that of Pure Negative Chi. Each transformation is instantaneous, and costs the character nothing.

1. Demon Form: A heavy-duty combat form. This is the character's natural form and it will automatically assume it if knocked unconscious.

Demon Form Attribute Bonuses: Human (3D6 each) +10 to P.S., +8 to P.E., +6 to P.P., +6 to Spd., +2 to M.E.

Natural Body Armor: The bony plates of a demon provides a natural Armor Rating (A.R.) of 17.

S.D.C.: Base of 40 S.D.C., but the character can invest more Chi so that every point of Chi gives the demon an additional point of S.D.C.

Chi: Whatever is left after the Infernal has invested in S.D.C. (the base, 40 S.D.C., is also taken out of the character's Chi.).

Demon Form Appearance (determined by the player character): Six to eight feet (1.8 to 2.4 m) tall and from 400 to 600 pounds (181 to 272 kg). The demonic looking character is covered in bony plates with horns and fangs (1D10 damage from ram or bite attacks), as well as with spines and barbs jutting out from the knuckles, wrists, elbows, shoulders, knees, and ankles.

Horror Factor: 14

2. Human Form: Earlier, before the Reformed Demon decided to abandon its Infernal duties, the character could form into any imaginable human form. Now, however, with a goal of becoming human, the character must settle on one permanent human appearance.

Human Form S.D.C.: Base of 30 S.D.C., but the character can invest more Chi, up to a total of 40, so that every point of Chi gives the Reformed Demon an additional point of S.D.C.

Chi: Whatever is left after the character has invested in S.D.C. (**Note:** the base 20 S.D.C. is also taken out of the character's Chi.).

Human Attributes & Bonuses: Roll 3D6 for all eight attributes, +1D6 for P.S. and Spd.

Human Form Appearance: The character looks like an ordinary human. **Note:** The Reformed Demon will have to select ONE appearance and stick with it.

3. Pure Negative Chi Form: Invisible to all, except those who can detect Chi, and intangible, the Pure Negative Chi Form can drift through the flow of Chi, or instantly teleport to any location known by the Reformed Demon. However, if the Pure Negative Chi Form remains in any area where there is a flow of Positive Chi, it will immediately be under attack (as if attacked by a Positive Chi assault of the same intensity as that of the flow of Chi).

While in Chi form, the character can perform any known Chi Mastery Abilities.

Amount of Chi While in Pure Negative Chi Form: Total Base Chi.

Pure Negative Chi Form Appearance: An invisible entity of Negative Chi. Can only be sensed or detected by those with the power to sense Chi, or see the supernatural.

Reformed Demon Requirements, Base Numbers & Bonuses:

Attribute Requirements: None

Alignment Requirements: The character is trying really, really hard to attain enlightenment, which means he would like to be principled, scrupulous or Taoist. However, coming out of thousands of years of evil and devious behavior, it's more realistic for the character to be aberrant, anarchist or unprincipled with aspirations of becoming more good with time.

Base S.D.C.: Varies with form.

Base Hit Points: None, Reformed Demons are made of pure Negative Chi.

Base Negative Chi: 5D10+75

Base P.P.E.: None, they are made of pure Negative Chi.

Starting Age: Start with a base of 1,000 Years, then add the roll of percentile dice (1D100) times 100 years for the Infernal's approximate age.

Reformed Demon Spirit Advancement Bonuses: The character isn't really advancing, since the Infernal is already a fully mature demon. Instead the "advancement" involves the character's humanizing process, which actually means giving up certain abilities and powers!

1st: No Advancement Bonuses. Combat bonuses are as per martial art form and level. Reformed Demons start being immune to Horror Factor and are +6 to save vs possession and +2 to save vs magic.

2nd: Reduce the natural A.R. of its demon form by one point. Add one point to the physical beauty of the human form. Reduce horror factor of the demon form by two points.

3rd: Add one Positive Chi Mastery ability. The character, while in human form, can now flush the body of Negative Chi and refill it with Positive Chi. While charged with Positive Chi, the character can not transform.

4th: Vulnerable to horror factor, but +5 to save. The character is now only +3 to save vs possession.

5th: Add one Positive Chi Mastery Ability, but also loses one Negative Chi Mastery Ability (player's choice).

6th: The character loses the ability to transform into Pure Negative Chi! Roll 6D6 and trade in that number of Chi, permanently, for the character's hit points!!

7th: Add the Zenjorike Power, *Discorporate*.

8th: Add one point to physical beauty in human form. Reduce horror factor of the demon form by two points and A.R. two points.

9th: The character loses the ability to transform into Demon (or any other) form. The character is well on the way to becoming permanently human.

10th: Special! A Reformed Demon who reaches this level is transformed into an ordinary human! All special transformation powers, demon attributes, bonuses, and magical knowledge is permanently lost! The character starts life again as a *first level* character of any O.C.C. he or she desires to follow!! All Attributes must be rerolled (+2 bonus on M.E., P.E. and P.B.; appears to be around 20 years of age — lives and dies as a normal human)! The character has only a hazy memory of the prior demonic existence, but remains +1 to save vs possession and horror factor.

Reformed Demon Human Martial Art Abilities: Take Liang Hsiung Kung Fu, at 10th level of advancement. Liang Hsiung, the martial art form based on demon combat, describes the Reformed Demon's combat abilities perfectly. However, the Reformed Demon receives **none** of the *Body Hardening Techniques* and *Demon Hunter Body Hardening Techniques* that usually come with the form.

Reformed Demon Human Negative Chi Mastery Abilities. The character starts out with **all** the *Negative Chi Abilities* (including advanced).

Also select two (2) *Positive or Negative Chi Mastery Abilities* (including advanced).

Reformed Demon R.C.C. Skills:

Chinese Language: Stage 4/Classical Chinese literacy.
Tiao Qi, the game of Chinese Checkers (+15%).
Xiang Qi, the game of Shogi (+10%).
Wei Qi, the game of Go (+5%).
W.P. Ancient: Select One

Torment (Special!): The character is a master of the demonic art of torture. Virtually any piece of information, or a confession to any crime (whether or not the victim is guilty), is possible with just four melee rounds (one minute) of torment. Victims of this torment must roll to save vs psionic attack (actually a save vs Mental Endurance). **Note:** Should one of the Reformed Demon's ex-colleagues discover that the character has used this skill, it will likely result in a one-way trip to eternal torment back in hell. **Note:** This and all skills known as a demon are lost when the character becomes completely human.

Reformed Demon Secondary Skills: The Reformed Demon, being an Infernal creature, has no true human skills (O.C.C. Skills). Most acquired skills are gained by long years of observation. Select four Secondary skills. **Note:** All are lost when the character becomes completely human.

Communications: None
Computer: None
Cultural/Domestic: Any
Cultural Games: Any
Electrical: None
Espionage: Any
Mechanical: None
Medical: None
Military: None
Physical: None
Pilot Skills: None
Science: Any
Swindler: Any
Technical: Any
Temple: Any
W.P. Ancient: Any
W.P. Modern: None

Reformed Demon Finances: The character starts out with no money, and no material possessions, other than a single set of clothing scrounged from trash cans.

Magic

Psychic Character Classes

Mang Wu P.C.C. (Blind Mystic)
Fang Shih P.C.C. (Geomancer)
Tao Shih P.C.C. (Immortalist)
Wu Shih P.C.C. (Chi Arcanist)

Like the characters in **Beyond the Supernatural**, or some of the characters in **Rifts**, P.C.C. characters have some kind of extraordinary P.P.E., or Potential Psychic Energy, which can be used in the pursuit of magic or the arcane. All these characters are either skilled in magic or have some control over the forces of psychic phenomenon (ESP/psionic powers). See **Beyond the Supernatural** for descriptions of other contemporary Psychic Character Classes (P.C.C.s) and for additional psychic abilities.

Blind Mystic P.C.C.

Mang Wu

In **Mystic China** the blind have a special relationship with the spirit world and are able to perceive things hidden from the sighted. For example, where a blind mystic may not see ordinary people, the movement and approach of ghosts, the living dead, infernals (demons), and other entities of Pure Negative Chi, will be perfectly obvious.

However, players who are thinking of taking a blind mystic character should strongly consider the disadvantages. Remember! The character really is blind! No matter how many special abilities he might have, it really doesn't compensate for the fact that he can NOT see the text of a book, read signs, look at a computer screen, read an instrument panel, recognize a face, judge distance, tell direction (not well anyway), or see a physical obstruction/danger right in front of him! The character can't read at all, not even braille, which can makes matters very difficult. There is no way that the character will ever be able to drive a car or do a thousand little things that most sighted people take for granted every day.

Blind Mystic Requirements & Base Numbers:

Attribute Requirements: I.Q. 8 and P.P. 8.
Alignment Requirements: None
Base S.D.C.: 25
Base Hit Points: Standard (P.E.)
Base Chi: Standard (P.E.)
Base P.P.E.: Most of the character's P.P.E. has been expended in gaining their psychic powers. Roll 2D6 for remaining P.P.E.

Blind Mystic's Advancement Bonuses:

1st: Immune to all horror factors based on sight alone (obviously), but is vulnerable to horror factors based on descriptions, sounds, smells, touch and other sensations. +2 to save vs horror factor and +2 to save vs possession. Sees supernatural beings (invisible or otherwise), sees magic energy (including enchanted weapons, foods, scrolls, etc.) and sees Pure Negative Chi (and the beings or places that possess it).

2nd: +1 to save vs magic.

3rd: Add 1D6 to S.D.C. and select one additional P.C.C. related skill.

4th: Recognizes possession of others by supernatural or Chi forces — 40% +5% per each additional level of experience.

5th: Select one additional secondary skill and is +1 to save vs psionic attack.

6th: +2D6 to Chi.

7th: Add 1D6 to S.D.C. and select one P.C.C. related skill.

8th: +1 to save vs possession and +1 to save vs horror factor.

9th: Add 1D6 to hit points and select one additional P.C.C. related skill.

10th: +1 to save vs magic.

11th: Select one additional secondary skill.

12th: +1 to save vs possession and +1 to save vs horror factor.

13th: Select one additional P.C.C. related skill.

14th: +2D6 to Chi and +1 to save vs psionic attack.

15th: Add 1D6 to hit points and 1D6 to S.D.C.

Blind Mystic's Combat Penalties: Whenever the character is "blind" in combat, either because an opponent is not "visible" by his Chi, or if the character is unable to use the Third Eye, a Chi Kata, or some other mystic means of detection, then there are serious combat penalties. They are not as bad as they might be for a sighted person because the blind mystic has some experience at fighting blind. Note that a common tactic for the character is to try to grab onto the attacker and change the combat to wrestling where there are no penalties. Penalties for fighting blind:

-3 to parry in close combat.

-4 to dodge in close combat.

-7 to dodge long-range attacks.

-4 to strike in close combat.

-7 to strike if attempting to throw or shoot.

-2 to pull punch.

-2 on initiative.

-1 to roll with punch/fall or impact.

Running(speed is half. Movement any faster is likely to cause a stumble and fall (roll 1D20 to avoid/dodge obstacles). A stumbling fall or bumping into an obstacle will cause one point of damage. Running into an obstacle at half speed will cause 1D4 damage and the character loses one melee action. Slamming into an obstacle at full tilt will cause 2D4 damage and the character loses two melee actions.

Blind Mystic Martial Arts: The character is limited to martial arts that offer the **Blind Man Kata** (which the character must take as his first special Kata). Select one of the qualifying martial arts on the following list:

Ba Gua Kung Fu (Eight Trigrams)
Bok Pai Kung Fu (Crane Style)
Han Yu Kung Fu (Chi Katas)
Hsing-I Kung Fu (Mind Shaping)
Mien-Ch'uan Kung Fu (Cotton Fist)
Shao-Lin Kung Fu (Classic Style)

Blind Mystic P.C.C. Skills:

Chinese Language: Stage Zero (Special!): The character knows the spoken language only and is completely ignorant of any written characters, except braille.

Sculpture/Identify Features by Touch (Special!): The ability to memorize facial, hand, and body features by touch and render them in sculpture. **Note:** It takes a blind mystic about fifteen minutes to do a rough clay "sketch" of a person. A roll on the sculpture skill determines the quality and whether the item is recognizable as a specific person. **Base Skill:** 22% +4% per level of experience.

Language Dialects: Chinese (+10%)
First Aid
Play Musical Instrument (+10%)
Swimming
Wrestling

Blind Mystic P.C.C. Related Skills: Select five from the following list.

Communications: Basic Radio Only. **Note:** Special instruments are required! The character can't see the read-out/instruments on most equipment.

Computer: Operation Only. **Note:** Only works when computers are outfitted with a voice output device.

Electrical: Basic Only

Espionage: Disguise, escape artist, imitate voice, palming, pick locks, pick pockets, and wilderness survival only.

Mechanical: Any. **Note:** Since the character can't read manuals, attempting to repair unfamiliar things will take up to twice as long as usual and is -20% on skill performance. This is not a problem if the model is something the character has already taken apart and rebuilt.

Medical: None

Military: None

Pilot Skills: None

Science: Any. **Note:** Because of the difficulty in obtaining books on tape, or in braille, there is a -15% penalty any time the character needs to do research or reference work.

Swindler: All (+5%)

Technical: Any. **Note:** Blind Mystics usually like to take photography, since it allows them a chance to "document" the world, and ask questions about it later, when the pictures are developed (-10% on skill proficiency and quality).

Temple: Any, except Feng Shui (Geomancy).

W.P. Ancient Chinese: Any

W.P. Modern: None

Secondary Skills: Select three from the following list. Because learning so many things is much more difficult for a blind mystic, many of the usual choices for secondary skills are not available.

Cultural/Domestic: Possibilities are bonsai, cooking, gardening, fishing, playing a musical instrument, poetry, sewing, sing.

Cultural Games: Any. **Note:** To play Tiao Qi, the game of Chinese Checkers, the character will need a special game set where the marbles of the various players each have a different feel.

Physical: Acrobatics, athletics (General), body building, climbing, gymnastics, prowl, running, and swimming: advanced are all possible, but -10% skill proficiency.

Finances:

Cash: Start with $15,000 in equipment, personal items, or savings.

Income: In most societies the blind mystic can take advantage of state support systems, or charities, which will provide a place to live (usually in a dormitory-style building), regular meals, and an allowance of about $25 per week. Otherwise, the character can always make a living as a fortune-teller or spiritual advisor, pulling in at least $500 per week.

Special Gear: The character starts out with a complete set of clothing and personal possessions, a flexible cane (for feeling obstructions while walking), a musical instrument, a braille "recorder" (like a little manual typewriter that can be used for writing braille notes), and a high-quality micro-cassette recorder.

Special Abilities of the Blind Mystic's Third Eye

As a compensation for the lack of sight, the character has developed a sensitive *Third Eye*, capable of "seeing" the forces of Chi, magic, the undead and other spectral forms, and into other, parallel realms and worlds. Just how sensitive this Third Eye is, at any given time will depend on how much Chi the character spends on the act of concentration.

1. Chi Sight: This is the "default" condition that occurs whenever the character concentrates. Any entities of strong Negative Chi (more than 12 points) within 20 feet (6.1 m; in any direction) will be noticed, but only with a "bad feeling," not with any detail or real vision. In addition, the character can "feel" the Chi present in anyone or anything within five feet (1.5 m). Cost in Chi Points: None, the character can do this simply by concentrating.

2. Sense Chi Movement: The blind mystic is sensitive to the exact movement of Chi within 12 feet (3.7 m). This means that the amount and type of Chi in any person nearby will be known to him. The mystic can actually sense the flow of Chi around him. In feeling the movement of Chi and seeing its aura, the character can sense the movement of bodies and limbs, including hands and feet, well enough to engage in close combat with no penalties. Cost in Chi Points: One per melee round (15 seconds).

3. Eye of Chi: Extending the Chi perception outward, the blind mystic "sees" everything in terms of Chi, up to 50 feet (15.2 m) away. He perceives the Chi as an aura of energy. Items that do not contain Chi and which are not "illuminated" by a strong flow of Chi (2 points or greater), will remain unnoticed by the blind mystic. Cost in Chi Points: Two per minute (four melee rounds/60 seconds).

4. Spirit Sight: By concentrating for one melee round (15 seconds) the character can "see" an entity, Infernal, ghost, dragon or any other type of supernatural creature. Even before the mystic "sees" the creature he can recognize it by its Chi and P.P.E. emanations. Ironically, the blind monk will always see the being for what it really is. For example, the character would "see" a Spirit Creature shape-shifted into human form, a demon disguised by magic, or a possessing/occupying entity inside another person's or animal's body. In addition, the mystic can sense whether the supernatural being has Negative or Positive Chi, whether it is weak or strong in power, and malevolent or benign. Cost in Chi Points: Four per minute (four melee rounds/60 seconds).

5. Other World Eye: The character can see into the realm of spirits and ghostly entities, where the dead often wait before they move along to Hell. The blind mystic can attempt to identify the past identity of any ghost based on a few clues. For example, the character can tell the gender, and the rough height, weight, age and personality of the ghost's former living identity. Cost in Chi Points: Eight per melee round (15 seconds). **Note:** The sensitivity of a character's Third Eye is sometimes even more powerful when they are sleeping. For this reason, blind mystics will occasionally get prophetic or vivid dreams where they seem to "see" events far removed. G.M.'s option to use, but use it sparingly and with care.

6. Mediumship: Chinese seances are usually noisy affairs, where the whole family is invited to attend, and everyone from ancient grandparents to the tiniest children usually show up. Mediumship gives the character the power to conduct a *seance* where the spirits of the dead may be summoned forth and questioned. Unlike Western Mediums who invite spirits into their own bodies, the blind mystic channels spirits into the body of a willing subject, never himself.

Each Blind Mystic will have a "spirit guardian" who is well known to the character. This helpful guardian is always the first summoned during any seance. This is usually an ancestor or the spirit of another blind mystic. After the guardian is summoned, it then serves as a spirit guide, either describing things in the after-life, or conveying questions to other spirits and presenting the answers. A seance is used primarily to speak with the spirits of the dead and is not a means of predicting the future, gathering arcane knowledge, or local gossip.

Only rarely are any other spirits allowed to possess the body of the mystic's volunteer subject. Other than the voice of the subject changing, there are no other outward signs during the seance. While observers are carefully warned NOT to touch the floor during the seance (they usually crowd onto beds and table-tops — only the blind mystic and the subject have their feet on the floor). There is no danger unless the spirit guardian is endangered by malevolent entities. **Note:** If the usual spirit does not show up, or some other entity comes first, the character will know there is *big trouble* and would be well advised to immediately stop the seance. Cost in Chi Points: One point for each melee round (15 seconds) that the seance continues.

7. Blind Mystic's Divination (Mo Ku): Mo Ku means "Touch Bones," the Blind Mystic foretells the future of a person by feeling the bones of their hands and fingers. As with all types of divination, Mo Ku results more in a series of warnings and vague impressions than of any definite or absolute view of the future.

As Kevin Siembieda states in **Beyond the Supernatural**, "The Game Master should NEVER predetermine the outcome of a game, or any event in a game." However, since the Game Master has insights in what may lie in store for a character's future, it's possible to see what the choices are in some of the more likely crossroads, and give *hints* as to dangers that lie ahead.

Typically the blind mystic senses the potential interference by powerful supernatural forces (including Enlightened Immortals) in the present or near future. The feeling will be particularly strong if the subject has been observed or approached by the supernatural force within the last day. He can also tell if the character is, or ever has been, possessed.

Furthermore, because the blind mystic has years of practice at reading hand bones and manipulating the hands of those who seek divination, the character has become expert at identifying certain things. For example, he can tell from calluses exactly what kind of manual labor a character routinely performs (ditch-digging, fighting, writing, gardening, etc.), and can also get a good sense of the character's age, physical condition (P.E.), general alignment (good, selfish or evil), and physical strength (P.S.); an ability similar to the psionic power of see aura. Base Chance of Success: 50% +5% per level of experience.

Note: The blind mystic can NOT use Mo Ku to do self-divination, it only works on others. **Duration:** 1D6 minutes. **Base Skill:** 42% +2% per level of experience. Cost in Chi Points: Two

Fang Shih P.C.C.

Geomancer

The *Fang Shih*, or "Direction Scholar," is a specialist in the ancient art of *Feng Shui*, China's version of geomancy.

They are undoubtedly the most respected, most highly paid occult scientists in **Mystic China** and around the world, where the demand for Fang Shih services are rising. In Hong Kong in particular, no respectable business would consider starting construction without consulting the opinion of a local Fang Shih as to the local flow of Chi.

As player characters, Fang Shih are capable of controlling flowing Chi, a talent that can be of enormous benefit when battling Infernals and other entities of Negative Chi.

Fang Shih Requirements & Base Numbers:

Attribute Requirements: I.Q. 9 and P.P. 8.
Alignment Requirements: None
Base S.D.C.: 25
Base Hit Points: Standard (P.E.).
Base Chi: Standard (P.E.).
Base P.P.E.: Part of the character's P.P.E. has been expended on innate psychic abilities, but there is still a reserve of 3D6+10 points that can be used in spell-casting.
Fang Shih Advancement Bonuses:

1st: +1 to save vs magic, +3 to save vs possession, +2 to save vs horror factor. Initial geomantic spells include *Convert Chi to P.P.E., Convert P.P.E. to Chi,* and *Sense Ti Chi, Draw Confining Arc of Chi,* and *Draw Flowing Spiral of Chi.*
2nd: Select one additional W.P.
3rd: +1 to save vs possession, +1 to save vs horror factor.
4th: Select one additional P.C.C. related skill and add geomantic spells: *Draw Knot of Obstruction, Draw Chi Barrier,* and *Draw Alternate Line of Natural Chi.*
5th: +1 to save vs magic.
6th: Select one additional W.P.
7th: Select one additional P.C.C. related skill, and add geomantic spells: *Draw Cage of Chi, Draw Spiral Line of Chi,* and *Draw Wall of Chi.*
8th: Add 2D6 to S.D.C. and +1D6 to P.P.E.
9th: Add geomantic spells *Draw Tangle of Chi* and *Draw Chi Entity Trap.*
10th: Add 1D6 to hit points and select one additional P.C.C. related skill.
11th: +1 to save vs possession, +1 to save vs horror factor.
12th: Select one additional W.P.
13th: Add geomantic spells *Draw Yin-Yang Symbol* and *Command/Control Dragon.*
14th: Add 1D6 to hit points and add 2D6 to S.D.C.
15th: +1 to save vs magic and +1D6 P.P.E.

Fang Shih Martial Arts: Because the character needs to know *both* the art of moving with Chi (Chi Katas) and Chi Mastery, there are only four possible martial art forms available. Select any one of the following:
- Ba Gua Kung Fu (Eight Trigrams)
- Hsing-I Kung Fu (Mind Shaping)
- Mien-Ch'uan Kung Fu (Cotton Fist)
- Tai-Chi Ch'uan (Exercise Style)

Fang Shih P.C.C. Skills:
- Advanced Feng Shui/Geomancy (+25%)
- Land Navigation (+20%)
- Chinese Language: Stage 4/Classical Chinese Literacy
- Chinese Classical Studies (+10%). **Note:** Specializes in the occult and Feng Shui writings. Able to date, authenticate, and recognize the value of old inscriptions and manuscripts within his area of specialty.
- Artistic Calligraphy (+5%)

Fang Shih P.C.C. Related Skills: Select four other skills.
- Communications: Any (+5%)
- Computer: Any (+5%)
- Cultural/Domestic: Any
- Cultural Games: Any
- Electrical: Basic Only
- Espionage: Any
- Mechanical: None
- Medical: First Aid or Paramedic Only
- Military: None
- Physical: Any
- Pilot Basic: Any
- Pilot Advanced: None
- Pilot Related Skills: None
- Science: Any (+5%)
- Swindler: Any
- Technical: Any (+5%)
- Temple: Any
- W.P. Ancient Chinese: Any
- W.P. Modern: Any
- W.P. Military: None

Fang Shih Secondary Skills: Select any three from the previous list. These do not get the advantage of the bonus listed in parentheses. All secondary skills start at base skill level.

Fang Shih Finances:

Cash: $85,000, which can be used to buy any initial equipment, or can be used as savings.

Wages: No money problems for most Fang Shih. People are constantly in the market for a talented geomancer and they'll pay top dollar for geomantic services. In the U.S. the rate is flexible, but $50 per hour would be considered the minimum and $500 per hour is not unheard of. In Hong Kong it would be more like $850 Hong Kong dollars per hour. Scheduling a couple of appointments each day (a busy schedule, because sometimes several hours of research are required), could result in $2,000 to $6,000 per week.

Special Fang Shih Gear: Aside from a set of clothing (usually high quality and includes several expensive business outfits), the character will always inherit a *Lo Pan* (Geometer's compass) from his teacher. A Fang Shih will also have a suitcase filled with items that can be used to "fix" Chi problems, including six inexpensive eight-sided Yin-Yang mirrors, six beaded curtains with expanding curtain rods, six sets of wind chimes, and three dozen pre-printed good luck charms (gold ink on red paper).

Geomantic Spells of the Fang Shih

In weakness, a Fang Shih coerces lines,
in strength, a Fang Shih entreats lines,
in perfection, a Fang Shih follows lines.

from Liu Ken Feng Shui Ti Nei Chuan,
("Liu Ken's Secrets of Feng Shui")

From the point of view of the Feng Shui, manipulating the flow of Chi with magical spells is really a crude way of doing things. Yes, there are times when one is in a hurry and there is no alternative. But when time allows, Fang Shih can affect Chi without expending P.P.E, or even Chi. Of course, before bending the lines of Chi, they must first be identified exactly.

There are three essential elements to measuring in the task. First, the character must know the correct date, both in terms of the calendar and in terms of the cycles of the moon. Second, it's important to know what time it is (this doesn't need to be exact, it's okay to be a half hour early or late). Finally, the character needs to be able to consult the *Lo Pan*, or "Geometer's Compass."

Each Lo Pan has a magnetic compass in its center. At the outermost edge it is divided into 365.25 units representing the days of the year (and the extra day of every fourth year). The Lo Pan is also calibrated for the time and date, as well as for certain *secret* measurements passed down to members of the various schools of geomancy.

All this is important because of the great *sixty-year cycle of Chi*. In ancient times it was discovered that Chi flows through the Earth in a very exact manner and that it follows a cycle of sixty years. With a Lo Pan and accurate measurements of the date, time, and place, a Fang Shih can determine exactly how Chi will flow through any given area.

Even though the character can perform the spell, sense Ti Chi, and mystically "feel" the flow of Chi, calculations based on the Lo Pan are much more accurate! Once measurement is complete, the character can then take steps to influence, control, or alter the flow of Chi. Here are some possibilities:

Fix Bad Feng Shui. Usually done in a home or business, the Fang Shih looks for disruptive flows of Negative Chi, or areas where Positive Chi is sluggish or stopped altogether. Most problems can be fixed by recommending a few furniture changes (moving the position or alignment of beds, stoves, couches, etc.), or minor architectural changes (usually this involves either rehanging doors, so they open the other way, or changing the shape or size of windows). If the changes seem too expensive, the Fang Shih will "patch" the flow of Chi by installing Yin-Yang mirrors, wind chimes, or beaded curtains.

Diverting Lines of Chi is a temporary change that will only last for about two hours. This is usually just a matter of moving objects in the area. Understanding how the Chi flow is going to behave, the character can move a piece of furniture or a large stone and create a small area (usually a pathway, about five feet/1.5 m wide, leading downstream from the point of change) where Chi does not flow, or where the flow of Chi is doubled.

Diluting Lines of Chi. There are times when the Fang Shih may simply want the flow of Chi to be lessened. The simplest way to do this is by fitting a curtain of strings, each fitted with small objects, usually of glass beads, across the line of Chi. As the Chi flows into the curtain it creates ripples and eddies, such that the area shielded by the curtain loses half or more of its normal Chi. The best kind of curtain is one made of glass beads, but its possible to make one out of just about any material. Only lasts for about two hours.

Reflecting Lines of Chi. Again, changes only last for about an hour. A mirror is used to reflect Chi, usually causing a line to be either bent, or reflected back upon itself. **Note:** Demons are very superstitious about these mirrors and will go out of their way to avoid them.

Additional Geomancy Magic: The character starts with the ability to cast *Convert Chi to P.P.E.*, *Convert P.P.E. to Chi* and *Sense Ti Chi*, *Draw Confining Arc of Chi*, and *Draw Flowing Spiral of Chi*. See Fang Shih Advancement Bonus Table for determining additional magic with experience. **Note:** Fang Shih are restricted to using *only* geomantic spells.

Tao Shih P.C.C.

Immortalist

The focus of the Tao Shih is that of an educated mage who is obsessed with the power of the written word and the inheritor of the Taoist Mystic tradition.

They do not cast spells directly, but they are experts in *storing* spells in the written characters of *Celestial Calligraphy*. Because a great many Chi Magic spells work only for the caster of the spell, Celestial Calligraphy is the only way to give magical protection to others. Anyone can activate paper-inscribed Celestial Calligraphy simply by setting fire to the paper and holding it while the written characters burn.

Basically, this character is on the way to becoming an Immortal and learning the secrets of Internal Alchemy.

Tao Shih Requirements & Base Numbers:

Attribute Requirements: I.Q. 14.
Alignment Requirements: None
Base S.D.C.: 15
Base Hit Points: Standard (P.E.)
Base Chi: Standard (P.E.)
Base P.P.E.: 6D6
Tao Shih Advancement Bonuses:

1st: +2 to save vs magic, +2 to save vs possession, and +1 to save vs horror factor.
2nd: Select one Mudra of Self-Possession.
3rd: Add 1D6 to S.D.C. and 1D6 to P.P.E.
4th: Select one new P.C.C. Related Skill.
5th: Add 1D6 to P.P.E. and +1 to save vs magic

6th: Select one Mudra of Protection.

7th: Add 1D6 to S.D.C. and +1 to save vs possession.

8th: Select one Mudra of Evocation.

9th: Add 1D6 to P.P.E. and +1 to save vs horror factor.

10th: Add 1D6 to hit points and select one additional P.C.C. related skill.

11th: Add 1D6 to P.P.E. and +1 to save vs possession.

12th: Select one Mudra of Self-Possession.

13th: Add 1D6 to S.D.C. and 1D6 to P.P.E.

14th: Select one Mudra for the Manipulation of Objects.

15th: Add 1D6 to P.P.E. and +1 to save vs magic.

Tao Shih Martial Arts: All *Tao Shih* are students of Hsien Hsia Kung Fu, and are prohibited from studying any other martial art form. Advancement takes place normally.

Tao Shih P.C.C. Skills:

Chinese Classical Studies (+15%). **Note:** Specializes in ancient magical writing. Can date, authenticate, and recognize the value of old manuscripts within the specialty.
Wei Qi, The Game of Go (+10%).
Chinese Language: Stage 4/Classical Chinese Literacy (+5%).
Chinese History (+10%)
Detect Ambush (+5%)
Land Navigation (+5%)
Radio: Basic Communications
Artistic Calligraphy (+10%)
Wilderness Survival
W.P. (Ancient Chinese): One of Choice.
W.P. (Modern): One of Choice.

Tao Shih P.C.C. Related Skills: Select eight other skills.

Communications: Basic Radio Only.
Computer: None
Cultural/Domestic: Any
Cultural Games: Any (+5%)
Electrical: Basic Only
Espionage: Any
Mechanical: Any, but only as Secondary Skill.
Medical: Paramedic only (+5%).
Military: None
Physical: Any (+5%)
Pilot Skills, Basic: Any (+5%)
Pilot Skills, Advanced: None
Pilot Related Skills: None
Science: None
Swindler: Any (+5%)
Technical: Any +10% in any language or dialect they select.
Temple: Any
W.P. Ancient Chinese: Any
W.P. Modern: Any
W.P. Military: Any

Tao Shih Secondary Skills: Select any four from the previous list. These do not get the advantage of the bonus listed in parentheses. All secondary skills start at the base skill level.

Tao Shih Finances:

Cash: Start with $25,000 to purchase initial equipment and/or for the character's personal savings.

Income: Tao Shih are rarely pressed for money. They are often supported by a Taoist temple and the local congregation who value the character's learning and knowledge. All that is expected of the character is that they participate in seasonal celebrations and ceremonies, occasionally assist in funeral services and to help protect them from demons and mystic forces. Combining their regular stipend and the occasional "tip" from wealthy worshippers and adventurers, means the character gets around $300 to $700 per week.

Special Tao Shih Gear: *Tao Shih Travelling Kit.* Since so much of the Tao Shih's art depends on writing and writing supplies, this canvas shoulder bag (or briefcase, if preferred) is designed to contain most of what might be needed in a compact form.

The travelling kit includes:
One *Wu Tsa Tsu* Spell/Magical Journal.
Five inksticks, one each of black ink, blue ink, gold ink, red cinnabar ink and white ink (water soluble).
Two inkstones, one large and one small.
One bottle of purified water, for mixing inks.
10 Chinese brushes of various sizes.
50 sheets of ordinary paper.
10 sheets of parchment paper.
20 slips of each of the ten colored joss papers (200 joss slips total).
500 $10,000 bills of "Hell Money"
5 small packages of wooden matches (100 matches per package),
One brass offering bowl (for incense, or for burning without touching).
Two scented candles.
One folded silk work cloth (the size of a tablecloth),
Two Peachwood Wands.
One small bottle of Cinnabar paint. **Cost:** $1,000

Initial Spells of the Tao Shih

Roll percentile and consult the following table. Then select whatever spells are allowed from the listing of the Chi Magic spells. **Note:** Most geomantic spells and some others, can NOT be rendered into Celestial Calligraphy. However, the Tao Shih can still read these spells and can transcribe them into a book or other writing.

01-10 All the spells from first, second and third levels, *except for the geomantic spells*, for a total of 21 spells.
11-20 Six spells each from the first, second and third levels, plus one spell each from the 4th through 6th levels, for a total of 21 spells.
21-30 Five spells each from the first, second and third levels, plus two spells each from the fourth through sixth levels, for a total of 21 spells.
31-55 Four spells each from the first four levels (4 from 1st, 4 from 2nd, etc.), plus one spell each from 5th through 9th levels, for a total of 21 spells.
56-75 Three spells each from the first five levels, plus two spells each from levels six through 8th, for a total of 21 spells.
76-80 Two spells each from the first eight levels, and one spell each from the 9th through 11th levels; a total of 19 spells.
81-85 Three spells each from first, second and third levels, and one spell each from 4th through 13th levels, for a total of 19 spells.
86-90 Four spells each from first and second levels, plus one spell each from third through 13th level, for a total of 19 spells.
91-95 Two spells each from first through sixth levels, and one spell each from 7th through 13th levels, for a total of 19 spells.
96-00 Two spells each from first and second levels, and one spell each from 3rd through 15th levels, for a total of 19 spells. No Living Chi spells allowed.

Tao Shih Magic & Magical Writing

Note: The Tao Shih can not cast spells directly. The *written* spell can be activated by burning the paper it is written on. Potency of the spell is equal to the experience level of the Immortalist Calligrapher at the time it was written.

1. Sense Magic & Sense Magic Writing. By touching any object, or any living creature, the Tao Shih can get a sense of whether or not magic is contained, active, or bound up inside of it. The Tao Shih also has the unique ability to sense the subtle aura around a piece of writing that warns of potential magic, understanding that some piece of magical information is included, even if the writing itself is not magical. **Range:** Touch

2. Read & Acquire Magic. Tao Shih are constantly seeking out ancient books, manuscripts or inscriptions that might contain magical spells or information about magic.

Once a Tao Shih has successfully deciphered a written spell, the character can always transcribe it into another form. Whether or not it can be used as Celestial Calligraphy depends on the specific spell (see Chi Magic spells), but there will be no need for any additional dice rolls. **Note:** Since Tao Shih do NOT automatically receive any spells as they gain new levels of experience, the ONLY way to gain new spells is by finding them in written form. **Base Skill:** 82% +4% per level of experience.

3. Books of the Tao Shih. Unlike other types of mages, the Tao Shih is a writer of magic and devotes a great deal of time creating special *Wu Fa* ("Magical Arts") books. Since a *Wu Fa* volume can only hold about forty spells, Tao Shih will find themselves putting together a larger and larger collection as they advance their knowledge. For travelling purposes, the Tao Shih usually carries a *Wu Tsa Tsu*, a magical journal, which includes notes for a dozen or so spells and room to make notes and to transcribe up to two dozen new spells.

If, for whatever reason, the Tao Shih does NOT have access to a book, notes, or other references, then the only way that a spell can be transcribed or formed into Celestial Calligraphy is if the character can reconstruct the spell. That requires a feat of memory that is not certain and the player character has to roll under this skill. **Base Chance of Reconstructing a Spell:** 24% +2% per level of experience (-10% if totally unfamiliar with the spell).

Tao Shih's Inscribing Celestial Calligraphy

Celestial Calligraphy, is sometimes known as Thunder Writing and is the art of writing magical Chinese characters. It is a method of storing a spell of *Chi Magic* into a series of mystical characters on paper. Burning the paper with the magically inscribed characters will activate the spell.

Choice of Ink. There are five ink pigment colors, each of which is considered to generate a different "active element."

1. Black Ink is strong in the element of water. Used for manipulating Negative Chi.

2. Blue Ink is strong in the element of wood. Used to focus perception, sense or vision.

3. Gold Ink is strong in the element of earth. Used for manipulating magical power/energy (P.P.E.).

4. Red Cinnabar Ink is strong in the element of fire. Used for manipulating or Evoking Positive Chi.

5. White Ink is strong in the element of metal. Used for healing or for altering organisms.

Choice of Paper. Each spell calls for a different kind of paper, which corresponds to one of the five elements and/or Positive or Negative Chi.

1. Matte Black (non-reflective): The element of water in a Positive Chi aspect. When used as a paper charm, it is usually hidden away as a source of secret protection.

2. Glossy Black (reflective): The element of water in a Negative Chi aspect. If any spell or magic is to involve one of the Yama Kings of Hell, or any of their Infernal servants, this is the appropriate paper.

3. Blue Paper: The element of wood in a Positive Chi aspect. Used for summoning or communicating with Immortals, Heavenly Deities and other spirits of Positive Chi.

4. Green Paper: The element of wood in a Negative Chi aspect. The paper most associated with geomantic magic and the manipulation of the flow of Chi.

5. Red Paper: The element of fire in a Positive Chi aspect. Commonly used all over the world as a symbol of good luck and the most common color for paper charms. Generates an explosive or outwardly moving component to a spell.

6. Pink Paper: The element of fire in a Negative Chi aspect. Considered to be the opposite of explosive, so that imploding or absorbing forces are generated.

7. Gold Paper: The element of earth in a Positive Chi aspect. Another popular color for paper charms, it is associated with wealth. In magical spells, it adds a component of forging, molding, or changing physical objects.

8. Yellow Paper: The element of earth in a Negative Chi aspect. Used in spells of protection or warding, especially against entities of Negative Chi.

9. Silver Paper: The element of metal in a Positive Chi aspect. As a paper charm, it represents good health. Often used with curative or healing spells.

10. White Paper: The element of metal in a Negative Chi aspect. Associated strongly with ghosts, souls, entities and departed spirits.

神 安 平 協 氣 志

Other Forms of Writing

Characters can also be carved into hard surfaces. For example, Celestial Calligraphy can be inscribed into a piece of jade or stone. It can also be painted on solid surfaces (this is generally done with Red Cinnabar Paint), or simply sketched in dirt or sand (usually using a Peachwood wand).

Choice of Script. The following eight different styles of script are only a small portion of the hundreds of secret or coded magical scripts that can be found in ancient manuscripts.

1. Yang Script. A square style of calligraphy with sharp angles and blocky characters. Usually used in conjunction with Positive Chi. Usually used in paper charms.

2. Yin Script. Rounded characters, which are said to be able to bind in Negative Chi. Typically used in communications with Infernals and the Yama Kings of Hell.

3. Cloud Script. This is the script that most Tao Shih will use in rendering spells into Celestial Calligraphy. It appears to flow smoothly, like western handwriting (cursive).

4. Constellation Code. A secret set of cryptograph, known only to Tao Shih. While they can be used for spells, they are also used for messages between Taoists and Taoist Temples. Entirely made up of dots connected by straight lines, each referring to some constellation in the heavenly night sky.

5. Vortex Script. Confined in the loops and swirls of these characters are stored a bit of P.P.E. Used for containing magical energies.

6. Pen Tshao. This is the mystical script of the Chinese Alchemist. There are thousands of characters, each with special meanings, that can be used to describe the components, procedures and effects of different elixirs and other compounds.

7. Eminent Spirits of Purity Script. Stop rain, raise wind, raise thunder, raise hail, stop fog.

8. Brilliant Jade Character Script. At most, the character will be able to recognize these magical runes for what they are. It is so very secret that only one or two characters have ever been translated by outsiders. Spells found with this script are usually of extraordinary power, but impossible to decipher.

Releasing Joss–Using Celestial Calligraphy

Most spells contained in Celestial Calligraphy are released by burning. Since the Chi Magic is released into whoever is holding the burning paper, it will be as if that character cast the spell. Some spells are intended to be used as ashes. In this case, the Joss is first burned in a metal bowl, and then mixed with water or other fluid, and then consumed.

Paper Charms of Celestial Calligraphy

Although the magic is very weak (the amount of P.P.E. is so small it won't even be noticed by a Wu Mage), these bits of paper confer small amounts of influence over a long period of time. Each takes about an hour to create and should be designed for use in a particular place.

1. Good Luck. In a household or building, the charm serves to change the balance of luck ever so slightly. Perhaps the result might be a +1 to save (vs just about anything) just once a day. Over time, this charm renders accidents less likely to happen, and when they do happen, they are less serious than they could have been.

2. Encourage Positive Chi. Over time the area will build up a slight increase in the flow of Positive Chi, but never increasing it more than a single point.

3. Good Health. The Positive Chi of the area will tend to scatter into any living bodies, therefore increasing healing and health by a tiny margin (perhaps an extra point of healing per day or +1 to save vs disease or poison).

4. Appease Ghosts. Immediately after the paper charm is put up, a quantity of Hell Money is burned. Rather than going to the afterlife, the transformed Hell Money sticks to the charm. Afterwards, the charm serves to attract ghosts who will take a few bills of the ghostly Hell Money and (hopefully) go away satisfied. Ghostly entities and minor spirits stay away.

5. Repel Demons. Generally done in Yin Script, the charm is usually a written notice warning demons of dire consequences if they remain in the area. Most demons loudly scoff at such foolishness, but these superstitious creatures (especially lesser demons) will think twice about hanging around and causing trouble.

Tao Shih Knowledge of Mudra

With a solid understanding of meditation, the character has also mastered some Mudra (five total) and continues to learn more.

Mudra of Self-Possession: Take the *Mudra of Tranquility and Collection* and the *First Mudra of Unmoving.*

Mudra of Protection: Take the *Mudra of Silent Contemplation* and the *Mudra for Protection from Magic.*

Mudra of Evocation: Take the *Mudra for the Collection of Alms.*

Mudra for the Manipulation of Objects: None to start.

Wu Shih P.C.C.

Chi Arcanist

The Wu Shih (more commonly the character is just called "Wu") are the Chinese equivalent of sorcerers.

Instead of cultivating psychic powers, Wu learn to save their inner resources and view their hoarded P.P.E. as a battery with which to power spells of Chi Magic.

Wu are also attuned to the world of Chi. In fact, they usually come to know about magic through their early experiences with the martial arts, where they will have mastered at least one ability that allows them to control Chi. **Note:** See the *Arcanist/Mage P.C.C.* in **Beyond the Supernatural** for other useful information that can also apply to Wu Shih.

Wu Shih Requirements & Base Numbers:

Attribute Requirements: I.Q. 12, M.E. 9, and M.A. 9.
Alignment Requirements: None
Base S.D.C.: 20
Base Hit Points: Standard (P.E.)
Base Chi: Standard (P.E.)
Base P.P.E.: 6D6+10
Chun Tzu Advancement Bonuses:

1st: +2 to save vs magic, +1 to save vs possession, +1 to save vs horror factor.
2nd: Add 1D6 to hit points, add 1D6 to P.P.E.
3rd: Add 1D6 to Chi and +1 to save vs magic.
4th: Add 1D6 to P.P.E. and +1 to save vs possession.
5th: +1 to save vs horror factor.
6th: Add 1D6 to S.D.C. and add 1D6 to Chi.
7th: Add 1D6 to P.P.E. and +1 to save vs possession.
8th: Add 1D6 to hit points and +1 to save vs horror factor.
9th: Add 1D6 to Chi and +1 to save vs magic.
10th: Add 1D6 to hit points and add 1D6 to S.D.C.
11th: Add 1D6 to P.P.E. and +1 to save vs possession.
12th: Add 1D6 to Chi and +1 to save vs horror factor.
13th: Add 1D6 to S.D.C.
14th: Add 1D6 to Chi and +1 to save vs magic.
15th: Add 1D6 to P.P.E. and +1 to save vs possession.

Wu Shih Martial Arts: All *Wu Shih* are retired martial artists. That means they devoted years to the study of a martial art form, but left it behind in the pursuit of magical power. As a result, each *Wu Shih* is *permanently stuck* at third level and cannot, under any circumstances, advance beyond that level! The character does NOT gain any experience in any martial art while progressing as a *Wu Shih.* Select any one martial art form from the following:
Bok Pai Kung Fu (Crane Style)
Hsing-I Kung Fu (Mind Shaping)
Pao Chih (Animus Development)
Snake Style Kung Fu (She Shen)
Tai-Chi Ch'uan (Exercise Style)

Wu Shih P.C.C. Skills:
Chinese Language: Stage 4/Classical Chinese Literacy.
Chinese Classical Studies (+10%)
Artistic Calligraphy
Research (+15%)

Wu Shih P.C.C. Related Skills: Select four from the following:
Cultural/Domestic: Any (+10%)
Cultural Games: Any (+5%)
Technical: Any (+10%)
Temple: Any (+5%)

Wu Shih Secondary Skills: Select any four from the following:
Communications: Basic Radio Only
Computer: Operations or Programming only.
Electrical: Basic Only
Espionage: Any
Mechanical: Any, but only as secondary skill
Medical: Any
Physical: Any
Pilot Skills, Basic: Any
Science: Any
Swindler: Any
W.P. Ancient Chinese: Any
W.P. Modern: Any

Wu Shih Finances:

Cash: Start with $5,000 to purchase initial equipment and/or for the character's personal savings.

Income: Since the character is so devoted to such an esoteric study, any kind of steady income is difficult. However, since the Wu is extremely literate in ancient Chinese, he is often able to pick up freelance work as a translator, researcher, or as a reference expert (at a bookstore, library or university). Such jobs are full-time and pay $250 to $600 per week.

Special Wu Shih Gear: Other than a set of clothing and personal effects, the Wu starts out with no other gear.

Wu Shih Magic & Spell Casting

1. Sense Magic. All Wu have attuned themselves to magical sensitivity. That means that most magic, magical items, or magical forces will be detectible. It's also possible, if the character spends at least one full melee round of concentration, to determine if a person or an object has been magically enchanted. Note that the most a Wu will notice is the presence of the magic and a general sense of how powerful the magic is (minuscule, low, moderate, powerful or super-powerful). **Range:** 120 Feet (37 m).

2. Read/Acquire Magic. Wu are intensely interested in any book, manuscript or inscription related to magic. By learning to read all available magical scripts, including those of Celestial Calligraphy, the character can attempt (roll under skill on percentile) to determine the function of any written spell or magical procedure.

Once a spell has been successfully deciphered, the Wu character can then attempt to cast it. Casting requires an additional roll against the Wu's skill proficiency. However, if the spell casting succeeds, then the character can add that spell to his/her list of known spells. **Note:** Since Wu do NOT automatically receive any spells as they advance in experience, one way to gain new spells is to find them in written form and decipher them (another is to be taught them). **Base Skill:** 25% +3% per level of experience.

Initial Spells of the Wu Shih: Roll percentile, consult the following table, then select whatever spells are allowed from the listing of the Chi Magic spells. **Note:** If the result says "No Living Chi" or "No Geomantic" spell allowed, then none of those can be chosen for the character's initial selection of spells. The character can, however, attempt to learn these spells later on, in the same way that any spells are learned by an arcanist/sorcerer.

01-10 All the spells from first and second levels, for a total of 16 spells.

11-30 Six spells each from the first and second levels, plus one spell each from the third through sixth levels, for a total of 16 spells.

31-55 Four spells each from the first four levels (4 from 1st, 4 from 2nd, etc.), for a total of 16 spells.

56-75 Three spells each from the first four levels, plus two spells each from levels five and six, for a total of 16 spells.

76-80 Two spells each from the first seven levels, and one (1) from the eighth level, for a total of 16 spells. No Geomantic spells allowed.

81-85 Four spells each from first and second levels, two spells each from third and fourth levels, and one spell each from fifth, sixth and seventh levels, for a total of 15 spells. No Geomantic spells allowed.

86-90 Three spells each from first through third levels, two spells each from fourth and fifth levels, and one spell each from sixth and seventh levels, for a total of 15 spells. No Geomantic Spells allowed.

91-95 Two spells each from first through sixth levels, and one spell each from seventh through ninth levels, for a total of 15 spells. No Geomantic Spells allowed.

96-00 One spell from each level, for a total of 15 spells. No Living Chi or Geomantic spells allowed.

Chi Magic

Mystic China is a world flowing with Chi, thus it's only logical that the creators of Chinese magical tradition would have turned their attention to ways of manipulating and controlling Chi. From the Dynasty of the Legendary Sage Emperors, over four thousand years in the past, thousands of Wu Shih have built on that magical heritage. Of the multitude of spells, those in the following list have withstood the test of time and are considered reliable for teaching to ambitious apprentices.

Players of **Beyond the Supernatural** and/or **Rifts** will find Chi Magic pretty familiar. As with those systems that use *Invocation Magic*, each magic spell (with one exception) requires the expenditure of a special kind of energy, called P.P.E. (Potential Psychic Energy). The more powerful the spell, the more P.P.E. required.

The main difference between Chi Magic and that of the systems based on pure P.P.E., is that Chi Magic is designed to exploit the Chi that flows through the natural world. Since there is Chi in all living things (including the bodies of those who cast spells), Chi Magic can be sometimes more efficient than invocation magic (it costs fewer P.P.E.), but this is balanced out by the fact that many Chi Magic spells are useless without Chi and others are relatively weak.

Mystic China P.C.C.s & Chi Magic

Three of the P.C.C.s in *Mystic China* are capable of using Chi Magic. First, there is the *Wu Shih*, who is the equivalent of the Arcanist in **Beyond the Supernatural**, and who can directly cast any of the spells described here. He/she is even capable of learning and manipulating invocation spells.

Second, the *Fang Shih*, or "Direction Scholar," can cast spells, but only "Geomantic Spells," all of which are used for manipulating the flow of Chi.

Third, *Tao Shih*, the inheritors of the Taoist Mystic tradition, do not cast spells directly, but are experts in *storing* spells in the written characters of *Celestial Calligraphy*. Because a great many Chi magic spells work only for the caster of the spell, Celestial Calligraphy is the only way to give magical protection to others. Anyone can activate paper-inscribed Celestial Calligraphy simply by setting fire to the paper and holding it while the characters burn.

Then, of course, there are the non-player characters. Many Immortals, Infernals, and quite a few mystic creatures (especially dragons) have control over magic, and some have a wider range of spells than those described here.

Silence of the Mind: Casting Chi Magic

Unlike Western spells, where the magic is mostly spoken invocations, the Chi Magic of China is based on the *mind's* power to manipulate the forces of Chi. Therefore, silence spells and other means of suppressing the spoken voice are useless when it comes to stopping Chi Magic.

On the other hand, there are several spells designed to frustrate those who use Celestial Calligraphy. Since releasing a stored spell requires burning the paper upon which it is written, spells of *non-ignition* have the same effect on Celestial Calligraphy that silence spells have on spells of invocation.

Sources of Magic & P.P.E.

The major source of power for Chi Magic spell casting is the sorcerer's own innate reservoir of P.P.E. While this usually suffices for lower level spells, the spell caster will need considerably more than his own personal P.P.E. to cast the more powerful, higher level spells. Here are some alternative sources of Potential Psychic Energy (P.P.E.).

Drawing P.P.E. from magic artifacts and containers. Certain mystic artifacts, as well as practical devices created by users of magic, can be "tapped" as a portable source of extra P.P.E. A user of Chi Magic can also draw on portable P.P.E. containers, no matter how the item was created. In other words, a *Wu Shih* can use the P.P.E. batteries created by invocation magic, or the P.P.E. stored by a *Tao Shih* in a script of Celestial Calligraphy, or the P.P.E. stored in the mystic Vajra created by other *Wu Shih*.

Drawing P.P.E. from Chi. The Chi magic spell, "Convert Chi to P.P.E.," can give a hefty boost in overall P.P.E. This is also handy if the character has either Dragon Chi or Dark Chi, which are the Chi Mastery abilities that let one tap into the flow of Chi permeating an area.

Drawing P.P.E. from Dragon Lines. For the *Fang Shih*, or geomancer, P.P.E. is always flowing in a living stream along the Dragon Lines (i.e. "ley lines"). However, it requires the character's special knowledge and ability to concentrate enough energy to yield even a modest amount of P.P.E. from such lines of energy. Unless given assistance by a *Fang Shih*, other spell casters will rarely be able to tap Dragon Lines.

Drawing P.P.E. from special sources. There are mythic creatures in the world of **Mystic China** who command vast sources of P.P.E., including dragons and Yin tigers. They are usually very reluctant to share, but it is possible that a fast-talking spell caster might be able to manage a "loan" of P.P.E.

Drawing P.P.E. from other living creatures. In the magic of **Beyond the Supernatural**™ and **Rifts®**, P.P.E. is often drawn from the life force of humans and other creatures. Not so in **Mystic China**. Chi Magic is a delicate manipulation of Chi, and drawing on P.P.E. from any living thing (even from a willing or enthusiastic volunteer), creates a violent feedback of Chi — thereby destroying the spell. The P.P.E. for Chi Magic cannot be drawn from any other living creature! Likewise, group spell casting, such as *ritual* or *ceremonial* magic, is impossible with Chi Magic.

Drawing P.P.E. from Geomantic Events or Confluences. Nexus points, as discussed in **Beyond the Supernatural** and **Rifts,** don't yield much P.P.E. in Mystic China. Likewise, the extreme surges of magical energy (P.P.E.) during such events as an equinox, a solstice, lunar eclipse, or a partial solar eclipse do NOT seem to occur in **Mystic China**. This is probably because the Chinese dragons, who are known to live on geomantic energy, consume all the excess P.P.E. from these events.

Spells of Living Chi

Just as many of humanity's technological innovations are simply copies of the natural abilities of animals, so the inventors of Chi Magic designed spells that replicated the powers of the supernatural creatures. This is especially true in the case of spells that create *Living Chi.*

For example, most Chinese dragons can generate living clouds of Chi, which continue to be a living part of the creature even while outside the body. A cloud of smoke or fire stays under the direct control of the dragon, who can make it move, spread out, contract, rise or fall and, when the dragon wills it, be sucked back into the body. This Cloud of Living Chi must be *invested* with Chi before it is released, but is often recovered when the Living Cloud is taken back into the body.

The great drawback of all Living Chi is that the character always runs the risk of losing whatever Chi is invested when the Living Chi is destroyed if cut off or dissipated, or if the Living Chi is consumed by some other being.

Let's say, for example, that a spell caster has exhaled a Living Chi Cloud through a keyhole with the intention of flooding the room on the other side. If something blocks the keyhole after the cloud has been sent into the room, or if the character is pulled away before having a chance to withdraw the cloud, then all the Chi invested in the cloud will be lost.

Types of Living Chi

Depending on the magic spell involved, Living Chi can be created in any of the following forms:

Living Chi Cloud. The most simple kind of Living Chi takes the form of a cloud, or gas, exhaled by the spell caster. The more Chi that a character puts into the Living Chi Cloud, the larger the volume of the cloud. When the character retrieves the cloud by inhaling, the remaining Chi is recovered. Physical attacks are usually completely useless against Living Chi Clouds. However, very strong winds of gale, tornado or hurricane force can scatter layers of Living Chi Clouds, effectively destroying one point of Chi per melee round.

Living Chi Animus. An Animus is created by combining Chi with the magical *aura* of the character. This creates the *Animus*, which might be thought of as a character's "living aura." The Animus is typically part of the character like his real aura and offers physical and/or magical protection like a suit of mystic armor. More advanced versions can be unleashed from the body to defend and fight attackers and may possess special powers (attacks are generally equal to those of its creator). These advanced forms of Animus possess one of the five elements and represent an even more powerful extension of the character's magical self. All Animus will always attempt to defend the physical body of their creator (of which they are an extension), even if the character is rendered unconscious or the Chi spirit is absent.

Living Chi Simulacrum. A Simulacrum is a kind of artificial person constructed magically out of Chi and the aura of the spell caster. Both the *Chi Clone* and the *Immortal Child* are examples of simulacrums that appear as real, solid, physical beings, but each simply dissipates when their magic is used up.

Living Chi Cache. As we've seen, most types of Living Chi are withdrawn back into the spell caster's body, allowing the Chi to be reabsorbed. A Living Chi Cache is the Chi equivalent of a trap. Designed to masquerade as ordinary Chi and to be unknowingly "swallowed" by an enemy spell caster. It can be a vicious Trojan Horse, containing some kind of offensive magic intended to "explode" in the belly of the enemy.

Magic Combat

Magic Attacks per Melee Round: Unless otherwise noted, each spell of Chi Magic requires one full melee round of concentration. The spell must be started at the beginning of a melee round, but the spell will not be actually released/activated until the beginning of the *next* melee round. Some higher level spells, 11th and above, may take longer to invoke. See the individual spell for details.

Saving Against Magic: *Saving against magical attacks.* When threatened by a direct magical attack where the spell caster is directly powering the offensive magic, characters can usually roll to save vs magic. This includes magic illusions, charms, curses, etc. Roll better than the spell caster's roll to strike on a twenty-sided die like a mystical parry. Defender can add in their P.E. bonus to this saving throw.

Saving against Chi Magic. Roll 12 or better to save.

Saving against Celestial Calligraphy. Roll 10 or better to save. Since the Chi Magic contained in written form is weaker than the Chi Magic of the focused mind, the saving throw is easier.

Saving against Demon/Infernal Magic: Roll 14 or better to save. The magic of Infernal Lords may require a 15 or 16 to save.

Saving against Dragon/Immortal/Deific magic. Roll 16 or better to save.

Saving against the physical effects created by magic. Look at it this way. If you are threatened by a forest fire, what do you do? Run! It really doesn't matter if the fire was created by a lightning ball spell or a real lightning strike. Regardless of whether the fire was caused by magic, the match of an arsonist, or just some careless tourist dropping a cigarette, the resulting fire is no longer magical, so a save vs magic no longer applies. So, if the threat from a spell has resulted in a physical manifestation such as fire, an energy bolt, a lightning strike, or impact from a solid object, there is no save vs magic. Instead the character should attempt to dodge or otherwise evade the attack.

Cancelling/Interrupting Chi Magic: Because the P.P.E. is not actually expended until the release or activation of the spell, it's possible to stop it at any time without loss. So, for example, if the invocation is interrupted, or if things have changed so the spell is no longer necessary ("gee, I think our sixteen attacks in the *first* melee round killed it"), the spell can be stopped before it is cast without penalty.

Once a spell has been released, all the P.P.E. is expended. However, a spell caster can always shorten the duration of a spell, effectively dispelling it at any time.

Chi Magic from a Western Arcanist Perspective

Western Mages, like the Arcanist from **Beyond The Supernatural** and the Ley Line Walker, Mystic, Shifter and Techno-Wizard and other men of magic from **Rifts**, will find the study of Chi Magic intriguing, but very difficult (progress at one-third their normal speed in gaining experience and rarely exceeding 6th level). However, from a role-playing system point of view, the two types of magic are very compatible, since both use the same P.P.E. system.

As far as using Wizards from **Revised Heroes Unlimited** or **Palladium Fantasy**, check out Kevin Siembieda's *excellent* rules for adaptation to the P.P.E. system in the **Rifts Conversion Book**.

Chi Magic Spells for Western Mages. There are two ways that Western Mages can attempt to learn Chi Magic. In the first case, they can attempt to master the basics of Chi, usually by engaging in a year-long combined course in the martial arts, meditation, and Feng Shui. The other approach is to attempt to convert Chi Magic spells into spells of "invocation."

Converting Chi Magic spells into Spoken Invocations

Assuming that the Western Mage has some kind of reference, either a book containing a description of the spell, or the cooperation of a *Wu Shih* or *Fang Shih*, it's possible to try converting most spells of Chi Magic into *spoken invocations*. However, this typically requires 1D4 months of study plus one month for every level of the spell itself. For example, a 5th level spell will take 1D4+5 months of study to translate into a spoken invocation. Note that geomantic spells and spells that create Living Chi can NOT be converted into spoken invocations.

Table of Spell Learning/Conversion (Optional)

Roll percentile for each time a Western Mage attempts to either learn a spell of Chi Magic or attempts to translate it into an invocation spell.

01-11 Half-Success! The desired spell is learned, but it's not nearly as efficient as it should be and requires twice as much P.P.E. as usual to cast. Another eight months of study might rectify the problem.

12-34 Nothing! Failure to learn the spell. Try another period of study.

35-40 Catastrophic Failure! The character doesn't learn the spell and all the character's P.P.E. is drained away for 1D4 weeks!

41-44 Feedback Failure! Not only does the character not learn the spell, but their understanding of all their spells is shaken. As a result, the character has to review all the spells known to him, spending one hour per spell refreshing his memory. Until a particular spell is reviewed, it can't be cast!

45-49 Chi-Draining Failure! All the Chi in the character's body is drained away. It takes no less than a week of rest and meditation to get the body back to normal and restore the Chi.

50-89 Success! The character learns the new spell and is able to cast it perfectly.

90-95 Accidentally Opens a Mystic Portal! Some kind of gateway, dimensional Rift, or other magical doorway is opened inadvertently. It will take 1D6 melee rounds before the spell caster can compose himself enough to close it. During that time, he or others can pass into the mystic portal to another world or dimension, and *things* from other worlds may come through from the other side! They may or may not attack the sorcerer.

96-00 Complete Success! Not only does the character learn the new spell, but insight is also gained into the operation of Chi Magic. Consequently, the character can learn to cast one other *Mystic China* spell of the same or lower level in half the normal study time. This bonus spell is automatically perfect, do not roll on this table for random results!

Celestial Calligraphy for Western Mages

Any Western Mage can detect the magical power (P.P.E.) contained within a piece of Celestial Calligraphy. Learning how to release the magic is simple. All a Western Mage needs is five minutes of instruction from an expert or prior knowledge through the study of Oriental magic lore/history. An hour or two worth of research in the library of any serious and experienced arcanist/mage should provide all the necessary tricks and secrets for releasing the paper versions of Celestial Calligraphy.

However, learning how to release spells by burning bits of paper and being able to actually figure out Celestial Calligraphy are two very different things. In order to learn how to read, much less create, Celestial Calligraphy, a character would have to spend no less than *five years* of study, first in arcane aspects of the Chinese written language and then in the secrets of the Thunder Script itself (assuming, of course, that a Tao Shih can be found who would be willing to teach a Westerner their mysteries).

An Alphabetical List of Chi Spells by Level

Level One
Chi Mask (3)
Convert Chi to P.P.E. (1 P.P.E. or 6 Chi)
Convert P.P.E. to Chi (1)
Convert Positive Chi to Light (1)
Create Sparks (2)
Sense Chen Chi (1)
Sense Ti Chi (1)§
Sense Wei Chi (1)

Level Two
Chi-Gung Invocation (6)
Convert Positive Chi to Heat (3)
Draw Confining Arc of Chi (4)§
Exhale Obscuring Smoke (4)*
Fill Object with Chi (5)
Reverse Chi (2)
Sense Infernal Influences (2)
Turn Away The Dead (6)

Level Three
Cure Negative Chi Disease (7)
Disperse Chi (9)
Draw Flowing Spiral of Chi (8)§
Exhale Burning Cloud (6)*
Inscribe Celestial Calligraphy (6)
Replenish Vajra (5)
Sense Alchemical Aura (4)
View Ghost Drama (8)

Level Four
Draw Knot of Obstruction (10)§
Exhale Electrostatic Fog (8)*
Invoke Chi Zoshiki (9)
Live on Negative Chi (8)
Open Window on Afterlife (12)
Ward Body (6)
Purify Ingredient (8)

Level Five
Circle of Non-Ignition (12)
Draw Chi Barrier (12)§
Empower Vajra (10)
Enter/Exit Tung Tien (12)
Exhale Poison Cloud (10)*
Fly with Stream of Chi (16)
Hsieh Chang – Malignant Miasmal Disease (8)

Level Six
Chi Chu – Accumulation of Morbid Chi (12)
Draw Alternate Line of Chi (15)§
Exhale Cloud of Acid (12)*
Freeze Mudra (16)
Mind Walk Spell (18)
Transmute Object into Chi (20)

Level Seven
Bring Forest to Life (30)
Detach Living Gas Cloud (18)*
Draw Cage of Chi (20)§
Evoke Animus of Pure Chi (34)*
Ignite Positive Chi (22)

Level Eight
Dispel Animus (30)
Draw Spiral Line of Chi (25)§
Enter Realm of Yama Kings (40)
Evoke Animus of Elemental Wood (65)*
Exorcism (28)

Level Nine
Control/Enslave Creature of Pure Negative Chi (50)
Draw Wall of Chi (30)§
Entice Disembodied Entity (45)
Evoke Animus, to create of Elemental Fire (70)*
Hsieh Chu Wu-Malignant Epidemic Possession (52)
Invoke Third Eye (40)

Level Ten
Evoke Animus of Elemental Metal (75)*
Inflict Mudra of Immobility (64)
Draw Tangle of Chi (80)§
Mask of Demon (60)
Sense Yuan Chi (50)

Level Eleven
Bring Wood to Life (100)
Create Vajra (50+)
Draw Chi Entity Trap (100)§
Evoke Animus of Elemental Earth (85)*
Temporarily Restore Youth & Vitality (90)

Level Twelve
Evoke Animus of Elemental Water (90)*
Impose Moving Area of Non-Ignition (100)
Ride the Yin Tiger (200)*
Spit Dragon Pearl (125)
Summon and Control Infernal Entity (200)

Level Thirteen
Control/Enslave Through Negative Chi (300)
Chi Clone (200)*
Chi Cache (100)
Detach Animus (200)

Level Fourteen
Draw Helix of Dragon Summoning/Control (800)§
Evoke Immortal Child (300)*
Open Hell Gate (300)
Weep Beans of Life (400)

Level Fifteen
Draw Yin Yang (2,000)§
Enter Divine Realm of Jade Emperor (500)
Remove Heart (700)

Chi Magic & Celestial Calligraphy

The number in parentheses is the number of P.P.E. required to use the magic.

* An asterisk next to a listing indicates that the spell produces a type of "Living Chi." Spells of this nature require the spell caster to expel some or all of their Chi from their bodies. A risk of any spell of this type is that the character's Chi can be lost or destroyed.

§ An § indicates a "geomantic" spell. These are spells designed to manipulate the flow of Chi. Fang Shih (geomancers) have only geomantic spells.

Level One

Chi Mask

Range: Self
Duration: Twenty melee rounds (5 minutes) per level of experience.
Saving Throw: None
Cost: Three P.P.E.

Used to change the appearance of the caster's Chi. Instead of seeing the character's true Chi, those capable of detecting Chi will see the false "Chi mask." The spell caster can decide if the Chi will either appear to be zero or any amount of Positive or Negative Chi. While the spell can be cancelled at any time, the caster must define the exact Chi appearance when the spell is first cast. **Note:** If the person disguised by *Chi Mask* uses his real Chi or has his Chi damaged, the amount of Chi displayed by the mask will not change.

As Celestial Calligraphy: Doesn't work unless the spell caster understands the spell completely (roll on the above Spell Learning Table after the appropriate time of study). **Blue ink on green paper.**

Convert Chi to P.P.E.

Range: Self
Duration: Instant
Saving Throw: None
Cost: One P.P.E. or six points of Positive or Negative Chi.

A desired amount of Chi contained in the character is instantly changed from Chi to P.P.E. The exchange rate is one point of P.P.E. for every six points of Chi. Any remaining Chi (what's left over after dividing by six) will not be changed and will remain as Chi.

As the Chi is converted to P.P.E. it must be expended in one of the following three ways.

First, it can be used to replenish any or all of the character's lost P.P.E. (but no more than the character's usual base P.P.E.).

Second, the P.P.E. can be diverted into a spell — however, the spell must be cast immediately (within two melee rounds) after the conversion.

Third, if the P.P.E. is not immediately used by the spell caster, or if the amount of P.P.E. being channeled exceeds a container's capacity, then the P.P.E. will dissipate into the surrounding area.

For example, a character who has been drained of P.P.E., but who has twenty-six Chi remaining, can cast this spell at a cost of six points of Chi. After the cost for the spell, there are twenty points of Chi left. Divide by six, and the character ends up with three points of P.P.E. and two points of Chi remaining.

This is also a sneaky way of eliminating some of the body's Negative Chi, since either Negative or Positive Chi can be converted into P.P.E.

As Celestial Calligraphy: Unless the character releasing the spell is properly prepared (i.e. trained and ready to direct the spell), then ALL the character's Chi will be converted into P.P.E. **White ink on green paper.**

Convert P.P.E. to Chi

Range: Self
Duration: Instant
Saving Throw: None
Cost: One P.P.E.

Each point of P.P.E. converted turns into six points of Chi. The caster determines how much of their P.P.E. will be converted, and whether the conversion will be into Positive Chi or Negative Chi.

For example, a character with eight points of P.P.E. and no Chi remaining, spends one P.P.E. on activating the spell, leaving seven points. Then, converts three points of the remainder, so he ends up with eighteen points of Chi and four points of P.P.E.

As Celestial Calligraphy: Unless the character releasing the spell is properly prepared (i.e. trained and ready to direct the spell), ALL the character's P.P.E. will be instantly converted into Chi. **White ink on green paper.**

Convert Positive Chi to Light

Range: Self
Duration: One melee round per point of Chi.
Saving Throw: Standard
Cost: One P.P.E.

The spell caster's Chi is magically converted into bright sunlight, making it seem as if light were radiating from every bit of exposed flesh. The quality of the light is such that it seems as if a window were thrown open directly to the sun.

Within 10 feet (3 m), all humans will find it difficult to see and will squint and shield their eyes (-3 on initiative and -2 to strike, parry or dodge).

Within 30 feet (9.1 m), all creatures of darkness, vampires, and others vulnerable to sunlight, will be affected (blinded and/or burnt as per their natural limitations; blinded beings are -8 on all combat rolls). Creatures that can be damaged by sunlight, when first confronted by the radiant light, will have to save vs horror factor of 14. Damage is as per usual for such beings.

Within 90 feet (27.4 m), everything will be clearly lit, as if by full daylight (the light is not blinding). The spell will continue until the caster cancels it, or until all their Chi is gone.

As Celestial Calligraphy: Unless the spell caster understands the spell, it will continue to work until ALL the character's Chi is burned up. **Red ink on silver paper.**

Create Sparks

Range: Self
Duration: Four melee rounds (one minute) per point of Chi.
Saving Throw: None
Cost: Two P.P.E.

By setting up a magical interference between the Chi in the body and the Chi of the environment, the caster can generate sparks at the tips of his fingers. Although these are relatively harmless (at a touch they can inflict one point of damage per melee round maximum), they can be used as illumination (limited to about 10 feet/3.0 m), start fires (50% chance when used on combustibles), or to ignite any flammable substance (90% likelihood) by touch.

Since the spell burns up the caster's Chi (Positive Chi or Negative Chi is fine), it stops when the character runs out of Chi.

The color of the sparks is a sign of the Chi in the area. Sparks are pure white only when there is no Chi flowing at all. In the presence of Positive Chi the sparks are blue. In an area of Negative Chi the sparks turn green.

As Celestial Calligraphy: Unless the character releasing the spell knows what it is and concentrates on creating the sparks, nothing will happen. **Gold ink on red paper.**

Sense *Chen Chi* – Living Vitality

Range: Eighty feet (24.4 m)
Duration: Four melee rounds (one minute) per level of experience.
Saving Throw: None
Cost: One P.P.E.

The spell caster senses the "living vitality" aspect of a creature's Chi. This is the Chi equivalent of a medical diagnosis and can be particularly helpful for any character with healing skills. The following three things can be detected:

The health of the character. One can tell if someone has a disease, as well as if they are just getting sick or recovering from an illness. With a full melee round of observation on any one creature, the spell caster can tell the seriousness of the disease, whether or not it is life-threatening, if it is communicable (catchy!), and if the problem is natural, Chi or magic based.

The injuries of the character. With a glance, the character will know who has been injured or is still recovering from injury (i.e. whether they are healing lost S.D.C. and/or hit points). If examined for a full melee round, it will be possible to determine if the injuries were serious (hit points) or just superficial (S.D.C.) and roughly how much of the character's vitality was lost (half, a quarter, etc.)

The presence of poison. Anyone currently under the influence of a poison or a magic potion will be instantly noticeable. However, to see if a character is recovering from a poison, or if a delayed-action poison is present, a full melee round's examination is needed.

As Celestial Calligraphy: Works even if the character doesn't understand the spell, but the ignorant won't be able to figure out what the different kinds of emanations actually mean, just that people with emanations are sick or injured. **Blue ink on silver Paper.**

Sense *Ti Chi* – Earth/Dragon Energy (Geomantic)

Range: One Hundred feet (30.5 m).
Duration: Four melee rounds (one minute) per level of experience.
Saving Throw: None
Cost: One P.P.E.

Provides a sense of the "Earth" or "Dragon" Chi energy that flows through the world. This provides a more detailed picture of the Chi world than received by those with Chi Mastery Abilities (they only pick up the amount and type of Chi).

Flow of Chi. The character can feel the *Chi Wind* as it blows along any area. This instantly conveys the amount of Chi, whether it is Negative or Positive, and the direction of the current (which way it is flowing). In addition, the character can sense magical Chi lines (created by geomantic spells) up to one hundred feet (30.5 m) away from the disturbance they cause in the flow of Chi.

Earth Chi Flow. By touching the earth or a piece of rock or stone embedded in the earth, the character can feel the underground flow of Chi. Also, a solid piece of concrete, if it touches the earth, can be used as a "conduit" to feel the flow of Chi in the earth, even if the character is fifty stories up in a skyscraper. In addition, the presence of any Earth Dragons, even those a mile (1.6 km) away, will be instantly obvious.

Sense Nearby Chi. If a wall, ceiling, or floor, is relatively thin (less than a foot/30 cm thick), then the spell caster can touch that surface and tell what the flow of Chi is like in the adjoining area.

As Celestial Calligraphy: Doesn't work unless the character understands the spell. **Blue Ink on Gold Paper.**

Sense *Wei Chi* – Internal Fire

Range: Eighty feet (24.4 m).
Duration: Four melee rounds (one minute) per level of experience.
Saving Throw: None.
Cost: One P.P.E.

The spell caster can sense the "internal fire," or Chi, in any creature, object, or disembodied entity. It is similar to what is sensed by those who have Chi Mastery, but *Wei Chi* does not reveal whether or not someone is a Chi Master, or has any kind of Chi abilities. While the spell is in effect, the caster can detect the following:

Chi Quantity. The amount of Chi in any creature or object.

Chi Type. Whether any source of Chi is charged with Negative Chi or Positive Chi.

Creatures of Pure Chi. All sources of disembodied Chi, or entities of Pure Chi (usually invisible), or the Chi given off by any invisible or hidden sources.

As Celestial Calligraphy: Works even if the character doesn't understand the spell, but the ignorant will simply see different kinds of glowing for Positive and Negative Chi, and may not be able to figure out how to relate the brightness of the glow to the amount of Chi or the color to good and evil. **Blue Ink on Pink Paper.**

Level Two

Chi-Gung Invocation

Range: Self
Duration: Two melee rounds per point of Chi.
Saving Throw: None
Cost: Six P.P.E.

Chi fills the body, resulting in a toughening of the skin so that blades cannot cut it and arrows cannot pierce it. The character's "natural" Armor Rating (A.R.) goes up to 16 and the S.D.C. is an additional 40 points for the duration of the spell. In addition to being resistant to sharp blades, sword points and jagged glass, the character is also resistant to flame, fire and flame throwers (half damage). Magic, psionics, poison, drugs, bullets, and explosives do full damage.

As Celestial Calligraphy: Works regardless of the caster. **White ink on silver paper.**

Convert Positive Chi to Heat

Range: Self
Duration: Varies according to Positive Chi expended.
Saving Throw: Standard
Cost: Three P.P.E.

The Chi in the body of the spell caster is converted into heat, in any one of the following three forms:

Internal Heat. Keeps the body of the caster pleasantly warm, no matter what the outside temperature or environment. Consumes one point of Positive Chi every twenty melee rounds (every five minutes). During this time the character is impervious to cold.

External Heat. The body radiates heat, so that the body's internal temperature extends out for another three or four feet (0.9 to 1.2 m) outward. Snow or ice will melt as if exposed to sunlight on a hot summer day. Anyone standing nearby will be comfortably warmed up. Consumes one point of Positive Chi every four melee rounds (every minute). During this time the character is impervious to normal cold.

Boil Liquids. The heat is channeled by touch (usually through a fingertip), so that the character can cause liquids to boil. Note that the liquid, no matter how flammable, will not ignite from the heat of the spell (although, if flammable, the touch of any flame or spark will ignite the liquid). Consumes one point of Positive Chi every melee round.

As Celestial Calligraphy: If the spell caster doesn't understand the spell, then it automatically generates *internal heat*, and will continue until ALL the character's Chi is used up. **Red ink on silver paper.**

Draw Confining Arc of Chi (Geomantic Magic)

Range: Touch
Duration: Ten minutes per level of experience.
Saving Throw: None
Cost: Four P.P.E.

Drawing an invisible line in the air (using hand gestures), the spell caster creates a sort of Chi dam that slightly alters the flow of Chi in an area. The arc is slightly curved and no more than 20 feet (6.1 m) long. It can either arc inward, so it "cups" the flow of Chi and gathers extra energy, or outward, so it "deflects" the flow of Chi, creating a bit of a dead space. Once the spell expires, the line fades away and Chi resumes its normal flow in the area.

Arc of Gathering Chi. If done so that the bowl faces the flow of Chi, the Chi will tend to accumulate inside the arc. The spell caster can arrange it so the amount is either doubled (in about a 20 foot/6.1 m wide area), or tripled (in a small, 5 foot/1.5 m wide area). For example, if the characters are in an area with a flow of four points of Positive Chi, the arc can create a small pocket of 12 Positive Chi points (triple), but the area would only be five feet (1.5 m) in diameter (the size of a closet). If the Chi is only to be doubled (8 points of Positive Chi), the area would be much larger, 20 feet (6.1 m) in diameter, the size of a meeting room.

Arc of Deflecting Chi. If done so that the bulge faces the line of Chi, the area inside will be shielded from the flow of Chi, Positive or Negative. About three-quarters (75%) of the flowing Chi will avoid the protected area. For example, in an area where 20 points of Negative Chi flow by, the area protected by the arc would only experience 5 points of Negative Chi.

Not available as Celestial Calligraphy.

Exhale Obscuring Smoke (Living Chi)

Range: Self
Duration: Up to 4 melee rounds (one minute) per level of experience.
Saving Throw: None
Cost: Four P.P.E.

The caster fuses the Chi with the element of water in the lungs to produce a dense smoke. Victims caught in the cloud will be unable to see anything beyond the cloud and their impaired vision means they can see no more than three feet (0.3 m) away, and then only blurry shapes. Victims in the cloud will be -5 to strike, parry and dodge.

However there is more to this cloud than just dense smoke. This is the first of a series of *Clouds of Living Chi*. The cloud that the character exhales is still a part of him/her, because it is made of up Chi "borrowed" from the character's body. Since the cloud is a part of the character, the spell caster can do all of the following:

Sense of Touch. While not as sensitive as fingers, the spell caster can "feel" the shapes and locations of anyone inside the cloud, as well as any surfaces that the cloud touches.

Invest Living Chi. The size of the cloud is determined by the amount of Chi invested in it by the character. Each point of Chi (Positive or Negative) contributes enough Living Chi Cloud to fill an area about ten feet wide by ten feet long, by ten feet tall in volume (1,000 cubic feet – 28.3 cubic meters – a little more than 3×3×3 m). So, for example, 20 points of Chi could be used to engulf an area 100 feet long, 20 feet wide, and 10 feet tall (20,000 cubic feet – 566 cubic meters – a little more than 30×6×3 m).

Expand and Contract. The cloud can be expanded to its maximum size (as defined by the amount of Chi invested), but it can also be compacted, and shrunk down to a tenth of the maximum, at will.

Cloud Movement. The spell caster can shape, move and manipulate the cloud, although relatively slowly. The cloud can only move with a Spd. of 4 (about 60 feet/18.3 m per melee round), and must always be in contact with the spell caster. Also, the cloud must stay in one piece and any "chunks" that get cut off (by a closed door, etc.) will dissolve.

Retract Cloud. At any time, until the spell expires, the character can pull the cloud back in, inhaling it, and retrieve any Chi that is left in it. If the cloud is cut off, or destroyed, or if the character keeps it out once the spell is over, then the Chi is dissipated, and the character will have to recover his lost Chi in one of the usual ways.

As Celestial Calligraphy: Doesn't work unless the character releasing the spell has had detailed instructions and knows how to manipulate Living Chi. **White Ink on Green Paper.**

Fill Object with Chi

Range: Touch
Duration: Permanent
Saving Throw: None
Cost: Five P.P.E.

An item, such as a weapon, is filled up with either Positive or Negative Chi. Once filled, the item becomes "solid" to entities of Pure Chi. For example, ordinary daggers, arrows and bullets could do no damage to an entity of Pure Chi, since they would pass through without contact. However, if one of those daggers, arrows or bullets were filled with Chi, they would inflict their usual damage, direct to the entity's Chi!

Also, if an item is filled with Chi, it can be used to accompany a character along on a *Mind Walk* (see Zenjorike), or can be taken with a character who is in Pure Chi Form. In either case, the actual physical object will be left behind and the character carries the "Chi Aspect" of the thing, which still does its regular damage.

Chi: In addition to the cost of casting the spell, the spell caster must also expend the Chi necessary to fill the object. The amount of Chi needed to fill an object depends on its size. Small items, like daggers, bullets, arrows and shuriken take only one point of Chi. Medium sized objects, like swords and spears, take two points of Chi. Larger objects, anything twenty pounds (9 kg) and over, usually require three points of Chi for every twenty pounds (9 kg) of mass.

As Celestial Calligraphy: Doesn't work unless the character releasing the spell has had detailed instructions. **Red ink on gold paper** for filling with Positive Chi, **black ink on gold paper** for filling with Negative Chi.

Reverse Chi

Range: Self
Duration: Instant
Saving Throw: Standard
Cost: Two P.P.E.

Changes the spell caster's Chi, so that Negative Chi will instantly become Positive Chi, or vice versa. There is no Chi gained or lost in the reversing process.

As Celestial Calligraphy: Works whether or not the caster understands it, automatically changing the character's Chi to the opposite type. **White ink on green paper.**

Sense Infernal Influences

Range: 80 feet (24.4 m)
Duration: Four melee rounds (one minute) per level of experience.
Saving Throw: None
Cost: Two P.P.E.

The spell caster becomes aware of the presence of creatures associated with the Yama Kings of Hell and any other entities who associate with the dead, or with the souls of the dead. Ordinary humans, no matter how evil they may be, or those who are infected with Negative Chi, are NOT detected by the spell. Here are some of the things that might be detected with *Sense Infernal Influences:*

Any opening or gateway to an Infernal place, such as one of the Hells of the Yama Kings, will be instantly recognized. The direction of an Infernal portal that is currently being used by an Infernal entity can be sensed from a much greater distance (up to one mile/1.6 km away).

Any Infernal creature or entity, such as a demon, a creature of Pure Negative Chi, or any servitor of the Yama Kings of Hell.

Undead or Living-Dead Immortals will also be detected.

As Celestial Calligraphy: It always works, even for those who don't understand the spell, but an ignorant caster may not understand what the different glowing auras mean. **Blue ink on glossy black paper.**

Turn Away The Dead

Range: Up to 60 feet (18.3) away.
Duration: Instant effect.
Area Affected: Circle, up to 20 feet (6.1 m) in diameter.
Saving Throw: Standard
Cost: Six P.P.E.

The utterance of this spell will turn/repel up to 1D6 animated dead per level of experience. This means that those creatures affected will turn and immediately leave the area without harming the spell caster or anyone nearby. The dead turned will not come back for 24 hours. The magic affects "animated" dead and corpses that are magically manipulated, but will NOT affect undead, vampires or Living-Dead Immortals, or any corpse actually possessed by a disembodied entity or Infernal. For example, if used against a group of undead animated by a Brass Snake, it will affect all of the corpses except the one actually occupied by the Brass Snake.

As Celestial Calligraphy: Works whether or not the caster understands it. **Black ink on yellow paper.**

Level Three

Cure Negative Chi Disease

Range: Self
Duration: Instant
Saving Throw: None
Cost: Seven P.P.E.

The spell caster is instantly healed of any and all Negative Chi illnesses and diseases. Works to cure any ailments inflicted by Advanced Negative Chi Mastery (Che Anemia – *Hsueh Chi*, Demon Chi Possession – *Kuei Chi*, and Rising Chi Cough – *Ou Ni Shang Chi*) as well as any spell or curse that passes on a Negative Chi sickness (specifically *Hsieh Chang* – Malignant Miasmal Disease, *Chi Chu* – Accumulation of Morbid Chi and *Hsieh Chu Wu* – Malignant Epidemic Possession).

As Celestial Calligraphy: For one person, the Celestial Calligraphy works in the usual way. However, it is possible for the Celestial Calligraphy version of *Cure Negative Chi Disease* to be used on a group of people. First the paper is burned in a metal bowl (preferably brass or bronze), with care taken that no one touches the metal or the burning paper until it is completely reduced to ashes. Then some purified liquid (water will do fine) is mixed in with the ashes. Each afflicted person then swallows a single mouthful (there should be enough for up to twenty people). Used in this fashion, the cure takes about twenty-four hours. **Red ink on silver paper.**

Disperse Chi

Range: Touch
Duration: Special, see below.
Saving Throw: Standard
Cost: Nine P.P.E.

This magic scatters the Chi contained in any person or thing, so it is drained away into the surrounding area. All the Chi will be gone, so the character or item will be down to zero Chi. Although it's usually used as an attack spell, Disperse Chi can also be used to remove harmful Negative Chi. If used on oneself or a willing subject, then no saving throw is required.

As Celestial Calligraphy: The area of effect (person/thing or area) must be defined when the Celestial Calligraphy is first inscribed. If designed to work on a person or object, but the caster doesn't understand the spell, it automatically disperses the Chi of the caster. **Gold ink on red paper.**

Draw Flowing Spiral of Chi (Geomantic Magic)

Range: Touch
Duration: Ten minutes per level of experience.
Saving Throw: None
Cost: Eight P.P.E.

An invisible line is drawn as the spell caster walks around in a spiral, about 20 feet (6.1 m) in diameter (although, if confined to a small room, the spiral could be as small as 8 feet/2.4 m across). If the Chi is to be drained away, then the spell caster should start on the outside and gradually walk in a spiral inward toward the center. If the spiral is to draw Chi into the area, then the spell caster starts at the center and walks the spiral line outward. Here are the four possible ways of drawing a Chi Spiral:

Spiral of Draining Negative Chi (Counter-Clockwise). The natural flow of Negative Chi in the area will start swirling around counter-clockwise, following the spell caster's line. This has the result of channeling most of the Negative Chi down, into the invisible magical hole at the center of the spiral. The Negative Chi downstream of the area, for about 100 feet (30.5 m), will end up empty of Chi or, if the flow is particularly heavy (20 points of Negative Chi or more), with just a trickle of about a tenth of the usual flow.

Spiral of Propagating Negative Chi (Clockwise). The Chi in the area (Negative or Positive), swirls around in an clockwise funnel, so that Negative Chi is drawn up, from the center of the spiral. Usually, this results in an increase of between 4 and 24 (4D6) points of Negative Chi within the area of the spiral. If the area affected is flowing with Positive Chi, then the Negative Chi will cancel out Positive on a one-for-one basis.

For example, say a Spiral of Negative Chi Propagation is used in an area where six points of Positive Chi was already flowing and 14 points of Negative Chi were drawn upward. The Positive Chi would negate six of the Negative Chi, leaving a net of eight points of Negative Chi flowing in the immediate area. Note that this only works if there actually is some Negative Chi just below the area of effect. Trying to do this on the 2nd floor of a building, where the next floor down is flowing with Positive Chi, is useless.

Spiral of Draining Positive Chi (Clockwise). The reverse of draining Negative Chi, where the Positive Chi in an area is drawn into an upward vortex; this can work inside or outdoors. For an area 50 feet (15.2 m) downstream of the spiral the Positive Chi is depleted to a flow of just a single point.

Spiral of Propagating Positive Chi (Counter-Clockwise). A reversal of Propagating Negative Chi, where the spell caster attempts to bring down a whirlwind of Positive Chi. The increase in Chi depends on where the spiral is drawn. Underground, where Chi is brought down from the surface or in a city crowded with buildings, the flow is usually from two to twelve (2D6) points of Positive Chi. Outdoors, in a wild area, the flow can be from five to thirty (5D6) points of Positive Chi. The Positive Chi within the spiral will cancel out an equivalent amount of Negative Chi, or add to any existing Positive Chi. This only works if there actually is a source of Positive Chi somewhere directly above the spell caster.

One other note. All this Chi, Positive or Negative, has to go, or come from somewhere. So the excess Chi will probably end up either upstairs (Positive), or at the next level down (Negative). Likewise, the Chi of either the upper or lower areas will be depleted of all the Chi propagated by a Chi spiral.

Not available as Celestial Calligraphy.

Exhale Burning Cloud (Living Chi)

Range: Self
Duration: Up to 4 melee rounds per level of experience.
Area Affected: Can exhale up to 20 cubic feet (a sphere 3.4 feet/1 m in diameter – or 0.57 cubic meters) of smoke, once per melee round.
Saving Throw: None
Cost: Six P.P.E.

Fusing Chi with the fire element in the body and then ejecting it out of the lungs, the spell caster is able to project a fiery cloud. Victims caught in the cloud will experience burning eyes (save vs pain to keep them open) and visibility will be cut to half the usual distance. Victims in the cloud will be at -2 on initiative and -3 to strike, parry and dodge.

In the first melee round of contact, extremely combustible objects (paper, newspapers, flammable liquids) have a 50% chance of igniting. Then, starting in the second melee round of contact, everything will begin to smoulder and extremely combustible objects will catch on fire. Characters who stay inside the cloud will take 1D6 points of burning damage for each melee round of exposure.

Sense of Touch. The spell caster can "feel" the shapes and locations of anyone inside or touching the cloud.

Sense of *Wei Chi*. The spell caster can sense the "internal fire" diffused throughout the body of any living thing inside the cloud or anyone touching the cloud from the outside. This reveals the type of Chi, Positive or Negative, and its amount. It can also be used to sense the presence of hidden sources of Chi.

Control Cloud. The cloud can be expanded or contracted and moved (Spd. 4) and shaped according to the whim of the spell caster. The size limit is the same as with all Living Chi Clouds: a 10 by 10 by 10 foot cubic volume (1000 cubic feet – 28.3 cubic meters – a little over 3×3×3 m) for each point of Chi invested. Retracting the cloud means the character can recover Chi.

As Celestial Calligraphy: Nothing happens unless the character knows how to invoke Living Chi. **White ink on green paper.**

Inscribe Celestial Calligraphy

Range: Touch
Duration: 10 minutes per level of spell to be stored.
Saving Throw: Standard
Cost: Six P.P.E.

The only way for a *Wu Shih* to create Celestial Calligraphy is by casting this spell (*Tao Shih* don't need to use the spell, since they create Celestial Calligraphy as an R.C.C. ability).

P.P.E. is expended twice during the casting of this spell. First, six points of P.P.E. are expended in order to initiate the Celestial Calligraphy. The spell caster then uses the appropriate materials (the correct colors of ink and paper) to write out a spell in Celestial Calligraphy. The amount of time required depends on the level of the spell; multiply the level times ten minutes for the total time needed for inscribing. The inscription of the characters for the Celestial Calligraphy must continue *uninterrupted* for the entire duration of the spell, or the spell will be spoiled and the P.P.E. lost.

Finally, once the Celestial Calligraphy is nearly complete, the spell caster must roll to save vs magic (12 or less on a 20 sided die). If the roll fails, then the Celestial Calligraphy is spoiled and the spell aborts (the six P.P.E. are also lost). However, if the saving throw succeeds, then the spell caster must add in the P.P.E. required for the stored spell (the usual amount to cast the spell) and the result is an active piece of Celestial Calligraphy that is triggered when it is burned.

Not available as Celestial Calligraphy.

Replenish Vajra

Range: Touch
Duration: Instant
Saving Throw: None
Cost: Five P.P.E.

Used by the spell caster to charge a Vajra P.P.E., and/or to fill it with Chi. In addition to the five P.P.E., the spell caster must also supply whatever additional P.P.E. and/or Chi that are to be channeled into the Vajra.

Not Available as Celestial Calligraphy.

Sense Alchemical Aura

Range: 120 feet (36.6 m)
Duration: Eight Melee Rounds (two minutes) per level of experience.
Saving Throw: None
Cost: Four P.P.E.

An ancient spell developed by Chinese alchemists in the Dynasty of the Legendary Sage Emperors (over 4,000 years ago). Using this spell reveals the faint glow of Chi that surrounds every living and non-living thing, coloring each aura with a tinge of color that gives away its nature. If a thing has two or more qualities that generate an alchemical aura, only the most powerful will be seen. Here are the colors that may be seen:

Light Purple – Alchemical Elixirs. Detects elixirs of immortality or other activated magical potions. The brighter the glow, the more powerful the elixir. Anyone who has recently consumed a magical elixir will also glow with this color, but very dimly.

Dark Purple – Enlightened Immortals. Anyone who has achieved, through Internal Alchemy, a step along the way to a Nine-Times Refined Elixir will glow with this unique shade. The more advanced the Immortal, the brighter the glow.

Light Blue – Alchemical Ingredients. This color signifies one of the magical ingredients so valued by the ancient alchemists. Natural materials, like the Divine Mushroom, chemicals, like Activated Cinnabar, and even artifacts, like Alchemical Touchstones, all glow with this color. Magical at the very brightest end of the scale, with a blinding blue-white glare, is the aura of the Three-Hundred-Year-Old Ginseng, or the Three-Thousand-Year-Old Living Ginseng (in **Rifts** this would include the Millennium Tree and the Planet Wormwood).

Dark Blue – The Color of Transformation. Anything undergoing transformation, such as chemicals being processed in a laboratory, glow with this color. However, the color also signifies someone, or something, who is recently transformed or transfigured by magical means.

Dark Red – Spell Magic. Magical items, characters currently commanding magical spells or artifacts, Living Chi, and anything charged with active magic will glow deep red. The item or spell must be charged with at least a point of P.P.E., or the glow will be too faint to be seen. The brighter the radiance, the more powerful the magic.

Pale Red – Celestial Calligraphy. Magical characters and writing, including talismans and other objects charged with magic-containing calligraphy, glow a pale red.

Dark Yellow – Dragons. A dark yellow glow, on the ground, over water, or in the sky, indicates the hidden presence of a dragon. An actual dragon would glow so brightly that nothing else would be seen, and there would be a dark yellow aura over everything in sight. Dragons who are in human form usually glow a dark blue (transformation).

Bright Yellow – The Ascended/Heavenly Messengers. This is the color associated with the Heavenly Court of the Jade Emperor, and with all deities.

White – Ghosts & Spirits. Any piece of a soul, or disembodied spirit, will softly emit a white light.

Black – Infernals. A glittering black sheen gives away the presence of Demons and other agents of the Yama Kings, or representatives of previous Hells.

Green – Poison. Actively poisonous substances glow green. However, in order for there to be even the hint of green, the material must be powerful enough to kill a person with a tiny amount in a few minutes. The more powerful the poison, the brighter the glow. Note that knockout poisons, non-fatal poisons, and drugs that are merely fatal after long use (arsenic, for example), do not register as green.

As Celestial Calligraphy: Works whether or not the caster understands it. **Blue ink on gold paper.**

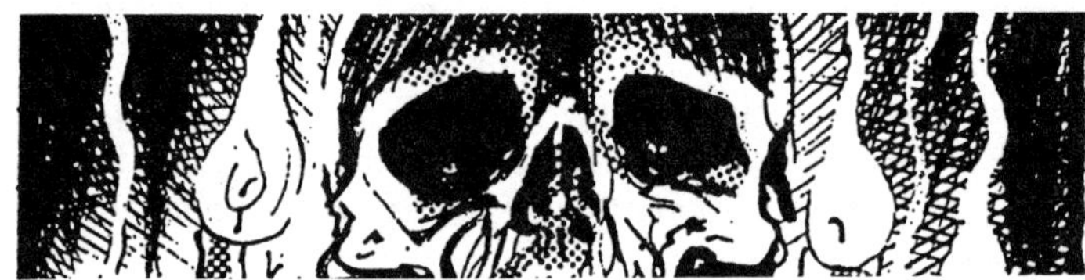

View Ghost Drama

Range: 50 feet (15.2 m)
Duration: Five minutes per level of experience.
Saving Throw: Standard (however, most ghosts will not resist the spell).
Cost: Eight P.P.E.

Characters with psychic sensitivity can often catch a glimpse of ghosts near places where someone has died, usually as a result of murder or violent accidental death. However, what is seen is usually just a few wisps or shifting shadows. This spell pours Chi energy into the scene of death, allowing observers to clearly see and hear the actual haunting.

According to the Chinese, ghosts are usually the *Hun* portion of the soul, the more primitive "body" piece that is left behind after the *Po* leaves for judging in the afterlife. Since the *Hun* is incapable of speech and is traumatized by the death, it simply goes through the motions of the few minutes leading up to the point of death and then repeats the same motions over and over again.

When illuminated by this spell, watchers will see the victim reenacting the scene of his own death, along with others on the scene, as well as all the physical elements that were there at the time.

In a play-test, the group's blind mystic spotted a ghost who seemed to be staggering down the side of a building. When the spell was cast, it was revealed that the character, who seemed to be wounded, was actually stumbling down the fire escape (which had been removed after the death), and being man-handled by two other men. One of the people, who was known to the victim, had clear features, and could be easily identified. The other person, who the victim didn't know, and seen only dimly in the dark alley. His features were too obscured for easy identification.

Remember that what is viewed is the ghost's own version of events, which may or may not be entirely truthful or accurate. For example, a murder victim who never saw the person responsible for stabbing him in the back will be unable to identify that person, so the figure will be in shadow to the point that even its gender is impossible to determine. The ghost can only point the finger at the person(s) he saw.

As Celestial Calligraphy: The user must have knowledge of how the spell works in order to activate it properly. **Blue ink on white paper.**

Level Four

Draw Knot of Obstruction (Geomantic)

Range: Touch
Duration: Five minutes per level of experience.
Saving Throw: None
Cost: Ten P.P.E.

The spell caster draws an invisible line, using hand gestures, enclosing an area. However, before closing the gap that finishes the area, a complex "knot" is drawn. All Chi attempting to cross the line, including entities of Pure Chi, will be drawn along it and end up in the knotted area. This knot prevents the entry or exit of any entities of Pure Chi. It also prevents entities of Pure Chi from teleporting into, or out of, the area. The natural flow of Chi is not obstructed by the ward, so the amount of Chi inside and outside the area should be the same.

The line must be free of gaps, or entities will be able to enter. So long as the entire area is enclosed, the overall shape can be anything (circular, square, triangular, etc.). If the spell caster is 5th level, or less, then the largest area that can be enclosed is about 20 feet (6.1 m) across. Higher level spell casters, those 6th level and higher (2nd level for *Fang Shih*) can add another five feet (1.5 m) of diameter for each level of experience.

Note that a demon who is barred from crossing the line while in Pure Negative Chi Form can easily change to physical form, step across, and then change back to Chi Form.

As Celestial Calligraphy: The user must know the working of the spell in order to cast it. **Gold ink on silver paper.**

Exhale Electrostatic Fog (Living Chi)

Range: Self
Duration: Up to 4 melee rounds per level of experience.
Saving Throw: None
Cost: Eight P.P.E.

The spell caster fuses the Chi with the body's element of metal and produces a cloud of electrical energy, which gives off sparks (blue sparks in a Positive Chi flow, green sparks where the flow is Negative Chi). Being caught inside the electrostatic cloud is frightening, since sparks go off constantly with loud pops and flashes, while hair stands on end and there is a strong smell of ozone. However, living things inside the cloud usually point of death and then repeats the same motions over and over again.

When illuminated by this spell, watchers will see the victim reenacting the scene of his own death, along with others on the scene, as well as all the physical elements that were there at the time.

In a play-test, the group's blind mystic spotted a ghost who seemed to be staggering down the side of a building. When the spell was cast, it was revealed that the character, who seemed to be wounded, was actually stumbling down the fire escape (which had been removed after the death), and being man-handled by two other men. One of the people, who was known to the victim, had clear features, and could be easily identified. The other person, who the victim didn't know, and seen only dimly take damage only when entering or leaving the cloud; and then only one point of damage.

It's not so harmless for electrical devices! The cloud will cause devices to explosively short out. Televisions and computer monitors implode on contact and any computer-based devices are temporarily rendered useless and take 3D6 damage per melee round. Automobiles, trucks, robotics, generators, and most industrial equipment will undergo severe damage, and will require many hours of electrical repairs. If the device isn't currently "turned on," then each can attempt a save vs electricity (12 or higher saves).

If the cloud comes into contact with very combustible items like paper, open containers of flammable liquids, gasoline vapor, etc., there is a very good chance of some spectacular pyrotechnics (75% chance).

Sense of Touch. The spell caster can "feel" the shapes and locations of anyone inside or touching the cloud.

Sense Tien Chi (Electrical Potential). The character casting the spell can sense *Tien Chi*, which is the type of Chi that's an ingredient of any electrical energy, as well as any source of electricity within the cloud, or touching the cloud. Power lines, extension cords, telephone wires, and other channels of electricity will be identifiable by their level of power and potential. Electrical storage devices, from "AA" cells to car batteries to high-tech (*Rifts*-style) nuclear generators can be sensed and identified by type and amount of charge. The internal electrical workings of machines, especially those that are operational, will also have a unique, recognizable "feel."

Close Electrical Circuit. It's possible for the character to bridge the gap between any electrical power source inside the cloud to any other object inside or touching the cloud. Jumping the gap to one target allows for 5D6 damage, once per melee round. It's also possible to shock everyone within the cloud by tapping an electrical plug, delivering 1D6 damage each per melee round.

Control Cloud. The cloud can be expanded or contracted and moved (Spd. 4) or shaped according to the whim of the spell caster. The size limit is the same as with all Living Chi Clouds: a 10 by 10 by 10 foot cubic volume (1000 cubic feet – 28.3 cubic meters – a little over 3×3×3 m) for each point of Chi invested. Retracting the cloud means the character can recover Chi.

As Celestial Calligraphy: Nothing happens unless the character knows how to invoke Living Chi. **White ink on green paper.**

Invoke Chi Zoshiki

Range: Self
Duration: Four melee rounds (one minute) per point of Chi expended.
Saving Throw: Standard
Cost: Nine P.P.E.

This is a magical version of the most powerful of the Arts of Invisibility. The character uses Chi to cloud the minds of observers, so that character can stand in full view, stare into the eyes of the enemy, and simply cease to exist! The character must use one point of Chi for every minute of disappearance. Obviously, this means it's a good idea to hide in a more conventional way before all Chi points are gone. Unlike those trained in the Arts of Invisibility, the caster of *Invoke Chi Zoshiki* is NOT shielded from a Chi Master's *Chi Awareness*, or from the spell Sense Chi.

As Celestial Calligraphy: Works whether or not the caster understands it. **White ink on silver paper.**

Live on Negative Chi

Range: Self
Duration: Four hours per level of experience.
Saving Throw: None
Cost: Eight P.P.E.

The spell attunes the character so that normal rest, recovery and healing can take place while the body is infected with Negative Chi. Note that as long as the body is under the influence of this spell it can not heal if filled with Positive Chi.

As Celestial Calligraphy: Works whether or not the caster understands it. **Black ink on silver paper.**

Open Window on Afterlife

Range: Touch
Duration: Four melee rounds (one minute) per level of experience.
Saving Throw: None
Cost: Twelve P.P.E.

The spell is cast on a mirror or a piece of glass, or even in a still pool of water or other liquid. At the beginning of the spell, the spell caster concentrates on the name or image of someone deceased. When activated, the Window on Afterlife shows the current situation of the soul, usually found in one of the Hells of the Yama Kings, or (if recently dead) in the *Shen Jing* (Transition Place) awaiting entry into the Hells. The Window is a one-way affair, so observers can see and hear, but can't be seen from the other side. It's possible to yell through the Window on Afterlife, but those on the other side will only hear faint, disembodied voices.

The duration of the spell is important, since it may take quite a while before anything can be seen within the window. That's because the spell must first *locate* the dead soul, something that depends on a variety of factors, including how long it has been since the soul departed the body. If the object of the spell is recently dead (within a month), then they will be located instantly; within 1D4 melee rounds. Those who have been dead longer, for up to three years, may take 2D6 melee rounds to appear in the window. For anyone who has been dead longer than three years, roll on the following table:

01-20 Success! The window opens up on the afterlife in 2D6 melee rounds.

21-60 Lengthy Delay. It takes 4D6+10 melee rounds.

61-75 Wrong Soul. After 6D6 melee rounds, the window finally opens, but has located the wrong spirit; probably someone with a similar name (if a name was used) or who closely resembles the dead person (based on the image used in the spell casting).

76-90 Overload. After a wait of 3D6 melee rounds there is a flash of light from the window and then the spell fades away.

91-00 There will be a wait of 20 melee rounds. After that, if the spell is still going, the window will open up onto a view of a crowded hall within the vast bureaucracy of the Yama Kings of Hell. Each desk is filled with stacks of scrolls and papers, and each chair occupied by an Infernal functionary (a demon in a clerk's uniform). One of the demons will look up, straight through the Window on Afterlife and will be heard to yell out, "I don't have time for this right now! Try again later!" At which point the Window will be dispelled.

If the soul of the dead person has been reborn, then all that will be seen is a light-filled tunnel indicating that they have departed from the realms of the Hells. Attempting to do the spell on someone not yet dead is not possible.

As Celestial Calligraphy: A *Tao Shih* can inscribe the characters for a Celestial Calligraphy version of Window on Afterlife, but only by drawing them directly on the surface of the glass or reflective surface with **blue ink.**

Ward Body

Range: Self
Duration: Ten minutes per level of experience.
Saving Throw: None
Cost: Six P.P.E.

Puts a layer of protection around any person or object, so as to prevent the entry of disembodied spirits or any other Chi-based interference; +6 to save vs possession of powerful beings +10 to save against lesser beings.

As Celestial Calligraphy: Works whether or not the caster understands it. **Red ink on silver paper.**

Purify Ingredient (Alchemical)

Range: Touch
Duration: Instant
Saving Throw: None
Cost: Eight P.P.E.

An old alchemical spell used to assure that the components of an elixir were pure and untainted. Can be used with most elements, chemicals, herbs, food, and even water. Removes impurities, including poisons in the substance. However, if the substance is itself a poison, then the purification will simply remove all non-poisonous impurities.

As Celestial Calligraphy: Doesn't work unless the caster understands it. **White ink on gold paper.**

Level Five

Circle of Non-Ignition

Range: 120 feet (36.6 m)
Duration: Three minutes per level of experience.
Saving Throw: None
Cost: Twelve P.P.E.

Creates a circle about 25 feet (7.6 m) in diameter, where fires can't be started. It becomes impossible to light a match, fire a bullet, or run an internal combustion (gas or oil) engine. Most importantly, characters with slips of paper containing Celestial Calligraphy cannot light them! Existing fires will continue to burn, but will quickly die down and will not spread.

As Celestial Calligraphy: Works whether or not the caster understands it, but will be centered around the spell caster unless properly controlled. **Gold ink on pink paper.**

Draw Chi Barrier (Geomantic Magic)

Range: Touch
Duration: Ten minutes per level of experience.
Saving Throw: None
Cost: Twelve P.P.E.

Drawing an invisible line in the air (using hand gestures), the spell caster defines a wall that blocks off the flow of Chi, and prevents any Pure Chi entities from passing through. If the line defines a closed area, then no Chi can flow into or out of the room. While creatures of Pure Chi can't pass through the barrier, they can teleport across/over it.

If the spell caster is 5th level or less, then the longest barrier that can be drawn is 25 feet (7.6 m) long. Higher level spell casters, those 6th level and higher (2nd level for *Fang Shih*), can add another five feet (1.5 m) of length for each level of experience.

Not available as Celestial Calligraphy.

Empower Vajra

Range: Touch
Duration: 3 minutes per level of experience.
Saving Throw: None
Cost: Ten P.P.E.

Used for the storing of spells in a Vajra. Each spell must be stored separately. Putting in the P.P.E. required for the stored spell is optional, but the ten P.P.E. required for the storage is mandatory. Bear in mind that the number of points on the Vajra (counting both ends) is the maximum number of spells that can be stored.

Not available as Celestial Calligraphy.

Enter/Exit Tung Tien; Caverns of Yin

Range: Touch
Duration: Four melee rounds (one minute).
Saving Throw: None
Cost: Twelve P.P.E.

In order to use this spell, the character must be somewhere underground or touching a natural wall of stone or rock; the rock must be at least ten feet (3.0 m) thick, or the spell will not work. Triggering the spell causes a fissure or crack to open in the rock (takes one full melee round to open). This opening will last for exactly two melee rounds (half a minute) and then will creak shut, closing up the rock as if there had never been a crack.

By entering the crack, characters will find themselves in the confusing tunnels of the great complex of caverns known as *Tung Tien*. Among other wonders, the caves lead to certain hiding places of Immortals, the realm of the White Tiger, the gathering places of the Earth Dragons, to the eternal forest of the Fu Sang Tree, and to vast underground swamps of Negative Chi.

From inside *Tung Tien*, the spell can be cast again (costing another 12 P.P.E.), opening a crack that opens to the place where the spell caster first entered. Or, if the spell caster has entered *Tung Tien* from other places at other times, the crack can lead to any of those other places.

As Celestial Calligraphy: Works whether or not the caster understands it. **Gold ink on green paper.**

Exhale Poison Cloud (Living Chi)

Range: Self
Duration: Up to 4 melee rounds per level of experience.
Saving Throw: None
Cost: Ten P.P.E.

All the previous Clouds of Living Chi (Obscuring Smoke, Burning Cloud, and Electrostatic Fog) came out the same whether they were generated by Positive or Negative Chi. However, starting on this level with the Poison Cloud, the appearance and powers of the cloud depends on whether it is charged with Negative or Positive Chi.

Either way, fusing the body's Chi with the element of wood generates a cloud of nearly transparent gas. Those who are inside the cloud or looking through it from the outside, will see that things are colored with a slight tinge of either green (if mixed with Negative Chi), or blue (Positive Chi). Those in contact with the gas will notice a slight antiseptic smell, like a doctor's office.

Sense of Chen Chi (Living Vitality). The spell caster does not "feel" either the physical shapes or the Chi of those inside the cloud. However, the spell caster can feel the *Chen Chi* of anyone inside the cloud, and tell whether they are healthy or ill, injured or healed, and poisoned or pure. For example, it might be learned of a character inside the cloud, "She seems to be recovering from a mild illness, in battle she seems to have lost about a third of her outer vitality (S.D.C.), but her inner vitality (hit points) are intact, and her blood is pure of contaminants."

Blue Poison Cloud – Positive Chi. The spell caster can choose which of those within the cloud are to be affected by the poison. Those afflicted (failing to hold their breath or save vs non-lethal poison) will be knocked unconscious. How long they'll be out depends on how much Chi was invested in the cloud. For each point of Chi, the character will remain unconscious for 1D6 melee rounds. Once a character is unconscious, the spell caster can pump more poison into their lungs, doubling the amount of time they'll remain unconscious.

Green Poison Cloud – Negative Chi. All within the cloud will be affected and those who fail to hold their breath or save vs poison, will take damage direct to hit points every melee round that they remain inside the cloud. The amount of damage depends on the strength of the cloud, which is determined by how many points of Chi were invested. For each point of Chi, the poison does 1D6 damage.

Precipitate Poison. The spell caster can, at will, cause some of the Living Chi Poison Cloud to condense into a liquid form. Usually this is done over a container of some kind of drinkable fluid (water, juice, beer, etc.), or on top of some kind of porous food (a boiling pot of rice, a loaf of bread, ice cream, etc.). The poison seeps in, so that the food or drink becomes a deadly poison. Each portion (enough drink for a cupful, or food for a small plate), costs one point of Chi to precipitate.

If at least 85% of the poisoned content/cup or plate is consumed, then the victim must save vs poison. A successful save means the victim suffers just stomach cramps and 1D6 of damage. Failure to save means the character will take 4D6 damage direct to hit points, as well as becoming violently ill for at least a full day (unable to walk or fight; reduce attacks per melee, combat bonuses, skill performance and spd. by 75%).

Control Cloud. The cloud can be expanded or contracted, and moved (Spd. 4) or shaped according to the whim of the spell caster. The size limit is the same as with all Living Chi Clouds: a 10 by 10 by 10 foot cubic volume (1000 cubic feet – 28.3 cubic meters – a little over 3×3×3 m) for each point of Chi invested. Retracting the cloud means the character can recover Chi.

As Celestial Calligraphy: Nothing happens unless the character knows how to invoke Living Chi. **White ink on green paper.**

Fly with Stream of Chi

Range: Self
Duration: Four minutes per level of experience.
Saving Throw: None
Cost: Sixteen P.P.E.

The spell caster attunes the Chi of their body so as to "hitch a ride" along with the natural flow of Chi in an area. Underground or indoors, the character can only fly in the direction of the natural flow of Chi, but can gradually fly higher or lower, adjusting up to 20 feet (6.1 m) of altitude every melee round. Outdoors, in areas strong with Positive Chi or where the moon is shining (providing counter-flows of Negative Chi), the character can change directions by matching the Chi flow at different altitudes.

Flight depends on the Chi in the area, as well as whether the spell caster is filled with Positive or Negative Chi. Flying underground or other places filled with Negative Chi is usually a pretty sluggish affair, with the character travelling as fast as the Chi flow, expressed as the Spd. Attribute. For example, if the flow of Negative Chi is 6, a spell caster will fly as fast as Spd. 6. Flying with Positive Chi is faster, so the character can fly at triple the Chi flow, measured by Spd., so if the Positive Chi flow is 6, the flight will be at Spd. 18.

As Celestial Calligraphy: Doesn't work unless the character releasing the spell has had detailed instructions. The Celestial Calligraphy must match the Chi of the area where flight is to take place, so **red ink on green paper** for an area of Positive Chi, **black ink on green paper** for an area of Negative Chi.

Hsieh Chang – Malignant Miasmal Disease

Range: Touch
Duration: Instant/Special
Saving Throw: Standard
Cost: Eight P.P.E.

This spell inflicts a disease or illness that has symptoms similar to malaria in that the victim develops alternating fever and chills, raging headaches, stomach upsets, weakness, and continuous fatigue (reduce attacks per melee, combat bonuses, skill performance and spd. by 75%, plus no initiative). This results in a continuous loss of Chi, such that the character will be at half strength within an hour of contracting the disease. Eventually, if not cured within a week or so, the character will start to lose hit points at a rate of 1D6 per day. Two months later, if the character is still ailing, attributes will start to falter. Losses to attributes are *permanent* and cannot be regained, even if the victim is later cured.

There are no medical procedures or drugs that can cure this magical ailment and victims may experience reoccurring symptoms for the rest of their lives. The only cure must be delivered by magical means or by Chi Healing.

As Celestial Calligraphy: Works whether or not the caster understands it, but the ignorant will release the sickness on themselves. **Black ink on silver paper.**

Level Six

Chi Chu – Accumulation of Morbid Chi

Range: Touch
Duration: Instant/Special
Saving Throw: Standard
Cost: Twelve P.P.E.

When the spell caster touches the victim, the spell changes the normal Chi/Biological mechanisms so as to disrupt the normal gathering of Positive Chi. After being infected, the victim will continuously gather Negative Chi instead of Positive Chi. This is pretty unhealthy for a number of reasons, not least of which is that a character can't heal from wounds without Positive Chi.

If the character starts out with Positive Chi, every time the body is in a place where Negative Chi flows, bits of the Positive Chi will be destroyed. Then, once all the Positive Chi is gone, the body will keep trying to fill itself with Negative Chi, all the way to the body's normal level of Chi.

The only possible cure for *Chi Chu* are Chi Healing (Positive Chi Mastery Ability) or magical means.

As Celestial Calligraphy: Works whether or not the caster understands it, but the ignorant will release the sickness on themselves. **Black ink on silver paper.**

Draw Alternate Line of Natural Chi (Geomantic Magic)

Range: Touch
Duration: Ten minutes per level of experience.
Saving Throw: None
Cost: Fifteen P.P.E.

By drawing an invisible line in the air with hand gestures, the spell caster diverts the natural flow of Chi from one place off into some other direction. For example, a flow of Negative Chi can be directed upward to flood a room that would normally be flowing with Positive Chi.

Another possibility is to have the line loop around and connect up with itself. This kind of loop doesn't last very long (one melee round per level of experience), but it builds up a tremendous amount of Chi. Every melee round of its existence it adds another lump of natural Chi to the loop. So, for example, in an area where there are four points of Positive Chi flowing, on the second melee round of the loop, there would be a flow of 8 points of Positive Chi, then 12 points on the third melee round, 16 points on the fourth melee round, and so forth.

If the spell caster is 5th level, or less, then the longest line that can be drawn is 20 feet (6.1 m) long. Higher level spell casters, those 6th level and higher (2nd level for *Fang Shih*), can add another five feet (1.5 m) of length for each level of experience.

Not available as Celestial Calligraphy.

Exhale Cloud of Acid (Living Chi)

Range: Self
Duration: Up to 4 melee rounds per level of experience.
Saving Throw: None
Cost: Twelve P.P.E.

Fusing Chi with the element of earth in the body, the spell caster then expels a Living Chi Cloud of Acid. If the character was originally charged with Positive Chi, the cloud will be bright yellow and easy to see through. Spell casters who start out filled with Negative Chi will generate a dirty-looking brown cloud of gas that also works like a Blinding Cloud.

Sense of Ti Chi (Earth/Dragon Energy). The spell caster does **not** "feel" either the physical shapes, or the Chi of those inside the cloud. Instead, all the *movement* of Chi as it flows through and around the cloud can be sensed. The character can immediately estimate the flow of Chi in an area, including both the quantity and direction. If the cloud touches a surface (floor, wall, ceiling), it's also possible to detect the Chi flow inside solid earth or rock, as well as the presence of any Earth Dragons.

Yellow Acid Cloud – Positive Chi. Does relatively little damage to living things, but inflicts massive corrosion on metals of all kinds. Damage to metal surfaces equals about 2D6 S.D.C. (2D6 M.D. in **Rifts**) for every square foot (0.1 square meter) of exposure, per melee round. Paint and other protective coatings are usually burned off in 1D6 melee rounds. Even materials magically protected experience some kind of rust or tarnish when exposed to the Yellow Acid Cloud.

Living creatures and organic material (wood, cloth, etc.) trapped inside a Yellow Acid Cloud must save vs poison each melee round or experience 1D6 damage of corrosion. If characters fail to hold their breath and fail to save vs poison, they take an additional 1D6 damage per melee round.

Brown Acid Cloud – Negative Chi. Smelling horrible and tasting worse, this dense smoke blinds all within it in two ways. First, characters inside the cloud will be unable to see more than a foot (0.3 m) away, and then, only blurry shapes. Those inside the cloud will be at -5 to strike, parry and dodge. Second, characters who attempt to see while engulfed in the cloud (i.e. opening their eyes) must save vs poison to avoid being temporarily blinded (lasts 2D6 melee rounds; -8 to strike, parry and dodge if blinded).

The cloud also does damage to living things in two ways. First, those who fail to hold their breath or save vs poison, will take 2D6 points of damage for every full melee round they are inside the cloud. Second, those in the cloud will have any exposed skin attacked, so they'll feel a stinging pain. Damage varies according to the amount of skin revealed, so a character with just hands and face exposed would take 1D6 of damage, but someone in a skimpy bathing suit would suffer 5D6 damage.

Finally, the cloud tends to cause things to rust and corrode, especially metal surfaces, as well as dissolving most natural (cotton, wool, silk) and artificial (nylon, acrylics) cloth and clothing.

Precipitate Acid. It's possible for the spell caster to condense some of the Living Chi Acid Cloud into liquid acid. Five Chi points of cloud will be concentrated into about a tablespoon of liquid acid — which, if dripped on a piece of metal (say, in and around a keyhole), the acid will burn through a chunk equivalent to 100 points of S.D.C. (equal to a deadbolt lock, see S.D.C. Table in *Ninjas & Superspies* or other Palladium rule books)! The liquid acid can be dripped directly on a target or, if preferred, into a glass container for later use. In **Rifts,** it inflicts one M.D. point.

Control Cloud. The cloud can be expanded or contracted and moved (Spd. 4) and shaped according to the whim of the spell caster. The size limit is the same as with all Living Chi Clouds:

a 10 by 10 by 10 foot cubic volume (1000 cubic feet – 28.3 cubic meters – a little over 3×3×3 m) for each point of Chi invested. Retracting the cloud means the character can recover the Chi.

As Celestial Calligraphy: Nothing happens unless the character knows how to invoke Living Chi. **White ink on green paper.**

Freeze Mudra

Range: 50 feet (15.2 m)
Duration: Permanent
Saving Throw: Standard
Cost: Sixteen P.P.E.

A rather specialized bit of magic, since it can only be inflicted on someone who is already performing a Mudra. The spell takes advantage of the Chi circulating through the Mudra and sets up a sort of "feedback loop," so the victim finds it impossible to leave the Mudra. Living victims (humans) can attempt to escape the effects of the spell once per day, but Infernals and Immortals will find themselves trapped until assisted by someone who can dispel the magic.

This famous spell was said to have been used in the aftermath of the Great Battle of Wu, where hundreds (perhaps thousands) of demons were permanently frozen into their ancient Mudra.

Not available as Celestial Calligraphy.

Mind Walk (*Meng Quia*)

Range: Self
Duration: Ten minutes per level of experience.
Saving Throw: None
Cost: Eighteen P.P.E.

The magical equivalent of the Mind Walk Zenjoriki Power.

The character's Chi spirit becomes free of the body and can move around in the realms of pure Chi. The body is left behind and the character becomes pure Chi, with no substance whatever. While in spirit form, the spell caster can see and hear normally, can use magic (half the body's P.P.E. goes with the Chi spirit), and can use any known Chi Mastery Abilities. **Note:** Unless some countermeasures are engaged, a character's body is completely vulnerable to any and all attacks, including possession by other Chi spirits.

The Chi of the Mind Walking character, whether positive or negative, can't be changed while out of the body. In other words, a character filled with negative Chi who does a Mind Walk will become a negative Chi spirit unable to perform positive Chi powers, and unable to change to positive Chi without revisiting the body.

Movement in spirit form is either by drifting or by teleportation, but the character can't do both at once. Drifting allows the character to slowly move from place to place, along with the flow of Chi, or at a maximum Spd. of 2.

Teleportation allows the character to move any distance instantly, simply by visualizing the destination. However, the act of visualizing requires that the character concentrate while motionless and inactive for four full melee rounds. Another limitation is that characters may only teleport to specific known places or people.

In addition to travelling in the Chi Energy of the material world, it is also possible to visit other realms, including the Transition Plane of the Newly Dead, the Hells of the Yama Kings, the Heavens of the Jade Emperor, and other places.

The Chi spirit is vulnerable to both Chi and magical attacks, but can attempt to parry or dodge Chi or save vs magic.

As Celestial Calligraphy: Doesn't work unless the character releasing the spell has had detailed instructions. **White ink on white paper.**

Transmute Object into Chi

Range: Touch
Duration: Permanent
Saving Throw: None
Cost: Twenty P.P.E.

An advanced version of the 2nd level spell, *Fill Object with Chi*. With this spell an object becomes something that, in addition to being filled with Chi, can also be completely changed into a Pure Chi Form. Therefore, when a character changes into Pure Chi, it is possible to take the item along. Then, when the character changes back to physical form, the object will also be there, in the flesh, no matter where it might be.

In addition to transmuting weapons, characters may also find it advantageous to empower clothing, tools, and other useful artifacts.

Chi: A bit more costly, in terms of Chi investment, than simply filling with Chi. Each object requires a minimum of five points of Chi and objects over ten pounds (4.5 kg) will require an additional five points of Chi for every additional ten pounds (4.5 kg) of mass.

As Celestial Calligraphy: Doesn't work unless the character releasing the spell has had detailed instructions. **Red ink on gold paper** for filling with Positive Chi, **black ink on gold paper** for filling with Negative Chi.

Level Seven

Bring Forest to Life

Range: 40 feet (12.2 m) in diameter, centered on the spell caster.
Duration: Special. The spell only works in darkness, twilight, or under heavy cloud cover. At the first glint of sunlight, the spell will dissipate.
Saving Throw: None, however, no tree can be *forced* to take human form, they must be willing.
Cost: Thirty P.P.E.

The spell caster must be standing amongst a grove or forest of trees before releasing the magic. Each tree within forty feet (12.2 m) will seem to be transformed into a living, breathing, human being. Each will appear different and unique, dressed differently, just as if the grove of trees were a small town filled with people; men and women, children and seniors.

While this would seem to be an incredibly powerful, high level spell, it is actually a relatively minor bit of magic. That's because it is the trees themselves who really do the changing. The magical spell is just a catalyst which empowers the trees to release their own stored Chi energy.

Any trees that are twenty years old, or younger, will not have accumulated the Chi necessary for the transformation. Those between the ages of twenty and forty will be transformed into children, who will start playing as if they'd never had the chance to play before. A tree between the ages of forty and sixty will seem to be a teenager. While those over the age of sixty will look like mature adults (remember, in Chinese terms, sixty is a great cycle, and the trees look at it as the benchmark for adulthood). Any tree over one hundred and twenty years will seem elderly, and will also have accumulated knowledge of Chi Mastery. As well as 100 to 600 points (1D6×100) of Positive Chi at their disposal. Finally, a tree that is six hundred years old is considered a "Great Master," and will be the equivalent of a Taoist Enlightened Immortal in attitude and power.

Trees that have recently depleted their Chi (for example, if they've been brought to life before, anytime in the last year), will be unable to participate in the spell. Also, not all trees will necessarily *want* to spend any time in human form.

Once the trees have been transformed into 'people,' they are likely to be very happy and curious, unless their grove is being threatened by lumberjacks or a new development, in which case they'll be rather somber. They will also be just as interested in each other as in the spell caster. Each has a name (tree names like *barren branch*, *rootless*, *early autumn*, and *straight bark*), and they all know each other by sight and by name.

Since each tree-person understands that this is a very rare event and that they might never have another chance to be a mobile human, they try to get the most out of the experience.

While marginally grateful to the spell caster, they can't be forced into doing anything. For one thing, any of them can change back to tree-form at will, and for another, attempting to move outside of the twenty foot radius (6.1 m) from the spell center causes them to instantly change back into trees (but not in their usual place, horror of horrors!). However, so long as they are entertained, the tree-people (at least some of them) will tend to be cooperative. They'll readily share information (they will remember everything that has happened in their grove, going back as far as their birth from a seedling) and they may even be willing to help with Chi Abilities.

As Celestial Calligraphy: Works whether or not the caster understands it. **Gold ink on blue paper.**

Detach Living Gas Cloud (Living Chi)

Range: One mile (1.6 km)
Duration: Ten minutes per level of experience.
Saving Throw: None
Cost: Eighteen P.P.E.

To be used in combination with one of the other spells that generates a Living Gas Cloud. By endowing the cloud with a long-range magical connection with the spell caster, it enables the character to control the cloud from up to one mile (1.6 km) away. Note that the enhancement spell must first be cast while the character is in physical contact with the cloud, not after the Living Gas Cloud has been cut off.

As Celestial Calligraphy: Nothing happens unless the character knows how to invoke Living Chi. **White ink on green paper.**

Draw Cage of Chi (Geomantic Magic)

Range: Touch
Duration: Ten minutes per level of experience.
Saving Throw: None
Cost: Twenty P.P.E.

The spell caster starts by drawing an invisible line around whatever is to be held in the cage. Usually this is done by walking around the prisoner or, if something very small is to be imprisoned, by moving the drawing finger around the small object. At the very end, when the circuit is complete, the spell caster should then draw a final piece of line connecting it to the imprisoned creature or object. Once complete, the Cage of Chi bars Chi and Chi entities from passing out of the area of confinement, even by means of a Chi entity teleport.

Since physical objects can readily pass in or out, the lines of the Cage of Chi are often etched along the physical walls of a box or other container. However, since the lines of a Cage of Chi only work where they were drawn, a Cage of Chi can not be moved.

If the spell caster is 5th level, or less, then the longest barrier that can be drawn is 20 feet (6.1 m) long. Higher level spell casters, those 6th level and higher (2nd level for *Fang Shih*), can add another five feet (1.5 m) of length for each level of experience.

Not available as Celestial Calligraphy.

Evoke Animus of Pure Chi (Living Chi)

Range: Self
Duration: Thirty minutes per level of experience.
Saving Throw: None
Cost: Thirty-Four P.P.E.

An invisible Animus is set up inside the spell caster, which serves as a kind of Living Chi Alarm. It is commonly used for defensive purposes to protect the spell caster while he is asleep, or when the character leaves the body in Pure Chi Form. The Animus is perpetually alert to all intrusions of both a physical and Chi nature, and either immediately wakes the character or contacts the Pure Chi Form if there is any threat. If left to itself, it will use any Chi Mastery Abilities that the character might have to defend the body. If facing a physical threat, the Animus will animate the body and use any defensive Martial Arts known by the character.

Sense *Wei Chi*. Through the Animus, the character can sense the "internal fire" of other characters, up to twenty-five feet (7.6 m) away. The spell caster senses the Chi type (Positive or Negative), amount and any hidden sources of Chi.

Animus of Pure Positive Chi. For each point of Chi invested, the Animus can automatically stop 1D6 points of incoming Negative Chi.

Animus of Pure Negative Chi. In any area where Negative Chi is flowing, the Animus *automatically* collects up a point of Negative Chi every melee round. This Chi can be used by the character in conjunction with any Chi Mastery Abilities, or with the casting of spells. However, when the Animus is absorbed back into the body, any excess points of Negative Chi (beyond the character's normal level) will be dissipated.

As Celestial Calligraphy: Nothing happens unless the character knows how to invoke Living Chi. **White ink on green paper.**

Ignite Positive Chi

Range: Twenty feet (6.1 m)
Duration: One melee round for every five points of Chi, to a maximum of eight melee rounds (two minutes).
Saving Throw: None
Cost: Twenty-Two P.P.E.

All the Positive Chi in the area is "ignited," so as to burst into the light of the sun. Every surface area, including the bodies of any characters within range, will radiate with light. Creatures of darkness and those vulnerable to sunlight, will be affected (blinded and/or burnt), taking double the usual amount of damage as long as they remain within the area. Within 200 feet (61 m) everything will be clearly lit, as if by full daylight.

Each melee round of the spell consumes five points of Positive Chi from the flow of Chi, or from any Chi items in the area. If the natural flow of Positive Chi is five or more, the spell can continue for the full duration (two minutes). However, if the only source of Positive Chi is a flow that is less than five, then the ignition spell will last just for a part of one melee round and the damage inflicted will be half.

Creatures that can be damaged by sunlight when first confronted by the radiant light must save vs a horror factor of 15.

As Celestial Calligraphy: Works whether or not the caster understands it. **Red ink on green paper.**

Level Eight

Dispel Animus

Range: Touch
Duration: Instant
Saving Throw: Standard
Cost: Thirty P.P.E.

When successful, i.e. when the animus fails to save vs the spell caster's magic, then the Animus and all the Chi held within the Animus, is instantly dissipated. The character who created the Animus will NOT regain the lost Chi.

As Celestial Calligraphy: Works whether or not the caster understands it, but only if the character happens to touch an Animus sometime during the duration of the spell. **Gold ink on red paper.**

Draw Spiral Line of Chi (Geomantic Magic)

Range: Touch
Duration: Ten minutes per level of experience.
Saving Throw: None
Cost: Twenty-Five P.P.E.

To cast the spell, an invisible spiralling line is drawn in the air, on the ground, or along the surface of any object (wall, ceiling, truck, tree, etc.). To picture it, imagine walking backwards, pointing your finger outward and turning the tip of your finger in a tight circle. If you were to leave a visible line, it would look something like a long spring or coil.

Once the line is laid out, the natural Chi in the area will tend to wind around it, funnelling inward to create a dense, fast-moving line of Chi or spiralling outward to spin the Chi away.

If entities of Pure Chi happen upon an active Spiral Line without warning, they'll tend to get sucked in, and spun out on the other end. It doesn't do any particular damage to the Pure Chi entities unless a Negative Chi entity ends up in a Positive Chi Spiral Line, but it is disorienting.

Spiral Line of Gathering Negative Chi (Counter-Clockwise, with the flow of Chi). The natural flow of Negative Chi in the area tends to wrap itself around the spiral line, speeding up and compacting as it goes. Within 1D6 melee rounds, the line will be pulsating with twelve times the usual flow of Negative Chi and speeding along at four times the normal speed.

Outside of the spiral line (for example, if the line goes along the center of a hallway, at the outside walls), the amount of Negative Chi is seriously depleted, so that only a tenth of the usual amount is found.

Although the magical line vanishes once the spell expires, it may take several hours to several days for the Chi to resume its normal flow in the area. If the natural Chi flow is 10 or less, the area will restore itself in 2D6 hours. If between 11 and 19 is the normal flow, then it takes 4D6 hours to reset itself. For areas where Chi is 20 or more, it takes 1D6 days for things to calm back down to normal.

Spiral Line of Repulsing Negative Chi (Clockwise, against the flow of Chi). Since the natural flow of Chi is against the Spiral Line, the Chi along the line tends to be spun out and away, leaving an area with only about a twentieth (1/20th) of the usual Chi.

Spiral Line of Gathering Positive Chi (Clockwise, with the flow of Chi). Drawn into a vortex line, the natural flow of Positive Chi in the area whips itself into a frenzied tube of rampaging Chi. Within 1D4 melee rounds the line will be pulsating with twenty times the usual flow of Positive Chi and speeding along at six times the normal speed. This effect tends to spread itself outward, so 10 feet (3.0 m) away the Chi is five times normal and moving at triple speed, and at 40 feet (12.2 m) away the Chi is twice the normal flow and moving at double speed.

When the magical line disappears at the end of the spell's duration, it will take several hours for the Chi to go back to normal. Usually, this delay is about 1D6 hours, but in mountainous areas or along a seashore it could be 3D6 hours.

Spiral Line of Repulsing Positive Chi (Counter-Clockwise, against the flow of Chi). When Positive Chi encounters this backwards-pointing spiral, it will tend to scatter away and create little whirlwinds of Positive Chi about twenty feet (6.1 m) away from the line. Right at the line, the Chi will be about half the normal amount. Out at the edges, Chi can double in the heaviest of the eddies.

If the spell caster is 5th level, or less, then the longest line that can be drawn is 20 feet (6.1 m) long. Higher level spell casters, those 6th level and higher (2nd level for *Fang Shih*), can add another five feet (1.5 m) of length for each level of experience. The line must be more or less straight (no sharp corners, or curves), and cannot be wrapped around back upon itself. The end point of a Gathering Spiral Line can be connected to some solid surface, which causes the Chi to be drained out in that direction.

Not available as Celestial Calligraphy.

Enter Realm of Yama Kings

Range: Touch
Duration: Four melee rounds (one minute).
Saving Throw: None
Cost: Forty P.P.E.

While the spell must be cast in an area of Negative Chi, there are no other restrictions on location. It creates a temporary gateway, or portal into the Hells of the Yama Kings. Unless the character is familiar with a particular location in the Hells, and the spell is successfully directed to that location, the "default" location of the gateway will be very near the point where souls first enter and await judgement, the *Shen Jing* (Transition Place).

The creation of the gateway will be instantly known and noticed by the Yama Kings, and by any Infernal denizens in the immediate area. **Note:** There is no "exit" version of this spell. If characters are foolhardy enough to enter the Realm of the Yama Kings, they will have to find their own way out.

As Celestial Calligraphy: Works whether or not the caster understands it. **Gold Ink on glossy black paper.**

Evoke Animus of Elemental Wood (Living Chi)

Range: Self
Duration: Five minutes per level of experience.
Saving Throw: None
Cost: Sixty-Five P.P.E.

With this magical Animus, the spell caster creates a twin presence, like another spirit within the body that is part Chi and part elemental wood. Depending on which type of Chi the character has at the start of the spell, the result could be either a Blue Animus (Positive Chi) or a Green Animus (Negative Chi).

At the time the spell is cast, the character must decide how much Chi to invest into the Animus. While it is true that the more Chi invested, the more powerful the Animus and all that Chi can be reabsorbed, there is always the possibility of losing the Animus along with the reservoir of Chi.

Sense of *Chen Chi* (Living Vitality). Through the Animus the spell caster can feel the *Chen Chi*, or living vitality, of humans and other living creatures within thirty feet (9.1 m), even in total darkness, or those obscured by smoke. From the *Chen Chi*, the character can determine whether one is healthy or ill, injured or healed, poisoned or pure. Sensing range is 30 feet (9.1 m).

Blue Animus – Element of Wood & Positive Chi. All Chi Mastery attacks based on Positive Chi are absorbed, while Negative Chi attacks are automatically defended as if by a Chi Defense of 1D6 for each point of Chi invested in the Animus.

Physical attacks, while not deflected, are slowed and absorbed by the Animus just as if they had to penetrate a layer of hardened wood armor. Thus, the character has extra S.D.C., one point for each point of Chi invested in the Animus. For example, if the Blue Animus were initially charged with 15 points of Positive Chi, then 15D6 of any incoming Negative Chi attacks would automatically be destroyed, and the first 15 points of damage from any physical attack would be absorbed by the Animus too.

Glowing Jade Animus – Element of Wood & Negative Chi. Absorbs all Chi Mastery attacks based on Negative Chi, so that the incoming Chi is added to the total Chi strength of the Animus. The Jade Animus is also a protection against magical attacks, absorbing spells equal to the amount of Chi invested. For example, if the Animus has 15 points of Negative Chi, then any spell using 15 P.P.E. or less would be absorbed and effectively negated!

If in contact (touch) with a *Living Chi Cloud of Acid*, any other Animus, or any other Living Chi thing made of the element of Earth, whether of Negative or Positive Chi, the character can use the Green Animus to consume 2D6 Chi points per melee round.

As Celestial Calligraphy: Nothing happens unless the character knows how to invoke Living Chi. **White Ink on Green Paper.**

Exorcism

Range: Self or one other.
Duration: Instant
Saving Throw: Standard
Cost: Twenty-Eight P.P.E.

This spell forces out any entity of Pure Chi, spirit, or supernatural being which has entered or is possessing the spell caster's body. Note that the disembodied creature will probably need to be subdued or rendered unconscious, so that the character can perform the spell without interference.

Once forced out of the host body, the possessive entity will usually attempt to find another nearby victim (within thirty feet/9.1 m). The first choice will be a body that is vacant, but anyone seriously depleted of Chi (zero, or just one point), could also be attacked.

As Celestial Calligraphy: Works whether or not the caster understands it. **Red ink on red paper.**

Level Nine

Control/Enslave Creature of Pure Negative Chi

Range: 30 feet (9.1 m).
Duration: One day per level of experience.
Saving Throw: Standard
Cost: Fifty P.P.E.

Like the Negative Chi Mastery Ability of *Enslave/Control Through Negative Chi*, this spell works on the weaknesses of any creature that is totally dependent on Negative Chi. If the victim of the spell fails to save vs magic, the spell caster can then give commands that must be obeyed, although the victim may attempt to pervert the *spirit* of the command, so long as the literal words are followed.

If the spell caster wishes to attempt enslaving the victim, then a *conditioning* routine must be followed. It starts with the spell caster saying something like, "I am your master! Obey me!" or "You will agree that you are mine to command!" and force the victim to agree. The spell caster must roll a twenty-sided for each of the enslavement commands and the victim can roll to

save vs magic each time. This process of forcing the victim to respond must be completed three times in a row in order to make the Enslavement *permanent.* If even one of the three attempts to enslave fails, the attempt at enslavement fails totally and the magic of control is also immediately dispelled.

Note that it is possible that the creature of Pure Negative Chi may succeed in resisting the enslavement, but may still answer as if the spell caster was successful. In other words, the Chi creature could attempt to convince the spell caster that the enslavement worked, just to get a chance at revenge.

As Celestial Calligraphy: Doesn't work unless the character releasing the spell has had detailed instructions. **Black ink on white paper.**

Draw Wall of Chi (Geomantic)

Range: Touch
Duration: Ten minutes per level of experience.
Saving Throw: None
Cost: Thirty P.P.E.

Standing in between a natural channel for Chi (in a hallway, a room, a gateway, a doorway, or an archway), the spell caster draws an imaginary line, using hand gestures, from one side of the channel to the other. Once the line is straight across the flow of Chi, it is magically empowered so that the line turns into a wall that blocks the channel from side to side and top to bottom. It's at that point that it starts to become a wall of Chi.

Each melee round the Wall of Chi grows as it absorbs all the Chi that would normally be rushing through the channel. Since it is gathering ALL the Chi that flows through the channel, the Wall usually starts out with ten times the amount of Chi in the normal flow. Then, in each succeeding melee round, another massive dose of Chi is added, again ten times the usual flow rate.

For example, take an area where five points of Positive Chi usually flow. Initially a Wall of Chi blocking that channel would contain 50 Chi. By the second melee round the wall would be 100 points, then 150, then 200, and so forth, with no limit except the duration of the spell.

Meanwhile, downstream of the Wall, the flow of Chi drops to nothing. This Chi drought eventually extends far off in the distance, as the flow of Chi rushes along without being replaced from behind. Eventually, of course, when the Wall of Chi expires or is dispelled, there will be a tidal wave of Chi.

If the spell caster is 7th level, or less, then the widest Wall of Chi will be 6 feet (1.8 m) wide. Higher level spell casters, those 8th level and higher (4th level for *Fang Shih,*) can add another two feet (0.6 m) of width for each level of experience.

Not available as Celestial Calligraphy.

Entice Disembodied Entity

Range: Touch
Duration: One day per level of experience.
Saving Throw: Standard
Cost: Forty-Five P.P.E.

Performed on a creature or an object, this spell is set up to lure unsuspecting creatures of Pure Chi or other disembodied entities, who are searching for a vacant host body. Once the spell is cast, the ensorcelled item sends out a psychic impression of a powerful but empty and defenseless body, ready for immediate occupancy. While the distance depends, in part, on the sensitivity of the victims, any entity of Pure Chi within one thousand feet (305 m) will clearly feel the psychic call. Once an entity enters the trap, the magic is immediately dispelled.

Once an entity has been enticed, it's up to the spell caster to react in some way, since this spell does nothing to delay the entity or to keep if from leaving.

As Celestial Calligraphy: Doesn't work unless the character releasing the spell has had detailed instructions. **Gold ink on red paper.**

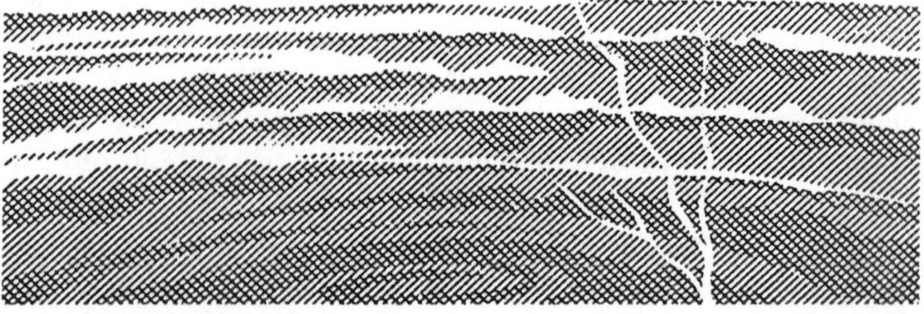

Evoke Animus of Elemental Fire (Living Chi)

Range: Self
Duration: Five minutes per level of experience.
Saving Throw: None
Cost: Seventy P.P.E.

Combining some of the character's Chi with the element of fire, the spell caster creates a fire-based Animus. If created with Positive Chi, the Animus will be constantly flaming, as if on fire, but if made with Negative Chi, it will simply glow ruby-red, as if super-heated. The more Chi that is invested in the Animus, the more powerful it will be and the brighter.

Sense *Wei Chi.* Through the Animus, the character can sense the "internal fire" of other characters, up to twenty-five feet (7.6 m) away. The spell caster senses the Chi type (Positive or Negative), amount and hidden sources of Chi.

Flaming Red Animus – Element of Fire & Positive Chi. All attacks based on flame or heat are harmlessly absorbed. The flames also create a kind of natural armor, so the Animus is A.R. 12, with an S.D.C. equal to the number of points of Chi invested. With a steady application of the flame (hold or grab), the Animus does 1D6 damage for every point of Chi invested in it. Anyone attempting to hold or grab the Animus will collect the same damage.

At the will of its creator, the Animus can be used to ignite easily burnable objects (paper, wood, flammable liquids). Objects touched will burst into flame immediately. Targets up to 20 feet (6.1 m) distant can be made to smoulder in just three melee rounds.

Glowing Ruby Animus – Element of Fire & Negative Chi. All attacks based on Positive Chi are automatically absorbed by the Animus (so long as the Animus is extended beyond the skin). The Animus will also keep the character toasty-warm, even in the coldest conditions, and will stop one point of any cold-based attack for each point of Chi invested in the Animus.

The Animus radiates intense heat. If a victim is held, or otherwise forced to stay within a foot (0.3 m) of the Animus, they'll receive 1D6 damage per melee round. If the Animus is invested with at least 25 points of Negative Chi, those that are too close (within three feet/0.9 m) must make a save vs heat (same as save vs lethal poison) to avoid being knocked unconscious by the extreme and debilitating temperature.

In the first melee round of contact, easily combustible objects (paper, newspapers, flammable liquids) have a 50% chance of igniting. Then, starting in the second melee round of contact, everything combustible will begin to smoulder, and easily burnable objects will catch on fire.

As Celestial Calligraphy: Nothing happens unless the character knows how to invoke Living Chi. **White Ink on Green Paper.**

Hsieh Chu Wu — Malignant Epidemic Possession

Range: Touch
Duration: Instant
Saving Throw: Standard
Cost: Fifty-Two P.P.E.

Very much like *Hsieh Chang – Malignant Miasmal Disease* previously described, except that the victim will be contagious. Each person touched by the victim must attempt the same saving throw vs magic (14 or higher). Failing means that the new victim also has the magical disease and will also, in about two days, become contagious.

Victims develop alternating fever and chills, raging headaches, stomach upsets, weakness, and continuous fatigue (reduce attacks per melee, combat bonuses, skill performance and spd. by 75%, plus no initiative). This results is a continuous loss of Chi, such that all the victims will be at half strength. If not cured within a week, victims will lose 1D6 hit points per day. Two months later, if the character is still ailing (and still alive!), attributes will start to falter. These last losses of attribute points are *permanent* and cannot be regained, even if the victim is later cured.

Effectively this spell can create a magical plague capable of wiping out an entire community of people. However, the risk of total extermination is usually limited to small, isolated communities, since any large city or anyone in touch with the larger world, will eventually attract the attention of those who *can* cure the thing.

Even so, the cure isn't easy. Only those with the power to cure with Chi, or who possess magic powers such as restoration or remove curse, can perform a cure. If the disease does spread, it may exhaust the resources of all the gifted healers in a community, though one can see how that may fit in with an evil plan.

As Celestial Calligraphy: Works whether or not the caster understands it, but the ignorant will release the sickness on themselves. **Black ink on silver paper.**

Invoke Third Eye

Range: Line of sight.
Duration: Twelve melee rounds (three minutes), plus four melee rounds (one minute) per level of experience.
Saving Throw: None
Cost: Forty P.P.E.

Otherwise known as the "Sight of the Blind Mystic," this spell allows the spell caster to see the forces of Chi, as if with Chi Mastery. Any spirits, ghosts or disembodied entities, as well as the special auras connected with dragons, Enlightened Immortals, and other special creatures will be visible.

As Celestial Calligraphy: Works whether or not the caster understands it. **Blue ink on white paper.**

Level Ten

Evoke Animus Of Elemental Metal (Living Chi)

Range: Self
Duration: Five minutes per level of experience.
Saving Throw: None
Cost: Seventy-Five P.P.E.

A Positive Chi Animus based on the element of metal, a Quicksilver Animus, will be very different from the electrically-charged Negative Chi version. As usual, however, the amount of Chi invested determines its total power.

Sense *Tien Chi* (Electrical Potential). With either version of the metal Animus, the character can sense electrical energy within thirty feet (9.1 m). Sensitivity ranges from the electrical current flowing through a person's nervous system, all the way up to high-tension power lines. It works in total darkness and through all electrically-conductive material (metals, etc.), but not through thick walls of natural insulators like wood or rubber.

Quicksilver Animus – Element of Metal & Positive Chi. The Animus makes it look like the character is covered in a thin layer of silvery-looking mercury. The material is very slippery, so the character has a +10 to escape from any holds, grabs or restraints. Acting as armor, the Animus has a natural A.R. of 15, and ten times as many S.D.C. as the Chi invested. In other words, an Animus invested with 12 points of Positive Chi will have 120 points of S.D.C. Unlike other Animuses, when the Silver Animus loses S.D.C. from physical damage, the equivalent amount of Chi is also lost. Thus, if the Animus of our example lost a Chi in battle, it would still return 3 points of Chi when reabsorbed.

Crackling White Animus – Element of Metal & Negative Chi. It looks as if the character is covered with thousands of tiny electrical sparks, giving the character total invulnerability to any lightning or electrical attacks. For every point of Chi invested in the Animus, the character can inflict 1D6 of electrical damage, merely by touch. Likewise, touching electronic devices will cause them to explosively short out, with televisions and computer monitors imploding on contact and any computer-based device taking double-damage (twice the 1D6 per point of Chi invested).

As Celestial Calligraphy: Nothing happens unless the character knows how to invoke Living Chi. **White Ink on green paper.**

Inflict Mudra of Immobility

Range: Forty feet (12.2 m)
Duration: Indefinite
Saving Throw: Standard
Cost: Sixty-Four P.P.E.

The spell forces the victim to adopt a *Mudra of Immobility*. Unlike most Mudras, this isn't designed to confer any special advantage, but merely to lock the body into an inescapable pose. As soon as the Mudra takes over, the character freezes into complete immobility, taking just one shallow breath of air every minute. Adopting this Mudra allows the character to go without food or water for the entire duration of the Mudra, without suffering any ill effects. However, the victim is also vulnerable to any and all physical attacks, with no chance to defend in any way.

Another use for the Mudra is conserving air when the character is in a place where air is in short supply. The amount of air required by the character is ten times less than normal or, to put it the other way, an oxygen supply would last ten times as long. Examples include being trapped in a cave or sealed room, or being dependent on the air tank in SCUBA gear or a space suit. If the air supply would last just twenty minutes for an ordinary person, it would support a character using this Mudra for two hundred minutes (that's three hours and twenty minutes)!

If the Mudra is cast on oneself, it can be dispelled at any time. In the short term, victims of the Mudra of Immobility are usually trapped until either the spell caster decides to release them, or someone comes along who can dispel the magic. However, after a day of being trapped, victims can attempt to save vs magic once per day.

As Celestial Calligraphy: Doesn't work unless the character releasing the spell has had detailed instructions. **White ink on silver paper.**

Draw Tangle of Chi (Geomantic)

Casting Time: Two minutes for every ten square feet of area (0.9 square meters).
Range: Self
Duration: Ten minutes per level of experience.
Saving Throw: None
Cost: Eighty P.P.E.

The spell caster draws a jagged line in the air, making sure that it consists of complicated twists, tangles, and snarls. Once complete (see Casting Time), the line serves to mess up the Chi flow, as well as the use of any Chi Mastery Abilities in the area. Entities of Pure Chi will find themselves completely snarled in the jagged lines and will be unable to move except by teleporting out of the area altogether. All Chi is affected.

There is really no limit to how big an area a Chi Tangle can cover, although after an hour of drawing (that would be 300 square feet/28 square meters), the character would have to save vs fatigue (roll 13 or better on twenty-sided, P.E. bonus okay) and, if the character failed, it would be necessary to start all over again.

The only uses of Chi that work in the area of the Chi Tangle are those that are strictly internal, such as Body Chi, Radiate Positive Chi, and Chi-Gung.

Not available as Celestial Calligraphy.

Mask of Demon

Range: Self
Duration: One hour per level of experience.
Saving Throw: None
Cost: Sixty P.P.E.

While the character appears *outwardly* normal, and not the least bit demonic, the character's Chi spirit is disguised to resemble that of a powerful Infernal. Those with Sense Infernal or Sense Alchemical Aura, or some other heightened Chi Senses, will immediately believe that the character is a demon, just masquerading in the character's true form.

Since the *apparent* Chi of the Infernal spirit is determined at the start of the spell, it's possible to use it to intimidate lesser Infernals.

As Celestial Calligraphy: Works whether or not the caster understands it, but if not understood the Chi spirit's appearance will be that of a Lesser Infernal. **Gold ink on pink paper.**

Sense *Yuan Chi* (Sense Age)

Range: 20 feet (6.1 m)
Duration: One minute per level of experience.
Saving Throw: None
Cost: Fifty P.P.E.

This spell enables the spell caster to accurately measure the age of any person or object under the age of 300 years. Items 300 to about 3,000 years old have a 10% margin for error in accuracy, over 3,000 to 10,000 20%, over 10,000 to 50,000 30%, and over 50,000 the margin for error is 40%. Aside from being able to figure out how old a person or animal (or Infernal) might be, the spell also gives a measure of the amount of years they are likely to have in their body. **Note:** The latter is not a matter of divination and there is no guarantee of any accuracy, but is more of a measure of a character's potential life-span.

As Celestial Calligraphy: Works whether or not the caster understands it, but those who are ignorant will only see a kind of aura around people and things, which will be sparkling if the person has a lot of life potential (like a baby or a small child), and with a bright glow for those of advanced age. Enlightened Immortals will be both sparkling and bright. **Blue ink on silver paper.**

Level Eleven

Bring Wood to Life

Casting Time Required: One half hour.
Range: Touch
Duration: Eight hours or until touched by sunlight.
Saving Throw: None
Cost: One Hundred P.P.E.

Some hefty piece of wood, like a plank, log, branch, etc. is magically transformed into a beautiful man or woman. Since the original weight of the wood determines the weight of the person (i.e. a 100 pound/45 kg piece of wood changes into a 100 pound/45 kg man or woman), the spell caster needs to find a piece of just the right size and weight.

As with the magic that brings a forest to life, this spell releases the Chi that is trapped inside a piece of wood, giving the spirit of the dead tree one last opportunity to live (the same piece of wood can never be brought to life more than once).

The woodling knows that it will only live for a short time, thus the resulting man or woman is most interested in pursuing pleasure. Laughter, song, dance, food and wine are desirable, but it is a desire for *love* that most motivates the animated lumber. While the spell caster can choose whether the wood will turn out as male or female, the exact appearance will depend on the type of wood. Pine wood will turn into very pale, fine-featured, delicate beings, while oak wood will tend to result in more voluptuous and sensual creatures.

Traditionally, this spell was used as a way of testing the character of apprentices, prospective students, and those who claimed to be following celibate vows. The ravishing beauty (P.B. 18+2D6) would appear to the prospective victim, obviously willing, as well as obviously good and innocent. Often they were also given a cover story to go along with the seduction, something like, "Alas! I have been condemned to marry one of the hideous Yama Kings of Hell! My only chance to escape is to find some mortal who finds me attractive. And it must be this night, or I will be sent into the darkness forever!" It wasn't surprising that a fair number of supposedly "pure" men were found to be in bed with large pieces of wood the following morning.

Not available as Celestial Calligraphy.

Create Vajra

Casting Time Required: Six hours per pair of points.
Range: Touch
Duration: Permanent
Saving Throw: Standard
Cost: Fifty P.P.E. per pair of points.

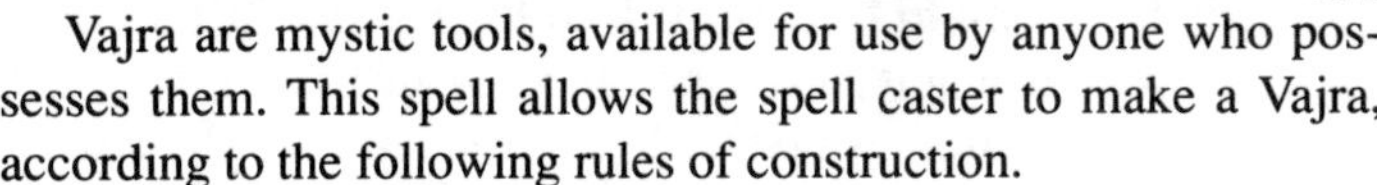

Vajra are mystic tools, available for use by anyone who possesses them. This spell allows the spell caster to make a Vajra, according to the following rules of construction.

The powers of a Vajra depends on the points or "tines," as in the tines of a fork, at each end. While the number of points can range from a single one on each end to a dozen or more, they must be in pairs. Thus, a Vajra with three points on one end must also have three points on the other end. The greater the number of tines, the greater the potential power of the Vajra. However, for each pair of points (Vajra must have the same number of tines on each end to be effective), it takes a full week of spell casting. That means a simple one-pointed Vajra takes just a week (280 P.P.E.), but a six tined Vajra takes six weeks to create and an investment of 1,680 P.P.E.!

Charge with Chi and P.P.E. A Vajra can "hold" both P.P.E. and Chi, simultaneously. The number of points (no matter what they are dedicated to do), determines the total storage capacity. Since Vajra are usually described by the number of points on one end, the "Three Point Vajra," below, actually has one pair of points (6 total):

One Point Vajra – 50 P.P.E. and 50 Chi
Two Point Vajra – 100 P.P.E. and 200 Chi
Three Point Vajra – 150 P.P.E. and 400 Chi
Four Point Vajra – 200 P.P.E. and 500 Chi
Six Point Vajra – 225 P.P.E. and 600 Chi
Seven Point Vajra – 250 P.P.E. and 700 Chi
Eight Point Vajra – 275 P.P.E. and 800 Chi
Nine Point Vajra – 300 P.P.E. and 900 Chi

Each additional pair of points allows for an additional 20 P.P.E. and 50 Chi.

The powers of a Vajra:

Absorb Chi. The Vajra is built to be self-powered and able to gather Chi from its environment. Two pairs of points (four total) must be dedicated to this function and they must be "tuned" to receive either Positive or Negative Chi. Once created, the tool will automatically gather Chi from the surrounding flow, at a rate of one point per melee round.

Chi Defense. The Vajra, when activated, will automatically defend whoever holds it from Pure Chi attacks. Each point dedicated to this function will destroy 2D6 points of incoming Chi, but the Vajra will consume one point of Chi each time the defense is used (obviously, if the Vajra runs out of Chi, the defense stops working). When first created, the Vajra is tuned to either Positive Chi (so it defends against Negative Chi attacks), or Negative Chi (defends against Positive Chi).

Passive Spell Containment. Virtually any spell can be stored in a Vajra. The number of spells that a Vajra can hold depends on how many pairs of points are dedicated to the task. One pair is able to contain one spell. Spells can be stored with their P.P.E. included so they can be cast regardless of other conditions, or as spells that draw on the Vajra's base P.P.E., or as spells that require the user to supply the P.P.E.

Active Spell Containment. Spells stored "actively" will instantly be cast whenever the Vajra is activated. Such spells require two pairs of points per spell level. Active spells in a Vajra are usually first or second level. Active spells always draw on the Vajra's base P.P.E.

For example, making Sense Chen Chi, a first level spell, as a Vajra's active spell would require just two pairs of points. Each time the Vajra were to be activated, so long as the P.P.E. cost of the spell was available (just one point, in this case), the spell would be triggered, so whoever holds the Vajra will be able to sense *Chen Chi*.

Secret Vajra Powers. All the above construction rules aside, there are ancient Vajra which seem to have none of the limitations of this spell and which seem to be empowered with any number of other abilities. For example, a Vajra has been discovered with but three pairs of points, containing hundreds of P.P.E., over a dozen spells and with an innate ability to drain Living Chi Clouds! Because of this it seems certain that there is a more advanced version of the Create Vajra spell waiting to be discovered, though no mortal has ever discovered it.

Not available as Celestial Calligraphy.

Draw Chi Entity Trap (Geomantic)

Casting Time Required: Twenty-Four Hours.
Range: Special
Duration: Indefinite
Saving Throw: Standard
Cost: One Hundred P.P.E.

Also called "the Demon Trap," it starts with the spell caster drawing a jagged line of invisible Chi, usually hundreds of feet long, winding all around, as well as up and down the central area of the trap. At the very center, to be inscribed in the last hour of the casting time, a snarl of lines is drawn around some solid object like a boulder, stove, engine block, etc. The first creature of Pure Chi to cross one of the jagged lines will find itself irresistibly drawn toward the central trap, unable to teleport, transform, or otherwise escape.

As far as saving vs magic, the creature must make the save before actually being drawn into the trap, when it first encounters the jagged line. If the Infernal or other creature of Pure Chi attempts to cross the line, it is too late and it will be drawn into the central trap immediately. Once inside the trap, there is no practical way for a disembodied entity to escape, unless released by its captor.

Not available as Celestial Calligraphy.

Evoke Animus of Elemental Earth (Living Chi)

Range: Self
Duration: Five minutes per level of experience.
Saving Throw: None
Cost: Eighty-Five P.P.E.

Depending on whether the Animus is built from Negative Chi, or Positive Chi, it will either take a yellow gaseous form, or a golden metallic form. The more Chi invested, the greater the potential power of the Animus.

Sense of *Ti Chi* (Earth/Dragon Energy). The *movement* of Chi, as it flows, is sensed by the character, who can tell the exact quantity, type (Positive or Negative), and direction. The presence of Earth Dragons, up to one mile (1.6 km) away, will also be detected.

Golden Animus – Element of Earth & Positive Chi. A shimmering gold foil seems to cover the character, as if with a layer of metallic paint. While it confers no S.D.C., it gives the character a natural A.R. of 17, which means any attack rolls 17 or less do NO damage! 18 and higher does full normal damage. The Animus is tremendously strong, having a base P.S. of 15, with another point of P.S. added for every two points of Chi invested.

For example, if the Animus has been invested with 20 points of Positive Chi, that will translate into an extra +10 to P.S. for a total of a P.S. 25. It will also enable the character to lift objects as heavy as 5,000 pounds (2265 kg) and inflict +10 damage in hand to hand combat.

Glowing Yellow Animus – Element of Earth & Negative Chi. A wisp of yellow gas surrounds the character, constantly giving off a mild smell of rotting eggs (sulfur). While the glowing yellow Animus provides no protection, it has the effect of a powerful corrosive acid on whatever it touches, except the character, of course. Damage to metal surfaces equals about 2D6 S.D.C. for each point of Chi invested in the Animus. Damage to organic materials, including living creatures, is 1D6 per point of Chi invested. In other words, a glowing yellow Animus created with 12 points of Negative Chi would do 24D6 (or a quick roll of 2D6×10+24) of damage to metal and 12D6 (1D6×10+12) damage to creatures of flesh.

As Celestial Calligraphy: Nothing happens unless the character knows how to invoke Living Chi. **White ink on green paper.**

Temporarily Restore Youth & Vitality (Alchemical)

Casting Time Required: Five minutes
Range: Self
Duration: Four hours per level of experience.
Saving Throw: None
Cost: Ninety P.P.E.

The character seems to lose all signs of old age. Skin will appear youthful and smooth. Hair becomes thick and rich, with the character's natural coloring. Upon casting, the spell caster determines how youthful the appearance will be. The one limit to the range of age is that the size of the character doesn't change in the illusion. So, even though the character can take on the appearance of a small child, it would be with the character's usual height.

Since the character's age hasn't really changed, posture and mobility problems caused by things like a bad back, rheumatism, or crippled legs will still exist and may give away the illusion.

As Celestial Calligraphy: Works whether or not the caster understands it, but those who can't control it will just end up looking about half their real age (seldom younger than 18). **White ink on silver paper.**

Level Twelve

Evoke Animus of Elemental Water (Living Chi)

Range: Self
Duration: Five minutes per level of experience.
Saving Throw: None
Cost: Ninety P.P.E.

The Animus is built of the character's Chi, along with the element of water. It is drastically different depending on whether it is created with Negative Chi (frozen form) or Positive Chi (liquid form).

Sense of Yeng Chi. In either version of the Animus, the character can touch the liquid of any body of water (spring, river, lake, ocean, etc.) and get an instant sense of the amount of Chi flowing along it. Not only at the surface, but also within the depths up to two hundred feet (61 m) away. The presence of any powerful Chi creatures (more than fifty points of Chi) within the water will also be noted. Finally, if there is a Water Dragon in that body of water, anywhere within fifty miles (80 km), the character will get an impression of whether or not the dragon is asleep and how far away it is.

Black Water Animus – Element of Water & Positive Chi. The Animus looks like nothing so much as a dark layer of water glistening all over the character. When touching any water that flows with Positive Chi, the Animus can absorb up to ten times the amount of Chi with which it was originally invested, at a rate of the flow of Chi per melee round. This temporary Chi can be used as a layer of protection, with each point of water-Chi adding another 2D6 points of S.D.C. to it. For every point of Chi invested in the Animus, it will provide an automatic 1D6 of protection against Negative Chi attacks.

While surrounded with this Animus, the character has no need to breathe normal air. Therefore, it's possible to remain submerged for as long as the Animus lasts.

Black Ice Animus – Element of Water & Negative Chi. A layer of ice seems to cover the character. Nearby objects are chilled by its presence and it can freeze whatever it touches. For example, a cupful of water can be frozen solid in just one full melee round, a gallon in two. The Animus makes the character invulnerable to all cold and cold-based attacks. Other attacks will have to penetrate an A.R. of 14 and an S.D.C. equal to five times the amount of Chi invested in the Animus.

As Celestial Calligraphy: Nothing happens unless the character knows how to invoke Living Chi. **White ink on matte black paper.**

Impose Moving Area of Non-Ignition: Neutralize Celestial Calligraphy

Range: Self
Duration: Five minutes per level of experience.
Saving Throw: None
Cost: One Hundred P.P.E.

The spell caster becomes the center of an area where fires can't be lit nor any chemical ignited, including gunpowder, gasoline, and even the ignition inside a car's engine. Obviously, this also means that slips of paper containing Celestial Calligraphy can't be used. The area extends fifty feet (15.2 m) around the character in every direction and moves as the character moves.

As Celestial Calligraphy: Works whether or not the caster understands it. **Gold ink on pink paper.**

Ride the Yin Tiger (Living Chi)

Casting Time Required: One Hour
Range: Self
Duration: One day for each level of experience.
Saving Throw: None
Cost: Two Hundred P.P.E.

The spell caster attempts to take on the traits of the mystic White Tiger. The most dramatic thing about the spell is that it changes the blood of the spell caster into a milky grey substance which is called *Yin Blood.*

Sense *Wei Chi.* The spell caster can sense the "internal fire" (Chi) diffused throughout the body of any living thing within sixty feet (18.3 m), revealing the Chi type (Positive or Negative) and amount. It also reveals the presence of hidden Pure Chi entities.

Change Positive Chi to Negative Chi. If the character started out with Positive Chi, then activating this spell turns it all into Negative Chi.

Yin Tiger Invisibility. While the blood is Yin, the character can become invisible at will. This form of invisibility cloaks the character even from Chi or magical means of detection.

Control Undead/Living Dead. While in Yin Blood form, the character can command any living dead or undead, and they will obey without question. It is possible for Undead Immortals, those who are aware of this power, to ignore the commands, but only by the use of powerful magic.

Shape Shift to Tiger Form. While filled with the Yin Blood, the character can change shape into the form of a tiger. The character's mass won't change, so a 100 pound (45 kg) character will be a 100 pound (45 kg) tiger. In tiger form the character cannot use any of his/her regular martial arts or combat skills, but will have five attacks per melee round, +4 to strike, +4 to dodge, and will do 4D6 damage with claws. It takes four full melee rounds (one minute) to change from human to tiger, or vice versa, during which time the character will be quite helpless.

Walk To Other Worlds. While the blood is transformed to Yin, the character can walk to the realm of the Yama Kings, to the Heavenly Court of the Jade Emperor, and to many other wondrous lands. It is also possible to walk to alternate worlds in this way (recognizes and uses dimensional Rifts, stone pyramids, etc.).

As Celestial Calligraphy: Works whether or not the caster understands it. **Gold ink on silver paper.**

Spit Dragon Pearl

Range: Fifty Feet (15.2 m)
Duration: Permanent
Saving Throw: None
Cost: One Hundred and Twenty-Five P.P.E.

The spell allows the character to spit out a pearl in the same way that a Water Dragon can. The more Chi invested, the larger the pearl. One or two points of Chi will yield a tiny, bead-sized pearl. At ten points of Chi, a Dragon Pearl will be about a half inch (1.3 cm) in diameter. It would take forty points to create a pearl a full inch (2.5 cm) in diameter. The color of the pearl depends on the type of Chi; so Positive Chi pearls are pearly white and Negative Chi pearls are pearly dark grey. Dragon Pearls, once created, are just as permanent as any real pearl and are indistinguishable from the real thing. However, any jeweler will recognize that they are extremely high quality and valuable.

Aside from simply creating the pearls, the other aspect of the spell is that they can be used as weapons, inflicting both physical and Chi damage when they strike. Spitting is done at +8 to strike and each point of Chi invested in the pearl equals 1D6 of physical damage. If someone is struck with a pearl (but only when it was first spit/created), they'll also suffer Chi damage, losing 2D6 points of Chi (Positive or Negative), for every point of Chi invested in the pearl.

As Celestial Calligraphy: Doesn't work unless the character releasing the spell has had detailed instructions. **Red ink on gold paper.**

Summon and Control Infernal

Range: Self
Duration: One day per level of experience.
Saving Throw: None
Cost: Two Hundred P.P.E.

The spell caster calls for a particular Infernal (by name), or a particular type of Infernal (by description), and pulls that demon out of the Hells of the Yama Kings. The Infernal appears before the spell caster and is compelled to obey any and all commands until the magic is dispelled. The spell caster can also command the Infernal to return to its Hell; something best done before the spell expires, as Infernals tend to get a little testy about such treatment from mere mortals. Only demon lords can resist this magic.

As Celestial Calligraphy: Works whether or not the caster understands it, summoning the nearest Infernal. **Black ink on glossy black paper.**

Level Thirteen

Control/Enslave Through Negative Chi

Range: 30 feet (9.1 m)
Duration: One day per level of experience.
Saving Throw: Standard
Cost: Three Hundred P.P.E.

An advanced version of *Control/Enslave Creature of Pure Negative Chi,*, that gives the spell caster the ability to attempt controlling anyone infected with Negative Chi. If the victim of the spell fails to save vs magic, the spell caster can then give commands that must be obeyed (although the victim may attempt to pervert the *spirit* of the command, so long as the literal words are followed).

If the spell caster wishes to attempt enslaving the victim, then a *conditioning* routine must be followed. It starts with the spell caster saying something like, "I am your master! Obey me!" or "You will agree that you are mine to command!" and forcing the victim to agree. The spell caster must roll a twenty-sided for each of the enslavement commands, and the victim can roll to save vs magic each time. This process of forcing the victim to respond must be completed three times in a row in order to make the enslavement last the duration of the spell! If even one of the three attempts to enslave fails, the attempt at enslavement fails totally and the magic of the control is also immediately dispelled.

Note that it is possible that the victim may succeed in resisting the enslavement, but may still answer as if the spell caster was successful. In other words, someone could attempt to convince the spell caster that the enslavement worked just to get a chance at revenge. An enslaved character can only escape enslavement if his/her enslaver lets him go, the spell duration elapses, or his enslaver is slain!

As Celestial Calligraphy: Doesn't work unless the character releasing the spell has had detailed instructions. **Black ink on white paper.**

Chi Clone (Living Chi)

Casting Time Required: One Hour
Range: Self
Duration: One hour for each level of experience.
Saving Throw: None
Cost: 200 P.P.E.

The character ends up being duplicated by a *Chi Clone* with all the spells, powers, abilities, strengths and weaknesses of the original spell caster. At the completion of the spell, the character's Chi spirit is automatically placed in the duplicate, leaving the original body vacant (most spell casters arrange for some kind of protection before starting the *Chi Clone* spell).

Not duplicated by the spell are the character's P.P.E. and Chi. The Chi, of course, will come along with the Chi clone, although the character may choose to leave some behind. However, it's up to the spell caster to decide how much of the remaining P.P.E. will be left with the original and how much will be put into the duplicate.

When the spell wears off or the clone is slain, the duplicate body disappears and the Chi spirit is instantly sent back to the original body (which, hopefully, will still be intact, unoccupied and alive).

Not available as Celestial Calligraphy.

Chi Cache (Living Chi)

Casting Time Required: Two Hours
Range: Self
Duration: Indefinite
Saving Throw: Standard
Cost: One Hundred P.P.E.

The idea is to give up a packet of Chi, so that it will be absorbed by a Living Chi and eventually swallowed by an enemy. Each Chi Cache is designed to be some kind of Trojan Horse, containing a nasty "surprise." There are two types, Spell Bombs and Negative Chi Contrivances.

Once the Chi Cache is complete it can stay inside the spell caster's body indefinitely. When the right opportunity comes along, the character can eject it, preferably directly into an enemy's Living Chi. It's also possible to send the Chi Cache out in any of the spell caster's Living Chi.

Finally, if the spell caster ever wants to disassemble the Chi Cache, it is possible to do so instantly, so that all the Chi invested and half the P.P.E. spent will be recovered.

Spell Bomb. The Chi Cache is constructed with a built-in spell which goes off as soon as the victim recovers their Chi. The spell caster has a choice of either building the P.P.E. into the spell (in which case the spell is guaranteed to go off, but it will cost the P.P.E. for Chi Cache, plus the P.P.E. for the spell), or the spell caster can just put in the spell hoping that the victim will have enough P.P.E. to activate it (if the victim doesn't have the necessary P.P.E., the spell won't go off).

Negative Chi Contrivance. Aside from the P.P.E. cost of the spell, the spell caster must also invest a number of points of Negative Chi into this Chi Cache. It is designed to work only when facing some kind of Living Chi made of Negative Chi. The idea is that the extra Negative Chi is allowed to be absorbed by the victim's Living Chi. Eventually the Living Chi is recovered by the victim, along with the Chi Cache. Then, whenever the victim gets around to switching their body from Negative Chi to Positive Chi, the Chi Cache's Negative Chi will go into attack mode. For every point of Negative Chi, 3D6 points of Positive Chi will be destroyed. Any remaining Negative Chi will then *activated* and each will do 1D6 damage direct to hit points, inside the victim.

Not available as Celestial Calligraphy.

Detach Animus

Range: Self
Duration: Indefinite (lasts as long as the Animus affected).
Saving Throw: None
Cost: Two Hundred P.P.E.

Used in combination with one of the *Evoke Animus* spells. This spell does two things: First, it allows the Animus to step away from the character's body, so that it can walk around freely. Second, the spell sets up a Chi-based psychic connection between the spell caster and the Animus.

Typically, a detached Animus travels by conventional means and would have to get back to the spell caster in order to return the invested Chi. They can squeeze through cracks and keyholes and allow physical and energy attacks to pass through them, but they are still capable of lifting and carrying objects. Here are some notes on particular cases:

Animus of Pure Chi. The Animus of Pure Chi is the only one capable of teleporting back to the character's body. All others must return by normal means (run, walk, via automobile, etc.) before the spell expires, or the character will lose all the Chi that was invested. No Animus of Pure Chi can carry an object or manipulate anything physical.

Quicksilver Animus (Metal), Golden Animus (Earth) and Black Ice Animus (Water). Each of these have a solid outer surface subject to physical attacks. Each appears to be a hollow structure, just a shade larger than the spell caster. This solid mass cannot be collapsed or squeezed down.

Glowing Jade Animus (Wood). Capable of draining Chi from other Living Chi made of elemental earth.

Black Water Animus – Element of Water & Positive Chi. This Animus, when detached from the body, loses one point of Chi for every full melee round that it is separated from water. So long as at least some part of it is in water, it's okay; even a foot in a stream or being outside in the rain will prevent loss of Chi.

As Celestial Calligraphy: Doesn't work unless the character understands the spell. **Gold ink on white paper.**

Level Fourteen

Draw Helix of Dragon Summoning/Command (Geomantic)

Casting Time Required: One Hour **Range:** Self
Duration: One day per level of experience.
Saving Throw: Standard
Cost: Eight Hundred P.P.E.

The spell caster draws an invisible line of Chi, inscribing a great helix (three dimensional spiral form) that is large enough to completely encompass a dragon. For each type of dragon (earth dragon, water dragon, etc.) there is a helix of a different design. Once completed, dragons will be summoned, starting with the nearest and moving outward until *one* either willingly answers the summoner or fails to save vs magic (a very unlikely event, since dragons have enormous bonuses to save vs magic).

Eventually, although it may take 3D6 hours, a dragon is likely to appear, probably out of curiosity. At this point a wise spell caster will NOT attempt to issue commands, but ask for "favors." However, once in the helix, the dragon can supposedly be forced to obey the commands of the spell caster. Dragons under the power of this spell will know full well what is happening to them and will hate it. They will also know that the simple way to be released is to arrange for the death of the spell caster. Therefore commands must be worded with extreme care, as the dragon will attempt to twist and pervert any spoken order.

A dragon may also attempt to resist every pronouncement by arguing, asking for clarification, or otherwise stalling. It isn't until the exact words of a command are repeated *three* times that the dragon feels truly compelled to obey without further delay.

There are also certain things that a dragon cannot be commanded to do. First, a dragon will not harm itself. Second, unless the dragon wishes to do so, it can't be forced into attacking or harming another dragon. Finally, a dragon may not violate the laws of the Divine Realm of the Jade Emperor, which, considering the arcane and complex nature of the Jade Emperor's power, means the dragon can pretty much choose whether or not to obey just about any given command.

Another example of the twisted and difficult nature of commanding a dragon is the other loophole in the spell. If the spell caster commands the dragon to do something that is impossible, or beyond the power of the dragon, and repeats the command three times, the spell will be terminated!

Note that dragons, convoluted creatures that they are, may pretend to be affected by a control dragon spell, even though they may have resisted the initial casting or after the spell wears off. In this case a dragon may take the opportunity to perform mischief, and turn the blame on the magic wielder.

Not available as Celestial Calligraphy.

Evoke Immortal Child (Living Chi)

Casting Time Required: Fifteen Minutes.
Range: Self
Duration: One hour per level of experience.
Saving Throw: None
Cost: Three Hundred P.P.E.

The casting of this powerful spell divides the caster's body and soul, so that a tiny replica of the character is created. The Immortal Child looks like a very young (perhaps four or five year old) version of the character, and is about one-fifth of the normal height of the spell caster.

At the time that the spell is cast, the entire Chi spirit of the character becomes invested in the Immortal Child, so that the original body is abandoned until the magic is dispelled (obviously, the spell caster should consider providing some kind of defenses for the body). Here are the powers of the Immortal Child:

Sense *Chen Chi* (Living Vitality). The Immortal Child can feel the *Chen Chi*, or living vitality, of all humans and other creatures within fifty feet (15.2 m), even in total darkness, or obscured by smoke. From the *Chen Chi*, it can be determined if the character(s) is healthy or ill, injured or healed, poisoned or pure.

Sense of *Ti Chi* (Earth/Dragon Energy). The *movement* of Chi, as it flows, is sensed by the Immortal Child, who can tell the exact quantity, type (Positive or Negative), and direction. The presence of earth dragons, up to one mile (1.6 km) away, will also be detected.

Sense *Wei Chi*. The Immortal Child can sense the "internal fire" diffused throughout the body of any living thing within sixty feet (18.3 m), revealing the Chi type (Positive or Negative) and amount. Also reveals the presence of any hidden Pure Chi entities.

Aura of Extreme Positive Chi. All Infernals, except for those of the very highest level (the Yama Kings and their direct emissaries), including all entities of Pure Negative Chi, will be repelled by the Immortal Child and will be unable to touch it, attack it, or even gaze upon it for more than a few seconds.

Take Pure Chi Form. The Immortal Child can instantly slip between physical form and a form of Pure Chi. In its Chi form, the Immortal Child can instantly teleport back to the spell caster, but NOT to anywhere else.

Flight and levitation. While capable of carrying small objects, the Immortal Child can't fly while lifting any more than about twenty pounds (9 kg).

Not available as Celestial Calligraphy.

Open Hell Gate

Casting Time Required: Fifteen Minutes.
Range: Self
Duration: Indefinite
Saving Throw: None
Cost: Three Hundred P.P.E.

Unlike the 8th level spell, Enter Realm of Yama Kings, the gateway produced by this spell is an open invitation for the forces of Hell to enter the world of mortals! No doubt originally created by some powerful Immortal, it is suspected that it was meant as a means to summon forth an invincible Infernal army, consisting of a horde of demonic forces capable of conquering the world.

In spite of the efforts of many *Wu Shih* to eliminate this spell from their teachings and sacred books, it still persists. There have even been records of the spell having been erased, or physically removed from certain collections of spells, only to have the spell reappear elsewhere in fifty or a hundred years time. It is also suspicious that, whenever a collection of magical writings has been burned, this spell often shows on a piece of scorched paper that has "fortunately" survived while most of the rest was destroyed.

If the character is familiar with the target location, there's a 50% chance that the Hell Gate can be opened to the exact point specified by the spell caster. Otherwise, it is said that the gate will open to wherever the Yama Kings will it. There are no restrictions on casting the spell and it will even work in an area of strong Positive Chi. Typically, 3D4 lesser demons will emerge from the gate or an emissary of a Yama King will appear to discuss "deals" and special arrangements (requiring a trade of services or valuables).

As Celestial Calligraphy: Works whether or not the caster understands it. **Gold ink on glossy black paper.**

Weep Beans of Life

Casting Time Required: One Melee Round.
Range: Self **Duration:** Special
Saving Throw: None
Cost: Four Hundred P.P.E.

The beans of life, which look exactly like tiny beans, are "wept" from the eyes of the spell caster, just as if they were tears. Each bean of life contains a huge quantity of Positive Chi and a mystic potential. Once created, a bean of life can be saved indefinitely.

Ordinarily a spell caster will produce only two beans in a single melee round, one from each eye. However, if the character has a real reason for sorrow, such as the death of a loved one, or the witnessing of a great tragedy, then the weeping can last for another one or two melee rounds. **Note:** Six beans is the absolute maximum!

Once created, anyone possessing a bean of life can use it in any of the following ways:

Using a Bean of Life as a Pill of Regeneration. Placed on the tongue, or in any open wound, the bean will instantly dissolve, filling the character with healing energy. Any character so treated will be perfectly healed and will gain an additional twenty-five years of youthful life and vitality.

Cracking open a Bean of Life. Smashing or breaking a bean of life (they have an A.R. 7 and 4 points of S.D.C.) means spilling out approximately 500 points of Positive Chi in a blinding flash of light. Any lesser Infernal creature within one mile (1.6 km) will be forced to return to its Hell or be faced with obliteration.

Planting a Bean of Life Above Ground: If planted in soil, sand, or even a crack in concrete, so long as it is in a place where there is direct sunlight (since the ultraviolet rays of the sun penetrate even thick clouds, it need not be a sunny day), and so long as the bean is then sprinkled with a little water, it will instantly take root and start to grow. Within one hour the bean will have generated a twelve-foot tall (3.7 m) beanstalk, brimming with pods and it's roots will have churned up good soil in an area twenty feet (6.1 m) across.

First Crop. The "crop" in the first hour results in about six bushels of "bean pods," with each pod containing eight beans. The beans from this first crop are tender, tasty, and ready to eat. A single bean has all the ingredients of a fully balanced daily diet and the plant produces enough in this first crop to feed 15,000 people. The beans remain juicy and edible for around twenty-four hours, after which they harden into ordinary beans.

Later Crops of the original beanstalk. The original vine will never again produce in quantity. However, if properly cared for (watered, etc.), it will produce one more pod of first crop beans every year. Even more remarkable, the soil around the beanstalk will become rich and fertile, capable of growing anything. The area of fertility increases a little more every year.

Second Planting. If the beans of the first crop are planted within twenty-four hours of the harvest, they will each grow to full size and present a harvest within one week.

Later Crops & Subsequent Plantings. At the end of the next full growing season, and for years to come, the crop yield will be rich and full.

Planting a Bean of Life below ground, in stone or concrete. If planted underground and sprinkled with a little water, the Bean of Life will instantly start to grow. If the bean was started in stone, rock, or any solid material (metal, concrete, etc.), it's roots will smash through that material, effectively pulverizing an area twenty feet (6.1 m) across and forty feet (12.2 m) deep. Meanwhile, the plant itself will grow ten feet (3.0 m) tall, but with white leaves and white pods. Only about one hundred pods will result, each with eight beans, but all the beans have the same properties as that of a first crop (see above). The beanstalk only lives for around eight hours, but for all that time, in an area one hundred feet (30.5 m) in diameter, there will be a flow of twenty-five points of Positive Chi circling around the plant.

Note that anyone carrying around a Bean of Life is likely to be noticed. Beans of Life have a distinctive Chi aura (purple and pink) and are highly sought after by Alchemists, Immortals and others in pursuit of power.

Not available as Celestial Calligraphy.

Level Fifteen

Draw Yin Yang Symbol (Geomantic)

Range: Touch
Duration: Ten minutes per level of experience.
Saving Throw: None
Cost: Two Thousand P.P.E.

The spell caster draws, using invisible lines of Chi, the *true* and ultimate Yin Yang Symbol. This great symbol of Taoism, the half black-half white, inward spiraling symbol of the Yin Yang, is more than a simple visual image. It is also a gateway. A gateway to the ***Hun Tun**, or the Primordial Chaos, the first nothingness that generated the Tao, which in turn created the universe!*

While there is much confusion about what might result from the actual performance of this spell, there is a clue in the two symbols that make up the name of Primordial Chaos. First, *Hun* is the symbol for a great, luminous cloud of insects. Second, *Tun* is the character for blunt and unenlightened confusion. On one thing all the ancient sources are in agreement, that the *Hun Tun* contains ALL the Chi required for the creation or destruction of the universe!

Note: In **Mystic China, Beyond the Supernatural** and **Heroes Unlimited**, this spell will release a plague of insects that will ravage 1000 square miles and unleash a dangerous demon lord (or evil alien intelligence) and hundreds of his demonic legions into the world (vampires are a likely pestilence). In **Rifts** this spell will release the *Four Horsemen of the Apocalypse*, regardless of whether or not they have recently appeared and been defeated (or in the alternative it may unleash a powerful, evil, alien intelligence).

Not available as Celestial Calligraphy.

Enter the Divine Realm of the Jade Emperor

Casting Time Required: Four hours
Range: Touch
Duration: One melee round per level of experience.
Saving Throw: None
Cost: Five Hundred P.P.E.

Opens a portal into the fabled realm of the Jade Emperor where the great bureaucracy of the gods controls and administers all the lives of all mortals.

Depending on who is present, there are a variety of possible "greetings" that await those who would catch a glimpse of the Jade Emperor's Realm.

If the major presence is that of a devout Taoist, or an Enlightened Immortal, or even a gathering of highly Principled characters, there will be little or no fuss. The gateway will simply open and characters will be free to come and go for as long as the spell lasts. However, if there are any Infernals (no matter how well disguised) or entities of Pure Negative Chi, or if the majority of those present are not of a good alignment, then at least two of the Guardian Deities will step out, blocking the way, and demand to know the business of those who would sully the steps of the Jade Emperor. Deadly combat, capture, enslavement and trouble can result.

Rumored to be unavailable as Celestial Calligraphy.

Remove Heart

Casting Time Required: Seven days.
Range: Touch
Duration: Permanent
Saving Throw: Special
Cost: Seven Hundred P.P.E.

A combination of spell casting and open surgery. The operation removes the heart of a character and transforms it into a magical gem with the appearance of a spherical, smooth, giant, ruby, about six inches (15 cm) in diameter. This gemstone is called the *Secret Heart* and it has an A.R. of 8, 20 S.D.C., and 6 hit points. The blood of the body is magically and continuously pumped through the Secret Heart, even though the body and heart may be separated by thousands of miles or actually be located in different dimensions. So, no matter what horrible damage is done to the character's body, the heart keeps pumping blood through it.

The spell is usually done on a willing volunteer (**Note:** it is impossible for spell casters to perform Remove Heart on themselves). Even though the character is willing, a saving throw vs magic (no bonuses allowed) must be made on each of the seven days of the spell casting. Should the character save vs magic on ANY of the seven times, the spell fails. If the spell fails on the first day, the character takes 6D6 damage direct to hit points, but can recover. If the spell fails on any subsequent day, then the victim suffers 3D6×10 damage direct to hit points and is likely to *die*.

It is also believed that there are four other spells related to Remove Heart: Remove Liver, Remove Spleen, Remove Lungs, and Remove Kidneys. Just as with the heart, each organ (or pair of organs) is removed and transformed into a crystal (blue for the liver, yellow for the spleen, white for the lungs, and black for the kidneys). In theory, a character who has had all these organs removed becomes invulnerable and Immortal. Not so, since brain damage, cancers that attack the nervous system, other ailments, psionic attacks, and magic can still kill the character. Likewise, even though it's much more difficult to kill the character in combat, that's just because there are fewer vulnerable targets. **Note:** See the *Heartless Immortals* description for more details. Being without a heart is roughly equal to partial removal of organs, including the bonuses listed there.

Not available as Celestial Calligraphy.

Chinese Alchemy

" ...then wrapped tightly in paper and thrown into a stream, the current would at once come to a halt. A door sealed with the elixir would not open, though ten thousand men should tug at it... Should one desire to ascend to heaven with all due speed, he should swallow the potion at once: death would immediately follow. But if one wished to prolong his stay among men, he should consume it little by little, and when at last it had all been taken, he too would then find himself to be an immortal... "

Michael Strickmann, "On the Alchemy of T'ao Hung-Ching" from **Facets of Taoism**.

Alchemy, whether in the east or the west, has always been the first of the experimental sciences. No matter what their country of origin, alchemists have always explored the principles of chemistry, physics and biology, along with lesser known sciences.

The only difference between Chinese and European alchemy is really a matter of goals and objectives. Where the western version of alchemy was obsessed with the idea of finding the "Philosopher's Stone" which could be used for changing base metals into gold, Chinese alchemy has always been focused on producing an "elixir" that could grant Immortality.

Since it is well known that Chinese alchemists have sought to cure old age, starting at least three thousand years ago, the question of "how," still remains. Here are three possible explanations for how *Elixirs of Immortality* might work, based on the idea of "death worms," and/or on the science of endocrinology.

Alchemy as a Cure for Death Worms

One theory of why Elixirs of Immortality work has to do with the toxicity of the formulas. Since all the early written works of alchemy were quick to recognize the deadly aspects of potions (they usually included cautionary notes, warning alchemists of the dangers from fumes and other hazards), the reasoning behind the consumption of poisons was that there was, within each body, something that would need to be killed in order to achieve immortality. A toxicity where a single drop is usually enough to kill a fifteen hundred pound ox, there are theories that the body must be shocked into a state *beyond death*, or that the poison triggers some supernatural healing ability in the body, which then goes on to reverse the aging process.

Consider **Victor Lazlo's** description of the evocation of a death worm:

"As my long-time readers are no doubt aware, I've seen enough wonders (and horrors!) in my investigations to have developed a certain reserve. So it is with some trepidation on my part that I tell you of one of the most shocking and disturbing experiences that I have ever witnessed. All the more startling because the creature I am about to describe is said to be just one of the ordinary inhabitants of my own body!

"This perturbing chapter of my explorations began harmlessly enough. I was in Hong Kong, enjoying a late-night snack of Dim Sum and Tea with Tommy Tung and some of his fellow Fang Shih. As it happened, the conversation turned to Chinese alchemy. Somewhat surprised by the reverence of their tone and the respect they seemed to have for that ancient humbug, I challenged them by saying the following,

"'Why did those men, otherwise so incredibly learned, dwell on the notion that potions of utter poison could somehow confer immortality? It would seem that any elixir consisting mostly of mercury and lead, would be nothing less than a suicide potion!'

"In the hush that followed my outburst, I was suddenly embarrassed. Hoping that I had not caused offense, I attempted to apologize.

"Surprisingly, smiles appeared around the table and, after a few conspiratorial winks, Tommy asked if I, as a scientist, would be interested in meeting a real alchemist. In spite of my skepticism (how easy it is for we of the western way of thought to fall into the habits of the closed mind!), I agreed.

"Within fifteen minutes I found myself in a cavernous basement and in the company of a woman I would judge to be at least eighty years old. While Tommy, the other Fang Shih, and the woman (seemingly the proprietor of this place) discussed matters in rapid-fire Chinese, I gazed around. Here were shelves containing several thousand ancient volumes, along with an equal number of jars and bottles, each neatly labelled. On antique tables stood instruments of brass, green glass and steel.

"Before I was able to get my bearings, the conversation ceased and the old woman approached. She had the practiced manner of a medical doctor, taking my pulse and looking into my eyes. Tommy explained that she needed to be sure that my Chi was steady before we were to proceed with the alchemical experiment.

"When I protested that I felt uncomfortable with the standard alchemical ingredients (Cinnabar, after all, is a most deadly concoction of mercury!) everyone laughed. With the exception of an herb that I could not identify, each of the ingredients of the draft that I was to consume were perfectly ordinary teas and spices, plus, of course, a pinch of ginseng.

"Once it was determined that the potion might be having its effect, I was seated in a chair with Tommy firmly grasping me from behind, my shoulders against the chair's back. Two others stood at my sides, holding my hands to the arms of the chair. Since all three were gifted in some form or other of the martial arts, I was discomforted to see that they each braced themselves quite rigidly, as if they were expecting to exert themselves against some monstrous force. Before proceeding further, I was told to look down. The old woman made sure that my gaze was firmly directed toward my own stomach.

"At this point I heard the scratchy noise of some sort of speaker system and a musical tape began to play. Although I am uncertain of the exact origin of the music, it definitely had much in common with the Tibetan chants I knew so well.

"Eventually, the rhythmic sound seemed to penetrate all the way through my body, seeming to vibrate deeply into my internal organs and resonate through my body's inner cavity. Keeping still and not allowing myself to move in time with that terrible music was one of the most difficult feats of my entire life.

"Just at the time when it seemed that I could no longer contain myself, I noticed something deeply disturbing. Something was moving under my clothing, as if some creature was emerging from my own navel!

"It was fortunate that my three friends were holding on so tightly, for I couldn't help but struggle, in a frenzy of fearful panic, as a horrible white worm poked its way free of my shirt.

"Blind, it was, and trailing a dozen or more tiny tendrils, each leading back under my shirt. It seemed to be moving in time with the music, but also to be straining against the tendrils, as if it too were somehow held or constrained. Although it seemed, at the time, to be monstrous in size, it was actually only about as wide as a button hole in my shirt.

"It was just at the point when it seemed that the dreadful worm might extend itself further that the music suddenly stopped. The worm instantly jerked itself back and I felt a sense of odd queasiness.

"At that point my friends saw fit to release me!

"Once free, I immediately ripped open my shirt, scattering buttons across the floor. In a fit I engaged in self-examination. Yet there was nothing there. Nor any sign that anything had ever been there, nothing but my own perspiration.

"After recovering from my experience, Tommy translated for the aged Alchemist (whose name I was never to learn), 'What you have seen, Mr. Lazlo, is but one of the Three Worms, the *San Chung*, that doom every mortal. It is the goal of the alchemist to kill the worms without killing the person. And to kill all the worms, since the three keep each other in balance. However, it is even more complicated than you might think, since eliminating the worms is not enough. No, there will remain another seven entities, what are called the Corpse Specters, or the *Qi Yin Shih*, who, unhindered by the worms, will quickly rot the body. It is the quest of the alchemist to find a formula that will kill all ten of the rotting entities, so as to avoid both age and death.'

"Do such horrors really exist inside our bodies? Is the vile worm that I beheld actually present and responsible for our body's natural aging process?

"In all honesty, I am unable to answer.

"It is more likely that I am all too suggestible and that I was merely hypnotized, or fooled by some trick or illusion. Yet, I have to admit, I find myself believing that the demonstration was a glimpse into a greater reality."

Excerpted from Victor Lazlo's **Splintered Souls & Broken Auras**, 1981. Author's Note: It's interesting that modern biology has just recently discovered built-in "self-destruct" mechanisms in each cell of the human body.

Alchemy as the Ancient Chinese Art of Endocrinology

Another possibility is that true Elixirs of Immortality are really complex and very advanced brews of hormones.

In researching this book, I've been constantly amazed by the scientific wonders of ancient China. One of the most stunning discoveries is how advanced the Chinese were in understanding and extracting human androgens, estrogens, pituitary hormones (gonadotrophins), steroids, etc. Considering that western science only "discovered" endocrinology in the 1920s, it's astonishing that "autumn minerals" (a crystallized form of steroids) were well known in China by 125 BC!

Since modern science has only been messing around with Endocrinology for only a few decades, it's entirely possible that Chinese alchemy, a subject of centuries of experimentation, may have come up with some practical answers regarding aging.

Guide to Chinese Alchemy

In many ways the return of the alchemists, banned for over a thousand years, is the most frightening of the recent developments in the world of **Mystic China**. Part of what makes this such a disturbing development is the fusion of ancient alchemy and modern technology. By using modern equipment and computers, contemporary alchemists now have a much greater chance of successfully brewing their mystic potions. In addition, with the use of computer simulations and safe laboratory techniques, the old dangers of dying (or being driven mad) from the mercury gas and other toxic chemicals, are much diminished.

Note that modern alchemists will hardly ever attempt to use their concoctions on themselves. No, they are all too aware of the heavy use of neuro-toxins, and out-and-out poisons in their creations.

Ten Great Known Books of Alchemy

The following reference books are well known and can be found in several "modern" (from 1850 AD to the present) editions. While some of these books are difficult to purchase, they can be located in libraries and specialty bookstores around the world, particularly in the Orient. On the other hand, earlier versions, or an original (written in the alchemist's own hand!) can be quite a valuable find. Costs can range from 3D4×10 dollars to 3D6×1,000 dollars depending on the buyer and the age, condition and completeness of the ancient tome.

1. Chien Ching. Translates to "Sword Scripture," but the full title is actually "Wondrous Scripture of the Perfected Immortal of the Ground Bourne, Essence of Stone and Radiance of Metal, on Storing the Effulgent-Spirits and Preserving the Body." Sort of a college-level course in alchemy, which includes most of the basics, along with quite a few introductory elixirs. However, none of its formulas for Elixirs of Immortality (there are a total of nine) seem to work properly, so experts suspect that the currently available editions are all defective.

2. Chou I Tsan Tung Chi. "The Concordance of the Three." This is a book of alchemical theory based on the sixty-four hexagrams of the I Ching. It is likely that this book will be needed in order to successfully interpret any formula that refers to one of the hexagrams.

3. Ho Tan Chieh Tu. "Rules for Timing in the Compounding of Elixirs." Since most formulas for Elixirs of Immortality are vague, or completely neglectful regarding matters of time (how long should it boil? how long should it steep? etc.), this is an important reference book.

4. Lien Hua Tsa Shu. "Assorted Arts of Refining and Transformation." More a book of chemistry than alchemy, the volume contains descriptions and directions for compounding many of alchemy's most important ingredients.

5. Shen Nung Pen Tsao Ching. Shen Nung Pharmacopeia, by Tao Hung Ching, circa 500 AD. Not strictly a book of alchemy, this volume contains critical information on ancient pharmacology, including the flora (herbs and roots), fauna and mineralia. An important tool for figuring out how to translate ancient ingredients into the proper names for contemporary items.

6. Tai Wei Ling Shu Tzu Wen Lang Kan Huan Tan Shen Chen Shang Ching. Which translates into; "Purple Writ in the Transcendent Script of Tai Wei, Supreme Scripture of the Wondrous Perfected on the Elixir of Lang Kan Efflorescence." Describes the preparation of a fourteen-ingredient pearl-like elixir, which is then planted so that it grows into a tree with circular (torus, or donut-shaped) fruit. The third generation descendants of this fruit (each generation undergoes a separate alchemical procedure, complete with incantations), when eaten in the precise way, will confer immortality. The book includes a mass of instructions, including details on the construction of all necessary equipment. Since the directions require vastly complex processes, as well as eighteen years of cultivation time, and none have *reported* success, very few alchemists have attempted to follow the procedure.

7. Tan Ching Yao Chueh. "Essential Formulas from the Alchemical Classics," by Sun Ssu Mo. This is the most well-known of all early books on alchemy. It includes a variety of procedures, along with several formulas for Elixirs of Immortality, as well as elixirs that can be used for creating artificial jade and pearl, and for curatives against fevers and poisons. **Note:** This is one of the few books that has been translated into English by a trained chemist (also see *Chinese Alchemy: Preliminary Studies* by Nathan Sivin, Harvard University Press, 1968).

8. Tan Fang Ching Yuan. The "Source-Mirror of Alchemical Formulas" is a guide to alternate ingredients, and alternate ways of doing things. Essentially it describes substitutes so that elixirs can be attempted when certain components are not available.

9. Tsan Tung Chi Wu Hsiang Lei Pi Yao. "Arcane Essentials of the Fivefold Categories, based on The Concordance of the Three." This book of alchemical theory is based on a variety of interpretations of the interplay of the five Chinese elements (Earth, Fire, Metal, Water, and Wood), but it is a jumbled mess of a book. Although most alchemists feel that it must contain some important clue, and believe that it is a valuable addition to any library, no one has come forward to describe exactly what is of value in this book.

10. Yen Tieh Lun. "Discourses on Salt and Iron," this volume is considered to be a very basic text on alchemy. It contains no formula for Elixirs, but it is an important reference book containing detailed descriptions of many of the most important processes for refining and purifying elixirs.

Ten Lost Books of Alchemy

Each of the following volumes are well known to alchemists, as well as antiquarians. They have each been mentioned numerous times in other books and sources, but each is considered "lost," and no copies have been seen within the last one hundred years. Any of the books listed here would be worth at least one million dollars to the right buyer, and may be considered priceless by any alchemists who are secretly studying the forbidden science. The costs of most typically range from 1D6× one million dollars to 3D6×10 million dollars depending on the buyer and the authenticity, age, condition and completeness of the ancient tome.

1. Chien Chieh. The book of "Sword Liberation" is rumored to contain secret methods of Sword Chi, along with a means of using Sword Chi for reversing the aging process.

2. Chih Hsuan Pien. Known as "The Guide to the Mystery," this volume is rumored to contain a complete guide to all the ancient magical spells of alchemy. Reputed to number in the dozens, these Chi-based spells are probably early versions of the spells currently known to Wu Shih and Tao Shih.

3. Chou Shih Ming Tung Chi. "A Record of Master Chou's Communications with the Unseen World." According to other sources, this book details how one can communicate on the special plane inhabited by Death Worms and Corpse Spirits. This book has also been listed as "forbidden" by several dynasties and is reputed to drive readers to a state of extreme delusion, or total madness.

4. Ho Tan Yao Lueh Hsu. "Prolegomena to a Resume of Essentials for the Compounding of Elixirs." Of all the lost books, this one seems the most likely to contain the missing secrets of ancient Chinese Endocrinology. Among other things, it is said to contain formulas for "restoring youth to the skin," "curing impotence," and "creating fertility in barren women." If discovered, it could provide a wealth of information, along with substantial material wealth to any modern pharmaceutical company. The value of such a book could reach several billions of dollars. An authentic volume has never been found.

5. Tai Chi Chen Jen Chiu Chuan Huan Tan Ching Yao Chueh. "Essential Instructions of the Perfected Immortal of the Grand Bourn (boundless realm) on the Elixir of Nine Cycles." Includes directions as to the collection of the five sacred mushrooms of Mao Shan (the mountain).

6. Tai Ching Chu Tan Chi Yao. "Collected Essentials on the Elixirs of Tai Ching." While this book is unlikely to contain any important formulas, it is considered to be of extreme historical importance. It may, in fact, record the early discoverers and pioneers in the field of alchemy.

7. Tai Shang Wei Ling Shen Hua Chiu Chuan Tan-Sha Fa. "Exalted, Life-Protecting Method for the Wondrous Transformation of Ninefold Cyclically Transformed Elixir." Supposedly, this book contains the formulas for a variety of elixirs, each of which replicates a particular power or ability of an Enlightened Immortal. If found, it would be highly coveted and incredibly expensive.

8. Teng Chen Yin Chueh. "Concealed Instructions for Ascent to Perfection." It is unknown whether this book is alchemical, or has something to do with mystic enlightenment. A tale from the early Chou Dynasty reports that the last known copy of the book was stolen by a "three-eyed demon."

9. Yu Ching Chin Ssu Ching Hua Pi Wen Chin Pao Nei Lien Tan Chueh. "The Golden Treasure Oral Formula for Preparing the Internal Elixir, Ching Hua's Secret Text in the Golden Box from the Jade Purity Heaven." Traditionally, the Elixirs of Immortality described in this book were designed to immediately elevate one to the state of a demigod.

10. Wei Fu Jen Chuan. "Life of the Lady Wei." Lady Wei Hua Tsun, who was probably practicing alchemy in the 2nd Century BC, is reputed to have discovered many secrets, and to have come up with a workable "unified theory" of Alchemy and Immortality. She was also reported to have created a separate branch of alchemy (Chi Chiu), which came up with the idea of vaccinating patients against diseases. It is suspected that certain court alchemists who were jealous of Lady Wei's genius, arranged to have all the copies of her book gathered up and destroyed. None are known to exist.

The Twenty Most Important Elemental Ingredients in Chinese Alchemy

01. *Chiang Fan* – Crimson Alum (Fe_2O_3)
02. *Chien* – Lead (Pb)
03. *Chin* – Gold (Au)
04. *Chu Sha* – Cinnabar (HgS)
05. *Hsi* – Tin (Sn)
06. *Hsiao Shih* – Epsom Salts ($MgSO_47H_2O$)
07. *Hu Fen* – White Lead ($Pb[OH]_2$)
08. *Hung* – Mercury (Hg)
09. *La* – Pewter (Sn-Pb alloy)
10. *Pai Shih Ying* – Quartz (SiO_2)
11. *Pai Yen* – Purified Salt (NaCl purified)
12. *Shih Hui* – Lime (CaO)
13. *Shih Liu Huang* – Sulphur (S)
14. *Shui* – Water (H_2O)
15. *Shui Yin* – Quicksilver/Mercury (Hg)
16. *Tieh* – Iron (Fe)
17. *Tou* – Brass (Cu-Zn alloy)
18. *Tung* – Copper (Cu)
19. *Yin Fen* – Powdered Silver (Ag)
20. *Yu Fen* – Powdered Jade ($NaAl[SiO_3]_2$)

The Twenty Most Important Organic Ingredients in Chinese Alchemy

01. *Chih* – Lard
02. *Chu Fu Ko Chih* – Subcutaneous fat from the back of a pig
03. *Chueh Fen* – Sparrow Feces
04. *Hsing Jen* – Apricot Pits
05. *Hu Chiao* – Indian Pepper
06. *Hua Shih* – Talc
07. *Ko Pu* – Clamshells
08. *Ku Chiu* – Wine Vinegar
09. *La Mu* – White Wax Tree Wood
10. *Luan Fa* – Human Hair
11. *Mei* – Plums
12. *Mi* – Honey
13. *Pang Hsieh* – Powdered Oyster Shell
14. *Su* – Butter Fat
15. *Suan Chiu* – Onion
16. *Tao Jen* – Peach Pits
17. *Tsu* – Rice Vinegar
18. *Wu Kung* – Dried Centipedes
19. *Wu Mei* – Prunes
20. *Yen Tsu* – Concentrated Vinegar

Ten Common Alchemical Terms

1. Ching Chiu. Used to describe alcoholic ingredients.
2. Hu. The word for a chemical boiler or cauldron.
3. Hsuan Chiu. Alchemical term for purified water.
4. Ko Ho Tan. The perfect laboratory site for compounding elixirs. Usually described as the west side of a ridge, next to a stream that flows east.
5. Lung Ku. It translates into the words, "Dragon Bones," but these are really ancient "prophesy bones." Any ox bone, left in the ground for at least one hundred years, is an okay substitute.
6. Tan. Term for Elixir or Potion.
7. Tao Kuei. A mysterious quantity, generally thought to be a "scoop" or a "dollop."
8. Tsao Wu. Phrase used to describe an Alchemist's Laboratory.
9. Wu. Used to describe something dried or powdered.
10. Yao. Term for herbs or drugs, usually connected with medicine.

Ten Legendary Alchemical Elixirs

1. Chih Shu Po Tzu. White Seeds of the Red Tree or Sapphire Essence Resurrection Elixir. According to all sources, this not only brings the dead to life, but also gives some kind of second sight.

2. Chin I. Liquified Gold or Golden Flower Elixir is one of the most famous Elixirs of Immortality. It is said to purify the soul as well as the body, such that those who take it will become simultaneously enlightened.

3. Chiu Chen Yu Li Tan. The Ninefold Perfected Jade Liquor Elixir. The special ingredient in this potion is said to be the Lang Ko mushroom, a purple fungus that grows on nine stalks. Although lost, it is said that the formula describes how to cultivate the mushroom. There is considerable debate on the subject. Many specialists believe that this is not an Elixir of Immortality, but rather a curative for a range of diseases.

4. Chiu Chuan. Nine-Times Cycles or Cyclically Transformed Elixir. Said to be a cure for demonic possession.

5. Chiu Huan. Nine Blossoms or Ninefold Metamorphosis Elixir, is the elixir of the famous thaumaturge, Tso Tzu. According to ancient sources, this elixir is designed to transform the subject into their ideal, perfect self; "...those pure of harmony, who have merged sense and essence, will be come forth from the spiritual furnace with a thousand pollutants burned away, transformed into the misty light of immortality..."

However, according to the same source, "...if the precious jewel is not guarded, then the Wondrous Metamorphosis Elixir will gather the spirit of the root, of previous incarnations..." In other words, there seems to be a danger that taking this elixir will cause one to revert to a primitive or even demonic state of existence.

6. Chiung Ching. Jade Essence or Grand Unity Jade Powder Elixir. Described as a cure for all "wounds and diseases, of both flesh, spirit and intellect."

7. Huang Shui Yueh Hua. Lunar Efflorescence of Sulphurous Solution or Beaming Moonlight Elixir. According to different sources this is either (1) a Greater Yin Elixir, which would mean it should offer immense powers over Negative Chi and possibly confer Undead Immortality, or (2) is an Elixir of Negative Chi. In any case, it certainly confers some great power over Negative Chi.

8. Lang Kan Hua Tan. Elixir of Lang Kan Efflorescence is said to transform those who consume it into entities of Pure Chi, or possibly, to transport them into some realm of the supernatural or of the afterlife.

9. Pi Cheng Fei Hua. Volatile Efflorescence of the Emerald Citadel or Radiance-Containing Brilliance-Emitting Elixir. Characters who take this formula are said to acquire a supernatural control over their own Chi, as well as blinding speed and dexterity.

10. Shui Yang Ching Ying. Virid Iridescence of Aqueous Yang, or Greater Yang Powder. It is said to release either (1) Positive Chi or (2) P.P.E. direct from the body of the user. It is unclear whether or not that which is released will regenerate normally or is permanently lost.

Common Side-Effects from an Elixir of Immortality (roll 1D6)

1. False Immortality. The victim will appear to lose all traces of age, becoming youthful looking within a matter of 2D6 minutes. For the next several days (3D6) the character will seem to be the picture of health and vitality. However, at the end of that period, the internal organs will suddenly age and fail, resulting in the death of the character.

2. Release of Death Worms, or the release of Corpse Spirits. Some, but not all of the character's normal complement of decaying entities will leave the body. The remaining entities, no longer held in proper check, will start to inflict the victim with a variety of tumors, seizures and other diseases. Speed and combat abilities are reduced by half, skill proficiency by -25%.

3. Swelling with Cold Morbid Chi (Hsieh Chi Leng). The character's body gradually loses all of its Positive Chi at a rate of 1D6 per day, and then starts to fill with Negative Chi. Since healing is impossible with Negative Chi, the character will undergo a gradual decline in health.

4. Possession by Demonic Forces (Kuei Chi). The elixir interferes with the victim's normal protective mechanisms, leaving the door open for possession (any bonuses to save are permanently lost and the character is -3 to save). A ghost or some other entity of Pure Negative Chi sets up inside the victim's body, and will gradually take control, eventually attempting to evict the victim's own spirit.

5. Mutation. By disturbing (but not killing) the Death Worms and Corpse Spirits, the victim starts to undergo a series of rapid, usually painful or destructive mutations; reduce P.B. and P.E. attributes by half and spd by 25%; G.M. can determine physical change in appearance (or can use the tables in **Heroes Unlimited** or **Aliens Unlimited**; optional).

6. Senility. The character will instantly lose 1D6 points from I.Q., and will continue to lose another point every month until the I.Q. drops down to two! Skill performance is a mere 10%, and gradually all memory will fade until the character is incapable of even remembering his or her own name!!

Mudra

By taking a rigid posture of the hand and the body, characters with the ability to perform Mudra channel *Chi* through their bodies. The list of Mudra that follows represents what is available to player characters. There are additional, powerful, secret Mudra practiced by various sects (for example, the Mudra of Tibet and India are more powerful than those of the Chinese).

List of all Mudra by Type

The number in parentheses indicates Chi Points needed to use the Mudra.

Mudra of Self-Possession
Mudra of Tranquility and Collection – *An Wei She Chu Yin* (0)
Mudra of Fearlessness & Banishment of Fear – *Shih Wu Wei Yin* (1)
Mudra of Appeasement – *An Wei Yin* (1)
Mudra of the Ceremony of Unction – *Kuan Ting Yin* (2)
First Mudra of Unmoving – *Yi Ting Yin* (1)
Second Mudra of Unmoving – *Er Ting Yin* (2)
Third Mudra of Unmoving – *San Ting Yin* (4)
Fourth Mudra of Unmoving – *Si Ting Yin* (6)
Fifth Mudra of Unmoving – *Wu Ting Yin* (8)
Thousandth Mudra of Unmoving – *Qian Ting Yin* (20)

Mudra of Protection
Mudra of Silent Contemplation – *Yun Yin* (0)
Mudra for the Deflection of Negative Chi – *Chi Di Yin* (2)
Mudra for the Deflection of Positive Chi – *Chi Feng Yin* (2)
Mudra for the Protection from Magic – *I Hui Yin* (4)
Mudra for the Reflection of the Dragon's Gaze – *Jing Long Yin* (4)
Mudra that Quenches Hellfire – *Huo Yin* (4)
Mudra of Subtracting Oneself from the Sight of Others – *Yin Hsing Yin* (8)
Three Smoke Mudra – *San Yan Yin* (6)
Five Smoke Mudra – *Wu Yan Yin* (12)
Eight Smoke Mudra – *Ba Yan Yin* (20)

Mudra of Evocation
Mudra for the Collection of Alms – *Qian Yin* (0)
Mudra for the Evocation of Healing Energy – *Huang Yin* (4)
Mudra of the Fulfilling of the Vow – *Shih Yuan Yin* (4)
Mudra for the Evocation of Power – *Chi Long Yin* (4)
Mudra of Terrible Anger – *Chin Kang Yin* (4)
Mudra for the Release of Restrained Chi – *Kai Chi Yin* (8)
Mudra to Prevent Errors of the Six Senses – *Liu I Yin* (8)
Mudra of Unification – *Hsieh Yin* (8)
Mudra of Communion with Spirits – *Shen Su Yin* (16)
Mudra for the Communion with the Yama Kings of Hell – *Chu Ti Yin* (20)

Mudra for the Manipulation of Objects
Mudra for the Handling of Jade or Jewels – *Ju I Chu Yin* (2)
Mudra for the Handling of Mystic Mirrors – *Ching Yin* (2)
Mudra for the Handling of a Reliquary – *Shuai Tu Po Yin* (2)

Mudra for the Handling of Mystic Vajra – *Chin Kang Chu Yin* (4)
Mudra for the Handling of Weapons of Power – *Chien Yin* (6)

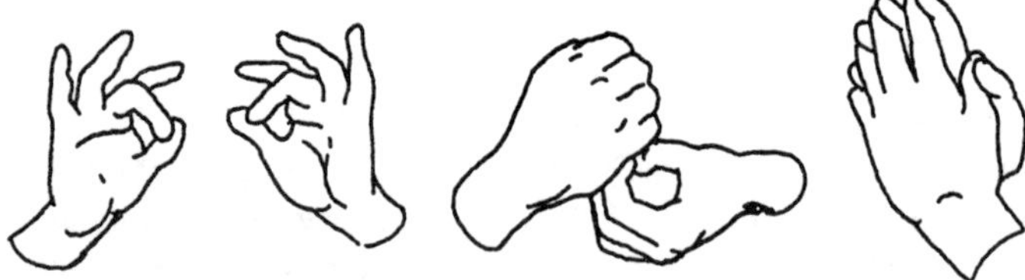

The Meditation Skill

In order to perform any Mudra, a character must have the skill of meditation. The *level of expertise* in meditation usually determines how long a Mudra can be maintained (duration; see Base Meditation Time below).

The skill of meditation involves engaging the mind and body, so that the body remains motionless, but without fatigue or pain, and the mind stays in a clear, calm and rested state. While meditating, a character recovers Chi, I.S.P., P.P.E. and other internal resources at an accelerated rate. Although it is not a substitute for sleeping, characters will usually feel alert and refreshed after any period of meditation. When in a meditative state, the character is, at a subconscious level, well aware of what is happening in the environment around him and can *instantly* leave the meditation position with no combat penalties. **Note:** Meditation is required for any character wishing to learn Mudra.

Base Meditation Skill: Regardless of the experience level of the character, any rolls based on meditation should use only the number provided by the character's Mental Endurance (M.E.) attribute.

Base Meditation Time (Duration): The amount of time that a character can continue to meditate:

At first level, duration is one hour +15 minutes at 2nd, 3rd, 4th and 5th levels.

At 6th level, the meditation time/duration jumps to *three hours*, +30 minutes for each *additional* level of advancement.

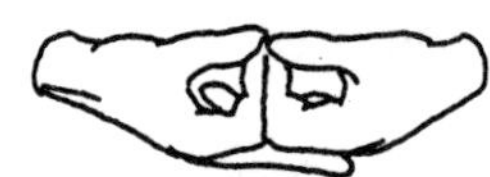

Explanation of Mudra and Mudra Terms

Meditation Time Required: This is the amount of "preparation time" that the character needs *before* the Mudra is activated. All Mudra require at least one full melee round before it can be used. If, at any point, the Mudra is interrupted, another full period of meditation time will be needed before the Mudra can be resumed.

Duration/Meditation Level: This is the duration of the meditation Mudra as related to the meditation skill. Duration can be less than one hour to several hours depending on the experience level of the character. In special cases, the duration of the Mudra may be extended to days.

Chi Required: Unless otherwise stated, the Chi expended by a Mudra can be Negative or Positive. However, only characters with at least one Negative Chi Mastery Ability can spend Negative Chi points on Mudra.

Range: This only applies to Mudra of Evocation. All others, including those of Self-Possession, Protection, and the Manipulation of Objects, are used on one's self or by touch.

Mudra of Self-Possession

Mudra that Tranquilizes & Collects
An Wei She Chu Yin

The first Mudra taught to any student of meditation. It works to calm the mind, lending peace to the user. If the character is hurt, or is missing Chi, I.S.P., or P.P.E., this Mudra will help the character recover the missing points at the usual rate.

In an area of Negative Chi, the Mudra will protect the body from losing any more Positive Chi, or from going further into Negative Chi (does NOT protect against Chi-based attacks, just from the drain of a natural flow of Chi).

Meditation Time Required: At 1st level it takes four melee rounds, then three melee rounds at 2nd level, two melee rounds at 3rd level. Any character who has attained 4th level or higher will be able to perform the Mudra in a single melee round.

Duration: Meditation Level (see meditation skill).

Description of Hand Positions: Requires two hands. Right hand, extended, open, with the palm turned slightly inward, while the left hand is facing palm outward with the forefinger bent to touch the inside of the thumb.

Chi Required: Zero.

Mudra of Fearlessness & for the Banishment of Fear
Shih Wu Wei Yin

Within two melee rounds of attaining this Mudra, a character's mind will be cleared of any disturbance, including those caused by horror factor or other traumatic experiences. Any penalties from these experiences will be negated. The character is immune to horror factor while the Mudra is maintained, as well as +5 to save vs magic and psionic attacks that induce fear, confusion, or panic.

Meditation Time Required: One melee round.

Duration: Meditation Level.

Description of Hand Positions: Requires two hands. Right hand, palm outward, left hand, palm upward.

Chi Required: One point

Mudra of Appeasement
An Wei Yin

Used to clear the body of unwelcome inhabitants, spirits and other attempts at *possession.* For each minute that the Mudra is maintained, all foreign entities must save vs banishment (12 or better on Twenty-Sided), or be ejected from the character's body.

Note: In **Rifts**, this would include symbiotes and parasites that have invaded the body in the last 48 hours. If banished, they leave the body without ill effect.

Meditation Time Required: Four melee rounds (one minute).

Duration: Half the usual meditation level.

Description of Hand Positions: Right hand, extended, cupped, with palm outward, while the left hand is facing palm outward with the forefinger bent to touch the inside of the thumb.

Chi Required: One point

Mudra of the Ceremony of Unction

Kuan Ting Yin

The Character is Immune to Possession while the Mudra is maintained. It is used to prevent the character's body from being invaded by any disembodied entities or other spirits. So long as the body maintains the position of this Mudra, no trespass is possible. This is especially useful for characters about to take a Mind Walk (Zenjorike).

Meditation Time Required: Four melee rounds (one minute).

Duration: Meditation Level.

Description of Hand Positions: Hands pointing upward, palms pointing together, with the forefingers and thumbs extended upward and touching, while the other fingers are folded with knuckles touching.

Chi Required: Two points.

First Mudra of Unmoving

Yi Ting Yin

Upon attainment of this Mudra, the character freezes into near-complete immobility, taking just one shallow breath of air every minute. Adopting this ability allows the character to go without food or water for the entire duration of the Mudra without suffering any ill effects.

Another use for this Mudra is conserving air when it is in short supply. The amount of air required by the character is six times less than normal (an oxygen supply would last six times as long). Examples include being trapped in a cave, or airtight vault, or being dependent on the air tank in SCUBA gear, etc. If the air supply would last twenty minutes for an ordinary person, it would support a character using this Mudra for 120 minutes.

Meditation Time Required: Eight Melee Rounds (two minutes).

Duration: At first level the character can remain in the unmoving state for three days, and will be able to manage another day for every additional level of attainment.

Description of Hand Positions: Requires two hands. Hands are open, palms upward, pointing toward each other, with the right hand holding the left, and with the tips of the thumbs touching.

Chi Required: One.

Note: During this Mudra, the character is aware of his surroundings as if in a dream, and cannot attack, move or communicate.

Second Mudra of Unmoving

Er Ting Yin

Used to recirculate the air inside the body, so the character doesn't have to breathe. Without air, underwater, buried underground, or in a poisonous or non-oxygen atmosphere, the character can refrain from breathing for as long as the Mudra remains in effect.

Meditation Time Required: Twelve melee rounds (three minutes).

Duration: Meditation Level.

Description of Hand Positions: Requires two hands. Hands are open, palms upward, pointing toward each other, with the left hand holding the right, and with the thumbs upward, and touching each other at the tips to form an opening.

Chi Required: Two points

Note: During this Mudra, the character is aware of his surroundings as if in a dream, and cannot attack, move or communicate. The character is still vulnerable to physical attacks and must end the Mudra to defend himself.

Third Mudra of Unmoving

San Ting Yin

Attaining this Mudra actually changes the body of the character. Inside, the blood slows and the organs of the body quiet, entering a state of suspended animation. Unable to move physically, the body's senses of sight, smell, taste, and touch also shut down; although the character can still hear loud sounds, like the voice of someone yelling nearby.

To an observer, it will seem as if the character turned to stone! Indeed, the skin takes on a stone-like texture, and becomes quite tough and durable. The exact appearance of this "stone" will depend on the character's chi. Characters brimming with Positive Chi (50 points or more) will appear to be polished black marble. A character with a modest amount of Positive Chi, between 15 and 49 points, will appear to be made of dark brown granite. Lesser amounts of Positive Chi will result in a skin that looks like baked red clay. A character with Zero Chi will look like grey slate. If the Mudra is attained while filled with a slight amount of Negative Chi (less than 10 points), then the appearance will be that of white marble with only tiny veins of grey. Finally, characters really charged with Negative Chi (10 or more points) will seem to be made of pure white quartz, faceted and gleaming.

Not only does the character look like rock, but the skin actually achieves the resistance of stone. Normal punches and kicks do no damage. Nor does the normal range of hot and cold temperatures.

Damage can be inflicted from those attacks penetrating the stone's Armor Rating of 16 (roll 17 or better to inflict damage). So the character can be hurt by hard impacts from hammers, chisels, bullets, electricity, fire, energy weapons, and explosions. However, the damage is always spread out and will seem to cause cracks that spread across the entire body. When the 120 S.D.C. of the stone surface is destroyed, the armor effect of the Mudra is gone, and the character's usual S.D.C. and hit points become vulnerable.

Meditation Time Required: Sixteen melee rounds (four minutes). **Also note:** It takes four melee rounds (one minute) to release the body from this particular Mudra.

Duration (Special): Up to one year per level of experience (indefinitely for Immortals and other superhumans).

Description of Hand Positions: Requires two hands. Hands are open, palms upward, pointing toward each other, with the left hand holding the right and with the corners of the thumbnails just touching.

Chi Required: Four

Bonuses of the Stone Surface: A.R.: 16, 120 S.D.C.

Fourth Mudra of Unmoving

Si Ting Yin

Similar to the Third Mudra of Unmoving, except that the character's spirit is set free in the same way as the *Mind Walk* Zenjorike ability.

Meditation Time Required: Twenty melee rounds (five minutes). **Also note:** It takes eight melee rounds (two minutes) to release the body from the Mudra.

Duration (Special): Up to one year per level of experience (indefinitely for Immortals and other superhumans).

Description of Hand Positions: Requires two hands. Hands are open, palms upward, pointing slightly forward and out from the body, with the right hand holding the left so the hands are crossed.

Chi Required: Six

Bonuses of the Stone Surface: A.R.:16, 120 S.D.C.

Fifth Mudra of Unmoving

Wu Ting Yin

Similar to the Third Mudra of Unmoving, except the character becomes like an immobile statue. However, instead of turning to simulated stone, this Mudra turns the character into the appearance of metal. It is also very different in that the body is continuously healed or repaired by whatever Chi, Positive or Negative, that flows through the area, protecting the body from damage.

Any character initially charged with Positive Chi will appear to be made of bright brass. Entering into the Mudra with Zero Chi means the character will take on a dull, dingy brass color. Being charged with a few points of Negative Chi results in a surface spotted with green tarnish. Any more than ten (10) points of Negative Chi and the body will be completely covered with mottled green and black tarnish.

Meditation Time Required: Forty melee rounds (ten minutes). **Also note:** It takes sixteen melee rounds (four minutes) to release the body from the Mudra.

Duration (Special): Up to five years per level of experience (indefinitely for Immortals and other superhumans).

Description of Hand Positions: Requires two hands. Hands are open, palms upward, the fingers interlinked, with the tip of the ring finger of the left hand touching the tip of the thumb of the right hand.

Chi Required: Eight

Bonuses of the Metal Surface: AR:16, 200 S.D.C. Regenerates S.D.C. with the Chi of the surrounding area each melee round. For example, in an area with a flow of three (3) Negative Chi, the body would heal any lost S.D.C. at a rate of three per melee round.

Thousandth Mudra of Unmoving

Qian Ting Yin

Warning! This is a self-destruct, suicide Mudra!! The idea is that the character, because of advanced age, or for some other reason, decides to voluntary exit to the spirit world, leaving the body behind as a permanent monument.

Meditation Time Required: One hour.

Important Note: There is no way for the character to retract the Mudra and return the body to its normal condition.

Duration: Permanent.

Description of Hand Positions: Requires a full body lotus position, as well as the positioning of the two hands. Hands are open, palms outward, fingers pointing upwards, wrists crossed and touching, left hand out, right hand closer to the body.

Chi Required: Twenty

Bonuses: The body becomes indestructible; effectively A.R. 20, 5,000 S.D.C. (or 50 M.D.C.) and is not affected by conventional weapons or the elements, only magic (or mega-damage weapons) will inflict half normal damage.

Mudra of Protection

Mudra of Silent Contemplation

Yun Yin

This is the second Mudra taught to all novices. By adopting this position, the character blocks out the noise and commotion of the outside world, allowing for complete concentration. It means that the character can be quietly alert and aware of what is going on in the immediate vicinity without having to break concentration.

For example, if a telephone started ringing in the middle of a Mudra of Silent Contemplation, it wouldn't interrupt the character's meditation. The character would, on some level, hear the telephone and would make a decision about whether to answer it or to let it keep ringing. If the character chooses to answer the phone, the Mudra would be ended and any benefits from the meditation/concentration/rest would cease. However, if the character chose not to answer the telephone, then the continued ringing would not bother the character in the least.

Meditation Time Required: One melee round.

Duration: Meditation Level.

Description of Hand Positions: Can be performed with either the right or left hand. The tip of the thumb touches the tips of both the ring and little fingers, while the index and middle fingers are extended next to each other (touching).

Chi Required: None

Mudra of Deflection of Negative Chi
Chi Di Yin

When used and directed at the incoming Negative Chi, the Mudra deflects up to 3D6 of the negative energy. It can be used once per melee round and the character can continue to move and fight (one-handed) while the Mudra is in use.

Characters adopting this Mudra can sense the direction of incoming Negative Chi, so the Mudra can be pointed in the correct way. However, if there is more than one source of Negative Chi, the character will only sense the largest source. Unless the character has some other warning, the Mudra can not be used against more than one stream of incoming Negative Chi.

Meditation Time Required: One melee round.

Duration: Meditation Level.

Description of Hand Positions: Can be performed with either the right or left hand. The tip of the thumb touches the tips of the middle and ring fingers, while the index and pinky fingers are extended toward the incoming Negative Chi.

Chi Required: Two

Mudra of Deflection of Positive Chi
Chi Feng Yin

The Mudra, when pointed at a stream of incoming Chi, can deflect up to 3D6 points of Positive Chi. It can be used once per melee round and the character can continue to move and fight (one-handed) while the Mudra is in use.

Characters adopting this Mudra can sense the direction of one source of Positive Chi, so the Mudra can be pointed in the correct way. However, if there is more than one source of Positive Chi, the character will only sense the biggest one around.

Meditation Time Required: One melee round.

Duration: Meditation Level.

Description of Hand Positions: Can be performed with either the right or left hand. The tip of the thumb touches the tips of the index and middle fingers, while the ring and pinky fingers are held together, pointing toward the incoming Positive Chi.

Chi Required: Two

Mudra for the Protection from Magic
I Hui Yin

Used to deflect any form of magical attack or effect. Once the Mudra is attained, the character can move and fight, but with only one hand (the other maintains the Mudra position). Useful against Chi Magic, Celestial Calligraphy, and most other forms of magic.

Meditation Time Required: Two melee rounds.

Duration: Meditation Level.

Description of Hand Positions: Can be performed with either the right or left hand. The tip of the thumb is simultaneously pressed against the tips of the middle, ring and little fingers, while the index finger is straight and extended.

Chi Required: Four

Bonuses: +4 to save vs ALL magic.

Mudra for the Reflection of the Dragon's Gaze
Jing Long Yin

This Mudra is used to turn away any form of living Chi, such as that expelled by dragons, demons, characters using Chi Magic, and by certain talented Immortals. This includes living Clouds of Chi, living Beams of Chi, or any attack/touch from an Animus. The living Chi will still engulf the character, but the character will not be actually touched or affected by it.

For example, if engulfed in a Cloud of Obscuring Smoke (see Chi Magic), the character will still be unable to see properly (the Mudra doesn't stop the smoke from gathering around the character). However, if engulfed in a Cloud of Burning Smoke, the character would take no damage and would feel none of the heat or other effects.

Meditation Time Required: Two melee rounds.

Duration: Meditation Level.

Description of Hand Positions: Requires two hands. Hands are placed back to back, fingers spread apart, with the ring fingers interlocked.

Chi Required: Four

Mudra that Quenches Hellfire
Huo Yin

While maintaining this Mudra, the character is immune from *supernatural/magical* flames, fires, burning or sparks, such as those generated by Infernals, or those created by magic. Provides no protection against *normal* fire or heat.

Meditation Time Required: Two melee rounds.

Duration: Meditation Level.

Description of Hand Positions: Requires two hands. The hands are cupped together with the little finger of the right hand held inside, the little finger of the left hand between the little finger and ring finger of the right hand. The thumbs are held together, forming a "lid" over the cup.

Chi Required: Four

Mudra of Subtracting Oneself from the Sight of Others – *Yin Hsing Yin*

This is a sort of invisibility where the passive, quiet nature of the character provides a natural concealment. Of course, the character isn't really invisible and can be seen, heard, smelled, or touched normally, it's just that the character seems less *noticeable*.

No attacks or other fighting moves are possible while maintaining the Mudra. So long as the practitioner sits quietly, without moving, and maintains the Mudra, he/she will be invisible to most others (75% chance of not being noticed). If the character is moving slowly the chance of detection drops to 50%. Normal movement negates all effects.

Another important aspect of this Mudra is that it conceals the Chi of the user, so the character blends in with the natural flow of Chi in the area. This means that the Mudra completely shields a character from detection by means of Chi. For example, entities of Pure Chi who are able to see Chi, will have no chance of detecting the character using this Mudra. It is particularly effective against demons, undead and other creatures of Negative Chi.

Meditation Time Required: Four melee rounds (one minute).
Duration: Half the usual meditation level.
Description of Hand Positions: Requires two hands. The right hand is open, palm down, a thumb's width above the left hand, which is a fist, thumb upward.
Chi Required: Eight

Three Smoke Mudra
San Yan Yin

Designed to protect the mind against any and all attacks. As long as the Mudra is in place, the character has a bonus against any kind of psionic or psychic attack, as well as any kind of direct mind-to-mind combat or communication. Not useful against any kind of physical attacks, and cannot be used while engaged in combat.

Meditation Time Required: Four melee rounds (one minute).

Duration: Meditation Level.

Description of Hand Positions: Requires two hands. Hands are extended outward, palms out, crossed at the wrists, with the left hand outermost, and the two pinky fingers linked.

Chi Required: Six

Bonuses: +4 to save vs psionics or mental attacks.

Five Smoke Mudra
Wu Yan Yin

Works as a kind of mystic "parry" that can be used in an attempt to deflect any type of physical attack. Physical weapons, bullets, punches, and kicks, as well as water or ice attacks can all be deflected. However, it is not useful against fire, electricity, explosives, air or gas attacks.

In use, the character rolls to parry any incoming attack. If successful (rolling greater than that attacker's strike roll), the attack seems to miss and the defender suffers no damage. **Note:** No attacks or other combat moves can be used while invoking the Five Smoke Mudra.

Meditation Time Required: Four melee rounds (one minute).
Duration: Half the usual meditation level.
Description of Hand Positions: Requires two hands. Hands are extended outward, palms out, crossed at the wrist, with the right hand outermost and the two ring fingers linked.
Chi Required: Twelve
Bonuses: +5 to magically parry (no other bonuses allowed, including P.P. bonus).

Eight Smoke Mudra
Ba Yan Yin

Another mystic "parry." For the duration of the Mudra, the character can deflect any and all kinds of energy attacks away from the body. Useful against fire, explosions, bursts of electrical power, lasers or other energy weapons, and even cold-based attacks. Note that the Eight Smoke Mudra does NOT offer protection against physical attacks.

Meditation Time Required: Four melee rounds (one minute).
Duration: One-Quarter of the usual meditation level.
Description of Hand Positions: Requires two hands. Hands are extended outward, palms out, fingers spread, with the tips of the thumbs and middle fingers touching, while the index fingers are crossed (right index finger in toward the body, left index finger away from the body).
Chi Required: Twenty
Bonuses: +5 to parry (no other bonuses allowed, including P.P. bonus).

Mudra of Evocation

Mudra for the Collection of Alms
Qian Yin

A temple Mudra, it is used simply to call attention to oneself, so that those who pass by will find their attention momentarily distracted by the sight of the character's begging bowl. Note that there is nothing that compels anyone to donate, the Mudra is simply an attention-getting device.

Meditation Time Required: Two melee rounds.
Duration: Meditation Level.
Description of Hand Positions: Requires two hands. The two hands are cupped together, palms upward, with the little finger of the right hand crossing the little finger of the left hand,

and the ring fingers touching at the tips. Usually clasping a begging bowl but the cupped hands are sufficient.

Chi Required: Zero.

Range: 20 Feet (6.1 m), plus 5 feet (1.5 m) per level of experience.

Note: Those distracted are -1 on initiative for that first melee.

Mudra for the Evocation of Healing Energy

Huang Yin

Note: Must be performed in an area of Positive Chi. This Mudra is ineffective in any area dominated by Negative Chi.

If performed in an area with Positive Chi, it will automatically cause Positive Chi to wash through the character's body. Negative Chi will be driven out of the body at a rate of one point per minute. Then, when the character is at Zero Chi, the body's normal Positive Chi will be filled, at a rate of one point per minute.

Once the Chi of the body is brought back to its full level, the body's natural healing mechanisms will then be stimulated. Hit points are the first to heal, at about one every five minutes. When hit points are returned to normal, the Mudra will then start to repair any missing S.D.C. at a rate of one per minute.

Meditation Time Required: Four melee rounds (one minute).

Duration: Half Meditation Level.

Description of Hand Positions: Requires two hands. First of all, the character must be in a seated in a meditation position. The hands are positioned so that the right hand is over the chest, palm up, fingers loosely pointing in toward the heart, while the left hand is on the ground, palm down, fingers slightly spread apart.

Chi Required: Four Positive Chi.

Range: Self

Mudra of the fulfilling of the Vow

Shih Yuan Yin

Prevents any creatures of pure Negative Chi, particularly demons, ghosts and any Infernal entities, from touching the character. This does not prevent the affected creatures from launching any sort of ranged attack (throwing objects, firing weapons), nor does it stop them from attacking by Chi or magic means. **Note:** Immortals of evil alignment will likewise feel reluctant to touch the character, but Immortals, unlike demons, can overcome the feeling.

The character, before beginning to meditate on the Mudra, can hold on to another object or character, with their right hand and extend the protection of the Mudra, so both are under its spell.

Meditation Time Required: Four melee rounds (one minute).

Duration: Half meditation time or, if the Mudra is extended to someone or something else, one-quarter of the usual meditation time.

Description of Hand Positions: One hand, the left, is held outward and open, with the palm outward, fingers only slightly bent and pointing downward.

Chi Required: Four Positive Chi.

Range: Self

Mudra for the Evocation of Power

Chi Long Yin

As soon as the Mudra is attained, a *pulse* or *throb* of power will be injected into the target of the Mudra. This is done by channeling the character's Chi through the Mudra which converts it into a healing energy. The effect of the Evocation of Power varies according to the target.

Used on a living thing or an entity of Pure Positive Chi, the Mudra will generate a sudden influx of energy which is enough to pull the creature out of sleep, unconsciousness, or any trance state. It will also inject a single point of Positive Chi.

Against creatures of Pure Negative Chi or Infernals, this Mudra is most painful. While it only destroys 1D6 of Negative Chi, any entity affected will feel as if it had just been hit with a massive electrical shock.

Machines and electronic devices will experience something like a "kick start" when hit with this Mudra. For example, if used on a stalled automobile, the Mudra will cause the engine to turn over at least once. A computer will "reboot" and if a television is working but the reception is bad, the Mudra will "kick" the picture into clarity. Any mystic devices, celestial calligraphy or talisman will be automatically activated by this Mudra. Note that the character using the Mudra has no control over this.

Meditation Time Required: Eight melee rounds (two minutes).

Duration: Instantaneous, although the character can hold off "triggering" the Mudra, once it has been attained, for the full Meditation Time.

Description of Hand Positions: Requires two hands. The hands are pointed away from the body, the fingers spread apart, with the tips of the thumbs touching each other, and the tips of the little fingers touching each other, such that the fingers of the left hand are inward and the fingers of the right hand are outward.

Chi Required: Four

Range: 6 feet (1.8 m), plus 1 foot (0.3 m) per level of experience.

Mudra of Terrible Anger

Chin Kang Yin

This Mudra contacts everyone within range with a direct mind-to-mind communication that the character is filled with some kind of justifiable rage or fury!

Animals react especially strongly. Canines, herd animals (cows, buffalo, deer, etc.), and most small creatures will instantly try to flee. Felines will be less likely to run in panic, but will definitely shy away and will become very cautious about approaching the character. Very intelligent animals (primates, elephants, dolphins, etc.) will be very aware of the anger, but may react in different ways.

Meditation Time Required: One melee round.

Duration: Instantaneous

Description of Hand Positions: Hands formed into tight fists, crossed and touching at the wrists, palms pointing outward.

Chi Required: Four.

Range: 30 feet (9.1 m), plus 3 feet (0.9 m) per level of experience.

Mudra for the Release of Restrained Chi

Kai Chi Yin

This Mudra is used to touch a creature or object which is suspected of containing some form of restrained Chi. It only works on Chi, or Chi entities, that are bound, confined, or otherwise restrained. Once the Mudra touches the object or creature, the Chi within will be free to either escape (if a spirit of some kind) or dissipate if it's just a bunch of loose Chi. Entities of Pure Chi who are deliberately possessing some creature or object can easily resist this Mudra.

Meditation Time Required: Eight melee rounds (two minutes).

Duration: Five minutes for each level of attainment.

Description of Hand Positions: Requires two hands. The hands are held together, palms touching and thumbs up with the left index finger pointing outward. The middle finger of the left hand is folded over the index finger of the right hand. Then the index finger of the right hand is inserted between the middle and index fingers of the left hand, and the middle finger of the right hand is inserted between the ring and little fingers of the left hand. Touching the object or creature with the tip of the left index finger is what releases the bound Chi.

Chi Required: Eight

Range: Touch

Mudra to Prevent Errors of the Six Senses

Liu I Yin

This Mudra allows the user to penetrate illusions, to glimpse entities of Pure Chi, and to see any spirit forms or ghosts. It does not allow the character to see anyone who has been rendered invisible by magical means, or to see those who have the power of invisibility (as in *Heroes Unlimited*).

Meditation Time Required: Four melee rounds (one minute).

Duration: One melee round (15 seconds).

Description of Hand Positions: Can be performed with either the right or left hand. The tip of the thumb is pressed against the middle joint of the middle finger, while the other fingers are extended stiffly away.

Chi Required: Eight

Bonuses: +6 to save vs illusions (magic and psionic).

Range: Self

Mudra of Unification

Hsieh Yin

Used on a body vacant of its spirit, or on someone who is missing some piece of their soul, this Mudra joins together body and spirit, or joins severed pieces of soul. When evoked, the Mudra reaches out to the separated spirit or the lost piece of the soul (either Po or Hun). These disembodied entities will then feel a call back to the body and sense the direction back to the body.

While no spoken communication is possible, the character performing the Mudra will be able to sense whether or not the lost spirit or soul piece is in distress (this is usually the case if it is somehow confined and unable to return).

It also works on *Astral Projection* (see **Beyond the Supernatural** or **Rifts**), even though it is not based on the same Chi principles as other spirit travel methods in *Mystic China*. In the case of astral projection, the Mudra of Unification serves to strengthen or repair the mystic cord and the astral self can easily find its way back to its physical body.

Meditation Time Required: Twelve melee rounds (three minutes).

Duration: Meditation Level.

Description of Hand Positions: Requires two hands. The hands are placed on opposite sides of the head or body of the target. The right hand touches with the tip of the thumb and (separately) with the the tips of the index and middle fingers held together. The left hand touches with tips of the thumb, index finger, and little finger all spread apart into a triangle.

Chi Required: Eight

Range: Touch

Mudra of Communion with Spirits

Shen Su Yin

Establishes a direct, mind-to-mind communication between the character and any spirits, ghosts, creatures of Pure Chi, or any other disembodied entities. The spirits will feel compelled to talk with the user of the Mudra. This is easily resisted, but the spirit will definitely notice the character and will not be able to ignore anything the character has to say.

The Mudra automatically protects the character, so that the communion link can not be used by spirits to attack or possess. The entities can't channel Chi or magical attacks through the Mudra.

Meditation Time Required: Four melee rounds (one full minute).

Duration: Meditation Level.

Description of Hand Positions: Requires two hands. The hands are formed into tight fists and pointed toward each other, so that just the tips of the knuckles of the middle fingers touch.

Chi Required: Sixteen

Range: 60 feet (18.3 m), plus 5 feet (1.5 m) per level of experience.

Mudra for the Communion with the Yama Kings of Hell

Chu Ti Yin

Using this Mudra is said to call to the rulers of the Hells, so that they will bear witness to whatever the character is seeing, saying and hearing. To most Infernals, undead, and evil Immortals, this is a particularly frightening course of action.

Of course, it is extremely rare for any of the Yama Kings of Hell to actually respond to the Mudra. In most cases, they don't even pay attention and simply let their bureaucratic underlings record the proceedings. However, since a permanent Hell record **is** created, Infernals will be extremely cautious about what they say and do while the Mudra is being performed. For example, where Infernals usually feel free to lie and make promises they never intend to keep, anything they say during the Mudra **must** be true.

Aside from forcing Infernals such as demons to speak truthfully and preventing false promises, the Mudra is also useful in either driving them away, stopping attacks, or getting them to behave politely. Mostly this is because the rules and laws of the various Hells are so complex and convoluted. From the point of view of a demon, since there's no way to really tell what actions are *legal* and *illegal*, it's better to do nothing when one's superiors are watching. Always fearful of their masters, demons get very, very nervous during this Mudra and will often spend the entire time talking about how wonderful it is to work for their Demon Overlord. They may also describe in detail their particular mission and how much they've accomplished, while making lengthy excuses for why they're not yet finished (boot-licking, in other words).

To intelligent undead creatures and certain kinds of Immortals, the attention of the Yama Kings is also unwelcome. That's because they're usually avoiding the fate that is in store for their soul or spirit. The last thing they need is to have their exact whereabouts revealed to the forces of Hell. Mindless flight is usually their instant reaction to this Mudra.

Note that the channel to the Yama Kings is a two-way affair. This means no matter how unlikely it may be, it is possible that one of the Kings may appear, Infernal servants may be dispatched to that location, or a gateway to Hell could be created.

It's also dangerous to perform this Mudra around certain Taoist elders and especially around drunken Taoist Immortals. Given the strange moods of these oddball eccentrics, it's entirely possible that they'll take the opportunity to bring up old arguments with the Yama Kings and then to start delivering insults and obscenities. Being a witness to the humiliation of a Yama King is not a good thing for mere mortals.

Meditation Time Required: Two melee rounds.
Duration: One-quarter usual meditation level/time.
Description of Hand Positions: Requires two hands. To be performed while seated, cross-legged on the ground. The right hand flat on the ground, palm downward, while the left hand is held in the lap, palm upward.
Chi Required: Twenty
Range: Varies

Mudra for the Manipulation of Objects

Mudra for the Handling of Jade or Jewels

Ju I Chu Yin

The character forms the Mudra while holding a piece of jade, a jewel of some kind, or a small piece of valuable jewelry (gold or silver is okay). This serves to illuminate the object, so that it becomes clearly visible in the spirit world and can be seen by ghosts, entities of Pure Chi, or other disembodied creatures.

Since many spirit entities and creatures of Pure Chi are unable to properly see objects in the material world, this Mudra allows the character to "illuminate" an object of value. Then it becomes possible for an object to be used as a bargaining chip with greedy or possessive creatures. Note that if the object is a cheap replica or a fake, this Mudra does nothing to disguise its value. While the Mudra works to highlight the value of an object, it will also clearly reveal a piece of junk for what it is.

Meditation Time Required: One melee round.
Duration: Meditation Level.
Description of Hand Positions: Requires two hands. The object balanced on the tips of the thumb, index, middle and ring fingers of the left hand (the digits should form a square), with the little finger touching the palm. The right hand is formed into a fist, with only the little finger extended to touch the top of the object.
Chi Required: Two

Mudra for the Handling of Mystic Mirrors

Ching Yin

Performing this Mudra allows the character to see whatever would normally be revealed in the glass of a mystic mirror without having to gaze into the mirror. It also allows the character to continue moving or fighting.

The Mudra does not interfere with any other power the mirror might possess, such as that of repelling entities or capturing demons.

Meditation Time Required: Two melee rounds.
Duration: Meditation Level.
Description of Hand Positions: The Mystic Mirror can be grasped in either the right or left hand, with the back of the mirror touching the palm of the hand. All five digits are spread apart and grip the edge of the mirror. Once the Mystic Mirror is grasped, the hand is brought up and into the center of the chest with the reflective surface facing outward.
Chi Required: Two

Mudra for the Handling of a Reliquary

Shuai Tu Po Yin

Where the other Mudra for the Manipulation of Objects is used to activate objects, this Mudra is specifically designed **not** to trigger or activate the object being touched.

When this Mudra is used to handle actual Reliquaries, containers used for the storage of either mystic artifacts or remains (either the polished bones or remaining ashes of someone who has died), then no saving throw is required. However, if the Mudra is being used to handle any other sort of object, the character will need to roll under the meditation skill to avoid activating the item.

Meditation Time Required: Eight melee rounds (two full minutes).

Duration: Meditation Level.

Description of Hand Positions: Requires two hands. The left hand grasps the object, thump pointing straight up, the index and middle fingers grasping but apart, and the ring and little fingers held together and extended outward. Then, when the object is fully held by the left hand, the right hand, flat palm up, with fingers together but thumb extended, slides under the object, providing most of the support.

Chi Required: Two

Mudra for the Handling of Mystic Vajra

Chin Kang Chu Yin

Allows the character to activate a mystic Vajra. Once the Vajra is turned on, the use of this Mudra lets the character direct and control its powers.

Meditation Time Required: One melee round.

Duration: Meditation Level.

Description of Hand Positions: The Vajra is held in the palm, with the fingers wrapped around the handle, but the position of the fingers is varied according to the number of "tines" or points on each end of the Vajra.

Chi Required: Four

Mudra for the Handling of Weapons of Power

Chien Yin

The only Mudra designed for use in a combat situation, it is used for activating or manipulating a special class of weapons. Characters performing this Mudra are capable of taking **defensive** actions, using their usual bonuses to parry & dodge. However, the character can perform no attacks. It is only the weapon that is aggressive. The bonuses, number of attacks per melee round, and damage are all dependent on the activated weapon — the character's usual bonuses are not to be included in any attacks.

Meditation Time Required: Weapon dependent.

Duration: Meditation Level.

Description of Hand Positions: If the weapon or the weapon's handle is small enough, the right hand should be above the left, with both hands grasping the weapon. The pinky finger of the right hand should be inserted between the index and middle fingers of the left hand, while the index finger of the left hand should be sandwiched between the ring and pinky fingers of the right hand. The knuckle of the right thumb should be aligned just above the tip of the left thumb. If the weapon is too large for this grip, then the hands should be positioned in the same way, but separately, so there is a gap between the ring and pinky fingers of the right hand, and a gap between the index and middle fingers of the left hand.

Chi Required: Six

Bonuses: Dependent on the Weapon

Immortals (Hsien)

Throughout the world of Mystic China there are many who have transcended the limits of mere mortal existence. Some, having achieved a measure of true enlightenment, are on their way to becoming fully realized beings — gods, if you will — who are destined for greatness. You'll find a complete description of the **Enlightened Immortals,** with details on the incredible powers they gain as they undergo their nine refinements of Internal Alchemy, at the end of this chapter. First, let's look at the results of those who seek immortality along a darker path. These "lost" Immortals are the vast majority who attempt perfection, some of which are evil and depraved, while others simply are misguided, often becoming the true villains of the world of *Mystic China*.

G.M. Note: The Stats for Immortals

To make matters easier for the Game Master, each of the "false pathways" to immortality is described with the following:

Typical Alignment: From this the Game Master can determine how best to use the Immortal in a campaign.

Typical Age: This is designed to let the Game Master roll up the Immortal's age; of course the Game Master can modify the result as is appropriate for the character and setting. Note that determining age usually involves rolling a number of dice, *then* multiplying the result and, *lastly*, adding the result of a roll on percentile dice. In general, the older the Immortal, the more awesome the level of power, and the more pervading his influence.

Temptation of Pathway: The usual reason or method used to get on this false pathway of Immortality.

Powers of Immortality: Note that not all the Immortals will necessarily have gained each of the powers described. It is up to the Game Master to decide just how powerful the character may have become. Also note that the powers listed in this section are not the only abilities the Immortal may have acquired. Elder Immortals have had hundreds, or even thousands, of years to pursue studies in magic (spell casting, geomancy, calligraphy, and others), mystic lore, and/or have acquired magic items and other *things* of power, not to mention gaining facility in a wide range of skills and combat abilities.

Weaknesses/Vulnerability: Each type of Lost Immortal should have some kind of defect or flaw which can be exploited by the player characters and enemies. Cryptic sayings from Enlightened Immortals, ancient legends, or the results of some kind of divination can be provided to the player characters as valuable clues to the weak points of their foes.

Note: Immortals are not intended as player characters, but as supernatural villains.

The Common Fear of all Lost Immortals

In the Chinese view of the afterlife, there is a rigid system of appointments and schedules. It is expected that the souls of mortals are to appear for their reckoning at the appointed time. The Lords of Hell (either the Yama Kings, or the darker forces that control the earlier realms of the dead) are displeased when these engagements are ignored. Thus, the Immortals fear these beings, for when they finally die, the Lords of Hell shall extract a terrible vengeance!

Those who attain an enlightened version of Immortality usually do so with the approval of the Heavenly Court of the Jade Emperor, which will politely send to the lords of the dead a *notice of cancellation*, long before one is due to appear.

For most Immortals who take *false* pathways, the longer they put off appearing in their designated afterlife, the more severe their punishment is likely to be. This is especially true for the Yama Kings, who will certainly exact revenge for every second that they have been kept waiting, but it's even worse for Immortals who were appointed to die over 2,000 years ago.

Before the Yama Kings were appointed to their posts, there was an earlier Hell, *Tai Yin* or "The Citadel of Night," where the *San Kuan*, or "Three Officials of the Damned," ruled (there are also mentions in ancient books of even more ancient Hells). It is only because of certain Immortals, whose names are still on the original calendars, that the elder lords of the dead have been kept from their retirement. It is something of an understatement to say that these ancient gods are displeased.

Therefore, bear in mind that no matter how terrible the power of any dark, Lost Immortal, there is an even more terrible fate waiting for them.

False Paths to Immortality

Here is a complete list of the *types* of Immortals, arranged by their appearance in this chapter.

- Yin Immortals (misguided)
- Immortals of Sleep (misguided)
- Undead or Living-Dead Immortals (usually evil)
- Alchemical Immortals (accidental, misguided or evil)
- Possessed Immortals (misguided or evil)
- Heartless Immortals (usually evil)
- Damned Immortals (usually evil)
- Ginseng Immortals (always evil)
- Companion Immortals (usually accidental)
- Enlightened Immortals (enlightened)

Yin Immortals

Immortality by the Excessive Conservation of Yin and Excessive Expenditure of Yang

If any pathway to Immortality *seems* enlightened and blessed by the gods, it is certainly that of the Yin Immortals. Although talent helps, virtually anyone with a sufficient dedication to the arts of Chi Mastery and Meditation can find incredible life-extension in this manner. However, trapped by their own skills and powers, such immortals end up spending vast amounts of their time gathering Chi, storing their residual Yin (Negative Chi) in the body, while needing to expend ever greater quantities of Yang (Positive Chi) in the maintenance of their aging bodies.

Ultimately, the Yin Immortals are on a nonstop treadmill. Stepping off, abandoning their rigorous meditation and Chi collection, for even twenty-four hours, can be fatal!

Often these Immortals seem holy or exalted, their good intentions obvious for all to see. They can be respected martial art teachers, Taoists, Blind Mystics, Hermits, or even Buddhist

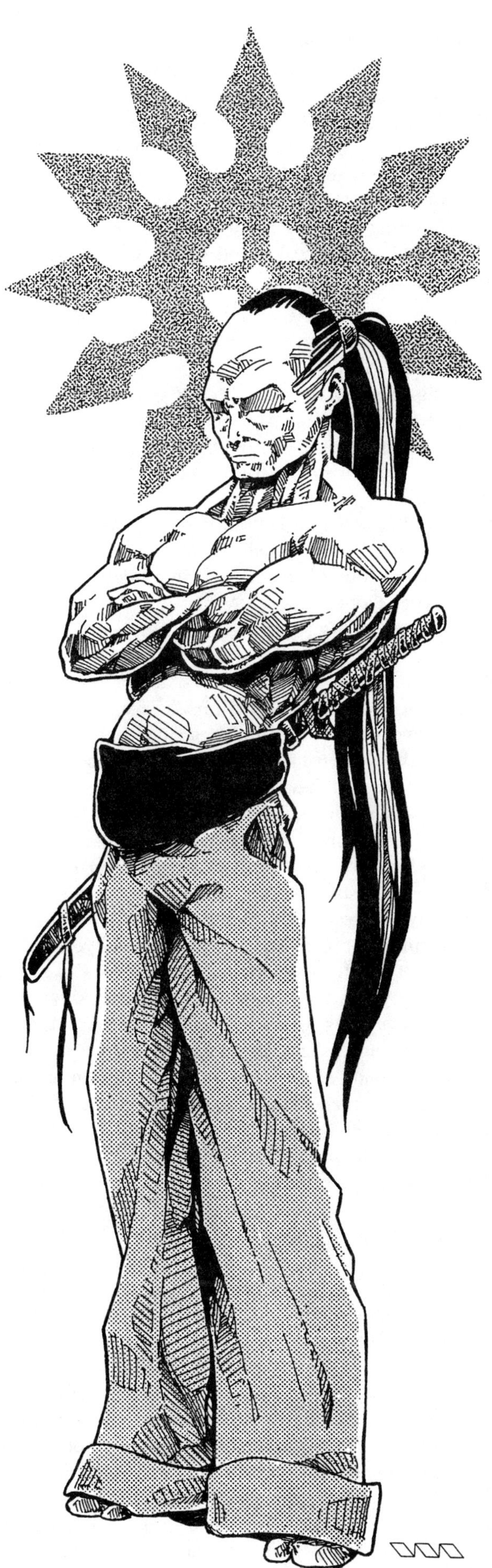

Monks. However, they have taken the wrong road on the way to Immortality, and it is extremely unlikely that they will last more than four or five hundred years.

Unfortunately for many young aspirants, Immortals who have discovered this particular false pathway are usually eager to pass their knowledge on to others. For the first couple of hundred years, they are enthusiastic about their new-found powers and see no reason why they shouldn't 'enlighten' others.

When the Yin Immortals finally discover that their "Immortality" is a false one, they usually take one of the following three courses of action.

One, most just retreat, bitter, and hope that there may be some plateau or level of stability. They never stop their meditation and fight death to the bitter end.

Two, a few Yin Immortals turn bad and, desperate in an attempt to cling to life, try whatever other pathways to Immortality they can find! Most are willing to become as evil as necessary in order to live forever.

Three, and rarest of all, are those who are genuine in their belief that enlightenment will inform their students of the wrongness of their pathway and then cease gathering Chi, allowing themselves to die and meet their fate in the afterlife.

Yin Immortals

Typical Alignment: Usually principled, unprincipled or aberrant.

Typical Age: From 101 to 500 years old (1D4×100, plus the roll of percentile dice).

Temptation of Pathway: Just the attractive notion, however false, of never having to die.

Powers of Immortality: While the Yin Immortals have limited special powers. Other than being able to *store* both Positive Chi and Negative Chi simultaneously and accumulate relatively large amounts of both, they usually have all the various *Chi Mastery abilities*, including those of Negative Chi. From the age of one hundred, they'll usually be charged with 201 to 300 points of Positive Chi (a percentile roll +200 points), and at least 51 to 150 points of Negative Chi (roll percentile dice and add 50 points), at any time. Because of the time they've had for learning and study, just about any powers and skills are possible.

Weaknesses/Vulnerability: The character is doomed unless the Positive and Negative Chi of the body is maintained.

The amount of time that the character requires to maintain their Immortality lengthens with each passing century. After 100 years they'll need to meditate at least three hours per day. Between 200 and 300, five hours per day. Between 300 and 400, eight hours per day. From the ages of 400 to 500, no less than twelve hours per day must be devoted to non-stop internal focus. Then, after reaching their 500th year, the Immortal must spend nearly all the hours of the day on mediation (12 +2D4 hours), and can only spend an hour or two per day on other pursuits, such as eating, napping, talking, and so on.

Most Yin Immortals also have a "Yin Lump" somewhere on their body; usually on the stomach, right above the navel. This lump starts out the size of a grape, but gets larger and larger with each passing decade. A very old Yin Immortal could have a basketball-sized lump! It is the container for the body's Negative Chi. Doing at least three points of damage to the Yin Lump disrupts the Yin Immortal's control over Negative Chi for up to 1D6 hours. Inflicting a full dozen points of damage to the Yin Lump opens it up inside the Immortal causing Negative Chi to flood the body, and preventing the character from using ANY kind of Chi Mastery for 2D6 hours.

Immortals of Sleep

Immortality as gained by the Mastery of the Art of Sleeping

You could call it the really lazy pathway to Immortality!

Sleep, according to certain Taoist Sages, is one of the most important tools for strengthening body, mind and spirit. Acknowledging this, the Immortals of Sleep have dedicated themselves to perfecting the ultimate "Art of Sleep."

First, they practice diligently, sleeping whenever possible, steadily increasing the depth of their slumber, and gradually lengthening their sleeping hours. Eventually, each Immortal of Sleep accomplishes the true sign of mastery, "The Profound Sleep," where they sleep for a minimum of fifty years without aging. In the course of the first Profound Sleep they also gain control over their sleeping minds, learning how to use dreams as a learning tool.

The Sleepers are often the most ancient of the Immortals but also have the most difficulty fitting in to society. This is because they only awaken for a few days, or weeks, between their great periods of sleep. Thus, they never really learn to fit in. Perpetual outcasts that are out of step with the times, they can appear to be extremely ignorant and often spend all of their waking time pretending to be homeless beggars or drunks.

By the way, although most consider this to be a false pathway to Immortality (because it is not enlightened), that may not be entirely true. The Immortals of Sleep do no real damage to themselves and cause no particular harm to others. Nor is there anything inherently evil about their peculiar habits. In fact, there are those who argue that the Immortals of Sleep are simply biding their time, waiting for some event in the distant future where all the sleepers will finally wake, and where their services against the forces of armageddon will ultimately prove to bring them into the fold of the Supreme Heaven of the Jade Emperor. Whether or not this is true remains a mystery.

Immortals of Sleep

Typical Alignment: Any, although selfish (anarchist or unprincipled) are most likely. Any character, regardless of alignment, could have the streak of lethargy required.

Typical Age: From 301 to 3,100 years old (3D10×100, plus percentile roll).

Temptation of Pathway: Many Immortals of Sleep are brilliant or very talented, but incredibly lazy. This pathway offers them a combination of an easy way into Immortality, plus the chance to get a lot of rest.

Powers of Immortality: Although it is rumored that the really ancient Immortals of Sleep control divine powers, the younger ones (those of less than two dozen centuries) generally have only the powers of Chi Mastery, Accumulate Chi and the Power of the Dreaming (described below).

Immortals who have slept through two Profound Sleeps (at least 100 years), will have attained mastery over ALL the Chi Mastery abilities, including both Positive and Negative Chi. After this point, Immortals of Sleep will usually alternate their places of sleep, first choosing a place of Positive Chi, and then, after a short waking period, seeking out some dark and gloomy (but restful) place of Negative Chi.

Special: Accumulate Chi. During the first few years of sleep, the Immortal gathers an additional 10 points of Chi each year. After twenty years, the rate of Chi acquisition slows and the Immortal only gains another 20 points for each decade (10 years) of continued sleep. Of course, over time that can be a monstrous amount, so an Immortal awaking from a 100 year nap, will be charged with an extra 360 points of Chi. The kind of Chi gained, Positive or Negative, matches the Immortal's state when falling asleep.

The Power of the Dreaming. Immortals of Sleep use their dreams as whole worlds of play, learning and experience. In their Profound Sleeps they live out entire lifetimes. Sometimes they experiment with Chi Mastery in these dream worlds of fantasy and adventure. Sometimes they have themselves being born into an imaginary family, growing up, marrying an imaginary spouse, having imaginary children and, after an imaginary death, watch the lives of their imaginary descendants as an imaginary ghost. The Power of the Dreaming also allows the character to see something of the "Waking World" (as they would call it). This is done not by leaving their bodies (their spirits never leave), but by somehow inviting the fragments of the dreams of others into their own dreams. However, this experience and knowledge of the Waking World is very limited. Psychic sensitives and mystics are the most likely candidates for dream fragments.

Weaknesses/Vulnerability: The biggest danger that an Immortal of Sleep faces is that they'll be accidentally buried or otherwise harmed during their lengthy slumber. Also, once an Immortal of Sleep has accomplished a "profound sleep," ordinary sleeping becomes impossible, so that any time they fall asleep they'll be likely to stay asleep for decades. Of course, the Sleeping Immortal's lack of awareness about the world around him, and the fact that he/she is awake only a short period every 50 years or so, may also be seen as a weakness.

Furthermore, it takes a great deal to rouse the character from a profound sleep that has lasted less than 40 years. Even telepathic or empathic communication is not likely to rouse the sleeper, but may enable the psychic to contact the Immortal's "dream" self and get advice or information. However, such contact will draw the character into the Immortal's imaginary dream world/life, and he may become embroiled as a character (friend or foe) in that imaginary place rather than waking up the Immortal, or getting useful information (the dream world will seem very real and the psychic could suffer mental or emotional trauma from adventures there).

Otherwise, they have no particular weaknesses.

Undead or Living-Dead Immortals

Immortality by Self-Mortification of the Flesh (Negative Chi)

The most common way of becoming a Living-Dead Immortal is by getting hooked on Negative Chi. When the body remains continuously charged with Negative Chi, it's not very healthy and some flesh eventually starts dying. Trapped into a cycle where there is less and less living flesh on the body, the Living-Dead Immortal turns to using even more Negative Chi as a means of strength and support. Eventually, nothing is left but a shriveled corpse supported by endless quantities of Negative Chi.

A more macabre way of becoming an Undead Immortal can come about accidentally. This can happen to powerful Negative Chi Masters who have the power to leave their bodies in spirit (Chi) form. If the character's spirit returns and finds the body has died during its absence, it's possible for the spirit to re-enter the body and re-animate it using the same techniques as those of the Living-Dead Immortals. However, although animated, and decomposition is slowed, the body is still *dead.* The spirit remains linked to the body through sheer force of will (and chi energy).

In addition, a character with powerful Negative Chi who becomes the victim of poison, a deadly spell, or some other slow-working, unavoidable means of death, may choose to go the route of the Undead Immortal.

The big problem with being an Undead Immortal is the character's permanent dependence on continual (and ever-increasing) supplies of Negative Chi.

Even though the constant assistance of Negative Chi keeps an Undead Immortal from expiring, the body tends to wither and dry out. If this process continues for too long, say, as long as five years, then the digestive system of the body will reach a point of no return, and the character will never be able to eat again. The problem is, what to eat? Unlike the so-called "vampires" of the west, Undead Immortals do not drink the blood of the living. Instead, they must consume flesh that is both easy to digest and rich in Negative Chi. While it's possible for an Immortal Undead to eat the raw flesh of other creatures, their system finds it very unpleasant (it tastes terrible!), and they can only handle tiny amounts (two or three bites per hour).

To really satisfy an Immortal Undead's need for food, human flesh is required. The closer the meat is to the Immortal Undead's own flesh, the easier it is to digest. So, for example, the meat of a chimpanzee would be more desirable than the meat from a cow. And, while human meat is satisfying to the Immortal Undead, the meat from a close "blood" relative is even better.

Under normal circumstances, very little food is needed; perhaps a pound (0.45 kg) per month. The bodies of those who have died of natural causes, or even the flesh of animals, will do quite nicely. However, if an Immortal Undead has been seriously wounded, or seriously depleted of Negative Chi (reaching zero or Positive Chi during combat), then a more substantial meal is required. In that case, the Immortal Undead will need the meat of an entire healthy corpse, such as the body of a young accident or murder victim, of the same gender as the Immortal.

Note that no Immortal Undead will immediately consume the flesh of a victim. The body should be buried underground, or stored in a place of constant Negative Chi for two to four days. Less than two days, and the flesh won't yet be filled with Negative Chi. More than four days, and the flesh starts to molder and loses the nutrients needed by the Immortal.

Typical Alignment: Usually evil; aberrant, miscreant or diabolic.

Typical Age: From 101 to 1,100 years old (1D10×100, plus percentile roll).

Temptation of Pathway: Very few choose to become Immortal this way. It usually comes about by accident or by the death of the character's body, and an unwillingness to accept the death.

Powers of Immortality: Eventually, as an Undead Immortal gains ever more experience with their new condition, they may discover any number of the following powers. However, there is no guarantee of the Undead Immortal discovering any particular abilities. There is no "Manual of the Undead," so each character may have a different set of powers (unless, of course, they encounter an even older Undead Immortal who deigns to teach his secrets; a rarity). Typically an Undead Immortal will have one to four (1D4) of the following:

1. Appear as Dead. No great trick here. Since an Undead Immortal really is dead, all that's necessary is to stop moving around, and stop breathing for awhile, and the result is a very convincing corpse.

2. Negative Chi Sensitivity. The senses of an Undead Immortal become quickly attuned to the flow of Negative Chi. In an area with Negative Chi, no matter how slight, the character can effectively "see" in total darkness, or through the shroud of a cloud or smoke (although being engulfed in a cloud of Living Chi, either from a spell caster, or a dragon, will blind the Chi senses). While tuned in to Negative Chi, the character can sense every movement of any nearby living creature (whether charged with Negative Chi, Positive Chi, or uncharged) — even those approaching from behind. If the Undead Immortal takes a mo-

ment (one melee round) to quietly sense the flow of Negative Chi, the movement of any Positive Chi-charged entity in the region of Negative Chi can be detected, even those who are miles away (provided the area of Negative Chi extends for miles). In an area of Positive Chi or no Chi, the Undead Immortal loses all of his special sensitivity and is dependent on the ordinary senses of the human body.

3. Negative Chi Mastery. The character gains complete control over Negative Chi, including the skills of Hardened Chi, Soft Chi, Find Weakness, Chi Overcharge, Fill with Chi, Chi Barrier, One Finger Chi, Fist Gesture, Dark Chi, Control Negative Chi, Negative Chi Polarity, and Chu Chi. With Negative Chi an Undead Immortal has one extra attack per melee round, is +2 to strike, and +4 to damage; these bonuses do not apply to physical combat, only Chi combat.

4. Dissolve to Pure Negative Chi. Once per day, the character can turn into a creature of Pure Negative Chi. The transformation lasts for 2D6 minutes. This means the body completely dissolves, leaving nothing behind! While in the Negative Chi state, the character can recover any lost Negative Chi, but only if in a Negative Chi environment. While in a state of Pure Negative Chi, the Undead Immortal is vulnerable *only* to Chi, magic and psionic attacks, and will be impervious to any physical or energy based attacks. The character can rematerialize in one melee round, but will be helpless against any attacks during that time.

If the Immortal Undead enters a Positive Chi area while in a state of Pure Negative Chi, the normal flow of Positive Chi will automatically *Chi Attack* the Undead Immortal. For example, if the environment is filled with 5 points of Positive Chi, then it will be the equivalent of an attack of *15D6 per melee round* against the character's Negative Chi. If, while in a Pure Negative Chi form, the character's Chi reaches zero, or a state of Positive Chi, then the character dies, and the bodiless soul will be released from its body.

5. Animate & Control Dead. By touching any corpse, human or animal, an Undead Immortal can attempt to fill it with Negative Chi and thereby animate it! If the corpse is fairly fresh and the brain is undamaged, it can be commanded to behave intelligently (or at least as intelligent as it was when it was alive); up to one body per level of experience can be commanded. Other corpses, with brain damage or badly decayed (one week in the heat will rot the brain, but it can keep for weeks if in a refrigerator or in snow), must be constantly controlled by the Immortal and only one such mindless being can be handled at a time. Any corpse animated by an Undead Immortal will be subject to any commands delivered with Negative Chi.

6. Control Other Undead Immortals: Some Undead Immortals can use the power to control the dead on each other (and traditional vampires and other undead beings). If this happens, it becomes a contest of wills where the elder, or the more recently fed, may have the advantage. Such battles of will are determined by each combatant rolling a sort of mental parry or dodge — the high roll wins. The recently fed are +1 and the elder is +2 (cumulative bonuses). Ties mean no effect; try again in a minute. This can be attempted once per minute (every four melee rounds). An Undead Immortal who falls under the control of another must obey his master, but a rematch of wills can be forced every two minutes (once every 20 minutes for undead who are not Immortals). This rematch will serve to break the hold of the original winner and a minute later, one or both can try to control the other again.

Note: When Undead Immortals are on the verge of defeat, they'll usually resort to using Negative Chi Mastery abilities, or direct physical combat, or both, to save themselves. Once one Undead Immortal has successfully controlled another, the mastery becomes permanent, and the loser turns into a slave, devoid of any freedom of will. All animated corpses and undead servants are subject to eventual decay and are usually vulnerable to the same things as an Undead Immortal.

Weaknesses/Vulnerability: The usual Western European means of dealing with undead, such as the sign of the cross, silver bullets, herbs like garlic and wolfsbane, and wooden stakes, are of no use when dealing with the undead of Mystic China. However, Undead Immortals definitely have their share of weaknesses, as seen by the following:

1. Positive Chi. Any area with a flow of Positive Chi works like a continual drain on the Negative Chi of the Undead Immortal. If unprotected (by, say, Divert Incoming Chi), a number of points of Negative Chi are lost every melee round equal to the flow of Positive Chi. This can be devastating!

2. Sunlight. A corroding influence on the undead, sunlight causes their flesh to burn. Superficial burns inflicted by morning or late afternoon sun does 1D6 damage for every ten minutes of exposure. The glare of noon time sun does 2D6 S.D.C. damage for every ten minutes of exposure. Of course, where there is sunlight there is usually Positive Chi, which means the Undead Immortal's Negative Chi is also being destroyed.

3. Water. While water itself does nothing to harm the Undead Immortal, being immersed in water that flows with Positive Chi is potentially fatal. If an Undead Immortal ends up in a stream, river, waterfall, ocean or lake where there is a powerful flow of Positive Chi, each melee round all the Positive Chi will turn into a *Chi Attack*, inflicting 3D6 points of damage for each point of Positive Chi flow. Chi damage is done directly to the Immortal's Negative Chi. No defense is possible and the Undead Immortal's only chance is to get out of the water before all the Negative Chi is gone.

Note that some waters, like stagnant pools, frightening looking swamps, sewers and certain underground currents, are filled with Negative Chi. In these waters an Undead Immortal can take a refreshing bath.

4. Decay. Every Undead Immortal must constantly battle the effects of their own decaying flesh. Each time an Immortal Undead slips up on their maintenance program (in other words, they go a year without eating properly), they'll slip down to another stage of decay. Likewise, each time an Undead Immortal takes serious hit point damage in combat, it can be disfiguring and inflicts another stage of decay (after all, the flesh does not heal). See the following table for full details regarding decay.

The Stages of Decay:

Perfection in Body. The body is perfect, indistinguishable from a living person, even to the point of being unaffected by the presence of Positive Chi. If properly maintained, with either daily meals of animal meat or weekly meals of human flesh, the Undead Immortal can stay this way forever. However, this is an extremely rare state since, once lost, it can NEVER be regained! As most Undead Immortals don't realize the peril of decay, at least not in the first few months of their new existence, there are very few who have maintained perfection.

Undead. Somewhat thinner than usual, with a very pale complexion. Otherwise, the Immortal will maintain the appearance he/she had when last alive, indefinitely (if they were plump before, they'll just be a little less plump now). If there are no wanderings out of a Negative Chi environment and the character feeds regularly, the body can sustain itself just from the background flow. Most Undead Immortals (80%) will first be encountered in this state.

Sparse. All the fat of the body is lost. Eyes and cheeks are sunken, limbs thin and bony. The Immortal Undead must channel 1D4 points of Negative Chi into the body every day.

Gaunt. If there is any color left in the hair, it turns totally white at this stage. The body looks like a skeleton covered in wasting muscles and pale flesh. The Immortal Undead must spend 2D4 points of Negative Chi on maintaining the body every day or it will degenerate down to the next stage.

Shriveled. All the hairs of the body turn a nearly-transparent white and half falls out. The body looks like a skeleton covered in pale, shriveled (mummy-like) skin. It is possible, with constant care and attention, that the Immortal could return the body's state to that of *gaunt*, but it will take 2D6 years of effort and regular feeding. The Immortal Undead must channel two points of Negative Chi into the body every day.

Emaciated. This is the point of no return because the Undead Immortal has lost the use of the digestive organs; there is no way to eat and no way to replenish the body. From this point on, any disruption to the character's system will cause another level of decay. Each day the Undead must spend two to four hours gathering the necessary quantities of Negative Chi.

Since the Undead Immortal has no way of knowing for sure that he's reached this stage, he'll often try to eat anyway. This is useless and unpleasant (nothing, not even the strongest spices, can cover up the revulsion and unpleasant taste of any food or drink). It may take him days or weeks to figure out the inevitability of his new condition. No matter what other precautions may be taken, within ten years the character will fall to the next stage of decomposition, *decayed*. If it happens that some attacker or intruder was responsible for the latest stage of decay, the rage and thirst for revenge will be nothing short of awesome!

Decayed. No spare flesh remains, just thin gristle. All the body's hair has fallen out and the skin color will turn a sickly greenish white. Since the internal organs are in a constant state of degeneration, the Undead Immortal emits a putrid stench, disgusting even to itself! Six to eight hours of every day must be spent in a place of powerful Negative Chi, supplying the body's ever-increasing need for artificial support. Again, there is nothing that can be done to prevent further decay. Within a decade the monster will become *Skeletal*.

Skeletal. Hollow and haggard, the Undead Immortal's body is dried up, and covered with a thin layer of brown leathery skin with patches of bone showing through here and there. Dried out, the smell is no longer a problem. Sometimes, because the taste buds have been destroyed, the Undead Immortal will start eating once again, but to no avail. They are incapable of digestion and no amount of food can restore them. The Undead Immortal must spend all but an hour of every day filling the body with Negative Chi.

Wasted. With all the bodily organs gone, including the brain, the head, and the eyes (the last four to go), the Undead Immortal's requirement for Negative Chi becomes enormous. Any attempt to venture into a place of Positive Chi is likely to be instantly fatal. Blind, deaf, and with none of the natural senses remaining, this pathetic remnant is totally dependent on its *sensation* of Negative Chi — can sense (and sort of "see" and feel the presence of) other characters, beings, objects and events occurring within the area covered by Negative Chi; otherwise -4 to strike, parry, and dodge.

Alchemical Immortal

Immortality from Ingesting a Formula of External Alchemy

One would think that most Alchemical Immortals started out as Alchemists, but this is totally wrong.

Alchemists are the wild-eyed geniuses who *make* alchemical elixirs of immortality. They are, however, rarely crazy enough to actually drink their own (highly toxic) potions. So most Alchemical Immortals are the result of a successful experimental elixir. One-out-of-a-thousand test subjects are fools who didn't die and the elixir of immortality actually worked. **Note:** For a lot more information on alchemy and Elixirs of Immortality, check out the chapter entitled, *Chinese Alchemy*.

Typical Alignment: Principled, unprincipled, miscreant or aberrant.

Typical Age: From 501 to 3,100 years old (5D6×100, plus the roll of percentile dice).

Powers of Immortality: Immunity to most poisons, drugs, illnesses, deprivations, fatigue and physical hardships. They have immense amounts of hit points and S.D.C. (P.E. attribute number x10, plus 6D6+36 S.D.C.). Furthermore, their P.E. is usually over 24 (roll 1D6+24). Otherwise Alchemical Immortals simply use their great age to learn skills, lore, magic, and other abilities.

Weaknesses/Vulnerability: Most have no particular weaknesses. Those who were originally alchemists or alchemist's assistants are likely to have continued their study of alchemy (and perhaps chemistry) and continued trying different elixirs. Many will become dependent on certain kinds of poisonous chemicals (mercury, lead, etc.), drugs or elixirs of ever-increasing potency. By the age of two hundred, these characters will be constantly consuming incredible amounts of deadly toxins. If deprived of them for more than a few days, the character may become weak or exhibit signs of withdrawal.

Temptation of Pathway: On the one hand, External Alchemy is probably the most difficult pathway to life extension. On the other, it's the only pathway to immortality where most find their way accidentally. Here are some of the people most likely to end up as an Alchemical Immortal (in case the Game Master wants to roll up an Alchemical Immortal, roll percentile for the number in parentheses):

Alchemist (01-02). Very, very few Alchemical Immortals are alchemists because the likelihood of coming up with a success-

ful and safe elixir, in the exact proportion for a particular individual, is remote. Of all the thousands of alchemists who have foolishly consumed their own experiments, only one or two succeed. Once an alchemist, always an alchemist, so it's likely that they'll still be working on discovering ever more powerful and exotic elixirs.

Alchemist's Apprentice (03-05). It's slightly more likely that an alchemist's apprentice might become immortal. Mostly because an alchemist might go through several dozen apprentices in the course of his career. The apprentice alchemist who becomes Immortal is very dangerous, since he/she knows something of the craft, but lacks the genius and discipline of their masters.

Alchemist's Sponsor/Employer (06-10). Since Alchemists need money (usually lots and lots of money), they often find themselves "employed" by powerful merchants, warlords, or the like. From the point of view of the sponsor, "I'll support you, protect you, get you the raw materials, equipment and experimental subjects that you require. In return, you will make me the beneficiary of your secret knowledge." This type of Alchemical Immortal is the most dangerous, since they started out rich, powerful, and with ruthless desires. Over the years they'll tend to get even richer, much more powerful, and even more brutal.

Alchemist's Relative/Servant (11-25). Those who live in the same household as an Alchemist run the risk of becoming an accidental Immortal.

Alchemist's Experimental Subject (26-65). For every few hundred experiments, there's always the possibility of success. In this case, the Immortal is some hapless soul from the bottom of society, desperate for money, a refugee, or some condemned prisoner.

A Foolish Adventurer (66-85). Some people will try anything, especially if it promises immortality, power or love. This type of character may have obtained, or been enticed to try, a potion that made such a promise. The result: an Alchemical Immortal!

Alchemist's Cadaver (86-95). Alchemists will often first try out a formula, especially those with the most dangerous ingredients, on a dead body. Or, there are alchemists who deliberately set out to animate the dead, or are keen on the subject of resurrection. In any case, the technique for bringing a body back to life may create Immortality as a side effect.

Accidental Ingestion (96-100). An Alchemist dies, a bottle gets mislabeled, or gets tossed in the garbage heap accidentally, where just about anybody can pick it up and drink it. Of course, for every Immortal that a random potion creates, there are dozens who just get sick, die, or worse.

Possessed Immortal

Immortality as Possession by Immortal Spirit

There are disembodied entities who, having lost their natural bodies, confer Immortality in exchange for a permanent position in a host body. Those who provide host duties become Possessed Immortals and gain a measure of the entity's powers along with the other benefits of eternal life, youth, and vitality.

Almost without exception, possessive entities are evil. Originally they were powerful monsters, corrupt dabblers in Negative Chi Mastery, or in forbidden forms of Chi magic.

The hosts who become Possessed Immortals usually fall into two categories. Those who are too stupid to figure out what has happened to them and those who figure it out, but who are evil or selfish enough to continue to play along with the Possessing Entities.

Typical Alignment: Usually unprincipled or anarchist, but could be of any alignment.

Typical Age: From 101 to 700 years old (1D6×100, plus a roll of percentile dice).

Temptation of Pathway: Those Possessed Immortals who deliberately enter into their state are usually tempted by the entity's promises of immortality and unlimited power.

However, most Possessed Immortals were simply dupes who thought they were grabbing a free drink or stealing a loose valuable.

Powers of Immortality: Exactly what powers the Possessed Immortal controls will depend on (1) how powerful the possessing entity is, and (2) how much power the Entity is willing to share. For example, entities often have powers similar to those of advanced Wu Shih, dragons, and even Infernals. The following powers are usually common to all Possessed Immortals:

Extraordinary Attributes. As part of the exchange, the entity usually boosts each of the character's physical attributes (P.S., P.P., P.E., P.B., and Spd.) by 2D6 each.

Ageless. The character seems to age only one year for every fifty. Most look youthful, vibrant and healthy. A Possessed Immortal who has lived 1000 years may look like a person in their thirties.

Chi Mastery. The character will be able to tap some of the entity's Chi (which will likely be 3D6 times 10) and use all the basic Chi Mastery Abilities (but not the advanced ones). However, the entity will first allow the body to exhaust all its normal Chi, and then NEVER allow more than half of the entities Chi to be depleted.

Entity Perceptions. Since the entity is always on the lookout for threats, and since it can see at great range in both the realm of Chi and in the realm of the spirits, the Possessed Immortal is almost always warned of any surprise attacks or hidden opponents. +4 on initiative, +2 to save vs horror factor, cannot be surprised by attacks from behind in close combat, gets an automatic parry, and can see beings of pure chi as well as ghostly spirits.

Unexpected Insights. From the point of view of the Possessed Immortal, it seems like "hunches" are always occurring at just the right time. Of course, these are actually the warnings and directions of the possessing entity, a being usually endowed with ancient secrets and hidden knowledge. The Game Master is the person who should deal out these hunches and flashes of insight. Such intuition should be reasonable. These are not psychic visions or divination, with details, just a feeling (don't open that door, don't trust that person, he's lying, wait here for a minute, bet on number seven, etc).

Weaknesses/Vulnerability: If the spirit can be lured out, abandoning its host, the character's body loses all its special powers and insight, and starts to revert to its true age at a rate of about fifty years per melee round.

Heartless Immortal

Immortality from the Removal of Bodily Organs

Check out the Chi Magic spell, *Remove Heart* (it's the last one listed, under 15th level). Heartless Immortals are those who have taken the knowledge of that spell and expanded on it so that all the vulnerabilities of the body are removed. This also involves the construction of a magical artifact: *The Secret Heart*, the place where all the vital parts of the Immortal's body can be stored.

The problem is, with the heart gone, the other organs are also destined for eventual decay. That means it's inevitable that the Heartless Immortal will have to preserve the rest of the body's organs in a similar way.

Each organ can be removed and stored in a separate "container," but it makes more sense to simply store everything in the Secret Heart. All of the organs are equally vital and vulnerable, so why defend more than one container if they can all be placed in one?

After all the vital organs are stored in the Secret Heart, the next most vulnerable part of the body is the brain. However, since the brain can't be removed, the solution is to permanently

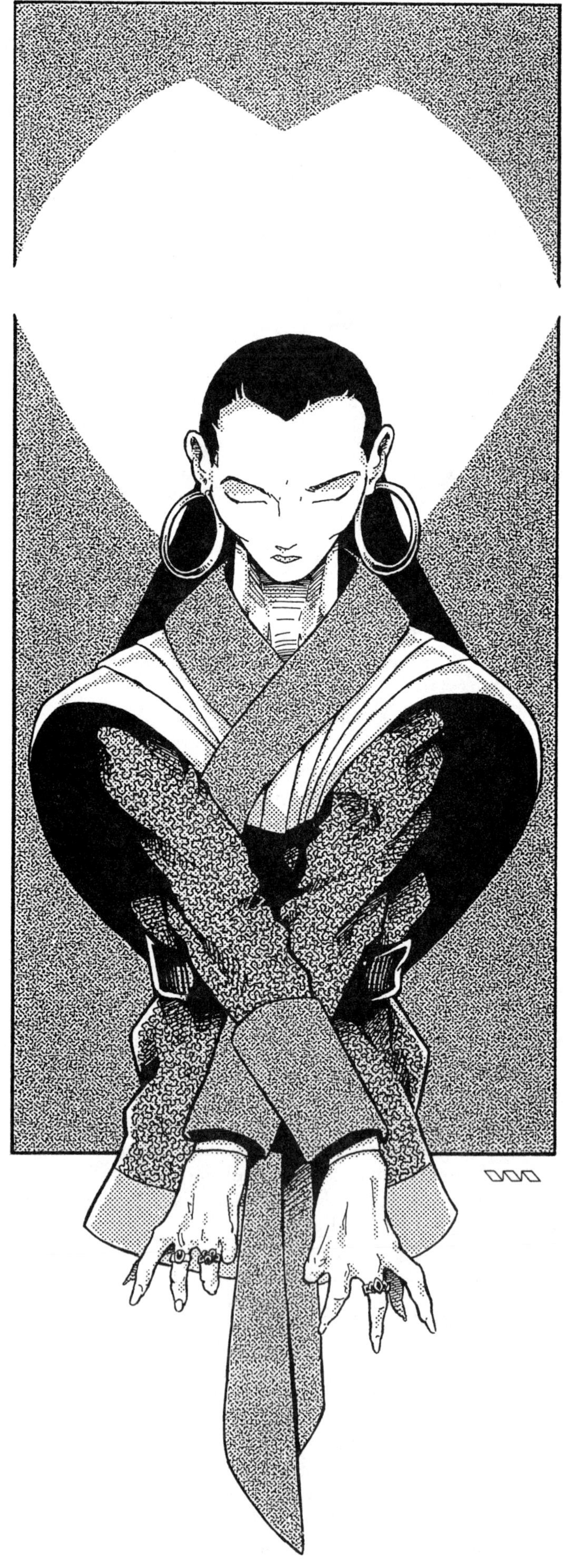

store the Chi Spirit of the character — permanently setting up its residence in the Secret Heart. Thus, the character's body is effectively a remote controlled robot. That way, even the destruction of the brain won't stop the character.

Finally, in the last magical enhancement to the Secret Heart, it is set up to automatically Tap Positive Chi. The idea is that even if the body is completely destroyed, the Secret Heart can start with as little as one shriveled cell and be able to *regenerate* a whole new body (sort of a super-fast grown clone).

One further detail. Where most Immortals are solitary and achieve their immortality on their own, the Heartless Immortal must get some kind of help in order to remove the heart and other organs from the body. That usually means the character is either (1) the client of some even more powerful Immortal, or (2) that the character is part of a cult in which loyal cult members perform the operation (it is likely that all the cult members recruit others for their particular brand of immortality).

Typical Alignment: Unprincipled, anarchist, aberrant, miscreant, or diabolic.

Typical Age: From 301 to 3,100 years of age (3D10×100, plus the roll of percentile dice).

Temptation of Pathway: Simply, the greed of being able to live forever.

Powers of Immortality: Other than making the character tougher to kill, the heart and internal organs are invulnerable because they aren't in the body! In addition, over time, the character can accumulate great knowledge, wealth, skill and power. Just how tough the character is depends on how far along the character has been in enhancing the Secret Heart (how many organs it contains).

Partial Organ Replacement. The character is impervious to diseases that may attack the heart, blood or internal organs, as well as being impervious to fatigue, +3 to save vs horror factor, +5 to save vs pain, +5 to save vs possession, +5 to save vs drugs and poison, and +2 to save vs magic potions. Weapons that pierce the skin have few vital organs to hit and do half damage.

Complete Organ Replacement. The Heartless Immortal has no vulnerable internal organs and so can only be killed by the destruction of the brain. Anything less, and the body will eventually regenerate, using the organs in the Secret Heart as a resource. The Immortal is impervious to the effects of disease, drugs that affect the body (sedatives, speed, etc.), fatigue, pain, and attacks/weapons inflict one-quarter their normal damage. The character is also impervious to possession, +8 to save vs mind controlling drugs and hallucinogens, +6 to save vs magic potions, +3 to save vs most types of magic, and a +6 to save vs horror factor.

Secret Heart Spirit & Regeneration. The character's Chi spirit is transferred to the Secret Heart, so even the destruction of the character's brain, or the removal of the entire head, will not be fatal. In fact, the character can completely regenerate within 24 hours, even if only a small piece of flesh remains. Eyeballs, limbs and body damage can be regenerated in 1D4 hours.

Secret Heart Chi Tap. After magically empowering the Secret Heart to tap into the forces of Positive Chi, the character becomes truly invulnerable. Complete regeneration can occur within 1D6 hours even if only a tiny piece of ash or a single cell remains of the original body. Lost limbs and body damage can be regenerated within 3D4 minutes! Meditation is required during the regeneration period.

Weaknesses/Vulnerability: 1. The main weakness of the Heartless Immortal is in their Secret Heart. Hold the Secret Heart, and the Heartless Immortal is helpless/paralyzed. Destroy the Secret Heart and thereby you destroy the Immortal! Obviously, the Secret Heart is the Heartless Immortal's most precious treasure and will be hidden with the greatest care and guarded with the most powerful defenses. In its natural state the Secret Heart has an A.R. of 8, 20 S.D.C., and six hit points. However, the Heartless Immortal will have spared nothing in layering other sorts of magical defenses and enhancements on the Secret Heart.

2. The brain. Unless the *Chi Spirit* of the Immortal is placed in the Secret Heart, destroying the brain will slay the Heartless Immortal! However, 97% will have their Chi Spirit reside in the Secret Heart.

3. Psionic attacks and mind control. Since the brain is vulnerable, the character is affected by psionics, most psychic phenomena, magic illusions, and powerful mind controlling drugs and magic elixirs (assuming the Immortal doesn't save against them).

4. Another weakness, not so dramatic, is that Heartless Immortals tend to lose all of their imagination and creativity. This means the character starts to become less and less like a person and more and more like a heartless robot. What happens is the pathways of the brain get so worn down that the Immortal finds it easier to go on "auto-pilot" for most things, lacks emotional response, and rarely does anything with conscious thought/control. This is particularly true for anything that the Immortal does on a regular basis, such as getting up, bathing, dressing in the morning, preparing and eating meals, etc. As a result, some will look like beggars or seem confused and forgetful. Most seem cold and uncaring about those around them.

Damned Immortals

Immortality Granted by a Demon Master

Infernals, dark gods and other powerful supernatural beings are continually on the lookout for ways to influence the living world. Many find it advantageous to cultivate powerful servants. From an Infernal's point of view, why should they be constantly searching for replacement vassals when humans can simply be turned into Immortal slaves? Even better, once their human servant has gone beyond their appointed mortal time (i.e.: is alive after they should have been dead), the Immortal servant becomes dependent, not just for life and youth, but as the only escape from the torment of their souls. Even if the character originally was righteous enough, or powerful enough to confront the demon (remember, Infernal Lords prefer powerful servants), sooner or later the character's immortal life becomes too dependent on the demon's support for him to challenge his master (to do so is to die). At that point, it becomes a simple matter of, "Do what I say, or die without my continued support."

Having made a pact, no matter what the reason or initial excuse, the Damned Immortal must eventually become the slave of the Infernal Master.

Typical Alignment: If they weren't of an evil alignment before, a few decades of living as the pawn of their Infernal Master definitely turns them that way. Typically miscreant, diabolic, or aberrant, but occasionally anarchist.

Typical Age: From 301 to 1,900 years old (3D6×100, plus the roll of percentile dice). Note that it's possible that a Damned Immortal might be older than this, but it would mean that the demon or Infernal who empowers the character would have to predate the Hells of the Yama Kings!

Temptation of Pathway: Demons and other powerful Infernals will try tempting the living with all sorts of promises. Mostly they'll tell the truth about the benefits of an agreement with them, stressing the fact that immortality and great powers are available for the asking. They soft-pedal centuries of servitude.

Powers of Immortality: Much of the power of a Damned Immortal depends on the power of their Infernal Master. For example, some Infernal Masters confer spells and talismans, where others offer Lesser Infernals as minions. Regardless of the type of Infernal Master, the following powers will eventually appear in the Damned Immortal simply from prolonged exposure to the life-giving energy handed over by the being they serve.

Superhuman. Almost immediately the character can feel the power of his or her dark union with the supernatural. The character's normal hit points are tripled, S.D.C increased by five times, the character has supernatural endurance (fatigues at one-third normal rate, is +1 to save vs magic, and is +5 to save vs drugs, poison, and disease), heals twice as quickly as normal humans, stops aging and "feels" young, powerful and vital.

Incredible Healing. After twenty-five years of service, the Damned Immortal is impervious to disease, +10 to save vs drugs and poison, +3 to save vs pain, +4 to save vs horror factor, and can regenerate 6D6 hit points or S.D.C. every ten minutes, and regenerate a lost limb or eye within seven days.

Call Infernal Master. After fifty years of service, a connection will grow between the Chi Spirits of the Damned Immortal and the Infernal Master. While not continuous, the Damned Immortal can attempt to "call" his Infernal Master at any time and will always be heard (of course, it's up to the Infernal to decide whether or not to respond). The same bond also allows the Infernal Master to spy on the Damned Immortal at any time, without fear of detection.

Negative Chi Mastery. Within two hundred years, Damned Immortals will absorb the Negative Chi Abilities of their Infernal Masters. At first this will include *Negative Chi Attack, One Finger Chi, Fist Gesture,* and *Dark Chi.* Other Chi Mastery abilities can also be gained, depending on the aptitude and dedication of the Immortal and the power of his master.

Transform to Pure Negative Chi. After five hundred years of exposure to the Infernal Master's energies, the Damned Immortal will be able to transform into a creature of Pure Negative Chi. This means the body completely dissolves, leaving nothing behind! While in the Negative Chi state, the character can recover any lost Negative Chi, but only when in a Negative Chi environment. The Immortal is vulnerable only

to Chi, magic and psionic attacks, and will be impervious to any physical or energy based attacks while transformed into Pure Negative Chi. The character can rematerialize in one melee round (15 seconds), but will be helpless against attacks during that time. If the Damned Immortal enters a Positive Chi area while in a state of Pure Negative Chi, the normal flow of Positive Chi will automatically *Chi Attack* the Immortal at a rate of 3D6 points of damage to Negative Chi for every point of Chi flow in the area.

Demon/Infernal Shape. A side-effect of the continuous influx of Infernal energy into the Damned Immortal is that their Chi Spirit will gradually take the shape of their Infernal Master. After one thousand years, this eventually gives the Damned Immortal the power to change shape at will, into the demonic form of their Infernal Master. The change takes one full melee round, during which the character can do nothing else.

Ironically, this ability to shift to demonic form signifies that the Damned Immortal will not be valuable as a servant for very much longer. After another 1D6×10 years, the Damned Immortal will lose the ability to shift *back* to human form. At that point, the Infernal Master will likely have little or no use for the Damned Immortal.

Weaknesses/Vulnerability: There are no special vulnerabilities of Damned Immortals other than their link to supernatural beings. However, the politics of their Masters may see the characters used as pawns and fodder in their Masters' rivalries. Furthermore, if their Infernal Master should be slain, the Immortal will lose ALL of his unnatural powers, shrivel up and die!

Ginseng Immortals

Immortality from the Capture of a Living Ginseng

The mystical ginseng plant, once it reaches the age of three thousand years, attains sentience and develops amazing powers of life and regeneration. Usually it uses these powers to protect itself and its offspring, and sometimes those innocents who call upon it for help. However, if the Living Ginseng is captured by trickery or magic, its captor can "harvest" pieces of the plant's flesh and become a Ginseng Immortal.

In appearance the Living Ginseng (or Mystical Ginseng) looks like a larger version of an ordinary ginseng root. Never weighing more than sixteen pounds (7.2 kg), the mystical root is a constant, radiating source of Positive Chi. One root is a source of 600 points of Positive Chi (or the equivalent of 300 P.P.E.)!

Keeping a Mystical Ginseng captive is relatively simple. It can't escape so long as it is bound in metal. Usually, one end of a copper or iron wire is twisted around the root and the other end of the wire fastened to something solid. However, contact with metal causes the Ginseng constant, neverending pain. Anyone touching the Ginseng (as well as psychic sensitives) will be able to hear its continuous sobbing and feel some of its torment.

Another source of wealth and power is attained by planting the *rootlings* of the Living Ginseng. These tiny tendrils are cut off (up to twenty can be "harvested" every week) and planted in a controlled environment indoors; if grown outdoors, they'll attempt to escape. After just a few weeks of proper sun, soil and water, the rootlings become the equivalent of Three Hundred Year Old Ginseng Root and each tiny living plant, a child of the Living Ginseng, can be chopped up and sold for around $60,000 for a variety of mystical and alchemical purposes.

Typical Alignment: Must be evil, because of the continual torment to the Living Ginseng. Usually miscreant or diabolic.

Typical Age: From 501 to 3,100 years old (5D6×100, plus the roll of percentile dice).

Temptation of Pathway: As long as the character controls the Living Ginseng, immortality, eternal youth, virtual invulnerability (natural A.R. 17 and double hit points and S.D.C.), and the power to grant these things to others is assured.

Powers of Immortality: Merely holding the Living Ginseng confers youth and vitality, so the character will look and feel like someone in the prime of life, regardless of his true age. *Pieces sliced from the Living Ginseng (an act of incredible cruelty) can be used for the following:*

Instant Regeneration. Eating an ounce (28 grams) of meat taken from the body of the Living Ginseng will spur the character's body into regenerating any damaged or missing body parts. If the character is not injured or ill, eating an ounce will, for the next twenty-four hours, enable the character to *instantly* heal from any wounds. The thrust of a sword or the impact of a bullet will do normal damage, but the damage will be healed instantly! In addition, the character will be impervious to disease and +3 to save vs poison and drugs.

Life-Giving. A cup of Living Ginseng Tea, made from a peel of the outer flesh of the mystic root, cures any ailment or disease, even those brought on by extreme old age.

Resurrection. Injecting a solution of Mystical Ginseng (made by dissolving two ounces/57 grams of Living Ginseng flesh into pure alcohol) into the heart of someone recently dead (within three days of death) will restore the person to life within minutes.

Weaknesses/Vulnerability: Whenever the Ginseng Immortal goes a full day without *touching* the enslaved Living Ginseng, they will resume their normal appearance and will start to age normally.

Separation from the Ginseng, whether by the magical plant's release or death, will end the character's Immortality. However, the character will not abnormally age or die, but will simply return to the age and condition he/she was before the Mystical Ginseng was enslaved.

Companion Immortals

Immortality as Consort to a Fallen Deity

There are a few Fallen Deities who have lost much of their powers of divinity and have been stranded in the world of mortals. Merely the continued presence of one of these divine entities is enough to confer youth and vitality on any mortal being. To confer immortality, the Fallen Deity needn't do anything at all, other than to occasionally touch his or her Companion Immortal.

In some cases the Companion Immortal is a lover, serving as the deity's sweetheart and assistant in the world of mortals. In other cases, where the deity has fallen into senility or insanity, the Companion Immortal is more of a guardian.

Note that some of the Fallen Deities and their Companion Immortals are not even human. For example, there are stories of a goose goddess who lost her worshippers, but who gained a gander lover of her own kind. Since they are inseparable, the two have remained together for over three thousand years, even enduring several periods of captivity.

Typical Alignment: Any, but usually unprincipled or anarchist.

Typical Age: From 501 to 5,100 years old (5D10×100, plus the roll of percentile dice).

Temptation of Pathway: Aside from the obvious benefits of hanging around with a divine being, Companion Immortals are often seduced by the incredible beauty and sexual attractiveness of the deity.

Powers of Immortality: Most of the powers available to the Companion Immortal are a matter of what the Fallen Deity can be talked into doing (and what powers are still within his/her grasp). Since a deity is capable of casting spells, or manipulating the weather, or whatever, then the Companion Immortal may be able to persuade the deity to do those things. Otherwise, except that the Companion Immortal never ages and may be healed and magically protected by the deity, he or she only has whatever powers, skills, knowledge, wealth and influence gained in their long years of life and experience (which can be considerable).

Weaknesses/Vulnerability: Physically, the Companion Immortal is just as vulnerable as any other mortal being. However, as long as the Fallen Deity is feeling protective, it is pretty dangerous to be seen as the Immortal's enemy. Often driving a wedge between the Companion Immortal and their deity is the only practical way to attack the Immortal. If the character falls from the deity's graces, he/she can lose the power of immortality and the protection of the god.

Ti Hsien: Enlightened Immortals

Immortality by the Pathway of Internal Alchemy

The Immortals, holding dice-sticks;
Sit gaming in a fold of Tai Mountain...
Cinnamon wine brims in jade cups;
The River God serves sacred fish...
A million miles are nothing;
Riding Chi through space...

after Tsao Chih's Ballads of the Immortals

All the previously described Immortals have taken false paths. Each, with the possible exception of the Immortals of Sleep, have only delayed their fate, and are doomed to eventually die.

Not so for the Enlightened Immortals. Taking the pathway of enlightenment, of illuminating the mind so that it sees the true state of the universe, is to create a spirit that can never truly die.

Once the mind has become enlightened, there is no way to actually die. Although the character can be killed, the soul will be returned to Earth for another cycle of reincarnation, where the reborn character will eventually regain any lost memories. So, having mastered that first lesson, each Enlightened Immortal is moving along a pathway toward complete self-mastery, a pathway that may lead across different lifetimes or involve living for hundreds of years at a time.

Internal Alchemy. For the Taoist, having a *spirit* that never dies is not enough. The goal is for the *body* to also live forever, so that an Immortal's final ascension to the Heaven of the Jade Emperor will be a total union of the physical, mental and spiritual. This desire for corporeal perfection has led the Enlightened Immortals to study the secrets of Internal Alchemy, of *Nei Tan* (as opposed to *Wei Tan*, External or Chemical Alchemy). This process of Internal Alchemy is related to the advanced techniques of Yoga in that the organs of the body are controlled by the mind, and so that breathing, digestion, and the purification of the blood all become different "reactors" used to refine the chemical elements of the body.

Ultimately, the objective of Internal Alchemy is the creation of an *Elixir of Immortality* — inside the body! Once created, the elixir assures the Enlightened Immortal of eternal life and prevents the body from weakening or aging. However, the mere freedom from death is not enough for the Enlightened Immortal! No, it is only the first step in a lifetime, or lifetimes, in which the Enlightened Immortal continues to advance. Each of these advancements is described as a "Refinement of the Elixir of Immortality," and there are nine steps possible. The process is only finished, and the Immortal finally withdraws from the world of mortals, when the advancement progresses beyond the ninth refinement. Note, however, that many Enlightened Immortals have taken special vows that they will NOT ascend until all other enlightened beings have the opportunity to do so. In other words, they promise to continue to walk among the world of mortals until some final armageddon.

Typical Alignment: Usually unprincipled or anarchist.

Temptation of Pathway: A desire for spiritual immortality.

Powers of Immortality: Each *Refinement of the Elixir of Immortality* will result in the discovery of yet another set of Powers of Immortality (see the following). Note that none of the powers are ever forgotten, but that Immortals generally prefer to exercise the powers they've just recently discovered.

Weaknesses/Vulnerability: None. Even if the physical body of the Enlightened Immortal is killed, the Immortal's spirit/soul will be reincarnated, and will, as they grow up in their new family, eventually recover all their previous memories and powers.

First Time Refined Elixir of Immortality

When the Immortal achieves the *First Time Refined Elixir*, there is no longer any need to fear death. The character can live an indefinite period of time without suffering from old age and, if killed, will soon be reborn.

Typical Age: Usually from one hundred to two hundred and fifty years old.

Apparent Age: Those who are cultivating this refinement of their internal elixirs will appear vigorous, but still old. From the age of one hundred to one hundred and fifty they'll look about fifty, and sixty or so in the later years.

Powers of Enlightened Immortality: The character will acquire all the Powers of *Zenjorike*, plus the following:

Perpetual Reincarnation. Rebirth means that the character's soul is wiped of all memories and is returned to the world as a fetus in the belly of a pregnant woman. Once reborn, the Immortal will initially appear to be a perfectly normal, and healthy, baby. However, even as a toddler the character will seem wise.

Seemingly by coincidence, other Enlightened Immortals will constantly have encounters with the youngster and the new parents. One may even settle nearby and become the child's friend and mentor. Starting at around the age of ten, the elder Immortals will arrange for the child to experience bits and pieces of the character's memories from the previous life. Then, by the age of seventeen, the character will recover the final piece of the soul containing his/her lost memory.

Once the memories are recovered, the character will regain ALL the skills, abilities, powers and knowledge possessed before his/her premature death. While the character must redo any Refinements of the Elixir of Immortality, the ones that had been accomplished before will present no particular difficulty and it's possible to do about one per month, until the character has caught up to his/her previous level of enlightenment.

Second Time Refined Elixir of Immortality: Riding the White Crane

Perfecting the Immortal's control over Chi has always been a feature of the elixir's second refinement. In times of old, this always meant that the Enlightened Immortal would become intimate with the White Crane, ancient China's symbol of the purity of Positive Chi. It also meant that the Immortal, having become acquainted with the White Crane, could then call upon the great bird for transportation. Unfortunately, the White Crane has not responded to the calls of Immortal since sometime in the 1950s.

Typical Age: From two hundred to three hundred years old.

Apparent Age: The character seems to be aged somewhere between fifty and sixty.

Powers of Enlightened Immortality: Most Immortals will have gained *Chi Mastery Skills* even before attaining the First Time Refined Elixir. However, with the *Second Time Refined Elixir* the character achieves absolute mastery over both Negative and Positive Chi, not only gaining all the Chi Mastery Skills, but also the *Unity of Chi, the Yin* and *the Yang*. That means the character can host *both* Negative Chi and Positive Chi in the body simultaneously, and use both reserves of Chi at the same time. In other words, the character can do double the normal amount of Chi operations, one using Positive Chi and the other using Negative Chi.

Third Time Refined Elixir of Immortality: Riding the Chi Lin

This stage of personal development is known as the *Refinement of Light*, or as the *Immortal Circulation of Light*. Traditionally, the creature with the greatest control over light has been the *Chi Lin*, a name which some translators have turned into the English word, "unicorn." Immortals who have passed through the third refinement can call the *Chi Lin* at any time, for assistance, or for transportation.

Typical Age: Generally, at least three hundred years old.

Apparent Age: The character doesn't look any older than fifty.

Powers of Enlightened Immortality: Eye Contact Divination. The Immortal can look into the eyes of any mortal being and focus on the character's entire past (as if the Immortal has just lived that life), the character's present (all the character's current woes, hopes, desires, and pleasures), as well as see one or more of the character's pathways into the possible future. It takes a full melee round (15 seconds) and the mortal being examined will experience a part of the Immortal's perceptions, getting a "triple whammie" from getting their past, present and future lives flashed to them. The mortal will be stunned for the next 2D6 melee rounds (half combat abilities, bonuses and speed).

Note that the Immortal is unlikely to perform this act without gaining some kind of permission from the mortal. In the way of Enlightened Immortals, the explanation isn't likely to be very clear, and the Immortal will probably only ask something like, "Would you like to know what I think about your potential?" or "With your permission, I'd like to look into your beautiful eyes."

The Immortal will rarely offer specific information about what he/she has seen, other than comments like, "You have survived many trials and have grown strong, do not let your rage destroy all you have built." Or, "Don't allow these recent sorrows to crush your spirit. Look to light and embrace friendship." Or, "The path you contemplate will only lead to sorrow. Search your soul for the true path." Or, "You have a bright future." And so on.

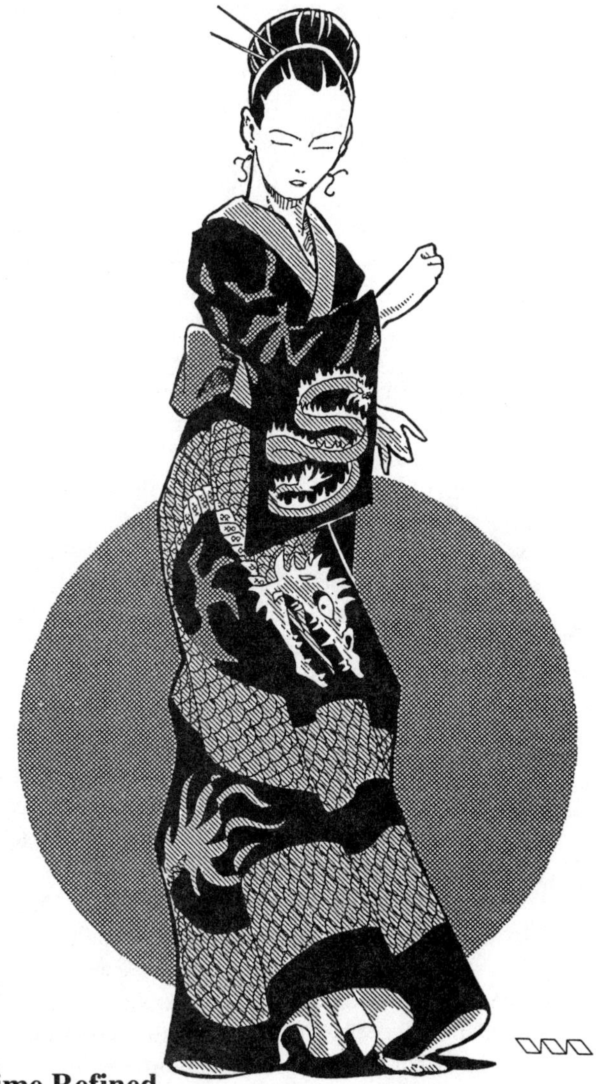

Fourth Time Refined Elixir of Immortality: Riding the Dragon

This stage is known as Dragon-Riding, since Enlightened Immortals are supposed to seek out each of the Dragon Kings, giving each a present and receiving a present from each in turn. The Enlightened Immortal will also sense the presence of lesser dragons, and will make a point of paying each a polite visit, or at least making a small offering (for example, burning incense at the base of a dragon's mountain). Even Enlightened Immortals, who delight in insulting deities and demons, and to whom even the Yama Kings of Hell are an object of contempt, always treat dragons with grave courtesy and respect. An Immortal does not *command* a dragon, but rather *requests* the dragon's attention, aid, or assistance.

Typical Age: Four hundred to five hundred years of age.

Apparent Age: Looks like a healthy person in their forties.

Powers of Enlightened Immortality: At this level of attainment, the character can form a living cloud within the lungs, mixing (internally) Chi with aspects of one of the Four Dragon Kings. This cloud, which is formed in the lungs in a single melee round, can be exhaled to cover an area of up to two hundred feet (61.0 m) in diameter. **Note:** The size and shape of the cloud is completely controllable by the Immortal. In all cases, the cloud can last one minute for every fifty years the Immortal has lived (including previous lives). A new cloud can be created every other melee round (every 30 seconds), with as many as two of each.

The Dragon King of the West's Gift: The Noxious Cloud of Living Chi. The Immortal exhales a cloud of vile-looking yellow-green gas. The gas reduces visibility to less than an arm's length and tastes horribly acidic. Chi, or P.P.E., expended in or against, the cloud is instantly absorbed, negating magic spells, wards and attacks. At the will of the Immortal, the gas can become one of the following: *Poisonous:* Characters can attempt to hold their breath or save vs poison; those who fail to do either will take 3D6 damage direct to hit points! *Corrosive:* All non-magical metals will be scarred with 1D6 points of rust and corrosion damage every melee round. *Or acidic:* All living creatures and organic material take 1D6 points of damage every other melee round. **Note:** If used in the **Rifts RPG** setting, all damage can be S.D.C. or M.D. depending on the wishes of the Immortal.

The Dragon King of the East's Gift: The Pearly Cloud of Living Chi is a dense, impenetrable cloud which totally obscures vision. The cloud looks, feels, tastes, and smells just like a normal cloud of water vapor, just incredibly thick. If desired, the Immortal can turn the cloud into a knockout gas (save vs non-poison; 16 or higher), which will render all victims unconscious for 3D6 melee rounds.

The Immortal can also condense the pearly vapors, creating a substance which looks like the glossy inside of an oyster shell. This "condensation" can be done on any non-moving object within the cloud (totally at the Immortal's control). Objects covered will have the look of pearl and be coated with a hard shell. This substance has an A.R. of 13, and the Immortal can apply 40 S.D.C. to it every melee round. For example, the Immortal could choose to coat two objects, a bronze helmet, and a ballpoint pen, putting 35 points of S.D.C. on the helmet, and 5 points of S.D.C. on the pen! Obviously, this can be used as a sort of additional armor to protect friends, allies and innocents. The pearl coating disappears either when all S.D.C. has been depleted or after 24 hours, whichever comes first.

The Dragon King of the South's Gift: The Flaming Cloud of Living Chi. The Immortal can breathe out a cloud of living fire, which seems to be made of roaring flames (horror factor 14). Visibility inside the cloud is reduced to about half normal, but it's still possible to see through the flames. At the Immortal's direction the living fire cloud can be hot enough to ignite wood (does 3D6 damage per melee to all people inside, plus any possible fire damage), or simply pleasantly warm. All the flow of Chi, both Positive and Negative, within the cloud can be controlled by the Immortal and the changes in the flow will last for at least a full day after the cloud is dissipated.

The Dragon King of the North's Gift: The Funereal Cloud of Living Chi. Upon being expelled, the cloud takes the form of a black mist which will feel deathly cold to any touched by it. All ghosts, entities of Pure Chi, and other ethereal presences will become visible within the cloud and be subject to the will of the Immortal!

Another power of the funereal cloud is that it is capable of *dissolving down the Chi* of any person it envelops. The victim's Chi is then held within the funereal cloud and can be either reconstituted by the Immortal, or withdrawn (breathed back) into the Immortal. While those in this state are not harmed, they will feel none of the passage of time and (from their point of view) will cease to exist until the Immortal chooses to exhale the funereal cloud once again and change them back into their physical form.

Fifth Time Refined
Elixir of Immortality: Riding the Phoenix

Oriental people regard the Phoenix as the symbol of control over the five elements, and it will pay a visit to the Enlightened Immortal sometime during this stage of development. From the Phoenix, the Immortal learns how to control the five elements with Internal Alchemy, including the trick of combining aura and elemental to create an *Animus*.

The Animus takes the form of the character's body, but is larger, so it looks like a version of the character which is just slightly taller and wider than he really is. When the Immortal is moving about, or in combat, the Animus forms around him to create the equivalent of a suit of magical armor, moving in exact coordination with the Immortal. Note that there are Chi Magic spells that can create an Animus, but they are inferior to the Animus of the Phoenix.

Typical Age: Five hundred or more years of age.

Apparent Age: The character looks around thirty years old.

Powers of Enlightened Immortality: Controlling one's Internal Alchemy, so as to generate an *Animus* of elemental energy. Each time the Animus fills the body, the Immortal must choose which of the five elements it is to represent. When activated, it seems like the character is glowing with a soft aura, as if surrounded by a fuzzy layer of light. Each elemental version of the Animus confers different powers, as follows: **Note:** In all cases, the Animus lasts for five minutes for every fifty years the Immortal has lived (including previous lives). Only one Animus can be summoned and used at a time. It can be canceled/dispelled in an instant, but calling forth a new or alternative Animus requires one melee round of concentration.

Green Animus of the Element of Wood. A soft green glow covers the Immortal, which serves to absorb any and all Chi or P.P.E. attacks directed at him. Any incoming Chi can be captured and used to restore any Chi the Immortal may be missing, or be immediately used with Chi Mastery.

Red Animus of the Element of Fire. A slight flicker of pulsating red seems to cover the character. While cloaked in this Animus, the character is invulnerable to fire, heat, or any energy based attacks (including mega-damage blasts). In addition, the Animus automatically protects the Immortal from any cold, or cold-based attack.

Yellow Animus of the Element of Earth. A wispy yellow fog clings to the Immortal, but this Animus has awesome strength, so the Immortal will be able to lift objects as if he had a supernatural P.S. of 25 (5,000 pounds/2265 kg) and do hand to hand damage with a +10 damage (in **Rifts,** the characters attack would inflict mega-damage).

White Animus of the Element of Metal. There will seem to be a glowing white aura about the character, and the Animus can stop or deflect any solid objects, especially those made of metal (such as bullets). The outer layer can also be used to conduct electricity, to the extent that even a bolt of lightning can be conducted across the Immortal without damage.

Black Animus of the Element of Water. A thin mist of black seems to flow around the character. By touching any living thing, the Immortal can use the Animus to manipulate the creature's Chi. Once contact is made, the Immortal can drain Chi, fill Chi, change the polarity of the Chi, or activate the character's Chi with any Chi Mastery ability.

Sixth Time Refined
Elixir of Immortality: Riding the Tiger

While in this stage of advancement, the Enlightened Immortal will be sought out by the White Tiger, or one of the White Tiger's minions. This is followed by a period, usually of a hundred years or more, when the Enlightened Immortal will spend time

away from humanity, wandering in wild places of forest, jungle, tundra and mountain.

Typical Age: Usually around six hundred years old.

Apparent Age: At this stage the character seems to regain a lost youth and can sometimes look as young as a teenager, but usually looks to be around twenty-five.

Powers of Enlightened Immortality: The gift of the White Tiger is the ability to change one's blood into a fluid of pure Yin (Negative Chi). In this state the Yin Blood of the Immortal is a milky grey and the flesh takes on a pale hue. **Note:** In most cases, the power lasts as long as the Immortal desires. No more than two of these powers can be used simultaneously.

Control Undead/Living Dead. The Immortal, while in Yin Blood form, can command any of living dead or undead, and they will obey without question. It is possible for Undead Immortals who are aware of this power to avoid the commands, but only by the use of powerful magic, or intense concentration; reduce all attacks and bonuses by half while concentrating to maintain a free will. (In **Rifts**, this power will affect all vampires, ghouls and undead, with the exception of the vampire intelligence).

Invisibility. While the blood is Yin, the character can become invisible at will. This form of invisibility cloaks the character even from Chi or magical means of detection, as well as mechanical sensors.

Self-Transmutation. While filled with the Yin Blood, the character can change shape, either to that of another creature, or even to take on the features and likeness of another person (never an inanimate object or plant). The new shape remains when the blood is shifted back to normal and the Immortal would have to go to the Yin Blood in order to change once again.

Walk To Other Worlds. While the blood is transformed, the character can walk to the realm of the Yama Kings, to the Heavenly Court of the Jade Emperor, and to many other wondrous lands. It is also possible to walk to alternate worlds in this way. See other Palladium Books, such as **Rifts** and the **Palladium Fantasy Role-Playing Game** for some of the many possibilities (In **Rifts,** the character can use stone pyramids and create Rifts at ley line nexuses).

Seventh Time Refined
Elixir of Immortality: Entering the Court of the Yama Kings

According to tradition, this is the phase where the Enlightened Immortal is to be presented to the Yama Kings of Hell. However, for at least the last two thousand years there have been no such introductions. In fact, whenever they encounter any official emissaries of Hell, Enlightened Immortals act incredibly rude, and usually ask that some insulting message be passed along to one or another of the Yama Kings.

This falling out of great powers seems to be due to some practical joke that went terribly wrong. Ever since that time, the Yama Kings have maintained a dignified silence, and the Immortals have been acting like spoiled brats (I know, you'd think that thousand-year-old Immortals would be a little more mature, but that's the way it goes with Taoists).

Typical Age: No less than eight hundred years of age.

Apparent Age: Around fifty.

Powers of Enlightened Immortality: At this level an Animus can be detached from the body and be sent walking about independently. While the Animus is away, the Immortal usually sits in meditation, seeing through its eyes and controlling it by thought like a remote controlled robot extension of his self. The *Animus* can be dissolved at any time, whether it is in contact with the Immortal's body or not, and all the Chi remaining in the *Animus* will immediately return to the Immortal. **Note:** In all cases, the Animus lasts for ten minutes for every fifty years the Immortal has lived (including previous lives). Only one Animus can be summoned and used at a time. It can be canceled/dispelled in an instant, but calling forth a new, or alternative Animus requires one melee round of concentration.

Eighth Time Refined Elixir of Immortality: Entering the Heavenly Court

The Enlightened Immortal finally comes to the attention of the Heavenly Court of the Jade Emperor and will be formally invited to visit. For some reason, in most legends of meetings between Immortals and the Heavenly Court, the Immortal always manages to be offensive, embarrassing, or just plain insulting. Perhaps it's because true Taoists just have a problem with authority.

In any case, when it gets to the point in the proceeding where the Jade Emperor offers the Enlightened Immortal a position within the Court (which is, after all, the whole point of the invitation), the Enlightened Immortal will laugh uproariously, quite unable to take the offer seriously.

It is rumored that any Immortal who were to actually accept a position from the Jade Emperor would receive a gift called *The Seven Jewels*, which includes such things as a *Jewel of All Desires*, *An Alabaster Elephant*, and a *Sword of Knowledge*, along with a position of deification within the Heavenly Court.

In spite of the rejection of the potential gifts of the Jade Emperor, during the Eighth Refinement, The Immortal does make significant progress. This comes in the form of something called *The Immortal Child*. This small being, a miniature version of the Immortal, only about a foot and a half (46 cm) tall, becomes a second aspect of the character. Other than its voice, which is that of a child-like version of the Immortal's, it has exactly the same features as the Enlightened Immortal.

Once created, The Immortal Child lives within the body of the Enlightened Immortal, but is also able to exit the body. Eventually, when and if the Immortal ascends beyond the mortal plane, or discorporates permanently into the wider universe, the Immortal Child will be left behind, it's memories blank, to be reincarnated all over again. However, until that happens, the Immortal Child is like a second self endowed with special powers, but NOT with the other powers that have been gained by the Immortal up to this point. Nor does the Enlightened Immortal have the unique powers of the child.

Typical Age: Somewhere between the ages of seven hundred and eight hundred.

Apparent Age: Between thirty and forty.

The Immortal Child's Powers of Immortality: The Immortal Child possesses none of the special powers conferred by the Nine-Times Refined Elixir of Immortality, nor does it have any magical or Chi powers (even if the Enlightened Immortal had learned them before attaining immortality). However, the Immortal Child can perform any Martial Arts or Mudra that the Enlightened Immortal has mastered, plus the following:

Immortal Child's Connection. No matter where the Immortal Child goes, it will always be a part of the Immortal, and the two selves will always see each other as part of a whole person. The Immortal Child can always return to the Immortal's body instantly, from anywhere in the universe. Note that this is a one-way trick. The Immortal Child can teleport into the Immortal, but it can't teleport away from the Immortal or the Immortal teleport to it.

Flight & Levitation. The Immortal Child can fly, hover and levitate effortlessly, at tremendous speeds, and without ever tiring. Maximum flying speed is 100 mph (160 km).

Assume Chi Spectral Form. The main power of the Immortal Child is the ability to instantly become a spirit of Pure Chi — but NOT an entity of either Positive or Negative Chi. Instead, the Immortal Child rides the Chi of the universe as if it were a wave function. In this form the Immortal Child can perceive both the Chi forces and the physical world, but is intangible to beings from either of those spheres of influence.

Ninth Time Refined Elixir of Immortality: Nine Times Nine Selves

This final step effectively places the Enlightened Immortal among the ranks of the deities, ready to permanently discorporate (see Zenjorike). However, as an Enlightened Immortal might point out, "if there are still things to see in the world of mortals, why should I be in a hurry to leave?"

Despite this sentiment, most Enlightened Immortals are usually ready to stop wandering at this stage. Setting themselves up in some remote place, such as a cave, a mountaintop, or out in the desert, they use their new found power of *Ubiquity* to experience the world of mortals and other worlds as well. It is said there are many alternate worlds, and an Enlightened Immortal of this caliber can experience as many as eighty-one of them simultaneously.

Typical Age: No less than one thousand years of age.

Apparent Age: In this final stage, the Enlightened Immortal's appearance seems to depend on the perceptions of the viewer. The higher the viewer's progress toward enlightenment, the younger the Enlightened Immortal will appear. So, in a group of observers, a character who is well trained in Meditation might see the Immortal as a twenty year old, while the cynical businessman sees the Immortal as an eighty year old. In photographs, or on videotape, the Immortal will appear around sixty.

Powers of Enlightened Immortality: The Power of Ubiquity. Although there is still only one original Enlightened Immortal (and only one Immortal Child), the character can generate up to eighty-one (81, or 9x9) *replicas*. Each copy is identical to the original Immortal and possesses ALL the vast powers of Enlightened Immortality, except that the copies can't create other copies, and they don't come equipped with Immortal Children. While the Immortal can draw back any one of the copies instantly, reabsorbing it into his/her body, the copies are usually limited to the usual means of travel.

Infernals

Chinese Demons

There are three different classes of Infernals who fall under the dominion of the Ten Yama Kings of the Chinese Underworld.

First, there are those Infernals who wander the Earth in a disembodied form. Most are just pathetic scavengers blindly searching for an empty body to possess. However, some of these lost spirits act as agents for the Yama Kings or their Infernals, and the rest are subject to commands, should their services ever be needed by other Infernals.

The second class of Infernals are the servants of the Yama Kings. In numbers they range from the countless multitudes of the Brass Snakes and Iron Dogs, who can be found everywhere throughout the Yama Kings' realm, to the handful of special servants like the White Lead Leopards and the Black Steel Centipedes. They are not part of the organized hierarchy, but they willingly support the rulership of the Yama Kings. The appearance of an Infernal servitor in the world of mortals should be considered a dire sign, since they never willingly leave the Yama realm.

Finally, the *Infernal Demons* of the Yama Kings of Hell are those who rule and manage the ten hells of the Chinese Underworld. For over two thousand years the Yama Kings have ruled the afterlife, and they must have sufficient servants to cope with the hundreds of millions of souls in their care, as well as the paperwork that documents the lives and trials of each soul. The realm of the Yama Kings needs demonic torturers and guardians, but it also requires vast numbers of demonic bureaucrats. Any of the Infernal Demons of the Yama Kings are capable of visiting the mortal world, and some have even developed extensive networks of servants, administered by select Damned Immortals.

Note: Infernals with the ability, *Enter Realm of Yama Kings*, have the power to create a gateway back to their Infernal homeland from anywhere in the world of mortals. The ability *Exit Realm of Yama Kings* provides the power to create a gateway out of the Hells and into the mortal world.

List of Wandering Infernals
- Angry Po Spirits (Po Chien)
- Bodiless Ghosts (Kuei Hsien)
- Possessive Entities

List of Infernal Servitors
- Brass Snakes (Tou She)
- Iron Dogs (Tieh Gou)
- Quicksilver Monkeys (Hung Hou)
- Copper Pigeons (Tong Ko)
- Black Steel Centipede (Hei Lou Kung)
- White Lead Leopards (Hu Fen Pao)

Hierarchical List of Infernal Demons
- Listed from the top, downward, in order of rank.
- Demon Overlords
- Horned Ushers
- Sycophant Demon (Li Gui)
- Adjutant Demon (Jing Gui)
- Bureaucrat Demon (Guan Gui)
- Intermediary Demon (Huang Gui)
- Envoy Demon (Fu Gui)
- Warrior Demon (Chiang Gui)
- Attendant Demon (Ma Gui)
- Minion Demon (Chung Gui)

Wandering Infernals

Angry Po Spirit – Po Chien

According to Chinese myth, Po Spirits are created when someone dies in a state of unresolved emotion. After the death of the body, the soul splits into two pieces, the **Hun** which moves off into the afterlife, and the **Po**, which tends to stay with the body. Ordinarily the Po Spirit is an inoffensive entity, which may drift around for a time, but which eventually joins with the flow of Chi and (probably) merges back into the Tao.

However, if the character died in a state of extreme emotionalism, there's a chance that the Po will turn into an angry spirit. Lacking the logic, communication abilities and intelligence of the Hun part of the soul, the Po Spirit becomes driven to do something about its emotions, but has no real way of resolving things. Typical situations that create these spirits are when the character has been murdered and dies with the knowledge that the murderer is likely to get away, or when death takes place just when the character's help is desperately needed by some loved one.

Even when an Angry Po Spirit is identified, and player characters are willing to help, the fact that the Po part of the soul contains *none* of the character's communication skills makes things difficult. The Angry Po Spirit can not talk, even psionically or mind to mind, write, or even mime any information.

Angry Po Spirit

Horror Factor: 11

Alignment: None, per se. The entity is simply driven by whatever was bothering the character at the point of death.

Size: Human-sized

Weight: None

Armor Rating: None. Bodiless spirits are intangible and cannot be affected by any material weapons or attack.

S.D.C.: None

Hit Points: None

Negative Chi: 2D6

P.P.E.: Usually None, but occasionally they will retain 1D6 if their former living self was very powerful magically or psionically.

The Eight Attributes: Don't really apply.

Natural Abilities: One, and only one of the following abilities is provided to the ghostly entity (roll 1D6 for random selection):

1. Bio-Manipulation: Pain: The entity can inflict pain on those it touches. Victims who fail to save vs pain will find themselves racked with agony and somewhat crippled (-6 to strike, parry and dodge) for four full melee rounds (one minute). No actual damage is inflicted, but the entity can attack every melee round.

2. Electrokinesis: The ghostly entity can collect up a volume of static electricity and discharge it at various targets. The charge only does one point of damage, but it can be painful and, when used against sensitive electronics like computers, it may cause them to overload (1-50% chance). Also, by touching an electrical device, the spirit can make it turn on and off, and eventually cause a discharge or electrical short, which may cause serious damage.

3. Hydrokinesis: Liquids that are at least 75% water can be manipulated by the Po Spirit. They can either be whipped up into a one gallon water spout or splashed up to six (6) feet away. Boiling liquids (coffee, soup, etc.) are particularly hazardous and can cause up to 2D4 damage if hurled directly in the face and 1D4 on bare flesh (hands, legs, etc.).

4. Pyrokinesis: Entities with pyrokinesis are capable of generating a heated spark sufficient to set off most flammable objects. This is particularly dangerous around gasoline and certain chemicals.

5. Telekinesis: In this case, the entity is capable of picking up a small object (no heavier than one pound) and manipulating it. Note that the entity can only do one thing at a time with telekinesis, so it could either pick up a cigarette lighter or flick the lighter's ignition, but it couldn't light it while holding it. Objects can't be moved fast enough to do any serious damage (one point of damage when tossed or knocked over), but if the angry spirit could get in a position to *drop* a one pound object from a height of ten feet or more, it could inflict 1D6 damage.

6. Psychic Scream: The entity can "scream" in a psychic sense, making its misery and frustration audible to those who are sensitive to supernatural phenomena and psionics. Blind Mystics, Fox Spirits, demons, human psychics and even ordinary dogs will find the scream to be painful, disturbing and annoying; -1 on initiative and -10% on skill performance due to broken concentration.

Attacks per Melee Round: One

Bonuses: None

Special Ability: While the angry Po Spirit is incapable of performing a possession on its own, it is possible for others to capture it with Chi, magic or psionics, and to place it in a host body. Once inside a body, if there is no resistance, the Po Spirit can take charge and move around normally. Note that the entity retains the physical, combat, martial art, weapon proficiency, and pilot skills of the dead character, so it may be very adept at certain things. Likewise, the Po will have clear memories of the dead character's senses of taste and smell (visual and audio memories will be quite dim), so it may be able to recognize people from its past.

While in possession of a living body, the spirit can communicate a bit better, but is still consumed with anger and/or an urgency to find its murderer or help a loved one. It is aggressive and agitated, and will want to leave to "do what it must," usually without assistance from others. This means the spirit is uncooperative, secretive, aggressive and obsessed. Anybody who gets in the way of its obsession is likely to get hurt.

Driving an angry Po Spirit out of a body is quite easy, if it is done within two days of the possession. After that time, the Po Spirit will become more difficult to evict and getting rid of it may require an exorcism.

Bodiless Ghosts – Kuei Hsien

Found throughout the mortal world, Bodiless Ghosts are usually hapless wanderers unable to put an end to their own pointless existence. Entities usually end up as a bodiless ghost as a part of the torment meted out to them in the Courts of the Yama Kings. There are also a few who just slip through the cracks of the Yama Kings' bureaucracy, and are never properly retrieved for their underworld judgement.

Where Angry Po Spirits are made up of the inarticulate, "animal-like" portion of a soul, the Bodiless Ghosts start out as the **Hun**, the part devoted to thinking and language.

A few Bodiless Ghosts have been given "assignments" by demons and other Infernals. They are promised the chance for eventual redemption (a return to the Hells of the Yama Kings, where they can start back on the pathway to being reborn) in exchange for the accomplishment of some task. Most of these tasks consist of searching for something, a person, or event that is of interest to an Infernal. Since they seek those things that elude powerful Infernals, it's not unusual for years, decades, or even centuries of watching to be required. Bodiless Ghosts who have been given a task are generally also empowered with the one-time ability to summon their Infernal Master upon the job's completion.

Bodiless Ghosts

Horror Factor: 12

Alignment: Any, but usually selfish or evil.

Size: Human-sized

Weight: None

Armor Rating: None. Bodiless spirits are intangible and cannot be affected by any material weapons or attack.

S.D.C.: None

Hit Points: None

Negative Chi: 3D6

P.P.E.: Usually None, but those who have been given a task by an Infernal will have 2D6.

The Eight Attributes: Don't really apply.

Natural Abilities: See aura and sense Chi.

Psionics: None

Magic Abilities: None

Attacks per Melee Round: One

Bonuses: None

Special Attack: Possession! The only possible attack by a Bodiless Ghost is that of attempting to possess a living body. They don't have the power to overcome any healthy spirit, but they can slip into a vacated body, or sometimes push aside the spirit of someone who is on the brink of death or lost to depression.

Once a Bodiless Ghost succeeds in a possession, there are limitations to what it can do. Since only the **Hun** portion of the soul exists, it will be extremely clumsy when attempting any kind of combat or ability requiring physical dexterity (penalty of -5 in combat and -25% on all physical skills). It will also be completely unable to interpret the senses of taste or smell (in other words, the nose would still work and would still smell the unique odor of gasoline, but the mind would not be able to identify the smell). However, it is observant, curious, and articulate.

Possessive Entities

Regardless of its origin, a Chinese Possessive Entity has learned how to survive in its disembodied state by traveling from host to host, continuously draining enough energy to sustain its own miserable existence.

Where Angry Po Spirits and Bodiless Ghosts are each just a half of a soul, Possessive Entities have managed to keep their spirit intact. In most cases, this is done by a special ritual at the moment of death, or by making a deal with an Infernal Demon. A few start out as spirits who were simply exploring in Pure Chi Form and found themselves unable to return to their natural bodies.

In order to survive and to avoid the dissolution of their being into its two component parts, the Possessive Entity seeks to inhabit other bodies. In some cases they do this simply to restore lost Chi and P.P.E.. Other times, when they find an attractive host, they will try to stay in the body for an extended period.

They are capable of sensing Infernals of any kind, at great distances. When they find one they are quite slavish and will offer to do anything in exchange for a bit of demonic power.

Horror Factor: 14.

Alignment: Evil, occasionally anarchist. They are driven only by the need to survive and care nothing for their victims.

Size: Human-sized

Weight: None

Armor Rating: None; as bodiless spirits they are intangible and cannot be affected by any material weapons or attacks. Of course a host body suffers all the weaknesses and frailties that are typical of its kind.

S.D.C.: None

Hit Points: None

Negative Chi: 5D6

P.P.E.: 3D6

The Eight Attributes: I.Q. 3D6, M.E. 3D6, and M.A. 3D6, the others don't apply except when in possession of somebody else's body.

Natural Abilities: Sense Chi, sense Infernal influences, see aura, and possession of the dead.

Psionics: None

Magic Abilities: None

Attacks per Melee Round: Two

Bonuses: +2 to resist eviction from a possessed body, +1 on initiative, and +3 to save vs horror factor.

Special Attack: Possession! Usually this is done only on bodies that are missing their soul-spirit. However, the Possessive Entity can attempt to seize control of the body of an unconscious or emotionally weak character. In doing so, the Possessive Entity expends a point of P.P.E. and makes a single roll to strike. The victim, even if unaware of the attack, is allowed to save vs possession (adding in the M.E. bonus, if any). The victim needs to beat the entity's roll to resist the possession. Characters who are seriously depressed or schizophrenic are -2 to save. **Note:** For more information on possession, see **Beyond the Supernatural**, pages 163-164 and pages 192-193.)

When a Possessive Entity chooses to leave a body, or when on the verge of being forced out, it will usually "loot" the body of all available Chi and P.P.E. and flee.

Infernal Servitors

Brass Snakes – *Tou She*

Motionless, there is nothing at all threatening or horrifying about a Brass Snake. They look exactly like little brass figurines that are manufactured all throughout China, India and Southeast Asia, and sold worldwide as knickknacks and souvenirs.

It is only when Brass Snakes move, undulating their metallic body, that the observer's mind says, "No! Such a thing should not be!" and the horror factor kicks in.

The demonic snakes are totally fearless, silent, and empowered to understand all languages. They will usually only attack if commanded to do so by a more powerful demon, god, Immortal or powerful sorcerer.

The only proper habitat for a Brass Snake is one of the Hells of the Yama Kings. They can be found anywhere in the underworld (20% chance of encountering a group of 2D4), but huge numbers of them are concentrated in all the rivers, lakes and other waterways of the realm of the Yama Kings (70% chance of encountering 1D6×10).

Brass Snakes

Horror Factor: 10, applicable only when they move. Motionless Brass Snakes look like small brass figurines and have no horror factor.

Alignment: Considered anarchist or aberrant; most simply obey their Infernal masters.

Size: Small; no brass snake is more than three feet long. Most are around eighteen inches (0.5 m). They are also thinner than most real snakes.

Weight: 2D4+1 pounds

Armor Rating: 18

S.D.C.: 50

Hit Points: None

Negative Chi: 30

P.P.E.: 2D6+10

The Eight Attributes: I.Q. 1D6+3, M.E. 1D6+10, M.A. 1D6+10, P.S. 1D6+16, P.P. 1D6+16, P.E. 1D6+18, P.B. 1D6+6, Spd. 1D6+8.

Natural Abilities: See the invisible, prowl 50%, sense Chi, see aura, sense *Chen Chi* – Living Vitality, and Enter the Realm of Yama Kings (spell).

Special Ability: Brass Snakes have the ability to enter into any dead body, even one that is nothing more than a skeleton, and bring it to life under their control.

Psionics: None, but are naturally resistant to psychic manipulation: +4 to save vs psionics and magic charms.

Magic Abilities: None

Attacks per Melee Round: Two

Bonuses: +1 on initiative, +5 to strike, +6 to dodge; damage is 1D6+2 for bite, plus special attack.

Special Attack: Liquid Brass! If injected, victims experience a horrible searing pain that seems to spread as it moves through the blood of the body. The molten metal causes 1D6 damage direct to hit points every melee round, for 1D6 melee rounds, in addition to bite damage. Victims must also roll to save vs pain each melee round to avoid being completely overcome by the agony (cannot move, concentrate or perform skills for the duration of the poisonous attack plus 1D6 minutes). **Note:** Each brass snake can only inject liquid brass twice per day.

Iron Dogs – *Tieh Gou*

The main guardians of the Hells of the Yama Kings are the Iron Dogs, whose numbers are uncountable. They are brutally savage creatures who delight in tearing apart the damned, whenever and wherever they are found.

Those of true purity will never be harmed by Iron Dogs, since their function is to attack only those who have sinned, or who are condemned to an underworld punishment. However, the

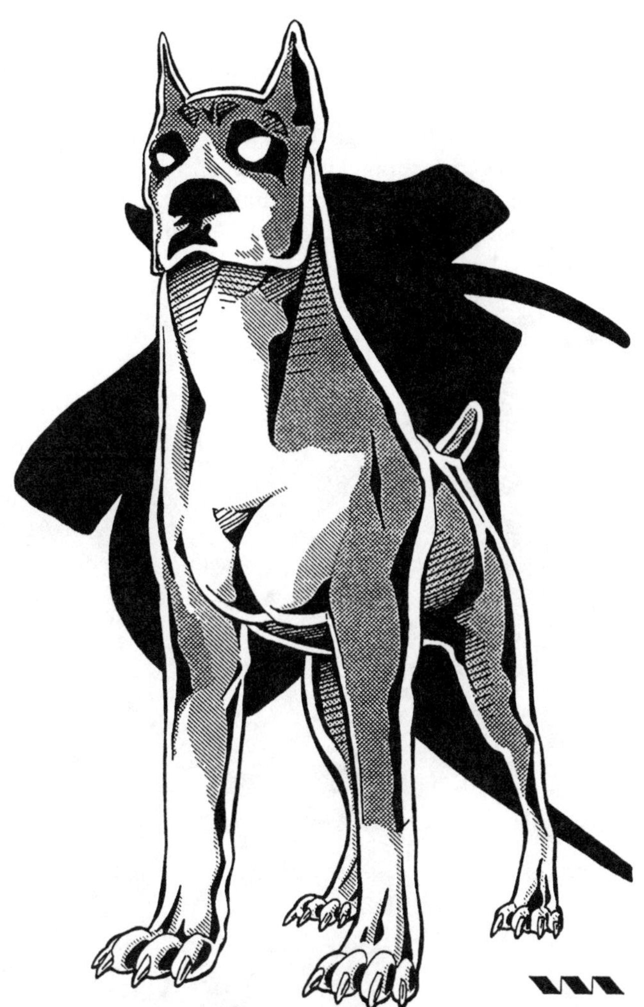

alignment of their prey won't prevent them from tracking and hunting anybody at the direction of their Infernal Masters.

Iron Dogs are more intelligent than ordinary canines and they are capable of speech, but not of imitating a human voice.

Iron Dogs

Horror Factor: 11

Alignment: Animal

Size: Medium-sized dogs.

Weight: 206 to 260 (6D10+200). They are made of pure iron, so they are much heavier than ordinary animals.

Armor Rating: 16

S.D.C.: 100 plus 2D6.

Hit Points: None

Negative Chi: 80

P.P.E.: 6D6

The Eight Attributes: I.Q. 2D6, M.E. 2D6, M.A. 2D6, P.S. 2D6+15, P.P. 2D6+10, P.E. 3D6+10, P.B. 1D6, Spd. 3D6+50.

Natural Abilities: Tireless running speed of 45 mph, leap lengthwise 20 feet (6 m; can only leap 6 feet/1.8 feet high), track by smell (80% in Hell, 50% in the natural world), nightvision (300 feet), see the invisible, see aura, sense Chi, sense *Chen Chi* – Living Vitality, sense Evil/Good, Enter Realm of Yama Kings, detect concealment 70%, and create fear.

Special Ability: Impose Appearance. While an Iron Dog cannot shape shift, they have the ability to force those who look upon them to see something else. This "something else" can either be an ordinary dog or a human, depending on what the Iron Dog wishes. Seeing the true form of the Iron Dog requires a roll to save vs psionic/mental manipulation.

Psionics: None

Magic Abilities: None

Attacks per Melee: Four

Bonuses: +1 on initiative, +4 to strike and dodge.

Each bite does 2D6+4 damage, a paw strike does 1D6 damage, a leaping pounce does 1D6 damage and has a 75% likelihood of knocking a human down (victim loses initiative and one melee action). A tripping attack by striking at a character's feet with its paws, or a blocking movement with its body, does no damage but has a 60% chance of knocking the character over (the victim loses initiative and one melee action).

Quicksilver Monkeys – *Hung Hou*

Possibly the most evil creatures in existence, since their entire reason for being is to cause pain and torment. They spend eternity either torturing those of the damned who are assigned to them, or turning on the weakest members of their own group when there are no other victims available.

Completely and utterly untrustworthy, no Infernal trusts them to carry out even the simplest mission. Unless a job calls for pure physical destruction and chaos, it's unlikely they'll be called upon. This doesn't mean Quicksilver Monkeys aren't intelligent. They are devilishly clever and can figure out the workings of complex puzzles, machines and weapons with astonishing speed. They are especially fond of human weapons and love using guns, explosives, or anything destructive. They are also quick to discover what mocking gestures, sounds and insults will most bother anyone around them and sly enough to pretend to be innocent, hurt, or pathetic; if that's what it takes to get in close to a potential victim.

Even though they are small, rarely more than two feet in height, they have tremendous physical strength (P.S. of at least 25). They are also capable of "melting" their bodies into pools of mercury and then reforming. They use this method to instantly avoid attacks or injury. They take no damage from bullets, punches, and similar kinetic attacks when liquified; they pass right through or whiz overhead. They can also use the "pooling," method to squeeze through cracks and under doors but spd. is a mere 3. To avoid an attack by "pooling" the demonic monkey must effectively roll a dodge. A successful roll means it turned into a pool of mercury before the attack struck its solid form and either missed or went through its liquid body without damaging it. Like any dodge, the creature uses up one melee action by "pooling" but can turn back to solid form in an instant to continue its assault.

The monkeys are not allowed to rove around through the Hells of the Yama Kings. Each of the Ten Hells has a special "jungle" where Quicksilver Monkeys are confined (3D6× 100 in an average group).

Quicksilver Monkeys

Horror Factor: 12, but 14 when grimacing or looking threatening.

Alignment: Diabolic

Size: Rarely more than two feet tall (0.6 m).

Weight: 95 pounds (43 kg) in metal form, or 25 pounds (11.3 kg) in flesh form.

Armor Rating: 8

S.D.C.: P.E. plus 110

Hit Points: None

Negative Chi: 6D6 plus 30

P.P.E.: 3D6 plus 15

The Eight Attributes: I.Q. 3D6+5, M.E. 3D6, M.A. 3D6, P.S. 5D6+20, P.P. 3D6+10, P.E. 4D6+5, P.B. 2D6, Spd. 3D6+5.

Natural Abilities: See the invisible, see aura, create fear, Enter Realm of Yama Kings, transform into a flesh and blood monkey, prehensile feet and tail, climb 90/80%, acrobatics 80%, and prowl 35%.

Quicksilver Monkeys can instantly melt into a pool of animated mercury. While in this state they can slither along, and squeeze through very small holes and crack, but move at a spd of 3. They can also form crude shapes, such as hands (usually with vile and impolite gestures) which are very flexible. Reforming themselves into Monkey form takes about three seconds.

Chi Mastery Abilities: Sense Chi, Sense *Chen Chi* – Living Vitality, **all** Negative Chi Abilities (including Advanced).

Psionics: Roughly one out of every twenty (5%) are the equivalent of Major Psionics.

Magic Abilities: None, but they are avid experimenters and they will attempt to set off any Celestial Calligraphy.

Attacks per Melee: Four

Bonuses: +2 on initiative, +8 to strike, +5 to parry and dodge, and +8 to save vs horror factor.

Special Attacks: Mercury Vapor. When seriously threatened, Quicksilver Monkeys are capable of generating a highly toxic vapor of gaseous mercury. Victims who breathe in the vapor will experience 2D6 damage direct to hit points! Damage will continue every melee round until fresh air is available to flush out the lungs. Note that the vile monkeys prefer not to use this attack, since it deprives them of the fun of inflicting pain by their own hands.

Copper Pigeons – *Tong Ko*

Copper Pigeons are frequently used as spies by the Yama Kings and Demon Overlords. They can be dispatched to observe activities in the realm of the Yama Kings or sent to the world of mortals, where their ability to transform into an ordinary pigeon makes them perfect snoops.

Copper Pigeons are a relatively recent addition to the Hells of the Yama Kings. Introduced by **Yen Lo Wang**, the King of the Fifth Hell, they are not entirely trusted by some of the other Yama Kings, nor are they regarded favorably by many lesser demons, who view them as yet another level of control over their lives.

Copper Pigeons

Horror Factor: 8, but only while in copper form.

Alignment: Aberrant — completely obedient to their demon masters.

Size: That of a pigeon.

Weight: In metal form, they weigh around fifteen pounds, but only eleven or twelve ounces when they take feathered form.

Armor Rating: 12 in Copper form.
Hit Points: None
S.D.C.: 15.
Negative Chi: 3D6 plus 15.
P.P.E.: 1D10+2
The Eight Attributes: I.Q. 1D6+1, M.E. 2D6, M.A. 2D6, P.S. 2D6+5, P.P. 3D6+5, P.E. 3D6+10, P.B. 2D6, Spd. 2D6+5 walking.
Natural Abilities: Fly at speeds up to 60 mph, extraordinary long-range vision (2 miles/3.2 km), nightvision (500 ft/152 m), see the invisible, see aura, sense evil/good, detect concealment, Enter Realm of Yama Kings, and Exit Realm of Yama Kings.
Chi Mastery Abilities: Sense Chi, Sense *Ti Chi* – Earth/Dragon Energy, and Chi Mask (allows a Copper Pigeon to appear to have the Chi of a normal bird).
Psionics: None, but highly resistant: +7 to save vs psionics.
Magic Abilities: None
Attacks per Melee: Two pecks with beak for 1D4 damage each.
Bonuses: +2 to strike, +2 to dodge when on the ground, +7 to dodge while in flight.

Black Steel Centipede – *Hei Lou Kung*

When the realm of the Yama Kings was established and other contestants for the rulership of the underworld were in full battle, it was the use of the Black Steel Centipedes that swung the balance in favor of the Yama. These gigantic creatures served as weapons of mass destruction and the one that remains on view is considered to be a clear reminder of the ultimate power wielded by the Yama Kings.

The one active centipede obeys only the commands of *Chuan Lun Wang*, the Supreme ruler of the Ten Hells of the Yama Kings. At one time there were at least nine others, one for each of the other nine Kings, but none of them have been seen in over 1,000 years. Of course, that doesn't mean they are not around or cannot be summoned if needed. It is rumored that Chuan Lun Wang can summon as many as three of these monsters.

Black Steel Centipede

Horror Factor: 18
Alignment: Evil predator; typically equal to aberrant.
Size: The one active Hei Lou Kung is roughly 2,000 feet long, with an average diameter of 150 feet. Its steel armor is over twenty feet thick on the body, but only six to eight feet thick covering the legs and pincers. **Note:** There are rumored to be much larger specimens (with 3× the S.D.C. and hit points), but these have not been seen since the establishment of the Yama Kings.
Weight: 3,000 tons
Armor Rating: 18
S.D.C.: 1D4×1000 (M.D.C. in **Rifts**)
Hit Points: 3D4×1000 (M.D.C. in **Rifts**)
Negative Chi: 225
P.P.E.: 8D6×10
The Eight Attributes: I.Q. 2D6+8, M.E. 2D6+10, M.A. 2D6, P.S. 2D6+40, P.P. 2D6+8, P.E. 2D6+10, P.B. 1D6, Spd. 2D6×10!

Natural Abilities: Can climb (90%) any surface, including walls and ceilings, at full speed and without stress from its immense weight. Bio-regenerates 1D6×10 S.D.C. or hit points per melee round, regenerates lost limbs in one hour, and is impervious to normal cold, heat, fire, disease and poison (magic versions do full damage). It can also turn invisible at will, see the invisible, nightvision 1000 feet (305 m), detect concealment, Enter Realm of Yama Kings, and Exit Realm of Yama Kings.

Psionics: Empathy, telepathy, see aura, sense good or evil, sense magic, and object read. 6D6×10 I.S.P.; considered a master psionic.

Magic Abilities: All first and second level spells.

Attacks per Melee: While the Black Steel Centipede is capable of attacking with 25 of its hundred claws every melee round, most targets (like humans) are too small for it to deliver more than three attacks per attacker.

Bonuses: +1 on initiative, +5 to strike, no bonuses to parry or dodge due to its size.

Damage: Claws do 3D6×20 damage, mouth pincers do 1D6×100 damage (mega-damage in **Rifts**; supernatural attributes and powers).

White Lead Leopards – *Hu Fen Pao*

Predating the Hells of the Yama Kings, the White Lead Leopards are the last remnants of an ancient order of assassins. Quite unlike any other Infernal Servitors, these creatures do not blindly obey. Instead they see their relationship with the Yama Kings as one of a contract. Thus, any assignment they accept must be justified according to the strict laws of both the Yama Kings and the Heaven of the Jade Emperor.

However, when one of the White Lead Leopards accepts a "contract," they will be eternally relentless in the pursuit of their assigned victim. No one is safe and there is no refuge. Because of their strict adherence to supernatural law, they even have the power to pursue their prey into the Heavenly realms, including into the High Court of the Jade Emperor.

There are but *seven* of these rare creatures left in all eternity, and each has become expert in a wide range of areas.

In appearance, whether in leopard or human form, each Hu Fen Pao seems to be made of a dull white metal with a surface marked with dark "spots" of corrosion. All seven of the White Lead Leopards live in the "Accidental City," which is part of the Ninth Hell, ruled by the Yama King, Tu Shis Wang.

White Lead Leopards

Horror Factor: 14

Alignment: Aberrant or principled. While they serve the forces of the underworld and often must do the bidding of evil creatures, the Hu Fen Pao are not necessarily evil and ALL live by a strict code of honor.

Size: Usually 10 feet (3 m) in length, including the tail.

Weight: Roughly 2,000 pounds (900 kg) in metal form or 400 pounds (180 kg) while taking the form of flesh.

Armor Rating: 15 in lead form or 8 in flesh form.

S.D.C.: P.E. attribute number plus 4D4×10.

Hit Points: None

Negative Chi: P.E. number times four.

P.P.E.: 7D6 plus 30.

The Eight Attributes: I.Q. 3D6+8, M.E. 3D6+10, M.A. 3D6+10, P.S. 3D6+20, P.P. 3D6+10, P.E. 3D6+10, P.B. 3D6, Spd. 3D6+60.

Natural Abilities: Tireless running speed of 45 mph, can leap 20 feet (6 m) lengthwise or straight up, track by sight 80%, track by smell 50%, prowl 60%, climb 60%, nightvision 300 feet (91 m), see the invisible, see aura, sense evil/good, Enter Realm of Yama Kings, and Exit Realm of Yama Kings.

Chi Mastery Abilities: All Negative Chi Mastery Abilities, Sense Chi, Sense *Chen Chi* – Living Vitality, Sense *Yuan Chi* – Sense Age, and Sense *Ti Chi* – Earth/Dragon Energy.

Psionics: Master psionic with the full range of psionic abilities!

I.S.P.: 3D6×10

Magic Abilities: Equivalent to 7th level Wu Shih.

Attacks per Melee: Six in human or leopard form; bite does 4D6 damage, each claw attack does 3D6 damage, plus any P.S. damage bonuses (in **Rifts,** supernatural P.S. and attributes).

Bonuses: +3 on initiative, +8 to strike, +5 to parry and dodge, +2 to pull punch, +6 to save vs horror factor, and +6 to save vs pain.

Special Skills and Abilities for use while in Human Form (Equivalent human level of experience is 5th):

12th Level Chi Hsuan Men Martial Artist, including four (4) Atemi Abilities (including advanced).
6th Level Shih Ba Ban Wu Yi Martial Artist, including fifteen (15) Weapon Katas.
Chinese Language: Stage 4/Classical Chinese Literacy.
Language Dialects: Chinese
Chinese Mythology – Taoist
Wei Qi, the game of Go (+18%)
Select eight (8) skills from the following list:
Communications: Basic Radio Only
Cultural/Domestic: Any
Cultural Games: Any (+10%)
Electrical: Basic Only

Espionage: Any (+20%)
Mechanical: Any, but only as Secondary Skill
Medical: First Aid or Paramedic Only
Military: Any
Physical: Any (+5%)
Pilot Skills, Basic: Any
Swindler: Any (+15%)
Technical: Any
Temple: Any
W.P. Ancient Chinese: Any
W.P. Modern: Any
W.P. Military: Any

Infernal Demons

All Infernal Demons, from the lowliest minion, to the exalted Demon Overlord, have the same basic range of powers and abilities, as follows:

The Typical Infernal

Horror Factor: Usually 14, but ancient and powerful ones and demon lords can have a high rating.

Alignment: Mostly diabolic, aberrant and miscreant, but there are a few who are anarchist or unprincipled.

Size: Infernal Demons can alter their size and weight at will, but they usually stand about nine feet tall (2.7 m) and weigh around 500 pounds (225 kg).

S.D.C.: None. Chinese demons are made of pure Negative Chi. However, Infernals can convert their Chi into S.D.C. and/or hit points when they assume a physical form.

Negative Chi: 6D6 plus 75.

P.P.E.: None. Infernals are made of pure Negative Chi. However it is possible for demons to "hoard" P.P.E.

The Typical Eight Attributes: I.Q. 3D6, M.E. 3D6, M.A. 3D6, P.S. 3D6+15, P.P. 3D6+10, P.E. 3D6+15, P.B. 2D6, Spd. 3D6+5.

Attacks per Melee: Four

Bonuses (in addition to attributes): +1 on initiative, +2 to strike, +3 to parry and dodge.

Standard Demonic Powers & Abilities

ALL Infernals, including the Yama Kings themselves, have the following abilities:

1. Assume Demonic Form. While in demon form, the Infernal has an Armor Rating of 17, a base S.D.C. of 40 (more are available in exchange for Negative Chi), horns, fangs, and spurs/spines/barbs (they inflict 2D4 damage each), as well as bonuses of +10 to P.S., +8 to P.E., +6 to P.P., +6 to Spd., and +2 to M.E.

2. Assume Other Forms. Infernals can take the form of a human, animal, or even inanimate object, but A.R. is reduced to 10 and S.D.C. is 20 (more are available in exchange for Negative Chi).

3. Enter and Exit the Realm of Yama Kings.

4. Possess ALL Negative Chi Mastery Abilities.

5. Sense Chen Chi – Living Vitality.

6. Torment (Special!): All Infernals are masters of the demonic art of torture. Virtually any piece of information, or a confession to any crime (whether or not the victim is guilty), is possible with just four uninterrupted melee rounds (one minute) of torment! Victims of this torment must roll to save vs psionic attack (actually a save vs Mental Endurance).

7. All Infernals are able to convert Chi to P.P.E. and vice versa (one P.P.E. point equals six Chi).

8. All Infernals have the following skills:

Chinese Language: Stage 4/Classical Chinese Literacy.
Tiao Qi, the game of Chinese Checkers (+5%).
Xiang Qi, the game of Shogi.
Wei Qi, the game of Go.

9. The ability to Manipulate/Control Undead.

10. All Infernal Demons can offer a version of Immortality to mortals, thereby creating a "Damned Immortal."

11. Bonuses: +1 to save vs magic, 1D4+3 to save vs horror factor, +2 to save vs pain, +8 to save vs possession, impervious to normal cold and heat, and are impervious to disease.

12. The abilities to see the invisible, see aura, and detect concealment.

Infernal Strengths

Most Infernals have ONE of the following strengths; roll 2D6 to determine which one. Roll twice for Horned Ushers and three times for Demon Overlords.

2. Possession of Servants in the World of Mortals. The Demon will have control over at least one Damned Immortal who will head a network of humans who owe fealty to the Demon.

3. Immense P.P.E.: 5D10 plus 20.

4. Combat Specialist: Add one additional attack per melee round, +1 on initiative, +2 to strike and parry, +5 to damage, and +5 to pull punch.

5. Extra Negative Chi: Add 1D6×10.

6. Extra Horror Factor: Add 1D4 to the base of 14 and is +1 to save vs horror factor.

7. Chi Mask (as Chi Magic Spell). Allows demons to conceal their true state of Chi.

8. One "Positive or Negative" Chi Mastery Ability.

9. Superb Demonic Form. The sharp claws, horns and similar parts of the demonic form do an additional +4 damage with every strike.

10. Torture Specialist. Demons able to inflict massive pain with incredible precision. Victims are -3 to save vs pain.

11. Range of Human Skills. Where most demons know (and care) nothing about the skills of mortals, this demon has made a hobby of learning a few from the human souls in its care. Select five of the following as Secondary Skills:

Communications: Any	
Cultural/Domestic: Any	
Electrical: Any	
Espionage: Any	
Mechanical: Any	
Science: Any	
Swindler: Any	W.P. Ancient: Any
Technical: Any	W.P. Modern: Any
Temple: Any	W.P. Military: Any

12. Roll for two additional Demonic Strengths.

Infernal Weaknesses

Most Infernal Demons have two weaknesses, but Horned Ushers and Demon Overlords only have one. Proctors, Lady Meng, and the Yama Kings have NO weaknesses. Roll 2D6 to determine weaknesses:

2. Secretly wants enlightenment.
3. Vulnerable to hangovers.
4. Unpopular with other demons (reduce M.A. by half).
5. Out-and-out coward.
6. Very ticklish.
7. Incredibly stupid (reduce I.Q to 3).
8. Outrageously superstitious.
9. Very unlucky, especially when gambling.
10. Sensitive to physical pain.
11. Has a guilty secret.
12. Roll two additional weaknesses.

Special Powers

Ordinary Infernal Demons have a 30% chance of having one of the following powers. Roll once for Horned Ushers, and twice for Demon Overlords. (roll 2D6):

2. Master Psionic. Has all psionic abilities and an I.S.P. equal to the Infernal's Chi.
3. Sense Ti Chi – Earth/Dragon Energy.
4. Sense Alchemical Aura.
5. All "Negative and Positive" Chi Mastery Abilities.
6. Natural Chi Zoshiki (Mystical Invisibility).
7. Teleport self at will, with 3D4+82% accuracy; perfect accuracy if the teleporter can see where he's going.
8. The Powers of exorcism and impervious to possession.
9. Disperse Chi. Allows the Infernal to disperse up to twelve points of Negative or Positive Chi from the local flow.
10. Sense Yuan Chi — Sense Age and See Aura.
11. Invulnerable to attacks from Positive Chi.
12. Wielder of Chi Magic. Knows all Chi Magic Spells!

An Infernal's Rank

A demon's rank is pretty much meaningless as a gauge of skill or power. Instead it is an indicator of how good the demon is at sucking up to its superiors.

01-60 Minion (Chung Gui). The vast majority of Infernals are "minions." No stronger, but no weaker than any other demon, Minion Demons are at the bottom of the social ladder and are usually ordered around by just about every other Infernal in the hierarchy.

61-75 Attendant (Ma Gui). Also known as "bootlickers," "brownnosers," and "toadies," these Infernals are recognized as being willing to take on extra duties and to snitch on their fellow demons in exchange for a small step up in status.

76-85 Warrior (Chiang Gui). In reality, all Infernals are considered "warriors," however, this "honorary" title indicates that the demon is ready to assume positions of greater responsibility and will be regularly assigned to combat and espionage missions.

86-90 Envoy (Fu Gui). Used as messengers and personal attendants by higher ranking Infernals. Envoys finally reach a rank where they no longer have to toil endlessly tormenting the damned.

91-95 Intermediary (Huang Gui). An Infernal who frequently represents Horned Ushers, Infernal Overlords, the Yama Kings or other great supernatural powers. They may engage in making pacts and contacts, negotiating settlements, act as harbingers of doom, or lead missions of combat and espionage, as well as direct minions.

96-97 Bureaucrat (Guan Gui). Assigned to the vast departments that handle the paperwork for the Yama Kings.

98-99 Adjutant (Jing Gui). Highly respected Infernals assigned to the personal staff of a Demon Overlord, a position that allows an Infernal the training necessary to advance in real power!

100 Sycophant (Li Gui). At this status level, the Infernal has become one of the members of a Yama King's Royal Court, is given a title and a special place of honor in ceremonies. Although the demon has no special powers, the character must exhibit intelligence and cunning. As a result, Sycophants are considered nearly equal in rank to a Horned Usher.

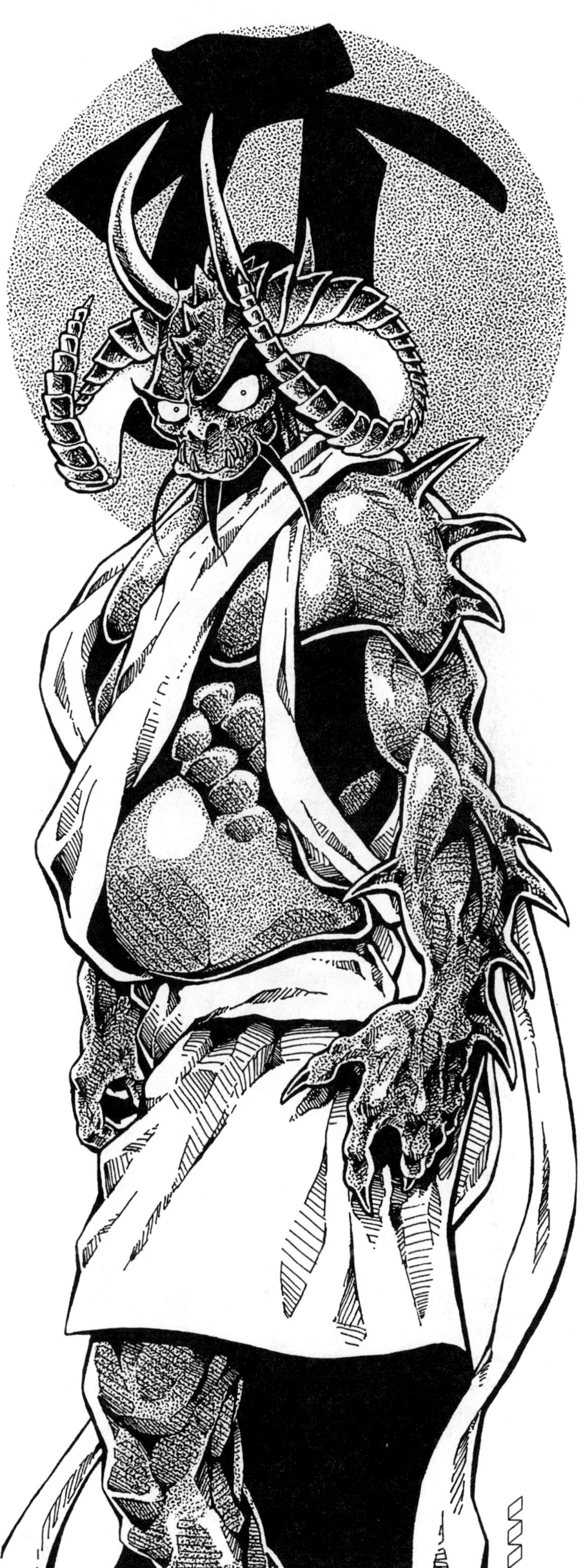

Horned Ushers

Horned Ushers are the personal retainers of the Yama Kings and primary assistants to Demon Overlords. They take their duties with utmost seriousness. They view all the Infernals below their rank with contempt and think of themselves as the only truly superior and dedicated Infernals. They believe that those of higher rank are merely lucky power mongers who lack serious discipline.

Typical Horned Usher

Horror Factor: 15

Size: Horned Ushers usually appear to be twice the size and weight of other Infernal Demons; 18 feet (5.5 m).

Alignment: Diabolic, miscreant or aberrant.

Negative Chi: 6D6 plus 100

Attacks per Melee: Five

Bonuses: +2 on initiative, +1 to strike, +4 to damage, +1 to save vs magic, +2 to pull punch, +3 to save vs pain and horror factor and +50 S.D.C. to human or animal form.

Note: All the previously described abilities, strengths, weaknesses, etc., apply; roll for them as usual.

Demon Overlords

Infernal Overlords are the officers and officials among the ranks of Chinese Demons. Each Overlord has responsibility over ten thousand demons. There are at least sixteen Demon Overlords assigned to each of the Yama Kings of Hell (one for each Yama King dungeon). Some of the Yama Kings started out as Demon Overlords.

Their powers are awesome, but they are constrained against using them against anyone in the world of men. Of course, they are allowed to "defend" themselves and may try to lure mortals into foolish attacks against them.

When visiting the World of Men, as the Overlords call Earth, they generally take human form and almost always appear as an aged sage. However, other possibilities and the whim of the Infernal could result in appearing as an ordinary animal (a dog or cat), a young person, or just about anything at all.

Typical Demon Overlord

Horror Factor: 16

Alignment: Always Diabolic, Aberrant or Miscreant.

Negative Chi: 6D6 plus 150.

The Eight Attributes: While the Overlord's I.Q. is at least 25 (3D6+22), all the other attributes are standard for Infernals; M.E. 3D6, M.A. 3D6, P.S. 3D6+15, P.P. 3D6+10, P.E. 3D6+20, P.B. 2D6, Spd. 3D6+5.

Level of Experience: Most Demon Overlords have the equivalent of 15th level experience in all regards to abilities, magic and skills.

Attacks per Melee: Six

Bonuses: +4 on initiative, +2 to strike, parry and dodge, +6 to damage, +2 to save vs magic, +6 to save vs pain and horror factor, +100 S.D.C. to human or animal form.

Note: All the previously described Infernal abilities, strengths, weaknesses, etc., apply; roll for them as usual.

A special Game Master's note about Overlords & Reformed Demons

If there is a Reformed Demon R.C.C. in the campaign, then it's likely that character's Demon Overlord should play a special part. The Overlord in charge of the rebellious character will be very interested in getting him/her back under control. After all, any success that a Reformed Demon may have tends to undermine the Demon Overlord's authority. Plus, losing control over one of their minions makes the Overlord look very bad in the eyes of the Yama Kings.

Since the laws of Hell prohibit the Demon Overlord from simply attacking, killing or capturing the escaped Reformed Demon, this leaves the Overlord with something of a dilemma as to how to get the rebel back without breaking the rules.

The solution is to "help" the Reformed Demon! After all, there's nothing illegal about giving assistance.

In what way?

The best way to get a Reformed Demon into trouble is to offer up opportunities for action. That way there will be plenty of chances for the Reformed Demon to screw up and plenty of chances for the Overlord to regain face. Thus, the manipulative demon will secretly arrange important bits of information, tips and rumors that may get the character in trouble, to find their way to him. For example, if there is a particularly cruel warlord on the loose somewhere in Mystic China, the Demon Overlord might want to tip the Reformed Demon off about certain "injustices" that are happening out in the world of men. Of course the Overlord doesn't really care about the suffering of the innocents, but if the Reformed Demon breaks *any* laws in bringing the Warlord to justice, or happens to kill the villain, then the Overlord will then be able to reclaim his subject. He may also send an emissary or intermediary to tempt or encourage rash thoughts and actions with dangerous consequences.

Note: I'd recommend figuring out the name and position of the Demon Overlord as soon as a Reformed Demon player character or NPC enters the campaign. Then, whenever it seems interesting, the Overlord or one of his servants can show up (probably charming and friendly), with genuinely helpful advice and information. In this role, the Demon Overlord should be endlessly patient and forgiving, overlooking any and all insults coming from the Reformed Demon or his companions, although if pushed too far by mortals, the Overlord may lash out at rude player characters. From the Demon Overlord's point of view, smiling under five hundred years of the character's abuse is better than the shame of the Yama Kings' scorn.

Yama Kings

When walking in the world of men, the Yama Kings nearly always take the form of blackened skeletons, garbed in their official robes and medallions of rank, complete with ornate headgear and signs of power. They will *never* appear without at least a dozen of their most powerful and fearsome servants in attendance. The appearance of a Yama King upon the Earth is a powerful sign of unrest and it will inevitably draw the attention of the Celestial Court of the Jade Emperor. The skies will always darken and lightning and thunder from above will accompany their every word and gesture.

Everyone who observes a Yama King visiting Earth will instantly know the King's name, of which hell he rules, and exactly the nature of the tortures normally inflicted by the King. There is no saving throw, but this is not something that triggers the horror factor or any supernatural pain or effect. It is as if each character simply "remembered" the information. Once the Yama King has departed the information will remain permanently fixed in the memories of those who observed him.

Yama Kings *never* take "direct" action upon themselves. It is beneath their dignity. Nor will they ever interfere in mortal affairs. If a Yama King appears, it is usually only to converse. Either they will have a message to deliver, or they may seek a particular piece of information, or it's even possible that a Yama King may approach a mortal with the offer of a deal for their services.

All ten of the Yama Kings will be covered in detail in the upcoming **Mystic China Sourcebook**. For the time being, here is a listing of just a few of the Yama Kings:

Chin Kuang Wang: King of the First Hell. Ruler of the Living Dead and those who have unfinished business in the mortal world. Chin Kuang's realm includes the Terrace of the Mirror of the Wicked, the *Hsieh Ching Tai*, where the condemned are able to see images of all the victims of every wrong they have ever committed.

Yen Lo Wang: King of the Fifth Hell. The foremost watcher of the world of mortals among the Yama Kings. Yen Lo has always been interested in creating new servants (the Copper Pigeons were his creations) and he is now taking a keen interest in computers and other aspects of modern technology. Included in his realm is the village of *Wang Hsiang Tai*, where the damned can see the misfortunes that follow their relatives after they have gone.

Tai Shan Chun Wang: King of the Seventh Hell. Second in command of the realm and heir-apparent to Chuan Lun, the supreme ruler. One remarkable thing about Tai Shan Chun is that he is one of those who came up through the ranks. At the time of the foundation of the Yama Kings, Tai Shan Chun was a low-ranking demon, one of the hundreds of thousands elevated from the previous version of hell. Taking advantage of the situation, with a combination of hard work and occasional treachery, Tai Shan Chun managed to pull himself up into the rank of Demon Overlord. Eventually, through masterful guile, Tai Shan Chun managed to overthrow the former 7th Yama, simultaneously gaining the support of the other nine Yama Kings.

Chuan Lun Wang: King of the Tenth Hell. Chuan Lun is the supreme ruler of the Hells of the Yama Kings and is also

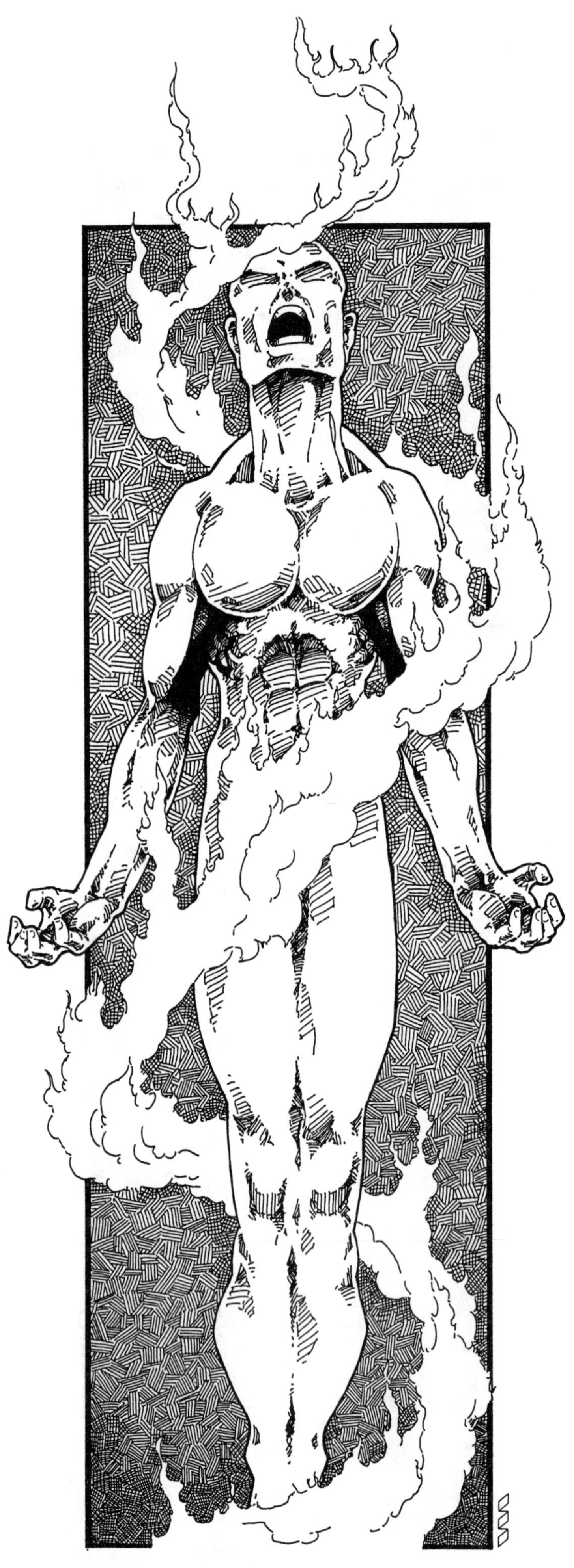

known as "He who turns the Great Wheel of Transmigration." Included in his realm is the great capital city of Feng Tu, where 24 administrative offices determine the fates of all departed souls.

Infernals Beyond the Reach of the Yama Kings

There were other realms in the underworld before the consolidation (some would say, before the conquest) by the Yama Kings. Most of these realms have been destroyed or absorbed into the realm of the Yama Kings. However, there are ancient places in the underworld that still operate under the Mandate of the Jade Emperor's Heaven.

While these "lost" underworlds are no longer a destination for most of the souls who depart the mortal world, they continue to operate for a dwindling number of ancient souls still undergoing punishment. Also, and this is a particular sore spot for the rulers of the old Hells, there are souls who they are obliged to "process," who have somehow continued to escape their fate. The missing ones are those who have become misguided Immortals, and their company is greatly desired.

Rebel Infernals

For one reason or another, there are Infernals who have escaped from the realm of the Yama Kings and fled into the world of mortals. Each of these dangerous Infernals may have dreams of worldly conquest, or long-term plans for forming a new underworld, or simply a desire to be left utterly alone (although most Infernals of this latter type simply migrate to other planes of existence, or plunge into the depths of outer space, and are not likely to be found anywhere on Earth). They can become dangerous forces of evil and villainy in the World of Men and are accumulate many mortal and Infernal enemies.

Martial Art Powers

Note: Only the *new* powers are described in **Mystic China**. The *Arts of Invisibility* and other powers listed below can be found in the **Ninjas & Superspies Role-Playing Game**.

Arts of Invisibility

Stealth
Hiding
Vanishing
Disguise
Escape
Mystic Invisibility

Atemi Abilities (Vital Points)

Healing
Neutral Atemi (Paralyze)
Blood Flow (Hit Point Attack)
Grasping Hand (Dislocate Joints)
Open Hand (Deafen or Stun)
Withering Flesh (S.D.C. Attack)
Dim Mak (Kills Chi)

Advanced Atemi — Tien Hsueh Abilities (New)

Enlightenment Strike
Blindness
Chi Block
Tien Hsueh Amnesia
Finger-Snap Tien Hsueh
Puppet Dance Tien Hsueh
Long-Distance Dim Mak

Chi Mastery

Chi Awareness
Chi Relaxation
Chi Combat
Chi Healing (Pos. only)
Dragon Chi (Pos. only)
Body Chi (Pos. only)
Hardened Chi (Pos. or Neg.)
Soft Chi (Pos. or Neg.)
Find Weakness (Pos. or Neg.)
One Finger Chi (Neg. only)
Fist Gesture (Neg. only)
Dark Chi (Neg. only)

Advanced Chi Mastery (New)

Radiate Positive Chi (Pos. only)
Heal the Mind (Pos. only)
Chi Weight Control (Pos. only)
Chi Overcharge (Pos. or Neg.)
Fill Object with Chi (Pos. or Neg.)
Divert Incoming Chi (Pos. or Neg.)
Control Negative Chi (Neg. only)
Negative Chi Polarity (Neg. only)
Inflict Negative Chi Illness (Neg. only)

Body Hardening Exercises

Chi-Gung
Dam Sum Sing
Iron Hand
Kick Practice
Stone Ox
Winter Training
Wrist Hardening

Demon Hunter Body Hardening Exercises (New)

Ao Dah Jong
Control Revulsion
Demon Wrestling
Eternal Clarity or Yung Chin
Feign Death/Coma/Unconscious
Laugh at Pain
Resist Chi Influence

Special Katas

Fortress Penetration
One Mind
Warrior Spirit
Five Principles
Windmill
Weapon Kata

Chi Katas for Mystic China (New)

Blind Man's Kata
Chi Ball Kata
Chi Defense Kata
Dragon Line Kata
Mending Chi Kata
Ying-Yang Kata

Martial Arts Techniques

Awareness
Breaking
Falling
Kaijutsu
One Life, One Shot, One Hit
Sword Drawing

Additional Martial Art Techniques (New)

Eight Horse Stomp
Light Body Climbing
Sword Chi Technique
Sung Chi
Shift Internal Organs
Vital Harmony

Zenjoriki

Calm Minds
Karumi-Jutsu
Mind Walk
Vibrating Palm

Additional Zenjoriki (New)

Discorporate
Mind Walk (expanded details)
Spirit Burst

Atemi/Ten Hsueh Powers

If you've ever hit the "funny bone" in your elbow or knee then you already know what **Tien Hsueh** (also known as "Atemi") is all about. A proper strike in the right area can paralyze a limb, disrupt the nervous system, or knock someone out altogether. These vulnerable points or "vital points" can be used to affect the body and mind in numerous ways.

Each Ten Hsueh ability can be used only with the martial arts form where the ability is available. In other words, if you get a Tien Hsueh ability through Ch'in-Na, you cannot use the ability with any other martial arts form.

Advanced Tien Hsueh Abilities - Supreme Control Over the Vital Points

1. Enlightenment Strike: In a two-handed move, the martial artist pushes his palms toward the victim, pulling the hands apart an instant before they would contact the face. The result is that the victim will instantly be freed from any possession spell or entity, Chi Control or mind controlling spell. The move uses up ALL the actions/attack of an entire melee round and must be done within striking distance from the victim.

2. Blindness: A precise two-finger strike to a point just below the victim's eyes. It causes a total blindness that persists for 1D6 hours! The roll is so difficult that the atemi expert must roll 14 or better to strike, with no bonuses allowed. A miss or if the victim manages to parry or dodge, means there is no damage or blindness. If the victim manages to roll with punch/fall/impact, then the blindness will only last 3D6 melee rounds! A blind character is -10 to strike, parry and dodge and must travel at half speed to avoid stumbling and falling (and possibly getting hurt).

3. Chi Block: This is a strike that disrupts the victim's ability to control his own Chi. Once disrupted, the victim is blocked from doing anything that requires Chi, including Chi combat, Chi magic, and even Chi-Gung Body Hardening. It will take 2D6 minutes of intense, uninterrupted concentration, or 1D6 minutes of continuous meditation for the victim to regain control over Chi.

A successful Chi Block requires a roll to strike of 10 or better, without benefit of attribute and combat bonuses. The opponent can attempt to parry or dodge and, if successful, will avoid any damage. If the victim manages to roll with punch/fall/impact, instead of the Chi Block, the character will lose 3D6 Points of Chi (Positive or Negative, whichever the victim is currently charged with).

Since the exact location of the "Chi Control Center" is different from person to person, the atemi expert must observe his opponent *before* attempting this attack. If the adversary is seen engaging in combat or in any form of Chi control, it will only take a single melee round to discover the exact spot. Otherwise, if the victim is simply engaged in normal activities (eating, walking, sleeping, etc.), the atemi expert will need to observe the victim for at least ten minutes.

4. Tien Hsueh Amnesia: This ability will not work in combat situations. Victims must either be willing and passive participants, or must be rendered unconscious before the Tien Hsueh Amnesia can begin.

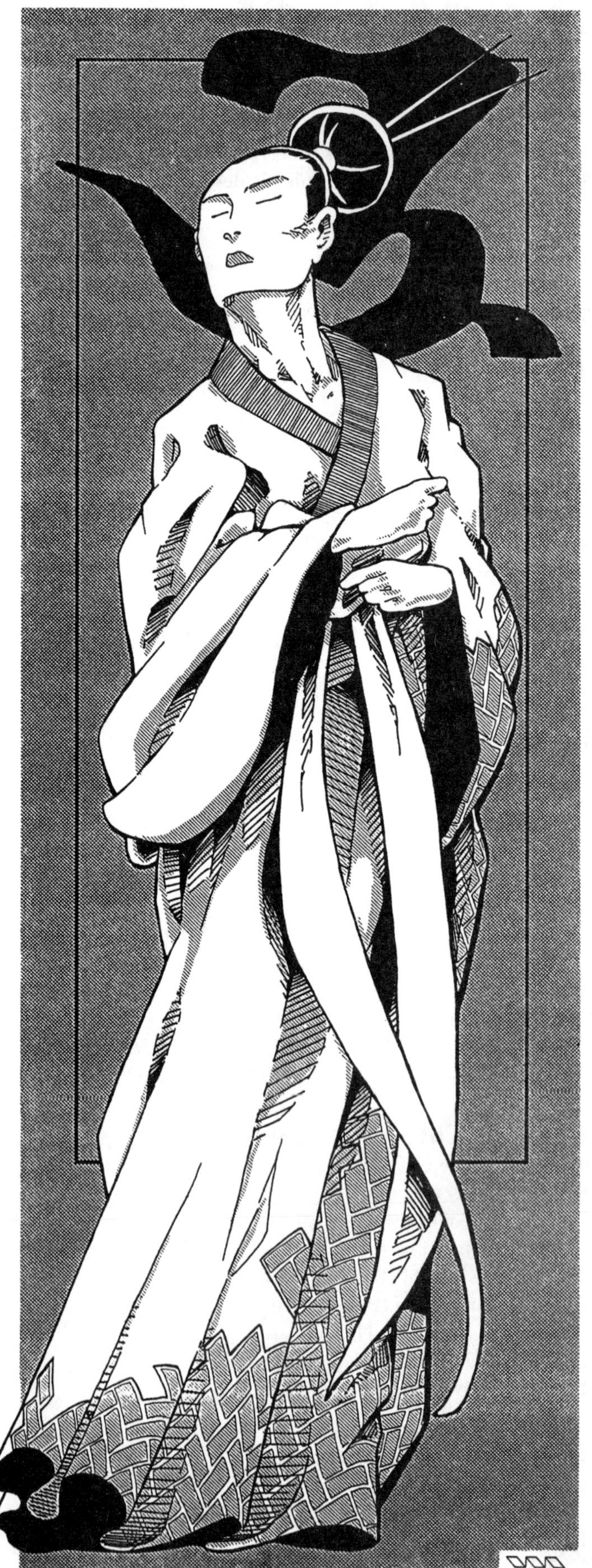

Short-Term Amnesia. If successful, the victim will forget all the events of the preceding 1D6+5 minutes. **Note:** The memories of the "lost" time will NEVER be recovered. It will be as if the character never experienced the events of that time period. This is the only Tien Hsueh Amnesia that is permanent. Traditionally, Short-Term Amnesia is done on those who have witnessed either the forbidden or the horrific, and when the victim volunteers to have his memory "erased" forever.

Alignment Amnesia. The victim remembers everything, including his or her name and previous life, but somehow "forgets" his/her alignment/moral view of life. To those who can detect alignment, the character will seem uncommitted and unformed, as if he had never figured out what alignment to become. Usually this is used as a means of infiltrating an enemy group (i.e.: it allows "good" alignments to sneak into evil groups, or "evil" alignments to pass undetected among principled and scrupulous). Lasts 1D6 days.

Full Amnesia. The victim remembers absolutely nothing from his or her life previous to the Tien Hsueh, nor any shred of identity. Although the character still has all his/her usual skills, abilities, and bonuses, he/she won't remember what they are (they just occur when needed). Because of the total loss of memory, the victim is easy prey for anyone who wants to "fill in" their memory. The amnesia lasts three hours per experience level of the character who caused the amnesia in the first place.

5. Finger-Snap Tien Hsueh: The sharp sound from this special "snap" of the fingers disrupts the victim's inner ear and he loses all sense of balance. Finger-Snap Tien Hsueh attacks must be made close to the victim, so the "snap" takes place no more than three feet (0.9 m) from the ears; closer is better. To succeed, the attacker must roll a natural 5 or better to strike, with no strike bonuses of any kind allowed.

After being affected by Finger-Snap Tien Hsueh, the victim can still think normally and perform most skills and other actions, but he cannot stand, walk or make sudden movements. If the character lays on the floor, is seated solidly, or stands with their back anchored against a wall, he will be comparatively okay. However, every time the character attempts to stand unassisted, walk, turn, or make a sudden movement, a wave of dizziness comes over him and he'll lose his balance and fall down. **Note:** Even when "propped up," the Finger-Snap victim is -3 on initiative, -7 to dodge and cannot kick, leap, or turn quickly without falling over.

There is no defense against Finger-Snap Tien Hsueh, except wearing noise-proof ear plugs or being in the middle of a rock concert or similar noisy environment. There is also no way for the victim to roll with punch/fall/impact. Recovery takes 3D6 minutes, although a *Healing Tien Hsueh* can cure the problem instantly.

6. Puppet Dance Tien Hsueh. The first step for the attacker is to get a good grip on the back of the victim's neck. This can be done with any sort of combat "grab" or just by moving a hand into place when the intended victim is unaware or helpless.

Once the attacker has a hand on the back of the victim's neck, it takes another roll to strike (normal bonuses allowed) and a single melee action for the Puppet Dance Tien Hsueh to be activated. The victim has one last chance to dodge/pull away, but there is no possibility of a roll with punch/fall/impact.

Mastering complete puppet control over his victim usually takes about one full melee round of experimentation with finger pressure. The puppet victim is completely aware but helpless. The attacker maintaining the puppet hold can manipulate his victim like a living puppet via pressure from his finger on the neck — the perfect hostage hold. The victim can be made to walk, skip, dance, open doors, or otherwise move around. The arms can be made to move, gesture, pick up or drop objects, scratch, point, etc. Even the face can be made to change gestures, with forced smiles, frowns, winking and blinking, mouth movements and the like. In fact, the only things the Puppet Dance can't do is get the victim to speak, although humming and grunting are possible. The victim can be forced to fight, but such actions will be terribly slow and clumsy. **Note:** The puppet has only two melee actions per round and has no combat or attribute bonuses available (natural rolls only). Skill performance is at -60%.

As long as the Tien Hsueh expert maintains the hold, the victim will be manipulated like a puppet. However, the attacker cannot perform any other Tien Hsueh, cannot use Chi, and will have difficulty in combat because he'll be distracted by the manipulation of his puppet (-1 attack per melee round, -2 on initiative and -2 to dodge). The attacker can continue to talk normally, walk around (with the victim), and use the other hand to fight, parry, shoot, or perform skills (one-handed of course).

Once the hold is released, the victim will be *instantly* back in charge of his/her own body and will remember (and resent) having been manipulated.

7. Long-Distance Dim Mak: Exactly like regular **Dim Mak** (see *Ninjas & Superspies*), except direct physical touch is no longer required. Unlike regular Dim Mak, where the attacker just needs to make a standard strike, a successful Long-Distance Dim Mak takes a full melee round of concentration (no other combat or Chi activities) and a roll to strike of a natural 15 or better (no bonuses allowed).

There are two ways that a Long-Distance Dim Mak can be delivered. First, if the victim is within *100 feet (31 m)* of the Tien Hsueh Master and in clear sight, the Dim Mak can be sent through the floor, wall, or any other solid object that both the victim and the attacker are touching; it will pass right through shoes, gloves or other protection.

The other possible delivery method is the telephone. If the victim can be made to stay on the line for the full melee round (15 seconds; while the attacker concentrates and says nothing), the Dim Mak can be delivered across great distances.Of course, the trick is to figure out some way to get the intended victim to stay on the phone for the fifteen seconds needed to focus the attack, because the attacker can't talk while concentrating. There are various tricks, including calling from a line with two phones and getting a confederate to talk to the victim, asking a question that will require the victim to make a very long answer, or just saying, "Oh, I have someone at the door, can you hold for a minute?"

Note: Recently certain Dim Mak experts have discovered that the telephone delivery method is not 100% certain. Upon investigation, they have discovered that it always works when the connection is through lines and wires. However, if somewhere between the Dim Mak attacker and the victim there is a microwave connection (some long cross-country lines), radio (mobile or wireless phone), a satellite link (trans-continental lines), or an optical cable (certain high-tech installations and some modern cities have replaced wires), then the Long-Distance Dim Mak can't work.

The build-up of concentration required to launch a Dim Mak attack gives the victim a chance to realize that they are in danger. Any character with any Chi Mastery will have their Chi Awareness "tickled" (the Game Master should say something like, "You sense some kind of change in the surrounding flow of Chi" or "You suddenly feel a dark cloud around you."). Characters with any psionics will get a "bad feeling" or a feeling of danger. Others should be allowed to roll under their M.A. on twenty-sided dice (no bonuses allowed) and, if successful, they will be aware that "something, you don't know exactly what, but something is definitely wrong."

Characters being attacked by Long-Distance Dim Mak can attempt to dodge, with all their usual bonuses, but only **if** they are aware of the direction of the attack or who is attacking. If the attack is successful, the victim can try to avoid the Dim Mak and any other damage by rolling with punch/fall/impact.

Note: Character's with good alignments will NEVER use Long-Distance Dim Mak. It's just too evil.

Chi

Chi is a fundamental "energy" that flows through the world. It comes in two flavors, or "polarities". **Positive Chi** powers living things and is usually associated with sunlight. **Negative Chi** is associated with the dead, darkness, and the light of the moon.

Chi: How It Works

If you're not familiar with the Chi rules first presented in **Ninjas & Superspies**, or if you need a refresher course, here are the main points:

Who has Chi? All living beings have Positive Chi. It's the energy of life that flows through the earth and through every living thing. Most physically fit, mentally healthy people will have a large amount of Chi. People who are sickly or mentally disturbed will have low amounts of Chi.

Why do all characters have Chi? While most people are unaware of Chi, there is one thing that everyone uses it for, healing! The body's tissues and blood must be flowing with a minimum amount of Chi in order to do any kind of repairs. A character must have at least one point of Chi in order to be healed from any damage. It doesn't matter how good the medical care is, a body without Chi can't heal itself. So, at zero Chi there is no recovery of S.D.C. or hit points.

How much Chi should characters from other games and non-player characters, have? Since P.E. (Physical Endurance) is the main "battery" of Chi, everyone's starting Chi is equal to their adjusted P.E. attribute number (after all skills and bonuses have been added in).

What happens to characters when they lose some of their Chi? Not much. As long as a character has at least one point of Positive Chi they'll heal normally and suffer no ill effects.

How do characters usually recover lost Chi? Anyone, so long as they have at least one point of Positive Chi left, can get

back all lost Chi simply by getting a full night's sleep. Interrupted sleep, where the character gets between four and six hours of rest, will result in recovery of only half the lost Chi.

What if the character has Zero Chi or Negative Chi? That's a problem! People with no Positive Chi remaining and with no Chi abilities, can't heal back their lost Chi. And, without Chi, the body can't heal itself. Even if a character is perfectly healthy, with full hit points and full S.D.C., a condition of Zero Chi or Negative Chi is harmful. Every week at zero or negative Chi, the character must roll to save against illness. The roll must be 15 or better on a Twenty-Sided dice (it's okay to use the P.E. bonus).

Sick characters will start to waste away, first losing just one S.D.C. per week, then one hit point per week, and finally, when they've dropped to zero hit points, they lapse into a coma and lose one point of P.E. per week. Even worse, the character must keep saving to avoid getting additional illnesses. When all the P.E. points are gone, the character dies.

How can characters recover from Zero or from Negative Chi? By getting help from anyone with *Chi Healing*. After a character recovers any Positive Chi, even a single point, then healing will start immediately, illnesses will disappear, and all lost Chi, hit points and S.D.C. will be recovered normally. Lost P.E. will come back at the rate of one point per week.

The Power of Chi Manipulation or "Chi Mastery"

Only characters with at least one Chi Mastery ability understand how to use the power of their Chi. Even then, characters must *focus their Chi* on a particular Chi ability before it can be used. Focusing takes one melee round action (about 3 seconds), but can be done during combat or at any other time. After the Chi is focused, the character can perform that one, particular Chi ability continuously. Switching from one Chi ability to another Chi ability means focusing the Chi once again and requires another melee action. Generally, a character can only perform one Chi ability at a time. Only those with the ability to "tap" Chi can continue drawing on a source of Chi while doing something else with Chi.

Any character with at least one Chi Mastery ability or any creature of pure Chi, *automatically* has the following three abilities: Chi Awareness, Chi Relaxation, and Defend against Chi Attacks (see **Ninjas & Superspies**, page 118).

Advanced Positive Chi Abilities

1. Radiate Positive Chi: The character emits light simply by releasing the primal nature of Positive Chi, that of the sun's energy. The Chi can be coming from the character or, if the character also has Dragon Chi, it's possible to fuel Radiate Positive Chi from another source. Note that creatures who are vulnerable/damaged by sunlight will have to do their own version of save vs horror factor (13; but only affects creatures of darkness). Here are the three possible ways of Radiating Positive Chi:

Radiant Eyes. The Positive Chi pours out of the eyeballs, turning them into miniature globes of sunlight. The beams act like the beam of a flashlight, pointing in whatever direction the character is looking. The light will NOT interfere with the character's vision and will even aid eyesight by providing illumination. The light will be bright enough to clearly illuminate objects up to 50 feet (15.2 m) away (a little better than an automobile's headlights). Creatures vulnerable to sunlight will be affected by the direct glare of the eyes just as if they were outdoors on a sunny day. **Cost:** Two points of Positive Chi per melee round.

Radiant Flesh. The entire character glows with a yellowish, sunny light, illuminating the area as if the character were a window thrown open to the sun. All creatures of darkness within 30 feet (9.1 m) will be affected and everything within that range will be clearly lit, as if by full daylight. **Cost:** Four points of Positive Chi per melee round.

Tide of Radiance. As with Radiant Flesh, the character will glow brightly and will illuminate an area up to 30 feet (9.1 m) in diameter. Even more significantly, all the natural Negative Chi of the area will be neutralized! Since the area around the character becomes effectively one of Positive Chi (although with only a fraction of a point of Positive Chi in the environment — too small an amount to be tapped by Dragon Chi), opponents who depend on a Negative Chi background can be at a severe disadvantage. **Cost:** The current level of Negative Chi plus four points in Positive Chi per melee round. For example, if the area has a malignancy of five points of Negative Chi, the character will have to spend nine points of Positive Chi per melee round to neutralize it.

2. Heal the Mind: By flooding the mind with a current of positive Chi, it's possible to attempt a curing of many mental illnesses. Note that a character can't do *self-healing* with this ability.

Saving Throw: The subject must roll a save vs psionic attack/insanity with no M.E. bonus. If the roll is successful, the healing fails. All attempts to Heal the Mind are automatically resisted by the subject, no matter how much he may want to be cured.

Cost: All types of Heal the Mind have the same cost, one point of Positive Chi per attempt.

Here are the three ways that Heal the Mind can be used:

Temporarily Healing Insanity. Heal the Mind cannot permanently cure such mental afflictions. However, it will temporarily stop the character from experiencing the usual negative effects of their insanity. For example, a character with a ghost phobia will not be affected by the phobic panic for as long as the healing lasts. Aside from the temporary relief from the symptoms of the insanity, this is also useful in that it allows some characters to come to their senses, realize that they have been acting irrationally and seek some kind of long-term help. **Note:** It's impossible to heal an insanity that a character is either born with, or comes about as a result of the character's own guilt/self-blame or self-hatred, even temporarily. **Duration:** 1D4 hours per level of the Chi Master.

Healing Induced Madness/Insanity. This *permanently* heals a character who has been driven Insane by some outside influence, such as results from physical and/or mental torture, drug induced hallucinations, illusions, and magic.

Healing Mental Manipulation/Damage. By restoring the mind to its proper state, any outside influences are eliminated. This includes changes brought about by hypnosis (for example, this will expose a post-hypnotic suggestion), suggestion, enslavement, or other forms of mind control and psionic manipulation.

3. Chi Weight Control: Transforming the Chi of the body into an equivalent amount of gravitational energy, the character can become either much heavier or much lighter. Chi Weight Control can be used anywhere, regardless of whether the environment is empty of Chi or has Positive or Negative Chi. Note that, while Chi Weight Control must be "turned on" at the beginning of the melee round, the character can "dial" their weight up and down during combat.

Increase Personal Weight. The character's personal weight can be increased from a few pounds all the way up to 20 times the character's normal weight! For example, a 150 pound (68 kg) character could suddenly weigh up to 3,000 pounds (1360 kg)!! Of course, if the character's weight exceeds the character's P.S. carrying capacity, it's no longer possible to walk around or perform kicks and leaps. Hand and arm movements and parries are unaffected. Dodges are at -2. One favorite technique is to turn on a massive increase in weight when falling on top of an enemy, when grappling an opponent or in an attempt to become unmovable. **Cost:** One point of Positive Chi per melee round.

Decrease Personal Weight. The character's weight is reduced as low as one pound (.45 kg). Note that the character's clothing and possessions are NOT affected. A favorite use of decreased weight is to lend greater distance to leaps and jumps, to be carried with ease and to lighten the load on vehicles. **Cost:** One point of Positive Chi per melee round.

Advanced Positive or Negative Chi Abilities

These are "universal" Chi abilities that can be used by characters with either Positive or Negative Chi. It doesn't matter which kind of Chi powers them, the effects are the same.

1. Chi Overcharge: This allows the character to "overcharge" the body with *double* the usual amount of Positive or Negative Chi. The Chi Overcharge will usually last one full day and will drain away immediately whenever the character falls asleep or is otherwise rendered unconscious. The excess Chi can be gained by either a full hour of meditation in the appropriate environment, where the right kind of Chi is available, or using either Dragon Chi (Tap Positive Chi) or Dark Chi (Tap Negative Chi). **Cost:** One point of Chi (Positive if the Overcharge is with Positive Chi, Negative if the Overcharge is with Negative Chi).

2. Fill Object with Chi. The idea is to fill up an object, usually a weapon of some kind, with Chi so that it becomes "solid" from the perspective of the flow of Chi. For example, creatures of pure Negative Chi are usually unaffected by daggers and arrows. However, if the dagger or arrow is filled with Positive Chi, then the weapon will do the usual amount of damage, direct to the creature's Negative Chi.

How long the object will stay filled with Chi depends on how it is handled. As long as it stays in physical contact with a creature filled with the same kind of Chi, the effect will last indefinitely. So a spear filled with Positive Chi will stay "charged" as long as it is held by the bare hand of a character filled with Positive Chi. The same spear, slung on a strap over the character's back, will only maintain its "charge" for an hour or so in a place of Positive Chi. In a place of Negative Chi, where the Chi of the environment is disrupting the Positive Chi of the spear, the Chi will *only last for one melee round per level of the character's experience.*

Another way of using Fill Objects with Chi is to use it as a way of making objects come along when characters Mind Walk (see Zenjorike power) or otherwise move around in Pure Chi Form (transforming the body, or leaving it behind). The "Chi Aspect" of the object can then be carried or used as an object of Pure Chi. For example, a creature of Pure Negative Chi could carry the Chi Aspect of a sword or gun and use it as a weapon, inflicting damage based on Negative Chi. When used in this way, the Chi Aspect of the object will last as long as it is held or in contact with the character.

Cost: One point of Chi per object, plus the amount of Chi used to fill the object.

The amount of Chi needed to fill an object depends on its size. Small items, like daggers, bullets, arrows and shurikens, take only one point of Chi. Medium sized objects, like swords and spears, take two points of Chi. Larger objects, anything twenty pounds (9 kg) and over, usually require three points of Chi for every twenty pounds (9 kg) of mass.

3. Divert Incoming Chi: By "grounding" a layer of Chi on the outside surface of the body, the character diverts all incoming Positive or Negative Chi harmlessly into the ground. This only works while the character has at least one foot on the ground (not while leaping, jumping, or doing fancy kicks), and it works in any environment (Positive or Negative Chi). It's also possible for the character to extend the grounding layer over one or two other people (two others is the maximum) or over some other object. In this case all the characters must remain in place, with all their feet firmly planted on the ground. **Cost:** One point of Chi (Negative or Positive) per melee round, or two points if one or two additional people are protected.

Negative Chi Mastery

These are abilities that rely on *Negative* or *Dark* Chi. One big disadvantage to being filled with negative Chi is that it prevents the character's body from healing; only positive Chi can heal. This is a particular problem if the character's hit points fall below zero. Unconscious, the character is unable to flush out the negative Chi. Then, unless there is some outside aid, the character has *no chance of recovery.* The only cure is to destroy all the negative Chi and replace it with at least a point of positive Chi.

Advanced Negative Chi Abilities

1. Control Negative Chi: You may have noticed in **Ninjas & Superspies** that there was no immediate horrible consequence to being infected with negative chi. It made healing difficult and depleted positive chi, thereby blocking the use of many chi-based powers. However, it didn't put the character in any danger, it didn't hurt, and it wasn't even particularly dangerous. After all, isn't that the way it should be? Shouldn't the good guys be able to walk away relatively unharmed?

Dream on!

Once a positive chi creature or character is infected with negative chi, they become vulnerable to a whole range of attacks. From the point of view of a Negative Chi Master, any character filled with Negative Chi is a hapless victim and a potential pawn!

To successfully manipulate the Negative Chi of another character, 1) the victim must already be infected with at least one point of Negative Chi, 2) the attacker must roll a four or better to strike against the victim, and 3) the attacker must be within 100 feet (30.5 m) of the victim. Characters with no powers over Negative Chi are helpless victims and cannot parry, dodge or roll to evade the Control over their Negative Chi. However, characters who have at least one Negative Chi Mastery Ability can automatically parry or dodge any Control Negative Chi attack.

Here are the three possible uses of Control Negative Chi, Activate Negative Chi, Enslave/Control Through Negative Chi, and Inflict Temporary Insanity Through Negative Chi:

Activate Negative Chi. The negative *chi* flares up, influencing the cells of the victim's body and does the reverse of healing, spreading brutal damage. Victim takes 1D6 damage directly to hit points for every point of Negative Chi infecting the body. For example, if the victim is already infected with four points of Negative Chi, then that character would take 4D6 points of damage, direct to hit points every time Activate Negative Chi was used. **Cost:** Each use of Activate Negative Chi costs one point of Negative Chi.

Enslave/Control Through Negative Chi. Weakened by the Negative Chi in their bodies, victims of this attack are vulnerable to another's will. While the victim can attempt to save vs psionic attack (M.E. bonus included), failure to do so means the character MUST obey any command, except those that are life threatening, and answer any questions truthfully when they are given by the Negative Chi Master.

If the character inflicting the Enslave/Control Through Negative Chi so wishes, it's possible to work on *conditioning* the victim into becoming his permanent slave. This will take some time and the victim's will must be completely broken before an enslavement is successful. Characters who are permanently Enslaved will *always* obey the commands of their master, even after being completely healed of any other Negative Chi effects. Note, however, that the victim will be well aware of the nature of the relationship and can attempt to secretly undermine the wishes of his master. However, such defiance can only be done behind his master's back, never to his face (always subservient in the presence of his/her master).

Cost: One point of Negative Chi per attempt. Once the Chi Master has control, there is no need to spend any more points.

Inflict Temporary Insanity Through Negative Chi. Negative Chi is used as a channel to strike at the victim's mind, flooding it with dark images and forcing the character to dwell upon all the nightmare things of his own worst fears. This is the equivalent of weeks of mental torment. The victim *always* gets a save vs insanity (M.E. bonus applies). **Cost:** One point of Negative Chi per attempt.

While it's possible to Inflict Temporary Insanity Through Negative Chi more than once, that's only because the victim has the chance of saving vs insanity and therefore being unaffected. Once an Insanity has been inflicted, there's no point in continuing, since only one insanity can be inflicted using this power.

Since nearly all Palladium RPGs, **Ninjas & Superspies, Beyond the Supernatural, Heroes Unlimited, Rifts,** etc., have *Insanity Tables*, the Game Master can simply use those rules to roll up the resulting insanity. If the Game Master prefers, the character will be inflicted with a gibbering fear of Negative Chi and anything related to Negative Chi, such that the character will run in panic whenever there is a threat of darkness. **Note:** Whatever Insanity the victim suffers, that same Insanity will afflict the character if and when they are ever again afflicted with Negative Chi Insanity. **Duration:** The effect of Temporary Insanity Through Negative Chi will last as least as long as the character is infected with Negative Chi. Once the character has purged the Negative Chi and returned to a state of healthy Positive Chi, the insanity will only last for 1D6 days.

2. Negative Chi Polarity (New!). By manipulating the Negative Chi of an area (**Note:** This functions **only** in areas filled with at least two points of Negative Chi), the character can change the Chi so that it becomes magnetic. After this is accomplished, any character, animal or thing of Positive Chi is pulled toward the source of Negative Chi, just like a piece of iron is pulled toward a magnet. **Cost:** Two points of Negative Chi per melee round.

The amount of pulling force exerted during Negative Chi Polarity depends on the Negative Chi of the area affected. Every point of Negative Chi in the area acts as a multiplier on the normal weights of all the victims. For example, a character who normally weighs 150 pounds (68 kg), drawn down in an area of five Negative Chi, will suddenly seem to weigh five times as much or 750 pounds (340 kg). If the character had a P.S. of 30 or so (able to carry 600 extra pounds/272 kg) he could still stagger around, but most characters would barely be able to drag themselves a few feet.

Negative Chi Polarity doesn't affect anything with zero Chi or those filled with Negative Chi. So, a character being dragged down by Negative Chi Polarity might still be able to fire off a gun and normal bullets would operate without being affected by the Negative Chi Polarity.

3. Inflict Negative Chi Illness - *Chu Chi*: By inflicting an accumulation of Morbid Chi upon a victim, it is possible to "infect" the character with Chi-based illnesses. Curing these ills is impossible with normal medicine. Only treatments using strong Positive Chi can cause a cure.

While Chi Illnesses are usually used against those with Positive Chi, they can be used with equal effect on characters or creatures of Negative Chi. In fact, some of those with Negative Chi are even more damaged by Chi Illness, because the cures usually require bathing in substantial amounts of Positive Chi — something fatal to many dark entities.

Unless the intended victim is already filled with Negative Chi, any Chi Illness is inflicted by physical touch. However, if the target is already contaminated with at least one point of Negative Chi, it's possible to Inflict Negative Chi Illness from up to 20 feet (6.1 m) away. Any victim can attempt to save vs illness (beat the Chi Master's attack roll, P.E. bonus allowed) to avoid the infection.

Once a victim receives a Negative Chi Illness, there's nothing the character who inflicted the disease can do about it. It must either run its course or treatment can be sought from those who deal in Positive Chi Healing.

Chi Anemia - Hsueh Chi. Once infected, by a successful strike, the victim will be unable to use Chi properly. Each use of a Chi ability will cost twice the number of points as normal! The victim, after two full days of infection, can attempt to save vs illness once per day (P.E. bonus okay). To infect a victim with Che

Anemia, the Negative Chi Master must roll ten or better to strike (on Twenty-Sided). **Cost:** Each touch of Che Anemia costs six points of Negative Chi.

Demon Chi Possession - Kuei Chi. To the victim, possession by Demonic Chi feels "as if stuck by a spear" in the chest. Until healed, there will sharp constricting pains with every breath and every few minutes the character will have to spit out blood. As long as the victim is affected, he/she will lose one attack per melee round and is -2 on initiative and -10% on skill performance. After one full day of infection, the victim can attempt to save vs illness twice per day (P.E. bonus okay). To infect a victim with Demon Chi Possession, the Negative Chi Master must roll ten or better to strike (on Twenty-Sided). **Cost:** Each touch of Demon Chi Possession costs ten points of Negative Chi.

Rising Chi Cough - Ou Ni Shang Chi. This nasty cough serves to trap the character's Chi, making it impossible to use any Chi Mastery abilities. It works by trapping a small amount of Negative Chi in the character's lungs which triggers a cough reflex. As the character coughs (the urge to cough is irresistible when the character attempts to manipulate Chi), the Chi accumulates in the lungs which swell up and cause more coughing. The victim, after two full days of infection, can attempt to save vs illness twice per day (P.E. bonus okay). To infect a victim with Rising Chi Cough, the Negative Chi Master must roll ten or better to strike (on Twenty-Sided). **Cost:** Each use of Rising Chi Cough costs eight points of Negative Chi.

Demon Hunter Body Hardening Exercises

A Special Thanks to Kevin Lowry, who play tested the first Demon Hunter character and provided the inspiration for this section!

While other martial artists are fanatical about conditioning, Demon Hunters are downright nuts! As with other Body Hardening Exercises, Demon Hunter Body bonuses can be used with *any* martial art form or in any kind of combat.

1. Ao Dah Jong. The idea is to inflict a lot of the potential damage on the character deliberately, so they'll be, 1) tougher, and 2) they'll be able to handle it when it happens in combat. For example, the character's shoulders are dislocated so he/she can learn to "pop" them back in without assistance. The bones of the hand and arm are also broken and broken again, so that they grow back stronger. **Bonuses:** +3 to save vs pain, with an additional +1 at 7th and 14th levels of experience, +2 to P.E. and +15 to S.D.C.

2. Control Revulsion. The character's training consists of being exposed to the most horrible, graphic, and disgusting sights, sounds, smells, tastes, and textures that the trainer can imagine. For example, not only would the character have to visit a morgue (preferably, immediately after it's been filled with several victims from a disaster like an airplane crash), but the character would be expected to sleep in a pile of bodies. The character develops a certain, shall we say, *resistance*, to horror factor. **Bonuses:** +4 to save vs horror factor and +2 to M.E.

3. Demon Wrestling. Like the standard wrestling skill (as in *Heroes Unlimited*), except that Demon Wrestling is tougher and filled with lots and lots of dirty tricks. Gouging, biting, and illegal strikes all take place in Demon Wrestling (no, the bonuses of conventional wrestling and Demon Wrestling cannot be added together!)

- Pin/Incapacitate on a roll of 18 or better at first level, on a roll of 17 or better at 4th level, 16 or better at 8th level, and 15 or better at 12th level.
- Crush/Squeeze does 1D6 damage or can crush/squeeze for pain such that the victim will have to save vs pain.
- +2 to strike with a gouge or other illegal move.
- +20% to Conceal Illegal Move. The character learns to surreptitiously deliver a gouge, jab, poke, or otherwise attack a pain sensitive area (victim must save vs pain). Also includes practice of acting innocent when accused ("who? me?").
- Feign Illegal Injury. The character learns to convincingly act like a foul blow did grievous pain and damage, complete with wincing, moans and groans, in a way designed to impress by standers and referees. +30%, with an additional +4% per level of experience (use with the M.A. roll for trust).
- Body Block/Tackle does 1D6 damage and opponent must dodge or parry to avoid being knocked down (loses initiative and one melee action if knocked down).
- +2 to roll with punch or fall, with an additional +1 at 5th, 10th and 15th levels of experience.
- +3 to P.S.
- +1 to P.E.
- +6D6 on S.D.C.
- +1 to save vs pain.

4. Feign Death/Coma/Unconscious. Sometimes it's a good idea to play dead. However, since demons tend to test their theories to extremes, playing dead or unconsciousness for a demon is pretty grueling. Typically the demon will poke, prod, twist, squeeze, toss, throw, scratch, and otherwise bedevil a body into sitting up and saying "alright, already!"

While in training, the character must spend hours playing dead while being badgered by a team of trainers. As a final examination, the character is tossed over a fence into a junk yard or some other area filled with vicious guard dogs. **Bonuses:** +2 to save vs pain, +1 to M.E., +1 to P.E., +5 to S.D.C., +1 to save vs horror factor.

5. Yung Chin or Eternal Clarity. A fancy name for learning how to drink a lot of booze without getting too drunk. Demons and many other vile creatures have less than savory habits, thus it's often easy to tempt them into either drunken binges or drinking contests. Not only can this lure creatures into making foolish wagers, but it also dims their ability to use Chi and slows their natural rate of Chi recovery.

This Body Hardening Exercise is meant to teach the character how to 'burn off' the effect of booze and recognize their own limits of drunkenness. After the training, the characters usually become 'professional' drinkers — they won't drink unless there is something specific to be gained by it. **Bonuses:** Resist the effects of alcohol at +20% with an additional +4% per level of experience. Penalties for drunkenness are *halved* and skills are only -6%. The character is also +1 to save vs poisons and drugs.

6. Laugh at Pain. Characters are conditioned to equate pain with humor. Gradually larger and larger needles are inserted in more and more painful parts of the character's body. When properly trained the character will be able to pull pieces of broken glass out of their own flesh while chuckling and cracking jokes. Not that it doesn't hurt anymore — it certainly does — it's just the character learns to laugh and joke about it. Which is something that's useful when attempting to intimidate or impress demons. **Bonuses:** +2 to save vs pain, +1 to M.E., +1 to M.A., and +8% with an additional +2% per level to intimidate when demonstrating resistance to pain & suffering (can be added to an M.A.%).

7. Resist Chi Influence. By practicing under waterfalls, at the edge of a cliff, deep underground, and in the middle of a freezing underground stream, the character conditions the body to ignore that natural tendency to be filled or drained of both Positive and Negative Chi. This results in a save vs Chi Attacks. 30% at first level +3% at each additional level.

Special Katas

Martial Artists practice Katas like dancers practice dance steps, memorizing and perfecting a series of moves until they become instinctively fast and accurate. These special routines are practiced over and over again until major bonuses are achieved.

The drawback of any kata is that it lacks flexibility and is only set up to do one thing well. Attack-oriented katas ignore the character's defenses and defense-oriented katas usually allow no attacks. Each kata is developed based on a specific martial art form and can only be used with that one form.

Kata's must always be performed *for an entire melee round.* Characters cannot slip in or out of a kata during a single melee round. There is no problem changing from one kata to another at the start of a new melee round.

Chi Katas for Mystic China

As with other Katas, the Chi Katas must always be performed *for an entire melee round.* Characters cannot slip in or out of a kata during the same melee round.

It is quite possible for a character to perform a Chi Kata, without having any other Chi Abilities. Likewise, a character can be charged with Positive Chi, be down to Zero Chi, or be infected with Negative Chi and still be able to perform any of the Chi Katas.

1. Blind Man's Kata. To use this Kata, the character must be blind, blind folded, in darkness/fog, or otherwise deprived of sight. The character engages in a series of sweeping circles and body movements by letting the subtle currents of Chi in the environment guide him/her. Without actually knowing the position of any opponents or "seeing" the combat, the character will sense the location and action of any attacker and automatically be in a position to parry, block or dodge any assault. It is also possible to use Chi Mastery and other skills simultaneously.

The only limitation is that the blind character cannot be the aggressor, only the defender. Thus, it is impossible to attack in any way while using the Blind Man's Kata. The blind character is able to parry, block, avoid, and counteract all opponents. All avoidance rolls are done with the character's usual bonuses, *plus an extra +1 bonus* from the use of this Kata. The only exception to the all-seeing operation of the Blind Man's Kata is an opponent with *no Chi at all.* Those characters with zero Chi are effectively unseen by the performer of the Blind Man's Kata and the character will be helpless against their attacks (-10 to strike, parry and dodge). Please remember, that's a pretty rare situation, since all living things have at least a bit of Positive or Negative Chi!

2. Chi Ball Kata. Stepping slowly forward, walking in synch with Chi flowing in the immediate area, the character works at gathering Chi, eventually pulling it together into a ball suspended between the character's hands. To an observer, it seems that the martial artist is slowly gathering an invisible substance like a mime artist, while simultaneously performing a circular dance step. On the other hand, anyone with the ability to perceive Chi will clearly see the ball of Chi energy being assembled by the character.

The Chi will be either Negative or Positive, depending on the environment and it doesn't matter whether the character has Positive Chi, Negative Chi, or no Chi at all.

Getting the ball started is the hard part. At first level, it takes four full melee rounds to get the ball formed. At third level, it only takes three melee rounds and at sixth level, just two melee rounds. From ninth level onwards, a character can start a Chi Ball in just one full melee round.

Once the ball has been started, it will contain an amount of Chi equal to the background Chi of the area. As soon as the Chi

Ball is released from the hands of the character performing the Kata (or, for that matter, if the character stops the Kata) the Chi Ball will start to unravel and will cease to exist within 1D4 seconds.

Once brought into existence, a Chi Ball can be used in the following ways:

Chi Ball Lens. Once a Chi Ball has been started, the character can look through it and see all the Chi in the surrounding area up to about 60 feet (18.3 m) away. Any creatures of Chi, the Chi inside any living beings, Chi flows or deposits, and the general amount of Negative or Positive Chi will be clearly seen through the Chi Ball. This sight continues no matter what else is done, so long as the character keeps performing the Chi Ball Kata and holds on to an intact Chi Ball.

Gathering Chi Ball. For each gathering melee round, the character adds an amount of Chi equivalent to the ambient Chi in the area. So, for example, if the background Chi is five points of Positive Chi, the Chi Ball will have five points of Positive Chi. After a second melee round of gathering, the Chi Ball will have 10 points, then 15 points, and so forth. The maximum that any character can gather is ten times the local Chi level, so the largest Chi Ball available in our example would have 50 points of Positive Chi. Once the maximum is reached, the character can continue the Chi Ball Kata indefinitely, maintaining the amount of Chi that has already been gathered.

Chi Ball Defense. As a shield against Chi attacks, the Chi Ball can be used against either the same kind of Chi or against opposing Chi. A Positive Chi Ball used as a shield against an attack of Positive Chi or a Negative Chi Ball used to block Negative Chi, will just get bigger, absorbing the excess. If the amount of Chi exceeds the maximum size for a Chi Ball, the extra Chi will be harmlessly expelled. On the other hand, if a Positive Chi Ball blocks Negative Chi, or if a Negative Chi Ball is attacked by Positive Chi, then the incoming Chi will destroy an equal amount of Chi in the Ball — destroying the Ball if the Chi is exceeded. If the Chi Ball is destroyed, the character will have to start the process of gathering all over again.

Note: As effective as a Chi Ball might be against Chi, it is totally useless as a shield from material attacks from fists or weapons.

Throwing or Inserting the Chi Ball. It's also possible to use the Chi Ball as a weapon, either tossing it at a target, or pushing it right into an opponent. However, due to the fragile nature of the Chi Ball, it immediately loses **half** of its Chi when released. Then, if thrown, it loses half of the remaining Chi within 15 feet (4.6 m), and all of the rest of the Chi after travelling 30 feet (9.1 m). So, if a Chi Ball containing 50 points of Positive Chi were inserted into a creature of Pure Negative Chi (it would require a successful Roll to Strike, with no bonuses), the creature would be infected with just 25 points of Positive Chi. If the Chi Ball where thrown at the creature, standing between 5 and 15 feet (1.5 to 4.6 m) away, the amount of incoming Chi would be just 13 points, or 6 points up to 30 feet (9.1 m) distant. Throwing a Chi Ball more than 30 feet (9.1 m) is useless, since it will dissolve beyond that point.

Because the Chi Ball is more impressive **before** it's thrown or inserted, many users of the Chi Ball Kata find it better to use the Chi Ball as a threat, rather than as an actual weapon.

Note: If a ball has been formed and discarded, then the character can continue the Chi Ball Kata, and another ball can be started immediately, without having to wait the usual 'start' melee rounds.

3. Chi Defense Kata: This fast-moving Kata is used in conjunction with physical combat. It involves weaving in and out of the currents of Chi that move through an area. By performing the Chi Defense Kata, the character has the chance to *dodge* any and all *Chi attacks*, including those from pure Chi, Hard Chi, Soft Chi, One Finger Chi, Fist Gesture, and Negative Chi Illness. Works against both Positive and Negative Chi attacks.

The character can continue to attack, defend, or just about anything else, except using other Chi skills and abilities. The Kata neither adds nor subtracts from the character's physical fighting skills while it is in use.

When using Chi attacks against someone in the Chi Defense Kata, the aggressor must roll to strike using only the bonuses that come with the Chi ability's Martial Art (i.e.: if the Chi Mastery skill was gained through the use of Tien-Hsueh, then only the strike bonus from Tien-Hsueh can be used). The user of the Chi Defense Kata then has to beat the strike roll, with no bonuses, in order to successfully dodge the Chi attack. Note that, unlike a normal dodge, dodging Chi attacks does **not** cost the character any melee round actions.

4. Dragon Line Kata: Using this Kata, the character attempts to follow the invisible Dragon Lines and flow of Chi in a surrounding area. The character will automatically be able to follow channels of Chi. Once on a channel, he/she can choose to move in the direction of greater Chi, less Chi, or Positive or Negative Chi. While in the Kata, the character moves at a normal walking pace and can also engage in combat without penalties.

5. Mending Chi Kata. By tuning into the Positive Chi of the area and moving in response to it, the character channels Positive Chi into the body, wiping out any Negative Chi and replenishing lost Positive Chi. However, the unique thing about the Mending Chi Kata is that it can be used to pull *Positive Chi out of a Negative Chi area*!

Although this seems unlikely, it's based on the fact that all Chi is really universal. Since all Chi flows in a complex manner, there is really no such thing as a place that contains one kind of Chi and not another.

How much Chi can be collected and how long it takes, depends entirely on the local Chi environment. If the environment contains Positive Chi, then collection is very quick; collecting a number equal to the area for every melee round that the Mending Chi Kata continues. For example, where Positive Chi is at four, the character can collect four points of Positive Chi per melee round.

Collecting Positive Chi from a Negative Chi environment is inversely proportional to the degree of Negative Chi. Or, to put it more simply, it takes as many melee rounds to collect one point of Positive Chi as there is Negative Chi in the area. For example, if the area has a background of three points of Negative Chi, it will take *three melee rounds* to collect *one point* of Positive Chi. When the negative Chi is six, it will take six melee rounds to collect each point of Positive Chi.

This is a **non-combative** Kata, so the character can neither attack nor defend while performing it. Likewise, the Kata requires total concentration, so no other skills or abilities, including Chi abilities, can be used simultaneously.

6. Yin-Yang Kata. Expert practitioners call this the "Give Over to the Tao Kata," because it feels like you're loaning your body to some other, greater, supernatural being. What makes it even stranger is the way it looks. While all the Chi Katas look like dances, the Yin-Yang Kata appears even more dramatic, with fast, modern-dance-like movements and the kind of leaps and kicks you'd expect to see at a ballet. Yet, while the body is engaged in this frenetic activity, the character's mind feels calm and subdued, submerged into the oneness of the Yin-Yang, seemingly like a distant observer. All actions, including strikes, parries, dodges, and rolls are done as normal, with neither penalties nor bonuses. The really weird thing about the Yin-Yang Kata is that attacks on supernatural beings, demons, creatures of Pure Negative Chi, and other things that would normally be immune to physical attacks, *take normal damage*, as if the attacks were based on magic or Chi (In **Rifts** all Yin-Yang Kata attacks inflict M.D. to supernatural beings and creatures of magic, but S.D.C. damage to all others).

Martial Art Techniques (Expanded Version)

Spectacular and secret martial art skills require years of dedicated practice under the most rare and talented instructors. Once learned, any of these skills can be used in conjunction with any martial art form.

1. Eight Horse Stomp: When performed outside on packed sand, dirt, or any hard surface, or inside on hard concrete or metal, the Eight Horse Stomp causes the equivalent of an earth tremor. The Eight Horse Stomp is not a kick and can NOT be used as a direct attack, even if a victim is underfoot.

Everyone, friend and foe alike, standing within one hundred feet (30.5 m) of an Eight Horse Stomp will have to save vs falling (roll with fall or impact) to avoid being thrown off their feet. Anyone with any kind of martial art or combat training will be unharmed, but ordinary folk have a 50% chance of incurring 1D4 damage from the fall. All who fall lose initiative and one melee attack/action. Only the character using the Eight Horse Stomp is certain to be unaffected by the tremor.

When performed in an urban area, an Eight Horse Stomp will likely set off more than a little disturbance. Burglar alarms, car alarms, and other kinds of motion sensitive devices will be instantly triggered. If done within twenty feet (6.1 m) of a tall building, every device within the building will be affected, no matter how many stories tall.

2. Light Body Climbing: Characters learn to time their breathing and movement to synchronize with the natural flow of Chi through Fire, Earth, Metal, Water and Wood (the five elements). As a result characters can climb, up or down, with the ease and speed of walking (roughly half their maximum Spd.). No skill rolls or saving throws are required for climbing while doing Light Body Climbing.

Light Body Climbing requires full concentration, so characters can not fight even to defend themselves. Nor can they use Chi, engage in magic, or do anything else that diverts the mind, except talk. This doesn't mean that the character will fall when doing other things, it just means they'll have to resort to conventional climbing skills. For example, they must roll vs the skill for every 20 feet (6.1 m) travelled when using the conventional climbing skill. Rappelling is not possible while doing Light Body Climbing.

Note: Characters must first have the climbing skill in order to use this special ability.

3. Sword Chi Technique: An ancient technique, where a martial artist focuses Chi through the hands and into the blade of a sword. This fills the sword with a portion of the wielder's Positive Chi. **Half** the character's Chi, rounding downward, is put into the weapon. Thus, a character with seven points of Positive Chi would channel three points into the sword. Attempting to do anything else with Chi, such as performing Chi Mastery, withdraws the Chi from the sword and ends the Sword Chi Technique. The character can't lose the Chi that's being concentrated in the sword, nor is there any loss of Chi in using the Sword Chi Technique. If the character stops using the technique, or drops the sword, then the borrowed Chi is instantly returned to the character.

Note that it's impossible to do any of the Sword Chi Techniques without a sword that is *known and named* by the character. In other words, the character can't just pick up any old sword and start doing Sword Chi. It doesn't work that way! Characters with Sword Chi should have a favorite weapon that can be drawn and used with Sword Chi instantly, without any other preparation.

It is possible to have other, stand-by weapons attuned for Sword Chi, but the character must spend at least a week practicing with any new sword, and must give that sword a unique name. Then, anytime the character wants to switch from the usual blade (even in mid-combat), it will take *one full melee round* of concentration before the character can invoke Sword Chi with the secondary sword.

Using Sword Chi Technique, the sword wielder can perform any of the following three actions:

Sword Chi Awareness. Concentrating through the sword, the user can sense creatures of Chi including anyone with over four points of Chi (Positive or Negative) within immediate sword range; less than 10 feet (3.0 m). This works even in total darkness, through opaque objects (curtains, bamboo screens, etc.), or against invisible opponents. The character can strike at them with no penalty.

Also, if facing a sword or other weapon that's filled with Chi from another wielder using Sword Chi Awareness, or an object that's been *filled with Chi* by Chi Mastery or Chi Magic, or an artifact filled with a Chi-using spirit, the character can also parry and dodge without penalty.

Sword Chi Damage. Opponents, such as creatures of Pure Negative Chi, demons, and other supernatural or magical beings, can be hurt by the sword's Positive Chi. The amount of damage inflicted on the opponent's Negative Chi is equal to the usual damage inflicted by the sword with the current Positive Chi level being the maximum. **Note:** In **Rifts, BTS** and **Heroes Unlimited,** the weapons do double damage to supernatural beings and creatures of magic.

Sword Chi Defense. Acting as a "ground," the sword automatically intercepts incoming Negative Chi attacks. Sword Chi Defense neutralizes incoming Negative Chi equal to the current charge of the sword.

An Example of Sword Chi Combat: Shen Xian is currently at 19 Positive Chi, so his damaged sword is charged with 9 points of Chi. His opponent is O Wai, a demon currently in bodily form, but magically invisible and charged with 30 points of Negative Chi. Shen Xian senses, through his sword, an entity of massive Negative Chi just a few feet away.

Shen Xian chooses to attack! Using his usual combat bonuses to strike the invisible intruder. A successful strike! The sword does 2D8 damage and Shen Xian has a +4 bonus to damage. The roll comes up 12 (+4), for a total of 16 points of damage to O Wai's S.D.C. The sword's Chi also does damage, but only enough to subtract 9 points from O Wai's Negative Chi, leaving 21. Remember, the sword was only charged with 9 points of Positive Chi.

The demon responds with a Negative Chi attack! By this point, O Wai knows that the sword contains at least 9 points of Sword Chi (although, from O Wai's point of view, it could be more). The demon uses 11 from his remaining Negative Chi for a Chi attack.

Shen Xian's sword automatically intercepts 9 of the incoming Chi, leaving 2 points that get through. For each point of Negative Chi that hit Shen Xian, he loses 3D6 of Positive Chi, so Shen Xian will lose 6D6 of Chi. There's a good chance that Shen Xian will lose his entire base of Positive Chi, at which point his Sword Chi will no longer function.

4. Sung Chi (resistance to fear): Comes from the term, Sung, which means looseness or relaxation. When used, the character is resistant to fear, horror factor, panic, and similar reacts. **Bonuses:** +5 to save vs horror factor, horrific illusions, hallucinations, nightmares, and magic or psionic induced fear. Applicable so long as the character retains at least one point of Positive Chi.

5. Shift Internal Organs: By exercising the internal muscles of the body, the character learns how to move things around inside the body cavity, enabling him to move vital organs out of harm's way! For example, a character can shift the heart out of the way of a blade or arrow point. If successful, the character can avoid all but one point of S.D.C. or hit point damage from a piercing wound.

This can also be used as a kind of sideshow carnival trick. The idea is to pierce oneself or have an assistant stab the character with thin knives or needles in places that ought to be fatal. Instead of dying, the character takes just a point or two of damage (usually to S.D.C.). **Note:** While Shift Internal Organs is pretty fast, fast enough for most hand to hand combat, it is NOT fast enough to dodge an *unexpected* gunshot or stab in the back.

To shift the organ out of the way in time to avoid damage, the character basically rolls a mental *dodge*. This dodge does not use up a physical melee action. The character is +5 to dodge/Shift Internal Organs under most combat circumstances; +9 when performing a "trick." Other dodge bonuses are NOT applicable. A failed roll means the internal organ was hit with a critical strike (double damage).

6. Vital Harmony: Taking control over the body's digestive system, the character creates a closed system. In other words, the character becomes much more efficient and requires far less food and water.

At first level, the character can go up to one week without food and water or, with a small supply of water (a small sip every day) up to three weeks without food. Each additional level allows the character to extend the time an extra day without water and an extra three days without food.

Vital Harmony also allows the character to more rapidly rid the body of poisons. Given sufficient water (a 100 pound/45 kg character will need about four glasses of water), the character can rid the body of virtually any toxin within one hour.

Zenjoriki (Xian Chi)

In the martial arts there are certain powers that defy conventional explanation. Call them supernormal, "Spirit Powers," or *Xian Chi* (the Chinese name). They are all Zenjoriki. Although the Xian Chi powers don't use Chi, most of them require that the character be charged up with at least one point of Chi (positive or negative). Only the power to discorporate can be performed when the character's Chi is zero.

1. Discorporate (Kai Tian): For a single melee round "action"(roughly 3 seconds),the character becomes immaterial. Or, as a Taoist Priest might say, the character becomes "at one with the entire universe" for that instant of time. This means the character will, for an instant, avoid any and all attacks and threats.

Unlike the power of Intangibility (see **Heroes Unlimited**), where a character is just molecularly rearranged, the Discorporated character more-or-less ceases to exist on the physical plane for a moment. So there is nothing that can harm the character.

Returning from the experience, the character is always fully invigorated (even Dim Mak will be dispelled — but, no, the character can't take anyone else along for the ride!), glowing with health, and fully charged with Positive Chi. **Note:** The character doesn't need to have any Chi at the beginning of a Discorporate, and can even have Negative Chi.

This is the first step in a character's road to the Taoist version of immortality. That is, at any time the character may choose to Discorporate *permanently*! However, while the character becomes one of the Immortals and ascends to another aspect of existence, the character is also **permanently out of the game!** Because time operates differently as the newly Immortal character absorbs the secrets (or becomes one with, depending on how you look at it) of the Tao, the character is out of the player's control.

Restrictions: No character should attempt to do Discorporation more than once per day. The problem is not the ability, but more a matter of the temptation. The character feels so fulfilled and loses so much sense of the importance of lowly material life, that it's necessary to *save vs temptation* anytime the character attempts Discorporation more than once per day! The player will have to save by rolling under 40% on percentile. A failure to make the roll means the character has departed and is lost to the players.

By the way, it is possible for "Evil" characters to acquire the Art of Discorporation. After all, anyone, even an Infernal, can become enlightened and "at one" with the Tao. However, characters who are fundamentally selfish or evil will likely be repulsed by the whole idea of discorporation — "What? Me, who is destined to rule the world? You expect me to give that all up for nothingness? That is madness!" For these characters, it usually doesn't take more than one experiment before they turn away from discorporation as a dangerous trap.

2. Mind Walk (Meng Qiao; New Material!): The character's spirit can leave the body and move about in the realms of pure Chi. While in this form, the character becomes pure Chi with no substance whatever.

While in spirit form, it is the character's embodied Chi that is travelling. The character can see and hear normally and can use any known Chi powers, but is completely invisible and insubstantial to normal beings in the material world. However, other Chi Masters (those with Chi Awareness) will be able to detect the Chi spirit. Communication, mind to mind, is possible with any person that the Chi spirit touches, or who possesses telepathy.

The Chi of the Mind Walking character, whether positive or negative, can't be changed while out of the body. In other words, a character filled with negative Chi will become a negative Chi spirit, unable to perform positive Chi powers and onto change to positive Chi without revisiting his/her physical body.

Movement while in spirit form is either by drifting or by teleportation, the character can't do both at once.

Drifting allows the character to slowly move from place to place, with a Spd. of 2. There are no restrictions either from objects or by directions with drifting and the character can move at the same speed while travelling in any direction or directly through any solid objects.

Teleportation allows the character to move a vast distance instantly, simply by visualizing the destination. However, the act of visualizing requires that the character concentrate, while motionless and inactive for four full melee rounds. Another limitation is that character may only teleport to specific *known* locations or people. One cannot teleport to a person or place he has never examined in person while in his physical form. A photograph or a description is not enough to form a focus for teleporting the Chi spirit.

Teleporting to Other Realms of Spirit. In addition to travelling in the Chi energy of the material world, it is also possible to visit other realms, including the *Transition Plane of the Newly Dead, the Hells of the Yama Kings, the Heavens of the Jade Emperor,* and other places. The basic Mind Walk is all that is required for these visits, but the character must have some way of knowing where to go. The best way is by the use of a guide, following another Chi Spirit to the new places. Another is simply to wander around.

Once a character has visited another realm as a Chi Spirit, it is possible to return using teleportation, but only to locations that the character has actually experienced.

Dangers: In some realms of Chi Spirit, the character will become "embodied." That is, the character will seem to be physically present in that place, even though the real body is very far away. These Spirit Bodies have advantages and disadvantages. Foremost among the drawbacks is that the character can't teleport while in a Spirit Body. It may be necessary to travel to some focus point, or to be "killed," or to otherwise dispel the Spirit Body, before the character can teleport back home.

While a Chi spirit the character can perform any known Chi powers just as if the character were present in his body. For example, the character could deliver a punch with the Hardened Chi power, delivering no physical damage but doing damage from the Hardened Chi only.

The Chi spirit is also vulnerable to Chi attacks. For example, any Hardened Chi, Soft Chi, Negative Chi Attacks, or One Finger Chi attacks directed against the Chi spirit will do damage directly to Chi. Chi spirits can parry or roll with punch against chi attacks (without physical and combat bonuses) but cannot dodge. Fist Gesture is the most deadly attack to Chi spirits since, if successful, it can completely destroys the Chi spirit. The Chi Spirit is also vulnerable to certain Chi Magic, as well as getting stuck in Chi Traps (which can be constructed by experts in Feng Shui), and other threats. **Note:** When a Chi spirit reaches zero Chi, it is dead with no hope of any recovery!

While a character's physical body is empty of the Chi spirit, it is completely vulnerable to any and all attacks, including possession by other Chi spirits. In addition, because the body is empty of all Chi during a Mind Walk, no healing is possible. After a body has been empty for two hours, it becomes possible that it will lapse into a coma (see the section on Coma and Death). For the first day, there is a 20% chance of a coma every hour. After twenty-four hours, there is a 60% chance of lapsing into coma every hour. All the normal risks (hit point loss, death) of coma will apply. Return of the Chi spirit will instantly cure the coma, but the effects of the coma will remain.

3. Spirit Burst: If charged with Positive Chi, the burst will seem like a brilliant flash of light, so bright that (for demons, anyway), it is like looking directly at the sun. On the other hand, if charged with Negative Chi, the burst appears to be a cold, deadly vortex of destruction.

In each case, the character becomes a pulsating nexus of Chi, something that no creature of pure Chi (dragons, demons, etc.) would dare to ignore.

With the flash of Positive Chi, anyone in the vicinity who is charged with Negative Chi (especially demons, being creatures of Negative Chi!) will instantly have 2D6 points of their Chi blown away. The next melee round, if the Spirit Burst is maintained, another 1D6 of Negative Chi will be destroyed, and so on until the Spirit Burst is relaxed, or until the creature of Negative Chi moves out of range (about 50 feet/15.2 m). Even when out of range of the Positive Chi radiation, Negative Chi beings will still be blinded if they try to look directly at the character who is generating the Spirit Burst.

On the other hand, if the Spirit Burst is based on Negative Chi, then anyone charged with Negative Chi will find themselves being *drained* by the vortex. In the first melee round each character with Negative Chi will lose 1D6 points of their Chi. The drain will continue, at 1D6 per melee round, as long as the Spirit Burst continues, and as long as the character stays in range.

The Negative Chi Vortex has an even more drastic impact on any creatures of Negative Chi, such as Infernals. In addition to losing 1D6 of Chi, any creature of Negative Chi will be *instantly transformed into pure Chi form*! Once in that form, if the creature stays in range of the Spirit Burst, things get even worse. First, the Negative Chi drain increases to 3D6 per melee round. Second, the disembodied creature of Chi will find themselves being pulled toward the vortex. If a creature of pure Negative Chi actually touches the vortex, it will be instantly consumed and destroyed; death is instantaneous. However, as long as some Chi remains in the creature, it is capable of moving away and out of danger.

The character who initiates the Spirit Burst gets no benefit from any of the Chi that is consumed, regardless of whether the Spirit Burst is based on Positive or Negative Chi.

Other beings charged with Positive Chi or who have zero Chi will be unaffected by the Spirit Burst. If a character has some kind of Chi ability, the Spirit Burst will be detectable. However, characters with no ability to detect Chi will be completely unaware of the phenomenon.

It doesn't matter if a Positive Chi burst is done in a place of massive Negative Chi or if the Negative Chi vortex is done where Positive Chi is overwhelming. Just remember the dots in the Yin-Yang symbol. Just as there is a dot of black in the thickest portion of white and a speck of white in the mass of black, so there is always a bit of Negative Chi in a place of Positive Chi, and vice versa.

4. Two Minds (Jing Chi): By deliberately separating the two parts of the soul, the character is able to do two things at the same time. In some circumstances, the character can even **be** in two places at once!

The Two Minds is based on the principle that the soul consists of two parts, the primary and the secondary minds. The primary is the *Hun*, "Cloud Soul," which is analytical and contemplative — the human consciousness. The secondary part is the *Po*, "Bone Soul," which is the instinctive, animalistic and aggressive aspect that acts on drives and desires rather than of thought. Split apart, the two pieces are capable of acting independently, just as if the character were suddenly split into two minds.

One of the most common applications of Two Minds is splitting into two parts when in combat. One part (usually the Po) controls the body's combat actions, while the other part (generally the Hun), works on tactical problems, yells out commands, or engages in simultaneous Chi combat.

However, the big thing to bear in mind is that the two parts of the soul are anything but equal. Each is a distinct aspect of the character, each with different parts of the character's skills, strengths and weaknesses. Here are the respective abilities, and disabilities, of the Hun and the Po:

Hun Abilities: Speech, analytical thought, deductive reasoning, cunning, compassion, mathematics, map-reading and direction finding, manipulation of Chi, and all thinking skills. All the "smarts" of the character usually end up in the Hun.

Hun Inabilities: Combat, martial arts, Chi recharging or gathering, danger sense, artistic sense, taste, and smell. Frankly, the Hun is a clumsy being, barely capable of walking, much less fighting.

Po Abilities: Combat (the Po can fight with all bonuses, from attributes, physical skills and martial arts), weapon proficiencies, pilot skills (if the character has pilot aircraft, the Po can turn on, fly, and land an airplane), Chi generation, and the senses of taste, scent, and esthetics.

Po Inabilities: Speech (in other words, the Po can't talk! It grunt, growls and shrieks like an animal), thinking skills, analytical thought/deduction, mathematics, Chi abilities, and control over emotions (very aggressive, extreme and reactionary, especial regarding feelings of anger, hate, and revenge. Thus the character may find it difficult to stop fighting or to show mercy).

Even more important than using Two Minds in a battle, is being able to use Two Minds in conjunction with Mind Walk. An ideal way of using it is to have the Hun self projected out as a spirit, and leave the Po behind to tend and defend the body. **Note:** Once split, the roles of the hun and po can't be reversed. So, for example, if the hun is off exploring the spirit world, while the po is in charge of the body, the character can't switch them around without bringing them back together and starting all over.

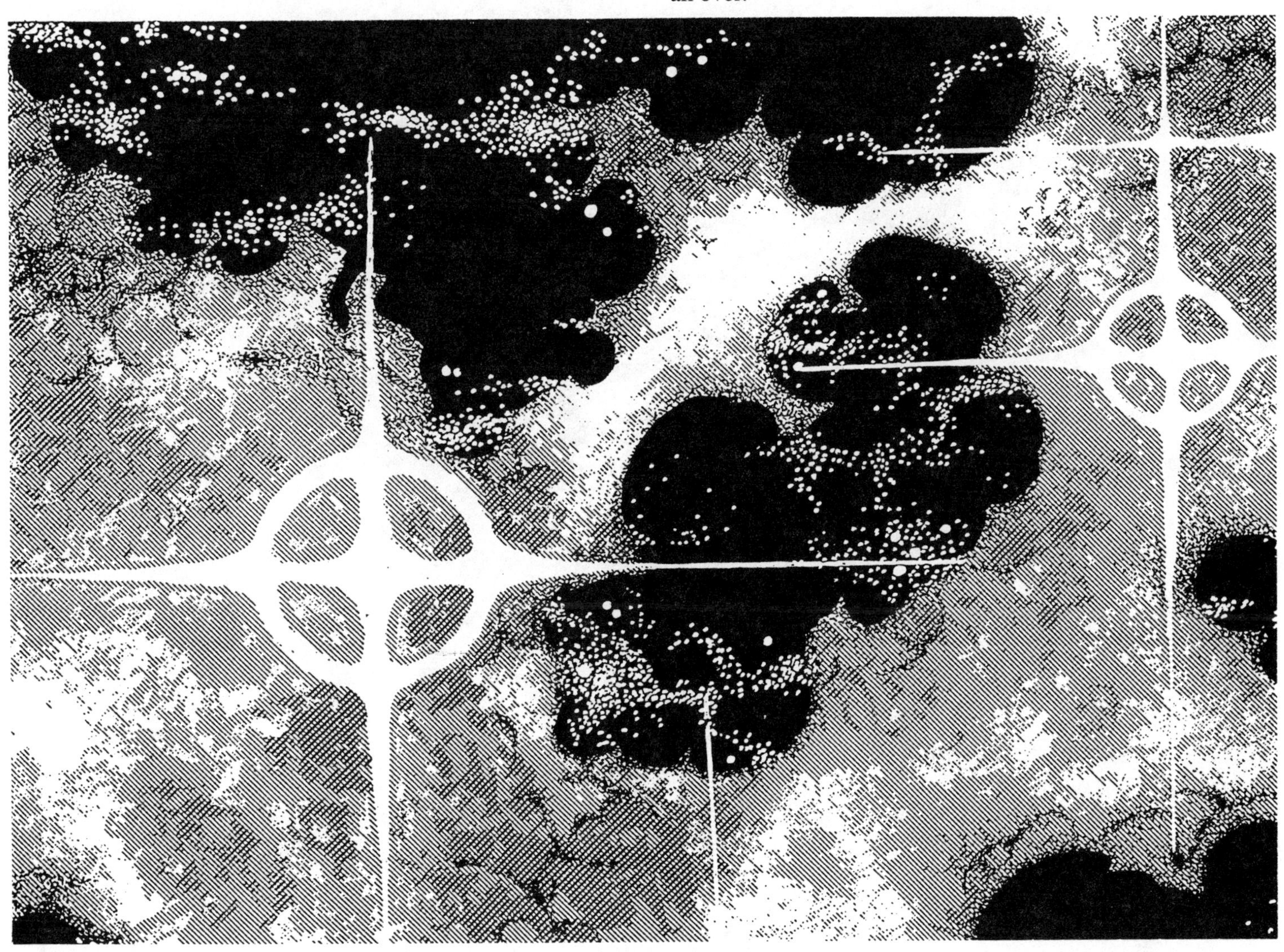

A Compendium of Mystic China Martial Arts

Listing of 29 Martial Art Forms

Note: Those marked with an asterisk are *new*. The others are duplicated from **Ninjas & Superspies**. 41 martial art forms of hand to hand combat are presented in **Ninjas & Superspies**.

* An Yin Kung Fu (Meditative/Mudra)
* Ba Gua Kung Fu (Eight Trigrams)
* Bak Mei Kung Fu (White Eyebrow)
Bok Pai Kung Fu (Crane Style)
* Chao Ta Kung Fu (Performance)
* Chi Hsuan Men (White Jade Fan)
Ch'in-Na (Seizing)
Choy-Li-Fut Kung Fu (Boxing)
Drunken Style (Pu Kung Fu)
Fu Chiao Pai Kung Fu (Tiger Claw)
* Gui Long Kung Fu (Dragon Spirit)
* Han Yu Kung Fu (Chi Katas)
* Hsien Hsia (Immortality)
* Hsing-I Kung Fu (Mind Shaping)
Kuo-Ch'uan Kung Fu (Dog Boxing)
Lee Kwan Choo (Non-Violent)
* Liang Hsiung Kung Fu (Demon Combat)
Mien-Ch'uan Kung Fu (Cotton Fist)
Monkey Style Kung Fu (Monkey Katas)
Pao Chih (Animus Development)
* Shan Tung Kung Fu (Black Tiger)
* Shih Ba Ban Wu Yi (Eighteen Weapons)
Pao Pat Mei Kung Fu (Leopard Style)
Shao-Lin Kung Fu (Classic Style)
Snake Style Kung Fu (She Shen)
Tai-Chi Ch'uan (Exercise Style)
Tien-Hsueh Kung Fu (Touch Mastery)
* Tong Lun Kung Fu (Praying Mantis)
* Triad Assassin Training (Automatic Pistols)

Martial Art Terms

Arts of Invisibility: These are special techniques of hiding and staying out of sight. Martial arts that offer arts of invisibility at first level include, Ch'in-Na, Drunken Style, Kuo-Ch'uan, Monkey Style, Pao Pat Mei, Snake Style and Tien-Hsueh.

Atemi or Tien Hsiuh Abilities: Powers requiring an intense understanding of the functions of the human body. Depending on the specific area of study, a Tien Hsiuh expert is capable of healing or damaging with nothing more than a light touch of the index finger. Those martial arts that offer Atemi at first level include An Yin Kung Fu (advanced), Bak Mei (advanced), Chi Hsuan Men, Ch'in-Na (advanced), Gui Long, Tien-Hsueh, and Praying Mantis (advanced). Those with "(advanced)" can also select from among the new *Advanced Atemi.*

Body Hardening Exercises: Many martial arts toughen the bodies of their students through a variety of extreme exercises. Even more extreme are the special exercises of the Demon Hunters. Martial arts offering body hardening at first level include, Bok Pai, Chao Ta, Chi Hsuan Men, Choy-Li-Fut, Drunken Style, Fu-Chiao Pai (Demon), Kuo-Ch'uan, Lee Kwan Choo, Liang Hsiung (Demon), Mien-Ch'uan, Monkey Style, Pao Pat Mei, and Shao-Lin. Those marked, "(Demon)," have the option of selecting from among the *Demon Hunter Body Hardening Exercises.*

Chi Mastery Abilities: All living things have chi, but only trained martial artists can tap its power. With Chi Mastery, a character learns to see chi everywhere, to tap its power, and to use it as a weapon or a tool. At first level, the following martial arts offer Chi Mastery Abilities: Ba Gua, Bak Mei (advanced), Hsing-I, Mien-Ch'uan, Pao Chih (advanced), Shan Tung (advanced), Snake Style, Tai-Chi Ch'uan, and Tien-Hsueh. Those marked "(advanced)" can select from among the new *Advanced Chi Mastery Abilities.*

Form: Martial arts are called "forms." A form is a complete fighting style. The forms in previous Palladium RPGs are Hand to Hand Basic, Expert, Martial Arts (general), and Assassin forms. There are 37 additional forms in **Revised Ninjas & Superspies** and 14 new forms here in **Mystic China**.

Typical phrases using the word are; "I'm going into Monkey form," and "The best parry bonus my character can get is by using my Xing, Eagle Claw form."

Katas (Specialty): A Kata is a practiced and formalized routine in the martial arts. Very often they are as graceful as a dance and can even be performed to music. The strength of a Kata lies in its repetition. The martial artist repeats the same sequence of moves thousands of times, until they become instinctive. Unfortunately, the weakness of Katas is also their routine, they are relatively inflexible. To use a weapon with any form it's necessary to learn a special weapon Kata. Only the following martial arts have Katas at first level: Ba Gua (Chi), Bok Pai (Chi), Choy-Li-Fut, Fu-Chiao Pai, Han Yu (Chi), Hsing-I (Chi), Mien-Ch'uan (Chi), Shih Ba Ban Wu Yi, Pao Pat Mei, Shao-Lin (Chi), and Tai-Chi Ch'uan (Chi). Note those with "(Chi)" also have the option of selections from the *Special Chi Katas.*

Martial Art Techniques: Unlike most special martial art abilities and powers, once a "Technique" is learned, it can be used anytime in conjunction with any martial art form. Martial art forms with techniques at first level include, Bak Mei, Gui Long, Kuo-Ch'uan, Lee Kwan Choo, and Shan Tung.

Mudra: While used mostly as a mystical source of power by monks, mystics, and those involved in arcane forms of meditation, they are also an important part of some martial arts, especially Tibetan. Among the martial arts listed here, only An Yin Kung Fu includes Mudra.

Types of Forms: There are several dual ways of describing a martial art form. A "soft" form uses circular deflecting movements, while a "hard" form uses straight muscular movements. "Internal" schools stress the supremacy of mental and spiritual training, while "external" schools work on improving the body.

Zenjorike: These are the mystic and inexplicable powers of the martial arts. At first level, only Fu-Chiao Pai (Karumi-Jutsu only), Hsien Hsia, Lee Kwan Choo, Snake Style, Tai-Chi Ch'uan and Tien-Hsueh have these powers.

Notes on The Martial Art Form Descriptions

Each of the Martial Art Forms is described in the same format. Here are some notes on each of the sections:

Entrance Requirements: The character's unmodified, original attributes must match the form's minimum attributes in order for the character to choose that form. Even to get a secondary form the character's originally rolled stats must meet the minimum, not the attributes *after* they've been improved by the Primary form's bonuses.

On the other hand, the character's alignment does not have to match the one required by the form. Why? Because a character may have studied the form in earlier years and then gone through a change of heart. However, if a character has a form that is incompatible with his present alignment, that means the character is considered a "traitor" to the form and will be hated, hunted or ostracized by its masters.

Attack Moves: Ways the character can move into combat, reduce the combat range, or somehow attack.

Attacks per Melee: Represents the maximum number of attacks per melee round (15 seconds) when using this form of marital arts at first level. It doesn't matter what kind of whiz-bang bonuses the character has, and it doesn't matter how many attacks per melee the character gets in another Form, this is the maximum first level attacks per melee, when using this Form. As the character advances in experience, he or she will gain additional attacks per melee round; these are indicated under *Level Advancement Bonuses*.

Bonuses gained from two or more forms of martial arts are *not* combined with each other, but remain separate and distinct from each other.

NEVER combine the bonuses of two or more "forms" for an overall bonus total. However, *skills* like boxing and wrestling are not considered "forms," and the bonuses can be combined or added to martial arts and to each other. Likewise, special training and powers *may* offer cumulative attribute, skill, and combat bonuses.

Basic Defensive Moves: Usually dodge, parry and automatic dodge. Almost every form, including the Agent Hand to Hand forms, has these three basic moves. **Note:** The one exception to the rule is Pao Chih, which has no moves to parry.

Character Bonuses: These are *one time only* bonuses. Players who receive *chi multipliers* should wait until the character is completely finished before using them.

Costume: A description of the average outfit worn in practice and training. It is also the outfit that's most comfortable for combat. Of course a character may wear anything convenient in the outside world.

Kung Fu outfits are very common. Rather than describe them over and over again, Kung Fu outfits usually consist of a long-sleeved, high-collared, front-buttoned shirt, matching loose-fitted pants, socks and soft-soled or running shoes.

Escape Moves: Methods of escaping combat or other dangers.

Level Advancement Bonuses: Certain bonuses are received automatically each time a character goes up in experience level. Note that bonuses apply only to their *own* form. In other words, a + 2 bonus to dodge in Tien-Hsueh is applied only when the character is fighting with the Tien-Hsueh form and not any other.

Martial Art Abilities and Powers: Depending on the form, these could come from Arts of Invisibility, Atemi Abilities, Body Hardening Exercises, Chi Mastery, Martial Art Techniques, Specialty Katas, and Zenjoriki. Characters can only select powers/abilities from the categories listed under their form. Thus, if Martial Art Techniques and Body Hardening are listed, the player can only choose from those two categories and not from any others. **Note:** The *Triad Assassin Training* is an exception in that it has **no** martial art powers or abilities.

Other Skills: Languages, cultural skills, survival skills, physical skills, oriental skills and philosophical training all start at first level. There is no bonus for getting the same skill more than once.

For example, let's say you manage to get two different forms, each with Chinese language, each with Tao philosophy, and each with climbing. Plus, you happen to get the same skills with your O.C.C. You still have just basic fluency in Chinese, standard Tao knowledge, and 1st level climbing.

Stance: This is the typical starting position of the form.

Weapon Katas: Using any weapon with a martial art form takes special training. Basically, it involves practicing and modifying all the regular moves of the form to accommodate the weapon. The only way to use a weapon not listed under weapon katas is to buy it using one of the Specialty Kata skills. Many forms have no katas and can't be used with weapons.

Important Note About Hand to Hand Abilities

The martial artists depicted in this game have devoted years of intense practice to "master" that particular form of combat. Consequently, they have developed a number of special techniques, punches, kicks, moves and/or skills and abilities that are *automatic to that specific martial art form.* These are noted under the categories of escape moves, basic defensive moves, advanced defenses, hand attacks, foot attacks, special attacks, holds/locks, and weapon katas. The character knows and can use **any and all** abilities/skills listed under each of these categories.

The martial arts abilities and powers are additional super abilities gained from years of study, practice and philosophy. Specific powers/abilities are often limited to use with a specific martial art form.

Quick Refresher on Martial Art Combat Moves & Damage:

While most of the moves in **Mystic China** can be found in any Palladium RPGs (**Beyond the Supernatural, Revised Heroes Unlimited, Rifts,** etc.), the following have only been described in **Ninjas & Superspies:**

Backflip: The backflip has been in Palladium systems before, but not as a combat maneuver. It involves throwing oneself backwards with the arms and shoulders, flipping the legs completely up, over, and back down on the ground into a standing position. The result is that one quickly moves backwards by a full body. Doing a backflip takes one full melee attack.

Backflip - Defensive. If used in place of a dodge, the character must roll over the opponent's strike roll using only the bonus to backflip. Failure to beat the strike means taking full damage *without a chance to Roll with Punch.* Success means avoiding the attack and escaping from combat.

Backflip - Escape. If used in place of a strike (when it's the back-flipping character's turn to strike) this removes the character from combat.

Backflip - Attack. This is especially useful against someone attempting some kind of back strike. Once the opponent is detected in the rear, the backflip moves one back into combat range. A backflip can also be used as a combined Strike against an opponent to the rear of the character. Use with either an Axe Kick, Snap Kick, or Backhand Strike. If striking with a Backflip use only the bonus to Backflip. Must be used as the first attack in a melee round. Cannot be used with death blow or knock-out/stun.

Automatic Body Flip/Throw: Certain martial artists can do a body flip/throw in place of a Parry. That means that instead of blocking or deflecting the blow, the character attempts to leverage the attacker's own force into a flip. Success requires beating the attacker's strike, using the bonuses for body flip/throw only. Failure means taking full damage from the attack without a chance to a roll with punch/fall/impact.

Critical Body Flip/Throw: Characters with Critical Body Flip/Throw can do critical strikes (double damage) by rolling a certain Natural number or better. Like a critical strike, this happens automatically. **Note:** Critical Body Flip/Throws never happen during Automatic Body Flip/Throws. The character can do one or the other, not both.

Cartwheel (Attack): Holding the body rigidly extended, the character rolls like a wheel using the arms and legs as spokes. Can be used to move quickly into combat range. A Cartwheel can also be used as a combined strike against an opponent to the rear of the character. Use with either an Axe Kick, Wheel Kick or Knife Hand. If striking with a Cartwheel use only the bonus to Cartwheel. Must be used as the first attack in a melee round. Cannot be used with death blow or knock-out/stun.

Choke: Simply, the attack involves grabbing someone by the throat. Normal Strike and Damage bonuses apply. Both hands must be used and the attacker can do no defensive moves, including Parries, Dodges, or Rolls, during a choke. In other words, the attacker just stands there and ignores all other attacks. Critical strike or knock-out/stun attacks from the rear can also be done to someone doing a choke.

Once a choke succeeds, the attacker can continue applying it as long as he likes, doing full damage every melee round attack. Damage is 1D6 done directly to hit points.

The victim of a choke attack can attempt to fend it off using normal defensive moves. However, if that fails, damage cannot be reduced by roll with punch/fall/impact or breakfall. The victim can continue to attack whoever is doing the choke, but that doesn't necessarily release the choke.

There are two ways to get out of a choke. The first is using brute strength. Everyone involved, the victim, any helpful friends, and the attacker, all roll twenty-sided and add in their damage roll bonus. High roll wins. If the attacker wins then the choke continues. If the victim or a helpful friend wins then the choke is released. The other way out is to use a Joint Lock to force the attacker to let go.

Combination Moves: Putting two or more moves together in a single action. Remember when using any combination move, no other automatic moves are possible, including automatic parry. Combination moves cannot be used as knock-out/stun or death blow attacks.

Combination Parry/Attack: Against one opponent, once per melee round, the character can simultaneously parry and attack. First, the character must roll a successful parry. If the parry works, then the character rolls to strike using either a Backhand, Knife Hand, or Palm Strike, or a hand weapon. No Strike or Damage bonuses allowed. The victim of a Combination Parry/Attack must use a melee round action to defend against it (automatic parry won't work). Uses up one melee attack.

Power Block/Parry: The character uses a powerful, damaging block against the opponent's strike. First roll for a successful parry. Then, if that works, roll for a Strike that does 1D6 Damage. No bonuses to strike or damage. The victim cannot parry, but can attempt to roll with punch/fall/impact.

Combination Strike/Parry: Against one opponent, once per melee round. Roll first to strike (using regular bonus). If successful then all attacks from that opponent for the rest of the melee round can be parried automatically. Uses up one melee attack.

Combination Grab/Kick: First roll to strike to grab the opponent with both hands. If that's successful, then roll to strike on a Kick Attack or Snap Kick. Critical Attack, does double damage. Strike and damage bonuses okay. Uses up one melee attack.

Reverse Turning Kick: This is the combination of a dodge and a kick. The kick can be either a Kick Attack or a Snap Kick. It's done in place of a Dodge, as a defensive move. First, make roll to dodge. If successful, then roll to kick. The opponent can defend normally. No bonuses to dodge, strike, kick or damage. Uses up one melee round attack.

Drop Kick: This is the combination of falling to the ground, a dodge and a kick. The kick can be either a Kick Attack, a Snap Kick, or a Crescent Kick. It's done in place of a Dodge, as a defensive move. First, make roll to dodge. If successful, then roll to kick. The opponent can defend normally. No bonuses to dodge, strike, kick or damage. Uses up one melee attack.

Note: Dodge (in combination). When a dodge is included as part of a combination move, it is a standard dodge. No other kinds of dodges or parries (including Automatic Parry) can be made at the same time. When used as part of a combination move, dodge bonuses can NOT be used!

Note: Parry (in combination). When a parry is included as part of a combination move, it is a standard parry. No other parries or dodges (including Automatic Parry or Automatic Dodge) can be used at the same time. When used as part of a combination move parry bonuses can NOT be used!

Disarm: Simply, getting rid of the opponent's weapon. It is basically a defensive move. Can be done as a Strike, during a hold, a joint lock, or during any one-handed grappling maneuver. Normally it takes a melee round attack. However, it can take the place of an automatic parry so long as it is the only automatic move made during that melee round attack. Disarm does not give the weapon to the attacker. True the item is forced out of the victim's grasp, but it is either knocked away or falls to the ground.

Handstand (Attack): The character flips over and stands on his hands. Can be used to move quickly into combat range. A Handstand can also be used as a combined strike against an opponent to the rear of the character. Use with either a Kick Attack, Snap Kick or Axe Kick. If striking with a handstand use only the bonus to handstand, not the bonus to strike. Must be used as the first attack in a melee round. Cannot be used with death blow or knock-out/stun.

Hold: Using both hands, the attacker grabs on to some part of the opponent's body and attempts to immobilize him. If the strike is successful then the victim is helpless until released. Holds do no damage. Neither the attacker nor the victim can attack, parry or dodge while hold is working. It's easy for the attacker to hold the victim so that some third character can attack unopposed or attack from the rear.

Getting out of a hold requires agility. Both the victim and the attacker roll twenty-sided and add in their P.P. bonus. The person doing the hold also gets to add in all his bonuses to hold and to strike. High roll wins. If the attacker wins then the hold continues. If the victim wins then the hold is released.

Arm Hold: This involves twisting the arm around the victim's back. Any items in the hand of the held arm can be easily removed.

Leg Hold: The victim is on the ground with the leg held up. There's no way for him to get up until the hold is released.

Body Hold: Any of a number of wrestling holds. The victim can be held on the ground or in a standing position.

Neck Hold: The victim is held around the neck from behind. This leaves the victim totally vulnerable to attacks from any other character.

Automatic Hold: Can be used with any other hold but as an automatic defense. If used, this is the only automatic move that can be used that melee attack. If it used in place of a parry/dodge, and if it fails (doesn't beat the attacker's strike), then the character takes full damage with no chance to Roll with punch/fall/impact or breakfall.

Joint Lock: These are advanced, one and two hand, versions of Holds. Unlike holds, locks make it impossible for the victim to escape unharmed once controlled. Holds do no damage, unless the victim gets hurt escaping. The victim is incapable of attacking, parrying or dodging while joint locked. The attacker, if using a one-hand lock, can continue to use the other hand for parries and strikes.

Finger Lock: One of the victim's fingers has been twisted around. The victim can choose to escape by sacrificing the finger. Doing this results in 1D4 damage, a save vs pain, and, of course, a broken finger.

Wrist Lock: A wrist is twisted away from the victim's body. The victim can escape by accepting a broken wrist, 1D6 damage, and a save vs pain.

Elbow Lock: Requires the attacker to use both hands. There is no escape for the victim. The attacker can not attack, parry or dodge while using this lock.

Automatic Lock: Can be used with any other lock but as an automatic defense. If used, this is the only automatic move that can be used that melee attack. If it is used in place of a parry/dodge, and if it fails (doesn't beat the attacker's strike), then the character takes full damage with no chance to Roll with punch/fall/impact or breakfall.

Katas and Specialty Katas: These are complex miniature martial art forms. They are designed to give the character large bonuses for specific moves, but at the cost of flexibility and many of the usual bonuses. See Specialty Kata section and individual Martial Art Forms for more information.

Kick Attack & Flying Jump Kicks: There are a whole range of foot-based attacks. Each kick attack works differently and does different amounts of damage.

<u>Kick Attack</u>: This is a conventional, karate-style, kick. It starts with bringing the knee, folded, up to chest level, then the foot is completely extended. Does 1D8 damage (or 2D4).

Snap Kick: A very short, very fast kick. Usually delivered low, striking the opponent somewhere below the waist. It works well in confined spaces and in grappling range but does relatively little damage (only 1D6).

Roundhouse Kick: By turning the body and swiveling the hips, there's tremendous power packed into this kick. Can be used only once per melee round, and no other kicks can be used in that melee round. Does 2D6 damage.

Wheel Kick: A damaging kick that involves sweeping the leg completely around the body. Cannot come right before or right after another kick. Does 1D10 (or 2D4+2) damage.

Crescent Kick: A swivel-hipped kick that sends the foot out on a sweeping arc. Does 1D10 (or 2D4+2) damage.

Axe Kick: A very high kick that goes up and over the opponent, coming down on the neck or shoulder. Can't be used in the same melee round with any other kicks. Does 1D10 (or 2D4+2) damage.

Backward Sweep: Used only against opponents coming up behind the character. Does No damage, it's purely a Knock-down attack. Cannot be Parried.

Tripping/Leg Hook: An attack on the opponent's legs. Does no damage, it's purely a knock-down attack. Cannot be parried.

Jump Kicks are performed by leaping completely off the ground and attempting to land foot-first on an opponent. Jump Kick can be used only by those skilled in hand to hand martial arts. The advantage of a jump kick is that it works as a critical strike and doubles the normal damage inflicted. The disadvantage of a jump kick is that no other attack may be performed in that melee round (all attacks for that melee are used up in the kick). The jump kick must be the character's first attack of that melee round. For the rest of the melee round, the character can only parry, dodge or move into position.

Jump Kick: Does 1D8 (or 2D4) damage and critical strike.

Flying Jump Kick: Must be made from long range. The character launches into the air, taking a position that will smash one foot into the opponent. Does 1D10 (or 2D4+2) damage and critical strike.

Flying Reverse Turning Kick: Must be made from long range. The extra twisting and turning of the body adds power to do 2D6 damage and critical strike.

Maintain Balance: Once some kind of knock-down attack has succeeded, while the character is starting to fall over, this is the last-chance attempt to recover. A successful roll (over the opponent's strike roll) means that the character will remain standing and able to continue fighting. If maintain balance is used then roll punch/fall/impact or breakfall can't be.

Circular Parry: The main idea here is that the martial artist can parry all attacks that come in, regardless of direction. So long as the defender is aware of the attackers, there's no limit to how many blows can be parried. Works like an Automatic Parry and takes no melee round attacks. During a Circular Parry the character can attack only once per melee round.

Somersault: This is an escape maneuver, used to get out of combat range. If used in place of a character's attack it means the character can leave the combat. If used instead of a parry or dodge, it means that the character must roll over the attacker's strike, using only the bonus to somersault. Success means avoid-

ing the attack and escaping from combat. Failure to beat the strike means taking full damage without a chance to roll with punch.

Special Moves: Here is a list of unique combat moves specific to particular forms. For more details, see the martial art form.

Ba Gua Kung Fu - Rotary Palm Strike and Sweep Kick.

Bak Mei Kung Fu - *Chum* Strike and *Chuk* Strike.

Bok Pai - Crane Fist.

Chao Ta Kung Fu - Impact Sponge and Fake Attack.

Choy-Li-Fut - Overhead Fore-Knuckle Fist, Uppercut and Roundhouse.

Drunken Style of Kung Fu - Stagger.

Fu-Chiao Pai - Power Block/Parry/Claw and Duo-Claw Strike.

Hsien Hsia Kung Fu - Two-Palm Push.

Lee Kwan Choo - Duo-Knuckle Strike.

Liang Hsiung - Punch/Spur Punch, Palm Strike/Palm Spike, Knee Snap/Knee Spike, Snap Kick/Snap Spike, Tripping/Leg Hook/Leg Spur, Gore, Double-Gore, Shoulder Ram and Elbow/Elbow Spike.

Mien-Ch'uan - Sticky Hand.

Shan Tung Kung Fu - Black Tiger Claw Strike.

Shih Ba Ban Wu Yi - Weapon Tap.

Snake Style - One-Fingertip Attack.

Tai-Chi Ch'uan - Push Open Hand.

Praying Mantis Kung Fu - Gou Strike, Negative Gau, Lau, Gou Combination, Gou Grip, Tsai Grip, and Hook at Eyes.

Triad Assassin Training - Pistol Whip.

Strike: Anyone attempting to hit an opponent must roll to strike. As with all combat rolls, a roll to strike is made with twenty-sided dice. Usually, after bonuses are added, the roll must be a 5 or better to hit. Rolling a 4 or less means a miss.

Human Fist (Punch): This is a conventional clenched-fist punch. Does 1D4 Damage.

Knife Hand: An open-handed strike with the blade of the hand. Does 1D6 Damage.

Fore-Knuckle Fist: The fist is clenched with the first joint of the fore-finger sticking out. Does 1D6 Damage.

Double-Knuckle Fist: A clenched fist with the fore-finger and index finger knuckles protruding. Does 1D8 (or 2D4) damage.

Power Punch: Winding out from the waist, this punch corkscrews out from the body for extra power. Common to many karate forms. Does 1D10 (or 2D4+2) damage.

Backhand: Usually used on an opponent coming up behind the character. Can be done without turning around. Does 1D4 damage.

Fingertip Attack: Usually used only to deliver Chi or Atemi based attacks. Does just 1 point damage.

Claw Hand: The hand is held in a claw position and used to rake the flesh of the opponent. Does 1D6 damage.

Palm Strike: An open hand strike done with the heel of the palm. Does 1D6 damage.

Double-Fist Punch: Both fists strike simultaneously for 2D4 damage. Cannot parry during this strike.

Knee: Does 1D6 damage.

Elbow: Does 1D4 damage.

Forearm: Does 1D4 damage.

Tripping/Leg Hook: This attack is not designed to do damage, just to knock an opponent off balance. See Kick Attacks.

Stun: A stunned opponent has no initiative and can take no action while stunned except defensively; -4 to parry and dodge. Plus the stunned character's Spd. and skill performance are reduced by half!

Damage Table (Martial Arts)

Hand Strikes:	
Backhand	1D4
Black Tiger Claw Strike	1D6+4
Claw Hand	1D6
Crane Fist	1D8
Double-Fist Punch	2D4
Double-Knuckle Fist	1D8
Duo-Claw Strike	2D6
Duo-Knuckle Strike	Shock/Stun Only
Fingertip Attack	1 Point Damage
Fore-Knuckle Fist	1D6
Gou Combination	3D6
Gou Grip	1D4
Gou Strike	2D6
Human Fist (Punch)	1D4
Knife Hand	1D6
Lau	1D4
Overhead Fore-Knuckle Fist	1D10
Palm Strike	1D6
Power Punch	1D10
Push Open Hand	Knock-Back
Rotary Palm Strike	1D6+Knockdown
Roundhouse	1D8
Two-Hand Push	Stun for two melee rounds
Uppercut	1D8

Foot Strikes:	
Kick Attack	1D8
Snap Kick	1D6
Roundhouse Kick	2D6
Wheel Kick	1D10
Crescent Kick	1D10
Axe Kick	1D10
Backward Sweep	No damage, Knock-down only
Sweep Kick	1D4
Tripping/Leg Hook	No damage, Knock-down only
Jump Kick	1D8, Critical Strike
Flying Jump Kick	1D10, Critical Strike
Flying Reverse Turning Kick	2D6, Critical Strike

Other Strikes:

Chuk	2D6
Elbow	1D4
Forearm	1D4
Knee	1D6
Pistol Whip	1D8

Note: 1D10 can be substituted with 2D4+2. 1D8 can be substituted for 2D4.

Here's a few important things to bear in mind when selecting Martial Art Forms.

1. Each form must be used separately. For example, if your character gets a + 2 to parry in Liang Hsiung Kung Fu, then that bonus can only be used when using Liang Hsiung Kung Fu. It can't be used when performing any other form.

2. The use of a weapon with a form, combining the form bonuses with the weapon skills, is only possible with a *Weapon Kata*. Some forms include weapon Katas, in others it's possible to get a specialty Kata skill in weapons. Each weapon Kata is designed for a specific form and can't be used with any other forms. There are many forms that have **no** weapon katas and **no** specialty katas. In these forms, the use of weapons with that form is impossible.

3. Receiving a skill more than once in different Martial Art forms does **not** provide any bonus or advancement. Remember, each bonus applies to that one, specific, martial art form.

An Yin Kung Fu (New!)

"Without meditation, studying the Buddha's teaching is like learning swordplay without so much as a stick in your hand, like learning archery with a splendid bow but not an arrow in your quiver!"

Shantung Peasant Monk,
to John Blofeld,
in *Bodhisattva of Compassion*

This is a Tibetan Buddhist martial art that emphasizes Meditation above all else. Characters learn combat strictly from a defensive point of view, since they are not supposed to be aggressive toward any creature.

Patience, silence and concentration are considered the hallmarks of any advanced student of An Yin Kung Fu. Any character with this martial art will have spent at least a year under a total *vow of silence*. During that year, no speaking, reading, or any form of entertainment was allowed, to the point where the character would spend most of the day staring at a blank wall. As a result, characters with this martial art form are exceedingly patient.

Entrance Requirements: Any alignments, but the character must have an M.E. of at least 10.

Costume: A simple cotton robe, belted at the waist with a piece of robe or cloth, with no ornamentation or decorations.

Stance: Unless a different Mudra is selected, the waiting stance is with the hands in the position of the *Mudra of Tranquility and Collection*, right foot extended and left foot back.

Character Bonuses:

Add + 5 to Chi

Add + 2 to M.E.

Combat Skills:

Attacks per Melee: Two to start.

Escape Moves: Roll with punch, fall or impact, maintain balance.

Basic Defensive Moves: Dodge, parry, and automatic parry.

Hand Attacks: Strike (Punch) and Palm Strike.

Foot Attacks: Kick Attack and Snap Kick.

Holds/Locks: Arm Hold

Weapon Katas: None

Modifiers to Attacks: Pull punch, knock-out/stun, critical strike.

Bonus Skills & Abilities:

Martial Art Abilities and Powers: Automatically receives *Mudra of Tranquility and Collection, Mudra of Silent Contemplation, Mudra for the Collection of Alms, Five Smoke Mudra,* and any other three *Mudra.* Also select one power from the *Atemi Abilities* (including advanced).

Language Skill: Tibetan

Training Skills: Begging, fasting, and meditation.

Philosophical Training: Meditative Buddhism.

Level Advancement Bonuses:

1st: + 2 to parry and dodge.

2nd: Select one additional *Mudra.*

3rd: + 2 to roll with punch/fall/impact.

4th: Select one additional *Mudra.*

5th: + 1 attack per melee round.

6th: Select one additional power from *Atemi Abilities* (including advanced) or one *Chi Mastery Ability.*

7th: + 2 to roll with punch/fall/impact.

8th: Select one additional *Mudra.*

9th: + 1 to strike.

10th: Select one additional power from *Atemi Abilities* (including advanced) or one *Chi Mastery Ability.*

11th: + 2 to parry and dodge.

12th: Select one additional *Mudra.*

13th: Double existing Chi.

14th: + 1 attack per melee round.

15th: Select one additional *Mudra.*

Why Study An Yin Kung Fu?

Primarily a form of meditation, with only basic combat skills, it is mostly defensive. However, for certain characters, the benefits of gaining a selection of *Mudra* outweigh the importance of fighting abilities.

Ba Gua (New!) Eight Trigrams Kung Fu

Ba Gua is among the most intellectual of all the martial arts. Analyzing the eight Trigrams of the *I Ching*, the creators have translated them into the "eight directions" representing angles of attack and defense; the "eight steps" of movement; and the "eight palms" of strikes and deflections.

The result is a graceful martial art, where the circular movement of Chi through the body is reflected in the circular movements of deflection and defense. All the attacks are likewise circular and are well suited to use with Soft Chi.

In order to achieve the grace and fluidity needed for true proficiency, students engage in an exercise called "Walking the Circle," where they spend hours stepping around, using their hands in coordination with their feet. In fact, anytime a character with *Ba Gua* has a few spare minutes, they should spend the time "Walking the Circle."

Entrance Requirements: I.Q. 11 and M.E. 10, but no alignment requirements.

Costume: Loose cotton tunic and pants.

Stance: *Ba Gua* discourages the use of stances, believing that they make the body too rigid. Instead, there are simply relaxed ways of standing, with the feet placed comfortably apart and hands open at hip level.

Character Bonuses:

Add + 10 to Chi

Add + 1 to M.E.

Add + 1 to P.E.

Combat Skills:

Attacks per Melee: Two

Escape Moves: Roll with punch/fall/impact, and maintain balance.

Basic Defensive Moves: Dodge, parry, and automatic parry.

Advanced Defenses: Circular Parry

Hand Attacks: Palm Strike, Knife Hand, Fingertip Attack, Backhand, Rotary Palm Strike (Special! Does normal damage but also works as a knockdown).

Basic Foot Attacks: Sweep Kick (Special! This low movement is designed to catch the opponent somewhere below the hip, but without sacrificing balance. 1D4 damage.), plus Backward Sweep and Tripping/Leg Hook.

Special Attacks: Body Flip/Throw, Disarm, Forearm, Combination Parry/Attack.

Holds/Locks: None

Weapon Katas: Optional, see *Pun Gung Bi*, below.

Modifiers to Attacks: Pull punch, knock-out/stun, critical strike.

Bonus Skills & Abilities:

Martial Art Abilities and Powers: Select two from among *Chi Mastery* and/or *Specialty Katas* (including Chi Katas). In addition to the standard list of Katas, here are two more distinctive *Ba Gua Katas* that may be selected:

Ba Gua Circle Kata: This is a highly defensive Kata that involves circling to cover all eight directions from attack. All parries for the entire melee round are made at + 3 and ALL attacks can be parried from any direction. In addition, one attack per melee round may be delivered that inflicts the normal damage with either a Knife-Hand or Backhand.

Pun Gung Bi Weapon Kata: Includes a special W.P. allowing the character to use *Pun Gung Bi*. These are paired weapons designed for use with the open palm techniques of *Ba Gua*. Easy to hide on the body, the character slips them on like rings, one on each middle finger. When using *Pun Gung Bi*, the Knife-Hand and Backhand strikes both do an additional 1D6 points of damage. Plus, the *Pun Gung Bi* can be used to parry sharp objects without damage to the hand.

Language Skill: Chinese (Mandarin dialect).

Training Skills: Feng Shui

Philosophical Training: Taoism

Level Advancement Bonuses:

1st: + 2 to parry and dodge, + 1 to hand strikes, + 1 to damage with hand strikes.

2nd: + 1 to rear attacks (Backward Sweep, Backhand Strike).

3rd: Select one additional *Chi Mastery Ability* or *Specialty Kata* (including Chi Kata).

4th: + 1 attack per melee, knock-out/stun on natural 19 or 20.

5th: + 1 to hand strikes and + 1 to damage.

6th: + 1 to parry and dodge.

7th: Select one additional *Chi Mastery Ability* or *Specialty Kata* (including Chi Kata).

8th: + 1 to rear attacks (Backward Sweep, Backhand Strike).

9th: + 1 attack per melee, knock-out/stun on natural 17 or better.

10th: Double existing Chi.

11th: Select one additional *Chi Mastery Ability* or *Specialty Kata* (including Chi Kata).

12th: + 1 to parry and dodge, + 1 to damage.

13th: + 1 to rear attacks (Backward Sweep, Backhand Strike).

14th: + 1 attack per melee, knock-out/stun on natural 16 or better.

15th: Select one additional *Chi Mastery Ability* or *Specialty Kata* (including Chi Kata).

Why Study Ba Gua Kung Fu?

Since it is one of the most "integrated" martial arts, combining internal Chi development with useful, but graceful, physical movements, this is a good all-around choice. Notably, this is the *Fang Shih's* most common martial art.

Bak Mei Kung Fu (New!) White Eyebrow Kung Fu

According to the traditional legends of the school, it was founded by a Taoist Priest who was known as much for being a failed spy and a traitor, as a teacher of martial arts (his name, Bak Mei, is really a nickname, "White Eyebrows," referring to the fact that his hair had turned white). This contradiction of naming the school after a man who betrayed it to the enemy is just one of the many contradictions within Bak Mei. In fact, one could say that Bak Mei is just one contradiction after another.

In fighting style, Bak Mei is also contradictory. Defenses are supposed to be soft and flexible, while attacks are taught as hard and destructive. So it is with Chi as well, since about half the Bak Mei moves call for Chi and the other half are purely physical.

Bottom line, Bak Mei expects students to display cleverness (what they call "wit"). After all, since there are no rules in combat and since circumstances always change, it is only with quick wittedness that one can prevail.

Entrance Requirements: Any alignments, but most are honorably aligned characters. Attribute requirements: I.Q. and P.P. 11 or higher. A high M.A. is also suggested but not required.

Costume: None

Stance: The right hand is extended only when the left leg is extended and vice versa. Initially, the hands are formed in a gripping position, as if the fingers were holding an invisible ball the size of the palm. All foot movements are designed around a triangular pattern, so every forward move is followed by a sideways move.

Character Bonuses:

Add + 5 to Chi

Add + 2 to M.A.

Add + 1 to P.P.

Add + 4 to Spd.

Add 10 to S.D.C.

Combat Skills:

Attacks per Melee: One

Escape Moves: Roll with punch/fall/impact, and maintain balance.

Basic Defensive Moves: Dodge, parry, and automatic parry.

Advanced Defenses: *Chum* (Special! This is a soft form of parry, where the opponent's hand or weapon is forced to sink down — like being gently pushed down in water. If successful, the opponent loses his next melee action/attack.), and Circular Parry.

Hand Attacks: Fore-Knuckle Fist, Strike (Punch), Backhand, Palm Strike.

Basic Foot Attacks: Crescent Kick, Backward Sweep.

Special Attacks: Death Blow and *Chuk* (Special! This sudden, violent thrust is supposed to bring the hand all the way in to some soft part of the opponent's body, where Chi is re-

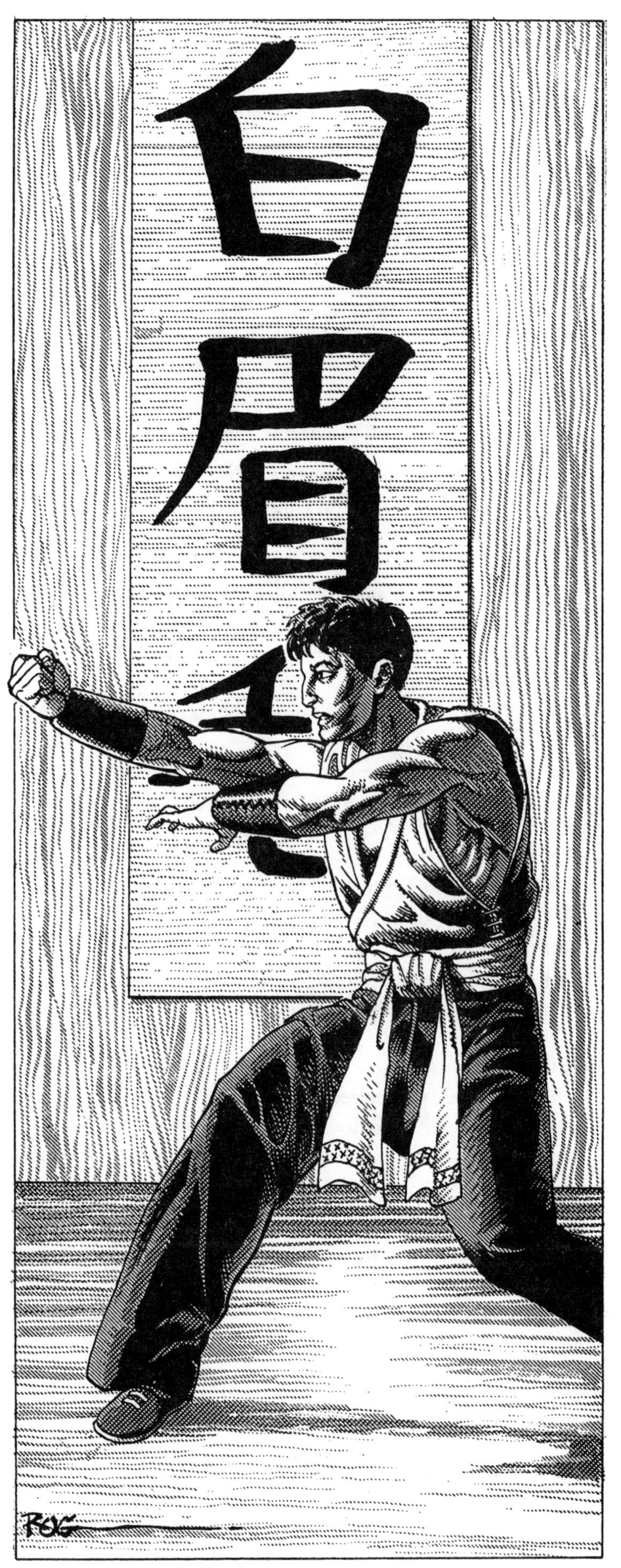

leased, simultaneous with a painful pinch or grip. If the character has a least one point of Positive Chi, the *Chuk* does 2D6 damage. Note that demons take double damage, 4D6, from this attack and will howl with pain when it happens to them.)

Holds/Locks: None

Weapon Katas: W.P. Whip (usually used with the Gieh Bian or Chain Whip).

Modifiers to Attacks: Pull punch, knock-out/stun, critical strike.

Bonus Skills & Abilities:

Martial Art Abilities and Powers: Select two from among *Atemi Abilities* (including advanced), *Chi Mastery Abilities* (including advanced), and/or *Martial Art Techniques.*

Language Skill: Chinese (Mandarin or Cantonese)

Training Skills: Prowl

Philosophical Training: Taoism or Buddhism.

Level Advancement Bonuses:

1st: + 1 to strike, + 2 to roll with punch/fall/impact, critical strike on natural 20.

2nd: + 2 to damage.

3rd: Select one additional *Atemi Ability* (including advanced), *Chi Mastery Ability* (including advanced), or *Martial Art Technique.*

4th: + 1 attack per melee.

5th: + 1 to *Chuk* (attack) and increase *Chuk* damage to 3D6, + 2 to *Chum* (defense).

6th: + 1 to strike, critical strike on natural 19 or better.

7th: Select one additional *Atemi Ability* (including advanced), *Chi Mastery Ability* (including advanced), or *Martial Art Technique.*

8th: Double existing chi.

9th: + 1 attack per melee.

10th: + 2 to roll with punch/fall/impact.

11th: Select one additional *Atemi Ability* (including advanced), *Chi Mastery Ability* (including advanced), or *Martial Art Technique.*

12th: + 2 to damage.

13th: + 1 attack per melee.

14th: Select one additional *Atemi Ability* (including advanced), *Chi Mastery Ability* (including advanced), or *Martial Art Technique.*

15th: Add one *Zenjorike Power.*

Why Study Bak Mei Kung Fu?

A form of some contradictions, with a major emphasis on Chi. Best suited for characters who are quick witted and clever.

Bok Pai Kung Fu
The Crane Style

Bok Pai, also known as the *White Crane Style*, is one of the major styles of Kung Fu. According to legend, a lama priest once witnessed a battle between a crane and an ape where the crane managed to win using the agility of its long legs, huge wings, and pecking movements. It is one of the more aggressive martial arts. Training is rigorous, involving years of practicing uncomfortable and complex stances, all designed to imitate the fighting position of the crane. Study of posture, balance, and energy circulation are all-important. There are many monasteries and martial art schools, as well as a large number of teachers available in Bok Pai.

A Bok Pai master entering combat, advances very slowly, preferring to meet the attacks of an opponent rather than rushing forward. Attacks can take the form of sweeping arm moves, rounded kicks and continuous turning movements. The form's main attack is the Crane Fist, a beak-like formation of thumb and fingertips pointed together, striking with a forward-and-down pecking motion.

The philosophy of Bok Pai can be summed up in four words; *sim* ("to evade"), *jeet* ("to intercept"), *chun* ("to penetrate"), and *chon* ("to destroy"). As a part of the training, all initiates are required to fight bouts on the *Mui-Fa-Jeong*, the "Plum Flower Stumps," which are a series of 36 pillars (like telephone poles) separated by four to eight feet (1.2 to 2.4 m) and driven into the ground. Combat actually takes place on the tops of the poles. Students may learn Bok Pai in Taiwan, Hong Kong or Singapore.

Entrance Requirements: No alignment or attribute requirements.

Costume: Silk Kung Fu outfit, preferably highly decorated.

Character Bonuses:

Add + 10 to Chi

Add + 2 to P.P.

Add + 4 to Spd.

Add + 10 to S.D.C.

Combat Skills:

Attacks per Melee: Two

Escape Moves: Roll with punch/fall/impact, and maintain balance.

Basic Defensive Moves: Dodge, parry, and automatic parry.

Advanced Defenses: Multiple Dodge and Circular Parry.

Hand Attacks: Crane Fist (SPECIAL! Beak-like formation of thumb and fingertips, does 1D8 damage), Backhand, Claw Hand, Palm Strike.

Basic Foot Attacks: Kick Attack, Crescent Kick, Axe Kick, Backward Sweep, Reverse Turning Kick (Combination Dodge/Kick).

Special Attacks: Death Blow, Body Flip/Throw, Critical Flip/Throw, Elbow, Forearm.

Weapon Katas: None

Modifiers to Attacks: Pull punch, knock-out/stun, critical strike.

Bonus Skills & Abilities:

Martial Art Abilities and Powers: You may select two (2) Abilities from among *Body Hardening Techniques* and *Specialty Katas* (including Chi Katas).

Crane Stance Kata (Special!) is a one-legged stance with one leg straight and the other bent so that the ankle is right at the knee. Arms are out-stretched, with elbows up and hands pointing down in a Crane Fist position. Cannot advance, retreat or dodge, and attacks are limited to the Crane Fist and Crescent Kick. Bonuses are + 4 to parry, + 6 to maintain balance, and + 2 to strike. In addition, bonuses count toward critical strikes (they don't have to be natural rolls).

Language: Chinese

Cultural Skills (Choose One): Gardening, Calligraphy, Chinese and Cooking.

Temple Skills: Fasting

Philosophical Training: Taoism

Level Advancement Bonuses:

1st: + 2 to Crane Fist Strike, + 1 to Crane Fist Damage, + 2 to roll with punch/fall/impact.

2nd: + 1 to strike, + 1 to damage, critical strike on natural 20.

3rd: + 1 attack per melee.

4th: Select one additional from *Body Hardening Exercises, Specialty Katas* (including Chi Katas).

5th: Critical strike on roll of natural 18, 19 or 20.

6th: + 1 to parry and dodge, critical strike on sneak attacks.

7th: + 1 attack per melee, + 2 to roll with punch/fall/impact.

8th: + 1 to Crane Fist Strike, + 1 to Crane Fist Damage, knock-out/stun on natural 19 or 20.

9th: Select one additional from *Body Hardening Exercises, Specialty Katas* (including Chi Katas).

10th: Double existing Chi, + 1 to parry and dodge.

11th: + 1 attack per melee, death blow on roll of natural 18 or better.

12th: Select one additional from *Body Hardening Exercises, Specialty Katas* (including Chi Katas), or *Chi Mastery Abilities.*

13th: + 1 attack per melee round.

14th: + 1 to Crane Fist Strike, + 1 to Crane Fist Damage.

15th: Add one *Zenjorike Power.*

Why Study Bok Pai?

A good combination of advanced martial art techniques and abilities. It's also balanced so there are solid attacks and defenses. Techniques work well in combination with other forms and katas. It is also a very beautiful style. No major disadvantages.

Chao Ta Kung Fu (New!)

Of all the martial arts, this is the only one whose main concern is looking good! That's because this martial art has been specially designed to produce performers for the Hong Kong film industry. A rough translation of *Chao Ta* would be "a million lucky punches," and it's mostly taught to aspiring martial art film stars.

Every year, hundreds of movies are produced in Hong Kong, and plenty of them have some kind of martial art scenes. While martial artists trained in conventional schools fill much of the need, those who study Chao Ta learn how to make things really look good on the big screen.

Any character who takes Chao Ta Kung Fu will always be able to land temporary work in Hong Kong. Unlike Hollywood, Hong Kong movies are made under budget and in a hurry. Shooting usually takes 6D6 days. The opportunities vary, but here's a table of possibilities:

01-25 Gofer. You "go for" photocopies, you "go for" sandwiches, you "go for" paper clips, and so on. It's not much, but it brings in enough to live on and it lets you get to know people in the business.

26-30 Assistant to the Grip. Your job gets a bit more complex as you help put up stage props, lighting, and all the equipment. It's hard work, but it pays pretty good.

31-55 Stunt Martial Artist. In mass action scenes, where dozens or even hundreds of martial artists are doing battle, you are one of the multitude. Unlike a real punching bag, you get paid pretty good for this work. However, you're main job is to get punched, kicked, shot and maimed realistically.

56-70 Extra Martial Artist. In most Hong Kong action pics, the bodies pile up like peanut shells, especially when the main character really gets moving. On average, you'll "fight to the death" every couple of days of shooting, simply wearing different outfits ("Tuesday we want you to wear a red headband, Friday come all in black, and next week... hmmm... we'll let you know when the next part of the script is finished..."). Pay is good.

71-75 Walk-On. You finally get to *say something*, instead of just grunting and kicking. Usually your line is "Hey! Stop it!" or "Give me your money!" or "Die, mutant pig!" or "We surrender!" At this stage there is usually a close-up of your death scene. Pay is very good.

76-80 Thug. Your character appears on screen several times before getting killed, usually as part of a group. There may be several speaking lines, and you'll be expected to look like you could actually win a few fights. Pay is good.

81-90 Minor Villain! At this point, you play a character who is actually named in the script (instead of "Thug #4 dies falling off roof"). You get sent to make-up and usually you are expected to perform something spectacular (right before getting bumped off). Pay is very good.

91-93 Major Villain! A definite step up, because you don't have to provide your own clothing. Practice snarling and cursing, not to mention getting beat up by all the real stars. A + 10% on all future rolls on this table. Pay is very good and work is regular!

94-97 Buddy Part! A great role, where you play one of the main character's best friends/relative/allies. The roll includes dialogue and a heavy-duty action scene, plus key screen credits! However, your main job is to die within the first half hour, usually horribly, at the hands of the villain. After your "death," you can continue to work the stunt crew for the rest of the shoot. The character enjoys a + 25% on all future rolls on this table. Pay is excellent!

98-00 Stardom Beckons! You get a real part in the movie, where your character is an important part of the action. If the movie is successful, the character will have a + 50% on all future rolls on this table! Pay for this job is excellent, and a future in film looks excellent!!

Entrance Requirements: All students must start out with an M.A. of 13 (a high P.B. is good too, but not required). There are no alignment restrictions.

Costume: Tailored silk Kung Fu outfit, tastefully decorated with embroidered dragons.

Stance: Graceful pose, looking tall, with legs straight and hands held loosely forward and fingers arranged artfully.

Character Bonuses:

Add + 1 to P.P.

Add + 1 to P.B.

Add + 2 to M.A.

Add + 3 to Spd.

Add 10 to S.D.C.

Combat Skills:

Attacks per Melee: Two

Escape Moves: Impact Sponge (Special! When successful, the character folds up, absorbing the blow, and falls down. This makes it *look* like maximum damage was done. The character loses one melee action (or more if he wants to feign serious injury; sometimes won't attack until the next melee round or until his opponent comes close to investigate). If successful, no actual damage is inflicted, otherwise damage is half. Roll with punch/fall/impact, maintain balance, and somersault.

Basic Defensive Moves: Dodge, parry, and automatic parry.

Hand Attacks: Strike (punch), Knife Hand, Power Punch, Backhand, Palm Strike, and Forearm Strike.

Basic Foot Attacks: Kick Attack, Snap Kick, Crescent Kick, and Reverse Turning Kick (Combination Dodge/Kick).

Jumping Foot Attacks: Jump Kick, Roundhouse Kick, Flying Jump Kick, and Flying Reverse Turning Kick.

Special Attacks: Body flip/throw.

Holds/Locks: Arm Hold, Leg Hold, Neck Hold.

Weapon Katas: W.P. Sword, W.P. Spear

Modifiers to Attacks: Fake Attack (Special! Delivering a blow with either hand or foot, putting every shuddering effort into making it *look* strong and powerful. Those who respond with Impact Sponge will take no damage. Anyone else takes half the usual damage from the attack, but it looks impressive), and pull punch.

Special Chao Ta Kung Fu "Acting" Katas:

Greased Lightning Kata (a rip-off of the Thai Kick Boxing Lightning Form): Double the character's normal attacks per melee round that are delivered in the first round, resulting in a blinding display of rapid-fire punches and kicks. However, all attacks are done at a -4 to strike, and do just *half damage*!

Kung Sao Kata: It literally means "forcing the crowd to cheer," and it involves holding back throughout a full melee round, building energy for one spectacular attack. While the attack can be with a normal punch or kick (in which case there's a + 3 chance of a knock-down), it is really designed to be used with the *Roundhouse Kick, Flying Jump Kick,* or *Flying Reverse Turning Kick.* When done properly, the result will be double the character's usual leaping distance and a + 4 to strike (normal damage; it's acting, remember).

Ni Huei Kata: This Kata, which translates to "Hiding the Lament," is a two-parter that starts only when your character gets hit by the enemy. The idea is for you to make it look like you've just suffered a horrible, super-serious hit, which *should*, by all rights, smash the life right out of you. The other half of the Kata is a combination of your posture and your expression, which tell the world (and the camera!) that you will *never* be defeated, and that something transcendental and awesome powers your mind and spirit to keep you from succumbing. The net result should impress opponents (and audiences) to the point where they believe their cause is hopeless (horror/awe factor 12)! In combat terms, the Kata confers a + 4 to roll with punch or impact, the rest is acting.

Bonus Skills & Abilities:

Martial Art Abilities and Powers: Select two *Body Hardening Techniques* and one of the three *Chao Ta Katas.*

Language Skill: Chinese (fluent in both Cantonese and Mandarin), also English and French.

Training Skills: Automatically receives the following two:

Body Building. The usual bonuses (+ 2 P.S./+ 10 S.D.C.), but with extra emphasis on toning and shaping the body for impressive looks.

Screen Acting (Special!). The character learns how to emote (express outward emotions on cue), to speak scripted dialog in a natural way, and how to appear graceful on camera. It also means learning how to work camera angles; blocking the star could mean instant unemployment. Roll for each screen appearance to avoid a bad acting job. **Base Skill:** 25%+ 5% per level of experience.

Philosophical Training: None

Level Advancement Bonuses:

1st: + 1 to dodge and parry, + 2 to roll with punch/fall/impact.

2nd: Select one additional *Body Hardening Exercise.*

3rd: + 1 attack per melee.

4th: + 2 to any "Fake" moves.

5th: + 1 to leap (add 5 feet/1.5 m to distance), + 1 to any Jump Attacks.

6th: Select one additional *Body Hardening Exercise.*

7th: + 1 attack per melee, + 2 to roll with punch/fall/impact.

8th: Select one additional Chao Ta Kata.

9th: Select one additional *Body Hardening Exercise.*

10th: + 2 to any "Fake" moves.

11th: + 1 to Leap (add 5 feet/1.5 m to distance), + 1 to any Jump Attacks.

12th: Select one additional *Body Hardening Exercise* (including Demon Hunter Exercises).

13th: + 1 to parry and dodge.

14th: Select one additional Chao Ta Kata.

15th: Select one additional *Body Hardening Exercise* (including Demon Hunter Exercises).

Why Study Chao Ta Kung Fu?

Because it's a way to get into show business! Also, if you're looking for a martial art that really "looks" spectacular, you can't get any better than this! While the intimidation factor may win a few battles, it's great for body building, and the training does allow students to defend themselves, Chao Ta isn't really all that effective in aggressive combat.

Chi Hsuan Men
The White Jade Fan (Exclusive)

One of the most ancient and strangest martial arts in existence. Even it's name, Chi Hsuan Men means "Unusual Style." Started in the 5th Century B.C. as a defense mechanism for the bureaucrat class of the ancient chinese dynasties. All the movements involve the use of "the white jade fan," actually a fan-like metal weapon used for both disarming opponents and poking.

The Chi Hsuan Men master will attempt to calm any enemy with both a relaxed pose and with friendly words. Then, preferably when the enemy is off-guard, the fan can be whipped out of the sleeves and used either to disarm or attack. Masters are extremely rare and usually train only one or two students at a time, treating them as apprentices.

Entrance Requirements: No attribute or alignment restrictions.

Costume: Prefer ornate traditional chinese gowns with sleeves that can wrap around the arm at least four times. Bright colors and ornate embroidery are favored. The traditional fan can be disguised as a normal fan and/or stored in a hidden sleeve pocket.

Stance: Almost at "attention," with legs only a foot apart and with hands crossed and fitted into sleeves.

Character Bonuses:

Add + 5 t o Chi

Add + 1 to P.E.

Add + 1 to P.P.

Add + 10 to S.DC.

Combat Skills:

Attacks per Melee: Two

Escape Moves: Roll with punch/fall/impact.

Basic Defensive Moves: Dodge, parry, and automatic parry.

Hand Moves: Strike (punch) and Fingertip Attack.

Basic Foot Attacks: None

Special Attacks: Death Blow, Disarm, PARALYSIS Attack (Vital Points)

Weapon Katas: W.P. White Jade Fan, W.P. White Jade Fan - Paired

Modifiers to Attacks: Pull punch, knock-out/stun, critical strike, and critical strike from rear.

Skills Included in Training:

Martial Art Abilities and Powers: Select two abilities from among *Atemi Abilities* and *Body Hardening Exercises.*

Languages: Chinese

Cultural Skills: Calligraphy and Go.

Philosophical Training: Confucianism

Level Advancement Bonuses:

1st: + 1 to roll with punch/fall/impact, + 2 to disarm, critical strike on natural 20.

2nd: + 1 to strike, + 1 to parry and dodge.

3rd: + 1 to disarm, + 2 to damage.

4th: + 1 to roll with punch/fall/impact, knock-out/stun on natural 19 or 20.

5th: + 1 to parry and dodge, + 1 attack per melee.

6th: + 1 to roll with punch/fall/impact, + 1 to disarm.

7th: + 2 to damage, critical strike or knock-out from behind, select one additional from *Atemi Abilities* (including Advanced Atemi) or *Body Hardening Exercises.*

8th: Death blow on roll of natural 19 or 20.

9th: + 1 to roll with punch/fall/impact, + 1 to parry/dodge, + 1 to disarm.

10th: Select one additional from *Atemi Abilities* (including Advanced Atemi) or *Body Hardening Exercises* (including Demon Hunter).

11th: + 1 attack per melee round.

12th: + 1 to parry and dodge, critical strike on natural 18 or better.

13th: + 1 to roll with punch/fall/impact, + 1 to disarm.

14th: Select one additional from *Atemi Abilities* (including Advanced Atemi) or *Body Hardening Exercises* (including Demon Hunter).

15th: + 1 to parry and dodge and + 2 to damage.

Why Study Chi Hsuan Men?

Aside from the rich tradition in this art, there is its common sense approach to battle. Attacks should be unexpected, should first make the opponent helpless, and then finish him off. One great disadvantage of Chi Hsuan Men is that it does not do well when dealing with multiple attackers. One of the rare arts that teaches Atemi.

Ch'in-Na
The Art of Seizing

One of the first arts that involved studying the nerves, tendons, joints and muscles of the human body. This is the ancient precursor to Aikido, Jujutsu and many other modern forms. Although Ch'in-Na is really a form of wrestling, its precise holds, strikes and locks can be disabling or deadly. The student spends equal amounts of time studying the body, sparring with fellow students and teachers, and meditating in solitude.

The Ch'in-Na master will always seek to grasp at the body's most vulnerable and fragile parts. Injuries inflicted include severed tendons, dislocated joints, and nerve damage. Usually this starts with a paralyzing attack followed by systematically inflicting damage on the helpless victim.

All Ch'in-Na masters conduct their classes in the strictest of secrecy. Students take a blood oath never to reveal the identity of any living Ch'in-Na artist (although deceased masters can be talked about and revered). Initial acceptance also requires the potential student to make a large cash gift (from $10,000 to $100,000). Even after "graduation," a Ch'in-Na student may be expected to continue offering yearly gifts of $1,000 to $5,000.

Entrance Requirements: Any alignments admitted but honorably aligned characters will tend to *avoid* Ch'in-Na (often anarchist). There are no attribute requirements.

Costume: None, prefer to remain inconspicuous.

Stance: Standing upright with forward foot facing forward and rear foot at a right angle, forward arm loosely extended, rear arm held just behind the body. Both hands at about waist level with palms held vertical and toward the center of the body, thumbs separate and fingers loose.

Character Bonuses:

Add + 5 to Chi

Add + 1 to P.S.

Add + 2D4 to P.P.

Combat Skills:

Attacks per Melee: Two

Escape Moves: Roll with punch/fall/impact, maintain balance

Basic Defensive Moves: Dodge, parry, automatic parry

Advanced Defenses: Combination parry/attack (every parry is an attempt to disable), and disarm.

Hand Attacks: Strike (Punch), Fingertip Attack, Claw Hand

Basic Foot Attacks: None

Special Attacks: Death Blow, Crush/Squeeze, Pin/Incapacitate, Choke, and PARALYSIS Attack (Vital Points).

Holds/Locks: Arm Hold, Leg Hold, Neck Hold, and Automatic Hold.

Weapon Katas: None

Modifiers to Attacks: Knock-out/stun, critical strike, and critical strike from rear.

Skills Included in Training:

Martial Art Abilities and Powers: Select two abilities from among *Atemi Abilities* (including advanced), and one from the *Arts of Invisibility.*

Languages: Chinese

Survival: Fasting

Philosophical Training: Taoism

Level Advancement Bonuses:

1st: + 2 to roll with punch/fall/impact, + 1 to strike, knock-out/stun on natural 20.

2nd: + 1 to parry and dodge, + 3 to damage, critical strike or knock-out from behind.

3rd: + 1 attack per melee, + 1 to maintain balance.

4th: Select one additional ability from *Arts of Invisibility, Atemi* (including advanced) or *Body Hardening Exercises.*

5th: + 2 to damage, critical strike on natural 18 or better.

6th: + 1 to parry and dodge, death blow on roll of natural 20.

7th: + 1 to maintain balance, + 1 to strike.

8th: + 1 attack per melee, select one additional *Ability from Arts of Invisibility, Atemi* (including advanced) or *Body Hardening Exercises.*

9th: + 2 to roll with punch/fall/impact.

10th: + 2 to damage.

11th: + 1 to maintain balance, + 1 to strike.

12th: Select one additional *Ability from Arts of Invisibility, Atemi* (including advanced) or *Body Hardening Exercises.*

13th: Add one *Zenjorike Power.*

14th: + 1 attack per Melee, + 1 to parry and dodge.

15th: + 1 to maintain balance and + 2 to damage.

Why Study Ch'in-Na?

The secrets of the body's weak points (Atemi) gives the power of pain over enemies. Any opponent falling under an attack risks permanent maiming. It's also discrete since a victim can be left without any visible signs of damage. A major disadvantage is the inability to deal effectively with multiple attackers.

Choy-Li-Fut Kung Fu

Created in 1838 as one of the many offshoots of Shao-lin Kung Fu. The form is very aggressive, concentrating on long hand techniques like roundhouse and overhand swings.

A Choy-Li-Fut master, when confronted with a fight, will immediately attack, plunging right into the middle of any group of opponents. Using the Circular Parry, he will fend off any attacks while lashing out with a flurry of hand strikes, snap kicks and back sweeps.

Instruction in Choy-Li-Fut is available in monasteries and martial art schools throughout China, as well as in Hong Kong, Taiwan and the United States. At least part of the training is spiritual, concentrating on Taoist thought, the building (though not the use) of Chi and in the humble practice of Taoist monks.

Entrance Requirements: No alignment or attribute restrictions.

Stance: See Bear Kata.

Costume: Kung Fu silk outfit.

Character Bonuses:

Add + 5 to Chi

Add + 2 to P.E.

Add + 1 to P.P.

Add + 3 to Spd.

Add + 10 to S.D.C.

Combat Skills:

Attacks per Melee: Two

Escape Moves: Leap and roll with punch/fall/impact.

Basic Defensive Moves: Dodge, parry, and automatic parry.

Advanced Defenses: Circular Parry

Hand Attacks: Strike (Punch), Knife Hand, Fore-Knuckle Fist, Backhand Strike, Overhead Fore-Knuckle Fist (Special! This special attack is so difficult that it's always done with a -4 to Strike. Does 1D10 or 2D4+ 2 damage.), Uppercut (Special! Like a boxing punch that comes from underneath, up into the chin. Does 1D8 damage), ROUNDHOUSE Strikes (Special! No Parries can be used during this attack. Does 1D10 or 2D4+ 2 damage.)

Basic Foot Attacks: Tripping/Leg Hooks, Snap Kick

Special Attacks: Elbow, Forearm

Weapon Katas: W.P. Pa-Kua Lance, W.P. Willow Leaf Double Swords (Paired), and W.P. "Eighteen" Staff

Modifiers to Attacks: Pull punch, knock-out/stun, critical strike, critical strike from rear.

Skills Included in Training:

Martial Art Abilities and Powers: Select two abilities from among *Body Hardening Exercises* and *Specialty Katas.*

Bear Stance Kata (Special). A solid two-legged stance where both legs are bent forward and both feet are pointed slightly outward. Arms are held in a wide wrestler-style position, with hands cupped forward in knife-hand position. Cannot retreat, circular parry, or dodge. Attacks are limited to Overhand Fore-Knuckle Fists, Backhand Strikes and Roundhouse Strikes. Bonuses are + 2 to parry, + 4 to maintain balance, and + 2 to strike.

Languages: Chinese

Temple Skills: Begging

Philosophical Training: Taoism

Level Advancement Bonuses:

1st: + 2 to roll with punch/fall/impact, + 1 to parry/dodge, + 2 to leap (add 4 feet/1.2 m to Leap Distance), knock-out/stun on natural 20.

2nd: + 1 to strike, + 1 to damage, critical strike or knock-out from behind.

3rd: + 1 attack per melee, select one additional *Body Hardening Exercise* or *Specialty Kata* (including Chi Kata).

4th: + 2 to leap (add 4 feet/1.2 m to leap distance).

5th: + 2 to damage, critical strike on natural 18, 19 or 20.

6th: + 2 to roll with punch/fall/impact, + 1 to parry/dodge.

7th: + 1 to leap (add 4 feet/1.2 m to leap distance), select one additional *Body Hardening Exercise* (including Demon Hunter Exercises) or *Specialty Kata* (including Chi Kata).

8th: + 1 attack per melee, + 1 to parry and dodge.

9th: Knock-out/stun on natural 18, 19 or 20.

10th: + 1 to leap (add 4 feet/1.2 m to leap distance), + 1 to strike.

11th: + 2 to roll with punch/fall/impact, select one additional *Body Hardening Exercise* (including Demon Hunter Exercises) or *Specialty Kata* (including Chi Kata).

12th: + 2 to damage.

13th: + 1 attack per melee.

14th: Select one additional *Body Hardening Exercise* (including Demon Hunter Exercises) or *Specialty Kata* (including Chi Kata).

15th: + 1 to strike, + 1 to leap (add 4 feet/1.2 m to leap distance).

Why Study Choy-Li-Fut?

A terrific action-oriented martial art. Capable of dealing with multiple attacks or multiple attackers with equal ease. Relatively few special abilities.

Drunken Style of Kung Fu
Pu Kung Fu

The idea behind the Drunken Style of Kung Fu is purely deceptive, all the moves can be performed while imitating a drunken stupor. Also called Ts'ui Pa Hsien for the "Eight Drunken Fairies Form."

Encountering a master seems to be nothing more than happening across an ordinary drunk. Wobbling unsteadily, stumbling to the ground, making uncertain hand movements and continuously singing or talking incoherently. All attacks and defenses seem to be pure accidents, with a hand outstretched at exactly the right time, a stumble to the left just in time to avoid a blow, and so forth. It is said that the greatest masters can leave their opponents completely defeated but without a clue as to anything other than "dumb luck" being the cause.

Drunken style may be humorous but it is also very difficult to learn. Years are spent practicing each small movement, along with the tremendous variety of foot and leg techniques. Secret schools are found only in Hong Kong and Singapore. Admission is by invitation only, and acceptance often means swearing allegiance to a particular Triad Society.

By the way, *Pu* is a Chinese symbol that means both "drink heavily" and "a group of friendly drinkers."

Entrance Requirements: No attribute or alignment restrictions.

Costume: No particular outfit. Practice is usually done in the character's normal street clothing.

Character Bonuses:

Add + 3 to M.A.

Add + 1 to P.E.

Add + 10 to S.D.C.

Combat Skills:

Attacks per Melee: Two

Escape Moves: Roll with punch/fall/impact, somersault (appearing accidental).

Attack Moves: Stagger (Special! Sort of a broken walk/fall into combat. A successful roll means entering combat distance and gaining initiative.), Roll, Backflip.

Basic Defensive Moves: Dodge, parry, automatic parry.

Advanced Defenses: Multiple dodge, automatic dodge, combination parry/attack, disarm, and automatic roll.

Hand Attacks: Strike (punch), Knife Hand, Backhand, Palm Strike.

Basic Foot Attacks: Kick Attack, Tripping/Leg Hooks, Snap Kick, Crescent Kick, Backward Sweep, Reverse Turning Kick (Combination Dodge/Kick), Drop Kick (Combination Fall/Dodge/Kick).

Special Attacks: Death Blow, Body Block/Tackle, Crush/Squeeze, Pin/Incapacitate, Choke, Combination Strike/Parry, Combination Grab/Kick, Knee, Elbow, Forearm.

Holds/Locks: Arm Hold, Leg Hold, Body Hold, Neck Hold

Weapon Katas: None

Modifiers to Attacks: Pull punch, knock-out/stun, critical strike, critical strike from rear

Skills Included in Training:

Martial Art Abilities and Powers: Select two from among *Arts of Invisibility* and *Body Hardening Exercises.*

Languages: Chinese (usually Cantonese).

Cultural Skills: Singing

Survival: Begging, disguise, and fasting.

Physical: Gymnastics, prowl, and swimming.

Philosophical Training: Taoism.

Level Advancement Bonuses:

1st: + 3 to roll with punch/fall/impact, + 2 to somersault/stagger/roll/backflip, knock-out/stun on natural 19 or 20, critical strike on natural 19 or 20, critical strike from behind.

2nd: + 1 to rear attacks (Backward Sweep, Backhand Strike), + 2 to parry and dodge.

3rd: + 1 to strike, knock-out/stun on natural 19 or 20.

4th: + 1 to somersault/stagger/roll/backflip, + 1 to roll with punch/fall/impact.

5th: + 1 attack per melee, + 1 to parry/dodge.

6th: Critical strike or knockout from behind (triple damage).

7th: + 1 to somersault/stagger/roll/backflip, + 1 to roll with punch/fall/impact.

8th: + 1 to rear attacks (Backward Sweep, Backhand Strike), Select one additional from *Arts of Invisibility* or *Body Hardening Exercises.*

9th: + 1 attack per melee.

10th: + 1 to roll with punch/fall/impact, + 1 to Rear Attacks (Backward Sweep, Backhand Strike)

11th: + 2 to somersault/stagger/roll/backflip, + 2 to Damage.

12th: + 1 to strike, death blow on roll of natural 20.

13th: + 1 to roll with punch/fall/impact.

14th: + 1 attack per melee.

15th: + 2 to somersault/stagger/roll/backflip, Select One (1) additional from *Arts of Invisibility* or *Body Hardening Exercises.*

Why Study Drunken Style of Kung Fu?

The perfect "hidden" form of martial arts, even the actual moves are disguised. Good all-around offensive and defensive actions along with a good number of secondary skills. Although the form is great against the unsuspecting, it's not as effective as other forms in straight combat.

Fu Chiao Pai
Tiger Claw Kung Fu

Inspired by the strength and power of the tiger, the Fu-Chiao Pai form is dedicated to building the strength and endurance of its followers. This is very much an external form, stressing offensive attacks, and a linear form, utilizing all kinds of solid, maximum-damage strikes.

A Master of the Tiger Claw Form will enter combat aggressively, leaping or charging the opponent as soon as possible. Once in combat, the master will try to keep in combat range, striking out with as many kicks as possible and using claw-type strikes only when the enemy comes too close.

Fu-Chiao Pai can only be learned at monasteries in remote locations in China and Tibet. In addition to standard practice and instruction, the student must also take at least one survival trip each year. These trips involve living alone in the wilderness, fasting, hunting (with bare hands) and living off the land.

Note: Students of Tiger Claw Kung Fu are rivals of the Black Tiger Kung Fu school. Mostly because their respective teachers do not approve of brawling; this means they throw insults at each other. A common term of abuse for those practitioners of Shan Tung is the insulting *Kao Hu*, which could mean "tiger cub," but is meant to mean "fierce baby sheep."

Entrance Requirements: No alignment restrictions. Requires a minimum M.A. 8, minimum P.S. 10 and minimum P.E. 8.

Costume: Silk Kung Fu outfit but often bare chested.

Stance: Low knee bends, feet more than shoulder-width apart. Hands outstretched in claw position.

Character Bonuses:

Add + 2 to P.S.

Add + 1 to P.P.

Add + 3 to Spd.

Add + 15 to S.D.C.

Combat Skills:

Attacks per Melee: Two

Escape Moves: Roll with punch/fall/impact, maintain balance, leap, backflip.

Attack Moves: Leap, roll, backflip.

Basic Defensive Moves: Dodge, parry, and automatic parry.

Advanced Defenses: Multiple Dodge, Power Block/Parry/Claw (Special! An attempt to simultaneously parry and Claw attack. Roll once for the parry, if successful then roll a second time to see if the strike is effective. Does 1D6 damage.).

Hand Attacks: Power Punch, Backhand, Claw Hand, Palm Strike, Duo-Claw Strike (Special! This is a special ripping attack that uses both hands. Using this attack means giving up the Automatic Parry for the entire melee round. Successful attack does 2D6 damage).

Basic Foot Attacks: Kick Attack, Tripping/Leg Hooks, Crescent Kick, Wheel Kick, Backward Sweep, Reverse Turning Kick (Combination Dodge/Kick), Drop Kick (Combination Fall/Dodge/Kick).

Jumping Foot Attacks: Jump Kick.

Special Attacks: Death blow, leap attack, combined strike/parry.

Weapon Katas: W.P. Claws

Modifiers to Attacks: Pull punch, knock-out/stun, critical strike, critical strike from rear.

Skills Included in Training:

Martial Art Abilities and Powers: Select two (2) Abilities from among *Body Hardening Exercises* (including Demon Hunter) and/or *Specialty Katas* (**not** including Chi Kata). **Note:** Karumi-Jutsu Zenjorike Power is received automatically.

Languages: Chinese

Cultural Skills: Gardening, Cooking

Survival: Fasting, Wilderness Survival, Tracking

Physical: Climbing, Gymnastics, Prowl, Swimming

Philosophical Training: Taoism

Level Advancement Bonuses:

1st: + 2 to roll with punch/fall/impact, + 1 to strike, + 1 to leap (add 6 feet/1.8 m to leap distance), critical strike from behind.

2nd: + 1 to damage, + 1 to parry and dodge.

3rd: + 1 attack per melee, critical strike on natural 18 or better.

4th: + 1 to leap (add 6 feet/1.8 m to leap distance), select one additional *Body Hardening Exercise* (including Demon Hunter) or *Specialty Kata* (including Chi Kata).

5th: + 1 to damage.

6th: + 1 to roll with punch/fall/impact, + 1 to parry/dodge.

7th: + 1 attack per melee, select one additional *Body Hardening Exercise* (including Demon Hunter) or *Specialty Kata* (including Chi Kata).

8th: + 1 to damage, + 1 to strike

9th: + 1 to leap (add 6 feet/1.8 m to leap distance).

10th: Select one additional *Body Hardening Exercise* (including Demon Hunter) or *Specialty Kata* (including Chi Kata). Death blow on roll of natural 19 or 20.

11th: + 1 attack per melee.

12th: + 1 to roll with punch/fall/impact, + 1 to parry/dodge.

13th: + 1 to leap (add 6 feet/1.8 m to leap distance).

14th: Add one *Zenjorike Power*.

15th: + 1 attack per melee, + 1 to damage.

Why Study Fu-Chiao Pai?

Tiger Claw Kung Fu is simply the most powerful of all the martial arts. Channeling the body's strength into doing the maximum physical damage to the opponent is what it's all about. The only weakness of the form is against multiple attackers.

Gui Long (New) Dragon Spirit Kung Fu

Gui Long seems to be the last surviving school from the mythical Warring States Period and is said to have been founded sometime in the 2nd Century B.C. In the myth of the style, the founder was *Hei Feng* ("Black Wind"), an epic swordsman who was eventually revealed to be the human form of a Feng Long, or Dragon of the air. It is even said that this dragon continues to watch over his human descendants.

Students are evenly divided between family members and those recruits willing to seek out a teacher. More like a long apprenticeship than a school, students are expected to live with their teachers for a period of no less than five years. They help with housework, caring for children, babies, and old folks, and more or less becoming one of the family.

While the student learns a full range of open hand (non-weapon) techniques, the main focus of Gui Long is on the *sword*, a discipline called *Chien Shu*. This goes beyond the mere manipulation of steel, since it is believed that all great swords are truly living things. If they were not created by a master swordsman with some living Chi, then it is up to the wielder of the sword to "bring the sword into life."

Entrance Requirements: Alignments must be either principled, scrupulous, unprincipled or (optionally) Taoist. Characters should start with a P.P. of no less than 11.

Costume: Quilted cotton jacket and pants, fitted for the individual's comfort but also so that it can serve as an undergarment for armor.

Stance: Sword hand should always be on the hilt of the sword, whether it is drawn or not. The other hand is open, fingers toward the ground, palm up and out. The forward foot (same side as sword hand) is flat on the ground, extended out, while the other leg is raised, with only the ball of the foot touching the ground.

Character Bonuses:

Add + 5 to Chi
Add + 1 to M.E.
Add + 2 to P.P.
Add + 2 to Spd.
Add + 10 to S.D.C.

Combat Skills:

Attacks per Melee: Three to start.

Escape Moves: Roll with punch/fall/impact, maintain balance, somersault, back flip.

Basic Defensive Moves: Dodge, parry, automatic parry.

Advanced Defenses: Multiple dodge, circular parry, power block/parry (does damage!), and automatic roll.

Hand Attacks: Strike (punch), Knife Hand, Palm Strike, and Backhand.

Basic Foot Attacks: Kick Attack, Snap Kick, Crescent Kick, and Backward Sweep.

Jumping Foot Attacks: Jump kick

Special Attacks: Death blow, leap attack, and flying leap attack.

Holds/Locks: Hand hold, arm hold.

Weapon Katas: W.P. sword

Modifiers to Attacks: Pull punch, knockout/stun, critical strike.

Bonus Skills & Abilities:

Martial Art Abilities and Powers: The character automatically receives an advanced version of **Chi Sword Technique**, from *Martial Art Techniques*, which will include *Sword Chi Healing*, *Sword Chi Resonance* and *Sword Chi Storage* (as below). In addition, select one more ability from among *Atemi Abilities* (including advanced) and/or *Martial Art Techniques*.

Sword Chi Healing. The patient should be kneeling, seated, or laying on the ground, relatively still. The sword is held over the patient by grasping the hilt of the sword in one hand. The other hand also grips the blade, but NEVER with bare fingers, using a piece of clean, pure white paper as a "sheath." When the point of the sword touches the patient, it creates a flow of

Positive Chi, generating one of three kinds of healing. First, if the patient is infected with Negative Chi, each point of the sword's Chi destroys one point of Negative Chi. Second, if the patient is at zero Chi, or has Positive Chi, and also wounded, the patient heals one point for every point of sword Chi. Third, if the patient is fully healed, but suffers from some kind of Negative Chi illness or affliction, then there is a 25% chance that the sword's Chi will cure the sickness (roll once). **Note:** Sword Chi Healing does NOT use up any of the sword's Positive Chi but it can only be done once per day.

Sword Chi Resonance. Starting with *Sword Chi Awareness* (see Sword Chi Technique in the Martial Art Techniques section for full details), the Gui Long practitioner is able to perceive something extra. Swords that have been attuned to *Sword Chi* have a different "vibration," thus it's possible for the character to sense the presence (but not exact location) of other significant swords at very long range (up to one mile/1.6 km distant). Aside from the general direction and distance to the other swords, the character will also get a relative sense of the "strength" of the other blades: more Chi, less Chi, or about the same as the character's own sword. It will also be shockingly clear if a sword is profanely charged with Negative Chi.

Sword Chi Storage. Unconsciously, but due to the character's training, the character "stores" a bit of Chi into their favorite sword. Over a week's handling, this builds up into a pool of 2D6 points of Positive Chi. This stored amount is always present and is added to the character's contribution when Sword Chi is activated.

Language Skill: Chinese (both Mandarin and Ancient dialects).

Training Skills: Calligraphy and Wilderness Survival.

Philosophical Training: Taoism

Level Advancement Bonuses:

1st: + 1 to strike, + 1 on initiative, + 1 to roll with punch/fall/impact, and critical strike on natural 20.

2nd:+ 1D6 to damage with any type of sword.

3rd: Select one additional from *Martial Art Techniques* or *Atemi Abilities* (including advanced).

4th: + 1 attack per melee.

5th: + 2 to maintain balance, somersaults, back flips.

6th: + 1 to parry/dodge, + 1 to roll with punch/fall/impact.

7th: + 1 attack per melee.

8th: Select one additional from *Martial Art Techniques* or *Atemi Abilities* (including advanced).

9th: + 1 to strike.

10th: Double existing Chi.

11th: + 1 attack per melee.

12th: Select one additional from *Martial Art Techniques* or *Atemi Abilities* (including advanced).

13th: Death blow on roll of natural 19 or 20.

14th: + 1 attack per melee.

15th: Add one *Zenjorike Power.*

Why Study Gui Long Kung Fu?

For those who seek the true experience of ancient weapon combat, and who understand that there is magic in the blade of a fine sword, this is the ideal martial art form.

Han Yu Kung Fu (New)

Although the name, *Han Yu*, translates to "The Secret Door," or "The Rarely-Found Gateway," this is one of the easiest to find of all the martial arts. No more remote than the nearest computer terminal or shopping mall, Han Yu Kung Fu is one of those martial arts that has truly kept up with changing times.

That's because the leaders of Han Yu have also grasped the magic of *franChising*. Springing up everywhere are upscale Han Yu "studios." Rather than presenting the introductory Katas as a martial art, they are advertised as "New Wave Exercise." Students learn to perform them to pop music, as if they were a fancy form of aerobics. There are even Han Yu T-Shirts, jackets and baseball caps, marketed to promote the school. This not only is making Han Yu into a household name, but it also attracts huge numbers of potential students.

All this came about when all the elderly teachers suddenly *disappeared* without a trace. It happened sometime in January of 1991, when Ko Deng, the senior teacher in this secret school, sent letters to all his foremost students, inviting them to accompany him on a pilgrimage to the shrine of the Han Yu founders.

Mysteriously, each and every one of the teachers proceeded to vanish, leaving no trace of any kind, nor any record of their travels — no government has any record of their exit or entry, there are no airline reservations, no hotel registries, nothing.

After a period of some confusion, the two best-known masters of their art, Mah Leigh Jiang (age 34), and her husband, Pieh Kih Jong Davis (age 29), took over the organization. They decided to take their favorite martial art into the modern age and immediately went on-line. Today, the two of them are enthusiastic participants in the worldwide Internet and prosperous entrepreneurs.

Entrance Requirements: Any, but most attractive to those who are honorably aligned. No attribute requirements.

Costume: Comfortable athletic shoes, loose blue jeans, and some king of long-sleeved shirt.

Stance: Feet shoulder-width apart, pointing forward with the knees just slightly bent. The shoulders are rounded forward a bit, so it looks like the character is slouChing. The hands are at waist level, positioned as if they were holding an invisible basketball.

Character Bonuses:

Add + 10 to Chi

Add + 1 to M.A.

Add + 2 to Spd.

Add + 5 to S.D.C.

Combat Skills:

Attacks per Melee: Two

Escape Moves: Roll with punch/fall/impact, maintain balance.

Basic Defensive Moves: Dodge, parry, automatic parry.

Advanced Defenses: Multiple dodge, automatic dodge, circular parry, disarm.

Hand Attacks: Strike (punch), Backhand, Palm Strike.

Basic Foot Attacks: Kick Attack, Reverse Turning Kick (Combination Dodge/Kick).

Jumping Foot Attacks: None

Special Attacks: Automatic Body Flip/Throw.

Holds/Locks: None

Weapon Katas: None

Modifiers to Attacks: Pull punch and knock-out/stun.

Bonus Skills & Abilities:

Martial Art Abilities and Powers: Select two from among the *Chi Katas* or *Specialty Katas.*

Language Skill: Chinese (Cantonese)

Training Skills: None

Philosophical Training: Philosophical Taoism.

Level Advancement Bonuses:

1st: + 2 to roll with punch/fall/impact and + 2 to parry/dodge.

2nd: Select one additional *Chi Kata* or *Special Kata.*

3rd: + 2 to parry, dodge and + 1 on initiative.

4th: + 1 attack per melee.

5th: + 1 to disarm and + 1 to maintain balance.

6th: Select one additional *Chi Kata* or *Special Kata.*

7th: + 1 to roll with punch/fall/impact and + 1 to parry/dodge.

8th: + 1 attack per melee.

9th: Select one additional *Chi Kata* or *Special Kata.*

10th: + 1 to disarm and + 1 to maintain balance.

11th: + 1 to parry, dodge and initiative.

12th: Select one additional *Chi Kata* or *Special Kata.*

13th: Double existing Chi.

14th: + 1 attack per melee round.

15th: Select one additional *Chi Kata* or *Special Kata*, or may add a first *Chi Mastery Ability.*

Why Study Han Yu Kung Fu?

If you're interested in a good martial arts oriented approach to Chi, this is your best choice. Combines good defensive combat techniques with the maximum possible Chi Katas. On the other hand, it's not very aggressive.

Hsien Hsia Kung Fu (New)

Harsh and uncompromising in its objectives, it's really no surprise that this martial art is considered to be on the verge of extinction. The name *Hsien Hsia* can be translated into "Great House of the Ancients," and fittingly describes the morgue-like quality of this ancient martial art's teachings.

Not helping this situation one bit are the traditional teachers of Hsien Hsia. They follow three rules when it comes to instructing their pupils:

1. Answer no questions. A dignified silence is the usual response, even to the most reasonable inquiries. If pressed, a teacher might respond, "All answers are contained within the teaching. A superior student will learn without causing annoyance."

2. Respect the Ancient Predecessors. In other words, stick to reading the texts and don't try to improvise. As the teacher would say, "Reading from the sacred texts is true. Any other teaching is false."

3. Change Nothing. Teachers of Hsien Hsia are convinced that everything about the school is perfect. Students *will* learn what is expected of them, when it is expected of them. Others are free to leave.

The point of this rigidity is that *Hsien Hsia* promises its students *Enlightened Immortality* through a course of Internal Alchemy. It may take many decades to achieve this state, but as the elders might say, "Those who are unsuitable are false, and not worthy of Immortality."

Students who undertake Hsien Hsia are absolutely prohibited from engaging in other martial arts. The use of any Chi Mastery or use of Chi of any kind is prohibited. According to the texts, "Idle indulgence in Chi trickery is false."

About half of all the teachings are the *Chi Chung*, or "Control of Breath," describing the *Tao Yin*, or "ancient breathing exercises." This means that students spend at least two hours a day simply practicing different techniques of breathing in and out.

All of this might lead you to assume that the teachers are themselves boring and colorless. *Nothing could be further from the truth!* Believe it or not, most teachers of Hsien Hsia are quite eccentric, funny and entertaining. Most are Taoists in alignment, and many of them have weaknesses for drinking, gambling and partying. The teachers simply believe that they should honor the style by teaChing it in the old way.

Entrance Requirements: No attribute restrictions. Anyone, of any alignment, with sufficient patience is acceptable.

Costume: Silk Kung Fu outfit with the jacket embroidered with the Chinese characters *K'ung* ("the void"), *Fa* ("the law"), and *Te* ("the Virtues").

Stance: Standing upright with head bowed down slightly, eyes half-closed, hands loosely open, one over the other, over the heart, with the palms pointing inward.

Character Bonuses:

Add + 20 to Chi

Combat Skills:

Attacks per Melee: One

Escape Moves: Roll with punch/fall/impact, and maintain balance.

Basic Defensive Moves: Dodge, parry, and automatic parry.

Advanced Defenses: None

Hand Attacks: Palm Strike, Two-Palm Push (Special! Hands are held together, palms outward, for a circular, gentle, push against an opponent. Does **no damage**, but stuns an opponent for two melee rounds! A stunned opponent has no initiative and can take no action while stunned except defensive, but is -4 to parry and dodge. Plus the stunned character's spd. and skill performance are reduced by half!

Basic Foot Attacks: None

Special Attacks: None

Holds/Locks: None

Weapon Katas: None

Modifiers to Attacks: Pull punch and knock-out/stun.

Bonus Skills & Abilities:

Martial Art Abilities and Powers: Start with the *Mind Walk* and *Calm Minds Zenjoriki Power* (no changes, no substitutions!).

Language Skill: Chinese (Mandarin dialect)

Training Skills: Calligraphy, Fasting, Prowl, Tracking, Wilderness Survival.

Philosophical Training: Taoism

Level Advancement Bonuses:

1st: + 1 to parry and dodge.

2nd: + 1 attack per melee.

3rd: + 1 to strike and + 1 on initiative.

4th: Add the *Two Minds Zenjorike Power.*

5th: Double existing Chi.

6th: + 1 to maintain balance.

7th: + 1 to roll with punch/fall/impact.

8th: + 1 to parry and dodge.

9th: Add the *Spirit Burst Zenjorike Power.*

10th: + 1 to strike and + 1 on initiative.

11th: + 1 to parry and dodge.

12th: + 1 to maintain balance.

13th: + 1 attack per melee.

14th: Add the *Discorporate Zenjorike Power.*

15th: Double existing Chi.

Why Study Hsien Hsia Kung Fu?

Inflexible, impractical, and mired down in rules, rules, rules, Hsien Hsia would seem to be a martial art to be avoided. However, in spite of the lack of combat skills, and the relative powerlessness of the form, it does offer the hope of attaining (eventually) Enlightened Immortality.

Hsing-I Kung Fu (New)

Hsing-I, which could be translated into "Mind Shaping," is one of the great secret martial arts. Ironically, it is hidden by being placed in plain view, since there are many schools of Hsing-I worldwide.

In the schools, where an introductory, combat-oriented version of the martial art is taught, students are told that there are no longer any teachers of *Shan Si*, or "Internal Engine." However, the students are always told of the legendary Chi arts of their forefathers and how the current form, the *Ho Pei*, the current external style, must be considered inferior to the internal cultivation of Chi. Promising students are carefully watched and those who show a true longing for the Chi secrets are eventually initiated into the hidden techniques of *Shan Si*.

Entrance Requirements: None

Costume: Simple Kung Fu outfit of silk or cotton.

Stance: Called *San Tsai Shih* ("Three Essentials"), the body is lowered considerably, with the knees bent so that the center of Chi will be strengthened. Weight is distributed so that 30% is on the front extended leg, and 70% on the other leg, which is behind.

Character Bonuses:

Add + 10 to Chi

Add + 2 to M.E.

Add + 1 to P.P.

Add + 5 to S.D.C

Combat Skills:

Attacks per Melee: Two

Escape Moves: Roll with punch/fall/impact, and maintain balance.

Basic Defensive Moves: Dodge, parry, and automatic parry.

Advanced Defenses: Circular Parry and Power Block/Parry.

Hand Attacks: Strike (punch), Fore-Knuckle Fist, Back-hand, and Palm Strike.

Basic Foot Attacks: Kick Attack

Special Attacks: Forearm

Holds/Locks: None

Weapon Katas: None

Modifiers to Attacks: Pull punch, knock-out/stun, and critical strike.

Bonus Skills & Abilities:

Martial Art Abilities and Powers: Take the *Hua Chin* Chi Mastery Ability as follows. In addition, select one (1) additional ability from among *Chi Mastery* and/or *Specialty Katas* (including Chi Katas).

Hua Chin (New): A special variation on *Chao Jin*, which can be used with either Positive or Negative Chi, is unique to Hsing-I. A combination physical and Chi attack, the *Hua Chin* can be used once per melee round, even in the midst of combat, with no preparation! Successfully doing the *Hua Chin* means that the force of the impact will inflict *two points of damage direct to hit points* and *destroy 1D6 of the victim's Chi*, in addition to the usual damage from the attack. It must be delivered with a *Fore-Knuckle Fist* or *Palm Strike*, not with a kick or any other attack. **Cost:** One point of Chi (Negative or Positive) for each Hua Chin attack.

Language Skill: Chinese (Cantonese or Mandarin)

Training Skills: None

Philosophical Training: Taoism

Level Advancement Bonuses:

1st: + 1 to parry, dodge and on initiative.

2nd: + 2 to strike.

3rd: + 1 attack per melee.

4th: Select one additional *Chi Mastery Ability* or *Chi Kata*.

5th: + 2 to roll with punch/fall/impact.

6th: + 1 to parry and dodge, add + 5 to S.D.C.

7th: + 1 attack per melee.

8th: Select one additional *Chi Mastery Ability* or *Chi Kata*.

9th: + 2 to roll with punch/fall/impact.

10th: Double existing Chi.

11th: + 1 attack per melee and death blow on roll of natural 18 or better.

12th: Select one additional *Chi Mastery Ability* or *Chi Kata*.

13th: + 2 to roll with punch/fall/impact.

14th: + 1 attack per melee, + 2 to Crane Fist Strike, and + 1 to Crane Fist damage.

15th: Add one *Zenjorike Power*.

Why Study Hsing-I?

A decent groundwork in the basics of hand to hand combat providing balance for a martial art that strongly emphasizes the building of great Chi and Chi abilities. No disadvantages.

Kuo-Ch'uan Dog Boxing Kung Fu

If ever there was a martial art that was downright silly, this is it! Dog boxing involves stupid-looking paw attacks from ground level, ridiculous barking and yipping noises, and the ability to walk around on all fours (or all threes). The reasoning behind this madness is that the moves often deliberately bait other martial artists, causing them to underestimate their opponents and therefore make mistakes.

A dog boxing expert, upon being attacked, may immediately fall to the ground and begin wailing as if terribly hurt. Then attacks are made only when the enemy continues to attack.

Students of Kuo-Ch'uan are sworn to secrecy when recruited into the school. They are not allowed to reveal their techniques, their teachers or even their fellow students. The school's public policy is to give demonstrations, but to make them ridiculous enough so that no one will take them seriously. For example, in any fight that is not serious, the Dog Boxer is supposed to lose deliberately. This helps keep future opponents off guard.

Entrance Requirements: No attribute or alignment restrictions.

Costume: None, loose fitting street clothes are preferred.

Stance: Starting position is usually squatting on the ground with elbows down, arms up and hands bent down; exactly like a dog begging for scraps while on hind legs.

Character Bonuses:

Add + 2 to P.S.

Add + 1 to P.E.

Add + 1 to P.P.

Add + 3 to Spd.

Add + 15 to S.D.C.

Combat Skills:

Attacks per Melee: Two

Escape Moves: Roll with punch/fall/impact, maintain balance, backflip, and somersault.

Attack Moves: Handstand, Cartwheel, Roll, Backflip.

Basic Defensive Moves: Dodge, parry, and automatic parry.

Advanced Defenses: Multiple Dodge, Combination Parry/Attack, Disarm, Automatic Roll, Breakfall.

Hand Attacks: Strike (punch), Knife Hand, Fore-Knuckle Fist, Backhand, Claw Hand, Palm Strike.

Basic Foot Attacks: Kick Attack, Tripping/Leg Hooks, Snap Kick, Wheel Kick, Backward Sweep, Reverse Turning Kick (Combination Dodge/Kick), Drop Kick (Combination Fall/Dodge/Kick).

Special Attacks: Death Blow and Combination Strike/Parry.

Weapon Katas: None

Modifiers to Attacks: Pull punch, knockout/stun, critical strike, and critical strike from the rear.

Skills Included in Training:

Martial Art Abilities and Powers: Select two abilities from among *Arts of Invisibility*, *Martial Art Techniques* and *Body Hardening Exercises.*

Languages: Chinese (Cantonese dialect).

Survival: Begging and Fasting.

Physical: Acrobatics, Gymnastics, and Prowl.

Philosophical Training: Taoism.

Level Advancement Bonuses:

1st: + 2 to roll with punch/fall/impact, + 2 to backflip/somersault/cartwheel/handstand, + 1 to rear attacks (Backward Sweep, Backhand Strike), critical strike from behind.

2nd: + 1 attack per melee, + 1 to parry and dodge.

3rd: Select one additional from *Arts of Invisibility, Body Hardening Exercises* (including Demon Hunter Exercises), or *Martial Art Techniques*, + 1 to Backflip/Somersault/Cartwheel/Handstand.

4th: + 1 to strike, + 1 to rear attacks (Backward Sweep, Backhand Strike), critical strike on natural 19 or 20.

5th: + 1 attack per melee, + 1 to parry and dodge.

6th: Select one additional from *Arts of Invisibility, Body Hardening Exercises* (including Demon Hunter Exercises), or *Martial Art Techniques.*

7th: + 2 to roll with punch/fall/impact, death blow on roll of natural 19 or 20.

8th: + 1 attack per melee, + 1 to parry and dodge.

9th: Select one additional from *Arts of Invisibility, Body Hardening Exercises* (including Demon Hunter Exercises), or *Martial Art Techniques.*

10th: + 1 to strike, + 1 to Backflip, Somersault, Cartwheel, Handstand.

11th: + 1 attack per melee, + 1 to parry and dodge.

12th: + 1 to roll with punch/fall/impact.

13th: Select one additional from *Arts of Invisibility, Body Hardening Exercises* (including Demon Hunter Exercises), or *Martial Art Techniques.*

14th: + 1 attack per melee, + 1 to parry and dodge.

15th: + 1 to strike, + 1 to rear attacks (Backward Sweep, Backhand Strike).

Why Study Kuo-Ch'uan?

Well, you've got to have a sense of humor to start with! The art is effective but not very glamorous. Better for defense than offense. Also one of the best martial arts for an espionage agent, especially because it also teaches the Arts of Invisibility.

Lee Kwan Choo

Lee Kwan Choo is a totally non-violent martial art. It is simply impossible to hurt anyone using it. The bonuses and techniques of the form may be introduced into other forms and katas but Lee Kwan Choo itself can not be modified.

Students learn to meditate while fighting. Techniques are ALL avoidance (Parry/Dodge) and leaping from combat. There are attacks in Lee Kwan Choo but they do NO DAMAGE. Lee Kwan Choo must be used alone; attempting to perform other forms will disrupt the delicate concentration required.

For example, while fighting in the Lee Kwan Choo style, the combatant would avoid all attacks. Suddenly, she will lash out with a devastating punch between the eyes of the opponent. In any other style this would be a killing blow, but here the fist gives a fraction of an inch from the victim. The defender would take NO DAMAGE, but the shock will cause a stun that lasts from 1 to 6 Melee Rounds.

Learning the art requires a retreat to a remote Tibetan monastery for the study of the meditative skills. While at the monastery, the student is expected to participate in all the domestic arts needed to produce the community's food and clothing, as well as helping in the ritual recopying of ancient manuscripts.

Entrance Requirements: No alignment or attribute restrictions.

Costume: Prefer a simple monk's robe.

Stance: Relaxed standing position, with arms loosely at the sides.

Character Bonuses

Add + 10 to Chi

Add + 3 to M.E.

Add + 3 to M.A.

Add + 6 to Spd.

Combat Skills:

Attacks per Melee: One

Escape Moves: Roll with Punch/Fall/Impact and Leap.

Attack Moves: Leap

Basic Defensive Moves: Dodge, parry, and automatic parry.

Advanced Defenses: Multiple Dodge, Circular Parry, Disarm.

Hand Attacks: Duo-Knuckle Strike (Special! Does Shock/Stun Only, NO S.D.C. or Hit Point Damage.)

Basic Foot Attacks: Snap Kick (Special: Shock/Stun Only! NO S.D.C. or hit point damage, only stun effects).

Weapon Katas: None

Skills Included in Training:

Martial Art Abilities and Powers: Select one ability from among *Body Hardening Exercises* and *Martial Art Techniques.* Also select one *Zenjoriki Power.*

Languages: Tibetan.

Cultural Skills: Gardening, Calligraphy, Cooking, Sewing, Wilderness, Survival, Fasting, and Mountaineering.

Philosophical Training: Tibetan Lore and Taoism.

Level Advancement Bonuses:

1st: + 3 to parry and dodge, + 3 to leap (add 4 feet/1.2 m to leap distance).

2nd: + 2 to strike, + 3 to roll with punch/fall/impact.

3rd: + 1 to parry/dodge, select one additional from *Body Hardening Exercises* or *Martial Art Techniques.*

4th: + 1 attack per melee and double existing Chi.

5th: + 1 to parry and dodge, + 1 to leap (add 4 feet/1.2 m to leap distance)

6th: + 1 to strike, + 2 to roll with punch/fall/impact.

7th: + 1 to leap (add 4 feet/1.2 m to leap distance), add one *Zenjorike Power.*

8th: + 1 attack per melee, knockout/stun on natural 18, 19 or 20.

9th: + 1 to parry and dodge, select one additional from *Body Hardening Exercises* or *Martial Art Techniques.*

10th: + 1 to strike, + 2 to roll with punch/fall/impact.

11th: + 1 to leap (add 4 feet/1.2 m to leap distance), select one additional *Martial Art Skill.*

12th: + 1 attack per melee, double existing Chi.

13th: + 1 to parry and dodge, + 1 to leap (add 4 feet/1.2 m to leap distance).

14th: + 1 to strike, + 2 to roll with punch/fall/impact.

15th: Add one *Zenjorike Power*, select one additional from *Body Hardening Exercises* or *Martial Art Techniques.*

Why Study Lee Kwan Choo?

In exchange for giving up the ability to injure, one receives the ability to shock and impress. As a purely defensive art it is hard to beat. It's also one of only four martial arts that teaches a Zenjorike ability at first level.

Liang Hsiung Kung Fu (New)

While the name, *Liang Hsiung* could be translated into "shining evil", or perhaps "brilliant barbarism," it's not because the school or its members are necessarily evil. It's just that the style, which some call *Demon Wrestling,* is based on how demons fight (and is arguably barbaric).

A close relative of *Liang Hsiung* is something called *Chi Ao Ti*, which was an ancient form of Chinese wrestling practiced in the 6th Century B.C. The *Chi Ao* combatants used horned headgear to ram and gore each other in arena-style combat.

Liang hsiung is a contemporary martial art that still relies heavily on medieval weaponry and on combatants who prefer to battle with horns and spurs/barbs and dagger-like blades and spikes of metal strapped to their bodies.

For example, there are two kinds of practice. The first is when the combatants strap on spurs/barbs/blades with dull points, wear a light helmet with horns and protective padding. In the second kind of *Liang Hsiung* practice, the participants don full sets of specially-designed *demon armor,* complete with points and sharp edges that tear through padding. Either way, once attired, practice involves using and avoiding the horns in head butts and the spurs in a variety of strikes and kicks.

Entrance Requirements: No limitations on alignment, although most students tend to be good, unprincipled or aberrant. P.S. should be no less than 12.

Costume: To modify street clothes, a set of spurs/spikes/blades are mounted on a leather strap and pulled on over knuckles, palms, elbows, shoulders, knees and ankles (the whole process takes just one melee round). Full combat attire means the character dons a full suit of armor, fitted with nasty looking horns, blades, hooked barbs and spurs with serrated edges.

Liang Hsiung Demon Armor. Modern outfits are made of composites, with a metal superstructure, providing an A.R. of 14 and 140 S.D.C.; -5% to prowl but reasonably light and maneuverable. Depending on how much money the character is willing to put into the armor, an A.R. 18 and 320 S.D.C. are possible. However, this armor is heavier and restricts movement: -15% prowl penalty and -5% on the performance of acrobatics, climb and other physical skills. Most prefer the lighter standard armor.

The helmet is sculpted to resemble that of a demon (extra charge for glowing eyes and mouth, or smoke generator in nostrils). Spurs are located at the knuckles (back of each hand), wrists (inside), elbows, shoulders, knees and ankles (outside).

Replacement Cost: $3,000 (add $1,000 for each additional A.R. point above 14 or for every extra 60 S.D.C).

Stance: Upright stance with legs together, one arm up, the other at waist, both hands held loosely with the forefinger pointing.

Character Bonuses:

Add +10 to Chi

Add +1 to P.E.

Add +4 to Spd.

Add +15 to S.D.C.

Attacks per Melee: Three

Escape Moves: Roll with punch/fall/impact, backflip, and maintain balance.

Basic Defensive Moves: Dodge, parry, and automatic parry.

Hand Attacks: Punch/Spur Punch (Special! If done bare-handed it does the usual 1D4 damage, but 2D4+2 if used with knuckle spurs). Palm Strike/Palm Spike (Special! If bare-handed, it does the usual 1D6 damage, but 2D6 if used with a wrist spur).

Basic Foot Attacks:

Knee Snap/Knee Spike (Special): Brings the knee up fast, usually for an attack to the groin or stomach. Typically does 1D4 damage, but 2D6 when used with a knee spur.

Snap Kick/Snap Spike (Special): Without armament it does 1D6 damage, but 2D6 damage when used with an ankle spur.

Tripping/Leg Hook/Leg Spur (Special): Usually a knock-down attack that does no damage, but does 1D6 damage and knock-down when performed using an ankle spur.

Special Attacks:

Gore (special): The character does a head slam into their opponent, doing 1D4 if unarmored or 2D6 with horns.

Double-gore (Special): A full thrust head ram, much like a bull's, does 2D4 damage unarmored or 4D6 if fitted with helmet and horns.

Shoulder ram (Special): Similar to wrestling's body block/tackle, except that the full impact is focused on the shoulder. Does 1D4 and knock-down if unarmored or 2D6 if wearing shoulder spurs.

Elbow/elbow spike (Special)! 1D4 damage if unarmored, but 1D10 (or 2D4+2) if wearing elbow spurs.

Holds/Locks: None

Weapon Katas: W.P. Demon Suit

Modifiers to Attacks: Pull punch, blunt impact (Special! When using the knock-out/stun or critical strike).

Bonus Skills & Abilities:

Martial Art Abilities and Powers: You may select two from among *Body Hardening Techniques* and/or *Demon Hunter Body Hardening Techniques.*

Language Skill: Mongolian

Training Skills: Prowl, Tracking, Horse Riding, and Wilderness Survival.

Philosophical Training: Taoism

Level Advancement Bonuses:

1st: +2 to palm strike, +1 to shoulder ram, +1 to gore/double-gore, +1 to damage.

2nd: +1 to strike and +1 to kick.

3rd: +1 to parry and dodge, +1 to roll with punch/fall/impact.

4th: Select one additional *Body Hardening Technique* (including Demon Hunter), and +1 to Shoulder Ram.

5th: +1 attack per melee round and +1 to gore/double-gore.

6th: +1 to parry/dodge and critical strike on natural 19 or better.

7th: +1 to strike, damage and on initiative.

8th: Select one additional *Body Hardening Technique* (including Demon Hunter).

9th: +1 to kick and +1 to shoulder ram.

10th: +1 attack per melee and +1 to strike.

11th: +1 to parry and dodge and +1 to gore/double-gore.

12th: Select one additional *Body Hardening Technique* (including Demon Hunter) or *Martial Art Technique.*

13th: Critical strike on natural 18 or better. +1 to Shoulder Ram.

14th: +1 attack per melee round and +1 to damage.

15th: Select one additional *Body Hardening Technique* (including Demon Hunter) or *Martial Art Technique.*

Why Study Liang Hsiung?

While antique in its reliance on armor, characters who enjoy the rough-and-tumble aspects of hand-to-hand combat will *love* the bashing-oriented techniques of Liang Hsiung. Plus, any characters who really want to "bulk up" will be pleased with a solid diet of Body Hardening Techniques. Totally weak on the Internal/Mystical end of things, but it is a lot of fun!

Mien-Ch'uan Cotton Fist Kung Fu

Like Japanese Aikido, Korean Yu-Sool, and Okinawan Taido, Mien-Ch'uan concentrates on internal, circular and deflecting movement. And like them, it also provides plenty of Chi training. However, unlike those forms, Mien-Ch'uan ignores the concepts of "fair play" and "honor" to concentrate on the all-important dictates of victory.

A master will approach any combat encounter cautiously, carefully evaluating the enemy's technique. Against hand-oriented artists, the response will be Sticky Hands (see below). For other martial artists, especially those who use a lot of kicking attacks, the Mien-Ch'uan master will keep to a constant sequence of Automatic Dodges and Circular Parries and hand strikes when its safe to do so.

Students do not choose to study Mien-Ch'uan, instead the masters choose the students. They prefer youths who are purely self-centered and who can be enticed by promises of power and profit. A master will always keep at least four apprentices around as servants.

Entrance Requirements: Limited to unprincipled, anarchist, and dishonorable alignments. No attribute minimums required.

Costume: Cotton or silk Kung Fu outfit.

Stance: Prefer a forward stance with legs bent and shoulder width apart. One hand extended loosely and held at the stomach in a fore-knuckle fist.

Character Bonuses:

Add +10 to Chi

Add +1 to P.E.

Add +4 to Spd.

Add +10 to S.D.C

Combat Skills:

Attacks per Melee: One

Escape Moves: Roll with Punch/Fall/Impact, Maintain Balance

Basic Defensive Moves: Dodge, parry, and automatic parry.

Advanced Defenses: Multiple Dodge, Automatic Dodge, and Circular Parry, Disarm.

Hand Attacks: Strike (Punch), Fore-Knuckle Fist, Backhand, and Palm Strike.

Basic Foot Attacks: None

Special Attacks: Death Blow, Combination Strike/Parry, Elbow, and Forearm.

Sticky Hands (Special): The "strike" for Sticky Hands involves the attacker touching the victim's hands. If successful, the victim is unable to defend against any kind of attack with the single exception of a Snap Kick that cannot do Critical, Knock-Out or Death Blow damage. Meanwhile, the attacker can do a normal number of Backhand and Palm Strikes per melee round. Escaping from Sticky Hands can only be done with a successful escape move such as a Roll or Backflip. Even this won't work if the Sticky Hands operator can beat the escape roll.

Weapon Katas: None

Modifiers to Attacks: Pull punch, knock-out/stun, critical strike, and critical strike from rear.

Skills Included in Training:

Martial Art Abilities and Powers: Select three abilities from among *Body Hardening Exercises*, *Chi Mastery*, and *Special Katas* (including Chi Katas).

Languages: Chinese

Cultural Skills (Choose Two): Gardening, Calligraphy, Poetry, Music (instrumental or singing), and Cooking.

Oriental: Geomancy

Philosophical Training: Taoism

Level Advancement Bonuses:

1st: +2 to roll with punch/fall/impact, and +2 to parry/dodge.

2nd: +2 to maintain balance and +1 to strike.

3rd: +1 to disarm, select one additional from *Chi Mastery* or *Special Katas* (including Chi Katas).

4th: Double existing Chi, critical strike on natural 18 or better.

5th: +2 to roll with punch/fall/impact, and +1 to damage.

6th: +1 attack per melee.

7th: +1 to maintain balance, select one additional from *Chi Mastery* or *Special Katas* (including Chi Katas).

8th: +1 to parry/dodge and +1 attack per melee round.

9th: +1 to roll with punch/fall/impact, add one *Zenjorike.*

10th: Double existing Chi.

11th: +2 to maintain balance and +1 to strike.

12th: +1 attack per melee, select one additional from *Chi Mastery* or *Special Katas* (including Chi Katas).

13th: +1 to roll with punch/fall/impact.

14th: +1 to parry/dodge and add one *Zenjorike Power.*

15th: +2 to maintain balance.

Why Study Mien-Ch'uan?

The secret moves of Mien-Ch'uan give powerful defensive advantages. While there are relatively few attacks, they are designed to be used without risk of personal damage. It's also one of the few arts to provide mystic Chi abilities.

Monkey Style Kung Fu

Monkey Style Kung Fu, sometimes referred to as *Tai Sing Pek Kwar*, is based on the movements of apes and monkeys. Each position imitates the clown-like flips, acrobatics, and loose body of the creatures.

To best understand the whys and wherefores of the Monkey form, just pay a visit to the Monkey House of the nearest zoo and spend some time watching. They have the ability to be completely relaxed yet constantly alert, they always roll smoothly away from attacks, yet they can turn and leap to attack instantly. They have the patience to watch and wait for an indefinite period to catch someone else off guard. Some of the monkey-imitation strikes include double-knuckle punches, slaps, arcing fingers and devious overhead raps.

A Monkey Style master will bare his teeth, make "ook" noises, and roll on the ground before entering combat. Responding to attacks, he'll roll and whimper and pantomime imaginary wounds, eventually appearing completely helpless. When the enemy has been lulled into carelessness or enraged, the master will leap or roll into a full-scale attack.

Instruction is available in China, Hong Kong, Singapore, and along the West Coast of the U.S. Many students work as street performers and acrobats while they take their training. Of the special Monkey Katas, usually only one set is taught to a student, the one which the instructor feels best suits the student's personality, body type and abilities.

Entrance Requirements: No attribute or alignment restrictions.

Costume: No special outfit. Some schools prefer Kung Fu outfits, others like loose karate outfits and still others use cut-offs and t-shirts.

Stance: The monkey stance is a low, bow-legged and off-center one, with the body slumped over and ready to roll forward or back at any time. Arms are held monkey-style, with elbows out and hands inward and loosely hanging down.

Character Bonuses:

Add +10 to Chi

Add +5 to M.A.

Add +1 to P.S.

Add +1 to P.E.

Add +10 to S.D.C.

Combat Skills:

Attacks per Melee: Two

Escape Moves: Roll with punch/fall/impact, leap, backflip, and somersault.

Attack Moves: Leap, Cartwheel, Roll, and Backflip.

Basic Defensive Moves: Dodge, parry, and automatic parry.

Advanced Defenses: Automatic Dodge, Disarm, and Breakfall.

Hand Attacks: Knife Hand, Fore-Knuckle Fist, Double-Knuckle Fist, Backhand, Claw Hand, and Palm Strike.

Basic Foot Attacks: Kick Attack, Tripping/Leg Hooks, Backward Sweep, and Drop Kick (Combination Fall/Dodge/Kick).

Special Attacks: Death Blow, Leap Attack, Body Block/Tackle, Choke, Knee, Elbow, and Forearm.

Holds/Locks: Arm Hold, Leg Hold, Body Hold, and Neck Hold.

Weapon Katas: None

Modifiers to Attacks: Pull Punch, Knock-Out/Stun, Critical Strike, and Critical Strike from Rear.

Special Katas: Choose one of the following, others can be added in place of Martial Art Abilities.

Drunken Monkey: Very similar to the bizarre imbalance and broken rhythm of the Drunken Style. All attacks are designed to look accidental. Includes an Automatic Dodge, +2 on all Parries, +2 on all hand strikes.

Lost Monkey: Works very much like a Dog Style maneuver. The Monkey artist stays on all fours and acts crippled. Then attacks are made from the floor. The only defense is a Multiple Dodge. Bonuses are +3 to Kick or Backsweep.

Tall monkey: Going almost to full height (but still keeping the legs slightly bent), the Tall Monkey uses long, sweeping arm movements much like those in the Crane Form. Defense is a Circular Parry (+2) and there is a +2 to Strike and a +3 to Damage.

Stone Monkey: A blindly aggressive Kata that involves walking with legs deeply bent, frequent leaps and acrobatic maneuvers. There are no parries or dodges. Bonuses include +1 Attack per Melee Round, +4 to Strike, +2 to Damage, and +2 to Roll.

Wood Monkey: Not really a Kata, but more of a ruse. The idea is to lay in a heap on the floor, pretending to be dead, asleep, unconscious, or badly wounded. Then, when the enemy is in range, it turns into a leap to the attack. Cannot move, parry, dodge or commit any other actions before the attack nor for the entire melee round of the attack itself. Two and only two attacks in the melee round of the trap. Any hand attacks are possible. Bonuses are +6 to Strike and +4 to Damage.

Skills Included in Training:

Martial Art Abilities and Powers: Select two (2) Abilities from among *Arts of Invisibility*, *Body Hardening Exercises*, or from among remaining *Monkey Katas* above.

Languages: Chinese

Survival: Begging

Physical: Acrobatics, Climbing, Gymnastics, Prowl

Philosophical Training: Taoism

Level Advancement Bonuses:

1st: +2 to parry/dodge, +2 to roll with punch/fall/impact, critical strike or knock-out from behind.

2nd: +2 to leap/backflip/somersault/cartwheel, +1 to damage.

3rd: +1 attack per melee and +2 to Breakfall.

4th: +2 to roll with punch/fall/impact, select one additional from *Chi Mastery Abilities, Monkey Katas, Arts of Invisibility* or *Body Hardening Exercises.*

5th: +1 to leap/backflip/somersault/cartwheel, and +1 to parry/dodge.

6th: +1 attack per melee and +1 to damage.

7th: +2 to roll with punch/fall/impact, knock-out/stun on natural 19 or 20.

8th: +1 to leap/backflip/somersault/cartwheel, select one additional from *Chi Mastery Abilities, Monkey Katas, Arts of Invisibility* or *Body Hardening Exercises.*

9th: +1 attack per melee and +1 to parry and dodge.

10th: +1 to roll with punch/fall/impact and critical strike on Natural 18 or better.

11th: +2 to leap/backflip/somersault/cartwheel and death blow on roll of Natural 20.

12th: Double existing Chi and +1 attack per melee.

13th: +1 to roll with punch/fall/impact and +1 to parry/dodge.

14th: +1 to leap/backflip/somersault/cartwheel, +2 to damage.

15th: Select one additional from *Chi Mastery Abilities, Monkey Katas, Arts of Invisibility* or *Body Hardening Exercises* (including Demon Hunter Exercises).

Why Study Monkey Style?

The combined flexibility and defensive power is hard to beat. On the other hand, it helps if the character doesn't take himself too seriously. Another great advantage is that the five Monkey Katas imitate forms that would require years of training to get separately.

Pao Chih (New)

As martial arts go, *Pao Chih* is almost totally non-athletic. Rather than focus on exercising the body, students are instructed to concentrate wholeheartedly on developing internally. Thus, they concentrate on the powers of *Chi* and, uniquely, on the creation/evocation of a personal *Animus.*

This Animus is a sort of Living Chi. An entity that takes the same shape of the character's body and moves with the character like a suit of living clothes or a shadow. Once evoked, the character can "see" through the senses of the Animus and use it as a means of performing Chi Mastery Abilities. Also, as the character grows in power (gains levels of experience), the Animus develops more and more useful features.

Mang I ("Blind Will") is the school's founder, the great, great grandson of the school's founder, or some charlatan who is passing himself off as the founder. The answer varies depending on who you want to believe. In any case, he is a mysterious figure, always appearing masked and cloaked, so that his (her?) true identity remains unknown.

Entrance Requirements: No alignments or attribute restrictions.

Costume: None

Stance: None

Character Bonuses:

Add +10 to Chi

Add +2 to M.E.

Add +5 to S.D.C.

Combat Skills:

Attacks per Melee: One

Escape Moves: Roll with punch/fall/impact.

Basic Defensive Moves: Dodge

Hand Attacks: None

Foot Attacks: None

Weapon Katas: None

Modifiers to Attacks: None

Bonus Skills & Abilities:

Martial Art Abilities and Powers: Select three from among *Chi Mastery* (including advanced) and the ability to Evoke Animus of Positive Chi.

Evoking the Animus. Each time the character wishes to create (Evoke) the Animus, it takes a certain amount of concentration. At first level, it requires at least four melee rounds (one full minute) to bring up the Animus. During Evocation, no other actions may be performed, nor can the Chi be used, not even for Chi defense.

Investing in the Animus. When the Animus is evoked, it must be given a certain amount of Chi from the character's own supply. As long as the Animus exists, the two "pools" of Chi are separate. The character can perform a Chi Mastery Ability, which would cost Chi from the body, or perform a Chi Mastery Ability through the Animus, which would subtract Chi from the Animus.

Duration of Animus. While inside the body, the Animus can last one hour for each point of Chi invested. Outside the body (at 10th level one develops the power to detach the Animus), the Animus can last one half hour for each point of Chi invested. **Note:** If the character knows another martial art, the Animus can be maintained while using the other form.

Abilities of the Animus. Inside the body, the Animus serves as a separate being, perpetually alert, and perpetually on guard to defend the character and the character's body (+3 on initiative).

If the character is asleep, unconscious, or absent (if the character's Soul-Spirit is missing), then the Animus will do whatever is necessary to protect the body. First and foremost, it will attempt to wake up/revive the character at the first sign of danger. If unsuccessful, it may take over the character's body to move it out of danger, dodge, or otherwise move toward safety.

Whatever Chi Mastery Abilities the character has are also possessed by the Animus. It will either perform those abilities at the direction of the character or, if left in charge of the character's body, it will use them to defend the character.

Reabsorbing the Animus. The character can instantly reabsorb the Animus, unless it is detached (although there are certain magical means to keep a character from absorbing it). When reabsorbed, the character regains all the remaining Chi of the Animus.

Language Skill: Chinese (Mandarin)

Training Skills: Calligraphy

Philosophical Training: Taoism

Level Advancement Bonuses:

1st: Use Animus to Block Negative Chi. For each point of Chi invested, the Animus can *automatically* (no preparation required) stop 1D6 points of incoming Negative Chi. For example, an Animus with three points of Chi can block 3D6 points of Negative Chi, every melee round. If the Negative Chi attack exceeds the defense, then the Animus will take the damage before the character's body.

2nd: Evoke Animus in three melee rounds. +1 attack per melee.

3rd: Animus can sense *Wei Chi*, the ability to sense the "Internal Fire" of Chi in beings and objects up to twenty-five feet (7.6 m) away. Senses Chi type (Positive or Negative), amount and location.

4th: Select one additional *Chi Mastery Ability* (including advanced).

5th Evoke Animus in two melee rounds.

6th: Animus can Absorb Positive Chi. If the Animus is missing any Chi (having less than the original investment), it can absorb Positive Chi from the environment at a rate of the flow of Positive Chi per melee round.

7th: Animus can sense *Chen Chi*. Through the Animus the character can feel the *Chen Chi*, or living vitality, of all humans and other creatures, within thirty feet (9.1 m), even in total darkness or obscured by smoke. From the *Chen Chi*, the character can determine whether a person or animal is healthy or ill, injured or healed, poisoned or pure.

8th: Evoke Animus in one melee round. +1 attack per melee.

9th: Select one additional *Chi Mastery Ability* (including advanced).

10th: Detach Animus. While the character remains in a still, meditative state, the Animus can "walk out" of the body, and then walk around in the world, using its Chi senses, and any of the character's Chi Mastery Abilities. Ordinarily, at this level, the Animus can only move at the character's normal Spd. However, it also has the ability to instantly teleport back inside the character regardless of range. If, for any reason, the character loses contact with the Animus (for example, he is knocked unconscious), the Animus will immediately return to the body. **Note:** The Animus cannot manipulate anything physical nor can it move through physical objects.

11th: Double character's existing Chi (the Animus' Chi still depends on how much the character wishes to invest).

12th: Animus can sense *Ti Chi*. The movement, or flow, of Chi is sensed by the Animus, which can determine the quantity, type (Positive or Negative), and direction.

13th: Select one additional *Chi Mastery Ability* (including advanced).

14th: Animus *Qing Ting*. Called the "Dragonfly," this gives the Animus the ability to move with the flow of Chi in the air, earth, water, wood, metal and even fire. Only works with the Animus detached, not while the Animus is in the character.

15th: Evoke Animus instantly.

Why Study Pao Chih?

Since virtually everything relating to combat is ignored, this isn't a very wise choice for anyone planning on an adventurer's lifestyle. On the other hand, it's the only non-magical way to evoke a personal Animus.

Shan Tung (New) Black Tiger Kung Fu

An athletic and dynamic martial art form, the Black Tigers or "*Gui Hu*," as they are sometimes known, believe in combining forceful action with an attention to the gathering and use of Chi.

Another strong teaching in *Shan Tung* is the "Theory of Multiple Enemies." This reinforces the belief that one should always deal with combat as if surrounded by enemies, including those who are hidden or unseen. At its extreme, those who believe in this theory are **always** suspicious and always assume that opponents are lurking nearby, waiting for a sign of weakness.

As bitter rivals to the *Fu-Chiao Pai* (Tiger Claw Kung Fu), those of Shan Tung believe themselves to be superior by virtue of their "Internal" training in Chi Mastery. If confronted with someone from the rival school, they are likely to remark, "How wonderful that you can leap such distances! It is too bad that your teachers neglect to instruct you in cunning, that you must spend so much time practicing to escape!"

Entrance Requirements: No alignment restrictions. Requires a minimum M.E. 8, P.S. 10 and P.P. 8.

Costume: Silk Kung Fu outfit, preferably in black, or a very dark color.

Stance: Low knee bends, feet wide apart, with one hand stretched, and the other pulled in to the waist, both in claw positions.

Character Bonuses:

Add +10 to Chi

Add +1 to P.S.

Add +1 to P.P.

Add +1 to P.E.

Add +10 to S.D.C.

Combat Skills:

Attacks per Melee: Two

Escape Moves: Roll with punch/fall/impact, maintain balance, leap, and backflip.

Attack Moves: Leap, roll, and backflip.

Basic Defensive Moves: Dodge, parry, and automatic parry.

Advanced Defenses: Multiple Dodge.

Hand Attacks: Backhand, Claw Hand, and Black Tiger Claw Strike (Special: This is a special ripping attack that requires giving up the automatic parry for the entire melee round. Successful attack does 1D6+4 damage).

Basic Foot Attacks: Kick Attack, Tripping/Leg Hooks, Crescent Kick, Backward Sweep, Drop Kick (Combination Fall/Dodge/Kick).

Jumping Foot Attacks: Jump Kick

Special Attacks: Death Blow, Leap Attack, and Combined Strike/Parry.

Weapon Katas: W.P. Large Sword (favors the *Chien* double-edged, straight-blade long sword).

Modifiers to Attacks: Pull punch, knock-out/stun, and critical strike.

Bonus Skills & Abilities

Martial Art Abilities and Powers: Select any one *Chi Mastery Abilities* (including advanced) and one *Martial Art Techniques.*

Language Skill: Chinese. In addition to the spoken language, all members of this martial art have been trained in the "Secret hand signs of the Black Tiger." This language of gestures and hand signs allows characters to signal their intentions, the movements of their enemies, and suggest tactics without making a sound.

Training Skills: Prowl and Tracking.

Philosophical Training: Legalism, Study of the Military Classics.

Level Advancement Bonuses:

1st: +1 to strike and critical strike from behind.

2nd: +1 to damage and +1 on initiative.

3rd: +1 attack per melee, critical strike on natural 18 or better.

4th: Select one additional *Chi Mastery Ability* (including advanced) or *Martial Art Techniques.*

5th: +1 to damage.

6th: +1 to roll with punch/fall/impact.

7th: Select one additional *Chi Mastery Ability* (including advanced) or *Martial Art Techniques.*

8th: Add +10 to Chi.

9th: +1 to damage and +1 to strike.

10th: Select one additional *Chi Mastery Ability* (including advanced) or *Martial Art Techniques.*

11th: +1 attack per melee.

12th: +1 to strike.

13th: +2 to damage and +1 on initiative.

14th: Add one additional *Chi Mastery Ability* (including advanced) or *Martial Art Techniques.*

15th: +1 attack per melee and +1 to damage.

Why Study Shan Tung Kung Fu?

By focusing on the development of Chi, and forceful combat moves, this martial art is certainly effective in any attack. However, those looking for a balanced approach to combat may be disappointed with the lack of attention to the defensive side of things.

Shih Ba Ban Wu Yi (New) Eighteen Weapons Kung Fu

Translating *Shih Ba Ban Wu Yi* into "Eighteen Kinds of Martial Arts Weapon Techniques" pretty much sums up what this martial art is all about. Students train with every traditional hand to hand weapon to the point where they can pick up a different weapon at random and use it with amazing prowess (+1 to strike and parry) with no combat penalties.

Initial practice is grueling, often taking ten to twelve hours a day for a full year. However, it does include practice in every one of the Chinese weapons listed in this book!

Entrance Requirements: Any alignments, but P.P. 10 and P.E. 9.

Costume: Kung Fu outfit, but always with at least two surprise weapons sewn or tucked into the material. In addition, for combat, one is expected to carry a main (overt) weapon and a hidden weapon, usually a chain or whip.

Stance: Upright, legs slightly apart, with hands loosely at the waist.

Character Bonuses:

Add +2 to P.P.

Add +2 to P.E.

Add +1 to P.S.

Add +20 to S.D.C.

Combat Skills:

Attacks per Melee: Three

Escape Moves: Roll with punch/fall/impact and maintain balance.

Basic Defensive Moves: Dodge, parry, automatic parry.

Advanced Defenses: Multiple Dodge and Circular Parry.

Open Hand Attacks: Strike (Punch), Knife-Hand, and Palm Strike.

Basic Foot Attacks: Kick Attack and Snap Kick.

Jumping Foot Attacks: Leap Attack (with weapon) and Jump Kick.

Holds/Locks: None

Weapon Katas: All 14 of the following Weapon Katas, which effectively means they can pick up virtually any ancient weapon and use it with deadly skill.

W.P. Axe

W.P. Blunt

W.P. Chain

W.P. Forked

W.P. Knife

W.P. Polearm

W.P. Spear

W.P. Staff

W.P. Large Sword

W.P. Short Sword

W.P. Whip

W.P. Small Thrown Weapons

W.P. Bow

W.P. Crossbow

Plus, choose four of the following as the character's *Paired* Weapon Proficiencies:

W.P. Axe - Paired

W.P. Blunt - Paired

W.P. Chain - Paired

W.P. Forked - Paired

W.P. Knife - Paired

W.P. Large Sword - Paired

W.P. Short Sword - Paired

W.P. Paired Short Sword & Axe

W.P. Paired Large Sword & Knife

W.P. Paired Short Sword & Knife

W.P. Paired Short Sword & Whip

Modifiers to Attacks: Pull punch, knock-out/stun, and critical strike.

Weapon Tap (Special): The attack does **no** damage, but makes a loud snap or bang by knocking the weapon against some part of the opponent's body or equipment. Getting a bang off a belt buckle, the skull, or a weapon is considered the most challenging. It adds +10% to any roll to impress or intimidate.

Bonus Skills & Abilities:

Martial Art Abilities and Powers: Select one *Specialty Kata* (no Chi Kata allowed).

Language Skill: Chinese (Mandarin)

Training Skills: W.P. in all the Katas described.

Philosophical Training: Taoism.

Level Advancement Bonuses

1st: +1 on initiative, +1 to strike, +1 to parry and dodge, and +2 to roll with punch/fall/impact.

2nd +2 to damage, critical strike on natural 19 or 20.

3rd +1 attack per melee round.

4th Select one additional *Specialty Kata* (no Chi Kata allowed).

5th +1 to strike and +1 to parry and dodge.

6th +2 to damage and +1 on initiative.

7th +1 attack per melee round.

8th Critical strike on natural 18-20 and knock-out/stun on natural 19 or 20.

9th Select one additional *Specialty Kata* (no Chi Kata allowed).

10th +1 to parry and dodge.

11th +1 attack per melee round.

12th +2 to damage and +1 on initiative.

13th +1 to strike.

14th +1 attack per melee.

15th Select one additional *Specialty Kata* (no Chi Kata allowed).

Why Study Shih Ba Ban Wu Yi?

Offers the full range of weapons that can be used in conjunction with a martial art. Excellent combat bonuses are offset by a lack of attention to Chi and other esoteric studies.

Pao Pat Mei
Leopard Style Kung Fu

As with the Tiger Claw Form, Pao Pat Mei is based on the fighting prowess of one of the great hunting cats. The difference between the two styles is like the difference between tigers and leopards. Where tigers rely on pure strength and power, the leopard must use quickness and accuracy. The tiger can afford direct contests of power, where the leopard must be more cautious and plan more carefully.

A master of Leopard Style Kung Fu will take the time to appraise an opponent before striking. There's not a lot of subtlety in this form. Every technique is dedicated to fast and deadly attacks.

Teaching is available only at remote monasteries in China, Vietnam, and Laos.

Entrance Requirements: No Attribute or Alignment restrictions.

Costume: Silk Kung Fu outfit.

Stance: Narrow stance with feet close together, one in front of another. Fists are held tight to the center of the chest, one on top of the other, almost touching.

Character Bonuses:

Add +2 to M.A.

Add +1 to P.S.

Add +1 to P.P.

Add +8 to Spd.

Add +10 to S.D.C.

Combat Skills:

Attacks per Melee: Three

Escape Moves: Roll with Punch/Fall/Impact

Attack Moves: Leap

Basic Defensive Moves: Dodge, parry, and automatic parry.

Advanced Defenses: Multiple Dodge and Combination Parry/Attack.

Hand Attacks: Strike (punch), Backhand, and Claw Hand.

Basic Foot Attacks: Kick Attack, Tripping/Leg Hooks, Snap Kick, and Backward Sweep.

Special Attacks: Death Blow, Leap Attack, Combination Strike/Parry.

Weapon Katas: None

Modifiers to Attacks: Pull punch, knock-out/stun, critical strike, and critical strike from rear.

Skills Included in Training:

Martial Art Abilities and Powers: Select two abilities from among *Arts of Invisibility*, *Body Hardening Exercises*, and *Specialty Katas*.

Languages: Chinese

Survival: Fasting, Wilderness Survival, and Tracking

Physical: Prowl

Philosophical Training: Taoism

Level Advancement Bonuses:

1st: +2 to parry/dodge, +1 to strike, +1 to roll with punch/fall/impact, critical strike on natural 20, critical strike or knockout from behind.

2nd: +1 attack per melee, +1 to Rear Attacks (Backward Sweep, Backhand Strike).

3rd: +1 to leap (add 3 feet/0.9 m to leap distance), +2 to damage.

4th: Select one from *Arts of Invisibility, Body Hardening Exercises,* or *Special Katas* (including Chi Katas).

5th: +1 to roll with punch/fall/impact, critical strike on natural 18, 19 or 20.

6th: +1 attack per melee and +1 to parry/dodge.

7th: +1 to rear attacks (Backward Sweep, Backhand Strike), and +1 to strike.

8th: Select one from *Arts of Invisibility, Body Hardening Exercises,* or *Special Katas* (including Chi Katas).

9th: +1 attack per melee round, +1 to roll with punch/fall/impact.

10th: Knock-out/stun on natural 20 and +2 to damage.

11th: +1 to leap (add 3 feet/0.9 m to leap distance), and +1 to parry/dodge.

12th: Select one from *Arts of Invisibility, Body Hardening Exercises,* or *Special Katas* (including Chi Katas).

13th: +1 attack per melee round and +1 to roll with punch/fall/impact.

14th: +2 to damage and +1 to strike.

15th: +1 to leap (add 3 feet/0.9 m to leap distance), +1 to parry/dodge.

Why Study Pao Pat Mei?

When it comes to quick and deadly, this is possibly the best of the martial arts. It's also relatively inflexible, offering few of the mind-oriented abilities.

Shao-Lin Kung Fu

This is the original version of Kung Fu (also called Gung Fu), and the martial art that spawned hundreds of derivative forms. It has shaped and influenced all the martial arts. It all started in the Shao-lin Temple in the Chiu Lien Mountains. For over a thousand years, students of the martial arts traveled there for training.

This continued until the reign of the 17th Century Emperor K'ang Hsi, when the Shao-lin monks responded to a call to put down an insurrection. 128 of the monks responded and managed to rout the enemy entirely. This was such an alarming display of power that the government eventually sent an army against the Shao-lin. Only five monks managed to survive the battle and burning of the temple.

Current Shao-lin training is available only in Taiwan and Hong Kong.

Entrance Requirements: No attribute or alignment restrictions.

Costume: Silk or cotton Kung Fu outfit.

Stance: A side stance, with one foot pointing toward the opponent, and the other on a right angle to the first.

Character Bonuses:

Add +2 to M.E.

Add +2 to P.S.

Add +1 to P.E.

Add +1 to P.P.

Add +10 to S.D.C.

Combat Skills:

Attacks per Melee: Three

Escape Moves: Roll with punch/fall/impact, and backflip.

Attack Moves: Leap and backflip.

Basic Defensive Moves: Dodge, parry, and automatic parry.

Advanced Defenses: Multiple Dodge, Combination Parry/Attack, Disarm.

Hand Attacks: Strike (Punch), Knife Hand, Double-Knuckle Fist, Backhand, Palm Strike.

Basic Foot Attacks: Kick Attack, Tripping/Leg Hooks, Snap Kick, Crescent Kick, Wheel Kick.

Jumping Foot Attacks: Jump Kick

Special Attacks: Death Blow, Leap Attack, Forearm Attack.

Holds/Locks: Arm Hold, Leg Hold, Body Hold, Neck Hold.

Weapon Katas: None

Modifiers to Attacks: Pull punch, knock-out/stun, critical strike, and critical strike from rear.

Special Katas: Dragon: Building energy and power throughout the melee round, but holding back until the very last chance to attack. The kata takes up the entire melee round and the only defense available is the Automatic Parry. All this energy turns the attack into a Critical Strike (Double Damage). The attack can be any hand strike, a Kick Attack, Snap Kick, or Crescent Kick.

Skills Included in Training:

Martial Art Abilities and Powers: Select two abilities from among *Body Hardening Exercises* and/or *Specialty Katas* (including Chi Katas).

Languages: Chinese

Physical: Gymnastics

Philosophical Training: Taoism

Level Advancement Bonuses:

1st: +3 to roll with punch/fall/impact, +2 to strike, critical strike on roll of Natural 19 or 20, critical strike from behind.

2nd: +1 to backflip/leap and +1 parry/dodge.

3rd: +1 attack per melee.

4th: Select one additional *Body Hardening Exercise* (including Demon Hunter Exercises) or *Specialty Katas* (including Chi Katas).

5th: +1 to roll with punch/fall/impact, +1 to damage.

6th: +1 to strike, knock-out/stun on natural 18 or better.

7th: +1 attack per melee, death blow on roll of natural 19 or 20.

8th: +1 to backflip/leap, select one additional *Body Hardening Exercise* (including Demon Hunter Exercises) or *Specialty Katas* (including Chi Katas).

9th: +1 to roll with punch/fall/impact.

10th: +1 attack per melee round.

11th: Select one additional *Body Hardening Exercise* (including Demon Hunter Exercises) or *Specialty Katas* (including Chi Katas).

12th: Critical strike on natural 18 or better.

13th: +1 to backflip/leap and +1 to damage.

14th: +1 to roll with punch/fall/impact and +1 to strike.

15th: +1 Attack per melee, select one *Additional Body Hardening Exercise* (including Demon Hunter Exercises) or *Specialty Katas* (including Chi Katas).

Why Study Shao-Lin?

A solid, combat effective form that stresses quickness and power. Bonuses can also be used with weapon forms.

Snake Style Kung Fu
She Shen Kung Fu

Snake Style Kung Fu seeks to tap into the Yin power of darkness, building up forces of the negative Chi.

The Snake Master will stand his ground in combat, swaying slowly from side to side, examining the opponent. When attacked, the response is to whip back or slump to the side. At the first sign of an opening, the master attacks with a single finger strike, channeling dark Chi into the enemy's body. This strike can leave the victim crippled, damaged or merely gasping for air. And a light stroke from the master can reverse all the damage.

Throughout the world there are less than fifty masters and students of Snake Style, each keep their training secret. To enter into their dark studios requires a blood oath of loyalty. Betrayal is rewarded with a sentence of death.

Entrance Requirements: Strictly limited to dishonorable and evil alignments. Requires minimum I.Q. 10, M.E. 12 and P.P. 7.

Costume: None, formal clothing preferred. However, Snake Masters tend to cultivate very long fingernails, up to 2 inches (5 cm), especially on the index fingers.

Stance: Upright, feet at right angles, slightly apart, hands held over chest, one cupping the other with index fingers extended.

Character Bonuses:

Double Normal Chi

Add +4 to M.E.

Add +4 to M.A.

Combat Skills:

Attacks per Melee: One

Escape Moves: Roll with punch/fall/impact.

Basic Defensive Moves: Dodge, parry, and automatic parry.

Advanced Defenses: Multiple Dodge and Combination Parry/Attack.

Hand Attacks: Palm Strike and One-Fingertip Attack (Special! Does absolutely no damage but serves to channel Chi attacks directly to Hit Points.).

Basic Foot Attacks: None

Special Attacks: Death blow and choke.

Weapon Katas: None.

Modifiers to Attacks: Pull punch, knock-out/stun and critical strike.

Skills Included in Training:

Martial Art Abilities and Powers: Select one ability from among *Arts of Invisibility* and *Chi Mastery*. Also select two *Zenjorike Powers*.

Languages: Chinese

Skills: Calligraphy and Geomancy

Philosophical Training: Taoism (Yin of the Yin-Yang)

Level Advancement Bonuses:

1st: +1 to roll with punch/fall/impact, +1 to strike, and critical strike from behind.

2nd: +1 to parry/dodge.

3rd: Select one additional *Arts of Invisibility Ability* or *Chi Mastery Ability* (including advanced).

4th: Double existing Chi, critical strike on natural 19 or 20.

5th: Select one additional *Zenjorike Power*.

6th: +1 attack per melee, death blow on roll of natural 20.

7th: Select one additional *Arts of Invisibility Ability* or *Chi Mastery Ability* (including advanced).

8th: +1 to roll with punch/fall/impact, and +1 to parry/dodge.

9th: Double existing Chi, critical strike on natural 18 or better.

10th: +1 attack per melee round.

11th: Select one additional *Zenjorike Power*.

12th: +1 attack per melee, +2 to parry/dodge, +1 to strike.

13th: Select one additional *Arts of Invisibility Ability* or *Chi Mastery Ability* (including advanced).

14th: Double existing Chi.

15th: +1 to roll with punch/fall/impact and +2 to damage.

Why Study Snake Style?

With two Zenjorike powers, Snake Style is by far the greatest mystic form in the martial arts. Deadly negative Chi attacks more than offsets the relatively weak physical moves.

Tai-Chi Ch'uan

The most common martial art form in the world. Tai-Chi Ch'uan is also the national exercise program of China, practiced by young and old every morning. It takes many years of study before it becomes a practical combat technique but the time is well used in the development of Chi.

A master will appear to move in slow motion. Never hurrying, always seeming to anticipate the opponent's attacks with gentle parries and an occasional open palm shove (see below).

Entrance Requirements: No attribute or alignment restrictions.

Costume: Loose cotton tunic and pants.

Stance: Rear leg bent slightly at the knee, forward leg a few inches off the ground, forward hand loosely outstretched, rear hand loosely at waist.

Character Bonuses:

Add +15 to Chi

Add +2 to M.E.

Add +2 to M.A.

Add +2 to P.P.

Combat Skills:

Attacks per Melee: Two

Escape Moves: Roll with Punch/Fall/Impact, Maintain Balance.

Basic Defensive Moves: Dodge, parry, and automatic parry

Advanced Defenses: Multiple Dodge, Automatic Dodge

Hand Attacks: Backhand, Push Open Hand, and Palm Strike (Special! Essentially a knock-down strike that also does 1D6 damage. Any victim failing to counter the attack will be knocked back a number of feet equal to the attacker's Chi — divide by 3 for number of meters.)

Basic Foot Attacks: Kick Attack, Snap Kick, Crescent Kick.

Weapon Katas: None

Modifiers to Attacks: Pull punch, knock-out/stun, and critical strike.

Skills Included in Training:

Martial Art Abilities and Powers: Select a total of three abilities from among *Chi Mastery* and *Specialty Katas* (including Chi Katas). You may also select one *Zenjorike Power.*

Languages: Chinese

Philosophical Training: Taoism

Level Advancement Bonuses:

1st: +2 to roll with punch/fall/impact, +2 to dodge, and critical strike from behind.

2nd: +2 to maintain balance and +1 to parry/dodge.

3rd: Double existing Chi.

4th: +1 to parry/dodge, critical strike on natural 19 or 20.

5th: Select one additional *Chi Mastery Ability* or from *Katas* (including Chi Katas).

6th: +1 to roll with punch/fall/impact, +1 to parry/dodge.

7th: Double existing Chi and +2 to strike.

8th: +1 attack per melee round and +2 to maintain balance.

9th: Add one *Zenjorike Power.*

10th: Select one additional *Chi Mastery Ability* or from *Katas* (including Chi Katas).

11th: Double existing Chi.

12th: +1 to roll with punch/fall/impact, +1 to parry/dodge.

13th: +2 to maintain balance, knock-out/stun on natural 19 or 20.

14th: Select one additional *Chi Mastery Ability* or from *Katas* (including Chi Katas), and +1 attack per melee round.

15th: Add one *Zenjorike Power* and double existing Chi.

Why Study Tai-Chi Ch'uan?

While far from the most powerful of combat forms, Tai-Chi nevertheless provides strong Chi power to its students.

Tien-Hsueh Touch Mastery (Exclusive)

To study Tien Hsueh, the Chinese art of "Touching Vital Points," requires a complete knowledge of human anatomy. The student becomes as familiar with the flow of blood, the workings of the body's organs, and, most importantly, with the nervous system, as any surgeon. So precise is this knowledge that a character can kill with the touch of a finger. Not merely kill instantly, but kill inevitably, so the victim will die hours or even days after the injury.

The teaching of Touch Mastery is highly restricted. Although it's masters control powerful organizations, there are never more than a dozen people who know the art in the entire world. Students must be born into the family of a master in order to be accepted. The result of acceptance is as likely to be death as training in the art. It can truly be said that the masters of Tien-Hsueh bury their mistakes. Once trained, a student will never be free of the control of the Touch Masters. Disobeying a command, failing in a mission, showing disrespect for a master, or revealing any of the secret arts will result in an automatic death sentence. The instant that student is condemned, the international organization will offer a "bounty" for the recovery of the corpse.

Entrance Requirements: Attribute minimums include I.Q. 11 and M.E. 8. Restricted to characters of diabolic (evil) alignment. **Note:** It is possible for characters to take this form and later go through an alignment change.

Costume: Traditional Chinese Silk Gown.

Stance: Upright stance with legs together, one arm up, the other at waist, both hands held loosely with the forefingers pointing.

Character Bonuses:

Double Normal Chi

Add +4 to M.E.

Add +2 to M.A.

Combat Skills:

Attacks per Melee: One

Escape Moves: Roll with punch/fall/impact

Basic Defensive Moves: Dodge, parry, and automatic parry

Hand Attacks: Fore-Knuckle Fist and Fingertip Attack

Basic Foot Attacks: None

Special Attacks: Paralysis Attack (Vital Points) and Dim Mak (Special)! This is the feared delayed death blow. Requires that the character take the Dim Mak Atemi Ability; see Atemi for more information.

Weapon Katas: None

Skills Included in Training:

Martial Art Abilities and Powers: Select a total of three powers from among *Arts of Invisibility*, *Atemi Abilities*, and *Chi Mastery.* Also select one *Zenjorike* **or** the *Long-Distance Dim Mak Advanced Atemi.*

Language Skill: Chinese

Special Skills: Geomancy

Philosophical Training: Confucianism

Level Advancement Bonuses:

1st: +1 to roll with punch/fall/impact, +1 to strike, critical strike or knock-out from behind.

2nd: +1 to parry and dodge.

3rd: Select one additional power from *Arts of Invisibility,* or *Atemi*, or *Chi Mastery* (including advanced).

4th: Double existing Chi.

5th: Add one *Zenjorike* power or two *Atemi* (including advanced).

6th: +1 to parry, critical strike or knock-out from behind (triple damage).

7th: +1 to roll with punch/fall/impact and +1 to strike.

8th: Double existing Chi and +2 to dodge

9th: +1 attack per melee, *Dim Mak* on roll of natural 18 or better.

10th: +1 to parry/dodge and add one *Zenjorike*, or two *Atemi* (including advanced).

11th: +1 to damage and +1 to parry.

12th: Select one additional power from *Arts of Invisibility*, *Atemi* (including advanced), or *Chi Mastery* (including advanced).

13th: +1 to roll with punch/fall/impact and add one *Zenjorike* or two *Atemi* (including advanced).

14th: +1 to parry and dodge.

15th: Double existing Chi.

Why Study Tien-Hsueh?

The most powerful of the "Internal" schools of the martial arts. Every effort is placed on the development of the mind and Chi energy. The exclusive teacher of the dreaded Dim Mak. Relatively weak in physical combat.

Tong Lun Kung Fu (New)
The Praying Mantis Style

This fast-moving form is one of the strangest of all the martial arts. It was created based on observations of the praying mantis insect, both as it catches its prey and as it fights others of its kind.

The most specialized movement of this form is the "Mantis Claw" (*Gou*), which experts practice endlessly. One exercise is to practice punching through the skin and flesh of a piece of meat (often a Tong Lun specialist will have a relationship with a butcher). An even more difficult exercise is to toss a piece of paper in the air and strike it sharply enough to tear or impale it (try it, it's a lot harder than it sounds). Another exercise (don't try this one at home) is to tap the corner of the eyeball between blinks, without doing any harm.

This is such a creative martial art, and innovation is so highly valued, that there are now dozens of competing styles, each with a whole series of new moves and counter-moves. One thing they all have in common is their desire for really close combat; to crowd in so close as to neutralize all the enemy's potential moves.

Entrance Requirements: Any alignment, but characters must have a P.P. of at least 11.

Costume: Cotton Kung Fu outfit, preferably with loose sleeves and pant legs.

Stance: Both arms are severely bent at the both the elbows and wrists, with the fingers pointing down and one hand extended further out than the other. Legs are apart, with knees slightly bent.

Character Bonuses:

Add +2 to M.E.

Add +1 to P.P.

Add +3 to Spd.

Add +5 to S.D.C.

Combat Skills:

Attacks per Melee: Three

Escape Moves: Roll with punch/fall/impact.

Basic Defensive Moves: Dodge, parry, and automatic parry.

Advanced Defenses: Combination Parry/Attack and Disarm.

Attack Moves: Strike (punch), plus ...

Gou Strike (Special): A close-in strike using the tips of the fingers to rip into the opponent. Always done with a -3 to strike, but a successful attack does 2D6+2 damage.

Negative Gou (Special): A backhand version of the above.

Lau (Special): This circular version of a Palm Strike does a bit less damage (1D4) but can **not** be blocked or deflected with either an automatic or circular parry.

Special Attacks: Death blow and Gou Combination (Special): Brings together the *Gou Grip*, followed by a rapid-fire

burst of *Gou Strikes*. Must be started at the beginning of the melee round and uses up all other actions (including parries) for the rest of the melee round. Does 3D6 total damage and if the victim does not succeed in breaking free (dodge), the martial artist can do the same damage again in the second melee round.

Basic Foot Attacks: Backward Sweep and Tripping/Leg Hook.

Holds/Locks: Gou Grip (Special): A sideways move and grip using the middle, ring and little fingers to grip and let the character grab on, inflicting 1D4 damage at the same time.

Tsai Grip (Special): A forward move ending in a full hand grip/hold that can be used as a Choke, Arm Hold, or part of a Combination Move.

Modifiers to Attacks: Pull punch, knock-out/stun, critical strike, critical strike from rear, and Hook at Eyes (Special! Does no damage, but can not be parried and forces the enemy to blink as the mantis claw darts at the eyes. A valuable intimidation attack.)

Bonus Skills & Abilities:

Martial Art Abilities and Powers: Select three from among *Atemi Abilities* (including advanced).

Language Skill: Chinese

Training Skills: None

Philosophical Training: None

Level Advancement Bonuses:

1st: +2 to roll with punch/fall/impact, critical strike on natural 19 or 20, death blow on roll of natural Twenty.

2nd: +1 to strike and +1 on initiative.

3rd: +1 attack per melee round and +1 to pull punch.

4th: Select one additional *Atemi Ability* (including advanced).

5th: +2 to damage.

6th: Critical strike on natural 17 or better.

7th: +1 attack per melee round.

8th: Select one additional *Atemi Ability* (including advanced).

9th: +1 to strike and +2 to pull punch.

10th: +2 to parry and dodge.

11th: Death blow on roll of natural 19 or 20.

12th: Select one additional *Atemi Ability* (including advanced).

13th: +2 to damage.

14th: +1 attack per melee round.

15th: Select one additional *Atemi Ability* (including advanced).

Why Study Praying Mantis Kung Fu?

While odd in its combat style, it can be used to effectively spread fear in the hearts of others. The form also offers extensive training in Tien Hsueh (Atemi).

Triad Assassin

A generation ago, recognizing that firearms were the wave of the future, the Triad bosses became dissatisfied with the traditional training of the various martial arts. They wondered if there might be some way to combine the discipline of martial art training with accurate and rapid gunfire.

In order to answer the question, they put out a challenge. Any martial art teacher who came forward with a workable improvement on weapons training, and was selected, would receive ten million dollars and would be commissioned to start a new school for Triad trainees.

Eight candidates came forward.

The selection process was simple. The Triads simply arranged for the eight to be placed in an abandoned eight story building, one on each floor. Whoever survived would be "selected." Twenty minutes later, the only survivor was then attacked by a strike force of six highly trained assassins (Triads don't spend that kind of money without being *sure* of their results).

Saih Wu Shen ("Arsenic Handshake Saih") was not only the winner, he had come out without a scratch on him. Ever since that day, Wu Shen has been the principle instructor of the Triad Assassin Program. It is said that his ability with a pistol is beyond human comprehension and that whatever mysterious martial art he originally studied gave him some strange sense of foreshadowing, so he is always waiting for those who would kill him.

While not a *traditional* martial art, Wu Shen's school has become an effective breeding ground for Triad henchmen and assassins. It's also the *only* martial art school that advocates the use of modern weaponry, and that integrates the use of firearms directly into martial art teaching. However, it is very specialized! Characters are trained only in the use of firearms and then only for automatic pistols. Moreover, the training is so precise that the weapon *must* be a 9 mm (or 9 mm Parabelum), with a clip/magazine that holds a minimum of thirteen rounds. Here are the preferred models:

Beretta Model 92 Double-Action (Italy) - 15 round magazine

Browning High Power (Belgium) - 13 round magazine

Glock (Austria) - 17 round magazine

Heckler & Koch VP70 (Germany) - 18 round magazine

New Nambu Model 57A (Japan) - 18 round magazine

PA15 MAB (France) - 15 round magazine

Pindad 9 mm (Indonesia) - 13 round magazine

Costume: Street clothing, preferably an expensive designer suit.

Stance: Upright stance with legs together, one arm up, the other at waist, both hands held loosely with the forefinger pointing.

Character Bonuses:

Add +1 to P.P.

Add +2 to Spd.

Add +5 to S.D.C.

Combat Skills:

Attacks per Melee: Two

Escape Moves: Roll with punch/fall/impact.

Basic Defensive Moves: Dodge, parry, and automatic parry.

Hand Attacks: Pistol Whip (Special): This is a special attack where the victim is slapped with the barrel of an automatic pistol. A successful attack does 1D8 damage.

Foot Attacks: None

Weapon Katas: W.P. Automatic Pistol; characters do not use the W.P. bonuses, instead use the ones listed here.

Modifiers to Attacks: None

Bonus Skills & Abilities:

Martial Art Abilities and Powers: None. Triad Assassin training offers no Martial Art Abilities or Powers.

Language Skill: None

Training Skills: None

Philosophical Training: None

Level Advancement Bonuses:

Note: Unlike the other Level Advancement Tables, the bonuses here are NOT cumulative. Instead, each level lists all the character's bonuses exactly. Works only with automatic pistols, which must be 9 mm, and with magazines of no less than 13 rounds.

1st: Two attacks per melee round.

+4 to strike with aimed shot, damage equals 2D6 per shot.

+2 to strike with burst shot, short burst does 2D6x2 damage, long burst does 2D6x5 damage.

+1 to strike with pistol whip and 1D6 damage.

+2 to roll with punch/fall and +1 to parry/dodge.

2nd: Ambidextrous Training Complete! Characters can fire with left or right hands with equal facility!

Two attacks per melee round.

+4 to strike with aimed shot, damage equals 2D6 per shot.

+2 to strike with burst shot, short burst does 2D6x2 damage, long burst does 2D6x5 damage.

+1 to strike with pistol whip and 1D6 damage.

+2 to roll with punch/fall and +2 to parry/dodge.

3rd: W.P. Automatic Pistol - Paired! The character can fire with a weapon in each hand, simultaneously, with great accuracy.

Four attacks per melee round (two for each hand).

+4 to strike with aimed shot, damage equals 2D6 per shot.

+3 to strike with burst shot, short burst does 2D6x2 damage, long burst does 2D6x5 damage.

+2 to strike with pistol whip and 1D6 damage.

+2 to roll with punch/fall and +2 to parry and dodge.

4th: Four attacks per melee round (two for each hand).

+5 to strike with aimed shot, damage equals 2D6 per shot.

+3 to strike with burst shot, short burst does 2D6x2 damage, long burst does 2D6x5 damage. Simultaneous burst (counts as two attacks) does 4D6x2 or 4D6x5 respectively.

+1 to strike with pistol whip and 2D4 damage.

+2 to roll with punch/fall and +2 to parry and dodge.

5th: Four attacks per melee round.

+5 to strike with aimed shot, damage equals 2D6+1 per shot.

+3 to strike with burst shot, short burst does 2D6+2x2 damage, long burst does 2D6x6 damage. Simultaneous burst (counts as two attacks) does 4D6x2 or 4D6x5 respectively.

+2 to strike with pistol whip and 2D4 damage.

+2 to roll with punch/fall and +2 to parry/dodge.

6th: Four attacks per melee round (two for each hand).

+5 to strike with aimed shot, damage equals 2D6+1 per shot.

+3 to strike with burst shot, short burst does 2D6+2x2 damage, long burst does 2D6x6 damage. Simultaneous burst (counts as two attacks) does 4D6+4x2 or 4D6x6 respectively.

+2 to strike with pistol whip and 2D4+1 damage.

+3 to roll with punch/fall and +3 to parry/dodge.

7th: Five attacks per melee round.

+6 to strike with aimed shot, damage equals 2D6+1 per shot.

+4 to strike with burst shot, short burst does 2D6+2x2 Damage, long burst does 2D6x6 damage. Simultaneous burst (counts as two attacks) does 4D6+4x2 or 4D6x6 respectively.

+2 to strike with pistol whip and 2D4+2 damage.

+3 to roll with punch/fall and +3 to parry and dodge.

8th: Five attacks per melee round.

+6 to strike with aimed shot, damage equals 3D6 per shot.

+4 to strike with burst shot, short burst does 3D6x2 damage, long burst does 3D6x6 damage. Simultaneous burst (counts as two attacks) does 6D6x2 or 6D6x6 respectively.

+3 to strike with pistol whip and 2D4+2 damage.

+3 to roll with punch/fall and +3 to parry/dodge.

9th: Five attacks per melee round.

+6 to strike with aimed shot, damage equals 3D6 per shot.

+4 to strike with burst shot, short burst does 3D6x2 damage, long burst does 3D6x6 damage. Simultaneous burst (counts as two attacks) does 6D6x2 or 6D6x6 respectively.

+3 to strike with pistol whip and 2D6 damage.

+3 to roll with punch/fall and +3 to parry and dodge.

10th: Six attacks per melee round.

+6 to strike with aimed shot, damage equals 3D6 per shot.

+4 to strike with burst shot, short burst does 3D6x2 damage, long burst does 3D6x6 damage. Simultaneous burst (counts as two attacks) does 6D6x2 or 6D6x6 respectively.

+3 to strike with pistol whip and 2D6 damage.

+3 to roll with punch/fall and +3 to parry/dodge.

11th: Six attacks per melee round.

+7 to strike with aimed shot, damage equals 3D6 per shot.

+5 to strike with burst shot, short burst does 3D6x2 damage, long burst does 3D6x6 damage. Simultaneous burst (counts as two attacks) does 6D6x2 or 6D6x6 respectively.

+3 to strike with pistol whip, 2D6 damage.

+3 to roll with Punch/Fall, +3 to parry and dodge.

12th: Six attacks per melee round (three for each hand).

+7 to strike with aimed shot, damage equals 3D6+3 per shot.

+5 to strike with burst shot, short burst does 3D6x2 damage, long burst does 3D6x7 damage.

+3 to strike with pistol whip, 2D6 damage.

+3 to roll with punch/fall, +3 to parry and dodge.

13th: Seven attacks per melee round.

+7 to strike with aimed shot, damage equals 3D6+3 per shot.

+5 to strike with burst shot, short burst does 3D6+3x2 damage, long burst does 3D6x7 damage. Simultaneous burst (counts as two attacks) does 6D6+6x2 or 6D6x7 respectively.

+3 to strike with pistol whip, 2D6 damage.

+4 to Roll with punch/fall, +4 to parry/dodge.

14th: Eight attacks per melee round.

+8 to strike with aimed shot, damage equals 3D6+3 per shot.

+5 to strike with burst shot, short burst does 3D6x2 damage, long burst does 3D6x7 damage. Simultaneous burst (counts as two attacks) does 6D6+6x2 or 6D6x7 respectively.

+4 to strike with pistol whip, 3D6 damage.

+4 to roll with punch/fall, +4 to parry and dodge.

15th: Eight attacks per melee round (four for each hand).

+8 to strike with aimed shot, damage equals 3D6+3 per shot.

+6 to strike with burst shot, short burst does 3D6x2 damage, long burst does 3D6x7 damage. Simultaneous burst (counts as two attacks) does 6D6x2 or 6D6x7 respectively.

+4 to strike with pistol whip, 3D6 damage.

+4 to roll with punch/fall and +4 to parry and dodge.

Why Study Triad Assassin Training?

The only martial art to focus on modern weapons. A character with this training and the right weapons is a deadly threat. On the other hand, there are no special powers or abilities, so it's pretty limiting in any other circumstances.

Introductory Scenario: An Outbreak of Alchemy

Game Master Note: This is suitable for any group of player characters, even those from other Palladium RPG systems. If desired, the location can be moved from Hong Kong to any other city with a suitable waterfront harbor. Likewise, the criminal organization described here can be changed to fit the Game Master's existing campaign.

Starting the Scenario

The Game Master should arrange for the player characters to be summoned to the harbor area, where construction workmen have discovered a very strange pair of bodies. Andrew Wu, the industrialist in charge of the harbor front project will meet the group at the gate to the construction site. He tells them the following as they walk toward the waterfront:

> "Come along, we don't have a whole lot of time. I've pulled a few strings, so you've got at least fifteen minutes to investigate before we call in the police. Basically, a couple of my workmen discovered a pair of bodies floating in the water. When you see the bodies, you'll understand why I wanted you to be here first. I don't know if it involves Feng Shui, magic or what, but there's definitely something supernatural about those bodies."

If the players ask, Mr. Wu can explain that there have been two other bodies washed up in the harbor in the last few weeks, but neither were at his construction site, and both of those other bodies were too decayed and disfigured for any identification.

When the player characters reach the water's edge, read the following:

> "You see a pair of bodies, each dressed in water-logged clothing, one in a business suit, the other in jeans and casual clothing. A pair of handcuffs connects the right wrist of one to the left wrist of the other. Another handcuff is attached to the chain between the two men, but it's other end is missing where there is a broken link in the chain. You then notice that there is something wrong with one of the men. The hands of the one on the left (in the suit) seem to be covered with tiny scales, and there is something like webbing between his fingers. Someone has placed towels over the heads of each of the bodies. What are you doing?"

Read the following if the features of the body in a business suit are revealed/uncovered:

> "Covering the skin of the man are hundreds of tiny scales. His scalp looks like a patchwork with a few clumps of short black hair remaining, but with most of it covered in scales. Even more grotesque, the man's mouth is open, revealing rows of needle-like teeth. Finally, there are two flaps, or gill slits, one on each side of the neck, each about four inches long."

If more of the body is revealed, it will be found that the scales cover the man's entire body surface and that the toes, as well as the fingers, have webbing between them.

When the other man's features, the one in jeans, is revealed, read the following:

> "Staring up at you, the dead man's eyes are not in the least bit human. Instead you see a pair of fish-like eyes, flat and silvery, each about three inches in diameter."

If the bodies are taken in for autopsy, it will be revealed that they died a few hours *before* being placed in the water. Both died of a massive breakdown in their internal organs. If questioned, the coroner will reveal the following:

> "Although I saw evidence of odd changes in the liver, kidneys, and reproductive organs, it seems like uncontrolled tissue changes in the lungs was probably the cause of death in both cases."

Game Master Information

From this point on, the adventure becomes a matter of doing detective work. A skilled Fang Shih should be able to figure out where the bodies were first dumped in the water. From that point, the characters should walk around for a few blocks, looking around alleyways, where any player character (or NPC) with the ability to detect spirits will see a ghost ...

Ghost Drama on the Stairs

In the alleyway behind the clinic, the ghost of one of the dead men is still replaying the events leading up to his death.

> "The ghost seems to be staggering down a set of stairs, starting from the third floor, and stumbling down, almost to the street. Although the fire escape is currently pulled up, the ghost staggers down as if it were extended down to the street."

The drama takes about a minute to play out, then it will start back at the beginning and go through the whole thing all over again. Repeated viewings will make it clear that the ghost is acting as if two people were helping him walk down the stairs.

Of course the place where the ghost starts down the stairs is the clinic where Ko has performed his "volunteer" service. Note that the day staff know absolutely nothing about Ko. In order to make the connection between the clinic and Ko it will be necessary to either keep an eye on the place until Ko returns, or somehow get Dr. Fung Dou Nan to reveal the connection (Fung will not give out Ko's name under any normal circumstances).

Triad Involvement

A local Triad (Chinese organized crime groups), the **Three Star Triad**, definitely knows quite a bit about the bodies. Both men were low-ranking Triad members, but the Triad isn't talking. That's because someone very high up in the organization has been "covering" for Ko right from the start. In fact, most of Ko's patients were actually Triad members.

William Davis Ko, Alchemist

Ko is a brilliant character who is a genius in contemporary chemistry. He has become insanely obsessed with ancient Chinese Alchemy ever since he "accidently" discovered an old book containing formulas that were similar to his own contemporary work.

Ko's "patients" have all been surprisingly cooperative. Those who return, after getting a taste of his treatment (they are amazed at how their wounds have healed in just a few hours!), come back again and again. Even more surprising, none of these low-level hoodlums have ever given Ko the slightest bit of trouble. They just keep coming back again and again, until they're finally killed by side-effects or mysteriously disappear.

Alignment: Anarchist. Ko tends to feel guilty about many of his actions, but he justifies himself by saying, "it is for the betterment of mankind that I do this." Actually, he knows that's a lie, but he can't help himself — he just has to find out more about the forbidden knowledge he's started to uncover.

Attributes: I.Q. 28, M.E. 23, M.A. 16, P.S. 7, P.P. 5, P.E. 12, P.B. 6, Spd. 5

Age: 48

Sex: Male

Ethnic Background: Han Chinese, born and raised in Taiwan.

Social Standing: Prominent scientist and businessman.

Weight: 175 pounds (79.3 kg).

Height: 5 feet, 5 inches (1.65 m).

Hit Points: 22

S.D.C.: 11

Chi: 24

O.C.C.: Research scientist/alchemist

Level of Experience: 8th

Level of Education: Ph.D. in organic chemistry, M.S. in biochemistry.

Occupation: President of Equitech Chemical.

Skills:

- Chemistry: Chinese Alchemical (78%)
- Chemistry: Advanced (98%)
- Chinese Language: Stage 4/Classical Chinese Literacy.
- Computer Programming (85%)
- Radio: Basic Communications (55%)
- Surveillance Systems (40%)
- Basic Electronics (60%)
- Paramedic (72%)

Disposition: Driven and fanatical in his research, Ko has seven children and three failed marriages. He's still on friendly terms with all his ex-wives and children, but he is barely aware of their existence. Likewise, he no longer visits, or even thinks about, his aging parents, his other relatives, or his old friends from his home town back in Taiwan.

Obsessions: Alchemy and the discovery of new drugs (through alchemy) that improve healing, resistance to disease and provide superhuman physical abilities.

Psionic Powers: None

Magic Knowledge/Powers: Lore concerning alchemy and magic chemicals and compounds.

Special Weapons: None. Ko is completely untrained in the use of any weapons, martial arts or fighting skills.

Criminal Record: None

Appearance: A rather drab looking guy with glasses and (usually) a bad haircut.

Corporate Assets & Money: As Chairman and major stockholder in Equitech Chemical he is personally worth around $11 million. The corporation provides him with a large laboratory budget, around $2 million a year, plus a salary of roughly $200,000.

Residence/Office: Ko occupies the top three floors of the Equitech Building. Floors 38 and 39 are his extensive personal laboratories staffed by sixteen assistants and technicians. The very top floor, the 40th (which was once outfitted as a luxury penthouse), is now a combination laboratory, library and arcanum. Other than the people listed below, he has had no visitors on the 40th floor for years. The rooftop, which is used as a helicopter pad for the company, can be reached by an elevator that doesn't stop at floors 38, 39 or 40. The entire building is equipped with a high-tech security system and at least three armed guards are on duty at all times.

A couple of nights a week, or when he's called, Ko takes over the office, posing as an herbalist, and disburses his elixirs to a variety of clients. Since Ko has a reputation of successfully treating knife and gunshot wounds without asking questions or making any report to the authorities, he's managed to build up a modest clientele among the criminal element.

Enemies: None. Of course his secret benefactor probably has powerful enemies, but, if they are even aware of Ko, they are likely to take a "wait and see" attitude, figuring that his dabbling in alchemy could be worth stealing.

Ko's Current Alchemical Research Directions:

Grand Unity Jade Powder Elixir: Of all Ko's experiments so far, this has been the most successful. When administered carefully, with proper restraint, even the most mortal wounds will be healed in just 1D6 hours. Of course, there is a 14% chance that the subject will die, but that's considered a pretty good success rate among Ko's medical clientele.

Radiance-Containing Brilliance-Emitting Elixir: Characters who take this formula seem to acquire a supernatural control over their own Chi (automatic defense vs Chi Attacks and the equivalent of the "Hardened Chi" Chi Mastery Ability), as well as blinding speed and dexterity (+4 to P.P. and +12 to Spd.). On the downside, it only lasts for 2D6 days, after which the characters permanently lose 10% of their Chi and 20% of their P.P.E.

Wonderful Metamorphosis Elixir: Still playing around with the exact formula (it seems that the elixir needs to be mixed in an exact proportion to match the chemical make-up of each subject), Ko has succeeded in transforming a series of victims into (roll 1D6):

1) Giant fish creatures who are capable of feats of telekinesis, telepathy and clairvoyance.

2) Scaled Men-Fish with very powerful bodies and whose fish-like eyes seem to see into a different world than our own.

3) Men with tiny scales, needle-like teeth, and webbed fingers, who recall nothing of their former names or identities.

4) Limbless, neckless beings, whose arms, legs and necks are withdrawn into their elongated bodies, and who seem to lose all capacity for breathing.

5) Subjects who grow gills, are capable of breathing above and below the water, and who are no longer able to eat anything but meat.

6) Those who are seemingly unaffected subjects and who have no outward signs of change, but who seem compelled to drown themselves whenever they are left alone around any volume of water as large as a bathtub.

Note: Unfortunately, since none of them have lived more than 48 hours after their metamorphosis, Ko is considering abandoning further research until he creates a better computer model of the elixir's function.

Jade Fountain Eye Medicine: Ko is somewhat puzzled by the modest success of this elixir. When used in moderation as eye drops, 81% of the subjects have become able to see in conditions of total darkness, apparently because they now have the capacity to see far into the ultraviolet range. Only 4% have died, although the remaining 15% have experienced the total destruction of their eyeballs; but were later "treated" with the *Wonderful Metamorphosis Elixir*, above, and cured.

Resurrection Elixir: This is currently Ko's most promising line of research. He has been distilling various substances from the bodies of his earlier victims and he has already tested over a dozen variations on this formula with varying degrees of success (roll 1D6)!

1) Mindless zombies with tiny scales for skin. They obey anything he tells them. Increase all physical attributes by 1D6, but reduce all mental attributes, attacks/actions per melee, combat bonuses and skill proficiencies by half.

2) Restored to perfect health, but remembers little about their past life (lose half their skills too).

3) Restored to health but exhibit tendencies toward sadism and evil; they have become beings of Negative Chi.

4) Returned to life, but the character can see into the spirit world — sees ghosts, spirits, and beings of Pure Chi. Tends to be a bit jumpy and paranoid. One-third report having nightmares about angry Yama Kings and Infernals.

5) Returned to life, but looks and feels 10 years older.

6) Returned to life and seems 100% okay!

Divine Dragon Elixir: Ko has only recently deciphered the formula for this next elixir and he's still running computer simulations to try to figure out what the stuff actually does.

Alliances & Allies

Someone powerful is behind Ko. There is no way he would have discovered as many secrets, nor could he have ever learned how to magically interpret some of the secret scripts unless he's been receiving some kind of magical or supernatural assistance.

Whoever is behind Ko's remarkable progress also has an involvement in at least one of the Triads. Not only has Ko and his company been "protected," but he always manages to find just the right patients when he needs new guinea pigs for his experiments. At least one of the following people, all of whom are in daily contact with Ko, works for someone else. **Note:** If desired, the Game Master can roll 1D6 to randomly determine which person is working for some evil manipulator:

1. George Mai: Ko's private secretary. George keeps Ko together, makes sure he makes it to important meetings, properly bathes and dresses, and takes care of a lot of the business.

2. Bo Nan Mihn: A refugee from Vietnam and Ko's personal chauffeur and bodyguard. Bo has extensive contacts with the Vietnamese underworld in Hong Kong. Bo is in constant electronic contact with other security elements of the company and can instantly call for at least four other officers for back-up.

He is a 4th level Bok Pai Kung Fu martial artist, with Crane Stance Kata, a Weapon Kata using knife, Chi Defense Kata, and the Chi-Gung Body Hardening Ability.

Attributes: I.Q. 12, M.E. 9, M.A. 10, P.S. 14, P.P. 15, P.E. 10, P.B. 11, Spd. 14

Weight: 130 Pounds (58.9 kg). **S.D.C.:** 28

Height: 5 feet, 6 inches (1.67 M). **Chi:** 23

Hit Points: 28 **P.P.E.:** 12

Bonuses: 3 attacks per melee round, +3 to strike with knife or Crane Fist, +2 to damage, and +2 to roll with punch or impact.

3. "Tony" Wong: For years Ko has been ordering all of his meals from his favorite restaurant, *The Golden Dragon*, a place just down the block. Over the years Tony, the delivery boy for the restaurant, has become one of Ko's only contacts with the outside world.

4. Amy Xian: She's Ko's closest scientific assistant. A whiz at chemistry, biology and computers, she's also well versed in ancient Chinese texts and scripts. Ms. Xian rarely comes up to Ko's Penthouse, but Ko usually spends at least an hour each day supervising the operations of Xian and the other lab workers.

5. Mung I Peng: Mrs. Mung is Equitech's chief accountant. During daily breakfast meetings, often with George Mai in attendance, Mung keeps Ko updated on the company's changing financial picture.

6. Dr. Fung Dou Nan: Dr. Fung has what one could call a "varied" medical practice in Hong Kong. Although he is on staff at a couple of hospitals, he also runs a small free clinic in a seedy neighborhood near the waterfront.

Jiang, the Laboratory Cat

Ko believes that the cat is nothing but an ordinary animal. Just something he keeps around in case a laboratory mouse escapes from a cage. In reality, Ko is partially under the cat's control! The cat is really a manifestation of a creature of Pure Negative Chi.

Jiang will exert control over Ko, keeping Ko fast asleep or unconscious, whenever there is a problem with an intruder. Jiang has already disposed of at least a couple of unwelcome guests without leaving a trace.

Cat Form: Appears to be an ordinary cat with white and black spots.

Horror Factor: None, as a cat.

Size/Weight: Cat shaped; about eight pounds (3.6 kg).

S.D.C.: 20

Hit Points: 28

Positive Chi: 35 Points

Natural Abilities: Two attacks per melee round, damage is 1D4 with claws or 1D6 bite, it can leap 5 feet (1.5 m), prowl 60%, swim 50% and climb 60/55%. The cat is also immune to chemical poisons and drugs, and can turn into a sixteen-legged form or Pure Negative Chi.

Bonuses: +2 on initiative, +1 to strike, +2 to parry, +6 to dodge, +4 to roll with punch or fall.

Sixteen-Legged Form: Looks like a scaled insect with two bulbous green eyes and green bristly hairs scattered across its body. Four long antenna, stick out of the top of the head, and the mouth is hidden in the throat.

The front two legs are very thin, but long and tipped with poison injectors. The next two legs are heavier, and equipped with three-part pincers capable of lifting and manipulating objects (it can, for example, pick up a pistol, aim and fire accurately). Immediately behind the heavy grippers are another pair of poison injectors, designed so they can rapidly stick into anything that's being held by the claws. The rest of the legs are all for locomotion.

Horror Factor: 8 when unseen (there's something really creepy about the sound it makes when crawling around; no prowl ability). 15 when visible.

Size/Weight: Less than 3 feet long (0.9 m) and 40 pounds (18 kg).

Armor Rating: 14
S.D.C.: 45
Hit Points: 28
Negative Chi: 45 Points
Natural Abilities: Can climb on all surfaces (like an insect) at full speed, turn invisible at will, has poison injectors, immune to chemical poisons and drugs, and can turn into cat form or Pure Negative Chi within one melee round.
Attacks per Melee: Four
Bonuses: +2 on initiative, +6 to strike, +9 to parry, +11 to dodge, +2 to damage, and +6 to roll with punch or fall. Damage from pincers is 1D6 or by poison injectors (see as follows).
Special Attack: Paralytic Poison! If the victim fails to save vs poison, the injection causes a kind of paralysis where a character can see and hear normally, but is unable to move except at a slow crawl; 10% of normal speed, only one melee action per round, and no initiative. Each dose means the effect will last for 4D6 minutes, with cumulative results.

Pure Negative Chi Form: An energy being.
Horror Factor: None
Negative Chi: 85 Points
Natural Abilities: All Negative Chi Mastery Abilities.
Attacks per Melee: Five
Bonuses: +1 on initiative, +4 to strike, +6 to parry, +3 to dodge.

And who, pray tell, is the master of Jiang, the cat? Obviously, someone very powerful has decided that Ko bears watching, or that Ko's experiments are either very valuable and/or very dangerous. Someone powerful, perhaps inhuman, is pulling Ko's strings.

The identity of the puppet master is up to the Game Master and, given the nature of **Mystic China**, it's probable that the there may be several intermediaries between Ko and whoever is ultimately responsible. The force ultimately behind it all can be an Immortal, Infernal, dragon, powerful sorcerer or alchemist, Triad Crime Lord, Capitalist Entrepreneur, madman or any number of other people or supernatural beings.

Experience Levels per O.C.C.

Antiquarian & Capitalist O.C.C.s
1 0000-1,900
2 1,901-3,800
3 3,801-7,600
4 7,601-15,200
5 15,201-23,200
6 23,201-32,200
7 32,201-43,200
8 43,201-58,200
9 58,201-83,200
10 83,201-113,200
11 113,201-152,200
12 152,201-192,200
13 192,201-242,200
14 242,201-292,200
15 292,201-342,200

Blind Mystic P.C.C.
1 0000-1,950
2 1,951-3,900
3 3,901-7,800
4 7,801-15,600
5 15,601-23,600
6 23,601-33,600
7 33,601-36,600
8 36,601-56,600
9 56,601-78,600
10 78,601-108,600
11 108,601-148,600
12 148,601-198,600
13 198,601-248,600
14 248,601-298,600
15 298,601-348,600

Chun Tzu O.C.C. & Jian Shih O.C.C.
1 0000-2,100
2 2,101-4,200
3 4,201-8,400
4 8,401-16,800
5 16,801-24,000
6 24,001-34,000
7 34,001-47,000
8 47,001-65,000
9 65,001-90,000
10 90,001-120,000
11 120,001-160,000
12 160,001-210,000
13 210,001-260,000
14 260,001-310,000
15 310,001-360,000

Nei Chia Wu Shih O.C.C.
1 0000-2,000
2 2,001-4,000
3 4,001-8,000
4 8,001-16,000
5 16,001-24,000
6 24,001-33,000
7 33,001-44,000
8 44,001-64,000
9 64,001-84,000
10 84,001-104,000
11 104,001-144,000
12 144,001-194,000
13 194,001-244,000
14 244,001-294,000
15 294,001-334,000

Demon Hunter O.C.C. & Wai Chia Wu Shih O.C.C.
1 0000-1,800
2 1,801-3,600
3 3,601-7,200
4 7,201-14,400
5 14,401-21,400
6 21,401-31,400
7 31,401-41,400
8 41,401-55,400
9 55,401-80,400
10 80,401-110,400
11 110,401-150,400
12 150,401-200,400
13 200,401-250,400
14 250,401-300,400
15 300,401-350,400

Fox Spirit R.C.C.
1 0000-3,000
2 3,001-5,000
3 5,001-10,000
4 10,001-20,000
5 20,001-30,000
6 30,001-50,000
7 50,001-80,000
8 80,001-120,000
9 120,001-170,000
10 170,001-230,000
11 230,001-300,000
12 300,001-380,000
13 380,001-470,000
14 470,001-600,000
15 600,001-800,000

Fang Shih, Tao Shih & Wu Shih P.C.C.s
1 0000-2,200
2 2,201-4,400
3 4,401-8,800
4 8,801-17,700
5 17,701-25,700
6 25,701-35,700
7 35,701-50,700
8 50,701-70,700
9 70,701-95,700
10 95,701-135,700
11 135,701-185,700
12 185,701-225,700
13 225,701-275,700
14 275,701-325,700
15 325,701-385,000

Reformed Demon R.C.C.
1 0000-2,500
2 2,501-4,000
3 4,001-9,000
4 9,001-20,000
5 20,001-30,000
6 30,001-45,000
7 45,001-65,000
8 65,001-90,000
9 90,001-120,000
10 120,001: Special!

Book & Reading List

Beats me how many books I've read in preparation for **Mystic China**. A couple of hundred, at least. Along the way I've come across a few that are genuinely worthwhile or just fun to read. Here are my picks:

Blofeld, John, **Taoism, The Road to Immortality**. 1985, Shambhala Publications, Inc. The best primer on Taoism I've ever seen, written by one of the few Westerners ever to actually visit the living practitioners of Taoism, and functioning Taoist Temples, back in the 1930s. I'm also very fond of his **I Ching** book and his biography, **The Wheel of Life**, is wonderfully entertaining.

Bloomfield, Frena, **The Book of Chinese Beliefs**. 1989, Ballantine Books. Very readable, very enjoyable. Instead of the boring academic stuff, the author describes how real people in Hong Kong relate to their ancient magical beliefs.

Bordewich, Fergus M., **Cathay, A Journey in Search of Old China**. 1991, Prentice Hall Press. A personal account of a six-month meander around some of the most obscure parts of contemporary China, always with an attempt to find some of the ancient mysteries.

Carradine, David, **Spirit of Shaolin**. 1991, Charles E. Tuttle Company, Inc. Surprisingly, the movie star (*Kung Fu*, *Death Race 2000*, etc.) writes a pretty good martial arts book, and he keeps the reader entertained with a fair number of stories.

Hoff, Benjamin, **The Tao of Pooh** and **The Te of Piglet**. 1982 and 1992, Dutton. If you're a fan of A.A. Milne's *Winnie-the-Pooh* (and what Taoist wouldn't identify with a Bear of Little Brain?), then these books are the perfect introduction, or maybe the perfect advanced directions, to Taoism (Tiddely pom).

Huanzhulouzhu, **Blades from the Willows**, translated by Robert Chard, 1991, Wellsweep Press. Huanzhulouzhu ("the Master of the Pearl-Rimmed Tower") is the pseudonym of Li Shanji (1902-1961), author of dozens of fantasy serialized novels (one, *Swordsmen of the Sichuan Mountains*, was originally published in fifty volumes!).

Hughart, Barry, **Bridge of Birds, Ten Skilled Gentlemen** and **The Story of the Stone**. Three wonderful fantasy novels, with at least a couple of neat role-playing ideas on every page.

The I Ching, available in many translations, based on a variety of Chinese versions. I find myself at a loss to recommend one version from the dozens that are currently available. So let me tell you about three of 'em. Richard Wilhelm's version is the classic, and might be more useful in a fantasy campaign. John Blofeld's is clear, complete, concise, and well-written, probably best for the beginner. Finally, Kerson Huang, a particle physicist, has come up with a excellent *I Ching* for readers who are into computers.

Mind-Dao, Deng. **The Wandering Taoist**. 1983, Harper & Row. A book that reads like a novel, but tells the story of the author's upbringing in a remote Taoist monastery. Required reading for anyone interested in the mystic aspects of the martial arts. Highly recommended for the mythic background and texture of Chinese martial arts and thought.

Porter, Bill, **Road to Heaven, Encounters with Chinese Hermits**. 1993, Mercury House. I was delighted to learn, contrary to what everyone had believed for the last thirty years, that Taoist Hermits are still holed up in the mountains of China. A first-hand account, accompanied by wonderful photographs.

Sawyer, Ralph D., **The Seven Military Classics of Ancient China**. 1993, Westview Press. Includes most of the books described in the Chun Tzu O.C.C. section, including a nice translation of *Sun Tzu's Art of War*. The best all-around reference book on both the lives, the tactics, and the sneakiness, of the military geniuses of Chinese history.

Schipper, Kristofer, **The Taoist Body**. 1993, University of California Press (translation of *Le Corps Taoiste*, 1983, Librairie Arthéme Fayard, Paris). The very best modern-day description of the religion of Taoism.

Temple, Robert, **The Genius of China**. 1986, Simon & Schuster (in Britain the title is *China: Land of Discovery & Innovation*). A beautifully illustrated, easy to read, description of 3,000 years of Chinese inventions. You name it, from advanced mathematics, to glow-in-the-dark paint, to mechanical engineering, chances are, the Chinese invented it first.

Walters, Derek, **Feng Shui**. 1986, Simon & Schuster. The most readable, most useful, and most beautiful of all the dozens of books that are available on Chinese Geomancy.

If you prefer video entertainment, you might want to track down a couple of movies: **Big Trouble in Little China** and **Chinese Ghost Story**, two of my favorites.